The Penguin Book of Japanese Short Stories

THE
PENGUIN BOOK
of

JAPANESE
SHORT
STORIES

Introduced by
HARUKI MURAKAMI

———

Edited and with Notes by
JAY RUBIN

PENGUIN BOOKS

PENGUIN CLASSICS

UK | USA | Canada | Ireland | Australia
India | New Zealand | South Africa

Penguin Books is part of the Penguin Random House group of companies
whose addresses can be found at global.penguinrandomhouse.com.

This translation first published in Penguin Classics 2018

005

Introduction copyright © Haruki Murakami, 2018
Selection and editorial material copyright © Jay Rubin, 2018

The Acknowledgements on pp. 515–18 constitute an extension to this page

Set in 11.25/14.75 pt Adobe Caslon Pro
Typeset by Jouve (UK), Milton Keynes
Printed and bound in Great Britain by Clays Ltd, Elcograf S.p.A.

ISBN: 978–0–141–39562–3

Contents

Contents

MEN AND WOMEN

NATURE AND MEMORY

Contents

Contents

Contents

Introduction

From Seppuku to Meltdown

I once heard the story that when jazz drummer Buddy Rich was being admitted to a hospital, the nurse at the front desk asked him if he had any allergies. 'Only to country and western music,' he replied. In my case, my only allergy is to Japan's so-called 'I novel' – the form of autobiographical writing that has been at the forefront of Japan's modern fiction since the turn of the twentieth century.

To tell the truth, from my teens to my early twenties, I read hardly any Japanese fiction. And for a long while I was convinced that, with a few exceptions, early modern and contemporary Japanese literature was simply boring. There were many reasons for this, but foremost among them may be that the novels and stories we were assigned to read in school were pretty bad. My 'I-novel allergy' was also quite strong back then (these days, to be sure, it has become less intense), and since you can't hope either to make your way through or to understand modern Japanese literature if you're going to avoid its constitutional predisposition to producing 'I novels', I made a conscious effort while young to avoid going anywhere near Japanese literature.

Reading is, of course, a supremely personal – even selfish – activity. Each person consumes reading matter in accordance with his or her own likes and dislikes, which no one else can pronounce simply to be right or wrong, proper or warped. People have an innate right to read the books they want to read and avoid the books they don't want to read. It is one of the few precious liberties granted to us in this largely unfree world (though, to be sure, many situations arise that complicate the matter).

At the same time, however, viewed in purely dietary terms, a balanced intake of information and knowledge plays an important role in the formation of a person's intellect and character, and though no one has the right to criticize me for having spent a lifetime consuming books in my own lopsided way, I can't help feeling that it's nothing to be proud of. Having become a Japanese novelist (once and for all), I may have something of a problem on my hands in saying that I know hardly anything about Japanese fiction – which is a little different from Buddy Rich saying he doesn't listen to country and western music.

This is why, after passing the age of thirty, I made an effort to read as much Japanese fiction as I could. Thanks to this I discovered quite a number of truly interesting works later in life but recall very few from those impressionable teen years I spent in the 1960s. At the urging of friends, I read several works by Ōe Kenzaburō (b. 1935), who was the young people's hero in those days. I remember having read classic figures such as Akutagawa Ryūnosuke (1892–1927) and Natsume Sōseki (1867–1916) back then, but I was never able to warm to such supposedly representative Japanese literary giants as Shiga Naoya (1883–1971), Kawabata Yasunari (1899–1972) or Mishima Yukio (1925–70). For some reason I can't put my finger on, I was never able to keep myself immersed in their style. I'd often give up partway through a work and toss it aside. They and I were probably just temperamentally incompatible; unfortunately, it seems, they were not 'novelists for me'. I don't mean to call into question, of course, their talent or the importance of their works. What should be called into question, I strongly suspect, is my own lack of understanding.

Speaking personally, then, I learned practically nothing about novelistic technique from my Japanese predecessors. I had to discover on my own how one goes about writing fiction. This was probably a good thing in the sense that I didn't have a lot of baggage to carry with me.

I was thirty when I debuted as an author, and almost forty years have shot by in the meantime (hard as that is to believe), but I confess that, with only a few exceptions, I have not kept close tabs on young authors who have followed me into the literary world. This is not to say that I have been avoiding their works or have no interest in them, just that I have been narrowly focused, heart and soul, on doing what I want to do rather than making the effort to read and learn from other people's writings.

James Joyce said something to the effect that imagination is memory, and he was absolutely right. Our memories (the wellspring of imagination) take shape while we are young, and once we pass a certain age, it's rare for them to undergo any major change.

All of this may add up to nothing more than a long-winded excuse for why I know so little (or next to nothing) about modern and contemporary Japanese fiction. I hope I have made myself clear on that point. And if I'm not mistaken, I would guess that most readers of this book of English translations know as little about modern and contemporary Japanese fiction as I do (or nothing at all). At least in my approach here, I'd like to go on that assumption.

Which is why, in this introduction, I am not standing a step above you as your guide to Japanese literature but taking a position on the same level as you so that together we can think about how best to approach this anthology. Let's just say that you are being guided through a foreign town by someone who lives in the country and speaks the language but who doesn't know that much about the geography or history.

To tell you the truth, I'm reading most of the stories included here for the first time in my life. I had previously read only six of the thirty-five – including my own! And many of the rest I had never even heard of.

I'm not making excuses, but this has enabled me to encounter the works with a fresh attitude devoid of suppositions or bias or attachments, which may be all to the good. It's always an interesting experience to chance upon the unknown. If I hadn't had this opportunity (which is to say, if I hadn't had this task presented to me), I might never have come across these works.

One thing I would like you to keep in mind is that the works collected here are by no means all universally recognized modern masterpieces. Some, of course, could be characterized as 'representative' works, but, frankly, they are far outnumbered by stories which are not. We also find here quite old works and very new works arranged literally side by side, like an iPod and a gramophone on the same shelf of a record store. The only way to find out what the editor had in mind when he made this selection is to ask the man himself (see the Editorial Note following this introduction), but in any case an individually edited anthology like this tends to give priority to the editor's intentions and taste over generalized principles of impartiality and conventional practice, and we have to make our way through the book following his lead. Another point to keep in mind is that, while the book includes a number of stories translated here for the first time, the choice of works has been largely limited to pieces that have already appeared in English.

In any case, this is certainly an unconventional selection of works by an unusual assortment of writers. Seeing this line-up, the average Japanese reader might find him- or herself puzzled. 'Why is *this* story in here? And why is *that one* missing?'

This is precisely why reading through this collection has been so fresh and interesting for someone like me with my spotty background in Japanese literature. Now and then I'd be quite astounded at the different and strangely compelling ways the fiction of my own country could be grasped. Above all, I found my curiosity piqued: 'What's coming next?'

Japan has long had a custom of selling *fukubukuro* (literally, 'good luck bags' or 'lucky grab bags') on New Year's Day, sealed bags offered by retailers with no indication of what they contain. One bag will normally hold an odd mix of items, the combined value of which is guaranteed to be far more than the bag's selling price. People have been known to wait in long queues at major department stores for these popular mystery bargains to go on sale, and to fight over the chance to buy them, anticipating the annual thrill of taking them home and discovering what's inside. Probably more than the satisfaction of getting a bargain, it's the mystery that must make these grab bags so irresistible. (I myself have never bought one.)

The comparison may not be apt, but the *fukubukuro* was the first thing that popped into my mind when I finished reading this book, which offers the same kind of mysterious and unpredictably rewarding experience. I hope readers will open the bag and enjoy what they find inside.

Now let's look at the stories in each thematically organized section of the book.

Japan and the West

This section features three of the most famous modern Japanese writers. All three of their works depict wealthy intellectuals bewildered by the great differences between the cultures of Japan and the West. Two of the three, Nagai Kafū (1879–1959) and Natsume Sōseki (1867–1916), had the experience of studying abroad. Sōseki lived in England for two years on a Japanese government grant which required him to do research on English-language pedagogical methods. Kafū spent four years in America, supposedly studying business at his father's behest, after which he went to France for nearly a year. In those days, study abroad was a privilege permitted only to the richest or most elite members of Japanese society.

Kafū had originally hoped to go to Europe and found much about American life that set his nerves on edge, so when he finally got to France, he plunged into the free life he found there like a fish returned to water, but this only added to the difficult psychological adjustments he had to make once he was home again in Japan. The story included here, 'Behind the Prison' (*Kangokusho no ura*, 1909), describes the clash between the ideal world he sought and the depressing reality in which he found himself confined. His search for the Japanese equivalent of the decadent, sophisticated free life he had experienced in Paris led him to the cafés and bordellos and strip joints he found in Tokyo's seamier 'low city' neighbourhoods. He saw himself as an outsider, a fugitive from Japan's elite circles. In Japan at that time, the freedom of spirit that he sought was to be found only in such places. Resigning in 1916 from the professorial post he had held for six years, he declared himself a lowly 'scribbler' (*gesakusha*), rejected marriage after two brief flirtations with the institution, took no regular employment, sought no position of authority, and spent his life freely pursuing his whims.

Sōseki, by contrast, though he shared many of Kafū's cares, spent his life among the chosen. His deeply serious nature overwhelmed him while he was studying in London and led to a serious nervous breakdown. Ordered home by the Ministry of Education, he was awarded a professorship at Tokyo Imperial University, the nation's premier educational institution (for men only). While teaching, he published fiction on the side (to calm his frazzled nerves, it is said), and when his writing attracted a large audience, he left his academic position to become staff novelist for the *Asahi shinbun*, the most authoritative newspaper of the day, where he serialized novel after novel. His career as a professional novelist lasted a mere ten years, but all his works attracted an enthusiastic following and in many ways set the course for modern Japanese literature. *Sanshirō* (1908; the title is the protagonist's given name) excerpted here, is one of his important mid-career novels, and it happens to be my favourite among his works. It vividly depicts the confusion and bewilderment of a country boy coming to the city for the first time, and in so doing conveys the conflicts between traditional lifestyles and Western culture. What

Sanshirō feels is more or less what all young people of the time experienced – the same thrills and confusion and joys and depression.

Tanizaki Jun'ichirō (1886–1965) did not have the experience of studying abroad, but he constructed the foundation for his sophisticated literature during the liberal, urbane period known as 'Taishō Democracy' (the brief time of peace between the Russo-Japanese War of 1904–5 and the war with China that began in 1931 and led into the Second World War). He was born into a well-to-do family, but had to withdraw from school and go to work when his father's business went bankrupt, though with the help of a teacher who recognized his academic talents he managed to advance to higher school. The novella included here, *The Story of Tomoda and Matsunaga* (*Tomoda to Matsunaga no hanashi*, 1926), depicts an individual whose personality is split between East and West. Although it's a bizarre tale put together in the form of a mystery, it is a well-wrought allegory, with just enough plausibility to convey with a certain poignancy the confusion and turmoil of intellectuals of the day who were unable to commit fully either to their Eastern or their Western side. It was serialized in the magazine *Shufu no tomo* (The Housewife's Friend) in 1926, the year the Taishō Emperor died and the age changed from Taishō to Shōwa, literally a historical turning point.

What we see in these three works is primarily the cultural state of Japan prior to the Second World War, when the country was actively importing Western culture while taking severe measures to preserve the 'national polity' known as the Emperor System and striving to fulfil the motto 'Rich Country, Strong Army'. The situation changed dramatically after Japan's defeat and the US occupation of the country, but even today the clash of systems Eastern and Western goes on in different forms. This sometimes gives rise to interesting stimuli, and at other times to a profound sense of depression.

If I may add a personal note concerning Tanizaki, when I received the 'Tanizaki Prize' in my mid-thirties, I had the opportunity to meet Tanizaki's widow, Matsuko, at the award ceremony. She was quite advanced in years but still energetic. She made a point of coming over to me to say how much she had enjoyed the novel of mine that had received the prize, *Hard-Boiled Wonderland and the End of the World*. I felt honoured to be awarded a prize in the name of Tanizaki, a writer I greatly admired.

The first time I visited the offices of the *New Yorker*, I was shown around by the then editor-in-chief, Robert Gottlieb. When we got back to his office, I noticed he had three copies of Tanizaki's *The Makioka Sisters* (*Sasameyuki*, 1944–9) on his shelf and asked him why that should be. 'I do it so people will ask me that question,' he said with a smile. 'Then I can tell them what a great book I think it is and, if they show interest, I can give them a copy.' How pleased Tanizaki would have been to hear that.

Loyal Warriors

This section contains two stories about seppuku, or hara-kiri, as it is often referred to in the West, the practice of ritual suicide by disembowelment associated with the samurai warrior class. Mori Ōgai's 'The Last Testament of Okitsu Yagoemon' (*Okitsu Yagoemon no isho*, 1912) deals with an Edo-period (1600–1868) samurai who follows his lord in death, while Mishima Yukio's 'Patriotism' (*Yūkoku*, 1961) depicts seppuku against the background of the Incident of 26 February, a coup staged by young army officers in 1936. The samurai writes his testament with almost perfunctory detachment while the young officer's performance of this distinctive form of suicide rises to erotic intensity.

The original point of seppuku was to slice open one's own stomach and, if possible, pull out the intestines so as to demonstrate to one's lord or to the people of one's world the purity of one's intent. It was an honourable method of suicide permitted only to the warrior class. It could be practised as an imposed form of punishment or as a voluntary expression of will. In either case, medically speaking, it was a terribly inefficient means of ending one's life. It took a long time and was tremendously painful. Slashing a carotid artery or stabbing oneself in the heart was a far easier death. Precisely because it was so inefficient and painful and time-consuming, most likely, the samurai warriors clung to this form of dying in order to put their courage and resolution on display (though in later years, it is true, so as not to prolong the agony, the individual would more often have a second ready to lop his head off from behind as soon as he had jabbed the blade into his abdomen).

To be a samurai – a member of the elite military class – meant that one had to be prepared to take one's own life at any moment if the occasion should arise. Nor would it be any exaggeration to say that the heritage of continued psychological tension has had an obvious impact on the society. Occasions calling for the physical slicing open of the belly may have ceased to exist, but the readiness to commit seppuku would still seem to be functioning as an aesthetic influence on the Japanese psyche. In the world of the contemporary salaryman and bureaucrat, one often hears a person say 'I've got to cut my belly open' or 'They're gonna make me cut my belly open' to mean he is going to take responsibility for something.

As an elite army officer, Mori Ōgai (1862–1922) was an intellectual with a cosmopolitan sensibility nurtured by a period of study in Germany, but still, when he heard the shocking news that General Nogi Maresuke (1849–1912), hero of the Russo-Japanese War, had cut his stomach open (and his wife took a dagger to her chest) to follow Emperor Meiji into death, he was deeply moved, and as Nogi was being laid to rest, Ōgai wrote 'The Last Testament of Okitsu Yagoemon'. Okitsu was a historical figure who actually ended his life with seppuku, and he may have left some sort of testament to explain his actions, but the 'testament' we have here is probably Ōgai's fictional creation. Presented in the form of a simple, practical document, it reeks with a suppressed bloodiness from beginning to end. Because it is written in a formal Chinese style often used in official documents, the story is probably not read by many Japanese nowadays, but in it we see Ōgai's cool, clean late style. Ōgai knew General Nogi well and must have felt deep sympathy for his manner of death. He went on to write several more pieces on samurai who follow their lords into death, most notably 'The Abe Family' (*Abe ichizoku*, 1913), a particularly sanguinary tale. We might note here that Natsume Sōseki, the other giant of Meiji-period letters, was also inspired by Nogi's suicide to write his best-known novel, *Kokoro* (1914).

Mishima Yukio (1925–70) used to say that 'Patriotism' had no real-life models, but it is generally held that there *were* people who *could have been* Mishima's models. In fact, there was a military couple who actually took their own lives like the couple in the story. But Mishima would almost certainly have found it unbearable to see his idealized, purified literary image of Lieutenant Takeyama Shinji's heroic seppuku and his wife Reiko's self-immolation reduced to the level of sheer realism. No reader who reaches the end of 'Patriotism' is thinking about whether or not the story has real-life models. Surely there are readers who are drawn to the beauty of the world depicted in the piece as well as readers who feel only revulsion. In either case, one cannot help but recognize Mishima's thoroughgoing purification of a single idea as an outstanding literary accomplishment.

In 1970, nine years after he wrote 'Patriotism', Mishima died committing seppuku in a patriotic act of grieving for the fate of his nation. I was twenty-one years old at the time, watching the surrounding events on television in the university dining hall and wondering what I was seeing. Even after it finally dawned on me what this was about, I was unable to discover any urgent 'meaning' in Mishima's act. If it taught me anything, it was that there existed a huge gulf between bringing an idea to a literary apotheosis and doing it as an act in the real world.

Men and Women

Of the six stories in this section, five are by women. What could this extreme imbalance mean? That women are more suited to writing about relations between the sexes? Or more simply that it's too hard for male writers to create accurate images of women and female psychology? Or that the long history of male-centred society in Japan has produced female writers whose gaze possesses a sharper critical spirit? Or perhaps all of the above?

Tsushima Yūko (1947–2016) was one year old when her father, the famous writer Dazai Osamu, died in a lovers' suicide. She grew up in the home of a single mother, and she herself, after her divorce, raised her children virtually on her own. It is a scene from this kind of life that we see depicted in fine detail in Tsushima's story 'Flames' (*Honō*, 1979), which is very much in the 'I novel' style. Blood passed from mother to child; a man who abandons his wife and child; a child's wordless outbreak of fever without clear cause or outcome: all are linked to the brilliant (and deadly) final explosion in the night sky.

Kōno Taeko (1926–2015) was born in Osaka in the very last year of the Taishō period (1912–26). A great admirer of Tanizaki, she steeped herself in his modernistic tendencies. 'In the Box' (*Hako no naka*, 1979) is a very strange story. The (almost meaningless) nastiness or eccentricity of the woman portrayed here seems like something that would never occur to a man but which might inspire a woman to say, 'Stuff like this happens all the time.' No men appear in the story, and I suspect that the very absence of men is, conversely, part of the message. All kinds of things seem to be going on in this box.

Nakagami Kenji (1946–92) is the first name that would come to mind if I were asked, 'Whose was the strongest literary voice to appear after the Second World War?' He unfurls his unique world before us with a powerful style that all but nails his characters and scenes to the page, his stories set against forceful images of his home area, Kishū (southern Wakayama Prefecture). I was surprised to find, when I met him and spoke with him face to face, that he seemed far gentler and more sensitive than I had imagined from his works. That he fell ill and died at the height of his powers is greatly to be regretted. In 'Remaining Flowers' (*Nokori no hana*, 1988), a young man lies naked with a blind woman in the darkness. Everything comes from the fertile earth, turns to bone and goes back to the earth. What emerges from the darkness returns to the darkness – a most impressive work.

Yoshimoto Banana (b. 1964) is the second daughter of the famous poet and critic Yoshimoto Takaaki (1924–2012). She made her literary debut in 1987 with the novel *Kitchen* (*Kitchin*), which won a great following among young readers and became a bestseller at home and abroad. Her early works paint a vivid panorama of the lives of young women using a natural style that seems to slip through space. 'Bee Honey' (*Hachihanii*) appeared in Yoshimoto's short-story collection *Adultery and South America* (*Furin to nanbei*, 2000). The female protagonist leaves Japan owing to marital difficulties and goes to stay with a friend living in Buenos Aires. As she becomes acquainted with the customs and history and people of her temporary foreign home, she begins to have a clearer, more externalized view of herself in the context of her daily life in Japan. This would seem to have all the ingredients for a murky tale, but the author's quiet, matter-of-fact sensibility can be strangely persuasive. This is Yoshimoto Banana's unique world, without a hint of the old dictates regarding what constitutes 'literature'.

Ohba Minako (1930–2007) was born in Tokyo as the daughter of a naval surgeon and spent her girlhood in Hiroshima Prefecture, where her father was posted. Her experience of the atomic bombing at the age of fourteen exposed her to horrific scenes that became a kind of take-off point for her fiction. Her dry, precise style is utterly devoid of ornamentation, and she has been highly praised for the way she uses it to whittle the world down to sharply rendered fragments. In 'The Smile of a Mountain Witch' (*Yamauba no bishō*, 1976), the ancient Japanese legend of the *yamanba* or *yamauba*, a mountain-dwelling hag with supernatural powers, becomes a device for laying bare the life – the often performative life – of a normal contemporary woman. More often than not, the 'supernatural beings' perceived by us are nothing more than images of ourselves reflected in a dark mirror. Many women may recognize an aspect of their own lives in the author's 'mountain witch'. The image of a woman who becomes a hobgoblin in the mountains but is perceived as an ordinary housewife when she lives among people is one of the most important motifs for the feminist Ohba.

Enchi Fumiko (1905–86) debuted as a dramatist but in her sixties she became widely recognized as a novelist when her stories for girls won great popularity. Daughter of the famous scholar of the Japanese classics Ueda Kazutoshi (or Ueda Mannen; 1867–1937), Enchi herself was deeply learned in the Japanese classics and produced a critically praised modern Japanese translation of the great eleventh-century novel *The Tale of Genji*. The narrative of 'A Bond for Two Lifetimes – Gleanings' (*Nise no enishi: shūi*, 1957) is propelled by translated passages of the classic gothic short story 'A Bond for Two Lifetimes' from the collection *Tales of Spring Rain* (*Harusame monogatari*, 1808) by Ueda Akinari (1734–1809), who is best known in the West as author of the ghost story on which is based the 1953 Mizoguchi Kenji film *Ugetsu*. I had no idea of the connection to Enchi when I used Akinari's 'A Bond for Two Lifetimes' as a structural element in my novel *Killing Commendatore* (*Kishidanchō-goroshi*, 2017). Akinari's classic story becomes the vehicle through which two men – the husband she lost in the war and the old professor who presses her for sexual union – reach out in the darkness for the flesh of Enchi's female protagonist. But what is the true form of each? This is an extremely well-made – and frightening – story, and I recall Suzuki Seijun's 1973 television adaptation of it, *A Mummy's Love*, as a particularly good one.

Nature and Memory

Abe Akira (1934–89) became a full-time novelist in 1971 at the age of thirty-seven after some years of writing in his spare time while directing radio and television programmes. Most of his works concentrate on his family and daily life in the 'I novel' style, and he is often identified as a member of the so-called 'Introverted Generation' of generally apolitical writers active in the 1960s and 1970s. Nothing special happens in 'Peaches' (*Momo*, 1971). We simply observe the author examining an old memory of his in this contemplative variant of the 'I novel' sometimes known as a 'mental-state novel' (*shinkyō shōsetsu*). The way the author brings his five senses into play, however, is quite vivid. It's like watching an old black-and-white film gradually taking on colour as the author's memory assumes concrete shape on the page. The weight and fragrance of the peaches piled into an old pram, the chill of the night air, the croaking of frogs and the creak of the pram's wheels are all immovable parts of the scene the writer brings back again and again. But then one day he begins to have grave doubts about his memory, and he is thrown into confusion. This fine work is an excellent example of one of the more important forms of Japanese fiction.

Ogawa Yōko (b. 1962) made her authorial debut in 1988, almost at the same time as Yoshimoto Banana, and the two attracted attention as women writers with a new sensibility. Ogawa has continued ever since to tell her stories at her own steady pace, and her quiet but solid style has won the support of many readers. Every neighbourhood has its own house of mystery where a mysterious individual lives, and local children are irresistibly drawn to it. There was one in my neighbourhood, and I'll bet there was one in yours, too. In 'The Tale of the House of Physics' (*Butsuri no yakata monogatari*, 2010), Ogawa turns her story into a tunnel that brings you back to that mystery house of your childhood. The piece is remarkable for the storyteller's tender-hearted, low-angled point of view.

Kunikida Doppo (1871–1908) was a Meiji-period contemporary of such literary giants as Mori Ōgai and Natsume Sōseki, but in scale he was more of a 'minor poet', perhaps a Turgenev to their Tolstoy and Dostoevsky. A devout Christian in his early twenties, Doppo turned to Wordsworth as a guide to the natural world and supported himself as a magazine editor and war correspondent. He is best known as the writer of *Musashino* (1898), an essay-like description of the natural beauty of the rural Musashi Plain that surrounded Tokyo in those days, his fresh, new style leading the way for Japan's developing naturalistic fiction. In 'Unforgettable People' (*Wasureenu hitobito*, 1898), the author sketches a series of scenes and characters in a manner that still strikes us as lively today, the images rising before us despite the intervening decades. The story's final twist is effective as well. I suspect that neither Sōseki nor Ōgai was capable of fashioning a sharp, little piece of this type.

The next story in this section called 'Nature and Memory' is a simple sketch I dashed off when it came to me out of nowhere – and promptly forgot about. Though I may have forgotten its existence, I'm delighted as a writer to know that the editor of this anthology liked it enough to pull some strings to include it here, and though I still find it a little puzzling (and perhaps wanting as a piece of literature), I'm pleased to think that the reader may enjoy it as well. As with much of my writing, 'The 1963/1982 Girl from Ipanema' (*1963/1982-nen no Ipanema-musume*, 1982) uses one of my favourite pieces of music to recall a certain mood and time; Stan Getz's marvellous solo on the famous track is something I will never tire of listening to.

Born in Tokyo in 1954, Shibata Motoyuki was a professor of English and American literature at the University of Tokyo for many years, but now devotes all his time – and incredible energy – to translating, writing and magazine editing. Translating American literature and introducing it to a new audience is his primary focus, and his work in the area has done much to change the very idea of translation in Japan. I have worked closely with him for over thirty years as a teacher and coach on my own translations. Without his considerable efforts, Japanese readers would not have their current broad access to such progressive American contemporary writers as Paul Auster, Steven Millhauser, Steve Erickson, Laird Hunt, Stuart Dybek, Barry Yourgrau and Rebecca Brown. He has many fans who choose to read certain writers only because he has translated them. Shibata is constantly writing essays on American literature, and on rare occasions he ventures into writing fiction himself. The short, sketch-like 'Cambridge Circus' (*Kenburidji-sākasu*, 2010) is subtly balanced between fiction and essay, captivating the reader with its fresh gaze, wry humour and narrative skill.

Modern Life and Other Nonsense

Uno Kōji (1891–1961) is thought of as an 'I novelist' who was primarily active in the Taishō period. 'Closet LLB' (*Yaneura no hōgakushi*, 1918), one of his very early works, straddles the line between masochistic self-study and parodic humour, drawing us ever deeper into sympathy for the miserable protagonist, who has graduated from the university but can't find what he wants to do with his life. He thinks he may have found it, but his high ideals are unaccompanied by genuine ability, his conceit unsupported by talent or perseverance. Where Natsume Sōseki described the life of an upper-class idler in his novel *And Then* (*Sore kara*, 1909), Uno's protagonist is a very different kind of idler, having nothing to do with the upper class. He spends his days lying in his boarding-house closet, living in his dreams and despising the inability of those around him to appreciate his superior intellect. I guess you could just say, 'There are lots of people like that even now,' and that would be the end of it.

Genji Keita (1912–85) won great popularity in the 1950s and 1960s publishing lots of entertaining 'salaryman stories' for commercial magazines. His career overlapped with the period during which Japan's economy experienced a rapid expansion and the necktie-wearing mid-level employee known in Japan as a 'salaryman' was the star. The often humorous style with which he depicted the earnest struggles of these people who gave their all for the company day after day (usually with little to show for it) aroused the empathy of readers, many of whom found themselves in similar situations. Now that Japan's famous 'economic miracle' is a thing of the past, there are probably not many readers who turn to Genji Keita these days. The qualities that make any one age 'contemporary' gradually fade and disappear with the passage of time. I suspect, though, that young readers of our day would find something quite fresh and engaging in this rather old-fashioned story, 'Mr English' (*Eigoya-san*, 1951). It's just a guess.

Betsuyaku Minoru (b. 1937) is well known as a dramatist. He was born in Manchuria when it was under the rule of the Japanese Empire and lived there until the end of the war. His theatre of the absurd in the manner of Samuel Beckett was especially popular among young audiences in the 1960s and 1970s. He also wrote many works of fiction, among which there were a good number of fable-like stories for children – or pieces which at least took the form of stories for children. 'Factory Town' (*Kōba no aru machi*, 2006) is one of those. It was written for a radio programme that featured readings of newly created fairy tales. Reading it reminded me that in the old days (which is to say, when I was a kid) there were lots of factories all around belching thick, black smoke. You don't see those any more now that manufacturing has grown less central to industry and people's attitudes towards the environment have changed. Nowadays, you'd never hear anyone say, 'That smoke makes me feel a sort of power rising up inside me.'

Many women writers are active in the current Japanese literary scene – to the extent that the presence of male writers has begun to pale by comparison – and Kawakami Mieko (b. 1976) is one of the new writers who stand close to the central core of this scene. She is one generation down from the writers who appeared in the 1980s and early 1990s, such as Ogawa Yōko, Yoshimoto Banana and Kawakami Hiromi (not that these women constituted a 'group' of any kind). The way I see it, her fiction is marked by a sharp linguistic sensitivity (before she turned to fiction, Kawakami was a poet) and a relatively relaxed working out of the story. The combination of sharpness and slowness gives rise to a unique groove. If you let yourself go with the groove, you will (often) find an unsettling twist waiting to take your breath away at the end. Kawakami wrote 'Dreams of Love, Etc.' (*Ai no yume toka*) in 2011 and made it the title work of a volume of stories published in 2013. Having been drawn to the piano playing of a neighbouring middle-aged housewife, where is the story's female protagonist headed? At first glance just a cosy little slice of everyday life in a quiet, peaceful-seeming neighbourhood, the story soon has an ominous presence hovering over it.

Hoshi Shin'ichi (1926–97) is the writer who introduced the short short story to the Japanese literary world. With only a few exceptions, he spent his life writing stories that end after a very few pages, and the style made him famous. Mori Ōgai was his grand-uncle, and his father was president of a pharmaceutical manufacturing company, a post which Hoshi himself briefly held. In my view, the most outstanding features of Hoshi's work are its sharp wit and the clever devices he employs to surprise the reader. I remember how much I enjoyed his works when I was young. To be quite honest, though, a lot of his stories give the impression of following a fixed pattern, which is probably the unavoidable fate of any author who writes plot-driven stories – in high volume – as Hoshi did. For years, it is said, he used to complain that 'It's not fair for a writer like me to be paid by the page like a novelist,' and I can see his point. This was probably why he had no choice but to produce a spate of short works such as 'Shoulder-Top Secretary' (*Kata no ue no hisho*, 1973).

Dread

As something of an heir to Natsume Sōseki, Akutagawa Ryūnosuke (1892–1927) left behind several outstanding works that represent Japanese literature of the Taishō period (1912–26), but early in the succeeding Shōwa period (1926–89) he suffered a nervous breakdown and committed suicide. Akutagawa's style underwent some major changes in the course of his career, but one consistently perceptible feature is a kind of evanescent beauty that floats like a light in the surrounding darkness. With his precise, fine-grained style, he was able to capture that light for the briefest of moments. In his early years, he tended to write tales based on the Japanese classics. His masterpiece, 'Hell Screen' (*Jigokuhen*, 1918), is one of those. Written when Akutagawa was in his mid-twenties, it has lost none of its stylistic brilliance.

Sawanishi Yūten (b. 1986) is the youngest author represented in this anthology. He made his literary debut in 2011 and, while pursuing an academic career, has continued to produce a constant flow of strangely flavoured pieces that appear in literary magazines. 'Filling Up with Sugar' (*Satō de michite yuku*, 2013) tells the story of a woman whose mother is dying from a disease called 'systemic saccharification syndrome'. It begins: 'The vagina was the first part of her mother's body that turned to sugar', which has to be the most intense opening of a piece of fiction I've read in recent years. The situation of a daughter caring for her terminally ill mother is relatively common in fiction, but the author is clearly borrowing it as a device to create the mother's fictional disease (one hopes it *is* a fictional disease) and thus to drive his quietly narrated story in surrealistic directions. The reader may find the end of the story quite shocking.

Uchida Hyakken (1889–1971) was one of several talented 'disciples' of Natsume Sōseki and a good friend of Sōseki's single most famous disciple, Akutagawa Ryūnosuke. He taught German at college level for many years, was happy in his cups and enjoyed the free life he found as a writer. Many readers still turn to Hyakken for the lively, amusing essays in which he displays his somewhat idiosyncratic view of the world. He wrote a lot, partly as a result of having lived so long, and I count myself an avid reader of the bizarre world he depicted. His many short stories can be reminiscent of Sōseki's *Ten Nights of Dream* (*Yume jūya*, 1908). Instead of the sharp neurotic edge we see in Sōseki's dream world, however, Hyakken presents us with an almost folksy, often humorous banquet of ghosts and goblins. 'Kudan' (*Kudan*, 1922) one of Hyakken's best and most representative stories, is a piece that only he could have created. The title is written with a character that combines the elements for 'human being' and 'cow', displaying in written form the hybrid creature from Japanese mythology at the story's centre. The title alone is enough to give me the creeps.

Disasters, Natural and Man-Made

I'm not sure you can say that Japan has an especially large number of natural disasters, but there have certainly been many destructive earthquakes, volcanic eruptions, tsunamis and typhoons wreaking havoc on the islands since ancient times, and we have always lived with a sense that such natural disasters are close at hand and are something for which we have to brace ourselves. This sense of fear and awe towards nature seems to be part of our genetically inbred mentality. By contrast, we have little experience in our history of the kind of man-made disaster that comes with invasion from abroad – until of course, that is, atomic bombs were dropped on Hiroshima and Nagasaki and a plane bearing General Douglas MacArthur landed at Atsugi Naval Airbase in the summer of 1945. Another overwhelming man-made disaster struck Japan as a by-product of the Tōhoku earthquake of 2011, when the natural disaster led to the meltdown of the Fukushima nuclear power plant. Surely these tragic events have given rise to more than one kind of mental rebooting of us Japanese. As both citizens and writers, we will have to pay close attention to the direction this rebooting may take.

The Great Kantō Earthquake, 1923

A massive earthquake struck the Tokyo-Yokohama area on 1 September 1923, killing over 140,000 people. Here we see one brief record of the experience written by Akutagawa Ryūnosuke. Little more than a fragmentary personal memoir that might have come from a diary entry, 'The Great Earthquake' (*Daijishin*, 1927) gives us the kind of stunning graphic – and at the same time strangely quotidian – detail that could only have been written by someone who was actually there. We see in Akutagawa, too, the posture of the professional writer who wants to leave a record of the gigantic disaster captured from several angles by his practised eye. Among his non-fictional pieces we find this:

> Precisely because it was so huge, this earthquake greatly shook the hearts and minds of us writers as well. Through the earthquake, we experienced intense love and hate and pity and anxiety. Writers always deal with human psychology, but in most cases it is psychology of the most delicate kind. Now there may be added emotions that swing more wildly and trace a bolder line.

From a piece entitled 'The Effect of the Disaster on Literature' (*Shinsai no bungei ni atauru eikyō*, 1923), this reflects what we writers who have lived through more recent disasters in Japan have been feeling deeply.

'The Great Earthquake' was not published until 1927, after Akutagawa's death, as part of his series of sketches entitled 'The Life of a Stupid Man' (*Aru ahō no isshō*), but it is included here as an introduction to the very strange story he published the year after the earthquake, 'General Kim' (*Kin shōgun*, 1924). Until I read 'General Kim' in this collection, I had no idea Akutagawa had ever written such a piece, and no one I know had ever read it. It depicts events surrounding Japan's military invasion of the Korean peninsula in 1592, but what is surprising is that it takes the Korean point of view. The story can be seen as entirely fantastical, but it admits as well of a political reading, giving us an apparent glimpse into Akutagawa's dual nature. Many of the adaptations Akutagawa wrote of classic stories and old tales were better realized than 'General Kim', but this little-known short piece has its own special quality.

The Atomic Bombings, 1945

Ōta Yōko (1903–63) was a Hiroshima native. She had been active in Tokyo since before the war as a writer of the 'women's school', as female writers were pigeonholed in those days. Then she experienced the atomic bombing of the city when she chanced to be at home with her mother and she recorded in painful detail the horrendous scenes she witnessed as they were happening. 'Hiroshima, City of Doom' (*Unmei no machi, Hiroshima*) is a chapter from her novel *City of Corpses* (*Shikabane no machi*, 1948). Her manuscript contained harsh criticisms of the American military, for which the Occupation authorities in Japan initially suppressed the work. The book contains many gruesome descriptions that can be painful to read and were undoubtedly more painful to write, but in this world there are things that can only be recorded for posterity, feelings that can only be conveyed and scenes that can only be described in written form. For those of us who make writing our profession, reading through such a work from beginning to end is both a valuable experience and an opportunity for soul-searching.

At one point in Ōta's book, the author is speaking with a naked boy whose entire body is burnt and festering after he was exposed to the radioactive blast near ground zero. He tells her, 'I may be dying. It could really happen. I'm in such pain,' to which she responds, 'Everybody may be dying, so buck up.' The weirdly humorous logic of such a dialogue could never appear in an ordinary fictional world.

Seirai Yūichi was born in Nagasaki in 1958 and grew up near the location of ground zero. He wrote while working at Nagasaki City Hall, and in 2001 his novella *Holy Water* (*Seisui*) was awarded the Akutagawa Prize, an event that launches the career of many a young writer. In 2010, he became head of the Nagasaki Atomic Bomb Museum. 'Insects' (*Mushi*) was included in the volume *Ground Zero, Nagasaki* (*Bakushin*, 2006). The author was of course born after the war, but his works narrate the fictional memories of people who experienced the atomic bombing of his city. History consists of the communal memories of value to our society that someone must hand down lest they fade into oblivion or get rewritten to suit someone else's agenda. The author here focuses on the desperate struggle between God and man from the point of view of a little insect, his narrator a descendant of pre-modern Japan's hidden Christians. The insect itself sounds 'dopey and amiable' when it asks the wounded protagonist, 'Are you still alive?' in the Nagasaki dialect.

Post-War Japan

Kawabata Yasunari (1899–1972) is one of Japan's most representative writers. He won the Nobel Prize in 1968 and, like Ernest Hemingway, died by his own hand a few years later. 'The Silver Fifty-Sen Pieces' (*Gojussen ginka*, 1946) was included in a collection of his short-shorts called *Palm-of-the-Hand Stories* (*Tenohira no shōsetsu*, 1971). In the transition from pre-war to post-war Japan, practically everything underwent dramatic change. The story focuses on silver fifty-sen pieces to give gentle, quiet and, perhaps we might say, middle-class expression on the page to these many changes. Near the end, it is unobtrusively revealed that the narrator's mother died in the firebombing of Tokyo and that there is 'not a single dog left in the whole burnt-out neighbourhood'. This little piece may be seen as an example of genuine literary art.

Nosaka Akiyuki (1930–2015) made a huge splash in the literary world and beyond with his 1963 novel *The Pornographers* (*Erogotoshitachi*), which graphically and humorously depicts a professional pornographer going about his business. I remember how much I enjoyed the book back then when I was a teenager. Until that point, Nosaka had been nothing more than a weird guy in Blues Brothers-style dark sunglasses contributing frivolous pieces to men's magazines and making outrageous pronouncements in the mass media, but all at once he was recognized as a capable and highly idiosyncratic novelist. Still, it was with the publication in 1967 of two heart-wrenching stories based on his wartime experience that he showed himself at his best: 'Grave of the Fireflies' (*Hotaru no haka*) and 'American Hijiki' (*Amerika hijiki*). Just a boy during the war, Nosaka continued to carry with him the memories of his harrowing wartime experiences and to embrace a kind of nostalgia for a Japan that possessed nothing but the scorched earth with which the bombs had left it. He labelled himself a member of the 'burnt-out ruins school' and continued to excoriate the hypocrisy of post-war Japanese society and the shallowness of its prosperity.

After graduating from college, Hoshino Tomoyuki (b. 1965) wrote for the *Sankei shinbun* newspaper until he left in 1991 to become a full-time novelist. 'Pink' (*Pinku*, 2014) deals with a state of impasse reached by Japan after the war. The two elements of peace and economic prosperity that supported post-war Japan have reached a dead end, and an abnormal weather pattern deals a further blow to the situation. At a loss, the young people try to give rise to a new wave by immersing themselves in a whirling 'tornado dance' movement, and they become trapped into still more violently self-destructive activity. This is a fantasy, of course, but the story contains real elements that cannot be dismissed as mere storytelling. The generation of Nosaka Akiyuki, author of 'American Hijiki', had an archetypal landscape in mind of Japan transformed into a plain of smoking ruins. My own generation had an image of rapid economic growth and idealism in the 1960s. But Hoshino's generation may have no such archetypal image worth writing about. To that extent (perhaps) the dystopian landscape is all the more urgent and vivid.

The Kobe Earthquake, 1995

I – Murakami Haruki, the author of this introduction – was born in 1949 and spent my boyhood in Kobe. When a huge earthquake struck the Kobe area in 1995, killing almost six and a half thousand people, I was living in Cambridge, Massachusetts. The sight of black smoke rising from the city that I saw on *CBS This Morning* filled me with a frustrating sense of my inability to do anything to help from far away. The house of my parents – the house I grew up in – was left leaning at a strange angle.

If there was one thing I could do, it was to write stories about the earthquake once the situation had settled down. Five years later, I published a book of interrelated short stories called *after the quake* (*Kami no kodomotachi wa mina odoru*) in which I decided the stories would (1) not describe the earthquake directly, and (2) not set the action in Kobe, but would (3) describe a number of changes that people had undergone because of the quake. I don't know if these stories served any purpose, but to me at the time this seemed like the best thing I could do. 'UFO in Kushiro' (*UFO ga Kushiro ni oriru*), originally written in 1999, is one of those stories. What kind of effect did the Kobe earthquake have on faraway Hokkaido?

The Tōhoku Earthquake, Tsunami and Nuclear Meltdown, 2011

The last three stories take their material – or background – from the triple disaster that devastated much of north-eastern Japan on 11 March 2011: the gigantic earthquake, the nightmarish tsunami and the 'unforeseeable' meltdown of the Fukushima nuclear power plant, which continues even now, seven years later. What should we novelists learn from this event? What should we take from it? What form should we put it into? A very long time will no doubt be required to find the answers to these questions, a search that will involve both tasks that require great urgency and tasks that require us to settle in for the long haul.

Saeki Kazumi was born in 1959 in the city of Sendai in one of the prefectures hardest hit by the disaster, Miyagi. He started writing fiction while still working as an electrician and made his literary debut in 1984. He takes his material from the real-life events around him and creates his fictional world with a quiet, controlled style all his own. Asbestos he inhaled in the course of his electrical work seriously compromised his health. 'Weather-Watching Hill' (*Hiyoriyama*, 2012) is a documentary account of the disaster. Saeki himself was on the scene when it happened, but rather than narrating it from his own point of view, he lets others recount their experiences, giving form to their individual humanity and lifestyles, and quietly letting them convey their own shock and sadness and their approaches to recovery. We cannot tell how much of the account is fiction and how much fact, but the distinction hardly matters in the face of such a reality.

Matsuda Aoko (b. 1979) was a theatre actor until she made her literary debut in 2010. 'Planting' (*Māgaretto wa ueru*, 2012) appeared in a special issue of the literary journal *Waseda bungaku* entitled *Ruptured Fiction(s) of the Earthquake* (*Shinsai to fikushon no 'kyori'*) and containing fiction about or set against the Tōhoku disaster. This is a surrealistic story. Makiko calls herself Marguerite, disguises herself with glasses and a light brown wig tinged with white, paints wrinkles on her forehead and follows instructions by planting in the garden all the many items sent to her by her employer. This is her job. But the things she has been instructed to plant gradually change from beautiful flowers to ugly things and then dirty things and finally to nothing but fear. One can interpret this allegory in any number of ways, but if we take it to refer to the psychological state induced by the earthquake, then the earthquake itself might become one gigantic, inseparable allegory.

The tale that Satō Yūya (b. 1980) spins out of the earthquake (and the power-plant meltdown it led to), 'Same as Always' (*Ima-made-dōri*, 2012), is another dark allegory. Most people will struggle almost painfully to keep irradiated food and water out of the mouths of their children. Some have gone so far as to leave the contaminated area or even move abroad. For the mother who is the protagonist of this story, however, the situation is the perfect opportunity for her to secretly murder her child. She can hardly believe her good luck, and she blithely goes on feeding radiologically contaminated food to her baby. This is a story that leaves a terrible aftertaste in which dystopia has ceased to be dystopian. Are we shown any way out, whether in real-world or literary terms?

Murakami Haruki

Editorial Note

Most nationally defined literary anthologies are arranged chronologically, perhaps on the assumption that they will be read primarily in college courses, where the anthology is meant to comprise a pocket history of the nation's literature over a predetermined period. This book is designed more for general readers who are looking for a good read when they open the book and don't much care how Japanese literature may have developed in the period covered, which in this case can be loosely termed the modern period. The arrangement is intended to suggest the general tone or subject matter of the story groups, so that someone hoping to be amused will turn to something under the heading 'Modern Life and Other Nonsense' rather than 'Dread' or 'Nature and Memory' or 'Disasters, Natural and Man-Made'.

The last-named group does have a chronological arrangement, however, illustrating how Japanese writers have reacted to some of the worst disasters in the modern period, but it can be read in any order. I can imagine readers who wish to know more about Japan's unique experience of nuclear weapons heading straight for the two stories about the atomic bombings, in which I would call attention to the second story, 'Insects', set in the culturally distinctive city of Nagasaki, which tends to be overshadowed by Hiroshima's position as the first victim of such American ingenuity.

The following list, based on the original form of each piece, is provided for those wishing to read the stories in chronological order:

Kunikida Doppo, 'Unforgettable People' (1898)
Natsume Sōseki, *Sanshirō*, Chapter 1 (1908)
Nagai Kafū, 'Behind the Prison' (1909)
Mori Ōgai, 'The Last Testament of Okitsu Yagoemon' (1912)
Akutagawa Ryūnosuke, 'Hell Screen' (1918)

Uno Kōji, 'Closet LLB' (1918)
Uchida Hyakken, 'Kudan' (1921)
Akutagawa Ryūnosuke, 'General Kim' (1924)
Tanizaki Jun'ichirō, *The Story of Tomoda and Matsunaga* (1926)
Akutagawa Ryūnosuke, 'The Great Earthquake' (1927)
Kawabata Yasunari, 'The Silver Fifty-Sen Pieces' (1946)
Ōta Yōko, 'Hiroshima, City of Doom', chapter from *City of Corpses*
    (1948)
Genji Keita, 'Mr English' (1951)
Enchi Fumiko, 'A Bond for Two Lifetimes – Gleanings' (1957)
Hoshi Shin'ichi, 'Shoulder-Top Secretary' (1961)
Mishima Yukio, 'Patriotism' (1961)
Nosaka Akiyuki, 'American Hijiki' (1967)
Abe Akira, 'Peaches' (1972)
Betsuyaku Minoru, 'Factory Town' (1973)
Ohba Minako, 'The Smile of a Mountain Witch' (1976)
Kōno Taeko, 'In the Box' (1977)
Tsushima Yūko, 'Flames' (1979)
Murakami Haruki, 'The 1963/1982 Girl from Ipanema' (1982)
Nakagami Kenji, 'Remaining Flowers' (1988)
Murakami Haruki, 'UFO in Kushiro' (1999)
Yoshimoto Banana, 'Bee Honey' (2000)
Seirai Yūichi, 'Insects' (2005)
Ogawa Yōko, 'The Tale of the House of Physics' (2010)
Shibata Motoyuki, 'Cambridge Circus' (2010)
Kawakami Mieko, 'Dreams of Love, Etc.' (2011)
Matsuda Aoko, 'Planting' (2011)
Satō Yūya, 'Same as Always' (2012)
Sawanishi Yūten, 'Filling Up with Sugar' (2013)
Hoshino Tomoyuki, 'Pink' (2014)
Saeki Kazumi, 'Weather-Watching Hill' (2014)

All of the above are independent stories except the excerpts from Sōseki, Ōta and the 1927 Akutagawa. Sōseki wrote many short stories, but none that reflects the scale and intensity of his novels. Chapter 1 of his 1908 novel *Sanshirō* comes close to being a self-contained story while suggesting the author's grasp of his time and society. The novel *City of Corpses*, from which 'Hiroshima, City of Doom' is taken, overshadows Ōta's other work and stands as the foremost literary documentation of the bombing of Hiroshima. One segment from an episodic story of Akutagawa's is used here as a preface to his bloodthirsty tale 'General Kim', inspired by the 1923 earthquake.

Tanizaki's novella of 1926, *The Story of Tomoda and Matsunaga*, may seem out of place in a book of short stories, but its hyperbolical alternating condemnation and celebration of both Japanese and Western culture demanded inclusion. Having first encountered it during my study of pre-war literary censorship in 1984, I had hoped to introduce it to the English-speaking world in this collection, but now readers have two means of access to this startling work, as noted in Further Reading.

One potential drawback to compiling a historical anthology of a nation's literature is that the editor is likely to feel obligated to include certain works or writers because of their generally recognized 'importance' in the developmental scheme of things without regard to his/her own personal response to the work. The reader of this collection can be assured that all the works here have been chosen because the editor has been unable to forget them, in some cases for decades, or has found them forming a knot in the solar plexus or inspiring a laugh or a pang of sorrow each time they have come spontaneously to mind over the years.

The poet Alan Shapiro reminds us of Eugenio Montale's phrase 'the second life of poetry' in characterizing the interplay of life and literature.[1] Especially when choosing more nearly contemporary works, I have asked colleagues to send me stories they felt compelled to translate because they have found them reverberating in their own lives. Kunikida Doppo may be seen as the father of the modern Japanese short story, but he is included here primarily because I have found his 'lone figure on the sunlit beach' to be one of my own 'Unforgettable People' since I first encountered it in 1965.

I have many people to thank for their help in the long, fulfilling process of compiling this anthology, many of whom doubled as both advisers and actively involved translators: Paul Warham, Richard Bowring, Geraldine Harcourt, Eve Zimmerman, Michael Emmerich, Noriko Mizuta, Phyllis

Birnbaum, Ted Goossen, Royall Tyler, Hitomi Yoshio, Rachel DiNitto, Richard Minear, Brian Bergstrom, David Boyd and Angus Turvill. I picked many other brains along the way, most notably those of Motoyuki Shibata, Howard Hibbett, Davinder Bhowmik, Ted Mack and Ted Woolsey. Maeda Shōsaku devoted endless hours to comparing the translations with the originals, as he has done since he first wrote to me in 2007. I literally can't thank him enough. Simon Winder made working with Penguin a delight again, Maria Bedford kept some indispensable gears spinning, and Kate Parker made the editorial process more epiphanic than I had hoped it would be. In his thorough, informative introduction, Murakami Haruki has gracefully acceded to his role as elder spokesman for modern Japanese literature. My thanks to him. And thanks to my wife, Rakuko, for always being there.

No anthology can include everything. The reader is referred to Further Reading for some of the excellent collections that are available.

Jay Rubin

Note

1. Alan Shapiro, *In Praise of the Impure* (Evanston, IL: Northwestern University Press, 1993), p. 13.

Further Reading

For Japanese names, spelling and name order are as in the given English publication.

Short Fiction by Individual Authors in this Volume

Japan and the West

Tanizaki Jun'ichirō, *The Gourmet Club: A Sextet*, trans. Anthony H. Chambers and Paul McCarthy (Tokyo: Kodansha International, 2001)

——, *Red Roofs & Other Stories*, trans. Anthony H. Chambers and Paul McCarthy (Ann Arbor, MI: University of Michigan Press, 2016) [containing an earlier translation of *The Story of Tomoda and Matsunaga*]

Junichiro Tanizaki, *Seven Japanese Tales*, trans. Howard Hibbett (New York: Knopf, 1963)

——, *The Secret History of the Lord of Musashi and Arrowroot: Two Novels*, trans. Anthony H. Chambers (New York: Knopf, 1992)

——, *The Reed Cutter and Captain Shigemoto's Mother: Two Novellas*, trans. Anthony H. Chambers (New York: Knopf, 1994)

Nagai Kafū: Edward Seidensticker, *Kafū the Scribbler: The Life and Writings of Nagai Kafū* (Stanford, CA: Stanford University Press, 1965) [containing Seidensticker's translation of a number of Kafū's short stories and novellas]

Natsume Sōseki, *The Tower of London*, trans. Damian Flanagan (London: Peter Owen, 2005)

——, *Sanshirō* [novel excerpted here], trans. Jay Rubin (London: Penguin, 2009)

Further Reading

———: Marvin Marcus, *Reflections in a Glass Door: Memory and Melancholy in the Personal Writings of Natsume Sōseki* (Honolulu: University of Hawai'i Press, 2009) [containing translations of Sōseki's semi-fictional short pieces]

Sōseki Natsume, *Ten Nights of Dream, Hearing Things, The Heredity of Taste*, trans. Aiko Itō and Graeme Wilson (Rutland, VT: Tuttle, 1974)

Loyal Warriors

Mori Ōgai, *The Incident at Sakai and Other Stories*, ed. David Dilworth and J. Thomas Rimer (Honolulu: University of Hawai'i Press, 1977)

———, *Youth and Other Stories*, ed. J. Thomas Rimer (Honolulu: University of Hawai'i Press, 1994)

———, *Not a Song Like Any Other: An Anthology of Writings by Mori Ōgai*, ed. J. Thomas Rimer (Honolulu: University of Hawai'i Press, 2004)

Yukio Mishima, *Death in Midsummer and Other Stories*, trans. Geoffrey W. Sargent, Donald Keene, et al. (New York: New Directions, 1966)

———, *Acts of Worship*, trans. John Bester (Tokyo: Kodansha International, 1989)

Men and Women

Yuko Tsushima, *The Shooting Gallery and Other Stories*, trans. Geraldine Harcourt (New York: New Directions, 1997)

———, *Territory of Light*, trans. Geraldine Harcourt (London: Penguin, 2018)

Kōno Taeko, *Toddler-Hunting and Other Stories*, trans. Lucy North (New York: New Directions, 1996)

Kenji Nakagami, *Snakelust*, trans. Andrew Rankin (Tokyo: Kodansha International, 1998)ww

———, *The Cape and Other Stories from the Japanese Ghetto*, trans. Eve Zimmerman (Berkeley, CA: Stone Bridge Press, 1999)

Banana Yoshimoto, *Lizard*, trans. Ann Sherif (New York: Grove Press, 1995)

Enchi Fumiko: *Rabbits, Crabs, Etc.: Stories by Japanese Women*, trans. Phyllis Birnbaum (Honolulu: University of Hawai'i Press, 1982)

Nature and Memory

Yoko Ogawa, *Revenge: Eleven Dark Tales*, trans. Stephen Snyder (New York: Picador, 2013)

Kunikida Doppo, 'Five Stories by Kunikida Doppo', trans. Jay Rubin, *Monumenta Nipponica*, vol. 27, no. 3 (Autumn 1972), pp. 273–341

——, *River Mist and Other Stories by Kunikida Doppo*, trans. David G. Chibbett (Tokyo: Kodansha International, 1982)

Haruki Murakami, *The Elephant Vanishes*, trans. Alfred Birnbaum and Jay Rubin (New York: Knopf, 1993)

——, *after the quake: stories*, trans. Jay Rubin (New York: Knopf, 2002)

——, *Blind Willow, Sleeping Woman*, trans. Philip Gabriel and Jay Rubin (New York: Knopf, 2006)

——, *Men without Women*, trans. Philip Gabriel and Ted Goossen (New York: Knopf, 2017)

Modern Life and Other Nonsense

Uno Kōji, *Love of Mountains: Two Stories*, trans. Elaine Tashiro Gerbert (Honolulu: University of Hawai'i Press, 1997)

Keita Genji, *The Lucky One and Other Humorous Stories*, trans. Hugh Cortazzi (Tokyo: Japan Times, 1980)

Hoshi Shin'ichi, *The Spiteful Planet and Other Stories*, trans. Bernard Susser and Tomoyoshi Genkawa (Tokyo: Japan Times, 1978)

Dread

Ryūnosuke Akutagawa, *Rashōmon and Seventeen Other Stories*, trans. Jay Rubin (London: Penguin, 2006) [containing an extensive Akutagawa bibliography]

——, *Mandarins*, trans. Charles De Wolf (Brooklyn, NY: Archipelago Books, 2007)

Uchida Hyakken, *Realm of the Dead*, trans. Rachel DiNitto (Normal, IL, and London: Dalkey Archive Press, 2006)

Disasters, Natural and Man-Made

Akutagawa Ryūnosuke: See under 'Dread' above

Ōta Yōko: *Hiroshima: Three Witnesses*, trans. Richard H. Minear (Princeton, NJ: Princeton University Press, 1990) [including Ōta's novel, *City of Corpses*, excerpted here]

Seirai Yūichi, *Ground Zero, Nagasaki*, trans. Paul Warham (New York: Columbia University Press, 2015)

Yasunari Kawabata, *House of the Sleeping Beauties and Other Stories*, trans. Edward G. Seidensticker (Tokyo: Kodansha International, 1969)

——, *Palm-of-the-Hand Stories*, trans. Lane Dunlop and J. Martin Holman (San Francisco: North Point Press, 1988)

——, *The Dancing Girl of Izu and Other Stories*, trans. J. Martin Holman (Washington, DC: Counterpoint, 1997)

——, *First Snow on Fuji*, trans. Michael Emmerich (Washington, DC: Counterpoint, 1999)

Murakami Haruki: See under 'Nature and Memory' above

Short Fiction by Other Writers

The titles here are listed alphabetically by the author's surname.

Dazai Osamu: Phyllis Lyons, *The Saga of Dazai Osamu: A Critical Study with Translations* (Stanford, CA: Stanford University Press, 1985)

Osamu Dazai, *Crackling Mountain and Other Stories*, trans. James O'Brien (Rutland, VT: Tuttle, 1989)

——, *Self Portraits: Stories*, trans. Ralph F. McCarthy (Tokyo: Kodansha International, 1991)

Edogawa Ranpo, *Japanese Tales of Mystery and Imagination*, trans. James B. Harris (Rutland, VT: Tuttle, 1956)

Yoshikichi Furui, *Ravine and Other Stories*, trans. Meredith McKinney (Berkeley, CA: Stone Bridge Press, 1997)

Izumi Kyōka, *Japanese Gothic Tales*, trans. Charles Shirō Inouye (Honolulu: University of Hawai'i Press, 1996)

——, *In Light of Shadows: More Gothic Tales by Izumi Kyōka*, trans. Charles Shirō Inouye (Honolulu: University of Hawai'i Press, 2005)

Kurahashi Yumiko, *The Woman with the Flying Head and Other Stories*, trans. Atsuko Sakaki (Armonk, NY: M. E. Sharpe, 1998)

Kenzaburō Ōe, *Teach Us to Outgrow Our Madness*, trans. John Nathan (New York: Grove Press, 1977)

Yokomitsu Riichi, *Love and Other Stories of Yokomitsu Riichi*, trans. Dennis Keene (Tokyo: University of Tokyo Press, 1974)

Anthologies

The titles here are listed chronologically.

Modern Japanese Literature, ed. Donald Keene (New York: Grove Press, 1956)

The Heart is Alone: A Selection of 20th Century Japanese Short Stories, ed. Richard N. McKinnon (Tokyo: Hokuseido Press, 1957)

Modern Japanese Stories, ed. Japan Quarterly Editorial Board (Tokyo: Japan Publications Trading Company, 1961)

Modern Japanese Stories: An Anthology, ed. Ivan Morris (Rutland, VT: Tuttle, 1962)

The Shadow of Sunrise: Selected Stories of Japan and the War, ed. Shōichi Saeki (Tokyo: Kodansha International, 1966)

Contemporary Japanese Literature: An Anthology of Fiction, Film, and Other Writing Since 1945, ed. Howard Hibbett (New York: Knopf, 1977)

Rabbits, Crabs, Etc.: Stories by Japanese Women, trans. Phyllis Birnbaum (Honolulu: University of Hawai'i Press, 1982)

This Kind of Woman: Ten Stories by Japanese Women Writers, 1960–1976, ed. Yukiko Tanaka and Elizabeth Hanson (Stanford, CA: Stanford University Press, 1982)

The Shōwa Anthology: Modern Japanese Stories: 1929–1984, ed. Van C. Gessel and Tomone Matsumoto (Tokyo: Kodansha International, 1985)

The Atomic Bomb: Voices from Hiroshima and Nagasaki, ed. Kyoko and Mark Selden (Armonk, NY: M. E. Sharpe, 1989)

Japanese Women Writers, ed. Noriko Mizuta Lippit and Kyoko Iriye Selden (Armonk, NY: M. E. Sharpe, 1991)

Monkey Brain Sushi: New Tastes in Japanese Fiction, ed. Alfred Birnbaum (Tokyo: Kodansha International, 1991)

New Japanese Voices: The Best Contemporary Fiction from Japan, ed. Helen Mitsios (New York: Atlantic Monthly Press, 1991)

The Oxford Book of Japanese Short Stories, ed. Theodore W. Goossen (Oxford: Oxford University Press, 1997)

Tokyo Stories: A Literary Stroll, ed. Lawrence Rogers (Berkeley, CA: University of California Press, 2002)

The Columbia Anthology of Modern Japanese Literature, vol. 1: *From Restoration to Occupation 1868–1945* and vol. 2: *From 1945 to the Present*, ed. J. Thomas Rimer and Van C. Gessel (New York: Columbia University Press, 2005 and 2007)

Digital Geishas and Talking Frogs: The Best 21st Century Short Stories from Japan, ed. Helen Mitsios (Boston: Cheng & Tsui Company, 2011)

More Stories by Japanese Women Writers, ed. Kyoko Selden and Noriko Mizuta (Armonk, NY: M. E. Sharpe, 2011)

March Was Made of Yarn: Reflections on the Japanese Earthquake, Tsunami, and Nuclear Meltdown, ed. Elmer Luke and David Karashima (New York: Vintage Books, 2012)

Ruptured Fiction(s) of the Earthquake, ed. Makoto Ichikawa, David Karashima et al. (Tokyo: Waseda Bungaku kai, 2012)

Islands of Protest: Japanese Literature from Okinawa, ed. Davinder L. Bhowmik and Steve Rabson (Honolulu: University of Hawai'i Press, 2016)

A Tokyo Anthology: Literature from Japan's Modern Metropolis, 1850–1920, ed. Sumie Jones and Charles Shirō Inouye (Honolulu: University of Hawai'i Press, 2017)

Periodicals

Descant, no. 89 (Summer 1992)

Granta, no. 127 (Spring 2014)

Monkey Business: New Writing from Japan [any edition]

Review of Contemporary Fiction: New Japanese Fiction, vol. 22, no. 2 (Summer 2002)

Note on Japanese Name Order and Pronunciation

Unless otherwise indicated, all Japanese names that appear from the Contents onwards are written in the Japanese order, surname first. The writer of the Introduction is known in Japan as Murakami Haruki. His name has been given in the Western order on the cover and title page because of its greater familiarity in the West. Following Japanese practice, the four writers in this volume with traditional literary sobriquets – Doppo, Sōseki, Kafū and Ōgai – are referred to by those rather than by their surnames.

Below are some guidelines for pronouncing Japanese names and terms.

Every *a* is long, as in 'father', *e* is pronounced as in 'bed' and *i* sounds like 'ee'. Three-syllable names tend to have a stress on the first syllable. Thus 'Natsume' is pronounced 'NAH-tsoo-meh', 'Taeko' is 'TAH-eh-ko' and 'Aoko' is 'AH-o-ko'. Two-syllable names are evenly stressed, hence 'Uno' is pronounced 'oo-no'.

Macrons have been included to indicate long syllables but have been eliminated from the place names Tōkyō, Kyōto, Ōsaka, Kōbe and Kyūshū, and from familiar words such as 'shōji' and 'Shintō'. Following the practice in past English publications, Ohba Minako's surname is spelled 'Ohba' rather than 'Ōba', whereas the long *o* appears with the standard macron in 'Ōgai' and 'Ōta'.

Apostrophes have been used to indicate syllable breaks in the names 'Jun'ichirō' (rather than 'Ju-ni-chi-rō') and 'Shin'ichi' (rather than 'Shi-ni-chi').

JAPAN AND THE WEST

TANIZAKI JUN'ICHIRŌ

The Story of Tomoda and Matsunaga

Translated by Paul Warham

I

Five or six years ago, on 25 August 1920 to be precise, I received a letter from the old province of Yamato, from a woman I had never met by the name of Shigeko. I am able to specify the date here because, even after all these years, I still have the letter in my possession. I don't normally bother to read the many letters that arrive on my doorstep from people I don't know, most of them from bookish young men and women desperate to share their love of literature. When I'm busy I simply bundle them up and leave them to languish unread in a corner of my study, but something about this letter filled me with a strange urge to open it right away. It had been addressed not in pen but with an ink brush, and the sender's name and address were in a hand that had about it an unmistakable air of old-fashioned elegance and grace: *Mrs Matsunaga Gisuke, Yagyū Village, Soekami District, Yamato Province.* One look at the envelope was enough to assure me that it contained something more than yet another letter from a young woman with literary aspirations.

The letter is a long one, but I will not let that prevent me from quoting it here in its entirety. Its contents go to the very heart of the story I have to tell.

Dear Sir,

I hope this finds you in good health despite the oppressive heat. Allow me to introduce myself. I am the wife of Matsunaga Gisuke, a resident of the village of Yagyū in the province of Yamato. I have never had the pleasure of making your acquaintance, and I realize that it must seem the height of bad manners for me to be troubling you with an unsolicited letter in

3

this way. I hope you will be kind enough to bear with me as I attempt to describe the curious sequence of events that has led me to write to you now.

I married into the Matsunaga family in 1905, when my husband was twenty-five and I was eighteen. As the eldest son, my husband had been away in Tokyo for several years before we were married, and had recently graduated from Waseda University. His family has farmed the land in this village for many generations, and even after our marriage he did not have any particular work to occupy him. For the first six months or so we lived a happy and peaceful life together. In the winter of that year, however, my husband's elderly mother passed away, and his behaviour began to change in a quite distressing manner. He took to bemoaning the fate that had left him to grow old here in the countryside. He left home whenever he could, travelling to Kyoto and Osaka at every opportunity in an attempt to lift himself out of his depression. Things continued in this way until the summer of 1906, when I was expecting our first child. Quite suddenly, he announced with an air of unshakeable resolve that he was leaving to go abroad, and that he planned to spend a year or two travelling in the West. Of course, I was appalled; the whole family was. We did everything we could to remonstrate with him, and opposed his idea in the strongest terms. But alas, our efforts were in vain. Nothing we said had the slightest effect on his determination to leave.

I heard from my husband not once in all the time he was away. None of us heard from him for more than three years. I was struggling to bring up our daughter on my own, wondering what on earth had become of him, when he returned in the autumn of 1909 just as suddenly as he had left. Although he has never been seriously ill, my husband has always been of a somewhat weak constitution. His appearance now suggested that his time overseas had seriously impaired his health. He was pale and sickly, and suffered a severe nervous breakdown not long after he came home. For the next few years, until the end of spring in 1912, he lived a quiet life here with us in the country. He showed great tenderness to me and doted on Taeko, our daughter. Little by little, his health began to mend and his nervous condition improved. But then it happened again, in the summer of 1912. Once again, he gave no explanation as to why he had to leave, and refused to tell me where he was going. All he would say was that he would be back again in two or three years and that there was no need to worry about him while he was gone. Whatever happened, he said, I should make no attempt to trace him. Even if I did, he said, I would never find him. And so he left again, asking me to look after the house in his absence and to take care of our daughter while he was away. I could do nothing but follow his instructions and wait for his return.

As on the previous occasion, he came home during the fourth year[1] after his departure, in the autumn of 1915. Once again, he came back looking ashen and drawn, and exhibiting the symptoms of a serious nervous condition. He apologized for having stayed away so long and for all the pain and worry he had caused me. He became emotional and prone to tears, and displayed an uncommon devotion to his wife and child. Gentleness and compassion marked everything he did, and he began to show signs of a new interest in religious matters. In the spring of 1917, the three of us – myself, my husband and Taeko, by this time twelve years old – made a pilgrimage to the thirty-three Kannon temples.[2] Perhaps as a consequence of his new-found piety, my husband seemed to regain much of his strength soon after.

He settled back into his quiet life in the country, and seemed much more at ease. I began to allow myself to contemplate our future with happiness, and to hope that everything might work out for us after all. But when the summer of 1918 arrived, he left again, setting off for parts unknown and giving no explanation beyond the same few words with which he had left us before. It was nearly four years since he had returned in the autumn of 1915. Another three years have passed since then. Next year will be the fourth since he left home, and I am consoled by the expectation that we shall see him home again before the year is out. All I can do is wait and hope. I have no way of knowing where he is or what he is doing.

I consider myself blessed to have married my husband, undeserving as I am. Together with our two daughters (our second child turns two this year), I continue to wait patiently. I certainly would not wish to suggest that he leaves home because he has grown tired of his wife. He has his reasons, I am sure: commitments and circumstances of which I know nothing. When he is at home he is always gentle and considerate. Even when he has had to leave home, he has always done so with tears in his eyes, begging me to wait for his return. I do not want to give the impression that I resent my husband's behaviour. In normal circumstances, I should be content to live with things as they are for as long as necessary.

Unfortunately, however, our elder daughter, Taeko, has been suffering from pleurisy since the winter of last year. Recently, her condition has become serious, and I cannot escape the thought that each day might be her last. It breaks my heart to hear her feverish little voice begging day after day for a glimpse of her father. I am at my wits' end.

The family attempted to trace my husband the last time he left home, but to no avail. We have been no more successful this time. Suspecting as before that he might have gone abroad, we made enquiries overseas as well as throughout Japan, but we found no clue to his whereabouts, and heard nothing to suggest that anyone matching his description had been seen in Tokyo, Kyoto or Osaka. When I remember what my husband said before he left – that we would never find him, no matter how hard we tried – I must confess that the whole affair strikes me as somewhat strange.

My husband was carrying very little luggage the last time he came home. Apart from his clothes, he had just one small travel bag with him. He took the same bag with him when he set out again nearly four years later. He guarded it zealously, of course, while he was with us in the country, and was adamant that no one else should touch it. I had no intention of prying into my husband's private affairs, but his inexplicable conduct had stirred a curiosity in me that I was powerless to resist. I knew even as I did it that I was committing an unforgivable breach of trust, but I could not help myself, and I did allow myself, just once, to take a peek inside. I found a gold signet ring with an amethyst setting, a seal inscribed with the name Tomoda, and a postcard, along with several dozen really rather lewd photographs of foreign women in a variety of poses. These I assume he must have collected as a souvenir of his travels in the West. The postcard was addressed to a Mr Tomoda Ginzō, care of the Café Liberté, Ginza Owari 3-chome, Kyōbashi, Tokyo. The only other name on the postcard was yours, in the space set aside for 'sender's name'. I remember that the card was written in pen, in a flowing hand, and was dated 7 May 1913. It read along the following lines: 'Sorry about the other night. How did things turn out regarding the matter we discussed? Looking forward to your reply.' Your name is familiar to me, of course, from magazines and newspapers, but Tomoda Ginzō was a name I had never seen or heard before. I have no idea why my husband should have had Mr Tomoda's postcard and seal in his possession, or why he was carrying with him a ring that must surely have belonged to someone else, as it was clearly much too large for his own finger. The more I consider the facts, the stranger they seem.

Please forgive me for having written at such length. Is it possible that you might be acquainted with my husband, Matsunaga Gisuke? The postcard I found in his possession made me wonder if Tomoda Ginzō might be an alias he was using for some reason. Such are the circumstances that have prompted me to write to you now. I hope you will make allowances for my confused state of mind. As I have said, I am not interested in hunting my husband down. If you do happen to know him, however, please let him know that I have been in touch and inform him of our daughter's illness. I am sure he would prefer to hear the news this way rather than directly from me. If you are not acquainted with anybody by the name of Matsunaga Gisuke, perhaps you do know a Mr Tomoda? If so, perhaps you would be kind enough to tell me what you know about him and how I might get in touch with him. I hope you will forgive me for making such selfish demands on your time with regard to a matter which is surely no concern of yours. I am afraid I can think of no alternative but to rely upon your kindness and beg you to take sympathy on my predicament.

I am enclosing a photograph of my husband, in case you might recognize him. It is a picture of the three of us, taken during our pilgrimage to the thirty-three Kannon. My husband normally hates to be photographed, but on this occasion he agreed to have a picture made as a souvenir of our trip. He was thirty-seven at the time, and turns forty this year.

I should be grateful if you were able keep the contents of this letter to yourself, but I understand that circumstances might make that difficult. Please feel free to proceed however you see fit. I do hope you will let me know if you have any information at all that might help.

Respectfully yours,
Matsunaga Shigeko

The letter had been posted on 23 August and reached Tokyo two days later, when it was delivered to my house in Aoyama on the morning of the twenty-fifth.

I tend to sleep late and I was still in bed when the post arrived. The letter unfurled across my pillows as I read. I need hardly say that its contents piqued my curiosity. But I was struck by Shigeko too. Here, I felt, was a woman who possessed a refinement that is all too rare these days. As I have said, her letter was written in an elegant and feminine hand, inscribed neatly on to a scroll of paper that was several feet long when unrolled to its full length. Her husband's family, she wrote, had been farmers for generations, but this was clearly a well-established country family of some pedigree, and Shigeko herself obviously came from quite a cultivated background as well. She couldn't have written an elegant letter like this otherwise. I rewound the scroll and sat back to read the letter for a second – and then a third – time.

And then there was the photograph she had enclosed, of the two parents and their young child. I picked it up and took a closer look. It was a postcard-sized picture, a full-length shot that showed them dressed for pilgrimage, sedge hats in hand, the daughter between her parents. Their faces had come out looking very small, and it was hard to get more than a vague impression of their appearance, but Matsunaga Gisuke – Shigeko's husband – looked much older than the letter had led me to expect. 'He was thirty-seven at the time,' she had written, but he looked to be in his early forties at least. He was a thin, gangly man with angular features and sunken, unhealthy-looking cheeks. It was not a pleasant face to look at. There was a glimmer of sharpness in his eyes, perhaps, but nothing to give the impression that this was an educated man who had been to university and then spent time in the West. To look at him, you would never have imagined he was anything but an ordinary country bumpkin. I didn't need to dredge up old memories. One look was enough to assure me that I had never met the man.

The name meant nothing to me either. I did know a Tomoda Ginzō; that much was true. But the Tomoda I knew looked nothing like the man in the photograph. It was inconceivable that they were the same person.

Standing next to her husband was Shigeko herself, with a serene expression on her face and a quiet air of grace and dignity about her. Her photograph did nothing to spoil the impression I had formed of her from her letter – even if she was not exactly what you'd call a beauty. The picture was the work of a provincial photographer, and the old-fashioned way the picture had been touched up made her look somewhat lifeless and doll-like. Still, there was something about her. Perhaps it was just my imagination, but I thought I could detect real intelligence in that oval face of hers – in her small, tight-lipped mouth and clear, gentle eyes. The pilgrim's clothes she was wearing heightened the effect. She looked like the kind of pilgrim you might expect to see on the stage – the picture of feminine elegance and refinement. Taeko, the daughter, seemed a sweet enough little thing, but she really had come out looking like a doll and it was impossible to say which parent she resembled most.

The letter and the photograph in front of me, I considered the details of the case. Naturally it struck me as odd that a man I had never met should be carrying a postcard from me inside his travel bag. But that was not all. Shigeko had no way of knowing this, but the truth was that the postcard wasn't the only thing in the bag I had seen before. I was also familiar with the amethyst ring and the pictures of European women. In fact, unless I was much mistaken, everything in the bag – the ring, the photographs of the women in 'lewd' poses, and the seal – all of it belonged to the man I knew as Tomoda Ginzō. Tomoda had been wearing an amethyst ring for as long as I had known him – more than ten years now. Indeed, I had seen him just a few days earlier, and I felt sure I had seen the ring then too, its stone glinting away as always on the ring finger of his left hand. And his fondness for taking photographs of foreign women was well known. He had a huge collection of them, which I had seen myself several times.

All the evidence suggested that even if I had no personal connection with Matsunaga myself, a connection of one kind or another must exist between him and Tomoda. I decided to ask him about it the next time we met. No doubt he could help clear things up.

Now that I came to think about it, it occurred to me that I knew remarkably little about Tomoda. We had been friends for years, but I didn't know what line of business he was in or even where he lived. When we met, it was often by chance. I couldn't recall that either of us had ever visited the other at home. I couldn't even say for certain whether he was married or single. I suppose it may seem strange for two men to be friends for more than ten years and still know so little about each other, but in fact the phenomenon is far from uncommon among drinking companions who hardly meet at all except to go carousing together. My relationship with Tomoda existed on precisely this level.

I couldn't think that I had ever had occasion to write to him about anything of substance, but I was prepared to believe that we had exchanged brief messages by postcard from time to time. The card Shigeko had found inside her husband's bag must have been from me. It was a long time ago now and I couldn't be absolutely certain of the details, but I seemed to remember that the Café Liberté had been a favourite haunt of ours around that time. It was rare for more than a couple of days to pass without my seeing Tomoda there at least once. It made sense that I should have sent messages there when I needed to get in touch with him; after all, I didn't know where he lived.

As for the 'other night' I had mentioned in the postcard – it was impossible for me to say for sure after so much time what this was an allusion to, but it was probably something pretty unsavoury. Most likely I had been referring to arrangements we had made to go out womanizing together or something along those lines. In those days Tomoda knew a place up in the Yamate district of the Yokohama Bluff called Number 10, where white girls were available, and from time to time a select number of Tomoda's drinking companions – me included – were allowed to accompany him there.

The establishment operated inside a somewhat forbidding-looking European-style building that bore a certain resemblance to a nobleman's mansion, and it was not easy for Japanese customers to get inside. But Tomoda was a regular, and with him there to vouch for us the doors to this wonderland were opened wide. Naturally this filled the rest of us with admiration – among the pleasure-seeking crowd who gathered at the Café Liberté, Tomoda was considered an extremely useful person to know. He would send word to tip us off whenever an interesting new girl arrived. I must just have received one of these messages when I sent this postcard. I must have arranged to accompany him to Number 10 and was writing to make sure he was still free to go as planned. It is hard to think that I would have written to him about anything else.

I was soon on intimate terms with the girls at Number 10, and before long I took to going there alone. Even so, I was almost certain to find Tomoda there whenever I went. The establishment was run on an impressive scale, inside a spacious European-style residence with a huge number of rooms.

The girls came and went, but seven or eight of them were generally there at any given time. The house was run along the same lines as most other bordellos staffed by white girls: a dance floor and bar on the ground floor, and the girls' rooms upstairs. Customers would typically spend some time dancing with a girl or getting to know her over a drink downstairs first. Often when I was sitting with a drink Tomoda's voice would boom out behind me. 'Well, well, well! Look who's here,' I'd hear him say, chortling as he came up behind me and slapped me on the back.

Occasionally, I arrived to find no sign of him. 'Is Mr Tomoda not here this evening?' I'd ask.

'He could be upstairs,' someone would reply, and then – right on cue – in he would waddle like some sumo wrestler, his flabby bulk swaggering down the staircase.

Tomoda was enormously popular with the girls, which may have had something to do with the way he liked to throw his money around. He was stout, almost corpulent, and must have weighed at least 165 pounds. He spoke fluent English and French, and was blessed with natural wit and charm. His every movement and expression showed him to be a sophisticated man of the world. In those days he was the only Japanese customer who could outdo the foreign clients of the establishment. I never heard any of the girls address him as 'Mr Tomoda' – at Number 10, he was just plain 'Tom'.

'You act as if you own the place,' I ribbed him once.

'Well, maybe I do,' he replied matter-of-factly, raising his champagne glass and surveying the clutch of women around him with a glow of self-satisfaction.

I said earlier that I didn't know what Tomoda did for a living, but I remember now an odd rumour that began to circulate around this time, prompted by the remarkable amount of time that Tomoda spent at Number 10 and the air of confidence he exuded whenever he was there. The story was that Tomoda, despite pretending that he was just another customer, might in fact be the owner – that he had secretly put up the capital for the place and was now running the whole operation. I don't remember who started the rumour, but once the suggestion had been made, I couldn't help thinking that it sounded plausible enough.

As far as I knew, there was nothing to prove the rumours wrong. On the contrary – there was plenty of evidence to support them. What about all those photographs, for example? All of them featured girls who worked at Number 10, or who had worked there in the past. How had he managed to collect so many of them? Tomoda's explanation was that he took each girl aside as soon as she arrived and talked her into it in the privacy of one of the rooms upstairs. But it was hard to believe that he would have been able to get away with this game of his – if, indeed, a game is all it was – without some special connection to the place, no matter how much money he spent and how much the girls seemed to like him. Maybe he really was the owner – perhaps he was admitting as much by showing me his photographs. Perhaps with me at least he was making no attempt to keep it a secret. Hadn't he told me once: 'You know, the next time you need to get in touch, you'd be better sending a card to Number 10. It'll reach me quicker that way.' And so at some stage I had started to think of him as Number 10's owner, or at least its main investor.

But perhaps at this point I ought to go back over the chronology. The postcard Shigeko had found in her husband's bag, addressed to Tomoda care of the Café Liberté, was postmarked 7 May 1913. This dated it to a time during the first few years of the Taishō era when Tomoda's favourite haunts were the Café Liberté in Tokyo and Number 10 in Yokohama. By the time Shigeko's letter to me arrived in August 1920, however, both the Café Liberté and Number 10 had long since shut down.

Not that I had lost track of Tomoda; he was merely operating from a different set of headquarters. In Tokyo: the Café Plaisantin, in the Ginza; in Yokohama: Yamate Number 27, on the Bluff. It probably goes without saying that the Plaisantin was a café much like the Liberté, and that Number 27 was a brothel very similar to Number 10, staffed once again by white girls.

The whole of the Yokohama Bluff was reduced to rubble in the Great Kantō Earthquake of 1923, and not a trace of the house remains today. In those days it was seven or eight blocks up from the Gaiety Theatre, a few streets in on the right as you walked in the direction of Honmoku. The foreign settlement was an area of lush greenery, quiet even during the daytime; the whole district had a foreign and exotic air about it. Number 27 lay on an especially secluded street, hidden behind almost wild, over-grown trees that shielded it from the prying eyes of passers-by. The house had been built around the time the port of Yokohama was opened to foreign trade in the 1860s. Before it became a house of assignation it had no doubt served as the home of some prominent foreigner.

In layout and scale, it was very similar to Number 10. It was quite luxu-riously decorated inside, but from the outside the size and age of the building combined with its desolate surroundings to give the place an eerie air. In fact, it looked a little haunted. The girls were all fresh-faced new arrivals – there were no survivors from Number 10. Almost the only constant from those days, in fact, was Tomoda himself. To my eyes at least, he showed every sign of having a special connection to the place. Once again, he had amassed a collection of photographs, this time featuring the girls from Number 27.

But something struck me as strange now that I thought about it. When had he moved from one place to the other? Suddenly, the link between the two eras was no longer clear in my mind. I could have sworn that I had been seeing Tomoda more or less regularly the whole time, but now that I tried to trace my memories back, I realized there was a period when we had lost touch for two or three years; perhaps three or four. Number 10 had closed down in 1915 or 1916 – of that much I was fairly certain. But by then Tomoda had already been missing for some time. It must have been around October 1915 that I heard the girls asking after him. 'What's happened to Tom? He never comes to see us any more.' He stopped coming to the Liberté around then. Time passed, and the Café Liberté shut down too. A year or so later the Café Plaisantin opened a few blocks over towards Shinbashi.

It was there that I bumped into Tomoda again one night at the end of 1918 or in January 1919. Some time that winter, anyway. I remember an icy wind whistling through the bare branches of the trees. And then – the more I think about it, the more the memories come back – I remember making some remark to him that night at the Plaisantin about how dull things had been in Yokohama since Number 10 closed down.

Tomoda grinned. 'I thought you novelists were supposed to be observant,' he said. 'There's a new place open in Yokohama now. Just like the old Number 10.' And that very same night – or was it a little later? – he took me to Number 27 for the first time.

But the reader has perhaps already been struck by the same suspicions that began to occur to me once I had thought things through this far. Namely, that the relationship between Tomoda and Matsunaga went far deeper than I had at first assumed.

According to the letter, Shigeko's husband had returned home for the second time in the autumn of 1915. He had remained in the country till the summer of 1918, when he left home again. And for precisely this period – between the autumn of 1915 and the summer of 1918 – I had no recollection of having seen Tomoda once. The whole thing started to seem very strange indeed.

I tried to think back to the first time I met him. It must have been around 1908 or 1909. I forget now who it was that introduced us. Perhaps we weren't introduced at all, and just fell into conversation one night when we were both drunk. The details escape me, but I'm pretty sure that our first meeting took place at the Café Kōnosu, which in those days was located in Koamichō in Nihonbashi. Again, though, it was no longer clear to me when we had moved from the Kōnosu to the Café Liberté. As I remember it, Tomoda had simply stopped coming to the Kōnosu at some stage, only to reappear just as suddenly at the Café Liberté a few years later. After so many years, I couldn't say for sure exactly how long Tomoda had been missing. But Shigeko's husband had returned home in the autumn of 1909 and left again at the beginning of the summer of 1912. The chronology was remarkably similar. A table of the two men's movements would look something like this:

Period One   *Summer 1906–Autumn 1909*
    Matsunaga Gisuke travelling in the West
    Tomoda Ginzō appears for the first time in the Café Kōnosu
    towards the end of this period

Period Two   *Autumn 1909–Spring 1912*
    Matsunaga Gisuke at home in the country
    Tomoda Ginzō whereabouts unknown

Period Three   *Summer 1912–Autumn 1915*
    Matsunaga Gisuke whereabouts unknown
    Tomoda Ginzō active at the Café Liberté and Number 10

Period Four   *Autumn 1915–Summer 1918*
    Matsunaga Gisuke at home in the country
    Tomoda Ginzō whereabouts unknown

Period Five   *Summer 1918–Present (1920)*
    Matsunaga Gisuke whereabouts unknown
    Tomoda Ginzō active at the Café Plaisantin and Number 27

For Periods One and Two, my memories of Tomoda Ginzō's movements were far from clear. But unless I was seriously mistaken, it seemed safe to assume that the same four-year cycle had been in operation all the way from 1909 to the present. Whenever Matsunaga was at home in the country, Tomoda's whereabouts were unknown. And during the periods when Tomoda was active in the Tokyo-Yokohama area, Matsunaga was nowhere to be found.

I lay in bed pondering the strange details of the case. I felt compelled to consider matters further. I drew up a mental chronology similar to the one I have just sketched out above and went over it carefully. I picked up Shigeko's letter and read it over again several times. Everything seemed to point to the same conclusion. I could no longer be sure that Tomoda and Matsunaga were not the same person. I placed the photograph of the family in pilgrims' clothes on my pillow and peered at it again.

'Tomoda Ginzō might be an alias he was using,' she had written. Shigeko herself, then, clearly had her suspicions. But the impression I got from the old-fashioned retouched photograph she had enclosed was that Matsunaga bore no resemblance to Tomoda at all either in face or build.

Of course, it is not true that the camera never lies. People often look quite different in photographs, and pilgrimage clothes in particular might make a person's whole character appear quite different too, I suppose. But there was simply no way that someone as chubby as Tomoda could be made to look as thin as the man in this photograph. Tomoda was practically obese. Matsunaga, according to this photograph, was tall and slim. Tomoda's face was so round he looked as if his cheeks were about to burst. Matsunaga had sunken cheeks and a sharp, triangular face. They were a study in opposites: one of them jovial, the other gloomy. A person might put on weight and lose it again any number of times over the course of a lifetime, but Tomoda's appearance hadn't changed a bit in all the years since I first met him at the Kōnosu. And what about Matsunaga? What was it that Shigeko had said about her husband? 'Although he has never been seriously ill, my husband has always had a weak constitution.' Or the ring that was 'clearly much too large for his own finger'. These remarks made it clear that Matsunaga had been as thin as he was in the photograph for many years. She had also written that the family had made fruitless enquiries overseas as well as throughout Japan both times he had disappeared, whereas Tomoda lived at the centre of Ginza café society, and was always to be found at the Plaisantin, just as I had found him there the other night. If Tomoda and Matsunaga really *were* the same person, was it conceivable that this fact could have escaped detection for so long? And was this kind of brazen behaviour really what one would expect of someone like Matsunaga, whose last words to his wife before leaving had been to remind her that she had no hope of tracing him, no matter how hard she tried?

These were not questions I could answer on my own, however long I lay in bed pondering them. I would have to confront Tomoda and see how he reacted. I was busy with work that day, but I managed to finish it by the evening and set out that night for the Ginza, hoping to catch Tomoda at the Plaisantin. If he didn't show up there, I would go to Yokohama and look for him at Number 27. I knew from experience that Tomoda Ginzō was not a difficult man to find.

2

The Café Plaisantin was a well-kept little place, a touch above ordinary cafés. The only food they did was steak – but what a steak it was, grilled the English way over hot coals, a real rarity in Tokyo. The wine list was impressive, too. Many of the drinks behind the bar were available nowhere else. Naturally a café of this kind relied on a group of discerning regulars rather than passing trade, and the Plaisantin was normally a somewhat exclusive place, a favourite haunt of connoisseurs. Tonight, though, the café was abuzz with people who had been drawn in to escape the hot summer evening. I arrived at eight and sat for an hour over a steak and three glasses of French vermouth, waiting for Tomoda to appear. But there was no sign of him. At the tables around me, all I could see were strangers' faces.

I decided to give him till ten. I finished my vermouth and ordered a glass of amontillado. The name may be familiar from Poe's story 'The Cask of Amontillado', but I suspect most people in Japan don't know what amontillado really is. In fact, it was only recently that I had tasted this remarkable wine for the first time myself. It was Tomoda who had introduced me to it.

'Try some of this,' he said one night as the waiter brought over a bottle I had never seen before from one of the shelves by the bar. 'Genuine amontillado. Ever tried it?'

'No. I've heard of it, of course.'

'This,' he said, as he poured me a good-sized sample, 'is the real thing, from Spain. Look at the colour. It's a work of art.' He gestured in the direction of the clear, amber liquid in the glass in front of me. 'Regular sherry is much darker than this; cloudier. Look how clear it is. That's the colour sherry is supposed to be. The stuff you've been drinking all your life is an English imitation. They add sugar to sweeten it. But there's no need for tricks like that with this stuff. This is the natural sweetness of the grapes – nothing more, nothing less.'

'It's wonderful! I've never tasted a sherry like it!' I was captivated by the colour. The drink was perfectly balanced, the delicate sweetness of the fruit rounded out by the gentlest hint of bitterness. A warm southern breeze seemed to rise from the glass in my hand.

'But where do they get it from? This stuff can't be easy to find.'

'You're not kidding. I take the credit for this. I found it in Yokohama at a place called the K. Trading Company. They had two dozen bottles of it stashed away in the warehouse. I gave one dozen to the bar and kept the rest for myself. For personal use only.' He was starting to sound rather pleased with himself.

I thought of Tomoda again now as I sipped my drink. My doubts about him were growing all the time. I was too close to have noticed it before, I suppose, but now I was forced to admit that this friend of mine – this man I had always assumed to be living such an uncomplicated life – was shrouded in mystery like no one else I knew. What had he been doing in the years before I knew him? How old was he? Where had he gone to school? I cross-examined myself on my friend's past and couldn't answer a single one of my own questions. Tomoda had always been a bit slippery when it came to subjects like these, giving strangely evasive answers that could be taken either as yes or no. He spoke such good English and French, was so comfortable with Western manners, and was such a con-noisseur of European food and drink, that I had always assumed he had spent time in the West. But now I came to think of it, I realized I had never actually heard Tomoda say so himself. He had occasionally mentioned his adventures in Shanghai, but I had never heard him talk about Paris or London.

'Where did you learn to speak English and French so well?' I asked him once.

'Just picked it up. When you spend as much money on foreign girls as I do, the language side of things pretty much takes care of itself,' he said, as if fluency in two foreign languages was nothing worth making a fuss about.

'You must have spent a lot of time in Europe, I suppose . . .'

He just laughed. 'You don't have to go to Europe to find foreign women, you know. Who needs Paris when you've got Yokohama? Or Kobe? Or Shanghai?'

This time I wasn't going to let him wriggle out of it so easily. 'If he's not here by ten,' I thought, 'I'll go to Yokohama myself. I'll get to the bottom of this somehow.' I ordered a second glass of amontillado.

'On your own tonight, sir?' The waiter took a sherry glass full of the amber liquid from a silver tray and set it down in front of me. He had been working at the Plaisantin for as long as I could remember.

'Afraid so. No takers at all tonight. You seem to be doing all right, though – this place is packed.'

'It's this summer weather, brings in all kinds of people. More trouble than they're worth, some of them.'

'I don't think I know a single person in here tonight. To tell the truth, I was hoping I might bump into Tomoda. But I've been waiting for nearly two hours now and there's still no sign of him.'

'Maybe he's up at Number 27, sir?' The waiter grinned and turned to look at the clock over the bar. 'It's only half past nine. Still a bit early for Mr Tomoda.'

'I wonder. Maybe he's not coming in tonight at all. In that case, I'll have to go on the attack and head out to Yokohama myself.'

'What is it, sir? Another interesting new arrival?'

'That's exactly what I want to ask him myself. I don't know – I've been getting a bit tired of Tokyo recently.'

'Why not give him a bit longer? He hasn't been in for a couple of days. I think we're about due for a visit.'

No sooner had the boy spoken than the front door swung open.

'The man himself!' I shouted as Tomoda came in. His magnificent bulk made its way across the room toward us, resplendent in a linen suit and an English-made straw hat. He was dressed in white from head to toe. The only thing that stood out was his red drinker's face.

'Hey!' he shouted, raising a hand in our direction and clicking his fingers the way I'd seen foreigners do. He pushed his way through the crowd, his shirt flapping over his protruding belly, and eventually plopped himself down in the chair opposite mine.

'Good evening, Mr Tomoda. We were hoping you might drop in,' the waiter said.

'What do you mean? Who was?'

'Well, I wouldn't say I've been sitting on the edge of my seat, exactly. Just getting a bit bored here on my own, that's all,' I said, as nonchalantly as I could, trying to cover up the waiter's unfortunate remark. My gaze fell naturally on the back of Tomoda's hand as it rested on the table. The amethyst ring was there as usual, glinting at me from the plump ring finger of his left hand.

'Bring me a pink gin, will you?'

'That's a bit of a departure for you, isn't it?' I said.

Tomoda hardly ever touched gin or whisky. Normally, he drank wine – claret, champagne, hock, sherry and cognac. He had nothing but disdain for British and American drinks. 'A cocktail is not what I call a drink,' he liked to say. 'A real drink should never be mixed. You want to taste the flavour of the drink itself, not some artificial concoction. The Americans know nothing about these things.'

'What, gin? No, I can't stand the stuff really. But there's nothing like gin and bitters when it's so absurdly hot. One glass is enough to cool you right down.'

'In that case, I think I'll have one myself.'

'But it has to be Old Tom. Dry gin's no good at all. Just a quick dash of bitters in a glass of Old Tom. Does the trick like nothing else.'

He took a handkerchief from his pocket as he spoke and used it to dab at the beads of perspiration on his face. Like most fat men, Tomoda sweated profusely. As always, he was wearing a stiff single collar, which was starting to wilt.

'Goodness, it's hot. You can't function in this weather. Yokohama's a bit better than this, at least.'

'Speaking of Yokohama, what's the news from Number 27? Any new arrivals?'

'As a matter of fact, something rather special came in from Shanghai just a few days ago.'

'Russian?'

'Portuguese, I think.'

'But they're not so different from Japanese girls, surely?'

'Watch what you're saying! They might have dark eyes and black hair like us but that's where the similarity ends. Everything else about them is completely Western. A Portuguese girl combines the best of both worlds. She's got the face of a Japanese woman – a really attractive Japanese woman, I mean – and the body of a European. Trust me, they don't come much better than that.'

'Hmm, I wonder. You've been known to get a bit carried away about these things.'

It wouldn't be the first time Tomoda had been guilty of exaggeration. He was always singing the praises of whichever girl happened to be his favourite. 'You've *got* to see this one,' he would say, 'she's fantastic.' Often, she turned out to be nothing like as remarkable as he had led me to expect.

'Nonsense! They've never had anything like this before.'

'Well, there's only one way to find out.'

'That can be arranged.'

'Shall we head over there now?'

Tomoda hesitated for a moment, looking about the room and putting his hand to the inside pocket of his jacket. 'I have a photograph,' he said.

'What, already?'

'You know me; I like to move quickly. I got her as soon as she arrived. Here – have a look.' He took the photograph from his wallet and cupped it in his hands for me to see.

'Now, then. Get a load of that body!'

'She's . . . still quite young, isn't she?'

'Eighteen – or so she says. Probably closer to twenty. Like what you see?'

'On this evidence, I like it very much. I should go and see for myself.'

Tomoda's chair swayed as he laughed. 'Funny. I thought you might say that.'

'Oh, by the way, that reminds me. I have something to show you, too.'

I decided to make my move while he was in a good mood. I reached into my jacket pocket just as he had done.

'Something to show me? And what could that be?'

'This.' I took out the picture of the Matsunaga family and set it on the table in front of us.

'What's this? Someone's pilgrimage snaps?'

I have never forgotten the expression that crossed his face at that moment. The instant he saw the picture he turned pale. He looked as though every hair on his body was standing on end. He didn't even pick up the photograph to get a closer look. His dull, drink-heavy eyes were suddenly wrenched open wide. I watched them flash as he fought to control his emotions. Waves of terror and anguish and loss washed over him. I didn't know what to say. At last, I heard a clink as Tomoda lunged for his glass and downed what was left of his gin in a single gulp.

'What's so special about it, then?' he finally said. His voice shook with an indignation he was struggling in vain to control.

'You don't recognize the people in the photograph?'

'No. Should I? Not really my crowd, you know.'

'Not ringing any bells at all?'

'Absolutely not. Why?'

Perhaps I was going about it the wrong way. I began to worry that I had taken him too much by surprise. I would never get to the bottom of the mystery if I made him angry. I decided to change tack, and continued more gently.

'Well, if you don't know anything about it, that just makes things more mysterious. The man in the photograph is from a village called Yagyū in Yamato. His name is Matsunaga Gisuke.'

'And what's so mysterious about that, exactly?'

'He went missing two or three years ago.'

'And? Are you a friend of his or something?' Tomoda growled.

'I've never met him – I thought *you* might know him.'

I remembered that Shigeko had asked me to keep the contents of her letter to myself. But I couldn't keep the truth from him now. Maybe I should suggest going for a stroll and talk things over with him outside. But the café was so crowded tonight. Next to our table a fan rattled and whirred. There was little risk that anyone would overhear what I had to say. And it would be easier to follow his reactions in a well-lit place like this. Quietly, I continued my account.

My lowered voice seemed to help Tomoda regain his composure a little. But as I spoke, he suddenly called the waiter over and asked him to bring some absinthe. He raised the drink repeatedly to his lips, nodding and grunting from time to time as I spoke. I have mentioned already that it was rare for Tomoda to drink anything as strong as gin – let alone absinthe. He was evidently looking to escape into an even more intoxicated state than he was in already. But his mumbled interjections grew more frequent and more involved as I continued my story, and I occasionally caught glimpses of genuine curiosity in his eyes.

'What a story!' he said when he had heard me out. 'You ought to write it up. It has the makings of a classic detective story!' He was more his usual self again now, banging his fist on the table and roaring his appreciation.

'What do you mean? You do know him after all?'

'No, I don't know the man. But I know the stuff in that bag of his. It was mine. All of it: the seal, the ring, the photographs, everything . . .'

'So how did he get his hands on them?'

'I had my bag stolen once. Let me see, when would it have been? If I had that postcard with me, it must have been around then, I suppose. My bag was taken while I was staying at the XX Hotel in Hakone. Probably the bag she found was mine too.'

'Shigeko said it was some kind of small carrying case.'

'That's right – one of those little box-like things. I don't remember the postcard from you, but the rest of it was definitely there. Money, too: two or three hundred yen. I lost it all.'

'Did they ever catch the thief?'

'I never reported it. I prefer not to deal with the police if I can help it. There wasn't that much money involved anyway. And those photos! How would it look if the police found those?'

'What about the ring you're wearing now?'

'This? A replacement. I had it made after the other one was stolen.'

He thought for a moment, then continued. 'It sounds funny, I suppose, having a ring stolen. The thing is, I hate thunder. It terrifies me. Whenever I hear thunder, I take off everything I'm wearing that's made of metal – watches, rings, anything. I remember there was a terrific thunderstorm that night in Hakone. I took off my ring and put it in my bag. Then I fell asleep and forgot all about it. Someone must have come in and swiped it while I was asleep.'

'You think this Matsunaga's a thief, then? It doesn't seem right, somehow. Shigeko's letter sounded so cultured. I don't know – I was imagining him as the head of a respectable family.'

'What about this leaving home every three or four years, though? A bit suspicious, don't you think? I can see how my photographs might appeal to an eccentric like that. And what about your postcard? That might have some value for a fan of yours, don't you think? . . . After it was stolen, it probably passed from hand to hand until it ended up with him. I don't know about the seal and the ring, though. That *is* odd.'

'Maybe he spent the money and kept everything else in the bag where he found it. He was probably worried the other things could be traced.'

'That's it! That must be the explanation.'

'Still . . . it's strange that he should have kept my postcard. He could have burnt it or torn it up or something.'

'I know!' Tomoda said with a laugh. 'The thief must be a fan of yours!'

'Oh, great!'

'You never know. Not all thieves are illiterate. Someone with a bit of education could probably make his way through one of your novels.'

'Marvellous. And is that what I'm supposed to tell Shigeko – that her husband is a thief? How's that going to make her feel? As if she doesn't have problems enough already. And besides, we don't have any proof.'

'Why not just say you don't know anything? It's not as though I'm desperate to get my property back.'

'But I'd have to tell her *something* about you.'

'Why?'

'Listen to what she says: "If you are not acquainted with anybody by the name of Matsunaga Gisuke, perhaps you do know Mr Tomoda? If so, perhaps you would be kind enough to tell me what you know about him and how I might get in touch with him."'

'Absolutely not! Out of the question! I want nothing to do with it.' Suddenly, Tomoda was shouting. The colour drained from his face again.

'But I can't tell her I don't know anyone called Tomoda Ginzō – what about the postcard?'

'All right. So tell her you do know someone called Tomoda Ginzō. You asked him about this Matsunaga person, and he knows nothing about him. And nothing about the articles in the bag either. The postcard may indeed have belonged to him once, but Mr Tomoda has no recollection of any of the other items. As far as he can remember he has never lost a seal and it is a matter of great mystery to Mr Tomoda how the seal and the postcard came to be in the possession of Mr Matsunaga. Yours sincerely, etc., etc. That's all you have to do. There's no need to go giving out people's personal details . . .'

'I'll have to do better than that. She won't be satisfied with such a vague reply. I can see how it might make things a bit awkward for you, but she's obviously managed to persuade herself that you and this Matsunaga are one and the same person. As far as she's concerned, Tomoda Ginzō is just an alias.'

'But look at us. It's not exactly a striking resemblance, is it?'

I gave the most good-humoured laugh I could manage. 'But she doesn't know that. She's never set eyes on you.'

'Here, let me see that photograph again.'

Tomoda held up the picture and looked at it closely. I saw fear flicker in his eyes again. Not as obvious this time, perhaps – but it was the same strange terror I had noticed before.

'So this is Matsunaga, is it? Look at the old fogey! I'm way younger than he is.'

'He was thirty-seven when that was taken. Turns forty this year, she says.'

'Four years older than me, then.' This was the first time he had ever volunteered such a straightforward piece of information about himself.

'You're thirty-six?'

'Born in 1885, the year of the rooster. Why? Don't I look it?'

'I don't know. I suppose your face does look around thirty-six. You're starting to go a bit thin on top, though.'

'It's the booze. Curse of the drinking man, I'm afraid,' he said, grabbing a handful of hair at the crown of his head. 'At the rate I'm going, I'll be totally bald before you know it. It's starting to get me down, to tell you the truth.'

'Even so, you still look a good four or five years younger than him. That much I can vouch for.'

'But it's not just our ages. Everything about us is different.'

'I know. You look nothing like him. That's the problem.'

'What do you mean, that's the problem?'

'If I could prove that you were the same person, maybe I'd be able to make some sense of this whole thing. As it is, I'm stumped.' I laughed again. But it was no laughing matter. For the more closely I studied the photograph of Matsunaga and his family and compared it with the man sitting in front of me, the more profoundly I was struck by the total lack of any resemblance between them whatsoever.

'Here's what we'll do,' Tomoda said, leaning across the table. 'We'll send her a picture. A photograph of me. To prove that her husband and I are two completely unrelated people who don't even look alike. What can she say to that?'

'You're right. That's the easiest way.'

'I'll put two or three good clear photographs in the post first thing tomorrow morning. You can send them to her, and say, "Here is what Tomoda Ginzō looks like. I am sure that one glimpse of these photographs will dispel any suspicions you may have. In light of this, I don't believe it is necessary to divulge any further information regarding Mr Tomoda's whereabouts or background." And that will be that.'

I had no choice but to follow this reasonable suggestion. We sat and continued to talk over still more drinks. From time to time I caught him stealing a glance at the photograph of the Matsunaga family, which I had deliberately left out on the table.

'What about it, then? Do you feel like heading over to Yokohama?' Tomoda said as he stood up. It was nearly eleven.

'I'd better not. I've got a lot on at the moment.'

'Come on – I'll show you the Portuguese girl.'

'I'd love to, but really. Another time, once I've cleared some of this work. You won't forget to send me those pictures, will you?'

'Don't worry. I won't forget – just don't go telling her anything I wouldn't. Agreed?'

We left the Plaisantin and walked together down the Ginza towards Shibaguchi. We both fell strangely silent as we left the café. Tomoda no doubt had things of his own to be thinking about. As for me – I had had far too much to drink that evening, and I was more intoxicated than I normally allow myself to become. My head spun as I went over our conversation, obsessively trying to make sense of it all. Who was he really, this man I knew as Tomoda Ginzō, stumbling down the street by my side at this very moment? His bag had been stolen, he said. Fair enough – that would explain everything. But what about the look of fear I had seen in his eyes when I showed him the photograph? Why had he felt the need to get so drunk, or at least act as though he were? And why was he so particular about keeping his identity and whereabouts a secret even though he knew he was under suspicion? The more I thought about it, the thicker became the cloud of mystery that enveloped him. Tomoda had said how suspicious it was that Matsunaga kept disappearing without a trace every three or four years. But if that counted as suspicious behaviour, then what about Tomoda himself? 'If I could prove that you were the same person, maybe I'd be able to make some sense of this whole thing,' I had joked. But of course, I hadn't really been joking at all. Even if they weren't the same person, it was still possible that they were somehow in cahoots. Perhaps Tomoda had met Matsunaga overseas. Perhaps they had been meeting in Tokyo at four-year intervals ever since, working together like shadows to carry out their nefarious schemes . . .

'Good night, then,' Tomoda said suddenly when we reached the tram stop at Shibaguchi. His tone was unusually brusque. He turned a corner and was gone, vanishing in the direction of Shinbashi Station.

Despite his assurances, I had my doubts whether he would really send me the photographs he had promised. Perhaps he had just been looking for a way out of our argument, I thought. But, in fact, they were delivered to my door by the afternoon post two days later. 'Identification photographs enclosed as promised,' his note read. 'I had thought that any recent photograph would do, but I couldn't find any suitable, so I had three new portraits taken specially. I am enclosing one full-length photo, one from the waist up and one of the face only. Together, they should be more than sufficient for our purposes. Please send all three photographs to Mrs Matsunaga without too much elaboration. I will thank you not to mention anything about my whereabouts or other personal details. I am not in the habit of giving out my address unless it is absolutely necessary. As I think I made clear the other evening, no purpose would be served by letting

Mrs Matsunaga know where I live. I see no reason why I should be inconvenienced any further for the sake of Mrs Matsunaga and her disappearing husband.'

The three photographs he had sent certainly served their purpose as identifying shots. Taken together, they told you everything you could want to know about his appearance, from his general build and character to the outline of his face and the shape of his skull. Every distinguishing mark was there in full view. But I couldn't help noticing that one thing was missing. Neither in the full-body picture nor in the upper-body shot was there any sign of the ring he always wore, although you could see his hands quite clearly in both. He must have made a point of taking it off. He had asked me specifically not to mention the ring in my reply to Shigeko. Surely this was the true reason why he had gone to the effort of having new pictures taken.

I put the 'identity photos' in an envelope together with my reply. As it happened, I was not able to follow Tomoda's instructions as closely as he would have liked. The sympathy I felt for Shigeko outweighed my feelings of friendship for him. I had my own doubts and suspicions, and although I knew that I might come to regret my actions later on, I decided that I couldn't simply push these thoughts to one side and lie to Shigeko now. My reply was even longer than her original letter to me. In it, I set down everything I knew that might help her get to the bottom of the mystery. I sent her all the evidence at my disposal: the chronological table showing how Tomoda and Matsunaga seemed to go missing in alternating intervals of four years, as well as a detailed report of our conversation at the Plaisantin. I also wrote: 'I don't know what you will make of the photographs I am enclosing, but I hope you will let me know if the man in these pictures resembles your husband in any way or if they contain any clue that might help you in your search. I will continue to look into things at this end, and will be happy to help in any way I can.'

A few days later, I received another long letter from Shigeko, full of thanks for my help. But in among all the formalities was a line that took me quite by surprise. For it was clear that the photographs I had sent had not been enough to dispel her doubts: 'The details you have been kind enough to provide have only deepened my suspicion that Tomoda Ginzō may be an alias used by my husband, Matsunaga Gisuke.' Her second letter was written in the same old-fashioned style as her first. This time I will summarize its contents. 'There is no doubt,' she wrote, 'that the pictures you were kind enough to send show a man quite different in appearance from my husband. But there is something about the eyes in that round face of his that reminds me of my husband. Perhaps my mind is playing tricks on me. My husband has always been thin. If, as you say, Mr Tomoda has always been rather stout, then my suspicions would seem to be quite unfounded. I cannot offer any solution to the mystery, but in spite of everything I can't shake the thought that they might somehow be the same person. If my husband were just four or five years younger – if he lost a few years, and gained a few pounds – perhaps this is how he might look. What height is Mr Tomoda, I wonder? My husband is a little over five feet and four inches. Do please let me know if you learn anything more of Mr Tomoda's background: where he comes from, what he does for a living, whether he has a family, his true age and whether there is any truth to the account of how he lost his bag. I realize that I am asking a lot. I hope you will understand my situation. Our daughter's condition shows no sign of improvement and she longs to see her father. I should be very much obliged if you would make Mr Tomoda acquainted with the details of the situation.'

I was stunned. Was her mind playing tricks on her, as she herself had admitted it might be? Or did Tomoda have some way of altering his appearance? Was such a thing even possible? I was more suspicious of him now than ever.

3

It was on the evening of the first or the second of September that I saw Tomoda again for the first time since receiving Shigeko's reply. This time we met not at the Café Plaisantin but at Number 27 in Yokohama.

I knew I was likely to find Tomoda at Number 27. That was my main reason for going there that evening, though I was careful to give the impression that I had just popped out of the house in search of a good time. As usual, I took a taxi from Sakuragichō through Yamashitachō to the front of the French consulate and up Yatozaka hill, arriving around nine at the front gate of the old house at the end of its dark and lonely back street. I reached up with my walking stick and rang the bell set high on the gatepost. From outside, the house looked deserted. A faint ringing sounded from a room some distance away on the other side of the tightly locked gate. The house itself remained silent. The sound of the far-off bell was eerie and unsettling, like the sound of a stone tossed into a deep ravine or a ghost moving around inside a deserted house. Eventually the establishment's Filipino houseboy came out to the gate and removed the iron latch with a heavy clank. He eased the gate back an inch or two and squinted out into the darkness to where I was standing in the light of the lantern that hung from the eaves.

'Hello? It's me.'

'Oh yes, sir, good evening.' Usually the boy spoke only English but with me he used his still slightly clumsy Japanese. Once he recognized me, he opened the gate just wide enough for me to squeeze through.

'Long time no see, sir.'

'It's been too hot for this kind of thing. But I hear a new girl's just arrived. I've come to have a look.'

'Yes, there is one you don't meet yet.'

'I hear she's a real beauty.'

'Yes, I think you will like.' His teeth flashed in the darkness, as white as the linen jacket he was wearing.

'I see I'm not the only one here.'

The shutters were all closed in spite of the heat, but a single sliver of light escaped from an opening in the dance-hall window.

'Who is it? Not Mr Tom by any chance?'

'Yes, sir. Only Mr Tom here tonight.'

'He might like a bit of company. Can we go in?'

Everything was going perfectly so far. I stepped into the corridor and knocked on the first door on the left, which led into the dance hall.

'Aha! So here you are at last . . .'

I entered the room to find Tomoda wearing a sailor's jacket and relaxing on a divan by the piano. Perched in his lap was a girl called Catherine, in a crimson crêpe de Chine dress that glowed like fire. Actually, it was only later that I realized how bright the dress was. At first glance it looked quite dark, thanks to the unusual lighting system in the room, which could be set to red, white or blue according to the mood of the moment. When I opened the door, the room was awash in warm red light. After the darkness outside, the soft light was probably just what my eyes needed, but I had other things on my mind and I flicked the switch to white as I entered.

'Ouch! What do you want to make it so bright for?' Catherine shrieked. She sounded drunk. Catherine was a petite, well-formed girl from England, the youngest of all the girls at Number 27 and a favourite with the clientele. Standing in front of her, in a dress of aqua-blue georgette, was Rosa. A girl I didn't recognize sat at the piano, wearing a citron-coloured organdy dress. This must be the new Portuguese girl. Her face was perhaps not quite as pretty as Catherine's, but her bare shoulders were uncommonly beautiful.

'It's all right. Let him have it as bright as he wants. He's come to see something very special tonight.' Tomoda's gaze darted between me and the Portuguese girl.

'Right on target,' I said in Japanese. 'Is this the girl in the photo you showed me the other day?'

'That's the one. Here, I'll introduce you.' Tomoda turned to the girl and switched to English. 'This gentleman here,' he said, 'is the famous writer Mr F. K. And this is Edna – a beautiful Portuguese young lady who's just come to us from Shanghai.'

'Are you really a writer?' Edna got up and came over to where we were standing.

'One of the most famous novelists in the country,' Tomoda said. 'If you're lucky, he might put you in one of his books. How would you like that?'

'Where were you in Shanghai?' I asked.

'The French Concession.'

'Working in one of the cafés?'

'Goodness, no. I was a nice girl in Shanghai.'

'So it's only since you came to Japan that you've turned naughty, is that right?'

'Really! Come on – let's have some champagne. A toast to new friends.'

This was Rosa's idea. Rosa was a thick-set and rather greasy-complexioned older woman whose best years were long behind her. Her arms were as big as my legs. She spoke fluent French and German, but unless I'm mistaken she was actually a Russian Jew. She was never going to be a popular choice with customers heading to the rooms upstairs, but she made up for this by the skill with which she squeezed drinks out of the guests as she made her way around the dance-floor bar.

'Good evening!'

I turned to find another young woman in white coming down the stairs.

'Hello, Flora! I didn't know you were here.'

'Things were so boring, I went upstairs for a nap. Boy – bring another champagne glass. Maria's gone off to Hakone with some American gentleman. He's taken her to stay at the Fujiya.'

'What about Emmy?'

'She's gone away somewhere too to get away from the heat. There's only the four of us left.'

'What is this anyway – some kind of police investigation?' Catherine swung her legs under her chair like a little girl, her champagne glass held high.

'Of course it is,' Tomoda said. 'Detectives and writers are one and the same.'

'What do you mean by that?' I said.

'You know – always asking questions, sticking their noses into people's affairs.' Was he being ironic? He was practically rolling in his chair with laughter.

'You know I didn't mean it like that. It's just – things are a bit quiet tonight, aren't they? Are you the only customer?'

'It's the summer. This business is dead when it's so hot.'

'It doesn't seem to stop you from coming every night.'

'I'm different. Most people like to get out of town, away from the heat. I'm happier here with the girls. And besides, I like having the place to myself. It's my own private paradise. Everyone else is in the doldrums and I'm just hitting my peak. I can do whatever I like, and there's no one to stop me.'

'Tom, Tom! We've finished the champagne. Why don't you buy us another bottle?' Rosa was up to her usual tricks.

'All right! And music! Come on, play us something!' Suddenly Tomoda lurched out of his chair. He took Catherine in his arms and lifted her into the air. She was still clutching her champagne glass, holding it out of harm's way in one hand as Tomoda stumbled on his heels and began to spin Catherine's crimson-clad body like a waterwheel, champagne glass and all.

'Wait, Tom! Stop it! Let me have my drink!' she squealed, pronouncing her words with a sharp edge that no Japanese woman could have produced.

Flora sat down at the piano and began to play. 'Come on, Tom – why don't you and Catherine dance a tango for us?'

'Your wish is my command. I say, K, have you ever seen me dance a tango?'

'I'm not sure I have.'

'Watch and learn. It goes like this.'

Still holding Catherine aloft, Tomoda gave her body one long swing and dropped her to the floor. No sooner had her feet hit the ground than she was up and dancing the tango hand in hand with Tomoda. I had seen Tomoda dance several times before, and I knew that he danced well. But this was the first time I had seen him dance a tango. Apart from in films, in fact, I don't think I had ever seen anyone dance a tango – not even foreigners. I could hardly believe what I was seeing. If I hadn't seen it with my own eyes, I would never have believed that any Japanese – not even Tomoda – could dance with such grace and skill.

He held the woman's slender body close, one hand clamped tight against her back. His left hand gripped her right and they lunged forward together, their arms entwined, hips swinging. At times their movements were slow, at other times fast. But no matter how frantic the tempo, her body never left his. They were fastened together, inseparable. She followed his every step, fell in with his every move. If he turned and swirled, she turned and swirled too. They were like two pieces of fabric sewn together to make a single piece of clothing – he the white outer layer, she the red inner lining. It was clearly not the first time they had danced together like this. Tomoda seemed to shake off his usual heaviness; his body seemed to lift off the ground as his spirits soared. As they twisted and twirled in time to the music, Catherine's feet hardly touched the floor. She had evidently shaken off all sense of time or place – had forgotten, even, that she was dancing at all – as she spun and swirled, clinging to Tomoda's breast, lost in a daze of intoxication. Their dancing grew wilder and more impulsive. They veered away from each other, one to the left, the other to the right, then came together again. He flung her away from him, caught her at an angle, then brought her upright with the tip of one finger, raising his arm like a man showing off a big fish he has just pulled from the water. She pirouetted five or six times on the spot, then fell back again, her face towards the ceiling. Her bobbed chestnut hair hung loose and shone in the light. Her champagne-flushed face turned crimson as the blood rushed to her head. Tomoda performed one dance after another, pausing only to gulp down a succession of different drinks between each dance. He was obviously quite intoxicated. He looked nervous and desperate to get drunk as quickly as possible, just as he had that night at the Plaisantin.

'No more! I'm finished!' He heaved a sigh and collapsed in a chair, pulling Flora down on to his knee. He held her close.

'What are you drinking, Tom?'

'Benedictine.'

'Here, let me try some.' Flora held her face under his glass and opened her mouth. She took the cigarette out of her mouth and thrust it between Tomoda's lips.

'Ugh! What kind of cigarette is this? It's so bitter!'

'If you don't like it, don't smoke it. I'll smoke it myself.'

'No, it's all right. Give it back, please,' Tomoda said, shaking his head and putting on his sweetest, most imploring tone of voice. And then he turned his glassy eyes to look at me. 'So what did you think of my tango?'

'It was quite something.'

'Quite something? What's that supposed to mean? Good or bad?'

'Good. Very good. Astonishing.'

'Astonishing! That's more like it. You'd better have a drink.'

'I don't know, I've had quite a bit already.'

'Quite a bit? Quite something? It's turning out to be *quite* a night for you, isn't it?' He laughed hilariously at his own joke.

'Where did you learn to dance like that, anyway?'

'It wasn't easy, let me tell you. It's not really something you can *study*, exactly – it's a question of application and practice. I served my time in every café, bar and cabaret I could find.'

'When was that?'

'Oh, a long time ago.'

'During your time in the West?'

'There you go again. I've told you before – unfortunately, I've never been to Europe.'

'But you didn't learn that in Japan, surely. It must have been while you were in Shanghai or somewhere like that.'

'Look out, here comes Inspector K again.'

I had been waiting for an opportunity to steer conversation to the topic that interested me, but with Tomoda apparently determined to play the fool, it wasn't easy. Rosa squeezed in next to him and Catherine stood behind them, draping her arms over the back of the chair and holding hands with Flora. Tomoda sat contentedly in the middle of this bouquet, occasionally leaning over to pass a drink to one of the girls. But I could tell he was still on his guard. Whenever he saw that I was about to speak, he leaped out of the chair before I could ask any awkward questions. 'Come on, Flora – the Apache!' Arms stretched wide, he lurched around the room in time to the music.

I should probably explain here that this peculiar behaviour was not unusual for him. Tonight was not the first time I had found him clowning around like this. In fact, he seemed to be in the middle of some game or other whenever I came. The girls were partly to blame, for the way they indulged his every whim – but the truth was that Tomoda seemed to enjoy horsing around like this more than anything else. He loved to be in a crowd, surrounded by noise, with the drinks flowing freely. As far as I knew, he had no regular relationship with any of the girls. He almost gave the impression that he wasn't interested in women at all. It was as though he had come just to pass the time. For a while, I suspected there might be something between him and Catherine but I never found any proof. When I asked the Filipino boy about it, he just shrugged. 'Mr Tom is a bit strange. He never has a woman. He likes taking all kinds of photographs and playing games, but that's all. Some people are funny that way.' I had witnessed this self-centred and unseemly wild behaviour of his too often in the past to be especially shocked by it now, but there was something almost abnormal about the way he was carrying on tonight. There was more to it than mere exuberance and the fact that no one was there to hold him back. He seemed anxious and pursued, as though he feared he might be caught at any moment.

Was this the explanation for his volatile behaviour – his drinking, his raucousness and his tendency to jump about the room at every opportunity? Was he trying to escape from something? Now that I thought about it, I realized that his antics had started when he saw my face. When I arrived, he had been sitting quietly, talking to the girls. Something about me terrified him. I seemed to cast a fearful shadow over him whenever I appeared.

'Tom! What *are* you doing?'

'Oh dear! Tom's drunk again!'

Flora had given him a shove and he had landed on his backside on the floorboards. He was slumped like a pot-bellied Billiken doll, his legs sprawled uselessly in front of him. The girls took him by the hands and tried to pull him up, but his belly was too much for them and he kept slithering back to the floor. Catherine brought a hat from somewhere and put it on his head. Rosa removed her bead necklace and hung it around his neck. He suddenly crossed his legs and began to pose like the Great Buddha. At length he managed to get to his feet, clutching at Flora for support and swaying from side to side, still mumbling incoherently about the 'Apache dance'.

But if Tomoda's tango had been quite impressive, his interpretation of the Apache was just outrageous. There was a blurred flurry of movement. He seemed to be trying to fling his poor partner in every direction at once, hoisting her aloft and tipping her back like a man practising his judo moves. Flora's bright red hair blazed across her forehead. Her dress had come undone at the seams, and I caught an occasional flash of bare flesh around her shoulders as she spun. But both the man and the women around him were too drunk to care how indecent they looked. The sight of them jabbering away in English and French made me feel as though I were somewhere else. In a bar in Paris, perhaps: anywhere but Yokohama, Japan. I was marvelling at the strangeness of it all when I became aware of Tomoda calling my name. He came up behind me and grabbed my arm.

'I'm drunk, K. Even more than usual. There's no holding me back tonight. Come on, get up and dance,' he slurred. He was speaking English even with me now. A strange hint of aggression lurked in his voice, beneath the cover of his intoxication.

'Too energetic for me. I'll leave that kind of thing to you.'

'I know what's on your mind.' There was a glimmer in his eye. He jerked his chin towards Edna. 'What do you think, then?'

'Not bad.'

'Amazing, isn't she? I told you so. Anyway, if you're interested, don't let me stop you.'

Edna sat slightly apart from the group in a corner of the room. She had been toying with a guitar but she had given up trying to compete with the noise and put the instrument down. She sat with her hands folded gracefully in her lap. As a new arrival, she probably wasn't used to the place yet. I watched her lean back in her chair, lost in thought, her dark eyes fixed on a point in space. In spite of her European clothes she had a certain seductive quality about her that reminded me of a Japanese geisha. I looked again at the swell of her round shoulders. The hands in her lap were of the same ivory white as her shoulders. The pink of her fingernails stood out against her pale skin.

'She has a certain serenity about her that I like.'

'Well if you like her, why don't you take her upstairs?' said Tomoda. 'I assume you'll be staying the night?'

'I don't know – what time is it? About eleven?' I glanced at my pocket watch.

'Oh, come on. It's not like you've got anything to hurry home to.'

'All right. I don't mind. But that's not really what I came for.'

'Ha! Why, what's the big deal?'

'Actually, there's something I need to talk to you about. I had a reply from Mrs Matsunaga.' I pressed straight ahead before he could change the subject.

'No doubt about it, she says. You're her husband. Despite the photographs, she's still convinced that you and Matsunaga are one and the same person. Must be woman's intuition or something.'

'Wait a minute! You'll give me a heart attack. Is this some kind of joke?' The whites of his eyes bulged as if he were struggling to swallow something stuck in his throat.

'I'm not making it up. That's what she said. And that's not all. She wants me to tell her everything about you. Where you're from, what kind of person you are. She wants details.'

'What the hell's her problem? Can't she see we look nothing like each other? And still she's suspicious? It's insulting to you, too.'

'Getting angry won't make any difference. Her husband vanished into

36

thin air. The poor woman's at the end of her tether. Someone like that is going to imagine all kinds of things.'

'Oh, you're no use. No wonder you're a writer – show you a damsel in distress and you start gushing sympathy.'

'I do feel sympathy for her, as it happens. Something in her letter appealed to me. The way it was written – so modest and refined, not like the modern style at all. If I were her husband and I read a letter like that, I'd be back home in no time.'

'What's stopping you? I'm sure she wouldn't know the difference.'

'Why don't you write to her yourself instead of making jokes about it? You could give her a few details about yourself, make it clear once and for all that you have no connection to the Matsunaga family. You could send her a copy of your family register.'

'Completely unnecessary.'

'Maybe for you. But what about her? Don't you feel even a little bit sorry for her?'

'I have no sympathy for that woman at all.'

'But if you leave things as they are, she'll become even more suspicious. Doesn't that bother you?'

'She can go to hell. I sent her the photographs and that's the end of it. I want nothing more to do with her. Let's talk about something else.'

'So what am I supposed to do? I don't want to let her down. She's relying on me. Not that there's much I *could* tell her even if I wanted to. I don't know anything about you either.'

Tomoda was glaring at me as if I had just threatened to kill him. 'What do you mean? You'd tell her more if you could?'

'I would. I've already told her everything I know.'

'Like what?'

'Like I said – everything I know. What we talked about the other night. How long I've known you, the ring . . . everything.'

At the mention of the word 'ring', his eyes flashed with rage. He raised his hand as if to strike me, and if we had been alone, I think he really would have. Instead, he started stomping about the room furiously, cursing under his breath.

'How could you? I should have known. Never trust the Japanese! Drinking buddies have a moral code. We don't go blabbing each other's secrets!'

'Hey! What are you talking about in Japanese?' Rosa shouted, her voice thick with drink. This was followed by the voice of one of the other girls. 'Yeah! Shut up! No Japanese allowed!'

'But everything's relative, even morals. I decided it would be more immoral for me to lie to her. And anyway, at the risk of making you even angrier, I'm starting to think she might have her reasons to be suspicious about you.'

'What do you mean?' Tomoda had been pacing up and down the room, but he stopped suddenly now as if a bullet had hit him.

'Think about it. We've known each other for years. But every few years you suddenly disappear and I don't see you at all. And the times that you *are* here match up exactly with when Matsunaga's away. I just didn't notice it until I read her letter. It seemed strange – so I wrote back to her, that's all, just giving her my impressions.'

'You mean to say you . . .' But Tomoda never got to finish whatever it was he was going to say. Somebody was playing with the switch that controlled the room's unusual lighting system. There was a click and the room turned red. Then another, and the room turned blue. Click! Click! Click! Suddenly, the room was plunged into darkness and we heard Catherine's piercing voice: 'If you two don't behave yourselves!'

'Tom! Stop talking in Japanese! It's so boring.'

'Yes, Tom! And why do you have to fight like that? You've had too much to drink.'

'It's all right. Calm down. Nothing's wrong. My writer friend here has been having problems with some crazy woman, that's all. I was just putting him straight on the matter. Isn't that right?'

'Exactly right, I'm afraid.'

Tomoda started to laugh hysterically and the lights began to flash again. But in the dazzle that accompanied every flick of the switch, I could no longer make out the expression on his face.

4

What became of Tomoda Ginzō after that? I know nothing of what happened next. From that night on, Tomoda stopped coming to Number 27 and the house itself closed down soon after.

The same thing had happened in 1915, the last time he disappeared. His lair back then had been Number 10, and this too was abandoned not long after he went missing. It could mean only one thing: Tomoda had entered his third period of obscurity. It remained to be seen whether his disappearance had anything to do with Matsunaga Gisuke. Nothing of note happened for nearly a year.

In October 1921, I received word from Shigeko informing me that her husband had returned to the family home in Yagyū. As on the previous occasions, he had been away a little over four years.

The joy the family felt to see him home again, the happy reunion of parent and child, husband and wife – all this and more was described at length in Shigeko's letter. I will leave the details to the reader's imagination. One thing I ought to mention concerns the daughter, Taeko, who had been so desperate to see her father. According to the letter, she had begun to shake off her illness soon after he came home and was now well on her way to a full recovery. One happy event followed another for the Matsunaga family.

Shigeko continued to write from time to time to inform me of Matsunaga's progress. I was the only person in whom she could confide about her husband's puzzling behaviour. Her letters gave me a glimpse of the kind of life he was living back in the country. It was clear that he had returned in much the same fashion as before. He had appeared without warning late one autumn afternoon dressed in Japanese attire, a single travel bag in his hand, looking exhausted and thin. He said nothing of where he had spent the past four years. He doted on his family and was given to tearful outbursts. Shigeko had promptly confirmed that the familiar items – the postcard, the photographs, the seal and the amethyst ring – were still in their usual place inside the bag. 'For the life of me, I cannot think why he still holds on to these things,' she wrote in one of her letters. 'Perhaps if I sent the photographs and ring to you, you might be able to tell me once and for all whether they are the same items you have seen in Mr Tomoda's possession. You must think it is absurd for me to persist in my suspicions now that my husband has come home. But how can I be sure that he will not leave again in another three or four years? If only I knew one way or the other. I sometimes look at the photographs you were good enough to send. Often the differences are so striking that it seems ludicrous to suspect they could be the same person. Mr Tomoda is so much younger-looking than my husband, and my husband is so frail and thin. At other times, though, I feel almost convinced that the similarities between them are real, and I become more suspicious than ever.'

It was early in the following year, towards the end of March 1922, that I took a trip to Kyoto and Nara. I had been in my hotel for several days when a letter arrived from Shigeko, who had seen an article in one of the papers that mentioned where I was staying. 'I understand you will be spending some time in Nara, which is only a few miles from us here. I would be so happy if we could meet. Yagyū is on the way to Tsukigase as you come from Kasagi Station on the Kansai Line. You may have heard of the famous plum blossoms at Tsukigase, which are at their best just now. If you came to see the blossoms, you would almost certainly pass through the village on your way. Would you take the time to stop by and give me a chance to thank you in person for all your help over the past two years? Also, I should like very much for you to meet my husband. It is selfish of me, I know, but I can't help wondering whether the mystery that has troubled me for so long might not be solved once and for all if you were to see my husband with your own eyes. He knows that I have written to you, but has never pressed me for details. I told him I wrote to say how much I had enjoyed your books. He seemed happy to hear that I was able to find some solace in your work while he was away.'

My curiosity piqued, I decided to pay her a visit at once – more for the sake of getting a glimpse of Matsunaga Gisuke than because I was interested in the famous blossoms. I left Nara at eight the next morning. Kasagi was the third station on the line. A bus ran from the station to Tsukigase, but it was no weather for sitting cooped up in a bus. Under a clear blue sky I set out on foot along the road that led the two or three miles to the village of Yagyū.

Several motor cars wheezed past as I walked, full of people on their way to see the blossoms. Clouds of dust kicked up by the passing buses sullied the clear air and spoilt the view a little, but I knew as soon as I started out that I had made the right decision. It is difficult to convey a sense of the happiness I felt as I walked through the Yamato countryside that spring day, but anyone who has had a similar experience will understand what I felt – the sense of wellbeing that was mine as I wound my way slowly along the path. The road I walked along must have been the prefectural road that passes through Tsukigase to Iga no Ueno. Yoshino aside, Yamato is flat country, with almost no real mountains or deep, secluded valleys. Bright, almost white roads criss-cross the terrain, linking scattered villages, crossing streams and skirting sloping hillsides. At first glance, it is some of the most ordinary-looking scenery in the world. But those peaceful, unpretentious fields were just made to be looked at on a spring day like this. There was beauty in everything, even in the most commonplace things: in the walls of the earthen storehouses off in the distance, in the thatched roofs, in the trees that lined the roads, in the paddy fields and bamboo groves. Everything danced before my eyes in the sunlight. My spirits soared.

I had on a thick winter coat and sweat soaked the back of my shirt as I walked. From time to time I stopped to admire the view. Somewhere in the distance a reddish mist floated across the foothills; birds twittered ceaselessly as they flitted by overhead. I had wandered into a painting of 'The Idyllic Village'. The legends of *The Peach Blossom Spring* must have been inspired by scenery like this, I thought. Sloping fields planted with tea stretched all around. The hillsides swelled, rising and falling in gentle feminine curves, the rows of tea plants glowing like velvet jewels in the sunlight. How magical it all looked! I quite forgot the purpose that had brought me here. I felt I could walk these hillsides all day without a hint of tiredness.

Yagyū turned out to be bigger than I had expected and I still had a fair distance to cover after I entered the village. But I knew the Matsunaga house was an old one and I recognized it as soon as I saw it.

Before I had even sent in my card, Shigeko herself was at the gate to meet me. She had been standing in the garden waiting. A girl of three or four toddled behind her. This was the second daughter, Fumiko, who had been born in August 1919.

'It's such a nice day, I just had a feeling you might stop by. What glorious weather!' She looked much like her photograph, with her long hair done up in an old-fashioned chignon, but with her cheeks blushing in the sunlight she looked at least a couple of years younger than thirty-five. As I had expected, she was well spoken and wore a simple silk kimono that suited her well.

The Matsunaga residence was a dark old house, more or less unchanged from the way it must have looked in the mid nineteenth century, when it would have been home to a prosperous local farmer. Shigeko led me into the parlour. 'My husband will be down in a few moments,' she said. We chatted comfortably while we waited. I began by asking her about her elegant handwriting, which had made such an impression on me when I received her first letter. Her formal education, she said, had ended after she graduated from a girls' school in Nara, but she had continued to read and practise calligraphy in her spare time after marrying into the Matsunaga family. I learned that her husband was a descendant of Matsunaga Hisahide, a samurai who had risen to prominence during the civil wars of the Middle Ages. The family had lived here for nearly four hundred years. The traditional script and style of her letters owed more to family tradition than her own personal preference, she said. She told me that in their early days together, before his mother died, Matsunaga used to rail against the family's old-fashioned ways. The time-worn customs had continued even after his mother's death, and for a while she wondered whether this was what had driven him away. But over the past decade his tastes had changed. He was much mellower now. Nothing pleased him more than to see his wife studying *waka* poetry[3] and reading the classics. Recently he had taken to setting her assignments, handing her verses from the Lotus Sutra to copy as calligraphy practice. He had apparently developed a taste for the Chinese classics himself, and often disappeared into the storehouse to rummage through a collection of texts that dated back to his grandfather's days. 'He's getting better all the time,' she said when I asked about her husband's health. 'But he's still not fully fit. He's been talking about another pilgrimage to the thirty-three Kannon this spring – it did wonders for him the last time we went.'

His weight was down to just ninety pounds. He had a weak stomach and rarely ate more than one meal a day. He almost never drank alcohol, and took great care over his health. In spite of his weak constitution, he had never been seriously ill. She didn't seem too worried about him: indeed, she said, people of his type were often the ones who lived to a ripe old age. And Taeko, thankfully, had made a full recovery since her father's return. She was living with relatives in Nara and studying at a girls' school there.

Shigeko seemed just like any other happy wife and mother as she responded quietly to my questions. She was much more relaxed and forth-coming than I would have expected from her letters. If she could only be assured that her husband was home to stay this time, there was no reason why she shouldn't live a quiet and peaceful life here in this beautiful vil-lage, her days as free from clouds as the spring skies outside.

She was less flustered than I had expected when I mentioned the travel bag. 'I wish you could see it, but there's no way I could bring it out while he's here,' she said. Instead, she gave me a detailed description and told me everything she could remember about the shape of the bag and the design of the amethyst ring. It was impossible to be certain without seeing it myself, but everything she said made it sound like a perfect match for the ring I knew so well. As we talked, there came the mournful sound of an invalid's unsteady shuffling in the corridor outside, and the master of the house entered the room at last.

A look of embarrassment crossed his face as our eyes met. He would be forty-two this year, but he looked nearer fifty. Thick wrinkles covered his neck and forehead. His hair was greying, his temples already white. His prominent Adam's apple quivered whenever he spoke. In fact, every bone in his body seemed to shake. He looked like a shrivelled tree draped with a kimono, or a puppet whose strings had become tangled and were in danger of snapping at any moment, sending him crashing to the floor in pieces. Poor Gisuke seemed to share such fears himself. He moved warily, as if his body were a fragile porcelain jar. Even after he sat down, he had to lean a hand on the tatami to support his unsteady torso. Any second now, I thought, he's going to totter over or have a dizzy spell and fall flat on his back. Clearly he was still reeling from the effects of what must have been a severe nervous breakdown.

Even the sharpness in his eyes that I had noticed in his photograph now looked like a symptom of his illness. They were the eyes of a brooding misanthrope or a man haunted by obsessive thoughts. Nothing in his appearance reminded me of Tomoda. The sharp, sallow face with its bristly whiskers, the croaking voice that emerged on the rare occasions when he could be coaxed into speech, the tobacco-stained teeth . . . I didn't have to look at him for long as he struggled to stay upright to know that he was not Tomoda. I got to my feet. I had seen enough.

'He's not always so quiet,' Shigeko said as she showed me to the door. 'He can be quite chatty when the mood takes him. He even asks about you sometimes. I'm afraid he's often like this with people he doesn't know well. I'm sorry. After you've come all this way . . .'

'Please, don't mention it. But I'm afraid I have to disappoint you. Your husband is not Tomoda Ginzō. You must have been mistaken when you said you saw some resemblance. I hope you'll take good care of him. He seems awfully frail.' A look of disappointment crossed her face as we parted. She stood at the gate as I walked away, following me with her eyes.

In the end, seduced by the fine weather, I spent the rest of the day touring the local sights. I continued to Tsukigase and on the way back stopped in at Iga no Ueno, a small but pleasant town where I visited the site of Araki Mataemon's famous vendetta and paid my respects at Bashō's grave. Later, I admired the bonsai plum trees at the Taiseirō inn, where I stayed the night.

5

'You're a writer, K – I'm sure you have all kinds of strange stories locked away inside that head of yours. But the tale I'm about to tell you is so bizarre that I hardly know where to begin, even though it's the story of my own life. By the time I finish, I expect you'll barely be able to believe what you're hearing.'

Tomoda Ginzō paused and downed another glass of cognac. I had run into him earlier that evening at the Café Sans Souci in Kobe. It was June this year, 1925, and this was our first meeting since that night at Number 27.

'I was born in the village of Yagyū, in the Soekami district of Yamato Province. I come from an old family – we're the direct descendants of Matsunaga Hisahide from back in the Middle Ages. My name as it appears on the family register is Matsunaga Gisuke. But I know what you're thinking. Who was the Matsunaga Gisuke you met two years ago? Patience. All will be revealed.

'In 1905, when I was twenty-five, I married a young woman by the name of Shigeko. This was no heart-warming story of young romance, by the way. I was just out of university and getting married was the last thing on my mind. But if you know anything about the way these old families operate, you'll understand the position I was in. I'd been head of the family since my father died. There was no way they would leave me alone to do as I pleased. Before long, the summons arrived from my mother, ordering me to come home from Tokyo and get ready to welcome Shigeko as my wife. Let's just say the prospect didn't exactly fill me with joy.

'The thought of spending the rest of my days in the middle of nowhere made me despair. I was a young man bursting with energy – how could I enjoy an empty life like that? I'm a born hedonist. And lazy too – there's nothing I hate more than the idea of honest toil. Anyway, for better or worse I didn't exactly have to worry about where my next meal was coming from. I spent most of my time daydreaming about escaping to a life of pleasure.

'I was in love with the city. I never made it as far as Tokyo, but from time to time I did manage to conjure up business that would take me to Kyoto or Osaka. I spent time and money galore in the pleasure quarters of Gion and Shinmachi. But eventually I'd had enough of geishas and teahouses and I started to look for other things to do. In those days, though, there *wasn't* much else. I started to get desperate. But then my mother died.

'It was as though a burden had been lifted from my shoulders. The worst of my troubles were over now, I thought. At last, I'm free. The family could nag and disapprove all they wanted, but I wasn't afraid any more. I itched to get away, free to go wherever I liked! And once I found a foreign country that suited me, I need never come back to Japan again! I decided to fulfil an old dream and set out for Paris.

'You know me today as a Japanese man who lives the life of a Westerner. And you know that wine and women mean everything to me. You could say that I've dedicated my life to these two essential items. One problem: I don't like Japanese drink, and I don't like Japanese women. I worship everything about the West.

'Probably it was my upbringing that was to blame – growing up in that old house in the country. Of course I was going to react against all the suffocating, old-fashioned traditions. A friend during my student days in Tokyo was another bad influence. He took me to Yokohama a couple of times, where I entered a dream world that few Japanese in those days had ever seen. It was my first glimpse into the world of the white man's pleasures. From that moment, I had nothing but contempt for Oriental tastes and traditions. It was all so gloomy – just like that old house in Yagyū. The idea of elegance and restraint disgusted me. It was the exact opposite of everything that was genuine and honest in life, of everything natural and spontaneous. It's not a culture for healthy young people with the energy and drive to make a life for themselves. Doddering old fogies put up with it because they have no choice. They force themselves to find meaning and pleasure in their tedious lives. But really it's nothing more than a sad and twisted mix of inhibition and self-deceit. Even when he does indulge in pleasure, the Oriental never really lets himself go. It's all so half-hearted.

'*Subtle*, they call it. *Suggestive. Refined.* What a lot of nonsense. It's a question of aptitude. Orientals just can't deal with a full dose of excitement. They're not up to it physically. Take singing. Here in the East, no one would dream of really opening up and belting out the loudest voice they can produce. It's more *refined*, you see, to sing in that lonely little whine. And women. When a woman is preparing herself to enter mixed company, does she do whatever she can to make herself attractive? Quite the opposite. She buries whatever charms she might have under several layers of sleeves and sashes. It's supposed to be more *alluring* that way, you see. Poppycock. The truth is that they *don't* because they *can't*.

'If they try to hit a high note, all that comes out is a thin falsetto squawk and they can't even hold that for long. And as for the women – the truth is that the Oriental woman doesn't have much to show off even if she wanted to. A muddy complexion and no curves at all. That's what I mean: they're just not up to it physically. But there's nothing they can do about it. They have no choice – and so they pretend that their way is more refined. Well, as soon as I realized what was going on, I started to despise the Orient. The people's yellow faces disgusted me. My problem, of course, was that I was no better – I had the same complexion myself. Every time I looked in the mirror I was reminded of my tragedy. Why had I been born into this land of yellow people? And the longer I stayed here, the yellower my face seemed to become.

'I dreamed of leaving this gloomy, lukewarm, spirit-sapping land behind me and escaping to the West. To a land where the voice soars free, singing songs of joy! No more of this stunted culture with its precious talk of elegance and subtlety and restraint. I wanted to be surrounded by people whose bodies looked more beautiful the less was left to the imagination. To the West! Where a world existed that was the very opposite of this land of subtle hints and things left unsaid – a world of strong colours, poisonous stimulants and alcohol that scalds the tongue. I longed to reach a place of extreme hedonism, where people pushed themselves to their very limits in pursuit of pleasure – a world of insatiable desires and unending intoxication. I set my sights on Paris, the quintessential heart of the sensual West I longed to find.

'I set off in the summer of 1906 when Shigeko was pregnant with our first child. Secretly, I'd resolved that I would never come back to Japan alive and I took steps to ensure that the family would be secure after I was gone. I'm sure she suspected the decision I'd made. She must have wept and cursed her luck. She knew now what a heartless man she had married. But she was powerless. She had no choice but to do what I said.

'To be honest, I did feel a slight twinge of remorse as the day of departure drew near. But all my doubts disappeared as soon as I boarded the ship. I didn't even have to wait till we got to France. The fun started as soon as we arrived in Shanghai. I fell in love in every port we visited. Forget about Paris, I thought, this is where I want to be! I'll make my home here with these wonderful women by my side. I said the same thing everywhere we stopped. In every city there was a new world waiting for me – stranger and stranger worlds like nothing I'd ever seen.

'My infatuation and intoxication grew deeper with every mile we travelled from Japan. When I reached Paris I threw myself wholeheartedly into a life of decadence. The bashful Oriental mind can hardly imagine the things I found there. Paris was a whirlpool of lust and desire – a dizzying vortex of excess, debauchery and sick perversions. It was everything I'd dreamed it would be – a paradise of sensual pleasures. I leaped in headfirst, desperate to be sucked into the whirlpool. I gave myself up to it, body and soul. A true hedonist is quite happy to pay with his life for pleasure. Alcohol, tobacco, gourmandizing and women: a hedonist would happily sacrifice his health and life to satisfy his appetite for these toxic pleasures. I plunged into an ocean of debauchery. I lived in the moment, resigned to the knowledge that each wave of pleasure might be my last. And these premonitions of mortality only made me more reckless.

Wine and women were more irresistible than ever, and I dived to the very depths of depravity.

'Within a year and a half of arriving in Paris, I realized that I'd become completely assimilated. I had become utterly Westernized, not just mentally but physically. Most people who travel to the West experience something similar, I suppose. But I can't believe that many have ever exhibited symptoms as extreme as mine – and within such a short space of time. My entire physique had changed. At first, I hardly noticed. But occasionally I'd run into other Japanese travellers, and none of them would recognize me as a compatriot. Some thought I was Italian. Others took me for a Spaniard. The true extent of the change I had undergone hit me when I was drinking with a girlfriend in a café one evening.

'A Japanese man was sitting at the next table and when I looked closely I realized I knew him. It was my old friend S. We'd been at university together and had been quite close at one stage. But he obviously didn't recognize me, even when he looked straight into my face. How odd, I thought. And then it dawned on me: I had changed so much that even my old friends couldn't recognize me. I cannot describe the happiness I felt at that moment. I walked over to his table, looked him in the eye, and spoke to him in French. Even when he heard my voice, he didn't recognize me. I was overjoyed.

'I raced home, my feet hardly touching the ground. I ran to my rooms and stood before the mirror in raptures, mesmerized by my own reflection. I remembered some photographs I had had made just before leaving Japan. I dug them out and compared them with my reflection in the mirror. What a contrast! It was incredible! Face, build, skin colour, the expression in the eyes . . . Was it really possible that a simple change of environment could alter a man so much in just a year and a half?

'I'd always been thin at home but I'd started to put on weight as soon as I boarded the ship. I'd been drinking night and day throughout the voyage, and by the time I arrived in France my clothes didn't fit me any more. So I knew I'd put on weight. But I hadn't realized until now just how radically this had changed me. It wasn't just that I looked different. As I looked at the photographs and compared them with the figure in the mirror before me, it would have been closer to the truth to say that I'd become someone else entirely. Matsunaga Gisuke, born in the village of Soekami in the province of Yamato, the descendant of Matsunaga Hisahide, was no more. He had vanished from the world and been replaced by someone else. The man I now saw before me was someone of no discernible race or nationality. You couldn't have said whether he was Japanese, Italian or Spanish. And this was me! This mysterious man was what I had become! A shiver ran through me. It was like something from one of those strange Western stories about doppelgängers. Except that in my case, I was the one who had turned into someone else. I felt possessed. I looked down at Matsunaga's photograph again. Was this really the man I had been just eighteen months ago? It was no surprise my friend hadn't recognized me. I hardly recognized myself.

'That moment made up my mind. I told myself: I am no longer Matsunaga Gisuke. Who was this man in the photograph – this spindly, gloomy-faced Oriental? I wanted nothing more to do with him. Our relationship is over, I said, and tossed his picture to the floor. A sense of joy welled up inside me like nothing I had felt before.

'I was Japanese no longer! I had been transformed into a Westerner! I was mad with joy. I clapped my hands and stamped my feet. I sang and danced around the room. Images came to me of Japanese food and clothes and customs. But they came to me not as memories of things I had experienced myself. They were like scraps of information I'd picked up about the lives of a faraway tribe. To get there you'd have to travel down to Marseilles and board a ship for the Orient. Eastward and eastward you'd sail, crossing the seas for six weeks or more until finally you reached a small island country called Japan, where the people have yellow faces and live in dark, gloomy houses. They speak in tiny, mumbling voices, and in the morning they sip miso soup out of wooden bowls coated in black lacquer. What a dank, colourless existence! And they don't even have any furniture in these shadowy houses. No beds, no chairs, nothing. They spend their lives down on the floor, crouching under low ceilings and sitting on their heels. Just imagining it made me feel claustrophobic. How suffocating! If the person I was now – I went by the name of Jacques Morin since leaving Matsunaga behind forever – if I had been dropped down into that world and forced to live like that again, I don't think I would have survived a single day.

'I know what you're thinking. What am I doing in Japan now? Why didn't I live out the rest of my days in Europe? You might well ask. The devil was toying with me again. As I told you, I was in love with Paris and the life I had there. It was a life of perfect indulgence – one pleasure after another, day after day after day. I had no intention of coming back – I expected to die there when the time came. And I kept getting fatter. At my peak, I weighed nearly 170 pounds. My skin got whiter all the time, the redness in my cheeks more and more pronounced. I was aglow with health. I had resolved to stay in Paris if it killed me. But, in fact, my new lifestyle seemed to be doing me no harm at all. I plunged deeper into the world of the senses – determined to drain the cup of pleasure to the last dregs. No matter how deeply I drank, it was never enough. If a man wants to be fit and healthy, all he needs to do is live the way they do in the West. Live life to the full. Your appetites are there to be satisfied. Have your fill, whether it's food or women you hunger for. The self-effacing Oriental philosophy of restraint just makes people weak.

'I was the living proof. Since I'd become Westernized and bulked up, I'd become the picture of health and vitality! And it wasn't clean living and a healthy diet that did it, that's for sure. It didn't seem to matter how I neglected my health: I got bigger all the time. What better evidence could there be for the benefits of positive living than the fine physique I had developed since I came to Europe? I was convinced I had made the right decision. I became reckless.

'How wonderful life was back then! A pleasant climate, wonderful food and not a care in the world. I enjoyed a string of successful love affairs. If I gambled, I won. I was sailing on an ocean of happiness with the wind set fair behind me – all I had to do was sit back and let the breezes blow me from one happy day to the next. I still had plenty of money. And even if I somehow managed to spend it all, there were plenty of ways for me to make a living, so long as I wasn't too proud to lower myself a little. This was Paris – even black Africans can live pretty well in Paris. And if it didn't work out, I was ready to die by the roadside. So there I was – optimistic and carefree and ready for whatever the future might hold. Or so I thought.

'That's when things started to go wrong. Just when I thought nothing could harm me, up jumped the devil and turned everything upside down. It was a beautiful day when it happened – a bit like one of those days you sometimes get in Japan as summertime fades into autumn. I was out for an afternoon stroll along one of the boulevards. Everything was perfect and I stopped for a moment to enjoy the view. I stood and looked up through the branches of the plane trees into the clear blue sky. And in that instant – and why, I've never known – I lost my balance. I started to shake. My vision blurred. I saw spots dancing across the sky. Then everything went dark and I almost fell over backwards. It ended in an instant, and before I had time to realize what was happening, I was back to normal again. I went on my way and forgot all about it. Until it happened again. And again.

'It was the same every time – I'd look up at something and suddenly my vision would swim. I became dizzy. I'd feel a sharp, heavy tug at my neck, as if I had a lead weight attached to the back of my head, pulling me backwards. Over time, it got worse. After a while, it didn't just happen when I looked up any more but sometimes when I looked down. One time I dropped a glove in the street. I bent down to pick it up and felt all the blood in my body rush to my head. The veins in my neck bulged and my whole face turned bright red like a boiled octopus. I could feel myself losing consciousness – any moment I was going to fall flat on my face. What the hell was happening? It was terrifying. I had no idea what was wrong. I tried to shrug it off and waited for it to pass. The occasional dizzy spell is nothing to worry about, I told myself. Anyone could have them. But it was no use. Soon it was happening every time I washed my hair or bent down to tie my shoelaces.

'The worst time was when I was eating a bowl of hot soup in a restaurant one day. It happened suddenly, as always. One moment everything was normal, the next I was in the throes of an attack. My face turned red and I could feel myself about to pass out. I thought I was going to collapse into my soup. Luckily I managed to pull myself back just in time; I came to my senses as my nose was about to hit the soup. But it was a shock. Maybe the soup was too hot. But if I was going to have an attack every time I bent my head to eat, I was going to have to be more careful where I took my meals from now on. Was I having a breakdown? Or was some horrible virus wreaking havoc with my brain?

'It was strange, but now I started to hear the voice of cowardice whispering in my ear. I'd made up my mind to die here if need be. And as far as I was concerned, nothing had changed. But these dizzy spells terrified me. My heart started racing, and I felt as though I were about to lose control completely. Cowardice creeps up on you. It eats away at your soul before you know what's happening. And when it strikes, it's irresistible. You might think you're ready to die, but there's no defending yourself against an attack of cowardice. "I don't mind dying" is not the same as "I am not afraid of death". The two conditions are perfectly compatible. You might not mind the idea of dying, but the fear remains.

'I found myself trembling at the slightest thing. What was wrong with me? I'd told myself I didn't mind dying – and now I was scared out of my wits by a little thing like this? But it didn't make any difference how I reasoned with myself. Suddenly, without warning, my whole body would start to shake and tremble. The colour drained from my face. I looked like clay. I was drenched in a cold sweat, unsteady on my feet. Sometimes it happened in the streets, in a crowd of people. All I could do was escape as quickly as possible. I'd make a mad dash for it, scampering home wildly like some lunatic, tugging out my hair in clumps. If it happened at home, I'd pound my feet against the floorboards and throw myself against the doors and walls. I picked things up and hurled them across the room. Eventually, I would dash to the washstand and douse myself with cold water.

'The palpitations grew worse and worse. My chest pounded as though my heart were going to explode. The attacks never lasted more than a few minutes, and after a few shots of brandy I usually felt more or less normal again. But I never knew when the next attack was coming. I lived in fear, a bottle of brandy constantly at my side.

'At first, these foolish attacks only happened when I was alone. So long as no one else noticed anything, it was easy enough to deal with the effects. But before long this changed too. In those days I was obsessed with a young chorus girl called Suzanne. We met as often as we could, and spent most of our nights and days together. And then, one evening, it happened. We met in our usual place, and were sitting back, exchanging sweet nothings on a chaise longue. Now, this Suzanne had pure skin as white as alabaster. And as I lay there admiring the arm in front of me, I was struck again by how beautiful she was. I'd spent many a happy hour in rapt contemplation of her skin before, but that night, for some reason, I was more bewitched than ever. I was transfixed by her pure white arm.

I allowed my eyes to move slowly up her arm to her shoulders. Ah, her shoulders! They were like nothing I'd ever seen – pale, shimmering perfection, even more sublime than her arms! I felt a shudder run through me. Every hair on my body stood on end. As the dazzle of her white skin flashed upon my optic nerve, I felt the world start to spin. I felt dizzy and there was a cold stabbing in my chest. Suddenly my sense of awe (How white her skin! How perfect!) turned to fear. My legs shook, as if I had made the mistake of looking down from the top of a cliff into the gaping abyss below. I know it sounds ridiculous to talk about a woman's pale skin as something terrifying. But it was so beautiful! And it belonged to the woman I loved more than anyone else in the world! This was enough to set anyone's heart hammering.

'"What's wrong? You're so pale," Suzanne said in a voice of tender concern. She slid over beside me. As she moved closer, her white skin loomed before my eyes. My terror reached a climax. I thrust away her hand and dashed to the washstand to throw cold water over my head.

'"Suzanne! Brandy! Quickly!" And that's the last I remember. One moment I was screaming for brandy, the next I was out cold.

'It pains me to think about it even now. To be blessed with such a wonderful woman and to be rendered incapable of enjoying the act of love with her! I fled her embrace and trudged back to my lodgings alone, cursing myself. The first thing I had to do was get through the following evening. We had an arrangement to meet again and I knew that any repetition of tonight's performance would mean the end. The best thing I could do was to finish the relationship myself as painlessly as possible.

'Not that I had tired of her. I knew she would be waiting for me and I could barely stop myself from rushing to see her right away. As soon as my attack had passed, her pure white skin, which had inspired such horror and revulsion the night before, once again took on the air of something magical. How could I have contemplated separating from such a wonderful woman? I was more in love with her than ever.

'I plucked up my courage and set out for her house, a prayer in my heart all the way. We managed to meet again several times in this way, but I suffered at least a mild attack almost every time. To make matters worse, it wasn't just her skin that set me off any more – anything pleasurable could act as a trigger. Once my excitement reached a certain pitch, it was all over.

'I'd drive myself on, climbing towards a peak of excitement – and then, suddenly, a valley of fear would open up and I'd come thudding down with a crash. When her burning lips drew close to mine, when she wrapped her arms around me as if she never meant to let me go, when we lay giggling and tickling each other in innocent play . . . My attacks always came at the worst possible moments. The greater the pleasure on offer, the worse the fear became: as if it were determined to shatter our happiness into pieces. Even when I didn't have an attack, the terrifying thought that it might happen again stopped me from enjoying myself. Here I was, a dedicated hedonist pledged to enjoy life to the full – and look at the state I was in! I'd lost the ability to practise my faith!

'Listen, K. Try to understand. Can you imagine the anguish I was facing every day? My life was a misery. The skies over Paris were as clear as ever. The sun still shone, and there were more beautiful women on the streets than you could count. But none of it brought me pleasure any more. It was torture. If I looked up at the sky my head spun. Go out in the sunshine, and the blood would rush to my head. The sight of white skin terrified me. I was inconsolable.

'My eyes were so bad by now that I couldn't stand the sunlight. I took to hiding like a mole in my gloomy room where no sunlight could penetrate. And then one day an image came into my mind of another room I'd once known. A room just as dark as this one, but somehow gentler and less oppressive. I remembered the old house back home in Yamato.

'It was only a few years since I'd left, but my memories seemed to come from the ancient past. I remembered the old life I'd led in that house for the first two decades of my life. The custom we kept up even now of lighting old-fashioned lanterns when we went to bed; the dreamy flickering light they made by your pillow. The smoke-blackened ceilings and main pillar of the dark bedroom. My wife's peaceful face in the shadowy lamplight, wrapped under the bedclothes and dropping off to sleep.

'What was I doing, thinking nostalgically of Japan like this? I tried to drive the thoughts from my mind. But the harder I tried, the more insistently the memories came back. I was overcome with sentimentality. I felt an indescribable longing for the past. And it wasn't just the old village.

'I thought back on the times I'd spent in the pleasure quarters. Memories of Gion and Shinmachi – the evocative twang of the shamisen, the delicate, lyrical songs sung with refinement and restraint. Everything I had once rejected; everything I had dismissed as self-serving lies and deceit. But now I discovered with a jolt that the memory of these things had a strange power to calm my ravaged nerves.

'But that wasn't the worst of it. I started to feel that white skin lacked something – a gentleness and sweetness and wholehearted sympathy I knew I could find only in a woman whose skin was tinged with yellow. I imagined the taste of miso soup in the morning. Pickles and rice, soup made from kelp stock, and raw sea bream arranged neatly on a tray. The simplicity and balance of the colours! I dreamed of the clean taste of Japanese food. I cursed myself as I did it. What was I thinking, longing for Japan shamelessly like a lovesick fool? What had happened to my pride?

'But it was no use. I couldn't stop the thoughts in my head. It was the same everywhere I looked. The tastes and fashions of the West seemed loud and vulgar to me now – shallow and without substance. I heard a voice constantly in my ear: *You are an Oriental. You'll never belong here. You can never become fully Westernized.* It followed me everywhere I went. Three times a day when I sat down to my meals, I would hear it taunting me again: *Give it up*, it would say. *You're not fooling anyone. You don't really think this stuff tastes good. You don't really like drinking from these glittering glasses and cutting up your food with metal prongs and saws. And look at that tablecloth and these porcelain plates. Oh, it's all very neat and hygienic, I suppose. But it's not exactly subtle, is it? Where's the depth to it? Wouldn't you rather eat with chopsticks from a set of lacquered bowls? Wouldn't that agree with you better? Don't you think it's slightly barbaric to hack at food with a knife and fork like this? It's closer to the way animals eat.*

'On and on it went, trying to tempt me back into my old ways. If I went to the opera, my evening would be ruined by a voice in my head that gave me no peace. *Oh, please! This is too much! I don't care how hard you try to pretend to appreciate European music, I refuse to believe that you enjoy this noise! You might fool everybody else – but you'll never fool me.*

'The voice never let up. It ridiculed me wherever I went. *Listen to them yelping up there, those sopranos and baritones you claim to find so wonderful. No more of this nonsense about "voice production" and "timbre". They sound like animals in pain. That ringing in your ears every time they hit a high note? That's your eardrum about to burst. Don't try to pretend. I know you're longing for the sweet songs of home. Those gentle songs are what will always be true music to your ears.*

'The constant chattering grew more and more insistent, until it wasn't a whisper any more and I could hear it as clearly as I could hear my own voice. *Look*, it said, *I'm telling you this for your own good. You've got to get out of here now. Go home to Japan! Too much brightness, too much whiteness – of course it's going to make you feel queasy after a while. It's in your blood – you're an Oriental. Living in the midst of this glare for so long is enough to give anyone a breakdown. It's no use trying to force yourself to love white women; it's just not in you. Your constitution won't allow it.*

'I did everything I could to resist the voice. But I could do nothing about the fear that gripped me tighter with each day that passed. By now, every aspect of my life in the West revolted me. I shuddered every time I had to walk past a high-rise building or get in a lift or drive in a car at high speed. The squeak of the solid floorboards under my feet, the pounding of the pavements . . . I was sick of being boxed in by covered-up walls in rooms with no natural wood. And the odours: the make-up, the perfume, the clothes, the food, the peculiar smell of the white race that seeped its way into everything. The merest whiff of it was enough to make me gag.

'All right, the voice said. *Enough. This country isn't the place for you, alive or dead. Just get on the ship. You'll start to feel better as soon as you leave these streets behind. Get on that ship and your fits and palpitations will melt away. You think I'm trying to trick you? Try it and see.*

'I could feel temptation tugging at my sleeve. Part of me was still appalled by the idea of going back. But all the time, I could hear a voice pushing me forward and urging me back home. *Get out of here! Run away! Quick!*

'I took passage on a steam packet. I stood on deck and watched the port of Marseilles recede into the distance. Half of me felt a rush of liberation; the other half felt as though I were being dragged away kicking and screaming.

'Do you remember the first time we met at the Café Kōnosu towards the end of 1908? That was just after I came home. I disembarked in Kobe and came straight to Tokyo without letting the family know I was back. I still had a bit of fight left in me. I couldn't face the thought of crawling back home and begging for forgiveness.

'I visited a few people I knew in Tokyo, but none of them recognized me. I decided to recuperate in a hot-springs resort and find some way of getting back to Europe. Then I met you and introduced myself as Tomoda Ginzō, the first time I had ever used that alias.

'But my recovery didn't go as well as I had hoped. In fact, my health was getting worse all the time. I lost my appetite and libido. I was reduced to teetotalism. Even the brandy I'd been using for a lift now only increased my fear.

'From the end of that year till the following autumn, I visited most of the major hot-spring resorts in Japan – Hakone, Ikaho, Beppu. Near the end, I went into seclusion in a place no one's ever heard of in the mountains of Shinshū. I lived like a Zen monk, miles away from any stimulation. But it did no good. I was wasting away – I could hardly muster the strength to walk. Climbing stairs exhausted me. "I can't take much more of this," I thought. I started to dream of home. If I could just make it back home, with my wife to take care of me, maybe I'd have a chance of recovery . . . Tears flooded my eyes as I remembered everything I'd left behind. An image came to me of the night three years earlier, when my wife and I had said goodbye.

'I could see her in front of me, sobbing silently, the tears streaming down her cheeks. And then I remembered – she'd been pregnant when I left home. Barring accidents, the child would be nearly four by now. I could picture the scene vividly: the little child with its arms open wide, calling out in a feeble voice for a father who never came home. And I seemed to hear my wife comforting the child she clutched to her breast: "There, there. It's all right, Daddy will be home soon."

'Waves of homesickness washed over me. Eventually, I could barely stand. I spent whole days in bed, shivering under the blankets. One day I held up the mirror I kept by my bedside, expecting to be horrified by how much weight I had lost. But what I saw was worse than that. The face that stared back at me wasn't mine at all.

'The hollow cheeks, the thick whiskers, that skin colour, those eyes . . . I had seen this face before. I had changed again. Matsunaga Gisuke was back!

'I felt a shock that was double what I'd felt that night in Paris. Without realizing it, I had been transformed from the man I thought I was. No – the man I *knew* I was: Jacques Morin, that man of indeterminate race and nationality, who could have been Japanese, Italian or Spanish. Tomoda Ginzō, as you knew him later. That was the man I had been until – when? As recently as the previous year, at least. And now I was transformed back into Matsunaga again. What did it mean? Which was the real me? And was there anyone else out there like me, blessed or cursed with a body that could change from one person to another within the space of twelve months?'

Impelled by some strange force, Tomoda Ginzō hardly paused to draw breath. He leaned in close and went on with his story.

'But that's not the end. All I wanted to do was go home and live out the rest of my life as a loving husband and father. One day, I would be buried there, in the earth that had borne me. But you already know what happened next.

'As Shigeko wrote in her letter, I spent the next few years – from the autumn of 1909 to the spring of 1912 – back in Yagyū living the quiet life of a country gentleman. It was dull, to be sure, but solitude and quiet were just what I needed. It did my nerves good and helped me to shake off the anxiety that had weighed on me so heavily for so long. The area is full of temples and sightseeing spots perfect for soothing the mind. The plum blossoms at Tsukigase in March, the Yoshino cherry blossoms in April, the wisteria in Nara in May, along with all the spring buds and fresh grasses . . . Together with my wife and daughter, I visited the temples of Nara in the spring sunshine: Nan'endō, Tōdaiji, Yakushiji, Hōryūji. And as the three of us stood together in the halls of those ancient temples, hands clasped in prayer before the holy images, I felt my emotions rise. This was where I truly belonged, here back at home in the East. My parents had paid their respects in these same temples. They, too, had prayed in front of these images. For generations, my ancestors had bowed their heads here in the same spot where I now prayed with my own family. I looked up at the face of the Buddha and imagined an unbroken line of ancestors stretching back through the generations, looking down on us as we prayed. I was moved to tears. All my anxiety was gone, and there seemed to be no reason why I shouldn't live the rest of my life here in this country.

'But of course, it's no secret what happened next. During the fourth year after my return I started to notice an unexpected change coming over me again. At my weakest, I'd weighed as little as ninety pounds. But I'd started to put on weight again – slowly at first, so that it was barely noticeable, until I was about 110 pounds. And then my tastes started to change.

'Living in the country, we never ate meat at home. Even our fish we rarely ate raw. Normally we stuck to a steady diet of miso soup, pickles, fruit and vegetables. For a time after I got back, this was just what I needed. But after a while my palate cried out for change. I longed for something rich and greasy. I couldn't go on eating the same meal three times a day. I felt I would starve.

'I would sigh as the familiar lacquer tray was set down in front of me again, and memories would assail me of the chateaubriand steaks and the steaming bowls of bouillabaisse I had enjoyed in Paris. I longed to eat till my stomach swelled. I wanted food that would burn my tongue and warm my blood. Hunger is an irresistible force: I knew that my whole life would start to crumble unless that hunger was satisfied.

'I set out for Nara or Osaka with nothing but food on my mind, determined to get my fill of nourishment. Turtle, eel, beef sukiyaki: I stuffed myself with all the food I could take.

'And then I tried drinking again. I ended my abstinence in a restaurant in Osaka, not without a sense of trepidation. I was worried that the taste of alcohol might trigger another breakdown. But nothing happened.

'I looked up. I looked down. I spun and I danced. I skipped and I jumped. No dizziness, no nausea, no hot flushes, nothing. Lifts? No problem. Whizzing along in a car was a pleasure. "I'm cured! I'm free! That awful cowardice has left me in peace at last!" I shouted for joy. And out of my intoxication that night was born a creature of insatiable appetites, with a heart that hungered for excess . . .

'After everything I've said, I'm sure you can guess what made me leave home again that summer. For all the same reasons as before, I started to loathe my quiet life in the country: the provincial dullness of the village, of Japan, the whole restrained Oriental approach to life.

'I started to think obsessively about Suzanne's white skin. I longed to breathe the gay night-time air of Montmartre. I wanted to live as Jacques Morin again. But this time I couldn't just set sail for Europe. I didn't have that kind of money any more. Several times I came close to going anyway.

I could always scrape together enough for a one-way ticket, I thought, even if it meant travelling third class. But after the disastrous end to my first trip, I didn't dare to leave with no money. My breakdown had taught me my lesson and I was in no hurry to have another.

'And I still had my misgivings, in spite of my contempt for the East. I was determined that the next time I left it would be forever. I would spend the rest of my life in Europe and never set foot on Japanese soil again. But I couldn't help worrying – a typical Japanese failing – that I might land in Europe with no money to buy drinks or food worth eating . . . I worried that my physical strength might start to weaken as it had before. What would happen if the panic and fear attacked me again?

'I told my wife I had to leave for three or four years and asked her to wait for me. *I'm not sure where I'm going*, I said. *But if I survive I'll be back.* I set out for Shanghai with just under two thousand yen in cash. I knew that it was possible to live a good Western-style life in Shanghai. In some ways, it was almost better than Paris.

'My original plan was to try Shanghai for a while and see how I reacted. If there was no relapse and no homesickness, I would find a way to get to Europe from there. I spent my two thousand yen in no time. But as luck would have it, a bewitching American girl I met there fell in love with me and I started working as her pimp.

'As you know, a pimp is like a cross between a kept man and a booking agent. She took me on and with the help of a couple of other girls we managed to get a shady little business going. I won't go into too much detail about our dealings, but suffice it to say that there are white working girls – the "white slaves" as they call them – in every port of the East, and that their employers know one another and cooperate closely. A lot of the girls are constantly on the move from one port to the next: Yokohama, Kobe, Tientsin, Shanghai, Singapore, Hong Kong. Some of the bigger businesses cover the whole network – the same house holding what you might call branch offices in every port.

'The thought of getting caught up in this world horrified me at first, but I was going to starve if I didn't find some way to make money and I wasn't really cut out for anything else. And besides, I thought, I might even end up enjoying it, surrounded by women and drink, doing whatever I wanted and earning a bit of money at the same time. It could be worse. I planned to stick it out for a couple of years and then wash my hands of it and leave for Europe once I'd saved enough money. Well, that was the plan.

'And that's how things stood when I came back to Japan in the spring of 1913. It was one of our old haunts that brought me over. Number 10 in Yokohama was up for sale and I came with a view to buying the property and setting it up as a branch of my Shanghai operations. Nostalgia was not what brought me back this time. I was here as the agent of a white-slave trader to do business in a particular Oriental market, which happened to be the port of Yokohama. I stopped using the Matsunaga name before I left for Shanghai and took to introducing myself by the alias I used at random the night I met you: Tomoda Ginzō.

'I'd half expected that my appearance might undergo the same changes as last time, and I suspected it was only a matter of time before I started to fill out again. I wasn't disappointed. After a year of heavy eating and drinking, I swelled out like a rubber ball. The little man who left Japan a mere hundred pounds came back to Yokohama weighing 170 – tying my old record! I marched proudly into Tokyo and that's when I met you again that night in the Ginza, at the Café Liberté.

'I'll leave it to your imagination to fill in what happened next. You're a novelist, and now that I've told you this much about my remarkable life, the rest of the plot pretty much writes itself. Essentially, my body has continued to undergo the same transformations every four years or so. I swing between two extremes – at my thinnest, I get down to ninety pounds; at my biggest, I weigh 170. As soon as my weight falls below a hundred pounds, I start to long for my gloomy old house in the country. I feel an aching nostalgia for pure Japanese culture. I grow sentimental, and I transform back into Matsunaga Gisuke – in looks, in build and in personality.

'I go home to Yagyū and take up my quiet, peaceful life again. But as my health recovers, my zest for life returns, too. The first thing to come back is my appetite – ravenous, insatiable and impossible to ignore. My libido is never far behind. Oriental culture starts to disgust me, and I feel my spirit revolting against the restrained life again. My weight begins to creep up. Before I balloon out to my full size, I run away from home. I cross over to Shanghai, pick up a few old contacts and start up in business again. Within a year, I am back to 165 pounds. I turn into Tomoda again and come back to Yokohama to set up a branch of my business here. I live as a businessman, looking after my interests in China and Japan. This has been my life for the past fourteen years – a series of changes that dates back to 1912.

'I know what you must be thinking. Why did I never go back to Europe? It wasn't financial restraints that kept me here; I made more than enough money. The world war that broke out in 1914 was one factor; that made immigration procedures more difficult. But the truth was that I had all the white women I wanted. It didn't make much difference where I was. Yokohama and Shanghai were like Paris to me. You've seen the photographs; you know what it was like. No restraints, no limits, no questions asked. I didn't *need* to become Jacques Morin again. I had everything I needed as Tomoda Ginzō, or "Tom" as the girls called me. In many ways, it was even better this way.

'And so, in spite of my good intentions, I never did make a clean break. I decided I preferred to stay and continue my work here rather than travelling all the way to Europe again. So when Number 10 closed down in 1915, I deposited the money I made from the sale with a bank in Shanghai. I withdrew it again four years later and invested it in Number 27. It must have been around that time that "Tomoda" started to appear for the third time at the Café Plaisantin in the Ginza.'

I had been sitting quietly, listening to him tell the remarkable story of his life, but at this point I interrupted him with a question. 'Were you running those places, too – the Plaisantin and the Liberté?'

'No. The Liberté just happened to be open for business at the same time as Number 10. Same with the Plaisantin; it just happened to coincide with Number 27. I had nothing to do with either of them. The waiters there didn't really know who I was or what I was doing, although a few of them probably had their suspicions.'

'But what were you doing in places like that anyway? I thought you'd want to avoid Japanese company as much as possible in your Tomoda phase.'

'Ah, yes. I knew I was forgetting something important. I had heard a rumour that you used to frequent the Liberté from time to time. It was in the hope of meeting you that I started to go there. I wanted to tell my story to a writer – the story of my life, which seems incredible even to me.

'The same goes for the things Shigeko found in my bag – the seal, the ring, the photographs, the postcard from you . . . What do you think they were there for? I used to sell everything I owned when it was time for me to turn back into Matsunaga, but I never let go of what was in that bag. And I wasn't holding on to them just as souvenirs.

'A man never knows when his number might be up, but I made sure that if anything happened to me in the country, my secret would still come out in the end. So why didn't I own up when you confronted me in the Plaisantin? You took me too much by surprise, suddenly whipping out that photo of us on our pilgrimage. I thought you must have seen through half of my secret already.

'At first, I was shocked. But then I started to resent you. And not just you. I was angry at Shigeko, too, for taking matters into her own hands by writing that letter. I had no idea she'd been poking around in that bag till I heard it from you. So if I seemed a bit stubborn that night, that's why.'

'And what about that night at Number 27? Was that just stubbornness too?'

'No. I was terrified. The news from home had triggered a relapse. I was suffering panic attacks and had a terrible premonition that I was going to start losing weight again. I managed to get through that night somehow thanks to the booze, but the next day I had a full-blown attack. My weight started to drop and twelve months later I was back in the country again.'

'And the man I met in Yagyū two years ago – that *was* you, I take it?'

'Yes, of course. Or perhaps not. Who can say?' Tomoda set down yet another glass of cognac. 'Maybe Tomoda and Matsunaga are really two different people after all. In terms of personality, they could hardly be more different. When one of them is around, the other is nowhere to be seen. They take turns possessing this fellow we call "me". That's the best explanation I've been able to come up with, anyway.'

He held out his hand with the amethyst ring. 'Look,' he said. 'I use the ring to monitor my weight. At the moment, I'm 100 per cent Tomoda. There's not a trace of Matsunaga in me. As long as the ring is wedged on like that, biting into the flesh so that you couldn't get it off my finger if you tried, I know my weight is holding steady at around 165 pounds.'

'So you're still travelling between Shanghai and Yokohama on business, I take it?'

'Yokohama's finished since the earthquake. I'm working out of Kobe this time. Sometimes I wonder, though – what will become of me in the end? How long can this go on? I'm forty-five this year. In another three or four years, I'll be Matsunaga again. Somehow I get the feeling that this time will be the last. I was in Yokohama more often than Shanghai last time around. I was worried that my attacks might start up sooner than usual if I went any further from Japan. And now I'm based in Kobe – even closer to Matsunaga's village.'

A sad expression came into his eyes as he spoke. But even so, Tomoda Ginzō still looked a good three or four years younger than forty-five to me.

NAGAI KAFŪ

Behind the Prison

Translated by Jay Rubin

My dearest Excellency,

Thank you for your letter. I have been back in Japan for nearly five months.

I was in the West, as you know, but I was unable to find any fixed employment or to earn academic credentials during my time there. All I brought home with me was my collection of concert, opera and theatre programmes, as well as my photographs and nude paintings of female entertainers. I am a full thirty years old now, but, far from being prepared to start my own family, I continue to while away my days in a single room on my father's estate, which is located behind the prison in Ichigaya. It has a rather imposing gate and a lush growth of tall trees. I'm sure you could find it easily just by asking for my father.

I will probably be here, doing nothing, for the time being. Indeed, I may have to spend the rest of my life like this. Not that I am surprised to find myself in this situation. The question of what I should do once I returned to Japan is the same old one that continued to trouble me even while I was lost in music or intoxicated by the lips of a lover, or gazing at the Seine in the evening from the shelter of spring leaves. I confess it was my inability to solve this painful problem, and not any irrepressible longing for art, that enabled a weakling like me to bear the loneliness of living abroad for such a long time. In a foreign country, so long as one's health is unimpaired, one need have no fear of starving. One can abandon all concern for reputation and answer newspaper advertisements to become a waiter, a shop assistant – anything at all. Without the hypocritical label of 'gentleman', one no longer feels the shameful need to deceive others. One gains opportunities to observe the hidden truths of society and to touch the genuine tears of life. Oh, but once one has returned to the land of one's birth – there is no place more constricting – one's surroundings no longer permit such freedom, and one can no longer simply transcend the demands of social position. Like a skiff on a fog-shrouded ocean, I had no clear way ahead of me, no plans for the future when I landed in the port of Kobe with its low shingled houses and its monstrously twisted black pines. Perhaps I could stay there in hiding, I thought, rather than return to Tokyo where so many people knew me. At that very moment, a heartfelt cry reached my ears, the deep, strong voice of someone ascending the crowded gangplank –

'Welcome back, brother!'

And who should appear before me, dressed in a university student uniform, but my very own younger brother! I had naturally lost touch with my father, especially during the past two or three years, but, greatly worried, he had contacted the steamship company, learned which vessel I had boarded and sent my brother to meet the ship.

Shamed by the extent of my father's efforts, I felt an instinctive urge to hide my face. At the same time, I was sick of parental affection. Why did my parents not simply turn their backs on a son who had proved himself so unfilial? And why did that son feel so threatened by his sense of gratitude towards his parents? Why, when he tried to force himself not to feel such gratitude, did he succeed only in filling himself with pain and dread? No, nothing in this world is as oppressive and debilitating as blood ties. Any other relationship – be it with friend, lover, wife; be it obligatory or constraining or difficult – is something one has consciously entered into at some point. Only one's ties with parents and siblings are formed at birth and are unbreakable. And even if one succeeds in severing such relationships, all one is left with is the unbearable agony of conscience. It is simply one's destiny. Your Excellency, I am certain you have seen sparrows that have built nests in the eaves of your home. No sooner do the young fly away from the nest than they escape forever from this fateful shadow. Nor do the parents make any attempt to bind their offspring's hearts with morality.

One glance at my brother, born of the same blood, his face so resembling my own, was all it took to fill me with an indescribably cruel emotion. In an instant, it seemed to sweep away the inexpressible nostalgia

I felt, along with the sorrow, the joy, the vivid sense of freedom of my wandering years, leaving nothing behind. Suddenly the air enveloping me seemed to grow still, as might be imagined in a medieval monastery, cold as ice and clear as a mirror.

'The six o'clock is an express train,' my brother said. 'Let's buy our tickets.'

I said nothing in reply. At Kobe Station all I did was stare at a few unrefined but voluptuous American girls buying bouquets from a flower vendor. After arriving at Shinbashi Station the next morning, I found myself being whisked by rickshaw to my father's estate behind the Ichigaya prison.

They held a little banquet for me at home that evening. My father turns sixty this year. He probably felt he had to give the party to keep up appearances regarding his son and heir, whatever the truth of the situation. They put me in the seat of honour before the *tokonoma* where a calligraphic scroll hung inscribed with a long string of Chinese characters that meant nothing to me. Sitting at the other end of the table were my mother and father. To my right was the brother who had been adopted into my mother's family to carry it on as pastor of a small church. To my left was my parents' youngest child, the brother who had met my ship, sitting there in his impressive uniform, its gold buttons gleaming. There were flecks of grey in my father's moustache, but his tanned face was more radiant than ever, and the added years only seemed to increase the youthfulness of his robust frame. My mother, by contrast, looked as though she had aged ten or twenty years during my absence. Now she was just a shrivelled-up little old lady I could hardly recognize.

I would want a wife or lover and, I dare say, my mother to remain eternally young and beautiful. When I saw her looking so aged, I could hardly lift my chopsticks to join in the feasting. Sorrow, pity and a mix of even stronger emotions struck me all at once: an intense desire to revolt against the fate that dooms us to perish.

Your Excellency, my mother was a young woman until I left for the West. People who didn't know us very well used to ask if she was my sister. She was born in old Edo and raised to be a great lover of the kabuki theatre, a skilled singer of *nagauta* ballads while accompanying herself on the shamisen. She also played the koto. Approaching forty, she could still sing that wonderful passage from 'Azuma Hakkei' with ease, the shamisen tuned up to the high *roppon* scale: 'Pine needle pins in her hair, she makes her way along the dewy cobblestones beside the Sumida River, writing brush in its case wet with ink . . .' And yet she was very restrained in her tastes. As far back as her teenage years she is said to have hated the colour red, and I never saw an under-kimono of hers that could be described as gaudy, even when the family's clothing was spread out to dry at the height of summer: perhaps a muted persimmon-coloured grid pattern, or a pale blue Yūzen print of plovers against white-capped waves. I'll never forget all the theatres she took me to in the arms of my wet nurse – the Hisamatsu-za, the Shintomi-za, the Chitose-za – where we would indulge in a rare treat of broiled eel on rice in our box seats. And those marvellous winter days in the warmth of the *kotatsu*, where she would spread out her colourful woodblock prints of such legendary actors as Hikosa and Tano-suke and tell me all about the old days in the theatre! Oh, the cruelty of time that destroys all things! If only I could stay forever and ever with my mother, Your Excellency, enjoying those magnificent pastimes! For her I would gladly ferry across the Sumida on the coldest winter day to buy her those *sakura-mochi* sweets from old Edo that she loved so much. But medicine? That is another matter. Not even on the warmest day would I want to go buy her medicine.

Never have I had it in me to surrender to those ancient articles of faith which mankind has been commanded to follow. Such precepts are too cruel, too cold. Rather than bow before them, how often have I cried out in anguish, wishing that 'I' and 'the precepts' could be united in a perfect, warm embrace! But having despaired of such an easy resolution, I determined that I would confront them head-on, that I would do battle with Heaven's retribution. My father is a stern disciplinarian, a diligent man, a fierce enemy of all that is evil. The day after I came home, he quietly asked me about my plans for the future. He wanted to know how I intended to preserve my honour as a man, to fulfil my duty as a citizen of the empire.

Should I become a language teacher? No, I could never presume to present myself as a teacher of French. Any Frenchman would know the language far better than I could ever hope to.

Should I become a newspaper reporter? No, I can imagine myself becoming a thief some day, but I am not so inured to vice that I would treat justice and morality as merchandise the way such people do. The scandal sheets *Yorozu chōhō* and *Niroku shinpō* present themselves as paragons of virtue, but any society reformed by them would be far darker than a society left wholly unreformed. I worry too much about this to sink to their level.

Should I become a magazine reporter? No, I am not losing sleep over social progress or human happiness to the point where I would stand up as an advocate for good causes. Nor am I the least bit bothered, as some journalists seem to be, by the cannibalistic, incestuous lives of animals.

Should I become an artist? No, this is Japan, not the West. Far from demanding art, Japanese society looks upon it as a nuisance. The state has established a system of education by intimidation and forces us to produce grotesque vocalizations that no member of the Yamato race has ever pronounced – T, V, D, F – and if you can't say them you have no right to exist in Meiji society. They do this primarily so that some day we will invent a new torpedo or gun, certainly not to have us intone the poems of Verlaine or Mallarmé – and still less to have us sing the 'Marseillaise' or the 'Internationale', with their messages of revolution and pacifism. Those of us with a deep-seated desire to devote ourselves to the Muses or to Venus must leave this fatherland of ours with all its stringent rules before we can begin to embrace our harps. This would be of the greatest benefit both to the nation and to art itself.

No, no, there is not a single profession in this world that will keep me alive for the days that remain to me. Should I become a rickshaw puller wandering the streets of the city? No, I have too great a sense of responsibility for that. Could I safely fulfil the demands of the profession by delivering my passengers uninjured to their destinations? And what if I became a manservant cooking rice? Mixed in with the countless grains, might there not be an invisible chip of stone that would tear my master's stomach, endangering his life? The more precise and subtle a human being's awareness, the less he can presume to take on any profession, however humble. First he must starve, he must freeze, he must numb the precision of his mind, he must be blinded by his own selfish desires. At the very least, he must ignore the teachings of the ancient sages. Oh, you who sing of how hard it is to make a living! How I envy you!

I turned to my father and said, 'There is nothing for me to do in this world. Please think of me as mad or crippled, and do not press me to live up to normal worldly expectations.'

For his part, my father would have found it a stain on the family honour were his son to become known as a reporter or a clerk or a servant or some other lowly worker. 'Fortunately we have a spare room,' he said, 'and food. You can just live here quietly and keep to yourself.' With that, he brought the discussion to a close.

These past few months, I have spent one blank day after another gazing out at the garden. The hot August sunlight casts the shadows of the luxuriant trees over the garden's broad expanse of green moss. Here and there patches of light break through the trees' black shadows, trembling with each passing breeze. I find the sight inexpressibly beautiful. A cicada cries. A crow caws. And yet the world, exhausted by the scorching heat, is as hushed as at night. A sudden shower strikes, but because the larger part of the sky remains blue and clear, I can see each thick thread of rain falling in the bright light. Each of the plants responds differently to the downpour, the delicate ones bowing to earth, the stronger ones springing upwards, the sound of the raindrops striking them varying from light to heavy depending on the thickness of their leaves. The shower symphony rises to a great crescendo with the rumbling bass drum of thunder that rolls through, to be followed by the gentle moderato of the green frogs' flutes and a final hush as sudden as the piece's opening. Then the entire garden – from the tiniest tree branches soaring aloft to the leaf tips of the *kumazasa* bamboo creeping among the ornamental boulders – is strung with crystalline jewels that lend a startling radiance to the mossy carpet, across which the massed trees' long, diagonal, cloud-like shadows drift until the evening cicadas call and twilight arrives. Around the time a wind chime begins ringing incessantly and the servants light our paper lanterns, from the street beyond the front gate comes the light clip-clop of wooden clogs and the laughter of young women. A student ambles along, chanting a poem, a harmonica sounds, and somewhere far away the pop of what must be fireworks. A street musician passes by, lamenting another broken heart to the twang of a shamisen. The night deepens . . .

The insect cries grow louder with each passing day. When I lie down to sleep at night, a terrifying din travels from the closed-off garden all the way to the space beneath the veranda outside my room. What power rules these tens of thousands of creatures, what makes them all unite in one voice to besiege me like this? I feel as if I am camped alone on a magnificent plain beneath an endless sky, waiting an eternity for the dawn to break, but when I open my eyes the dim lamp on my desk reveals that I am actually lying beneath a low board ceiling that might come crashing down at any moment, my body confined by suffocating colourless walls and blank sliding paper doors. Then a keen sense of the nature of life in Japan overwhelms me – so limited, so lacking in depth. The sudden clatter of raindrops against the ceiling sounds like someone trying to play a broken koto. I hear the night wind tearing through the trees above. But the sound lacks the depth of a lion's roaring in a dark valley, and I wonder if what I hear is the rustling of reeds on the shoreline of a great river flowing through a tropical plain. The insects cry without cease. They cry even after the break of dawn and the arrival of noon. And that is not all I hear. The rains fall day after day.

What a humid climate we have! I try closing all the shoji and lighting the charcoal brazier in the corner of the room, but my kimono is still so moist I can't help wondering if my skin will grow scales like some fishy creature's. The fine leather binding of *The Diary of Countess Krasinska*, given to me as a keepsake by Rosalyn when I left America, has been all but destroyed by mould. The lacquer shoes in which I danced with Yvonne in a Parisian ballroom have grown a ghostly white fur. Cruel stains have formed on the summer topcoat I spread on the grass when lying there with Hélène in the Bois de Boulogne.

I hear the sad calls of vendors wandering through the neighbourhood and the clatter of shutters being closed nearby as night falls. Oh, the nights in Japan! No words can describe their darkness! Darker than death, darker than the grave, cold, lonely. Shall I call it a wall of darkness – an indestructible barrier that cannot be pierced by any blade of rage or despair, that cannot be scorched by any flame of rancour or frenzy? I sit beneath the only spot of light in the whole room, a single oil lamp, reading and rereading the letters I exchanged with the people I knew in those days of joy, unable to read a letter to the end before having to press my face, in tears, against its pages. The cries of the insects fill the garden.

Eventually, however, it dawns on me that the intense cries of the insects have begun slowly to fade with the passing of each dark and lonely night. I find myself wearing a new padded *haori* over my lined kimono, the smell of the freshly dyed cloth oddly sickening to inhale. The rains have ceased. In contrast to the morning and evening chill, the sunny afternoons are frighteningly hot. The leaves have turned yellow, but how strange to watch them as they flutter down through the windless air on to the garden's mossy carpet in the harsh, summer-like sunlight. I feel the deep melancholy of the French poet who sang of the South American climate: 'Here the leaves scatter in the April spring.'

I go out to the garden one afternoon, a partially read book of poems in hand, and walk among the beds. The streaming rays illuminate each overlapping leaf of the plums, the maples, the other trees that grow in such profusion, casting their shadows like patterns on the mossy ground. Deep in this shade stands a gazebo. Beyond it is an unobstructed view of a flowering field. I sit to take in the immense blue sky at a glance. Thin white clouds spread across the blue from west to east as if painted with a brush, never moving however long I gaze at them. Countless dragonflies flit back and forth like the swallows one sees high in the summer skies of France. Multicoloured cosmos, taller than the gazebo, bloom in profusion beneath the harsh sun, spreading to all corners of the field, each of which is densely covered in low-growing *kumazasa* bamboo. Crimson amaranths seem to burst into flame. The Chinese bellflowers and asters retain their brilliant purple, but the white-flowered bush clovers are already past their peak and bow to the ground like the dishevelled tresses of a woman who has thrown herself down in tears, flowing towards my feet upon the gazebo's paving stones. In their dewy shadows, one or two surviving insects cry out in thin melodic strains.

Ah, this blue sky, this sunlight: mementos of a forgotten summer. How could one imagine it to be October, to be autumn? The barest hint of a breeze turns the pages of the poetry book on my knees until I have a clear view of the final stanza of Baudelaire's sad 'Song of Autumn':

> *Ah! laissez-moi, mon front posé sur vos genoux,*
> *Goûter, en regrettant l'été blanc et torride,*
> *De l'arrière saison le rayon jaune et doux!*

'Ah! let me, with my head bowed on your knees, / Taste the sweet, yellow rays of the end of autumn, / While I mourn for the white, torrid summer!'[1]

No matter what I see, even the most beautiful flower, I wonder if it is blooming only to make us think of the sadness to come when it has withered and died. The delightful intoxication of love, I can only believe, exists to give us a taste of the sadness to come after parting. And surely the autumn sunlight shines this beautifully in order to tell us, 'Know ye that the sadness of winter will be here tomorrow.' Now and then I become strangely agitated and, wishing to see the fading sunlight for even a few seconds longer, I leave to walk not just in the garden but through the gate and into the streets beyond. Ah, what scenes the autumn sun – the autumn sun of my birthplace – has shown me!

As I said at the beginning of this letter, my home is located behind the Ichigaya prison. When I began my travels nearly six years ago, this was a tranquil patch of countryside. 'You know,' I would tell the city girls, 'it's that place where the azaleas bloom.' Only then would it dawn on them which area I was talking about. Now, however, it is just another new district slapped together on the edge of Tokyo. All that is unchanged are the long prison embankment that looms over the narrow street and the life of the poor who toil here beneath it.

The first thing you see across from our front gate is the long, weather-beaten wooden fence enclosing the jailers' compound and then the horrible embankment itself, casting a shadow over the narrow street and topped by a spiky hedge, beneath which not even a weasel could burrow. The flanks of the embankment are covered by a prickly growth of frightful devil's thistle, one touch of which would cause your hand to swell in pain. On stormy September days, I would expect the wind to blow over the dilapidated fence around the jailers' compound, and, sure enough, the next morning, when the street was littered with tree branches, I would see pairs of prisoners chained together at the waist in orange jackets with numbers on their collars and wearing bamboo coolie hats, pulling up and repairing the fence under the supervision of uniformed, sword-bearing guards. Sometimes, too, at the height of summer, a gang of prisoners would mow the weeds on the embankment. Passers-by would stop and stare at them in silence, eyes filled with simultaneous loathing and curiosity.

The embankment runs in a long, straight line from both left and right until it curves sharply inwards at the centre, where it ends in a large black gate between two thick columns. The gate's heavy-looking doors are always tightly shut. No voices can be heard from the other side of the gate, and there is nothing to be seen from the outside except a narrow chimney poking up above a low tiled roof, and four or five skinny cedars. The trees stand some distance away from one another, which to my eyes suggests that even these unfeeling plants are being kept apart in the prison yard to prevent them from whispering together, plotting evil schemes under cover of darkness.

Where the raised embankment suddenly gives out some distance from the gate, the narrow street becomes a downward-winding slope, on one side of which, during my absence, some rich gentleman seems to have built a new residence upon high stone walls, while on the other side the road is lined with the same kind of rental tenement houses that have been there forever, like a row of boxes, one atop another, going down the hill. The prison embankment stands behind them like a blank wall, thanks to which no ray of sunlight has ever reached the tenements. Their wooden foundations are rotting and over-grown with moss, and insects have eaten holes through the bottom edges of the storm shutters standing outside each unit's front lattice door during the day. Two or three of the units invariably have barely legible 'For Rent' signs hanging from them. And always there are signs soliciting piecework. Often when passing these tenements on a cold winter evening, I have seen on a small window's torn, soot-smeared shoji the pale shadow cast by an oil lamp of a woman with tousled locks retying her obi. And on sultry summer evenings, peering through sparse reed blinds, I have had a clear view of the secrets of these people's households. How well I recall passing by here on afternoons when the prisoners' used bathwater would gush down the drain-age ditches below the tenements' windows, raising clouds of foul-smelling steam. It must be the same even now. Most shocking of all were the local housewives with scabrous babies on their backs, seizing the opportunity to make use of the hot water on cold, clear days, to wash things in the ditches as they chattered away with mouthfuls of crooked teeth, or in summertime scattering the stinking water on the road.

Behind the Prison

Shabby shops line both sides of the road at the bottom of the hill – a sweet shop, a hardware store, a tobacconist, a greengrocer, a firewood seller – among which a rice merchant and soy sauce dealer are the only good old-fashioned establishments with thick pillars that might arouse vague feelings of rebellion. Which is not to suggest a modern socialist reaction on my part, but merely a fantasy inspired by the traditional look of the houses and starring such popular stage heroes as Jiraiya or Nezumi Kozō. Oddly, there are two old stonemasons down here, and especially noticeable of late has been the increase in the number of home-delivery tempura shops and fishmongers, proof of the day-by-day increase in the number of tenements in the area. Upon a wooden counter disturbingly overgrown with green moss sits a shallow, round wooden sushi rice mixing bowl half filled with greasy water containing fish parts, shaved fish meat and rows of skewered shellfish that have been dried in the sun, almost all bearing price tags of ten sen or less. As far as I can see, the eyes of the dead fish are all stagnant and cloudy, the scales on their bellies have faded to a pale bluish white, and the chilled bloody edges of their sliced meat have lost so much of their freshness that the colours in each shop front are not only unpleasant but downright depressing. The sight of dripping blood used to terrify me whenever I passed a butcher's shop in the West, but here, to the contrary, the thought that this faded, cold fish meat is the only source of nourishment for the blood of most of my countrymen fills me with an inexpressible sorrow. All the more so when I turn the corner at the bottom of the hill near sundown and hear the hoarse voice of the old man at a stand there displaying nothing but fish bones and guts with a scarf tied over the top of his head and yelling, 'Get your *tai* guts cheap! Get your *tai* guts cheap!' He's surrounded by housewives with babies on their backs, the women all screaming at him to bring his prices even lower.

Above the sand-whitened tiled roofs, the evening sky's great expanse glows less red than a murky burnt sienna because autumn is nearing its end, casting shadows more intensely black than the dark of night. The narrow road is suddenly crowded with men most likely coming home from work – rather well-dressed gentlemen, military men on horseback, passengers in rickshaws. All move as black shadows, without a single light to be seen in the houses on either side of the road. Running with dizzying speed among them are children at play, waving sticks and other playthings.

I have seen men in Western suits stop at the fish guts stand by the roadside on their way home from the office before climbing the hill towards the back of the prison, carrying their purchases wrapped in bamboo sheathing. The sight brings to mind scenes of dinner in poor Japanese households.

The lattice door of a tenement unit clatters but shows no sign of opening, nor does the patched grey shoji behind it catch any lamplight from within. The threshold remains in darkness. One Western-suited gentleman steps out of his never-polished rubber-soled shoes, opens the shoji and steps inside to find his disabled old mother coughing beneath the window of the tiny three-mat room. The baby is squealing. Shocked to realize that night has fallen, the wife squats down like a frog on the kitchen floor, nervously trying to fill the lamp with oil. Alerted to her husband's homecoming by the sound of the opening door, she turns her colourless face towards him in the skylight's afterglow, loose hairs from her dry-looking bun floating off in all directions. Though not cold, she sniffles as she offers him a blank 'Welcome home'.

Instead of answering, the husband asks, 'You're only getting to the lamp now?' and he scolds her for her poor housekeeping. His old mother crawls out of her bedding on the floor and tries to intervene. Whichever side she takes, the results are the same and the argument blossoms. Just then the eight-year-old comes in wailing about the fight that sent him flying into the drainage ditch, and he has the mud-smeared kimono to prove it. Now the argument centres on him until the evening dishes line up beneath the dusky lamp – boiled beans, pickled vegetables, a stew of fish bones and scallions, and a rice tub smeared with dirty fingerprints. Gathered around their flimsy table, the family talk about uncle so-and-so, who showed up this afternoon wanting to know the cost of Mother's medicine in the spring. They talk about how the wife's father lost his job. They talk about their everyday expenses. The family's mouths were formed for only two purposes: to eat food and to complain endlessly about the hardships of life. Whether they are impoverished or not, it amounts to the same thing. The pure art of conversation for its own sake is lost on people like this. They have no need of language for anything other than seeking advice, complaining, harping on the same old stories and quarrelling.

*

Such are the scenes that have greeted me when I have strolled out of our front gate and up the road behind the prison in the hope of enjoying the autumn light. What grips my heart still more painfully are the tragic acts of animal cruelty I see on the road. Two or three freight wagons in a row drawn by emaciated horses over long distances, some loaded with bales of rice, others with timber or bricks or other heavy payloads, will be led through the rear gate of the prison at the top of the slope. Unfortunately for the animals, the open area in front of the gate rises at the same angle as the road itself, which causes the wheels of the turning wagons to dig into the soft, damp soil, and this makes it impossible for the exhausted horses to drag the wagons up and through the gate in a single effort. When this happens, the rough teamsters scream at the horses and beat them mercilessly with fallen branches. The men yank violently on the reins, and the horses clamp their white teeth on the bits in what seems like unbearable pain. Their manes bristle, their bloodshot eyes bulge and finally their forelegs collapse, bringing them down on the gravel surface. Everything on the narrow slope comes to a halt whenever this occurs, but far from being shocked, most passers-by stare open-mouthed in amusement. Here, then, is proof that cruelty to animals is an issue only to a few Christians, not a pressing problem for the whole of Japanese society. Is this a matter for grief or celebration? Witnessing these scenes only deepens my sense that the Japanese are a warlike people who are sure to defeat the Russians once again in the future.[2] Oh, patriots, set your minds at ease. As long as you can make a yellow man like me believe in the white man's Yellow Peril, you should feel free to go on cursing your wives, oppressing your children and giving three cheers for the empire with glasses held high. And so we declare: the age is still too young for us to worry that melancholy poets will begin giving voice to their ideals.

Slowly, gradually, I have come to avoid and even fear the prospect of venturing beyond the front gate. Yes, let me gaze in quiet solitude at the shifting autumn sunlight through the glass doors of my veranda.

Sadly, autumn is already beginning to fade. The intense sunlight that made the afternoons seem like summer has weakened now, and the sky is always thickly overcast. It looks like the frosted glass skylight of a large atelier, across which cloud curtains move, sending down pale refracted rays as soft as twilight. Shadows and colours seen in this light seem to have a transparent clarity that cannot be sensed in the blinding glare of the sun. The trees have lost their leaves, their crowns bare and bright, their slender black branches tracing innumerable upward-thrusting lines against the sky. Behind them, the gazebo's thatched roof and the field's withered grasses glow yellow through the black evergreens in the distance. Half hidden by the ornamental stones beyond the veranda, tiny golden chrysanthemums bloom like stars. From there to the far end of the garden spreads an unbroken velvet carpet of moss even more lustrous than in summer. Two or three wagtails, pecking at the tiny moss flowers, move across the carpet, flicking their long, pointed tails up and down. How sharply their grey feathers and the crimson leaves of the dwarf sumac bonsai upon a boulder contrast with the broad green lustre of the moss!

No wind blows. The shifting, cloudy autumn afternoon maintains its thick silence, giving the illusion that the outlines of objects have been obliterated, leaving only their colours. On occasion, a few remaining leaves will suddenly flutter down from a tree. This unexpected stirring of the air is like the deep sigh of some mysterious creature. When that happens, every single leaf in the garden – from the evergreens' lush needles to the clumps of chrysanthemums among the stones – resounds with an inexpressible sorrow and then, a moment later, reverts to silence. Atop the smooth moss: the wagtails again, the chrysanthemum blossoms, the bonsai's crimson foliage. Ah, the light of a dream, the thin overcast of departing autumn.

Excellency! Since yesterday I have been reading Verlaine's book of prison verse *Sagesse*:

> O my God, you have wounded me with love.
> The wound remains open, unhealed.
> O my God, you have wounded me with love . . .[3]

Excellency! Please come visit me once before the onset of winter. I am lonely.

NATSUME SŌSEKI

Sanshirō

Translated by Jay Rubin

He drifted off, and when he opened his eyes the woman was still there. Now she was talking to the old man seated next to her – the farmer from two stations back. Sanshirō remembered him. The old man had given a wild shout and come bounding on to the train at the last second. Then he had stripped to the waist, revealing the moxibustion[1] scars all over his back. Sanshirō had watched him wipe the sweat off, straighten his kimono and sit down beside the woman.

Sanshirō and the woman had boarded this train in Kyoto, and she immediately caught his eye. She was very dark, almost black. The ferry had brought him from Kyushu the day before, and as the train drew closer to Hiroshima, then Osaka and Kyoto, he had watched the complexions of the local women turning lighter and lighter, and before he knew it he was homesick. When she entered the car, he felt he had gained an ally of the opposite sex. She was a Kyushu-colour woman.

She was the colour of Miwata Omitsu. At home, he had always found Omitsu an annoying girl, and he had been glad to leave her behind. But now he saw that a woman like Omitsu could be very nice after all.

The features of this woman, however, were far superior to Omitsu's. Her mouth was firm, her eyes bright. She lacked Omitsu's enormous forehead. There was something pleasant about the way everything fitted together, and he found himself glancing at her every few minutes. Several times their eyes met. He had a good long look at her when the old man took his seat. She smiled and made room, and soon after that Sanshirō drifted off.

The woman and the old man must have struck up a conversation while he was sleeping. Awake now, Sanshirō listened to them.

Hiroshima was not the place to buy toys, she was saying. They were

79

much cheaper and better in Kyoto. She had to make a brief stop in Kyoto in any case and bought some toys near the Tako-Yakushi Temple. She was happy for this long-delayed return to her native village where her children were staying, but she was concerned about having to live with her parents now that the money was no longer coming from her husband. He was a labourer at the Kure Navy Yard near Hiroshima, but had gone to Port Arthur during the war.[2] He came back for a while when the war ended, but left again for Dalian because he thought he could make more money there. His letters came regularly at first, and money arrived every month, but there had been neither word nor money for the past six months. She knew she could trust him, but she herself could no longer manage to live in Hiroshima without work. At least until she learned what had become of him, she would have to go home to her parents.

The old man did not seem to know about the Tako-Yakushi Temple or care about toys. He responded mechanically at first. But the mention of Port Arthur brought a sudden show of compassion. His own son had been drafted into the army and died over there, he said. What was the point of war, anyway? If there were prosperity afterwards, that would be one thing, but people lost their sons and prices went up; it was so stupid. When there was peace, men didn't have to go off to foreign countries to make money. It was all because of the war. In any case, he said, trying to comfort her, the most important thing was to have faith. Her husband was alive and working, and he would come home soon. At the next stop the old man wished her well and stepped briskly from the carriage.

Four other passengers followed the old man out, and only one got in. Far from crowded to begin with, the carriage now seemed deserted. The sun had gone down: maybe that had something to do with it. Station workers were tramping along the roof of the train, inserting lighted oil lamps into holders from above. As though reminded of the time, Sanshirō started to eat from the lunchbox he had bought at the last station.

The train started up again. It had been running for perhaps two minutes when the woman rose from her seat and glided past Sanshirō to the door of the carriage. The colour of her obi caught his eye now for the first time. He watched her go out, the head of a boiled sweetfish in his mouth. He sunk his teeth into it and thought, she's gone to the toilet.

Before long, she was back. Now he could see her from the front. He was working on the last of his meal. He looked down and dug away at it with his chopsticks. He took two, three bulging mouthfuls of rice, and still it seemed she had not returned to her seat. Could she be standing in the aisle? He glanced up and there she was, facing him. But the moment he raised his eyes, the woman started to move. Instead of passing by Sanshirō and returning to her seat, however, she turned into the booth ahead of his and poked her head out of the window. She was having a long, quiet look. He saw how her side locks fluttered in the rush of wind. Then, with all his strength, Sanshirō hurled the empty wooden lunchbox from his window. A narrow panel was all that separated Sanshirō's window from the woman's. As soon as he released the box into the wind, the lid appeared to shoot back against the train in a flash of white, and he realized what a stupid thing he had done. He glanced towards the woman, but her head was still outside the window. Then she calmly drew it in and dabbed at her forehead with a printed handkerchief. The safest thing would be to apologize.

'I'm sorry.'

'That's all right.'

She was still wiping her face. There was nothing more for him to say, and she fell silent as well, poking her head out of the window again. He could see in the feeble light of the oil lamps that the three or four other passengers were all looking sleepy. No one was talking. The only sound was the ongoing roar of the train. Sanshirō closed his eyes.

'Do you think we'll be getting to Nagoya soon?'

It was the woman's voice. He opened his eyes and was startled to find her leaning over him, her face close to his.

'I wonder,' he answered, but he had no idea. This was his first trip to Tokyo.

'Do you think we'll be late?'

'Probably.'

'I get off at Nagoya. How about you?'

'Yes, I do too.'

This train only went as far as Nagoya. Their remarks could not have been more ordinary. The woman sat down diagonally opposite Sanshirō. For a while again the only sound was that of the train.

At the next station, the woman spoke to him once more. She hated to bother him, she said, but would he please help her find an inn when they reached Nagoya? She felt uneasy about doing it alone. He thought her request reasonable enough, but he was not eager to comply. She was a stranger, after all, and a woman. He hesitated as long as he could, but did not have the courage to refuse outright. He made a few vague noises. Soon the train reached Nagoya.

His large wicker trunk would be no problem: it had been checked all the way to Tokyo. He passed through the ticket barrier carrying only a small canvas bag and his umbrella. He was wearing the summer cap of his college with the badge torn off to indicate that he had graduated. The colour was still new in just that one spot, though it showed only in daylight. With the woman following close behind, he felt somewhat embarrassed about the cap, but she was with him now and there was nothing he could do. To her, of course, it would be just another battered old hat.

Due at 9.30, the train had arrived forty minutes late. It was after ten o'clock, but the summer streets were noisy and crowded as though the night had just begun. Several inns stood across from the station, but Sanshirō thought they looked a little too grand for him – three-storey buildings with electric lighting. He walked past them without a glance. He had never been here before and had no idea where he was going. He simply headed for the darker streets, the woman following in silence. Two houses down a nearly deserted back street he saw the sign for an inn. It was dirty and faded, just the thing for him and this woman.

'How about that place?' he asked, glancing back at her.

'Fine,' she said.

He strode in through the gate. They were greeted effusively at the door and shown to a room – White Plum No. 4. It all happened too quickly for him to protest that they were not together.

They sat opposite each other, staring into space, while the maid went to prepare tea. She came in with a tray and announced that the bath was ready. Sanshirō no longer had the courage to tell her that the woman was not with him. Instead, he picked up a towel and, excusing himself, went to the bath. It was at the end of the corridor, next to the toilet. The room was poorly lit and dirty. Sanshirō undressed, then jumped into the tub and gave some thought to what was happening. He was splashing around in the hot water, thinking what a difficult situation he had got himself into, when there were footsteps in the corridor. Someone went into the toilet. A few minutes later the person came out. There was the sound of hands being washed. Then the bathroom door creaked open halfway.

'Want me to scrub your back?' the woman asked from the doorway.

'No, thank you,' Sanshirō answered loudly. But she did not go away. Instead, she came inside and began undoing her obi. She was obviously planning to bathe with him. It didn't seem to embarrass her at all. Sanshirō leaped from the tub. He dried himself hastily and went back to the room. He was sitting on a floor cushion, not a little shaken, when the maid came in with the register.

Sanshirō took it from her and wrote: '*Name*: Ogawa Sanshirō. *Age*: 23. *Occupation*: Student. *Address*: Masaki Village, Miyako County, Fukuoka Prefecture.' He filled in his section honestly, but when it came to the woman's he was lost. He should have waited for her to finish bathing, but now it was too late. The maid was waiting. There was nothing he could do. '*Name*: Ogawa Hana. *Age*: 23. *Address*: As above,' he wrote and gave back the register. Then he started fanning himself furiously.

At last the woman came back to the room. 'Sorry I chased you out,' she said.

'Not at all,' Sanshirō replied. He took a notebook from his bag and started a diary entry. There was nothing for him to write about. He would have plenty to write about if only she weren't there.

'Excuse me, I'll be right back,' the woman said and left the room. Now, writing was out of the question. Where could she have gone?

The maid came in to put down the bedding. She brought only a single wide mattress. Sanshirō told her they must have two mattresses, but she said the room was too small, the mosquito net too narrow. And it was too much bother, she might have added. Finally, she said she would ask the receptionist about it when he came back and then bring another mattress. In the meantime, she stubbornly insisted upon hanging the single mosquito net and stuffing the mattress inside it.

Soon the woman came back. She apologized for taking so long. She started doing something in the shadows behind the mosquito net and eventually produced a clanking sound – probably from one of the children's toys. Then she seemed to be rewrapping her bundle, after which she announced that she would be going to bed. Sanshirō barely answered her. He sat in the doorway, fanning himself. It occurred to him that he might best spend the night doing just that. But the mosquitoes were buzzing all around him. It would be unbearable outside the net. He stood up and took a muslin undershirt and some underpants from his bag, slipped them on and tied a dark blue sash around his waist. Then, holding two towels in his hand, he entered the net. The woman was still fanning herself on the far corner of the mattress.

'Sorry, but I'm very finicky. I don't like sleeping on strange mattresses. I'm going to make a kind of flea guard, but don't let it bother you.'

He rolled his side of the sheet towards the side where the woman lay, making a long, white partition down the centre of the bed. The woman turned the other way. Sanshirō spread the towels end to end along his side of the mattress, then fitted his body into this long, narrow space. That night, not a hand nor a foot ventured out beyond Sanshirō's narrow bed of towels. He spoke not a word to the woman. And she, having turned to the wall, never moved.

The long night ended. The woman washed her face and knelt at the low breakfast table, smiling. 'Were there any fleas last night?'

'No, thank you for asking,' Sanshirō said gravely. He looked down and thrust his chopsticks into a small cup of sweet beans.

They paid and left the inn. It was only when they reached the station that the woman told him where she was going. She would be taking the Kansai Line to Yokkaichi. Sanshirō's train pulled in a moment later. The woman would have a brief wait for hers. She accompanied Sanshirō to the ticket barrier. 'I'm sorry to have put you to so much trouble,' she said, bowing politely. 'Goodbye, and have a pleasant trip.'

Bag and umbrella in one hand, Sanshirō took off his hat with the other and said only, 'Goodbye.'

The woman gave him a long, steady look, and when she spoke it was with the utmost calm. 'You're quite a coward, aren't you?' A knowing smile crossed her face.

Sanshirō felt as if he were being flung on to the platform. It was even worse after he boarded the train; his ears started to burn. He sat very still, making himself as small as possible. Finally, the conductor's whistle reverberated from one end of the station to the other, and the train began to move. Sanshirō leaned cautiously towards the open window and looked out. The woman had long since disappeared. The large clock was all that caught his eye. He edged back into his seat. The carriage was crowded, but no one seemed to be paying any attention to him. Only the man seated diagonally opposite him glanced at Sanshirō as he sat down again.

Sanshirō felt vaguely embarrassed when the man looked at him. He thought he might distract himself with a book. But when he opened his bag, he found the two towels stuffed in at the top. He shoved them aside and pulled out the first thing his hand chanced upon in the bottom of the bag. It was a collection of Bacon's essays, a book he found unintelligible at the best of times. The volume's flimsy paper binding was an insult to Bacon. Sanshirō had been unlucky enough to come up with the one book in the bag he had no intention of reading on the train. It was in there only because he had failed to pack it in the trunk and had tossed it into the bag with two or three others at the last minute. He opened Bacon's essays at page twenty-three. He would not be able to read anything now, and he was certainly in no mood for Bacon, but he reverently opened the book at page twenty-three and let his eyes survey its entire surface. In the presence of page twenty-three, he might try to review the events of the night before.

What was that woman, really? Were there other women like her in the world? Could a woman be like that, so calm and confident? Was she uneducated? Reckless? Or simply innocent? This he would never know because he had not tried to go as far as he could with her. He should have done it. He should have tried to go a little further. But he was afraid. She called him a coward when they parted, and it shocked him, as though a twenty-three-year-old weakness had been revealed at a single blow. No one, not even his mother, could have struck home so unerringly.

These thoughts only made him feel worse. He might as well have been given a thrashing by some stupid little nobody. He almost wanted to apologize to page twenty-three of Bacon. He should never have fallen apart like that. His education counted for nothing here. It was all a matter of character. He should have done better. But if women were always going to behave that way, then he, as an educated man, would have no other way to react – which meant that he would have to steer clear of them. It was a gutless way to live, and much too constraining, as though he had been born some kind of cripple. And yet . . .

Sanshirō shook off these ruminations and turned to thoughts of a different world. He was going to Tokyo. He would enter the university. He would meet famous scholars, associate with students of taste and breeding, do research in the library, write books. Society would acclaim him, his mother would be overjoyed. Once he had cheered himself with such dreams of the future, there was no need for Sanshirō to go on burying his face in page twenty-three. He straightened up. The man diagonally opposite was looking at him again. This time Sanshirō looked back.

The man had a thick moustache on a long, thin face, and there was something about him reminiscent of a Shinto priest. The one exception was his nose, so very straight it looked Western. Sanshirō, who was looking with the eyes of a student, always took such men to be schoolteachers. The man wore a youthful summer kimono in a blue-and-white splashed pattern, a more sedate white under-kimono and navy blue split-toed socks. This outfit led Sanshirō to conclude that he was a schoolteacher – and thus of no interest to anyone with the great future he himself had in store. He must be forty, after all – beyond any future development.

The man smoked one cigarette after another. The way he sat with his arms folded, blowing long streams of smoke from his nostrils, he seemed completely at ease. But then he was constantly leaving his seat to go to the toilet or something. He would often stretch when he stood up, looking thoroughly bored, and yet he showed no interest in the newspaper that the passenger next to him had set aside. His curiosity aroused, Sanshirō closed Bacon's essays. He considered taking out another book, perhaps a novel, and reading that in earnest, but finding it would have been too much bother. He would have preferred to read the newspaper, but its owner was sound asleep. He reached across and, with his hand on the paper, made a point of asking the man with the moustache, 'Is anyone reading this?'

'No, no one,' he said, looking sure of himself. 'Go ahead.'

This left Sanshirō, with the paper in his hand, feeling ill at ease. The newspaper contained little worth reading. He skimmed through it in a minute or two and returned it, properly folded, to the seat opposite. As he did so, he nodded to the man with the moustache. The man returned his nod and asked, 'Are you a college student?'

Sanshirō was pleased that the man had noticed the dark spot on his cap. 'Yes,' he answered.

'From Tokyo?'

'No, Kumamoto. But –' he began to explain, then stopped. There was no need to say that he was now a university student, he decided.

The man answered simply, 'Oh, I see,' and continued puffing on his cigarette. He was not going to ask Sanshirō why a Kumamoto student would be going to Tokyo at this time of year. Perhaps he had no interest in Kumamoto students. Just then the man across from Sanshirō said, 'Ah, of course.' That he was still sleeping, there could be no doubt. He was not just sitting there talking to himself. The man with the moustache looked at Sanshirō and grinned.

Sanshirō took the opportunity to ask, 'And where are you going?'

'Tokyo,' was all the man said, stretching out the syllables. Somehow, he no longer seemed like a middle-school teacher. Still, if he was travelling third class, he was obviously no one special. Sanshirō let the conversation lapse. Every now and then the man, arms folded, would tap out a rhythm on the floor with the front lift of his wooden clog. He seemed very bored, but his was a boredom that betrayed no desire to engage in conversation.

When the train reached Toyohashi, the sleeping man shot up and left the carriage, rubbing his eyes. Amazing how he could wake himself at the right time like that, thought Sanshirō. Concerned lest the man, still dazed with sleep, had alighted at the wrong station, Sanshirō watched him from the train window. But no, he passed through the ticket barrier without incident and went off like anyone in full possession of his faculties. Reassured, Sanshirō changed to the seat opposite. Now he was sitting next to the man with the moustache. The man moved across to Sanshirō's former seat. He poked his head out of the window and bought some peaches.

When he was seated next to Sanshirō again, he placed the fruit between them and said, 'Please help yourself.'

Sanshirō thanked him and ate a peach. The man seemed to enjoy them very much. He ate several with great abandon and urged Sanshirō to eat more. Sanshirō ate another one. They went on eating, and soon the two of them were talking like old friends.

The man remarked that he could well understand why the Taoists had chosen the peach as the fruit of immortality. Mountain ascetics were supposed to live forever on some ethereal essence, and peaches probably came closer to that than anything else. They had a mystifying sort of taste. The stone was interesting too, with its crude shape and all those holes. Sanshirō had never heard this particular view before. Here was a man who said some pretty inane things, he decided. The man spoke of the poet Shiki's[3] great liking for fruit. His appetite for it was enormous. On one occasion he ate sixteen large persimmons without ill effect. He himself could never match Shiki, the man concluded.

Sanshirō listened, smiling, but the only subject that interested him was Shiki. He was hoping to move the conversation a little more in that direction, when the man said, 'You know, our hands reach out by themselves for the things we like. There's no way to stop them. A pig doesn't have hands, so his snout reaches out instead. I've heard that if you tie a pig down and put food in front of him, the tip of his snout will grow until it reaches the food. Desire is a frightening thing.' He was grinning, but Sanshirō could not tell from the way he spoke whether he was serious or joking. 'It's lucky for us we're not pigs,' he went on. 'Think what would happen if our noses kept stretching towards all the things we wanted. By now they'd be so long we couldn't board a train.'

Sanshirō laughed out loud. The man, however, remained strangely calm.

'Life is a dangerous business, you know. There was a man called Leonardo da Vinci who injected arsenic into the trunk of a peach tree. He was testing to see if the poison would circulate to the fruit, but somebody ate one and died. You'd better watch out – life can be dangerous.' As he spoke, he wrapped the chewed-over peach stones and skins in the newspaper and tossed them out of the window.

This time Sanshirō did not feel like laughing either. Somewhat intimidated by the mention of Leonardo da Vinci, he had suddenly thought of the woman. He felt oddly uncomfortable and wanted to withdraw from the conversation, but the man was oblivious to his silence. 'Where are you going in Tokyo?' he asked.

'I've never been there before; I really don't know my way around. I thought I might stay at the Fukuoka students' dormitory for the time being.'

'Then you're through with Kumamoto?'

'Yes, I've just graduated.'

'Well, well,' the man said, offering neither congratulations nor compliments. 'I suppose you'll be entering the university now,' he added, as though it were the most commonplace thing one could do.

This left Sanshirō a little dissatisfied. His 'Yes' was barely enough to maintain the civilities.

'Which faculty?' the man asked.

'I was in the First Division – Law and Letters.'

'I mean at the university. Will you be in Law?'

'No, Letters.'

'Well, well,' he said again.

Each time he heard this 'Well, well', Sanshirō found his curiosity aroused. Either the man was in so exalted a position that he could walk all over people, or else the university meant nothing to him. Unable to decide which was true, Sanshirō did not know how to behave with the man.

As if by prearrangement, they both bought meals from the platform vendors in Hamamatsu. The train showed no sign of moving even after they had finished eating. Sanshirō noticed four or five Westerners strolling back and forth past the train window. One pair was probably a married couple; they were holding hands in spite of the hot weather. Dressed entirely in white, the woman was very beautiful. Sanshirō had never seen more than half a dozen foreigners in the course of his lifetime. Two of them were his teachers in college, and unfortunately one of those was a hunchback. He knew one woman, a missionary. She had a pointed face like a smelt or a barracuda. Foreigners as colourful and attractive as these were not only something quite new for Sanshirō, they seemed to be of a higher class. He stared at them, entranced. Arrogance from people like this was understandable. He went so far as to imagine himself travelling to the West and feeling insignificant among them. When the couple passed his window, he tried hard to listen to their conversation, but he could make out none of it. Their pronunciation was nothing like that of his Kumamoto teachers.

Just then the man with the moustache leaned over Sanshirō's shoulder. 'Aren't we ever going to get out of here?' He glanced at the foreign couple, who had just walked by. 'Beautiful,' he murmured, releasing a languorous little yawn. Sanshirō realized what a country boy he must appear; he drew his head in and returned to his seat. The man sat down after him. 'Westerners are very beautiful, aren't they?' he said.

Sanshirō could think of nothing to say in reply. He nodded and smiled.

'We Japanese are sad-looking things next to them. We can beat the Russians, we can become a "first-class power", but it doesn't make any difference. We still have the same faces, the same feeble little bodies. Just look at the houses we live in, the gardens we build around them. They're just what you'd expect from faces like this. Oh yes, this is your first trip to Tokyo, isn't it? You've never seen Mount Fuji. We go by it a little further on. Have a look. It's the finest thing Japan has to offer, the only thing we have to boast about. The trouble is, of course, it's just a natural object. It's been sitting there for all time. We didn't make it.' He grinned broadly once again.

Sanshirō had never expected to meet anyone like this after Japan's victory in the Russo-Japanese War. The man was almost not Japanese, he felt.

'But still,' Sanshirō argued, 'Japan will start developing from now on at least.'

'Japan is going to perish,' the man replied coolly.

Anyone who dared say such a thing in Kumamoto would have been beaten on the spot, perhaps even arrested for treason. Sanshirō had grown up in an atmosphere that gave his mind no room at all for inserting an idea like this. Could the man be toying with him, taking advantage of his youth? The man was still grinning, but he spoke with complete detachment. Sanshirō did not know what to make of him. He decided to say nothing.

But then the man said, 'Tokyo is bigger than Kumamoto. And Japan is bigger than Tokyo. And even bigger than Japan . . .' He paused and looked at Sanshirō, who was listening intently now. 'Even bigger than Japan is the inside of your head. Don't ever surrender yourself – not to

Japan, not to anything. You may think that what you're doing is for the sake of the nation, but let something take possession of you like that, and all you do is bring it down.'

When he heard this, Sanshirō felt he was truly no longer in Kumamoto. And he realized, too, what a coward he had been there.

He arrived in Tokyo that same evening. The man with the moustache never did tell Sanshirō his name. Nor did Sanshirō venture to ask it; there were bound to be men like this everywhere in Tokyo.

LOYAL WARRIORS

MORI ŌGAI

The Last Testament of Okitsu Yagoemon

Translated by Richard Bowring

My ritual suicide today[1] will no doubt come as a great shock and there will be those who claim that I, Yagoemon, am either senile or deranged. But this is very far from the truth. Ever since my retirement I have been living in a hut of the simplest kind that I built at the western foot of Mount Funaoka here in the province of Yamashiro. After the demise of my former master, Lord Shōkōji, the rest of my family moved from the castle town of Yatsushiro in the province of Higo[2] and are now living in Kumamoto in the same province. They will be very shaken when this testament reaches them from so far away. Nevertheless, I request that one of my neighbours send it to them at the first opportunity. I have for some years now lived the life of a Buddhist monk, but I compose this last testament because at heart I am still a warrior and thus deeply concerned about my posthumous reputation.

My hut is of so wretched an appearance that those who find me may even suppose that I committed suicide because of debts I could not pay before the end of the year. But I leave no debts. Nor do I propose to put anyone to the slightest expense on my behalf. In a box in the wall cupboard by the side of the *tokonoma* is some money that I have saved. Although it is but a trifle, I request most earnestly that it be used to pay for my cremation. I should deem myself most fortunate if you would also send a little keepsake with this note to those relatives in Kumamoto whom I have just mentioned – just a fingernail, perhaps, for I have shaved my head quite bare.

The three wooden memorial tablets which are standing in the *tokonoma* are for the three men I have served: my former master Hosokawa Tadaoki, Lord of Etchū, known as Lord Sōryū Sansai and in death as Lord Shōkōji; Hosokawa Tadatoshi, Lord of Etchū, known in death as Lord Myōge

Inden; and Hosokawa Mitsuhisa, Lord of Higo. I request that care be taken to burn the tablets in cleansing holy fire so that they may not be subjected to any disrespectful treatment. I end my life today, the second day of the twelfth month of the first year of Manji [1658], since it corresponds to the thirteenth anniversary of the death of Lord Shōkōji, who passed away on the second day of the twelfth month of the second year of Shōhō [1645].

As I wish the reason for my death to be understood by my descendants, I leave the following account.

It happened a full thirty years ago. In the fifth month of the first year of Kan'ei [1624], a ship from Annam arrived at Nagasaki. Lord Shōkōji had retired as a monk three years earlier. He gave me orders to purchase a rare article that he would be able to use in the tea ceremony, and so I set out for Nagasaki with a colleague. As luck would have it, a large tree of rare aloes wood had been imported. It was, however, in two parts – the bole and the upper branches – and a retainer who had been sent all the way from Sendai by Lord Date Gonchūnagon decided he must have the bole. I too had my eye on the same piece of wood and so we bid against each other and gradually forced the price up.

At this point my colleague said that even if it were our master's orders, incense wood was a useless plaything and we would be wrong to throw away a vast amount of money on it. He would prefer us to let the Date have the bole and ourselves to buy the upper branches. I could not agree, I told him. My master's orders were to go and buy a rare article, and the finest thing among these imported goods was undoubtedly this aloes wood. Of the two parts, the bole was obviously the rarest of the rare; only by buying the bole would we be carrying out our master's orders. To give in to the overweening pride of the Date and let them take the bole would be to bring the name of Hosokawa into disrepute.

My colleague laughed at me and said I was making far too much of this. If it were a question of whether we should give up or occupy a whole province or a castle, then of course we should fight the Date to the bitter end. But was this not just a piece of wood to be burnt in a brazier for the tea ceremony? To think of spending so much money on it was absurd. Were our master himself to bid for it, we as his retainers should actively try to dissuade him. Even if he had set his heart on getting the bole, to let him accomplish his desire would be nothing less than an act of gross flattery.

I was not yet thirty at the time and took offence at what he said, but managed to hold myself in check. His words sounded very wise, I told him, but my overriding concern was for the orders and requests of my master. If he ordered me to capture a castle, I would do so though it had walls of steel. If he ordered me to behead a man, I would do so though he were a devil. He had given me orders to buy something rare, and so I was duty bound to search for something unique. It was not for me to question or criticize my master's orders, provided they were not contrary to moral principles.

He ridiculed me all the more. I was right, he said. Had I not just declared that one should not do anything contrary to moral principles? If we were dealing with military equipment, he would not have minded spending an enormous sum of money, but to pay a price out of all proportion to the value of the wood was a sign of youthful imprudence, he said.

I knew the difference between military equipment and incense despite my age, I retorted. When Lord Taishō Inden was head of the family, Lord Gamō said that he had heard the Hosokawa possessed many excellent implements and would like to come and see for himself. The appointed day arrived. When Lord Gamō appeared, Lord Taishō Inden brought out swords, bows, spears and various kinds of armour to show him. Lord Gamō was somewhat surprised, but looked them over and then said he had really come to see the tea utensils. Lord Taishō Inden laughed. Lord Gamō had talked of 'implements', so he had shown him the kind of thing military families were usually known for, but if it was tea utensils he wanted to see, then he did happen to have a few of those as well. Only then did he bring them out. Could there be another such family in Japan which had devoted itself to military matters for generations and yet was also highly skilled in such arts as poetry and the tea ceremony? If one were to claim that the tea ceremony was a useless formality, then so were grand ceremonies of state and festivals in honour of one's ancestors. The order we had received this time was to buy a rare article for use in the tea ceremony – nothing more. This was our master's order and so we must carry it out even at the cost of our lives. Because my colleague had no feeling for the art of tea, he obstinately considered it unreasonable for our master to spend a great sum of money on incense, I replied.

He did not wait for me to finish. 'Of course I know nothing of the tea ceremony! Of course I am a stubborn warrior! If you are so skilled in a variety of arts, let's see your main accomplishment,' he said, jumping up. There in the inn he seized his sword from the rack in the *tokonoma* and swung at me out of the blue. My sword was hanging in the rack under the double shelves of the *tokonoma*, and as there was nothing else near at hand I parried his blow with a bronze vase that held a seasonal arrangement of lilies. Jumping aside, I reached for my sword, whipped it out and cut him down with a single stroke.

Without further ado, I purchased the bole of the aloes wood and brought it back to the castle at Kitsuki. The retainer from the Date clan had no choice but to buy the upper branches and take them to Sendai. Presenting the wood to Lord Shōkōji, I requested permission to commit seppuku. I had placed great store by my master's orders, I said, but in the process I had killed a samurai of whom he had need. He listened to my story and then told me he felt everything I had said was entirely understandable and that even if the wood turned out not to be valuable, there was no doubt it was the rare article he had ordered me to go and buy. I was therefore right to have felt the matter important. If we looked at everything with an eye to its utility there would be nothing left to value in the world, he said. What is more, he immediately kindled a piece of the wood that I had brought back. It was of rare quality and he named it 'Hatsune', or first song, from the ancient verse 'Each time we hear the cuckoo cry it sounds so new, always singing its first song'. He was full of praise that I had returned with an article of such quality. But the descendants of the man I had killed must not harbour any ill will, he said. He immediately ordered my colleague's son to appear, had sake brought out before us and made us swear that no grudge would be held on either side.

Two years later, on the sixth day of the ninth month of the third year of Kan'ei [1626], when the emperor went in progress to the castle at Nijō, he asked Myōge Inden for some of this fine incense and it was presented to him. The emperor was well pleased and I heard that he called it 'Shiragiku', white chrysanthemum, from the ancient verse 'Who can claim its match? A white chrysanthemum blooming after the autumn colours are gone'. The wood that I had brought had been graciously praised by the emperor himself and had become the pride of the family. I wept at such unexpected good fortune.

Having already decided to commit seppuku, however, I was secretly waiting for the proper time. Meanwhile, I was given special favours not only by Lord Shōkōji, who was in retirement, but also by the then head of the family, Lord Myōge Inden. In the ninth year of Kan'ei [1632], on the occasion of our transfer to another domain, I became a guard at Yatsushiro Castle, where Lord Shōkōji was in residence. I was also ordered to accompany him to the Capital. Thus, busy with many arduous duties, I saw the days and months pass by to no purpose. Then, in the fourteenth year of Kan'ei [1637], came the campaign against Shimabara and I requested leave from Lord Shōkōji that I might fight as a bannerman under his son. It was my intention to die in battle, but our lord's military prowess was such that the rebel leader, Amakusa Shirō Tokisada, was killed, and even insignificant servants such as myself were given rewards. So I lived on for many years, my long-cherished desire as yet unfulfilled.

However, in the eighteenth year of Kan'ei [1641], Lord Myōge Inden unexpectedly fell ill and died before his father. The Lord of Higo became head of the family. Then, in the second year of Shōhō [1645], Lord Shōkōji too passed away. Prior to this, in the thirteenth year of Kan'ei [1636], Lord Chūnagon of Sendai, who had prized the same incense wood we had divided, also died in his castle at Wakabayashi. The incense from the upper branches he had called 'Shibafune', firewood boat, from the verse 'Scorched by longing, I am a boat of firewood, loaded with the cares of the world, rowed on but only to be burnt'; and he had kept it as a treasured possession.

Then, in the second year of Keian [1649], the Lord of Higo suddenly passed away at the age of thirty-one. On his deathbed he worried that his son, Lord Rokumaru, might be too young to control so large a domain, and so he informed the shogun that he wished to return the domain to the shogun's direct rule. The shogun, however, remembering the family's loyalty since the days of Lord Taishō Inden, ordered that the seven-year-old Lord Rokumaru be confirmed as his successor.

I then requested that I might retire. I left Kumamoto and came here. But I still felt concern for Lord Rokumaru and, although I was not present, wished to pray for him that he might rule in peace, at least until he came of age. Thus, despite my intentions, I lived on for yet more years. Then, in the second year of Shōō [1653], Lord Rokumaru at the young age of eleven became Lord of Etchū. He was given the name Tsunatoshi and enjoyed the favour of the shogun. I was delighted to receive this news. Now I no longer had anything weighing on my mind and yet I felt it would be a pity for me simply to die of old age. I waited for this day, the thirteenth anniversary of the death of Lord Shōkōji, from whom I received so many favours and whom I now wish to follow after all these years. I know very well that to follow one's master into death is prohibited, but I do not expect to incur censure. I did kill my companion in my youth and should have committed suicide many years ago.

I have no friends I see regularly, but I have recently been on close terms with the monk Seigan from Daitokuji. I request most earnestly that my neighbours here show him this letter before sending it on to my home province. I have been writing this note by the light of a candle which has just gone out, but there is no need to light another. There is sufficient reflection from the snow at the window to enable me to cut across my wrinkled belly.

The second day of the twelfth month of the first year of Manji
Okitsu Yagoemon, his signature

MISHIMA YUKIO

Patriotism

Translated by Geoffrey W. Sargent

I

On 28 February 1936 (on the third day, that is, of the Incident of 26 February[1]), Lieutenant Takeyama Shinji of the Imperial Guard's First Infantry Regiment – profoundly disturbed by the knowledge that his closest colleagues had been with the mutineers from the beginning, and incensed at the imminent prospect of imperial troops attacking imperial troops – took his officer's sword and ceremonially disembowelled himself in the eight-mat room of his private residence in the sixth block of Aobachō in Yotsuya Ward. His wife, Reiko, followed him, stabbing herself to death. The lieutenant's farewell note consisted of a single sentence: 'Long live the Imperial Forces.' His wife's, after apologies for her unfilial conduct in thus preceding her parents to the grave, continued: 'The day that must come for a soldier's wife has come . . .' The final moments of this resolute husband and wife displayed the kind of heroism that is said to make even the most ferocious deities weep. The lieutenant's age, it should be noted, was thirty-one, his wife's twenty-three; and it was not half a year since the celebration of their marriage.

II

Those who saw the bride and bridegroom in the commemorative photograph – perhaps no less than those actually present at the lieutenant's wedding – had exclaimed in wonder at the bearing of this handsome couple. The lieutenant, majestic in military uniform, stood protectively beside his bride, his left hand resting upon his sword, his officer's cap held at his right side. His expression was severe, and his dark brows and wide-gazing eyes well conveyed the clear integrity of youth. For the beauty of the bride in her white over-robe, no comparisons were adequate. In the eyes, round beneath soft brows, in the slender, finely shaped nose, and in the full lips, there was both sensuousness and refinement. One hand, emerging shyly from a sleeve of the over-robe, held a fan, and the tips of the fingers, clustering delicately, were like the bud of a moonflower.

After the suicide, people would take out this photograph and examine it, sadly reflecting that too often there was a curse on these seemingly flawless unions. Perhaps it was no more than imagination, but looking at the picture after the tragedy it almost seemed as if the two young people before the gold-lacquered screen were gazing, each with equal clarity, at the deaths which lay before them.

Thanks to the good offices of their go-between, Lieutenant General Ozeki, they had been able to set themselves up in a new home at Aobachō in Yotsuya. 'New home' is perhaps misleading. It was an old three-room rented house backing on to a small garden. As neither the six- nor the four-and-a-half-mat room downstairs was favoured by the sun, they used the upstairs eight-mat room as both bedroom and guest room. There was no maid, so Reiko was left alone to guard the house in her husband's absence.

They refrained from taking a honeymoon trip, these being times of national emergency. The couple spent their wedding night at this house. Before going to bed, Shinji knelt formally on the matted floor with his sword laid at his knees, and bestowed upon his wife a soldierly lecture. A woman who had become the wife of a soldier should know and resolutely accept that her husband's death might come at any moment. It could be tomorrow. It could be the day after. But no matter when it came – he asked – was she steadfast in her resolve to accept it? Reiko rose to her feet, pulled open a drawer of the cabinet and took out what was the most prized of her new possessions, the dagger her mother had given her. Returning to her place, she laid the dagger without a word on the mat before her, just as her husband had laid his sword. A silent understanding was achieved at once, and the lieutenant never again sought to test his wife's resolve.

In the first few months of her marriage, Reiko's beauty grew daily more radiant, shining serenely like the moon after rain.

As both were possessed of young, vigorous bodies, their relationship was passionate. Nor was this merely a matter of the night. On more than one occasion, returning home straight from manoeuvres, and begrudging even the time it took to remove his mud-splashed uniform, the lieutenant had pressed his wife to the matted floor almost as soon as he entered the house. Reiko was equally ardent in her response. Within a month of their wedding night, she experienced true ecstasy, and the lieutenant, sensing this, was equally ecstatic.

Reiko's body was white and pure, and her swelling breasts conveyed a firm and chaste refusal. But, upon consent, those breasts were lavish with their intimate, welcoming warmth. Even in bed the young couple were frighteningly and awesomely serious, and they remained serious in the very midst of increasingly wild, intoxicating passion.

By day the lieutenant would think of his wife in the brief rest periods between training; and all day long, at home, Reiko would recall the image of her husband. Even when apart, however, they had only to look at the wedding photograph for their happiness to be once more confirmed. Reiko felt not the slightest surprise that a man who had been a complete stranger until a few months ago should now have become the sun about which her whole world revolved.

All these things had a moral basis, and were in accordance with the injunction in the Meiji Emperor's Imperial Rescript on Education that 'husband and wife should be harmonious'. Not once did Reiko contradict her husband, nor did the lieutenant ever find reason to scold his wife. On the god shelf downstairs, alongside the tablet from the Great Ise Shrine, were set photographs of their Imperial Majesties, the emperor and empress, and regularly every morning, before leaving for duty, the lieutenant would stand with his wife at this hallowed place and together they would bow their heads low. The offering water was renewed each morning, and the sacred sprig of *sakaki* was always fresh and green. Their lives were lived beneath the solemn protection of the gods and were filled with an intense happiness which set every fibre in their bodies trembling.

III

Although the home of Saitō Makoto, Lord Keeper of the Privy Seal, was in their neighbourhood, neither of them heard the gunfire on the morning of 26 February. The lieutenant's slumbers were first disrupted by a bugle sounding muster in the dim, snowy dawn, when the ten-minute tragedy had already ended. Leaping from his bed, and without speaking a word, the lieutenant donned his uniform, buckled on the sword held ready for him by his wife and hurried into the snow-covered streets of the still-darkened morning. He did not return until the evening of the twenty-eighth.

Reiko learned the full extent of this sudden eruption of violence only later, from the radio news. She spent the next two days alone, in tranquillity, behind locked doors.

In the lieutenant's face, as he hurried silently out into the snowy morning, Reiko had read the determination to die. If her husband did not return, her own decision was made: she too would die. Quietly she attended to the disposition of her personal possessions. She chose her sets of visiting kimonos as keepsakes for friends of her schooldays, and she wrote a name and address on the stiff paper wrapping in which each was folded. Constantly admonished by her husband never to think of the morrow, Reiko had not kept a diary and was now denied the pleasure of reading her record of the past few months' happiness and consigning each page to the fire. Ranged beside the radio were a small china dog, a rabbit, a squirrel, a bear and a fox. Smaller still were the tiny vase and ceramic water jar that stood there. These items comprised Reiko's only collection, but they were hardly worth giving as keepsakes or even having them included in her coffin. The thought seemed to increase the look of aimlessness and helplessness on each of the little china creatures' faces.

Reiko took the squirrel in her hand and looked at it. Her thoughts turned then to a realm far beyond these childish affections. She gazed up into the distance at the sunlike Great Moral Principle her husband embodied. She was ready, and happy, to be hurtled along to her destruction in that gleaming sun chariot. But now, for these few moments of solitude, she allowed herself to luxuriate in this innocent attachment to trifles. The time when she had genuinely loved these things, however, was long past. Now she merely loved the memory of having once loved them, and the place in her heart had been filled by more intense passions, by a more frenzied happiness. Never once had Reiko used the word 'pleasure' for those day and night joys of the flesh, the mere thought of which could set her heart to racing. Her lovely fingers retained the February cold and the icy touch of the china squirrel, yet beneath the repeating patterns on the taut skirt of her colourful *meisen* kimono, she felt a hot, fleshy moistness that defied the snows when she thought of the lieutenant's powerful arms reaching out towards her.

She was not at all afraid of the death hovering in her mind. Waiting alone at home, Reiko firmly believed that everything her husband was feeling or thinking now, his anguish and distress, was leading her – as surely as the power in his flesh – to a pleasant death. She felt her body could melt with ease into the merest fragment of her husband's thought.

Listening to the frequent announcements on the radio, she heard the names of several of her husband's colleagues mentioned among those of the insurgents. This was news of death. She followed the developments closely, knowing all too well that, as the situation became daily more irrevocable, an imperial ordinance could come down at any moment, and those who were initially seen as heroes fighting to restore the nation's honour would be branded as mutineers. No communication came from the regiment. Fighting might commence in the city streets, where the remains of the snow still lay.

Towards sundown on the twenty-eighth, Reiko was startled by a furious pounding on the front door. She hurried downstairs and pulled at the bolt with trembling fingers. The shape dimly outlined beyond the frosted-glass panel made no sound, but she knew it was her husband. Reiko had never known the bolt on the sliding door to be so stubborn. Her impatience only increased its resistance, and the door would not open.

Almost before she knew she had succeeded, the lieutenant stepped inside, his high-top boots heavy with slush from the street, and stood there on the concrete floor of the entryway, muffled in his khaki greatcoat. He turned to heave the door shut and drew the bolt before Reiko could do so. What did this mean? she wondered.

'Welcome home.'

Reiko bowed deeply, but her husband made no response. He had already unfastened his sword and was about to remove his greatcoat when Reiko stepped behind to assist him. The coat, which was cold and damp and had lost the odour of horse dung it normally exuded when exposed to the sun, weighed heavily on her arm. Draping it across a hanger, and cradling the sword and its leather belt in her arms, she waited while her husband removed his boots and followed him into the sitting room. This was the six-mat room downstairs.

Seen in the clear light of the lamp, her husband's face, covered with a heavy growth of bristle, was almost unrecognizably wasted and thin. The cheeks were hollow, their lustre and resilience gone. In normal good spirits he would have changed into comfortable old clothes as soon as he was home and urged her to make supper at once, but now he sat cross-legged at the low table on the matted floor still in his uniform, his head drooping. Reiko refrained from asking whether she should prepare supper.

After an interval the lieutenant spoke.

'I didn't know a thing. They didn't ask me to join. They were probably trying to be kind to me because I was newly married. Kanō, and Homma too, and Yamaguchi.'

Reiko pictured those high-spirited young officers, friends of her husband, who had come to the house on more than one occasion.

'An imperial ordinance may be sent down tomorrow. They'll be posted as rebels. I'll be in command of a unit with orders to attack them . . . I can't do it. I can't do a thing like that.'

He spoke again.

'They've ordered me off guard duty for one rotation. I have permission to return home for the night. Tomorrow morning, without question, I'll have to attack my friends. I can't do it, Reiko.'

Reiko sat erect with lowered eyes. She understood clearly that her husband had spoken of his death. The lieutenant was resolved. Each word, being rooted in death, emerged sharply and with powerful significance against this dark, unmovable background. Although the lieutenant was speaking of his dilemma, already there was no room in his mind for vacillation.

There was, however, clarity, like the clarity of a stream fed from melting snows, in the silence which rested between them. Sitting in his own home after the long two-day ordeal, and looking across at the face of his beautiful wife, the lieutenant was for the first time experiencing true peace of mind. For he had known at once that his wife divined the resolve which lay beyond his words.

'Well, then . . .' The lieutenant's eyes opened wide. Despite his exhaustion, they were strong and clear, and now for the first time they looked straight into the eyes of his wife. 'Tonight I shall cut my stomach.'

Reiko did not flinch.

Her round eyes showed tension, as taut as the clang of a bell.

'I am ready,' she said. 'I ask permission to accompany you.'

The lieutenant felt almost mesmerized by the strength in those eyes. His words flowed swiftly and easily, like the utterances of a man in delirium, and it was beyond his understanding how permission in a matter of such weight could be expressed so casually.

'Good. We'll go together. But I want you as a witness, first, for my own seppuku. Agreed?'

When this was said, a sudden release of abundant happiness welled up in both their hearts. Reiko was deeply affected by the greatness of her husband's trust in her. It was vital for the lieutenant, whatever else might happen, that there should be no irregularity in his death. For that, there had to be a witness. That he had chosen his wife for this was the first mark of his trust. The second, and even greater, mark was that though he had pledged they should die together, he did not intend to kill his wife first. He was deferring her death to a moment in the future when he would no longer be there to verify it. If the lieutenant had been a suspicious husband, he would doubtless have chosen to kill his wife first, as in the usual suicide pact.

When Reiko said, 'I ask permission to accompany you,' the lieutenant felt these words to be the final fruit of the education which he himself had given his wife, starting on the first night of their marriage, and which had schooled her to say what had to be said, when the moment came, without a shadow of hesitation. This assured him that his reliance on his own efforts had not been misplaced. He was not so self-satisfied as to imagine that the words had been spoken spontaneously by his wife out of love for her husband.

With happiness welling almost too naturally in their hearts, they could not help smiling at each other. Reiko felt as if she had returned to her wedding night.

Before her eyes was neither pain nor death. She seemed to see only a free, expansive plain stretching into the distance.

'The water is hot. Will you take your bath now?'

'Ah yes, of course.'

'And supper . . . ?'

The words were delivered in such level, domestic tones that the lieutenant came near to thinking, for the fraction of a second, that everything had been a hallucination.

'I don't think we'll need supper. But perhaps you could warm some sake?'

'As you wish.'

As Reiko rose and took a padded *tanzen* robe from the cabinet for after the bath, she purposely directed her husband's attention to the opened drawer. The lieutenant rose, crossed to the cabinet and looked inside. From the ordered array of paper wrappings, he read, one by one, the addresses of the keepsakes. There was no grief in the lieutenant's response to this demonstration of heroic resolve. His heart was filled with tenderness. Like a husband who is proudly shown the childish purchases of his young spouse, the lieutenant, overwhelmed by affection, lovingly embraced his wife from behind and planted a kiss on her neck.

Reiko felt the roughness of the lieutenant's unshaven skin against her neck. This sensation, more than being just a thing of this world, was for Reiko almost the world itself, but now – with the feeling that it was soon to be lost forever – it had freshness beyond all her experience. Each moment had its own vital strength, and the senses in every corner of her body were reawakened. Reiko raised herself on the tips of her toes as she accepted her husband's caresses from behind.

'First the bath, and then, after some sake . . . lay out the bedding upstairs, will you?'

The lieutenant whispered the words into his wife's ear. Reiko nodded in silence.

Flinging off his uniform, the lieutenant went to the bath. To faint background noises of splashing water, Reiko tended to the charcoal brazier in the sitting room and rose to begin the preparations for warming the sake.

Taking the *tanzen*, a sash and some underclothes, she went to the bathroom to ask how the water was. In the midst of a coiling cloud of steam, the lieutenant was sitting cross-legged on the floor, shaving, and she could dimly discern the rippling of the muscles on his damp, powerful back as they responded to the movements of his arms.

There was nothing to suggest a time of any special significance. Going busily about her tasks, Reiko was preparing tiny snacks to accompany the sake from odds and ends in stock. Her hands did not tremble. If anything, she performed this even more efficiently and smoothly than usual. True, there was a strange throbbing deep within her breast from time to time. Like distant lightning, it had a moment of sharp intensity and then vanished. Apart from that, there was nothing out of the ordinary.

The lieutenant, shaving in the bathroom, felt his warmed body healed at last of the desperate tiredness of the days of anguish, and filled – in spite of the death which lay ahead – with pleasurable anticipation. The sound of his wife going about her work came to him faintly. A healthy physical craving, submerged for two days, reasserted itself.

The lieutenant felt confident there had been no impurity in the joy they had experienced when resolving upon death. They had both sensed in that moment – though not, of course, in any clear and conscious way – that those honourable pleasures they shared in private were once more beneath the protection of a flawless morality entirely congruent with the Great Moral Principle and Divine Power of the nation. On looking into each other's eyes and discovering there an honourable death, they had felt themselves safe once more behind steel walls which none could destroy, encased in an impenetrable armour of Beauty and Righteousness. Thus, far from seeing any inconsistency or conflict between the urges of his flesh and the sincerity of his grieving patriotism, the lieutenant was even able to regard the two as parts of the same thing.

Thrusting his face close to the dark, cracked and misted wall mirror, the lieutenant shaved himself with great care. This would be his death face. He must leave no unsightly unshaved patches. The clean-shaven face gleamed once more with a youthful lustre, brightening the darkness of the mirror. There was even a certain elegance, he felt, in the association of death with this radiantly healthy face.

Yes, this would become his death face! Already, in actual fact, it had half departed from being the lieutenant's personal possession and become the bust on a dead soldier's memorial. He tried closing his eyes. Everything was wrapped in blackness, and he was no longer a living, seeing creature.

Returning from the bath, the traces of the shave glowing faintly blue beneath his smooth cheeks, he sat cross-legged on the mat beside the now well-kindled charcoal brazier. Busy though Reiko was, he noticed, she had found time to touch up her face. Her cheeks wore a colourful glow, and her lips were moist. There was no shadow of sadness to be seen. Truly, the lieutenant felt, as he saw this mark of his young wife's passionate nature, he had chosen the wife he ought to have chosen.

The lieutenant drained his cup and handed it to Reiko before refilling it. Never having tasted sake before, Reiko accepted it without hesitation and timidly brought it to her lips.

'Come here,' the lieutenant said.

Reiko moved to her husband's side and was embraced as she leaned backwards across his lap. Her breast was in violent commotion, as if sadness, joy and the potent sake were mingling and reacting within her. The lieutenant looked down into his wife's face. It was the last face he would see in this world, the last face he would see of a woman. He scrutinized it minutely, with the eyes of a traveller bidding farewell to splendid vistas he will never revisit. It was a beautiful face he could not tire of looking at, the features regular yet not cold, the lips lightly closed with a soft strength. Before he knew what he was doing, the lieutenant kissed those lips, and in the next moment he realized that, though there was not the slightest distortion of the face into the unsightliness of sobbing, tears were welling slowly from beneath the long lashes of the closed eyes and brimming over into glistening streams from the corners.

Soon the lieutenant urged her to move upstairs with him to their bedroom, but his wife replied that she would follow after taking a bath. Climbing the stairs alone to the bedroom, where the air was already warmed by the gas heater, the lieutenant lay down on the bedding with arms outstretched and legs apart. Everything was the same as always, even the time at which he lay waiting for his wife to join him.

He folded his hands beneath his head and gazed at the dark boards of the ceiling in the dimness beyond the range of the floor lamp. Was it death he was now waiting for? Or a wild ecstasy of the senses? The two seemed to overlap, as if the object of this bodily desire was death itself. Whichever might be true, the lieutenant had never before tasted such total freedom as he felt now.

A car sounded outside the window. He heard the screech of its tyres ploughing through the snow piled at the side of the street. Its horn reverberated between nearby walls. Listening to these noises, he had the feeling that this house rose like a solitary island in the ocean of a society going as restlessly about its business as ever. All around, vastly and untidily, stretched the country for which he grieved. He was to give his life for it. But would that great country, with which he was prepared to remonstrate to the extent of destroying himself, take the slightest heed of his death? He did not know, and it did not matter. His was a battlefield without glory, a battlefield where he could display deeds of valour to no one; it was the front line of the spirit.

Reiko's footsteps sounded on the stairway. The steep stairs in this old house always creaked, and he had fond memories of the sound. Many a time, while waiting in bed, the lieutenant had heard that sweet creaking. At the thought that he would hear it no more, he listened with intense concentration, striving to fill every moment of this precious time with the sound of those soft footfalls on the creaking stairway, each moment a sparkling jewel.

Reiko had wound a broad Nagoya obi around the waist of her yukata, its deep red muted in the room's dim light. The lieutenant reached for it, and with the aid of Reiko's hand, the obi fell away, slithering to the matted floor. The lieutenant moved to embrace her in her yukata, thrusting his hands beneath her arms, but when his fingers were enclosed by the warm flesh of her armpits through the yukata's open side slits, he felt his whole body burst into flame.

In a few moments the two lay naked before the glowing gas heater.

Neither spoke the thought, but their hearts, their bodies and their pounding breasts blazed with the knowledge that this was the very last time. It was as if the words 'The Last Time' were spelled out, in invisible brushstrokes, across every inch of their bodies.

The lieutenant drew his young wife close and kissed her vehemently. As their tongues explored each other's mouth, reaching into the smooth, moist interior, they felt as if the still-unknown agonies of death had tempered their senses to the keenness of red-hot steel. The death agonies they could not yet feel, the distant agonies of death, had refined their awareness of pleasure.

'This is the last time I shall see your body,' said the lieutenant. 'Let me look at it closely.' And, tilting the shade on the lampstand to one side, he directed the rays of the lamp along the full length of Reiko's outstretched form.

Reiko lay still with her eyes closed. The light from the low lamp clearly revealed the majestic undulations of her white flesh. Not without a touch of egoistic satisfaction, the lieutenant rejoiced that he would never have to see this beauty crumble with the passing years.

At his leisure, the lieutenant allowed the unforgettable spectacle to engrave itself upon his mind. With one hand he fondled the hair, with the other he caressed the magnificent face, implanting kisses here and there where his eyes lingered. The quiet coldness of the high, tapering forehead, the closed eyes with their long lashes beneath faintly etched brows, the set of the finely shaped nose, the gleam of teeth glimpsed between full, regular lips, the soft cheeks and the small, wise chin . . . these things conjured up in the lieutenant's mind the vision of a truly radiant death face, and again and again he pressed his lips tight against the white throat – where Reiko's own hand was soon to strike – and the throat reddened faintly beneath his kisses. Returning to the mouth, he laid his lips against it with the gentlest of pressures, and moved them rhythmically over Reiko's with the light rolling motion of a small boat. If he closed his eyes, the world became a rocking cradle.

Wherever the lieutenant's eyes moved, his lips faithfully followed. The high, swelling breasts were surmounted by nipples like the buds of a wild cherry, which hardened as the lieutenant's lips closed about them. The arms flowed smoothly downwards from each side of the breast, tapering toward the wrists, yet losing nothing of their roundness or symmetry, and at their tips were those delicate fingers which had held the fan at the wedding ceremony. One by one, as the lieutenant kissed them, each finger withdrew behind its neighbour as if in shame. The natural hollow curving between the bosom and the stomach carried in its lines a suggestion not only of softness but of resilient strength, and while it gave forewarning of the rich curves spreading outwards from here to the hips, it had in itself an appearance only of restraint and proper discipline. The whiteness and richness of the belly and hips were like milk brimming in a great bowl, and the sharply shadowed dip of the navel could have been the fresh impress of a raindrop, fallen there that very instant. Where the shadows gathered more thickly, hair clustered, gentle and sensitive, and as the agitation mounted in the now no longer passive body, there hung over this region a scent like the smouldering of fragrant blossoms, growing steadily more pervasive.

At length, in a tremulous voice, Reiko spoke.

'Show me . . . Let me look too, for the last time.'

Never before had he heard from his wife's lips so strong and unequivocal a request. It was as if something which her modesty had wished to keep hidden to the end had suddenly burst its bonds of constraint. The lieutenant obediently lay back and surrendered himself to his wife. Lithely she raised her white, trembling body, and – burning with an innocent desire to return to her husband what he had done for her – placed two white fingers on the lieutenant's eyes, which gazed fixedly up at her, and gently stroked them shut.

Suddenly overwhelmed by tenderness, her cheeks and eyelids flushed by a dizzying uprush of emotion, Reiko threw her arms about the lieutenant's close-cropped head. The bristly hairs rubbed painfully against her breast, the prominent nose was cold as it dug into her flesh and his breath was hot against her. Relaxing her embrace, she gazed down at her husband's masculine face. The severe brows, the closed eyes, the splendid bridge of the nose, the shapely lips drawn firmly together . . . the blue, clean-shaven cheeks reflecting the lamplight and gleaming smoothly. Reiko kissed each of these. She kissed the broad nape of the neck, the strong, erect shoulders, the powerful chest with its twin circles like shields and its russet nipples. In the armpits, deeply shadowed by the ample flesh of the shoulders and the chest, a sweet and melancholy odour emanated from the growth of hair, and in the sweetness of this odour was contained, somehow, the essence of young death. The lieutenant's naked skin glowed like a field of barley, and everywhere the muscles showed in sharp relief, converging on the lower abdomen about the small, unassuming navel. Gazing at the firm, youthful stomach, modestly covered by a vigorous growth of hair, Reiko thought of it as it was soon to be, cruelly cut by the sword, and she laid her head upon it, sobbing in pity, and bathed it with kisses.

At the touch of his wife's tears upon his stomach, the lieutenant felt ready to endure with courage the cruellest agonies of his seppuku.

What ecstasies they experienced after these tender exchanges may well be imagined. The lieutenant raised himself and enfolded his wife in a powerful embrace, her body now limp with exhaustion after her grief and tears. Passionately they held their faces close, rubbing cheek against cheek. Reiko's body was trembling. Their breasts, moist with sweat, were tightly joined, and every inch of the young and beautiful bodies had become so much one with the other that it seemed impossible there should ever again be a separation. Reiko cried out. From the heights they plunged into the abyss, and from the abyss they took wing and soared once more to dizzying heights. The lieutenant panted like the regimental standard-bearer on a long, hard march. As one cycle ended, almost immediately a new wave of passion would be generated, and together – with no trace of fatigue – they would climb again in a single breathless movement to the very summit.

IV

When the lieutenant at last turned away, it was not from weariness. For one thing, he was anxious not to deplete the considerable strength he would need in carrying out his seppuku. For another, he would have been sorry to mar the sweetness of these last memories by overindulgence.

Since the lieutenant had clearly desisted, Reiko, too, with her usual compliance, followed his example. The two lay naked on their backs, with fingers interlaced, staring fixedly at the dark ceiling. The room was warm from the heater, and even when the sweat had ceased to pour from their bodies they felt no cold. Outside, in the hushed night, the sounds of passing traffic had ceased. Even the noises of the trains and trams around Yotsuya Station did not penetrate this far. After echoing through the region bounded by the moat, they were lost in the heavily wooded park fronting the broad driveway before Akasaka Palace. It was hard to believe in the tension gripping the whole quarter, where the two factions of the bitterly divided Imperial Army now confronted each other, poised for battle.

Savouring the warmth glowing within themselves, they lay still and recalled the ecstasies they had just known, reliving each moment of the experience. They remembered the taste of kisses which had never wearied, the touch of naked flesh, episode after episode of dizzying bliss. But already, from the dark boards of the ceiling, the face of death was peering down. These joys had been final, and their bodies would never know them again. Not that joy of such intensity – and the same thought occurred to them both – was ever likely to be re-experienced, even if they should live on to old age.

The feel of their fingers intertwined – this too would soon be lost. Even the wood-grain patterns they now gazed at on the dark ceiling boards would be taken from them. They could feel death edging in, nearer and nearer. There could be no hesitation now. They must have the courage to reach out to death themselves, and to seize it.

'Come, let's make our preparations,' said the lieutenant. The note of determination in the words was unmistakable, but at the same time Reiko had never heard her husband's voice so warm and tender.

After they had risen, a variety of tasks awaited them.

The lieutenant, who had never once before helped with the bedding, now cheerfully slid back the door of the closet, lifted the mattress across the room by himself and stowed it away inside.

Reiko turned off the gas heater and put away the floor lamp. During the lieutenant's absence she had arranged this room carefully, sweeping and dusting it to a fresh cleanness, and now – if one overlooked the rosewood table drawn into one corner – the eight-mat room gave all the appearance of a parlour ready to welcome an important guest.

'We've seen some drinking here, haven't we? With Kanō and Homma and Noguchi . . .'

'Yes, they were great drinkers, all of them.'

'We'll be meeting them before long, in the other world. They'll tease me, I imagine, when they find I've brought you with me.'

Descending the stairs, the lieutenant turned back into this calm, clean room, now brightly illuminated by the ceiling lamp. There floated across his mind the faces of the young officers who had drunk there, and laughed, and engaged in innocent boasting. He had never dreamed then that he would one day cut open his stomach in this room.

In the two rooms downstairs, husband and wife busied themselves smoothly and serenely with their respective preparations. The lieutenant went to the toilet, and then to the bathroom to wash. Meanwhile Reiko folded away her husband's *tanzen*, placed his uniform tunic, his trousers and a newly cut bleached loincloth in the bathroom, and set out sheets of paper on the sitting-room table for the farewell notes. Then she removed the lid from the writing box and began rubbing the inkstick on the stone. She had already decided on the wording of her own note.

Reiko's fingers pressed hard upon the cold gilt letters of the inkstick, and the water in the shallow well of the inkstone darkened at once as if a black cloud had spread across it. She stopped thinking that this repeated action, this pressure from her fingers, this rise and fall of the faint scraping sound, was all solely for death. It was a routine domestic task, a simple paring away of time until death should finally stand before her. And yet, in the increasingly smooth motion of the inkstick rubbing on the stone, and in the rising scent of the thickening ink, there was inexpressible darkness.

Neat in his uniform, which he now wore next to his skin, the lieutenant emerged from the bathroom. Without a word, he sat upright on his heels at the table, took a brush in his hand, and stared undecidedly at the paper before him.

Reiko took a white silk kimono with her and entered the bathroom. When she reappeared in the sitting room, clad in the white kimono and with her face lightly made up, the farewell note lay completed on the table beneath the lamp. The thick black brushstrokes said simply:

'Long Live the Imperial Forces – Army Lieutenant Takeyama Shinji.'

While Reiko sat opposite him writing her own note, the lieutenant gazed in silence, intensely serious, at the controlled movement of his wife's pale fingers as they manipulated the writing brush.

With their respective notes in their hands – the lieutenant's sword strapped to his side, Reiko's small dagger thrust into the sash of her white kimono – the two of them stood before the god shelf and prayed in silence. Then they put out all the downstairs lights. As he mounted the stairs, the lieutenant turned his head and gazed back with astonishment at the sheer beauty of his wife's white-clad figure climbing behind him out of the darkness with lowered eyes.

They laid the farewell notes side by side in the *tokonoma* of the upstairs room. He wondered whether he ought to remove the scroll that was hanging in the *tokonoma*, but it had been written by their go-between, Lieutenant General Ozeki, and, moreover, it consisted of two Chinese characters signifying 'Ultimate Sincerity'. He therefore left it in place.

Even if it were to become stained with splashes of blood, he felt that the general would understand.

Sitting erect on his heels with his back to the *tokonoma* pillar, the lieutenant laid his sword on the matted floor before his knees.

Reiko sat facing him, a mat's width away. With the rest of her so severely white, the touch of rouge on her lips seemed remarkably seductive.

Across the mat that divided them, they gazed intently into each other's eyes. The lieutenant's sword lay before his knees. Seeing it, Reiko recalled their first night and was overwhelmed with sadness. The lieutenant spoke in a hoarse voice:

'As I have no second to help me, I shall cut deep. I might handle myself poorly, but please do not panic. Death of any sort is a fearful thing to see. You must not be discouraged by the sight. Do you understand?'

'Yes, I do.'

Reiko nodded deeply.

Looking at the slender white figure of his wife, the lieutenant experienced a strange rapture as he faced death. What he was about to engage in was an act in his public capacity as a soldier, something he had never previously shown his wife – a death that required as much resolve as entering the battlefield at a decisive moment, a death equivalent in weight and in quality to a death on the front line. He was about to show his wife his conduct on the battlefield.

The thought led the lieutenant to a strange momentary fantasy. A lonely death on the battlefield, a death before the eyes of his beautiful wife . . . in the sensation that he was now to die in these two dimensions, realizing an impossible union of them both, there was a sweetness beyond words. This must be the very pinnacle of good fortune, he thought. To have every moment of his death observed by those beautiful eyes – it was like arriving at death enveloped by a gentle, fragrant breeze. There was some special favour here. He did not understand precisely what it was, but this was a domain unknown to others, a special dispensation for him alone. In the radiant, bride-like figure of his white-robed wife, the lieutenant seemed to see a glorious vision of all those things he had loved and for which he was to lay down his life – the Imperial Household, the Nation, the Army Flag. However distant they might have been, all of these, no less than the wife who sat before him, had been presences observing him closely with clear and never-faltering eyes.

Reiko too was gazing intently at her husband, so soon to die, and she thought that never in this world could there be anything so beautiful. The lieutenant always looked handsome in uniform, but now, as he contemplated death with severe brows and firmly closed lips, he revealed what was perhaps masculine beauty at its most superb.

'It's time,' the lieutenant said at last.

Reiko bent low to the mat in a deep bow. She could not raise her face. She did not wish to spoil her make-up with tears, but the tears could not be held back.

When at length she looked up, she saw hazily through her tears that her husband was winding a strip of white cloth around the blade of his now unsheathed sword, leaving five or six inches of naked steel showing at the point.

Resting the sword in its cloth wrapping on the mat before him, the lieutenant rose from his knees, resettled himself cross-legged and unfastened the hooks of his uniform collar. His eyes were no longer looking at his wife. Slowly, one by one, he undid the flat brass buttons. The dusky brown chest was revealed, and then the stomach. He unclasped his belt and undid the buttons of his trousers. The pure whiteness of the thickly coiled loin cloth showed itself. The lieutenant pushed the cloth down with both hands, further to ease his stomach, and then gripped the white-wrapped blade of his sword. With his left hand he massaged his abdomen, glancing downward as he did so.

To reassure himself of the sharpness of his sword's cutting edge, the lieutenant folded back his left trouser flap, exposing a little of his thigh, and lightly drew the blade across the skin. Instantly blood welled up in the wound, and several streaks of blood ran down, glistening in the strong light.

It was the first time Reiko had ever seen her husband's blood, and she felt a violent throbbing in her chest. She looked at her husband's face. The lieutenant was looking at the blood with calm appraisal. For a moment – though aware that it was a hollow comfort – Reiko experienced a sense of relief.

The lieutenant's eyes fixed his wife with an intense, hawk-like stare. Moving the sword around to his front, he raised himself slightly on his hips and let the upper half of his body come down over the sword point. That he was mustering his whole strength was apparent from the angry tension of the uniform at his shoulders. The lieutenant aimed to strike deep into the left side of his stomach. His sharp cry pierced the silence of the room.

The effort was entirely his own, but the lieutenant felt as if someone else had struck the side of his stomach agonizingly with a thick iron rod. For a moment his head reeled and he had no idea what had happened. The five or six inches of naked point had vanished completely into his flesh and the white cloth he gripped in his clenched fist pressed directly against his stomach.

His consciousness returned. The blade had certainly pierced the wall of his stomach, he thought. His breathing was difficult, his chest thumped violently, and in some far deep region, which he could hardly believe was a part of himself, a fearful and excruciating pain came welling up as if the ground had split open and disgorged a burning stream of molten rock. The pain came suddenly nearer with terrifying speed. The lieutenant bit his lower lip and stifled an instinctive moan.

Was this seppuku? he was thinking. It was a sensation of utter chaos, as if the sky had fallen on his head and the world was reeling drunkenly. His will power and courage, which had seemed so robust before he made the incision, had now dwindled to something like a single hair-like thread of steel, and he was assailed by the uneasy feeling that he must advance along this thread, clinging to it with desperation. His clenched fist had grown moist. Looking down, he saw that both his hand and the cloth about the blade were drenched in blood. His loincloth, too, was dyed a deep red. It struck him as incredible that, amid this terrible agony, things which could still be seen could still be seen and things that existed still existed.

The moment she saw him thrust the sword into his left side and the deathly pallor fall across his face like an abruptly lowered curtain, Reiko had to struggle to prevent herself from rushing to his side. Whatever happened, she must watch. She must be a witness. That was the duty her husband had laid upon her. A mat's space away, she could clearly see her husband biting his lip to stifle the pain. The pain was there, with absolute certainty, before her eyes. And Reiko had no means of rescuing him from it.

The sweat glistened on her husband's forehead. The lieutenant closed his eyes and opened them again, as if experimenting. The eyes had lost their lustre and seemed innocent and empty like the eyes of a small animal.

The agony before Reiko's eyes burned as strong as the summer sun, utterly remote from the grief which seemed to be tearing her apart within. The pain grew steadily in stature, stretching upwards. Reiko felt that her husband had already become a man in a separate world, a man whose whole being had been resolved into pain, a prisoner in a cage of pain where no hand could reach out to him. But Reiko felt no pain at all. Her grief was not pain. As she thought about this, Reiko began to feel as if someone had raised a cruel wall of glass high between herself and her husband.

Ever since her marriage, her husband's existence had been her own existence, and every breath of his had been a breath drawn by herself. But now, while her husband's existence in pain was a vivid reality, Reiko could find in this grief of hers no certain proof at all of her own existence.

With only his right hand on the sword, the lieutenant began to cut sideways across his stomach. But as the blade became entangled with the entrails, it was pushed constantly outward by their soft resilience. The lieutenant realized that he would need to use both hands to keep the point pressed deep into his stomach. He pulled the blade across. It did not cut as easily as he had expected. He directed the strength of his whole body into his right hand and pulled again. There was a cut of three or four inches.

The pain spread slowly outwards from the inner depths until the whole stomach reverberated. It was like the wild clanging of a bell. Or like a thousand bells that jangled simultaneously at every breath he breathed and every throb of his pulse, rocking his whole being. The lieutenant could no longer stop himself from moaning. But by now the blade had cut its way through to below the navel, and when he noticed this he felt a sense of satisfaction, and a renewal of courage.

The volume of blood had steadily increased, and now it spurted from the wound as if propelled by the beat of the pulse. The mat before the lieutenant was drenched red with spattered blood, and more blood overflowed on to it from pools which gathered in the folds of the lieutenant's khaki trousers. A spot, like a bird, came flying across to Reiko and settled on the lap of her white silk kimono.

By the time the lieutenant had at last drawn the sword across to the right side of his stomach, the blade was cutting less deeply and had revealed its naked tip, slippery with blood and grease. But, suddenly stricken by a fit of vomiting, the lieutenant cried out hoarsely. The vomiting made the fierce pain fiercer still, and the stomach, which had thus far remained firm and compact, now abruptly heaved, opening wide its wound, and the entrails burst through, as if the wound too were vomiting. Seemingly ignorant of their master's suffering, the entrails gave an impression of robust health and almost disagreeable vitality as they slipped smoothly out and spilled over into the crotch. The lieutenant's head drooped, his shoulders heaved, his eyes were narrow slits and a thin trickle of saliva dribbled from his mouth. The gold markings on his epaulettes caught the light and glinted.

Blood was scattered everywhere. The lieutenant was soaked in it to his knees, and he sat now in a crumpled and listless posture, one hand on the floor. A raw smell filled the room. The lieutenant, his head drooping, retched repeatedly, and the movement showed vividly in his shoulders. The blade of the sword, now pushed back by the entrails and exposed to its tip, was still in the lieutenant's right hand.

It would be difficult to imagine a more heroic sight than that of the lieutenant at this moment, as he mustered his strength and flung his head back. The movement was performed with sudden violence, and the back of his head struck with a sharp crack against the *tokonoma* pillar. Reiko had been sitting until now with her face lowered, gazing in fascination at the tide of blood advancing toward her knees, but the sound took her by surprise and she looked up.

The lieutenant's face was not the face of a living man. The eyes were hollow, the skin parched, the once so lustrous cheeks and lips the colour of dried mud. The right hand alone was moving. Laboriously gripping the sword, it hovered shakily in the air like the hand of a marionette and strove to direct the point at the base of the lieutenant's throat. Reiko saw all too clearly how her husband made this last, most heart-rending, futile exertion. Glistening with blood and grease, the point drifted towards the throat again and again. And each time it missed its aim. The strength to guide it was no longer there. The straying point struck the collar and the collar badges. Although its hooks had been unfastened, the stiff military collar had closed together again and was protecting the throat.

Reiko could bear the sight no longer. She tried to go to her husband's aid, but she could not stand. She moved through the blood on her knees, and her white skirts grew deep red. Moving to the rear of her husband, she helped no more than by loosening the collar. The quivering blade at last contacted the naked flesh of the throat. At that moment Reiko felt that she herself must have propelled her husband forward, but that was not the case. It was a movement planned by the lieutenant himself, his last exertion of strength. Abruptly he threw his body at the blade, which pierced his neck, emerging at the nape. With a tremendous spurt of blood, the blade came to rest, its cold blue-tinged point thrusting upwards beneath the lamp.

V

Slowly, her socks slippery with blood, Reiko descended the stairway. The upstairs room was now completely still.

Switching on the ground-floor lights, she checked the gas jet and the main gas line and poured water over the smouldering, half-buried charcoal in the brazier. She stepped over to the full-length mirror in the four-and-a-half mat room and lifted its cloth cover. The bloodstains on the skirts of her white kimono looked like a bold, vivid pattern. When she sat down before the mirror, she was conscious of the dampness and coldness of her husband's blood in the region of her thighs, and a shiver went through her. She then devoted a great deal of time to her make-up. She brushed the rouge on generously to her cheeks, and to her lips she applied deep colour. This was no longer make-up to please her husband. It was make-up for the world she would leave behind, and there was a touch of the spectacular in her brushwork. When she rose, the mat before the mirror was wet with blood. Reiko was not concerned about this.

Returning from the toilet, Reiko stood finally on the concrete floor of the entryway. When her husband had bolted the door here last night, it had been in preparation for death. Now she stood immersed in the consideration of a simple problem. Should she leave the front door locked or unlocked? If she were to bolt the door, the neighbours might not notice their death for several days. Reiko did not relish the thought of their two corpses putrefying before discovery. After all, it would be best to leave the door unlocked. She released the bolt and drew the frosted-glass door partway open. At once a chill wind blew inside. There was no sign of anyone in the midnight streets, and stars glittered ice-cold through the trees in the grounds of the mansion across the street.

Leaving the door ajar, Reiko mounted the stairs. She had walked here and there for some time and her socks were no longer slippery. About halfway up, her nostrils were assailed by a peculiar smell.

The lieutenant was lying on his face in a sea of blood. The sword point protruding from the back of his neck seemed to have grown even more prominent than before. Reiko walked unconcerned through the pools of blood. Sitting beside the lieutenant's corpse, she stared intently at the face in profile where it lay on the mat. His eyes were opened wide, as if he were possessed by something. She raised the head in her arms, wiped the blood from the lips with her sleeve, and planted a farewell kiss on them.

Rising then, she took a new white blanket and a waist cord from the closet. To prevent any derangement of her skirts, she wrapped the blanket about her waist and bound it there firmly with the cord.

Reiko sat herself on a spot about one foot distant from the lieutenant's body. Drawing the dagger from her sash, she examined the transparent gleam of its blade and touched it to her tongue. The taste of the polished steel was slightly sweet.

Reiko did not linger. When she thought how the pain which had previously opened such a gulf between herself and her dying husband was now to become a part of her own experience, she saw before her only the joy of herself entering a realm her husband had already made his own. In her husband's agonized face there had been something inexplicable which she was seeing for the first time. Now she would solve that riddle. Reiko sensed that at last she too would be able to taste the true bitterness and sweetness of that Great Moral Principle in which her husband believed. What she had until now tasted only through her husband she was about to savour directly with her own tongue.

Reiko rested the point of the blade against the base of her throat and made a thrust. The wound was shallow. Her head blazed, and her hands shook uncontrollably. She gave the blade a strong pull sideways. Something warm flooded into her mouth, and everything before her eyes reddened in a vision of spouting blood. Encouraged by this, she plunged the point of the blade deep into her throat.

MEN AND WOMEN

TSUSHIMA YŪKO

Flames

Translated by Geraldine Harcourt

That evening, on the way to collect my daughter from day care, I encountered yet another funeral. It was on the street I always took from the station, inside an eye clinic where I used to go myself. Floral wreaths flanked the entrance of the old, low building, and from the open doors black-and-white curtains receded into the interior. There was no one on duty outside; perhaps the service was over.

The clinic had belonged to a dour old doctor. He had seemed to have no assistant or nurse, nor many patients. His office contained a jumble of medicine boxes, and its floor was on a slight incline. The funeral was most likely his, but perhaps not. Much as I would have liked to go in and ask, I didn't even pause outside.

I was encountering a lot of deaths. I've lost track of exactly how many funerals I came across on my regular routes; it surely can't have been all that many and yet, at the time, I couldn't shake the feeling that deaths lay in wait for me at every turn. And I couldn't help wondering what in the world they were trying to tell me, appearing like that, one after the other.

The weather was unsettled at that time of year, on the cusp between winter and spring. Some days brought a warm, moist wind that gusted from morning till night; others brought an inch or two of snow. It was a season when those who were ill were liable to slip away. My apartment was in an old neighbourhood where many households were elderly: I supposed that was bound to translate into these numbers. The local death rate that year had nothing to do with my having moved to the area. Why should it? Yet each time I met with another passing, my mind sought to link it with myself – to pin it on me.

The first had been at the flower shop directly across the street from the building where I lived. It was the owner who died. The neighbourhood association's black-and-white marquee went up in front of the shop. The funeral was a big one, with many wreaths. The shop reopened in less than a week. My daughter and I remarked that the middle-aged woman – evidently the florist's daughter – who now stood in the open shop front had red rims to her eyes, as though she'd been weeping moments before.

Then it was the old retired barber who lived above his shop next door to our building. For two days we had to thread our way among the easels holding floral wreaths on the pavement as we came and went.

It was when I noticed the next funeral, at a house near my daughter's day care, that I thought with a ripple of alarm, 'This is going too far.'

But there were more to come. Kobayashi, my former boss, died not long after that. He had been in the hospital for the better part of a year with cirrhosis of the liver. Suzui, who had replaced him when he took sick leave, broke the news to me one morning as I arrived at the library. Suzui attended the funeral that day, bearing a condolence offering with my name accompanying his own on the envelope. On his return in the late afternoon he told me it had been a good, simple funeral. But Kobayashi's domestic situation had apparently been complicated; there'd been two women present who could have been Mrs Kobayashi, and Suzui hadn't known whom to approach or how.

Even Kobayashi's death didn't particularly affect me – or, at least, not with sadness. There was an intervening layer of surprise and fear. I was starting to sense some obscure intent in this string of deaths.

And I continued to encounter still more funerals, days apart.

It was right about then that I was laid low by flu. Having felt unwell since I got up in the morning, by the evening I couldn't stay on my feet in the kitchen, and my temperature registered over 102. For a start, I lay down with my legs under the *kotatsu* quilt in the tatami room and consulted my daughter: 'Mummy's sick. I can't do a thing . . . I'm wondering what to do about you. Shall I call Mitchan's house and ask her daddy or mummy to come for you, so you can stay over, like you always do?'

About once a week she stayed over at the home of a playmate from day care. Mitchan's parents had talked me into this, initially to let my daughter have some breathing space, but gradually both she and I had come to count on these breaks. My husband Fujino had not responded to my third request to attend divorce mediation. His phone calls and letters had ceased, and he no longer showed himself in my daughter's vicinity. All signs of him seemed to have vanished from my life. One could call this a peaceful time, I suppose, but in fact I spent it on edge with something close to fear, because I no longer had any clues as to what to expect. In response to her mother's tension, my three-year-old daughter was having frequent fits of anger.

She took with alacrity to spending nights away, right from the start. The anxiety was all on my side, and more than once I woke up in tears, having dreamed I'd lost her in the middle of town somewhere. In time, though, I came to sleep deeply on those nights when I had the whole futon to myself, and I'd even begun to prompt her, 'How about going to Mitchan's tomorrow?' She needed no coaxing; she'd give a squeal of delight and start singing 'Mitchan's tomorrow, Mitchan's tomorrow' to a made-up tune.

When I'd ask her if I could pop in, she'd answer excitedly, 'You come too, Mummy. We can eat dinner together.' Which made me feel like joining in her song while doing a little dance.

When I found I was running a temperature of 102 and would be out of action for at least a day, my thoughts automatically turned to Mitchan's family. My mother lived not far away, but I couldn't let her know. I hadn't even told her how things stood with Fujino. I wanted her to think everything was fine and my daughter and I were positively blooming. My attitude to my mother was like my attitude to Fujino.

'It's okay, I won't go to Mitchan's, I'll stay with you. You're sick, aren't you, Mummy?'

That day, her face entirely failed to light up at the word 'Mitchan's'. In surprise, I pressed her: 'Are you sure? It's *Mitchan's*? I might not be able to take you to day care tomorrow. You'd have to stay at home all day.'

'I don't mind. Mummy, are you sick?' She peered at me as she repeated the question. She seemed fascinated by the idea. I nodded, took her hand, and put it on my forehead.

'It's hot. You're really sick.' Her eyes sparkled. She went on to touch my cheek, my lips and my hand, her expression showing signs of growing excitement.

I got up and gave her some bread and milk and cold sausage, then burrowed into the futon that I'd left down in the two-mat room and was asleep before I knew it.

I woke in the night to find a cleaning cloth on my forehead, dripping wet, and my daughter, still dressed, curled up asleep on top of the quilt. The lights and the TV were on.

We stayed in all the next day. I dozed, and she wiped my face with a towel, took my temperature, and brought me glasses of water which she poured into my mouth and on to the tatami; she also watched TV and napped contentedly, her head pillowed on my arm. We sipped rice porridge – invalid food – together. And that night she too ran a fever – nearly 104 degrees. It was my turn to minister with damp towels and mop her perspiring neck and chest.

The next morning, my own temperature being down to near normal, I took her on my back to see the doctor, who gave us both medicine. I knew I should at least stop to buy milk and eggs, but we came straight home and, after taking our respective medicines, went back to bed.

The following day, her fever too began to go down at last. But she had developed the diarrhoea that always followed a bout of illness. I put her in a nappy, long outgrown; even so, the futon and her lower body didn't escape soiling. The room was oddly cozy, filled as it was with our own warmth and the smell. Washing her nappies, which took me back, I fell into a stupor as if still feverish myself. But then it occurred to me that it was Saturday – I had a day off ahead, no permission required. The fridge had been empty since the previous day. In the evening, while my daughter slept, I did the shopping. In addition to milk, eggs and vegetables, I bought bananas. I remembered how, when she was a baby, I used to scrape a banana with the rim of a spoon and carry the mush to her mouth. I couldn't remember how big she had been at the time, though.

That night, I freshened us both up for the first time in three days, using hot water from the kitchen. First I sponged my daughter's face, neck and hands, then her chest and back. Then, holding her down with my left hand as she squirmed ticklishly, I gave her lower half a thorough sponging. After changing the water, I took off my top and began to sponge my neck and arms with a hot towel while she watched. When it arrived at my chest, she reached out timidly to touch my nipples. I paused and watched the movement of her hand. She tweaked a nipple then instantly pulled back in hoots of laughter. I had already hunched up with unexpected ticklishness, covering my breasts with my arms.

She rolled about giggling on the futon, then lifted her face. 'Can I do it again?'

After a moment's hesitation, I nodded. She took my nipple between her fingers, holding on this time and pressing harder, trying to squash it.

'Ow! Careful, you'll break it!'

I pulled away from her hand. Rather than pain, I was overtaken by chills. As a newborn baby, her sucking had sent the same chills through me: a shudder accompanied by a keen joy.

'Does it hurt?' she asked, eyeing my nipples uneasily.

'Well, of course. And if you break them off, they won't grow back.'

I quickly put my pyjama top on, flustered in case she'd noticed the sudden chills.

'Yes, they will,' she said. 'They'll come out again.'

'No way. And neither will the milk.'

'Is it all gone?'

'That's right. You used to drink lots, though . . .'

'I want some.'

My daughter's eyes were sparkling again.

'You can't. I told you, it's all gone.'

I stood up and escaped, laughing, into the kitchen. But once I'd put the lights out and we were both in bed, she reached out towards my breasts again and said, in a voice that held laughter, 'I'm a baby . . .'

'Aha. So you are – you're even wearing nappies.'

'Mewble mewble, mewble mewble.'

I had to laugh. 'That baby has a funny-sounding cry. More like a cat, I'd say.'

Breathless with stifled laughter, she went on: 'Mewble mewble, my tummy's hungry.'

'Wow, so this baby can talk already?'

'Mewble mewble. Want mummy mook.'

'There, there, hush now. It's all right, then, here you are.'

I pulled her to me with a grand gesture, tugged my top up to uncover my breasts and pressed her face to my nipple. She closed her mouth around it for a brief moment, but then started laughing shyly and took her mouth away. She left her cheek resting on my breast, all the same, and was soon sucking on the edge of my pyjama top instead. She never could go to sleep without a bit of cloth to suck, since she'd been a baby.

Towards daybreak, I had a dream.

I was on an outing, some sort of school picnic or factory tour, with a couple of dozen other people. These seemed to be classmates from my primary-school days, but they had grown up and were adult size.

We were being kept waiting for something on the landing of a drab staircase in an office building. Some drank fizzy drinks, some excused themselves to go to the bathroom. Thinking this was my chance, I began to change my clothes.

Next thing I knew, I was surrounded by shocked looks. I glanced down at myself, only to discover my right breast showing through a gap in my underwear. Startled, I tried to conceal it, but couldn't.

A voice snapped, 'What do you think you're doing? Shame on you!' There was a chorus of remarks: 'Put your clothes on. Now!' 'That's what you get for dithering.' 'How embarrassing!' 'What a place to choose.' 'Talk about clueless!' 'She's such a loser.'

While fumbling away, I was thinking sadly that they were right. Why hadn't I found some more secluded spot? I'd simply thought I could do a quick change while nobody was looking, but now what was I to do? My underwear and blouse had got all tangled up and I couldn't tell where the sleeves were or where to put my head. I'd probably have to take everything off before I could finish dressing. The more I fiddled about, the more my right breast showed itself.

The thought that I was not only upsetting everyone but would get left behind reduced me to tears.

A man gave my back an encouraging push. 'There's plenty of time, silly, why don't you go to the toilets? I'll follow you.' On shaky legs, I started to climb the stairs.

There was no one in there. My escort found a chair in the washbasin area and sat down, turning his back. 'Make it quick. There's no one here, you're okay.'

He was an old classmate whose name I'd forgotten but whose face was very familiar. From behind, he looked just like a bigger version of the child he had been.

'Very well.' Relieved by the quiet, I began undressing. I would be naked from the waist up, so I thought I'd better say something, and told the man, 'Don't look.'

He laughed. 'I'm really not that interested.'

'No, I suppose not.'

Reassured, I stripped to the waist and set to work untangling my blouse from my underwear. My arm brushed the man's shoulder; his skin was soft to the touch. Now that I looked properly, he too had nothing on. Though he was full-grown, his back was as smooth as a plump child's. Every time I moved, my hand or back or nipple brushed against his skin. I held my breath, bewildered by this turn of events. Everything before my eyes went dark except our skin, which had begun to glow. Though on the verge of screaming in fear, I was lost in wonder at the luminosity of our skin . . .

On waking in the morning, I noticed that my nipple was still a little sore. I glanced at my daughter asleep by my side and found myself taking a deep breath as the succession of deaths came back to me.

I was back at work at the library when I had a call from Fujino for the first time in three months and met him in a nearby coffee shop. He was letting his hair grow long.

He asked how I was; I answered I was very well.

'You want a divorce, right?' he continued. 'Are you going to insist on getting the family court to mediate?'

I nodded.

'For crying out loud . . . If you want a divorce that badly, let's get it over with. I just think it's a shame we couldn't have talked it over like reasonable people. It's exactly a year since we split up . . . and I've had enough. I'm worn out.'

I stared at him, stunned. I had been growing vaguely resigned to the possibility that I might end up still married to Fujino. However, I told myself not to believe him yet. He was a man of many moods.

But he had more to say that day: 'It's been tough on me too, toughest thing I've ever dealt with, but it was me who left, I guess, so I can't complain . . . Take good care of our little girl. Let's discuss the arrangements another time. Don't worry, you can have custody. I couldn't do anything for her anyway . . .'

With a wry smile, he drew a paper from the inside breast pocket of his jacket and handed it to me. It was the divorce form I'd sent him in the autumn. I had already filled my section out; now Fujino's side was also completed and bore his seal. The witnesses' section remained blank. 'You file it,' he said. 'I'll leave it to you.'

'But . . . are you sure?'

These feeble words were all I could come out with. It was so sudden. I couldn't take my eyes off the paper, and meanwhile I had lost all sensation in my body.

'Am I *sure*? Isn't this what you wanted? I'm doing what you wanted, that's all.'

'Thank you . . .'

Without being fully conscious of it, I had bowed my head. I wanted to put the same question to him again and again: was he sure, might we be making a huge mistake? I had indeed wanted a divorce all along, and yet, flying in the face of those wishes, I had an urge to huddle up to him and cry, 'Maybe we've got it wrong – weren't we hoping for something different?' All I did, though, was sit in front of him, my head lowered, in a daze.

Before he left, Fujino did some explaining: he wouldn't be able to repay the money he owed me for some time yet; he intended to pay child support when he could, but this too was impossible at the moment; he didn't want to let people down by abandoning his dreams of making a movie and creating a small theatre company. He got up to go.

'Sorry to call you out while you're at work.'

I murmured, 'No, *I'm* sorry . . .' with another bow of my head.

He paid for our coffees and disappeared from my sight.

So, it was true, then? I remained seated for some time, unable to move. The magnitude of what I was now certain to lose was overwhelming. Whatever our relationship may have been like for the past year, he was, after all, the man who had been closer to me than anyone else. The only man I'd ever wanted to share my true feelings with. I hoped he at least understood that I was entirely without hate or bitterness towards him. He might have felt the same way, for all I knew. I could only think that perhaps there existed a kind of bond that required both parties to believe themselves hated by the other. Both Fujino and I were flesh and blood human beings who didn't want our lives to end yet.

The thought left me even more drained of strength.

By now, the weather had turned consistently warm.

Late one night, I was woken by a loud boom. The building rocked. My daughter woke too, calling out tearfully. My heart was racing as we went up on to the rooftop terrace together to see what had happened. I scanned the streets: nothing looked unusual. But I could see people leaning out of windows here and there; clearly I wasn't the only one to have heard the explosion.

I searched further, hugging my daughter's head to me as she continued to cry with fright. What on earth had made that noise?

Suddenly, a shock that seemed to send cracks through our bodies hit the building, accompanied by a sharp flash. I shut my eyes and ducked involuntarily, then resumed the search. A much louder boom than the one I'd heard in my sleep resounded in the night; at the same moment, the sky flared red. I still had no idea what was happening, but the beauty of the red glow that spread and intensified as I watched took my breath away.

There was another blast and a new red glow lit the night sky. By now I'd forgotten my fear. The entire sky had a sunset tinge; a shower of sparks glimmered, and to the right a burst of light surged like an animate thing, while around it the sky was flushed with the lingering glow of the second explosion. The streets, too, were reddened by the sky.

A fourth and a fifth explosion followed, a little smaller, then everything fell quiet. The array of colours, however, was growing in complexity and beauty.

'Instead of crying, how about having a look? I've never seen such a pretty sky. It's fantastic.'

I tilted my daughter's face up to the sky.

'Ah! Mummy . . . ' Though still clinging to me, she gazed open-mouthed. The tear stains on her cheeks were reflecting the red light.

Once the blasts died down, the colours gradually faded, beginning furthest from where the explosions had occurred. Although we waited, there were no more to come, and the sky steadily darkened.

We stood on the roof until the sky returned to its original colour. We were both shivering.

In the paper the following day, I read that a small chemical factory quite a distance from our building had exploded due to spontaneous combustion, causing several fatalities.

It occurred to me that the glow in that night's sky had perhaps signalled the last of the deaths that had been happening around me. People had died in that light. Died in an instant, I didn't doubt.

I had the feeling that I finally understood what the series of deaths had been trying to tell me. The light of heat, of energy. My body was fully endowed with heat and energy. I couldn't help but see myself standing there last night, transfixed by the glowing red sky, never sparing the approach of death a thought.

KŌNO TAEKO

In the Box

Translated by Jay Rubin

It wasn't as if I'd had an unpleasant experience while I was out that day. I wasn't especially tired, either; in fact, I came back in a good mood. I stepped into the lift and pressed 'Door Close' and '3', but when I saw another woman rushing towards the closing door, I pressed 'Door Open'.

Hugging a large paper-wrapped package, she stepped through the re-opened door to join me in the lift, but she spoke not a word of thanks. Even so, once I had pressed 'Door Close' again, I might have asked this woman with her arms full 'What floor?' and pressed the button for her, but before I could do so, she said:

'Ninth floor, please.'

Without a word, I pressed '9', but I felt sorry I hadn't simply ignored her. It was her problem she had chosen to have her arms wrapped around such a big package: she shouldn't be imposing on other people that way.

I fumed over the woman's rudeness in the few breaths it took the box containing the two of us to rise to the third floor. When it stopped and the door opened, on an impulse I ran my hand over the rest of the buttons – from the '4' past her damned '9' with its light already glowing.

'There you go,' I said. 'I've pressed them all for you.'

Leaving her with these words and a panel full of glowing buttons, I stepped out of the lift.

'Of all the –' I heard behind me and turned to find the woman struggling to pull her keys from her handbag without losing her grip on the big package.

Usually if there were still people in the lift when I got off at the third floor, I would press 'Door Close' for them on my way out. People exiting at the second floor would often perform the same kindness for me. The door would eventually close on its own, but it took a very long time – so long you sometimes wondered if the door were broken.

If you pressed 'Door Close', the door would close right away. No one remaining in the lift would ever wait for the door to close automatically, and so it was a nice gesture for people getting off to not simply walk away but to press the button on their way out. 'Thank you', 'Thanks', 'I appreciate it': such phrases would naturally be exchanged in the process.

In taking my revenge on the woman by illuminating all the buttons, however, the one button I naturally chose *not* to press was the 'Door Close' button. I hurried away while the door remained open with the woman in full view. Now that she not only had her arms wrapped around that big package but also had her keys pulled halfway out, she would have to struggle to push the 'Door Close' button; otherwise, the door would seem as if it were never going to close and let her continue to the next floor. Even if the person getting out before her had not been me but someone else who failed to do her the kindness of pressing 'Door Close', she would have had no way around this struggle, but now she would face the same dilemma on every floor. Fourth floor, fifth, sixth, seventh, eighth: every time, the car would stop and the door would open for nothing. And the way the lift worked, even if you kept the 'Door Close' button pressed, when a number of buttons had been pushed the car would not bypass a floor. By the time she reached her destination, the woman would have had to repeatedly struggle to make the open door close or be kept waiting on every floor until the door closed automatically. 'There you go, I've pressed them all for you' – what a marvellous line!

The memory of that day would often come to me after that when I boarded the lift and pressed the buttons. Perhaps because I used the lift at irregular times and some days didn't take it at all, I never rode with the woman again. I had the impression that I had never encountered her before that day, but judging from the way she went straight for her keys while holding her big package, she was almost certainly a resident of the building. Apparently, although we both lived there, we always missed each other. These occasional thoughts about the woman made me more considerate than before whenever people boarded the lift after me – perhaps because I was ashamed of myself for having taken rather excessive revenge that day. And perhaps I wanted to believe that I was not usually like that: I had done what I did because the woman had been so ill-mannered. If people thanked me for letting them on, I would often ask them 'What floor?' even if they were not carrying anything.

That day, too, I asked 'What floor?' in a show of thoughtfulness.

'Ninth, please.'

Automatically, I pressed '9', but the person continued almost as if she had been waiting for this moment, 'Or if you like, press them all.'

I realized that I had not had a good look at the woman's face either that first day or now. Still, I couldn't let her get away with taking her revenge for that day by exploiting my act of kindness. Perhaps she realized that I would end up the loser either way – whether I pushed all the buttons from 4 to 8 again in compliance with her challenge or she managed to reach the ninth floor without incident.

'Fine, I'll do that.'

As I said this, I ran my hand up the button panel, which instantly lit up. That same moment, the lift came to a stop. I stared hard at the red button with its white-engraved 'Emergency'. Had the doors opened, I was planning to press the 'Door Close' button, announce 'I'll press this for you, too', hit the red button and slip out through the closing doors.

But the doors did not open. Normally, the doors opened right away even without the aid of the 'Door Open' button . . . I pressed 'Door Open', but still they did not open.

'We haven't reached the third floor yet,' the woman said behind me. 'The light is still on.'

Of course, she was right.

'Still,' the woman continued, 'it has definitely stopped, hasn't it? It must be broken.'

Perhaps I had thrown it off-kilter by hitting all those buttons at once so roughly.

'You can always use this if you're in a hurry,' I said, pointing to the emergency button and moving away from the panel to let her see it.

'No, I'm in no hurry,' she said with a wave of the hand, leaning against the back wall of the lift.

I, too, leaned back, giving her a view of my profile.

NAKAGAMI KENJI

Remaining Flowers

Translated by Eve Zimmerman

Without a break in the hot weather, all the flowering plants on the benches wilted. They held off watering them during the day, knowing the sun-heated water would just damage the roots. They tried hard to convince each other that withered flowers have a beauty all their own, but inwardly they sighed, hoping that someone would come up with an idea to save the potted flowers from the heat.

'I don't care any more. I've had that plant for years. Got lots of seeds from it, too.'

'Let me tell you, those seeds you gave me, they grew a different-coloured flower at my place. And they've never changed.'

The old women of the alleyway[1] waited for the sun to sink before they filled their buckets. First, they ladled water over the hot benches and then they watered the plants. The wilted blossoms would give off an accumulated scent of death that rose and permeated the air, mingling with the smell of the warm water.

Everyone else was mystified, listening to the complaints of the old women who were so pained by their potted plants roasting in the sun, but who couldn't think of a way to protect them. All you had to do, the younger people said, was move the plants indoors to a shady earthen entryway or stand a screen next to them. But none of the old women seemed ready to act on this advice. What was the point of having flowers if people passing by couldn't admire them?

'It won't do any good, not with the weather this hot.'

'You can't even use them for cut flowers. They won't last at all.'

Sitting down in the shade, the old women shared gossip and nodded to each other as if they were enjoying the sight of the flowers wilting under the white-hot sun.

In the middle of the heatwave, work began on a plan to widen the road by razing a house on the corner of the alleyway where the old women lived.

Rumours about the project had been circulating since way back, but when the people who lived in the houses that would be affected by it heard that the job had been scheduled, they began to hold regular meetings. Still, the old women didn't know what kind of promises had been made in return for razing the house on the corner. All they knew was that the project extended from the corner house almost to where they lived. First, a backhoe would come and smash the house, shaking it from the sides and top, followed by a bulldozer that would scrape away the pieces. Because the younger people at the meetings were making the decisions, the old women could do nothing but wait. In case showers of dust rained down from the shattered house, they soaked pieces of gauze in water and wiped down the leaves of the plants one by one.

The house on the corner was so dilapidated that if the men had tied a thick rope to it and pulled with all their strength, they could have brought it down. They didn't need any of the steel machinery that raised such a racket. The walls looked on the verge of collapse as if their insides were porous, and the roof sagged in the middle, seemingly unable to bear its own weight. The house belonged to an earlier time. The old women were the only ones who remembered that the roof dated back to the days when the mutual credit union funded new tiled roofs.

The house had originally had a roof made from cedar bark. In the old days, when the area produced timber, you could buy plenty of cedar bark for the price of a couple of roof tiles. It only made sense to use the materials at hand. The seams between the pieces of bark were fastened with wood and when the wood aged and warped, they held it in place with a rock the size of a baby's head. The house on the corner had looked like that, too.

Around the time cheap tiles appeared on the market and timber stopped coming down from the mountains, bark grew scarce and became more expensive, if you could find it at all. Someone recommended using tiles for the roof, claiming that they looked better. Local residents got together and created a credit union because nobody could afford to replace a roof on their own.

One of those who eventually won credit union funding was the occupant of the corner house, and so they changed the roof from bark to tiles. Some years later the roof began to sag as if, designed for cedar bark, it couldn't bear the extra weight. Tiles fell off in places, leaving gaps like missing teeth, and in other spots where tiles had worked loose, birds nested and grass seeds took root. Once no one was living in the house any more, the pace of its decline quickened. With one or two shakes of the backhoe's claw, the house crumbled silently in on itself as if it had been waiting to be struck.

Even though the house had been nothing but a shell, everyone predicted that demolishing it would raise clouds of dust and grime since it had stood on the corner for so long. But the house gave way easily as if it had never been there at all.

Once the corner house was razed, the view improved considerably. A dump truck went back and forth to the site, stacking the discarded boards and wooden pillars, and making trips to the incinerator. After they had started to level the soil, a rumour spread: what were clearly the remains of a man had been discovered in what was probably a large potato storage hole in the earthen floor of the house's storage closet. The rumour seemed to bubble up in the strong sunlight. Both those who spread the rumour and those who heard it kept their voices down. No one called the police. They left the remains in the hole and had labourers fill it in and smooth over the site with the bulldozer. In any case, these bones were old. And because the demolition job had gone to a contractor in the alleyway, they knew exactly what kind of people had been living in the house.

Instead of reporting it to the police and having them make waves with an investigation, the contractor judged it would be much better to bury the remains the way they were. The old women whispered among themselves, asking what good it would do to revisit the past just because some bones had turned up. What worried them more was the additional afternoon sun beating down on the plants now that the house on the corner was no longer there to provide shade.

His fate was like a piece of paper falling to bits.

The roughneck Jūkichi saw the woman in Nantō, where he split up with his mates. The bunch of them had moved on to this town in Ise when they were through at the logging camp in remote Miyagawa. Up at the camp everything had gone his way, the pay had been good and he'd won big at gambling. Now that he was carrying more money than he'd ever seen in his life, he could feel the winds of his hometown insistently calling to him as they all bounced from one labour camp to another like migratory birds.

He knew that once he got back home, there'd be nothing to do. All day long the old women of the alleyway would be sitting outside, gabbing in the sun. Maybe they'd been heading out somewhere but never made it, or they'd come back too tired to run any more errands. And who shat all those kids out? They boiled up out of the shadows chasing dogs and waving sticks at each other. It was that kind of town.

Before heading for the next work camp, Jūkichi and the others decided to take a boat to the island across from the old port in Ise, where transport ships used to anchor waiting for the winds to shift in their favour. They were still waiting for the boat to leave when Jūkichi noticed women coming and going, shoulders hunched against the cold, and this reminded him of his town at New Year.

When they went out drinking that night, Jūkichi got into a fight with his mates. The next morning at the inn one of them said they should patch things up and get going, but Jūkichi stayed under his quilt, covering his head. He felt too much at home to leave.

'You guys go. I'm staying.'

His friends tried to humour him. 'C'mon. It'll be a drag without you.'

This made Jūkichi want to work even less. One friend, fed up, tried to pull the quilt off Jūkichi, but Jūkichi held on to the top of it, so the other fellow lifted his quilt from the bottom.

'C'mon, you fucker. You wanna stay here 'cause that whore you had last night was so good?'

The workers stared at Jūkichi's crotch and howled with laughter. Finally, they gave up on trying to humour him and took off, but they told him where they were going, first up the river into the mountains, and if that was no good, they'd try a place even further along.

Jūkichi left the inn just after noon and wandered around Nantō. Everything about the town looked like home but felt different. He had to keep moving, like a dog in heat.

The woman was doing laundry in a washtub by the well. A patch of small chrysanthemums grew tall by the well like overgrown weeds, and fishermen's lanterns were scattered on the ground. It was an ordinary afternoon scene in a deserted fishing village, but there was something odd about the way the woman moved. Jūkichi stopped and stared at her.

In a squatting position, the woman felt for the pump handle, and when she located it, she stood and started pumping water. Extending her hand to check if water was coming out of the pipe, she then pressed the pump handle down again.

The woman's face was beautiful, and every inch of her soft flesh emanated the scent of womanliness, but she was blind.

The sight of her was almost too much for Jūkichi.

He spoke to her at once and took hold of the pump handle for her. At first she was startled, but when she realized that he was a passing stranger who had offered to help her out of pity and wasn't going to hurt her, she told him about herself in stops and starts.

Two days later Jūkichi took the blind woman back to his hometown. For a long while the house on the corner had sat vacant. Its last occupant was a well-known thief named Kenkichi. Hatching one crazy scheme after another, he had altered the house, cutting a hole in one wall for an escape route out back and building a storage closet that was concealed behind a fake wall. When Jūkichi arrived home with the woman, he had his friends and their followers clean the place from top to bottom.

The woman sat in a corner of the main room, looking like an empress doll on its display stand. She seemed to know just by listening that the rough Jūkichi was in his element when he ordered the pleasure-seeking young men around with a flick of the chin. She would turn towards sounds or voices, and tell Jūkichi whenever he spoke to her, 'Let *me* do that.' A drinking party filled that day and the next. Five days passed before Jūkichi found himself alone with her in the house. He felt he could never be too kind to her. In the darkened house, where his eyes were as blind as hers, the woman's soft flesh and her scent appeased the desire that welled up in him. Burying his face in the source of the woman's soothing nectar, now mingled with the stream of his own spent desire, he raised his face to hers when she let him know that she'd had enough. How, he urged her to tell him, could she live without being able to see?

'It's nothing,' she answered, 'I was born this way.'

When she grew impatient for Jūkichi to want her, the woman would take the lead. He was satisfied just to look at her during the day. The way the blind woman moved reminded Jūkichi of a beautiful bird with clipped wings. The sight of her feeling her way along a wall until she touched a pillar, then stepping down into her wooden sandals in the dirt-floored kitchen to wash something in the sink, or to see her sweeping the house made him feel as if the beautiful bird were stroking him all over and bringing him to ecstasy.

When the woman bumped into a pillar or tripped on the threshold, she became a caged bird beating its clipped wings against the bars, resenting its captivity. In those moments, Jūkichi would hold her, asking if it hurt or if she had injured herself. When he saw blood oozing from a wound, he caressed her until the pain ebbed. Bearing the pain while Jūkichi held her in his arms, the woman would reply, 'I'm fine. It doesn't hurt.' A touch or embrace from Jūkichi would bring a deep sigh from her lips, as if she could forget her limitations only at those moments. Once the woman was naked in Jūkichi's arms, her skin beaded with sweat, and he watched her cry out for joy, he would feel the beast within himself rising and he'd flip her over, determined to treat her roughly.

Jūkichi always had many friends, so when he and the woman were nestled close to each other during the day and friends showed up at the house, Jūkichi embraced the woman, taking advantage of her blindness. Like a bird owner proud of his bird's plumage and song, he was keen to show her off. He would undress her, press her to have sex with him in various positions, and even lifted her legs and hips so that his friends could see. Dissatisfied with just looking, the friends would gesture at their crotches, wanting to change places with him, because how would she know if it was a different man? But Jūkichi ignored them. The woman didn't notice anything while she and Jūkichi were at it; only afterwards she'd ask, 'Who's there?' as if she could faintly sense the presence of other men. Drawing her close to him, Jūkichi put his lips to her ear, whispering, 'There's no one here. It's just the two of us.' Though the woman guessed exactly what was going on, she nodded and pressed her cheek against Jūkichi's, seeming to feel secure when she entrusted the daytime world of seeing to him. Whispering endearments to her, he told her truthfully that she was the best woman he'd ever had and that her blindness made her a woman among women. Then he'd signal to his friends that it was time to leave. When he found himself alone with her in the darkness, though, his sight felt like a burden to him.

Once he'd taken up his new life with the woman from Nantō in the house on the corner, Jūkichi never went out to work. With his earnings from the logging camp and his big win at gambling, he held one long party for his friends, treating them all to sake. Day and night the house on the corner resounded with the loud voices of drunken young men and the warbling laughter of the heedless young woman. To the people of the alleyway, a bunch of young toughs drinking and carousing without doing a lick of work amounted to a public nuisance.

By that time, there wasn't a soul in the alleyway who didn't recognize Jūkichi's blind woman. People were surprised that she could laugh that way despite her hardships. She must be crazy about him, they said, and he must be incredibly good to her. But when it came to Jūkichi's gang, they could see trouble coming a mile away, so they avoided making friendly conversation with her.

In fact, they had no opportunity to strike up a conversation with the woman. Whenever she came to get water at the well or do the laundry, Jūkichi would be with her, carrying the bucket or the washtub, and he would wait by her side until she had finished. To them it seemed as if Jūkichi wanted to take over the woman's chores. But she resisted, telling him that a man shouldn't do this kind of work, that she'd always done it this way by herself, as if she could sense the gazes of the men and women of the alleyway who were watching them with bated breath.

She filled the tub and washed the clothes, making a soapy foam, then rinsed them. Pointedly, she was showing the others – and herself – that she was Jūkichi's woman. This made him feel strangely uncomfortable. Standing so close that he could touch her, he hung on her every move. Truly, the woman had the face of an empress doll. She moved with real elegance – and an erotic tinge – when she worked the pump, panting softly, then squatted down and washed the clothes with foam-covered hands. Cocking her head towards nearby sounds, she exhibited none of the gloomy demeanour of the blind but seemed all the more lovable to Jūkichi. She evidenced no more pain regarding her blindness than any of the sightless creatures that lived in the world.

Watching her, Jūkichi felt his body ache. It was clear that his thoughts were different from the woman's. He had no desire to settle down with her. Like a migratory bird that wanders far from home, he would drift from place to place, stopping where the money was good, where his friends were, and, if possible, where he could reach the woman easily. When the money piled up, he would skip work and spend his days doing nothing.

With no intention of starting a household or settling down, Jūkichi had taken the woman to live in his hometown because he'd been driven by a sense of rootlessness that bubbled up inside him whenever he finished one job, had money to burn and was on his way to the next job. But once he had the blind woman there with him, she brought his sense of rootlessness into sharp relief.

The way the woman moved – the way she moved her blind eyes, the way she moved her hands to touch things, the way she reached out to offer him a piece of food to eat – aroused him and spoke directly to his manhood as he touched her naked body. She trusted him, nestling up to him for comfort, and Jūkichi desired her.

Still, Jūkichi sensed that their bond would break when his money was gone. She stayed inside the house like a bird with clipped wings, serving as Jūkichi's companion, mixing with the friends who came to visit him and laughing cheerfully when she drank. The voices of the young men and the woman spilled out from the house, drifting down the alleyway with an ominous ring. As the days passed, Jūkichi and the woman both knew that the end was near. Throwing parties for his friends, Jūkichi used up all his wages and his gambling money. The day after the money ran out, he went to work at a timber yard, stacking logs. From that day on, Jūkichi was away from home all day.

The alleyway people watched as the woman, alone, drew water from the well and carried it back to the house, splashing it everywhere. The women were squeezed around the well, washing enough dirty clothing to keep a laundry in business, when they saw her come back with her bucket and begin to wash her clothes. She had no idea that a neighbour had moved aside to let her in, nor that she was splashing people when she couldn't aim the water from the pipe directly into the bucket.

The women of the alleyway watched her in silence. They warned each other not to speak to her, whether in sympathy or criticism. It was impossible for a blind woman to behave like a normal woman, especially in a place that was not hers by birth.

Jūkichi got home in the evening. The woman had worked hard to fill the tub, but she had left the bath unheated, she said, because she was afraid of fire. He warmed the water, took his bath and helped the woman with hers. It felt almost as if they were newly-weds. But Jūkichi knew his freshly washed clothes and his supper were the fruits of the woman's special efforts. They would have enough money as long as he stayed out working from morning to night, but he sensed that their new relationship would not last.

The woman's labours pained Jūkichi. In the darkened house he listened to her joyful cries and caressed her as if kneeling before her in worship, knowing all the while that the man inside himself was blind, too. Spinning down into an impenetrable darkness, this blind man became a solid mass that was thrust back up, turning molten with heat and then dissolving. If only he himself could be blind the way his fingers and skin and the thing between his legs were blind! In the darkness the woman cried out, enveloping Jūkichi as if she had been set free at last.

Not long after that, the people of the alleyway began to hear the woman's laughter when Jūkichi was out. They kept watch from a distance for fear of what terrible thing might occur.

Leaving in the morning for work and returning in the evening, Jūkichi looked the same as always. But someone reported that his friends were coming and going during the day while he was out. When the warble of the woman's laughter spilled from the house one day, the people of the alleyway perked up their ears and knew that she was crying out in pleasure. She must be doing it with Jūkichi's friends while he was gone.

The people of the alleyway sensed something ominous. When a woman took a lover, she was usually punished severely by her man. But in the case of a blind woman, the assumption would be that she had been forced even if she had been a willing partner. A man could easily chase the woman and pin her down, and because she couldn't run away when he threatened to stab her or tie her up, he could control her with a single word. If Jūkichi found out that the woman had a lover, he would come to this conclusion. He would hate his friends all the more for having betrayed him by taking advantage of her blindness, and he would exact harsh revenge. Holding their breaths, the people of the alleyway waited for disaster to strike.

People stopped seeing Jūkichi in the alleyway after that. Everyone thought he must have found a good job and left home for a while. Every day without fail, the sound of the woman's laughter spilled from the house in the early afternoon. The woman planted several miniature chrysanthemums by the side of the house around then. No one knew how she had come by them. What people really wanted to tell her was that she would meet a terrible end when Jūkichi learned she had a secret lover, but all they said was, 'You planted flowers – what a nice thing to do.'

These were probably the first words ever spoken to her by people who had been watching Jūkichi and the woman.

'I can't see the colours, but they smell pretty,' she responded, looking in the wrong direction before turning to the person who had spoken.

Jūkichi never came back. The woman's laughter continued. When the little chrysanthemum flowers opened and the scent drifted into the alleyway, the old women and the others complained that it gave them a headache; it was like the raw smell of Jūkichi and the woman having sex.

YOSHIMOTO BANANA

Bee Honey

Translated by Michael Emmerich

I was sitting in the plaza in front of La Casa de Gobierno, not feeling much of anything. There were a few men standing around, acting so suspiciously that it was obvious at a glance they were pickpockets. To my surprise, once I had indicated that I was on to them, giving each man a look that said, 'Yes, I can see you're a pickpocket,' they kept their distance. Now whenever my gaze met one of theirs he looked right back at me, as if we were acquainted. Was it that hard to make ends meet here, or were people just very laid back? I didn't get it . . . an odd city, Buenos Aires.

I had taken a seat at the edge of a bed of flowers to watch the pigeons and an old lady selling pigeon food. She didn't seem to have anything weighing on her mind. She had simply come to spend the day selling pigeon food. I guess that was more or less how I felt myself.

At the far side of the plaza, I could see the pink walls of La Casa de Gobierno – 'The Government House'. Madonna sang there in *Evita*, didn't she . . . God, how did I ever end up seeing a movie like that? . . . No sooner had this question occurred to me than I found myself remembering, once again. The rainy night when I rented the video and watched it in the living room. He came home in the middle of that awful movie. His right side was drenched – he said the wind had broken his umbrella. I brought a bath towel and gave his head and body a casual rubbing down, the way you might dry off a dog or a cat, then flopped back on to the sofa. The place smelled like rain, just from him having come in. Clear beads of water streamed down the windowpane. The road outside was quietly, blackly wet. It was an ordinary night, like all nights. He made a pot of coffee and handed me a cup. The cup itself we had bought together one Sunday, at an antique shop nearby. We had to make

a lot of turns to get there, and . . . that's right, there were flowers blooming, tons of them, all different colours, and the road looked white in the
sunlight, so I felt I was in heaven. Orange, yellow and pink flowers. Green
grass swishing in the wind. I had way too many memories – like standing
between two mirrors, staring into their distance. Our history together,
his and mine, had the near-infinite expanse of a world in miniature, and
now I was cut off from all of it.

I had come to visit a friend who lived in this city.

My friend was learning to tango when she and her dance instructor,
an Argentinian, fell in love and got married. Now she had a sort of business showing around visitors from Japan. She wasn't an official guide or
anything, but she seemed busy enough. She said she got paid at the end,
after the tour was over, like a tip. Her husband was away just then, touring
with some of his dance students, so I stayed at their house. My friend had
to take some people around during the daytime, and it was night by the
time she got back. I took it easy until she finished, day after day. It was
fun to be so free; I wished I could live that way forever. Recoleta was
especially nice, the part of town where she and her husband had their
house – lots of trees and grass – and I felt great just wandering around. I
walked and walked, trying to keep myself from thinking. Only when my
legs began to ache and my mind grew numb did I feel I was finally myself
again. A little wine at night was all it took to send me tumbling into bed.

For the time being this is fine, this is enough, I told myself night after
night, sprawled out on an uncomfortable sofa bed in a house that wasn't
mine, the unfamiliar sounds of an unfamiliar city ringing in my ears. I
have to give myself time, that's all I can do. Like a wild animal lying very
still in the darkness, licking its wounds, waiting, just waiting, nothing
else, to give its feverish body time to heal. The best thing for me right
now is to go on doing nothing like this, to let my spirit recover, little by
little, until I learn how to breathe again and can think seriously about
what to do.

'There's a procession of mothers wearing white scarves in the Plaza de
Mayo today, starting at two,' my friend said on her way out that morning.
'Watching it isn't exactly pleasant, but it makes me think about all kinds
of things every time. All kinds of things, really. I mean, this is recent

history we're talking about. I think you'll understand when you see them. You'll think about your own parents, too, back at home.'

So I made my way to this plaza, to witness the procession. Soon the mothers – old enough by now to be grandmothers – began to gather, arriving alone or in little groups, their white scarves tied over their heads. A few journalists were there to cover the event, and a few policemen. The pink walls of La Casa de Gobierno looked blurry under the cloudy sky. They mixed ox's blood into the paint to get that colour. Suddenly a tremendous flock of pigeons fluttered into the air, and the dozen or so old women in white scarves began slowly circling the plaza. Some old men walked with them, and there were a few others, presumably relatives. The women cradled old pictures in their arms. Photographs of grinning young men, young women dressed in their finest. Expressions so sweet and ordinary it was almost impossible to believe they had been swept up in something so terrible.

'Are you from Japan?' asked a middle-aged woman standing next to me. She looked as if she might be Japanese, and spoke in Japanese.

'Yes, I am.'

'I came to this country as an immigrant. We live in the suburbs. It was awful back then. All of a sudden we found ourselves living under the junta, just like that. Many people vanished. Students who had once dabbled in leftist politics, Peronists.[1] Participating in a demonstration, little things – that was all it took. Hardly any of them returned.'

She was Japanese, that was clear, but something about the way she was dressed, something in her expression and her make-up, gave me the sense that she had been away from Japan for a long time.

'I saw a movie about it once.'

How did I end up seeing such a disturbing movie? There were images of kidnapped students being corralled, half naked; students being raped; having hoses turned on them; being abandoned, blindfolded. Those parents walking in the plaza in front of me must have been at their wits' end then, unable to sleep at night; and yet they were living in their own homes as usual. During that period, these people lost something extraordinarily important, a sense of something, forever. Their sons and daughters lost their lives; they lost part of themselves.

'A military truck drove into the forest near our house one night,' the woman said. 'We were so scared we wouldn't even go outside. Soon we heard a horrible barrage of gunshots, people screaming and groaning, then another large truck came and it was quiet again. When we went into the forest the next morning, there was blood on the ground, all over. That's how thirty thousand people disappeared.'

I nodded without speaking, watching the procession.

It occurred to me that the pigeons and the pickpockets, the immigrant beside me, the tourists, we were all just *here*. You could tell, looking at them ambling around the plaza in their white scarves, that those mothers no longer thought their children might come home. Maybe this was their way of expressing the constant, unending frustration they carried in their hearts, of giving form to the time they had lived through, of refusing to let what had happened get lost in the oblivion of simply being here, like this, right now. Cradling pictures of their daughters and sons, the old women chatted among themselves. That made me feel the reality of it all the more. That's how it goes, I thought. This is time passing. This is the colour of sorrow.

Sorrow never heals. We simply take comfort in the fact that our pain seems to fade. How flimsy my own sorrow is, compared with what these parents feel. It has no real basis, none of this outrageous injustice to support it. It just keeps drifting on in its indistinct way. And yet that doesn't mean one is more valuable than the other, or deeper. We are all in this plaza together. I let myself imagine.

One morning, her son, at the height of his teenage cockiness, goes off to school as always, hardly taking a sip of coffee, long and lanky in his favourite jeans. To his mother, he looks the same as he always has, ever since he was a boy. That look is where all her memories reside – it's only natural. He never mentioned to her that he once participated in a demonstration, just for a little while, and maybe just because his friends were going. He never comes back. What would that feel like? No one can say for certain what happened until after the rash of political upheavals that follow in the wake of the coup d'état. No one tries to help, because everyone is too scared. Terrible rumours keep circulating, throwing her into confusion; there are no good rumours. Those fortunate enough to make it back from the internment camps live in terror, and the stories they tell make her hair stand on end . . . I was at high school when it happened, but it's too far away. This isn't a story of the Inca Empire. It didn't even take place during wartime. I was living in Japan then, living at home with my parents, rebelling against them, staying out until morning, doing things, when this happened, here, on this earth. It's too big, too much – I felt as if I might faint.

I thought.

Why, right now, here under this languid, overcast sky, are all these afternoons we live, theirs and mine, intersecting in this way, in this unremarkable plaza?

I noticed a plump woman among the circling mothers who looked like my own mother. The longer I looked at her, the more similar she seemed, except for the colour of her eyes. As I stared, I began to think she moved in the same way, too.

Whenever I caught a cold, my mother would mix up a drink for me, dissolving honey in hot water, adding a splash of whisky, squeezing in the juice of a lemon. She was still doing that for me when I was at high school. On one of those evenings when children were bleeding and being tortured here, I was being pampered by her. Maybe that is what this world is? Precisely *that*? For some reason, my mother called her drink 'bee honey'. No matter how many times I pointed out that it was really more like 'honey lemon', she said her name was better and kept it. I seemed to feel the hot, sweet taste of it filling my mouth. It's the same all around the world. A mother's scent. A whiff of the female body, and something heavy, sweet, endlessly deep. That scent was here now, filling the plaza, circling it, because there was no other outlet, going around and around.

'It's ridiculous! You can't break up over something like that!' My mother cried on the other end of the line. 'Married life lasts a long time, all kinds of things happen. Even if you do break up in the end, at least give it two or three more years.'

'I won't have a second chance if I get any older than I am now,' I replied.

'At your age, two or three years doesn't matter,' my mother said.

An unrelated scene came to mind: me pressing my face into the sofa, wailing, after our cat died; my mother running her hands roughly, but with a gentleness in the tips of her fingers, through my hair.

If only my husband no longer loved me! If only his love would simply vanish! If only his lover were a nasty, unpleasant woman! But in real life, things don't work out so neatly. He conveyed his love by calling me here every night since my arrival. He sounded unsure of himself, had none of the casualness of my mother's hands – was that the distance between us? I thought we had become a family, but in reality we were just two strangers doing our best to compromise. And yet I had a feeling I would back down that night, finally, urged on by all the years we had spent together; I would start wanting to tell him, when we talked on the phone, about the feelings that were churning inside me after seeing these mothers. It was so confusing . . . Tonight, holding this confusion inside, I would lie down once more on that sofa bed, in my friend's house. I had the feeling, though, having seen these mothers with my own eyes, not in a movie, not reading about them in a book, but seeing them, hearing their voices and noticing how their skirts swayed in the breeze, seeing how they laughed as they chatted – all that had come together inside me to form a core, something that could change me, just a little. Suddenly I saw myself, what I was like as a human being, from a place very, very far away.

A few other mothers, also dressed in black and wearing white scarves, had set up a stall on the far side of the plaza. I walked over. They were selling videos, pamphlets, postcards, T-shirts. A sign explained that the profits went to support their activities. I had picked up a T-shirt, planning to buy it, when one of the white-scarved mothers started talking to me. I wasn't sure what to do, since I don't speak Spanish, but a young woman nearby, probably a journalist, translated into English for me.

'She's saying that an "S" size might be better. People are wearing T-shirts kind of small these days.'

I couldn't help smiling. Such strength, and of course she had once had a child of her own . . . Mothers are mothers no matter what country they come from, after all, and that's a very sad thing to be. Will I ever become a mother myself? Will I ever be able to see these people, to think of them, in a different light? With nothing decided, everything seemed oddly renewed. I bought the T-shirt, said thank you and left the plaza behind.

OHBA MINAKO

The Smile of a Mountain Witch

Translated by Noriko Mizuta

Let me tell you about a legendary witch who lives in the mountains.

Her scraggly grey hair bound with a length of cord, she waits in her house for a man from the village to lose his way so she can devour him. When an unknowing young man wanders up to her lair and asks for a night's lodging, the owner of the house grins, a comb with missing teeth clamped between her own yellowed teeth that shine in the flickering lamplight. The eerie hag terrifies him and she says to him, 'You just thought, "What a creepy old woman! Like an old monster cat!" didn't you?'

Startled, the young man steals a glimpse at her from under his brows as he gulps down his millet porridge and thinks to himself, 'Don't tell me she's planning to devour me in the middle of the night!'

Without a moment's hesitation, the mountain witch tells him, 'You just thought, "Don't tell me she's planning to devour me in the middle of the night!" didn't you?'

Turning pale, the man replies, 'I was just thinking that with this warming bowl of porridge I finally feel relaxed and that my fatigue is catching up with me,' but his body goes as hard as ice and he thinks to himself, 'The reason she's boiling such a big pot of water must be that she's preparing to cook me in the middle of the night!'

With a sly grin, the old witch says, 'You just thought to yourself, "The reason she's boiling such a big pot of water must be that she's preparing to cook me in the middle of the night!" didn't you?'

The man becomes even more terrified. 'You accuse me wrongly. I was only thinking that I'm really tired from walking all day and that I ought to excuse myself and retire for the night while I'm still warm from the porridge, so that I may start out early tomorrow morning.'

But he thinks to himself, 'What a spooky old hag! This monster cat of a woman must be one of those old mountain witches I've heard so much about. That's how she can read my mind so well!'

Without a moment's hesitation, the mountain witch says, 'You just thought, "What a spooky old hag! This monster cat of a woman must be one of those old mountain witches I've heard people talk about. That's how she can read my mind so well!"'

The man becomes so frightened he can hardly keep his teeth from chattering, but he manages to shuffle along on shaky knees, saying, 'Well, I must excuse myself and retire for now –'

Practically crawling into the next room, he lies down on a straw mat without undoing his travelling attire. The witch follows him with a side-long glance and says, 'Now you're thinking that you'll wait for a chance to escape.'

Indeed, the man had stretched out in order to take her off her guard, hoping for a chance to escape.

These old mountain witches are able to read every thought that crosses a person's mind, and in the end the victim runs for his life away from the witch's abode. She pursues him relentlessly and the man keeps running. At least this is the form the classic mountain-witch tales assume.

They call them *yamauba* – 'mountain hags' or 'mountain crones' – but surely these witches cannot have been wrinkled old hags from birth? At one time they must have been babies with skin like freshly pounded rice cakes and the faint sweet-sour odour of the newborn. They must have been maidens seducing men with their moist, glossy complexions of polished silk. Like tiny pink shells, their shining fingernails must have dug into the shoulders of the men they suffocated in ecstasy between their swelling breasts.

For some reason, though, no tales have been handed down of tender, young mountain witches. The young ones can't remain shut up in the mountain fastnesses and instead they take up residence inside beasts or birds – cranes or foxes or snowy herons – which then become beautiful wives that live in human settlements, or so their stories have been transformed, it seems.

These metamorphosed animals who turn into human wives are always very intelligent and sensitive, but their fates are invariably tragic. After years of devoted service to their husbands, they revert to emaciated animals at the end, their fur or feathers dropping out as they flee back into the mountains. Perhaps these poor creatures, with all their bitterness and resentment, are the ones who become old mountain witches. After all, devouring may be the ultimate expression of affection. Does not a mother, full of emotion, often squeeze her child and exclaim, 'I love you so much I could eat you up!'?

Now, the woman I'm going to tell you about was an absolutely genuine mountain witch.

She died at the age of sixty-two.

At sixty-two, when her soulless naked body was cleansed with surgical spirit, her skin was glossy and youthful like the wax figure of a goddess. Her hair was half white, and on the mound beneath her gently sloping belly were a few strands of silver. And yet, around her calmly closed eyelids and her faintly smiling lips, there lingered the strange innocence and bashfulness of a little girl who is forcing a smile when she is ready to burst out crying.

She was a mountain witch among mountain witches, and though she longed for a dwelling in the mountains, she never lived in one. Instead, she spent her entire life in a temporary abode as a human woman in a human settlement.

She had been an old mountain witch ever since she could remember.

When still a tiny thing, she would be so engrossed in play she would often wet her pants. And when her mother came running, the little mountain witch would say to her, 'Oh, you naughty girl. You've got to tell Mummy in time before it's too late. We don't have any fresh undies for you today.'

At that, her mother would burst out laughing, so the little mountain witch would continue, 'I'm no match for this child! What can I say?'

When her father was late coming home at night and her mother glanced at the clock on the wall, the child would say, 'What in the world is he up to, coming home late night after night! He says it's work, but I know he's really staying out as late as possible because it's so boring at home. As if he's the only one who feels that way!'

At that, her mother would cast a wry grin and scowl at her, but before she could say anything, the little girl would exclaim, 'You foolish girl! Come on now, go to bed. Little children who stay up late never grow. They stay little forever and ever.'

Appalled at her daughter's ability to read her mind time after time, the mother would give in, saying, 'This child is very bright, but she really tires me out!'

When she was a little older and her mother brought her a new toy, the girl would say, 'This will keep her quiet for a while.' Annoyed, her mother would give her a look, whereupon the daughter would say, 'Why in the world does this child read people's minds all the time? She's like a mountain witch. People will probably come to dislike her as they would a mountain witch.'

Of course, her mother would blurt out such thoughts all the time, so the girl was merely parroting her mother's words.

When she started going to school, her mother was relieved to have time away from her daughter, but soon she noticed that the little girl had ended her habit of echoing people's thoughts and was growing quieter day by day. 'You're so quiet all of a sudden now that you're at school,' she said one day.

Her daughter replied, 'When I say what's on my mind, people give me nasty looks, so I'm just going to shut up. Grown-ups like it when kids pretend to be stupid and unaware of things, so I've decided to keep grown-ups happy from now on.'

Conscious of her unique accomplishment in having given birth to a mountain witch, the mother responded firmly, 'Go ahead and say whatever is on your mind. You don't have to pretend anything. You're a child, after all.'

But the girl merely regarded her mother with a disdainful smile.

The child received good grades at school for the most part. Whenever she did poorly on a test, she would tear it up and not show it to her mother. Her mother would complain when she did not finish the lunch she brought to school, so on days when she had little appetite, she threw her leftovers into a rubbish bin on her way home. To ward off suspicion, she would leave a little food in her lunchbox now and then and tell her mother, 'The teacher talked longer today, so I didn't have time to finish it.'

The child bloomed into maidenhood, but the family could not afford to buy her expensive dresses. When she and her mother went shopping, the girl would pick the dress she knew her mother found most appropriate and pretend that she really liked it. Putting herself in her mother's place, she would say, 'I think this is really sweet. If I wore something fancy at my age, people would think some rich old man was keeping me.'

On such occasions, her mother would look at her a little sadly, and on the way home, for no apparent reason, she would buy her daughter something way beyond her means. The girl would pretend not to notice her mother's impulse and act genuinely pleased.

The girl would assume whatever manner was expected of her as though it was what she herself wanted to do, not only with her family but with anyone she wanted to please. When they wanted her to laugh, she would laugh. When they wanted her to remain silent, she remained silent. When talkativeness was desired, she chatted merrily. With a person who considered himself intelligent, she would act a little stupid – though not *too* stupid, because that type of person usually thought it a waste of time dealing with very stupid people. And with stupid people, she would make a show of appreciating their simplicity.

Probably because she wanted so desperately to be liked by far too many people, she had to squander a frightening amount of mental energy every day. Before she realized it, she had become antisocial, reading books in her room all day, avoiding contact with others.

'Why don't you go out with your friends?' her mother would ask, to which she would answer simply: 'I get so tired . . .'

Her mother, too, found it tiring to be with her. It was a relief when her daughter was not around. She began to long for the day when her daughter would find a suitable young man and leave her. In other words, mother and daughter had arrived at that natural phase of life when they were ready to part.

The daughter knew that she was a burden to her mother – had known it all too well as far back as she could remember. She wanted to free her mother – and herself – as soon as possible. At the same time, somewhere in her heart she held a grudge against her mother, a grudge that was sometimes so strong she would feel surges of inexplicable rage. That is to say, she was going through the short, rebellious phase of puberty, but she realized that her hatred and anger were directed at the cunning ways of her mother as a same-sex competitor: her mother's despicable techniques of taking advantage of her motherly authority and of avoiding direct confrontation. With this realization came a sudden awareness of how much her mother had aged and how much she herself had matured.

As a mature girl, she naturally found a man

He was an ordinary, run-of-the mill sort of man. Like all men, he had been doted on by his mother, and so he firmly believed that because his mother was of the opposite sex, he was allowed to express himself as freely as he pleased with other women beyond all reason. When such a man matures physically, the woman with whom he shares his bed must be a substitute for his mother. She must be as magnanimous as a mother, as dignified as a goddess. She must love him as limitlessly and blindly as an idiot. And moreover, like a sinister beast, she must have a spirit possessed by evil. Fortunately, however, the daughter's man at least had the male characteristic of liking women.

The woman was gratified by the man and came to believe that she should reward him for this by exerting herself in every way to please him. This proved to be a monumental effort for her because, after all, every corner of his mind was transparent to her. Seeing into his heart was exhausting and stood in the way of her happiness.

First of all, the man wanted the woman to be constantly jealous, so she had to exert herself to appear that way. When another woman's shadow approached the man, she would have to act as though she thought of the other woman as a competitor, and the man would be satisfied.

'Don't ever leave me. I can't live without you. I'm helpless. I can't do anything when you're gone,' she would cry and cling to him. And as she spoke these words, she would have the illusion that she really was a weak, incompetent creature.

The man wanted the woman to evaluate other men as beneath their true worth. She had to close her eyes to other men's virtues and observe only their vices. He was not a total fool, however, and would not allow her to overstate the men's flaws. To please him, she had to render equitable judgements demonstrating an awareness of the others' shortcomings while concluding that, although the others might have certain virtues, they were finally not to her liking. Thus every little opinion she expressed had to be well thought out.

Strangely enough, the man tended to feel pleasure in his exclusive possession of a woman who was constantly being pursued by other men. Far from merely tolerating her pretended flirtations with other men, he tended to encourage them. Deep down, it seems, all men long to join the species we call 'pimps'.

There would be no end to a list of such examples, but at times the woman would forget to act jealous or to flirt with other men, or she would carelessly state her true womanly impressions of attractive men. At such times the man would become bored or think the woman lazy or thick-skinned or lacking in sensitivity. Even if the woman did succeed in behaving as he wished in everything, he would assert with the arrogant air of an all-knowing sage, 'Women are stupid, cowardly, unmanageable creatures, full of jealousy, capable only of formulating shallow ideas and telling small-scale lies. The word "man" can stand for all human beings, but a "woman" can only be fully human by clinging to her man.'

Thanks to this illogical treaty of inequality, the two managed to live somewhat happily, but eventually both the man and the woman grew old and the man reached the age when he would grumble all year long about one or another part of his body that had gone bad. He demanded that the woman worry about him all the time and said that, if it looked as though he was going to precede her in death, he would be so concerned about leaving her behind that he could not die in peace. In the course of dem-onstrating to him how agitated this made her, the woman became truly agitated and convinced herself that he might be seriously ill. Unless she truly believed this, she could not set his mind at ease, and if her man were not at peace, she herself could not attain peace. Thus, even though she hated the nursing profession so much that she would rather die than commit herself to it, she became a nurse the way a woman in desperate circumstances might sell her chastity. Seeing her in her new line of work, the man commended her, saying that nursing was the one profession most truly in keeping with a woman's instincts, that at least where nursing was concerned, women were blessed with an innate talent against which no man could compete.

Around that time, the woman became grotesquely fat. A few short steps were all it took to make her shoulders heave with every breath, like a pregnant woman. The obvious main reason for this was that she pos-sessed exceptionally healthy digestive organs that gave her an enormous appetite. In addition, she had the pitiful trait of wanting to make others feel good. Even if she did not desire a particular dish, she would eat what-ever people offered her in order not to disappoint them. Everyone thought that she just loved to eat; they would be deeply offended if she refused their food. On the other hand, her husband often boasted that he was a man of iron will. When he saw her eating and exclaiming, 'Here I go again!' he would ridicule her: 'You're such a weak-willed woman.' Even if someone put her heart and soul into cooking something to please him, he had the will power to refuse it outright if it was not good for his health, which is to say that his strong nerves allowed him to ignore another's feelings without shame.

His use of words such as 'strength of will', 'insensitivity' and 'laziness' so differed from hers that she would at times be overwhelmed by an acute sense of loneliness. She came to fear not only her husband but many of the others around her, as though she were surrounded by foreigners who spoke another language. Sometimes she dreamed of living alone in the depths of the mountains the way she had locked herself up in her room all day when she was a little girl, not playing with anyone.

In the mountains, there would be nobody to trouble her, and she would be free to immerse herself in her fantasies. The thought of getting even with all those who had tormented her in the human settlement made her heart race – all those who could keep wearing the expressions of happy heroes just because they were dull-headed, slow-witted and incapable of reading other people's minds. What relief it would give her to be able to say aloud to them like the legendary mountain witches, 'You just thought . . . didn't you?'! How good it would feel to slit the skin of her temples and let her horns grow out – horns that were itching to sprout but could not do so on their own!

When she imagined herself living alone in the mountains, she saw herself as a beautiful fairy, sprawled in the fields, naked in the drenching sunlight, surrounded by trees and grasses and animals. But once a familiar human being appeared from the settlement, her face would change into that of a demon crone. He would stare at her, his mouth hanging open like an idiot, uttering coarse, incoherent, self-righteous words that made her fly into a rage.

On such occasions, her husband would be sure to appear, dressed in shabby beggar's clothing, wandering aimlessly around the den of the transformed woman, and like a brat who has lost a fight, he would shriek, 'Without her to hide my unreasonable desires for me, I'm lost.'

Hearing his voice, she would look at her reflection in a mountain spring.

Half her face wore the smile of a loving mother, while the other half seethed with demonic rage. Half her mouth dripped blood as it tore and devoured the man's flesh, while the lips of the other half caressed the man where he lay curled up like a baby, sucking at the breast that hid his face.

Her obesity put increasing pressure on her blood vessels, causing hardening of the arteries. Parts of her body grew numb and she developed headaches and ringing in the ears. The doctor ascribed these symptoms to menopause. She received this diagnosis in her early forties and was forced to live with it for a full twenty years.

The man cited statistics proving that women, as a rule, were more durably constructed than men, their minds and bodies more robust, their lifespans longer, which was why he was sure to die before she would. The woman thought the reason men's lives were statistically shorter than women's might have something to do with the fact that men end their own lives in youth by participating in wars and other violent acts, but demonstrating this with statistics would have been too much trouble, so she kept quiet.

'It's true,' she said. 'Men have larger builds, but at heart they're more frail and sensitive. That's why all women love men.' She knew she was lying, but she also knew that the world would be a place of darkness without men. And so she spent several hours every day massaging the man where he said it hurt and making and feeding to the man the kind of delicate ground food that people give to little birds.

She knew full well that her own fat body with its hardened arteries would not last much longer, but she could think of no other way to live than to continue providing food for the little bird of a man who believed in his own frailty.

One morning, the woman studied herself closely in the mirror. Her face was covered with the deep wrinkles of a mountain witch, and her yellowed teeth were gapped and ugly as an aged cat's. White frost had fallen on her hair, and she felt chilling pain as though needle ice was ready to pop out all over her body.

She felt a faint numbness as if her body might belong to someone else. The stiffness tied in with the distant memory of her mother, who had died so long ago. The flow of her blood seemed to stagnate in places, and she felt herself growing dizzy. She drifted off momentarily, and when she regained consciousness she found her limbs paralysed, her mind dimming and parts of her body gradually growing colder.

On any other morning, she would have been up long ago preparing his breakfast, but when her husband awoke to find that she was still in bed (they had slept side by side for forty years), lying face down like a frog in rigor mortis, he sprang into action with a suddenness that belied his many physical complaints and carried her to the hospital. Surprisingly, the doctor who until the day before had written her off as a case of menopause now declared as if he were a different person that she had the symptoms of cerebral thrombosis and if luck were against her she would survive no more than a day or two. The man reacted with total confusion, but he managed to pull himself together and decide that the first thing he should do was send for their son and daughter, both of whom lived far away. The two children came immediately and with their father they knelt around their stricken mother, who had lost the power of speech.

The next two days and nights might well have been the best two days of her life. The three of them took turns rubbing her arms, rubbing her legs and even taking care of her down below without relying on the nurse.

Those two days went by without any sudden changes in her condition, either positive or negative, but her consciousness gradually dimmed until she could no longer recognize the people around her. Puzzled, the doctor said, 'Considering her weight, her heart is surprisingly strong. She may last longer than I expected.' When he told them about a case of cerebral thrombosis in which the unconscious patient lived for two years on nothing but intravenous feeding, the three members of the woman's family fell silent and gathered around her.

Soon the son said there was a limit to how long he could stay away from work. Since it looked as though there would be no changes in the immediate future, he would return home for the time being. The daughter's expression darkened, and she began to worry about her husband and children.

The poor man became anxious; he would not know what to do if his daughter left. He pleaded with her to stay on, sounding so helpless that the daughter, as worried as she was about her own family, reluctantly agreed to remain.

The daughter recalled the time when she had been critically ill as a child and her mother had stayed up for days watching over her. If it had not been for this woman who lay before her, unconscious, straying between life and death, she would not be alive today. She waited beside the bed, thinking this could be the last time she would ever see her, but when another two days had passed, she began to wonder how long her mother would remain in her present condition, unable to respond when spoken to, just a living, breathing corpse. At sixty-two, her mother was still too young in terms of the average lifespan to be departing this world, but everyone had to die sooner or later. Even if she were to pass on here and now, they should perhaps be grateful that she could go while being watched over by her husband and daughter.

The daughter felt strangely uneasy to think of the doctor's patient who had survived for two years on intravenous feeding. If her mother did that, was her father prepared to pay the medical expenses? And medical expenses aside, neither she nor her brother could possibly abandon their families in order to stay by their mother's bed.

Just then she thought of her own five-year-old daughter, whom she had left in the care of her mother-in-law. She herself had fallen ill and run a high fever at that exact age, nearly contracting meningitis. She recalled with strange clarity how her half-mad mother crouched, unmoving, by her pillow in their miserably untidy house. The memory led her, of all things, away from her mother, who lay moaning between life and death before her very eyes, and instead towards the imagined – unlikely but terrifying – possibility of her own daughter falling ill in her absence.

Unaware of her daughter's anxieties, the mother survived another two days, often fixing her empty eyes on points in space and emitting incomprehensible, animalistic moans. On the morning of the third day, the daughter woke feeling too weary to climb out of bed after a week of intensive nursing. It was a dull, gloomy morning, typical of the hazy weather of the cherry blossom season. She stared vacantly at the profile of her unconscious mother, whose quiet breathing continued as before, and whose sunken cheeks made her look, if anything, younger and more beautiful.

When the morning round had ended, the daughter thought of how soiled her mother must be, and she asked the doctor if she could wipe the patient down. He said he would instruct the nurse to do it and left the room. Soon the nurse came in and performed her duties as instructed in a businesslike manner, rolling the unconscious patient over as though she were a log.

Nervously, the daughter lent a hand. The patient was rolled over and stripped of her nightclothes soiled with perspiration and excrement. At that very moment, the mother opened her eyes wide and stared straight at her daughter, who stood facing her, helping to support her weight. She produced a faint smile as the light returned to her eyes. The radiance had the sad, momentary brilliance of a child's sparkler, and when it faded, the mother's eyes lost their light again. Saliva dribbled from the corner of her mouth, a spasm shook her throat, and the movement of her eyes came to a dead stop. It all happened in an instant.

Rattled, the nurse ran off to tell the doctor of this sudden change. He rushed in and started to perform artificial respiration. He also injected cardiac medication directly into her heart with a thick needle. He seemed more to be shaking a laboratory animal that had failed during an experiment than treating a living human being. In any case, the people around her were doing their best to restart her heart.

The woman died.

Or perhaps it would be more accurate to say that she summoned up her last ounce of strength to drown herself by washing her accumulated saliva down her windpipe.

In the last smile she exchanged with her daughter, she clearly read her daughter's mind. Her daughter's eyes were saying that she did not want to be tied down by her any longer. 'Mother, I don't need you to protect me any more. You've outlived your usefulness. If you have to be dependent on me, if you can't take care of yourself without being a burden to others, please, Mother, please disappear quietly. Please don't torment me any longer. I, too, am preparing myself so that I won't trouble my daughter as I am being troubled by you. I'm willing to go easily. That's right. It's what we ought to do. I never want to be the kind of parent who, for lack of resolve, continues to press her unwanted kindnesses upon her offspring.' This daughter of hers, this product of her husband and herself, possessed a twofold strength of will. Either she would overcome all temptation, exercise moderation and live robustly until the moment of her death at one hundred, or live arrogantly and selfishly to the end, retaining the energy to kill herself at eighty. In either case, the woman was satisfied with the daughter she had borne and raised.

Through her daughter's face, she saw the son who was not there, walking among the crowds of the metropolis. He was talking to her with a crooked smile on his face. 'Mother, I have incessantly chirping chicks at home. I myself don't know why I have to keep putting food in their mouths. But when I catch myself, I'm always flying towards the nest with food in my beak. I do it before I even think about it. If it were all right for me to stop carrying food to them and stick close by your side, the human race would have perished long ago. In other words, for me to do what I do for them is the only way I can prolong and preserve the warm blood you gave me.'

Next she saw her aged husband, who was standing nearby with his head drooping and a stunned look on his face. This happy mad old man was moved by the beauty of his wife's naked body and carried away by his own fidelity in having tended her to the very end. The greatest happiness for a human being is to make another happy. She was satisfied to see this man who had the ability to change any given circumstance into happiness, and she blessed the start of his life's second chapter. At the same time, she thought she heard the pealing of her funeral bells.

With her own hands, she drew her white shroud closed around her, right side over left. The wind rushed across the dry riverbed and she glanced back to see someone running with dishevelled hair. She asked the reason for this, speaking to another deceased traveller, a stranger who had joined her out of nowhere. 'A mountain witch is chasing him,' came the answer.

She felt the warm heart of a mountain witch suddenly beating again beneath her drawn-together shroud, and she smiled. The heart of the mountain witch kept up its healthy beating, but the blood vessels meant to transmit its powerful pulsing were completely closed, cruelly and solidly blocked.

The time had come for the spirit of the witch to return to the quiet mountains. The day had come for her to stand on a rocky ledge, letting her white hair stream in the raging wind, her eyes wrenched open like golden flames, her wild laughter echoing forever among the hills. Her transient dream of living down in the human settlement disguised as an animal had ended.

She shook her head, recalling the days she had spent dreaming of living alone in the mountains, and the old sorrow came back from girlhood when she had first begun to dislike human beings. Had she lived in the mountains all that time, she would have been a witch who captures and devours humans from the settlement below.

Which would have made her happier, she wondered: to live in the mountains and become a man-eating witch; or to live in the settlement with the heart of a mountain witch? It seemed to her now that it would have made no difference. If she had lived in the mountains, she would have been called a mountain witch. Living in the settlement, she could have been called either a fox spirit incarnate or an ordinary woman with a healthy mind and body who lived out her natural life. That was the only difference. It would have been the same either way.

Just before she took her last breath, it crossed her mind that her own mother must have been an absolutely genuine mountain witch as well.

Strangely enough, she died with the sweet, innocent smile of a baby on her lips, passing from this world in complete peace. Her daughter clung to her, sobbing, her tear-swollen eyes revealing an indescribable sense of liberation as she whispered, 'Mother, how beautiful you are in death! You must have been a truly happy woman.' The wide-open fish eyes of the woman's husband overflowed with tears as he mourned in silence.

ENCHI FUMIKO

A Bond for Two Lifetimes – Gleanings

Translated by Phyllis Birnbaum

Kneeling on the veranda, I called out through the patched and faded sliding door, 'May I come in, Professor?'

From within came a muffled grunt that could have meant either yes or no and the sound of shifting bedclothes. This was his usual answer. I softly slid open the door and went in, still wearing my overcoat.

As I had anticipated, Professor Nunokawa was lifting his rumpled head of white hair from his grimy pillow and groping for the large, thin book that lay at his side. Every time I came to take notes for him, I was bothered by the dirty fuzz on the coarse sheets and the strip of white fabric attached to the quilt's border. The maid Mineko, who looked after the professor, seemed to let many days go by without changing the linen. Even a young person in a fetid sickbed would look quite miserable: an old man lying in such a state seemed even more appalling.

My vague sense of pity for him had at some point changed into a genuine feeling of disgust for this wretchedness. The feeling grew with each breath I took of the sickroom's mouldy smell, but I gently enquired after the professor's health as I spread my notebook on the desk by the bed. Mineko had evidently made preparations for my visit by setting the faded old rosewood desk there before she went out to shop.

The professor had a hot-water bottle in his bed. The few pieces of charcoal in the small china brazier were forever going out, and the room became bitingly cold on days like today when the early winter rains might mix with snow. Following the suggestion the professor had made during our first session, I kept my coat on and sat through each meeting still dressed for the outdoors.

'Today we're going to do "A Bond for Two Lifetimes", aren't we?' The professor obviously didn't want to discuss his illness. He lay back and opened the thin book on his chest. A red pencil in his right hand, he looked at me by moving only his eyes behind his thick-rimmed spectacles. On the desk, I opened the same version of *Tales of Spring Rain* that the professor was holding.

'"A Bond for Two Lifetimes". From the beginning on page fifty-nine,' I said.

The professor was doing modern colloquial versions of Ueda Akinari's *Tales of Moonlight and Rain* and *Tales of Spring Rain*,[1] which would become a volume in a series of Edo literary masterpieces put out by the publishing company I worked for. I had undertaken to act as secretary for Professor Nunokawa, my former teacher, as he dictated; he was too sick to write by himself. Despite his illness, he worked on this colloquial translation with much enthusiasm, partly because he needed the money.

I had finished recording the nine gothic tales from *Tales of Moonlight and Rain* and the first four stories in *Tales of Spring Rain*, all dictated by the toothless professor through slackened lips, narrating slowly but almost without pause, like a silkworm spitting out thread. In *Tales of Spring Rain*, a work of Akinari's later years, the preface states:

How many days now have the spring rains brought this pleasing quiet? As always, I take up my writing brush and inkstone, and let my thoughts wander here and there, but I find nothing to write about. Copying the old-fashioned storytelling styles is a job for the amateur writer, but, living like a mountain rustic, what tales can I tell? I have been deceived into believing the things people have written about the past and the present, and, not realizing they were lies, have related these tales to others, thus deceiving them as well. Oh, well, perhaps it can't be helped. There will always be people who continue to tell false stories and pass them off as classics. So I might as well go on telling my tales while the spring rains fall.

When he says that 'copying the old-fashioned storytelling styles is a job for the amateur writer', the old author seems to dismiss the skilfully wrought style of his earlier *Tales of Moonlight and Rain*. Still, he continued to record his dark and unwieldy inner passions boldly and without restraint, employing historical personages, legends and popular tales. Many stories in *Tales of Spring Rain* diverge from accepted feudal morality, so, of course, the work did not become as popular as *Tales of Moonlight and Rain* and not many copies were handed down through the generations even in handwritten form.

Akinari passed his later years without his wife, who had died at an advanced age, and he had no children; in addition, he could no longer see out of his left eye. For a considerable period, he lived in a faintly illumined world, troubled by problems of food, clothing and shelter. Professor Nunokawa had established a reputation as a scholar of Edo literature. His oldest son had died during the war, and his wife had also passed away. His only daughter, who was married, hardly ever came to see him because of his uncompromising character and because she disliked having Mineko there. All that the professor had helping support him in his old age, without either pension or annuity, were a few of his old students who enabled him to continue revising manuscripts and doing this kind of scholarly dictation. I had not noticed as much while he was translating *Tales of Moonlight and Rain*, but by the time we got to *Tales of Spring Rain*, I was often struck by the similarity of Akinari's last years and Professor Nunokawa's present life. The professor's dictation often sounded as if it were seeping out quite spontaneously from an essential source at the very depths of his being.

The professor propped the book on his chest and began to speak slowly in the low voice people use to commence recitations of Buddhist prayers:

'One autumn in Yamashiro Province, all the leaves had fallen from the tall zelkova trees. The strong, cold wind blew down over the mountain village, making for an exceedingly lonely scene. There was a rich landowner whose family had lived in Kosobe village for many years. They owned extensive paddy fields in the mountains and lived in such comfort that, through harvests both good and bad, the family never had to worry.

'Thus the master of the house quite naturally whiled away his time reading books and made no effort to seek friends among the village people. Every day until late at night, he read books beneath his lamp.

'His mother would worry about this. "Shouldn't you be going to bed soon? Hasn't the temple bell already struck twelve? Father always used to say that if you stay up late at night reading books, you will wear yourself out and end up ill. When people enjoy doing something, they tend to immerse themselves completely in their own entertainments without being aware of what's happening. Then they regret it later." She thus offered him her views on the subject.

'He took her warning as a sign of motherly affection and, feeling grateful to her, resolved to be in bed after the clock struck ten. One night a gentle rain was falling, and amid the stillness that had settled in from early evening, no other sound could be heard. Consequently, he became so lost in his reading that, before he knew it, much time had passed. This night he forgot his mother's warning, and when he opened the window, thinking that it might be two in the morning, the rain had stopped, there was no wind and the late-night moon had risen.

'"Ah, what a quiet night it is! I should write a poem about this moment," he said and, rubbing an inkstick over the ink slab, he took up his writing brush. He put his mind to one or two poetic lines, and while inclining his head and trying to think of more, he happened to hear something like a bell ringing among the chirping of the insects, which until then he had thought to be the only sounds.

'Now he realized that this was not the first time he had heard the sound of this bell. Every night when he had been reading his books like this, he had heard the same noise. Strange that he should notice it only now. He stepped down into the garden, looking here and there to find the source of the ringing bell, until he reached the place where he thought the noise had originated, beneath a stone in the corner of the garden where there was a clump of unmown grass. After making sure the sound was coming from there, he returned to his bedroom.

'The next day he called his servants together and ordered them to dig beneath the stone. When they had dug down three feet, their shovels struck a large rock. Removing the rock, they saw what appeared to be a tub-shaped coffin with a stone lid on it. With a great effort, they lifted off the heavy lid, and, looking inside, they found a peculiar creature which now and then rang a bell it held in its hand.

'When the master, followed by the servants, came close and had a nervous look, they saw a seated form which might have been a human being and, then again, might not. It was parched and hard in appearance, shrivelled like a dried-up salmon, and bony. The hair had grown long and hung down to the knees. The master ordered a strong servant to step down into the coffin and carefully lift the thing out.

'"It's light, very light, like nothing at all!" the servant exclaimed when he had it in his hands. "It can't be an old man." He spoke loudly as if masking his fear.

'Even while the people were lifting the thing out, the hand kept ringing the bell. The master saw this and reverently clasped his hands in prayer, saying to the others, "This is what the Buddhists call 'entering a meditative trance'. While still alive, one sits down crosslegged in the casket and dies while doing Zen meditation. This is what must have happened to this person. Our family has been living in this place for over a hundred years, and since I have never heard anything about such an event, it must have occurred before our ancestors came here. Did his soul go to paradise and only his corpse remain here unrotted? What tenacity, to have his hand keep ringing the bell as before. Since we have dug him up, let's see if we can bring him back to life."

'The master helped the servants carry the thing, dried and hard like a wooden statue, into the house.

'"Be careful! Don't bump against a post and smash it," he cautioned them. They carried their fragile burden slowly and carefully, eventually depositing it in one of the rooms and gently covering it with quilts. The master brought over a teacup filled with lukewarm water and pressed a moistened cotton wad against the dried lips. Then, a black, tongue-like object slowly emerged from between the lips and started to lick them. Soon the thing was sucking eagerly at the cotton wad.

'Upon seeing this, the women and children raised their voices in terror, "How horrifying, horrifying! It's a ghost!" and ran out, refusing to come near again.

'The master, encouraged by the changes in the thing, treated the dried-up creature with care. His mother joined him in giving it lukewarm water, each time remembering to intone a Buddhist prayer. By the time some fifty days had passed, the face, hands and legs, which had been like dried salmon, regained their moisture bit by bit, and some body warmth seemed to have been restored.

'"Truly, he's coming back to life!" the master said, redoubling his care and ministrations. As a result, the eyes opened for the first time. The creature moved them towards the light though didn't seem to see clearly. When he was fed rice water and thin gruel, he moved his tongue and seemed to taste them. He behaved like an ordinary person you might find anywhere. The wrinkles on his skin, previously like the bark of an old tree, became less pronounced, and he put on more flesh. He could move his arms and legs more freely. He seemed to be able to hear, for when he became aware of the north wind's gusts, his naked body shivered as though he were chilled. When he was offered some old padded clothes, he put out his hands to receive the offering with great pleasure. He also developed an appetite.

'At the beginning, when the master had thought of the man as the reincarnation of a revered personage, he had treated him with respect and did not dream of giving him the unholy flesh of fish to eat. However, when the new arrival saw the others partaking of such food, he twitched his nostrils to indicate how much he hungered for it. And when a fish was put upon his tray, the guest ate with gusto, even gnawing at the bones and wolfing down the head. The master felt his spirits sink but he asked him politely, "You have gone into a trance, and it has been your unusual fate to return from the dead. To help us foster the spirit necessary to achieve enlightenment, please tell us what you can remember about how you managed to live for such a long time beneath the earth."

'The man just shook his head and said, "I know nothing," and looked stupidly into the master's face.

'"Even so, can you not at least remember when you went into the ground? What was your name in your previous life?"

'They questioned the man like this, but he could recall nothing. He became bashful, moved back, sucked his finger and was no different from any doltish peasant farmer from the area.

'All the master's efforts of the past several months and the exaltation of believing that he had restored some worthy cleric to life had come to nothing, and so he was thoroughly disheartened by this turn of events. Afterwards, he treated the man like a servant, and had him sweep and water the garden. Not seeming to mind such menial work in the least, the man was not lazy as he went about his chores.

'"Buddha's teachings are quite ridiculous. What has happened to all the piety that was supposed to have been strong enough to put him in a trance, sustain him in that state for over a hundred years buried in the earth, and get him to ring his handbell? There's no trace of nobility in his character. What's it supposed to mean that only his body has come back to life for no particular reason?" the master said, and thoughtful villagers joined him, knitting their brows in consternation.'

'Let's stop there for now.' At some point, the professor had turned on his side to rest. He listlessly put down the book that he had been holding.

'You must be tired. Shall I bring you some tea?'

'No,' he said, pursing his lips sourly. 'Has Mine come back? I must go to the bathroom. Could you call her for me?'

I got up very quickly and slid the door open, calling out in a shrill voice to Mineko. She was already back from her shopping and apparently somewhere in the kitchen. 'Mineko! Mineko! The professor has to relieve himself!'

The professor had problems with his bladder and urinated with difficulty. He usually used a catheter, but one time during his dictation he had felt the sudden urge and had ended up wetting himself, which was why I became a bit frenzied.

The rumour was that the professor had nicknamed Mineko 'Goddess of the Narrow Eyes'. When she came running in from the kitchen, with her slit-like eyes and flabby white flesh, I slipped into the adjoining family room. Mineko seemed to have been working on her knitting there. On the soiled cotton-print cover of the heated *kotatsu* table lay an unfinished red sweater with two or three knitting needles stuck in it. The room was cold. I slipped my hands into the heated *kotatsu* and listened to what was taking place in the next room. I guessed that Mineko was trying to slide the bedpan under the professor.

'There! Now a little more . . . lift yourself up a little more, that's it, now we're fine.' Breathing hard, she raised her voice as if issuing commands and then said bluntly, 'Professor, it's time you let Mrs Noritake go, isn't it . . . ? Well, isn't it . . . ? It's time you let her . . .'

'No. Not yet. We're just taking a break. You finish this up now.'

'Take your time,' I called to them. 'I'm organizing my notes.'

Instead of answering me, the professor yelled at Mineko, 'Ouch! Don't be so rough!' The insertion of the catheter's narrow rubber tube was obviously very painful. He groaned a few times and as soon as he fell silent, I heard a thin trickle of urine splashing into the bedpan through the tubing – a sound that expressed only too bleakly the meagre store that remained of the professor's life.

More than ten years had passed since I graduated from my women's college. Professor Nunokawa, who was a teacher there, favoured me a great deal by lending me books and having me help him with his research. During that time, with a boldness that astonished me, he would rub his body against mine, squeeze my hand and brazenly make advances, suggesting further intimacies. Since I was engaged to my husband at the time – he was later killed in the war – and was just about to get married, I took the professor's advances as the impudence of a middle-aged man. I found it altogether repugnant and was filled with contempt for him.

Looking back on the scandals that had brewed in those days over the professor's lechery – so inappropriate for a teacher – I now realized that his body must have been brimming over with the energies of a man in the prime of life. The professor called me Tamakazura in those days, after the daughter of one of Prince Genji's love interests.[2] I lost my husband little more than a year after my marriage. He had been a technical officer in the navy and was killed in an air raid on a naval port in Japan. I was now a bereft war widow with a young boy to look after, living a marginal existence in the ten years since the end of the war.

As a woman alone and working in those harsh post-war conditions, I encountered many brash advances from various men, of a sort even worse than Professor Nunokawa's. But I came to typify the saying 'A twentyish widow needs no more husbands'. I felt both my mind and body fully, naturally moistened and blossoming from the mere year or more of contact with my husband. Whether for good or ill, I had passed these months and years without the opportunity of marrying for a second time. Now past thirty and holding down a job in a publishing house, I might appear to others to be a woman as parched in body and soul as the dried-up salmon in the story. But deep within my being, I was nourished by the miracle of being able to embrace my husband in my dreams and of seeing his face quite vividly in the features of my small son.

As a result, I had recently begun to view the inevitable sexual aggressions of men with a sympathetic eye. When I realized that for the strong-willed Professor Nunokawa, who had in the past pursued me so tenaciously, life now amounted to putting all his energies into producing a paltry quantity of urine in the next room, my whole being shook, and I was brought very close to tears.

I was called in again and entered the room. Mineko had disposed of the bedpan and vanished behind the sliding door. It may have been my imagination, but the professor seemed to have more colour in his face as he leaned on the pillow with one elbow.

'What do you think of this story? It's interesting, isn't it?' the professor asked me, enthusiastically.

'Very much so. I didn't know that there was a story like this in *Tales of Spring Rain*. Was it taken from another source?'

'Of course it was.' The learned professor told me the story of 'The Attachment that Plagued the Trance', from *The Old Woman's Teatime Stories*, the apparent source of Akinari's tale. In 1652, a priest named Keitatsu of the Seikan Temple on Mount Myōtsū in Yamato-Kōriyama was about to go into his final meditative trance. Suddenly, he became infatuated with a beautiful woman visiting the temple and was unable to attain enlightenment. Fifty-five years later, still unable to subdue his own soul, he continued to ring his handbell and beat his drum.

'With its preface dating from the early 1740s, *The Old Woman's Teatime Stories* must have been written when Akinari was a child. In any case, since the work comes from that period, he wouldn't have been able to get a copy easily and so might have read it decades later. If Akinari had written this story in the same frame of mind he had been in when he wrote *Tales of Moonlight and Rain*, I think he might have described the part about the priest's infatuation with the beautiful woman in more detail.'

When I heard him say this, I lowered my eyes and thought that the professor might be expressing something of his own feelings here.

'Actually there's another story told about this in *A History of the Novel through Biography*, written by Tsubouchi Shōyō and Mizutani Futō in the Meiji period. In that book, Aeba Kōson tells of a man who had seen the manuscript of a work by Akinari called *A Tale of Rainy Nights*, which resembled this "A Bond for Two Lifetimes" but had quite a different ending. The two versions are similar up to the point where the bell sounds below the ground, but then *A Tale of Rainy Nights* goes on to say that the man who hears the bell himself digs the hole. There he finds an old Buddhist priest who had gone into a trance and had been reciting sutras with fierce concentration. The man helps the priest up to ground level, and under the light of the moon, they open their hearts to each other and discuss many matters. Even this format, religious questions and answers, was quite possible for Akinari.'

'But the version we're working on is more typical of Akinari, don't you think, Professor?' I objected.

As a form of fanatical faith, the story of a priest who had gone into a trance and recited the sutras with his whole heart but had retained his human shell for decades might have been a good object of criticism for the polemical Akinari. But for me, the latter part of the story that the professor was now translating into colloquial Japanese had a far more intense eeriness and profound sense of sorrow.

'Ha, ha, ha,' the professor laughed weakly, his sharp Adam's apple twitching. 'You want that to happen to you, don't you? That's perfectly natural. You'd like to have a marital bond that extends over two lifetimes.' It was the professor's nature, when he felt better, to come up with witticisms that were not exactly in good taste.

'I still have time, so if you're not tired, shall we go to the end of the story?' I edged up to the desk.

'Hmm, I suppose we can try. If we get through this, I can take it easy afterwards.' The professor lay down on his back again and opened the book on his chest. 'We did up to here, didn't we? "Truly, the teachings of Buddhism are useless. He entered the earth like this and rang his bell for over a hundred years. How pitiful that nothing is left but the bones."'

'Yes, that's where we left off.'

'Upon observing the dimwittedness of this man from the grave, the mother of the master of the house gradually changed her whole attitude towards life: "For these many years, I have thought only of avoiding suffering in the world hereafter. I have been extraordinarily generous in my almsgiving and charity at the temple. Morning and evening, I never fail to utter a Buddhist prayer. When I see this man with my own eyes, I feel I have been duped by a sly fox or cunning badger," she said, also sharing these views with her son.

'Save for visiting the graves of her parents and husband on their death anniversaries, she abandoned her religious duties. Not caring a bit for the opinions of her neighbours, she went off on moon-viewing picnics in the hills and fields, doing the same when the cherry blossoms bloomed; taking along her daughter-in-law and her grandchildren, she was concerned only with enjoying herself.

'"I spend time with my relatives often and pay more attention to the servants," the mother would tell people from time to time. "Occasionally I give them things. I now live in peace and ease, having completely forgotten that I used to be full of gratitude when given the chance to say my Buddhist prayers and listen to sermons." As if loosed from chafing restraints, she behaved in a youthful, lively manner.

'Although the disinterred man usually wore a vacant stare, he would grow angry if he didn't have enough to eat or if someone scolded him. At these times, he would get a furious look in his eyes and mutter complaints. The servants and the local people stopped treating him with even the slightest bit of reverence, and only his name, Jōsuke of the Trance, bore witness to the fact that he had entered into a trance and had come back to life. For five years, he stayed on as the family's servant.

'There was a poor widow in the village who was also regarded as rather stupid, and at some point she became intimate with Jōsuke of the Trance. He was seen diligently cultivating her tiny field and washing the pots and kettles in the stream out back. Since only special circumstances had forced the master to agree to employ Jōsuke and keep him for the rest of his life, once this state of affairs became known, everyone viewed him with a bitter smile and pushed for him to marry the woman. In the end, Jōsuke did become the woman's husband.

'The gossip flew:

'"He says he doesn't even know how old he is, but he seems to remember quite well what men and women do together."

'"Oh, now I see – there does seem to be a reason for Jōsuke's return to the world of the living. Everyone thought he had been down in that pit ringing his bell morning and evening because of a pious wish for Buddha's providence. So he actually was set upon coming back to our floating world of pleasure only to have sex, eh? What a noble desire that was!"

'The young people of the village went to great lengths to investigate how Jōsuke and the widow were carrying on. When they peeped in through the cracks in the dilapidated house's wooden door, it was no monster they saw cavorting with a woman. They returned home dispirited.

'"The priests are always preaching about the Buddhist law of cause and effect, but when we see such an example before our very eyes, our faith vanishes." This became the common talk among the people of the village, and not only there but in the neighbouring villages as well. People became negligent about making offerings to their temples.

'The one who worried about these changed attitudes more than anyone else was the chief priest of a temple with a long history in the village. It is a hopeless task for ordinary people in this debased world to fathom the mysteries of spontaneous Buddhist enlightenment, but the priest could not look away while Buddhist virtues lost their lustre because of events taking place before their very eyes. He resolved to investigate the circumstances in which Jōsuke entered his trance and at least to dispel the terrible confusion in the minds of these foolish men and women.

'He consulted the temple's death registry and questioned every elder of the village. Indeed, he made such efforts to learn the facts about Jōsuke's burial that he forgot to perform the required services at the temple. In his investigations, he learned that, after a disastrous flood in the village over a hundred and fifty years ago, when the houses and villagers were all washed away, the topography changed and a new branch in the river appeared, improving the water supply so that people started living there once again.

'Thus, where the village had been before the flood now corresponded to a place somewhere in the middle of the river. Since the hamlet now called Kosobe was formerly at the sandy bank of the river where no houses had stood, it was impossible to discover why the man's coffin had been buried there.

'"But if the holy saint had been trapped in the flood, water must have poured into his mouth and ears. Afterwards he would have dried up and hardened. Could that be why he turned into the dullard that Jōsuke is today?" Some people expressed such views with complete seriousness, while others mocked them. Meanwhile, the question of Jōsuke's past was no closer to an answer.

'The mother of the village headman had lived eighty long years, and she became quite sick. When she was near death, she summoned her doctor and said: "I am fully prepared to die now, though I have lived this long, unaware that my time was coming, because of the medicines you have given me. You have taken good care of me for many years, and I hope that you will continue to take care of my family after this. My son is almost sixty years old, but he is weak-willed and dependent. I often worry about him. Please give him advice now and then, and tell him not to let the family fortunes decline."

'The son, the village headman, heard this and smiled bitterly. To his mother he said, "I am already old enough that my hair has turned grey. Though by nature I am a bit dull-witted, I have listened to all you have taught me and will do my best for the family. Please don't worry about this ephemeral world of ours; just chant your Buddhist prayers to ensure that you achieve a grand rebirth in paradise."

'At this, the sick woman looked at the doctor in disgust. "Just listen to him, Doctor. You see the fool who has been such an affliction to me. At this point in my life, I have no intention of praying to the Buddha and being reborn in paradise. I am not particularly afraid that my lack of faith will cause me to be reborn into the animal realm with all its suffering. Having lived so long and observed all sorts of creatures in this defiled world, it seems to me that even cows and horses, so often the symbols for pain, don't actually lead a life of unrelieved suffering. In fact, they seem to enjoy happy and contented moments too. While moving among the ten worlds of our lives, we human beings are supposed to be far superior to cows and horses, but I can count on my fingers the number of pleasurable moments I've had. Driven on day after day, I've had less free time than any cow or horse! All year long, day in day out, we have to dye our clothes anew and wash them. In addition to such everyday tasks, if we neglect to pay tribute to our master at the end of the year, it means punishment, for us a calamity of the first order . . . And just when we are beset by anxiety, along come our tenant farmers, from whom we expect payments in rice, to grumble about their poverty. Ah, is there really a paradise? Where? When? My one deathbed request is that you do not bury my coffin. Take it to the mountain and cremate it without fuss. Doctor, please bear witness to this request. My last wish is that I not become like that Jōsuke of the Trance. Ah, everything is so tiresome. I don't want to say any more." She then closed her eyes and died a moment later.

'In accordance with this woman's last wishes, her body was brought to the mountain and cremated. Jōsuke of the Trance joined the tenant farmers and the day workers in carrying the coffin up the mountain, working as a substitute cremator until the coffin had been set on fire and the corpse had gone up in flames. He stayed there as the survivors picked out the tiny bones, so like white branches, that remained among the ashes and placed them in the urn. But his zeal was motivated only by his desire to get as much as he could of the rice with black soya beans that was distributed to the mourners at the end of the ceremony. When people realized this, they thought him a disgrace.

' "Forget about offering prayers to the Buddha in order to be reborn in the Pure Land. Take a good look at what's happened to Jōsuke," the villagers said, spitting at the mention of his name and admonishing their children not to follow his example.

'But some people countered with: "That may be true, but didn't Jōsuke come back to life and marry? This might very well be due to the beneficence of the Buddha, who wanted to fulfil his promise of a bond for two lifetimes between husband and wife."

'Jōsuke and his new wife – the former widow – sometimes got involved in terrible domestic rows, and afterwards she'd always go running to her neighbours. "What have I done to deserve such a worthless fellow for a husband? Now I long for those days when I was a struggling widow living on scraps. Why doesn't my former husband come back to life again the way this man has? If he were here, we wouldn't lack for rice or wheat, and we wouldn't be suffering to get even rags on our backs as we are now." She wept openly in fits of regret.

'Many are the strange occurrences in this world.'

When I finished taking notes, the brief winter day had already ended. Clearly exhausted, the professor had laid the open book face down on his chest and shut his eyes under the faint yellowish lamplight. He did not offer criticisms or expound on his perceptions, which normally would have completed the session after such a story. I thought about the hour or so it would take me to get home and, after a hasty goodbye, left the professor's house.

Professor Nunokawa's house was on the outskirts of Nerima, and in the autumn many of the trees in this area scattered scarlet leaves on the ground. For someone like me from central Tokyo, the site evoked nostalgic visions of the Musashi Plain. The bus route, however, was far off and to get to the train station I had to walk quite a while down narrow paths, which cut across fields and wound through clusters of trees and bamboo groves, a hard walk in summer and winter. If I went in the opposite direction, I'd come out on a main road and, even though the next station was a long distance away, I'd be able to walk through a bright stretch of shops and houses.

But I was accustomed to the first way and routinely went through the narrow paths in the fields even though it was dark. In the two or three days since my last visit, the daylight hours had grown much shorter, and I felt I should hurry. Burying my chin in the collar of my overcoat and holding my umbrella low, I trudged down the dark path as a light rain started to fall.

Because I had been taking notes until only moments before and had not exchanged views with Professor Nunokawa afterwards about the strange man in 'A Bond for Two Lifetimes', Jōsuke's lifelike figure was still floating vividly in my consciousness as if he were right there before my eyes. In the story, there was no mention of what Jōsuke had been like before he went into a trance, only that in his next life he had changed into a stupid country bumpkin and married a woman who had lost her husband. Did this part, with its 'bond for two lifetimes', come from some other source or was it an imaginative creation of Akinari's later years?

As Professor Nunokawa had stated, if the young Akinari had written this in his thirties, when he composed the gothic *Tales of Moonlight and Rain*, he would doubtless have woven a tale of quite startling eroticism. A pious priest is stirred by one glimpse of an unusually attractive woman just before he enters his final meditative trance. His blind attachment remains forever in his hand, ringing the bell, and he can never escape the wheel of rebirth. In comparison with what the young Akinari might have produced, the Jōsuke of this 'A Bond for Two Lifetimes' was so unkempt and stupid that, with only a slight shift, the whole incident could turn into a display of comic storytelling.

But the Akinari who had written this story must have already lost the sight in his left eye, and his old wife, Sister Koren, had probably passed away by then. He must have written 'A Bond for Two Lifetimes' during this period of loneliness and deprivation, half ridiculing and half fearing those smouldering, seemingly unquenchable inner fires of sexual desire, which remained no less strong than his impulse to create.

As a result, Akinari wrote a story of a man who might once have been a sage of high virtue with an enlightened understanding of the great questions of life and death; this man was reborn an illiterate simpleton who ended by using a woman's body to satisfy the sexual obsessions he had been unable to fulfil in his first life. With this story, Akinari might have been hinting at the weird, maggot-like squirming of sexual desire that remained within him in his dotage.

Twice in the story the author has an old woman, who longs for the afterlife, take this event as an opportunity to mock the Buddhist laws of cause and effect. In this scepticism he seems to despise the very nature of sex, which goes endlessly around and around in a vicious cycle, never sublimated by old age or by devotion to religion.

This reminded me of Professor Nunokawa himself, who had taken in the much younger Mineko. Stories were told about how she had already transferred ownership of the antiquated house to her name, presuming that the professor had not long to live. It was hard not to see similarities in Jōsuke's relationship with the widow.

While thinking over these matters, I had a sudden, unexpected recollection of the last time I had embraced my husband the night before he died in the bombing. I thought of how I had writhed in his strong arms, panting like a playful puppy, and had finally withered with the pleasures of a desire so strong that my body and soul seemed to vanish. More than mere memory, those sensations suddenly returned to my flesh. My very womb cried out in longing. Just then my foot slipped. I tottered two or three steps and came dangerously close to falling on my knees.

'Careful,' I heard a man's voice saying, and something took hold of the arm with which I was still clutching my umbrella. With this help, I just managed to right myself.

'Thank you very much.' I was out of breath.

'Sometimes the bamboo roots jut into the path around here,' the man said in a low, muffled voice. 'Are you sure you didn't drop anything?' He bent down to help me look.

He was right about where we were – on a path cut through a bamboo grove halfway between the professor's house and the station. I saw the light from a house flickering through the thick stand of bamboo. I could not make out the man's face in the dark, but he did not have an umbrella and his overcoat was wet. I held out my umbrella and asked him, 'Won't you come under?' Without reserve, he brought his body right up against mine.

'Cold, isn't it? And the rain makes it worse.' With a chill ungloved hand, he gripped my hand to help me hold the umbrella.

I could not see his face clearly, but from his voice and appearance he seemed rather old and down on his luck, yet the hand he put on top of my gloved one was soft like a woman's. I preferred men with strong, bony grips, like my dead husband's, and so I did not care for the softness of this man's. Strangely, I did not think of shaking him off and even felt the guilty pleasure of the cold softness of his palm slowly tightening around my glove. The man joined his outer hand to mine in carrying the umbrella and used the other hand to hold me around the shoulder. My body was completely encircled within his arms. We had to walk along entangled in this way.

In the darkness, I staggered frequently, and each time he adjusted his hold on me, guiding me like a puppeteer. Touching me on my breasts, my sides and other parts of my body, he would laugh, but whether out of joy or sadness, I could not tell. It struck me that he might be crazy, but that did not diminish the strange pleasure I took in his embrace.

'Do you know what I was thinking about when I slipped a minute ago?' I asked in a flirtatious voice that might have passed for drunkenness. He shook his head and embraced me so tightly that it became difficult to walk.

'I was thinking about my dead husband. He was killed by a bomb in a military air-raid shelter in Kure. I was in government housing a few blocks away with our child and survived. You know, I wonder if my husband thought about me before he died. Now, for some reason, I long to know how he felt before he died. My husband loved me, but being a soldier, he made a distinction in his mind between loving and dying alone. I genuinely admired my husband's magnificent attitude towards life, but, until the moment he died, did he really not see any contradiction between loving a woman and dying?'

The man did not answer my question, and as if to stop my words, he brought his cold lips against my mouth. Then, sadly kneading and shaking the flesh of my arms, he kissed me long and hard. As his cold tongue became intertwined with mine, I felt his sharp canine teeth against my tongue. They were obviously my husband's.

'Oh my dear, oh my dear, it's really you . . .' I called out as the man pushed me down in the grove, where the bamboo roots pressed hard against my back, and then he fell on top of me, all the while seeking my acquiescence. But his hands were indeed soft and cold, quite different from my husband's. Those hands bore down on my prostrate form and, as I resisted, tried to undo the buttons of my overcoat.

'I was wrong,' I declared weakly. 'You're not the one. You're not my husband.'

He remained silent and, seizing one of my flailing hands, forced my fingers into his mouth. Behind his cold lips, his canines were pointed, sharp awls, just like my husband's, which had passed painfully over my tongue so many times in the past. But the hands were different. My husband's hands had not been as fleshy and soft as a woman's. And his body also . . .

At that moment, out of nowhere, I recalled the musty, mildewed invalid's smell I had encountered upon entering Professor Nunokawa's room. Was this Professor Nunokawa? The moment the thought crossed my mind, my voice called out totally different words, while my body sprang up convulsively like some wild dog.

'Jōsuke, Jōsuke! This is . . .' Muttering these words, I ran full speed into the darkness.

When I emerged on to the brightly lit street in front of the station, my heart was still pounding from the vivid hallucination that had seized me on the dark path. A train had just arrived, and a crowd of men in black overcoats on their way home from work came pushing their way out of the narrow wicket, each appearing to emerge from the same mould. I stood to one side, observing them all pass through, and each one of them looked to me like an unblemished specimen of manhood. As a woman, I felt both envy and an excruciating tightness in the chest.

Jōsuke of the Trance was alive and well in these men. I had seen it for myself. More than the shameful hallucination I had just experienced in the darkness, this realization made my blood churn. It was an unnerving agitation that warmed my heart.

NATURE AND MEMORY

ABE AKIRA

Peaches

Translated by Jay Rubin

I know all too well that memory cannot be trusted, and I have surely heard this said by others. But I am constantly being shocked anew at how wildly deceptive memory can be. It beguiles us at every turn. I was taken by surprise again not too long ago.

Winter. Night. The moon.

I am a young boy and with my mother. We push a pram filled with peaches.

The single road connecting our town with the town on the west runs through open farmland, then rises and falls as it slopes gently downwards beyond an elevated stretch of sand dunes. It was a narrow, rock-strewn country road back then. On the slope there were no houses, only thick pine woods lining either side.

My mother and I make our way slowly down the hill. Soon we will come to the river at the bottom. The river runs to the sea. Beyond the river's wooden bridge, paddy fields stretch into the distance. The air throbs with the bull-frogs' heavy cries, the wet smacking of the mud snails. We are almost home.

I doubt if there has been a year in the thirty or more that have gone by since then when I did not recall that night scene. The image in my mind is always the same – if not so fixed as a painting, then perhaps more like some frames of underexposed film flickering on the screen. Especially on cold winter nights when I walk alone through the darkness with my coat collar turned up, the fragmentary memory of that night on the road comes back to me.

And each time, I have said to myself: *Oh yes, I remember that – odd how well I do remember that night.* The very words of this monologue, too, are the same, repeated year after year with all the intensity a second-rate actor would give them. And while I am busy congratulating myself on my stagecraft, the memory always slips away, its veracity untested.

But the scene needs more commentary.

My mother had taken me along to the neighbouring town that night to lay in a stock of peaches at an orchard or some such place. She could get better ones than at the local greengrocer's, and they would be fresh picked. It was probably worth making a special trip and buying enough to fill the pram.

Peaches. Fruit like pure, sweet nectar – nothing else. Easily bruised, quick to spoil. And each one heavy, almost unnervingly so. Filled with several dozen of these heavy peaches, the pram must have been more difficult to push than if it had held a live baby. And like the downy skin of a newborn, each could be scuffed and bruised in an instant if my mother did not push the pram slowly and carefully.

The darkness must have exaggerated the distance, long as it was. The night was cold and, up well past my bedtime, I must have been very sleepy. Partway down the hill, my mother stopped and wrapped her beige shawl around me.

More than the cold, it was my fear of the dark shapes arising one after another along the moonlit road that prompted her to do this. She probably had to cover my eyes with the shawl and walk along holding me against her.

Perhaps she had been careless enough to tease me about foxes along the way, and this was what aroused my fears, dark shadows or no. She had told me several stories of the foxes she had encountered as a little girl. My mother was born in Osaka at the turn of the century and she spent her childhood in the city, but on walks to the deserted countryside she would always hear the foxes crying, and people would say that they could cast a spell on passers-by.

Her stories must have come back to me one after another, the shawl around my head powerless to calm my fears. Why did she have to start talking about foxes *here*? I'm sure I wanted to get down the hill and among houses again as soon as possible.

But to walk any faster would have been out of the question. The pram would have bounced along the rocky road, damaging the peaches. I had been the baby in this pram until not long ago. Now it was only good for carting things. Most of the time, it stayed in the storage shed in the corner of the yard.

And so the young mother and her little boy, pressing close and sharing whispers, slowly pushed the old, little-used pram down the hill of the deserted country road. Bathed in moonlight, the one added the clip-clop of her wooden sandals, the other the soft padding of his tennis shoes to the creak of the pram's rusting wheels.

This, then, was the scene that had lived in the fondest part of my memory for so many years. In none of its details had I found anything to wonder at.

And then one day – in fact, just two or three days ago – as I was gazing blankly at the view from my window, it struck me with such force that, for a moment, I was unable to breathe. Peaches in the winter? Frogs and mud snails in the winter? How could I have failed to notice *that* until now? And, stranger still, what had inspired me – possessed me – at this one moment to seize upon the vital clue? For it was this that lay bare the hoax that memory had played on me year after year. Now, for the first time, I saw the wildly impossible connection that memory had made: carting a load of peaches on a cold winter night! Nowadays, perhaps. But back then? Unthinkable.

One after another, doubts began to overtake me. I would have to think it through from beginning to end. All right, then, exactly when was it? Why, in fact, were my mother and I walking down that hill so late at night? Were those really peaches in the pram? And if not, what were we bringing from the other town?

When it came to this, all I could be sure of was that one year, on one particular night, my mother and I had come down the hill on the road that linked our town with the next one. These unsubstantial facts were all that remained. Had it been peach season or shawl season? I did not know. I was far too young to have been alone – of that I was certain. But of that and nothing else.

We still had the pram that night, which meant I could not have gone past the first few years of primary school – or 'People's School', as it was called during the war. The one photograph that shows me in the pram – wearing a little white robe, my face a white mask of baby powder – was taken a month before my second birthday. If we were using the pram to cart things, it must have been falling apart, the hood broken, the water-proof cloth of the body peeling. Had I been so rough on it as all that? Had we thrown it in the storage shed because it was a wreck? And how about my age? I think I walked both to and from the other town, a goodly distance for me even now. My mother didn't have to carry me. Surely I had left kindergarten by then and was going to primary school.

This was probably true, because I seemed to recall that when we got home late that evening, my brother, who was at middle school, was very put out with my mother and me. By then the war was on, and my father, a navy man, was no longer at home. Even assuming there was a moon that night, the road should have been dark because of the blackout. Still, the war was in its early stages; the air raids had not really started. It was probably the summer or the winter of 1942. My brother, so annoyed with us then, had left home by the following year. That night, he was probably hard at work preparing for the Naval Academy entrance examination. He must have been angry at my mother for being so late with his dinner.

But even as I go on making one reasonable-sounding guess after another, I realize that my 'evidence' has no more validity than any other tricks of memory. Not a thing I have mentioned here is certain. Indeed, I can refute every item without even trying.

First, there is the old pram. How long did we actually have it around the house? When did we get rid of it? And how? By leaving it in a nearby field? Sending it to the junk shop? I have no definite answers. It could just as well have stayed in the storage shed during the war and even for a time thereafter. Then the hoax would have been so easy to play: I might simply have confused that night scene with a post-war episode of stocking up on something.

Far from my mother's leading me by the hand, it seems more likely that I was there to protect her, that the road was unsafe for a woman alone at night. By then I would have been in my sixth year of primary school or my first year of middle school. And we were wheeling not a pram-load of peaches, but of black-market rice or potatoes or sweet potatoes – or if I'm going to insist on a cold winter night – perhaps some New Year's rice cakes. Then again, fuel being as hard to come by as food, it might have been kindling or charcoal or scraps of coal with which to stoke our old-fashioned bathtub.

Under this kind of scrutiny, the lovely image of a mother and child slowly pushing a pram downhill on a moonlit night is suddenly transformed into something less charming – a suspicious-looking couple transporting black-market goods. We would then have had our reasons for moving about under cover of night.

But where does my scowling brother fit in? He should not have been there waiting for us. Following his demobilization after the war, he was almost never at home. And if it so happened that he was in the house on that particular day, he would have had no reason to be angry with us. If anything, he would have been grateful. And so it was not my brother, probably, but my father who was waiting for us. It was always my father who stayed at home. Or rather, as a former officer, waiting at home was the only job there was for him to do.

But no, this has to be wrong. Those were peaches, I'm sure of it. All I have to do to make the memory consistent is change the cold winter evening to a summer night. This casts doubt, of course, on my mother's wrapping her shawl around me and the feeling I have that she told me tales of foxes as we walked along. But literary tradition aside, there is nothing wrong with the subject of foxes in summer. Only the shawl is out of place.

As far as literary hoaxes go, the most obvious one is the moonlight that comes flooding into my so-called memory. I could easily have been led from an old story of the fox's cry on a cold winter night into yet another story that my mother probably told me around the same time.

It was a story about a distant relative of hers, a young girl, something that happened when my mother was herself a girl. Born with a bad leg, the girl was sent to a convent when the other girls her age were marrying. She was suspected of having stolen something from one of the other nuns, however, and the older nuns beat her cruelly. That day, or perhaps it was the next day, or a short time thereafter, the girl drowned herself in a pond. It happened on a moonlit winter night, my mother said, unfolding the bright scene of death before me.

Within the grounds of the convent – somewhere in Kyoto, or possibly Nara – there was a large pond, on the banks of which grew a giant plum tree. Its heavy, gnarled branches stretched out low over the water to the middle of the pond. It looked just like a bridge, my mother said, as though she had seen the tree herself. Dragging her bad leg, the poor young nun crawled quietly along the branch in her white robes as the moonlight flooded down. Then she fell and disappeared beneath the surface. The thing she had supposedly stolen was found some days later among another nun's belongings.

I suspect my mother embroidered rather freely on the story of the young girl's suicide but, child that I was, it moved me very deeply. More than the horror of her fate itself, however, what struck me was the fact that such a dark drama of an ill-fated life should be concealed somewhere out on the furthest branches of the bloodlines that connected me to others. Its ancient stage settings, like something out of the Nara or Heian past; the indistinct backdrop, like the ones in the shadow plays: these were what left an impression on me.

Is the image in my mind, then, of the same tradition as my mother's eerie tale? Did I create it for myself, as one often hears is done, by unconsciously fusing two wholly distinct memories into a single night's occurrence? Was this one of those 'beautiful recollections', a pack of lies put through a sentimental tinting job until it comes out 'like a little story'? It might well have been.

The memory I have (or seem to have) of pushing the pram down the hill with my mother is unique: it happened that once and never again. Her wrapping her shawl around me when we were out together was a common enough occurrence, however, and her storytelling was by no means confined to night-time walks. It could and did happen anywhere – at the dinner table, in my room, and probably most often while she was sewing.

At that age – be it summer or winter – I would most often walk with my mother at night on the way back from my aunt's house, which lay in precisely the opposite direction from the hill, in the town to the east. There was a river in that direction as well, but it was a river we followed for a while rather than crossed. The water's dark surface used to frighten me badly. My cousins had told me of a boy my own age who had fallen in when hunting crabs on the bank and had sunk into the mud and died. The story had an eerie epilogue, which the girls had eagerly supplied: on windy nights, you could hear the dead boy's sobbing from the riverbank.

I would hide my face in my mother's sleeve, trying not to see the faint glow of the river as we passed by in the dark. Here, too, there were few dwellings, and the road was lonely and hemmed in by pine woods, but once we left the river behind I felt safe. Sometimes my mother would stop to gather a few pine cones and put them in her basket. One night, she stopped walking quite unexpectedly and, instructing me to stay put, waded cautiously into the deep grass by the roadside. I watched until she squatted down, then waited, praying that no one would come from either direction.

Thus, while I was familiar with the road to the east from an early age, I passed the hill in the other direction late at night only that once. If I am right in recalling that those were peaches we carted, it could have been no later than shortly after the war broke out. While my father was away, my mother had part of the lawn dug up and four peach trees planted, three yellow and one white. They were mature trees and bore fruit the following year – in such numbers that my mother had to spend many evenings tearing up old copies of her ladies' magazines and pasting the pages together to make covers for the still-green peaches. Every summer through the war years and after, we had more peaches than we could eat, and she was kept busy giving them away to relatives and neighbours. We never had to buy any.

All of which leads me to believe that the night in question had to have been in 1942. The trip she made to buy that load of peaches may have given my mother the idea to plant her own trees. Or, possibly, having decided to grow peaches, she went to the orchard in the next town to see how it was done. But, in fact, where these questions are concerned, my memory tells me nothing at all.

What I do remember, however, as inseparably associated with the peach trees, are the face and voice of a man. It was he who had encouraged her to plant them, who actually brought the young trees and put them into the ground. And every year he would come with fertilizer, inspect and prune the trees, and have a long chat with my mother before he left. He was the son of a local landowner whose family had built and rented many houses here for several generations and who also farmed the land. He was 'the son', but he was of my mother's generation and by then was head of the household. He had often visited us before the war, too. My father bought our land from his father. Apparently, it had once been their water-melon patch.

My mother never invited the man in, but whenever he would drop over to say hello, bringing a bundle of vegetables at the peak of the season, she would serve him tea on the open veranda outside the dining room and sit nearby to talk. She left the care of the peach trees entirely to him, and the time would come when she would ask him to dig a bomb shelter as well. He could be asked to scoop the night soil, do any job. A round, ruddy man, he wore a cloth cap and a workman's waistcoat with a large pocket on the front. He had a loud, ringing laugh that he would suppress for no one.

The dining-room veranda was my 'territory'. On the cement floor underneath were kept bundles of firewood, bales of charcoal, dried tulip and hyacinth bulbs, cobwebbed flowerpots and a watering can. It was a sunny spot, and cats from other houses would come to stretch out there. I once saw a sick-looking cat eating weeds that had sprouted from cracks in the cement. They were long, slender plants with seed clusters like bonbons. I used to lie on the veranda, looking at all these things through the spaces in the planks.

One day, as the afternoon sun was fading from the veranda, the man and my mother sat there engrossed in conversation. It was just then that I came home from school.

Their talk was more light banter than anything serious.

'I know *your* type. You've done it all. With all sorts of women . . .' I heard my mother saying.

'No, not me, no . . .'

To hide his embarrassment, he laughed his ringing laugh, but he did not look at my mother. His eyes stayed fixed on the peach trees he had planted.

I was having my afternoon snack close by, and all at once I found myself listening to their every word. The banter continued for a time, but then my mother caught her breath.

'What? Would a woman dare to do such a thing?' I heard her say.

I knew nothing about sex at that age, of course, but I had some vague idea of what they were talking about, enough to know that it was a dangerous topic.

Not long afterwards, on a day when the smell of the peaches was stifling in the summer heat, I was in my room with my mother, listening to the broadcast announcing the end of the war. My father did not come back until September, too late for him to be served peaches. But the fruit that lay rotting on the ground continued to fill the garden and the house with its heavy, sweet perfume, and my father must have been aware of it long before he reached the doorway.

Still, what had my mother been talking about with the man that day? As I thought about it years later, their strangely forced repartee began to flare up, incandescent, a point of peculiar brilliance in my memory. Here was the landlord, a man with a reputation for debauchery, trying to laugh off indecencies that he had broached with reluctance, while on the other hand, there was my mother, increasingly serious to the point of catching her breath. Indeed, it was she, a woman in her prime left alone to guard the chastity of her marriage bed, who sought to draw out this kind of talk. The sharp contrast between the two of them struck my heart again and again: the man grown weary of women; the woman separated from her husband by years of war. As far as I could tell, her life had undergone no change, and it was precisely because of this that I recalled the scene as though witnessing a dangerous tightrope act.

I had been a child then, but surely I had said to myself: *My mother is a soldier's wife, not the kind of woman to enjoy such vulgar talk with another man.* But my skin, no doubt, had been feeling something a little different. I still liked to sleep with my mother in those days. And in the winter, especially, there were many opportunities to do so. At bedtime, of course, I would get into my own bed, but I would snuggle into hers after going to the toilet in the middle of the night. Too sleepy to chase me out, she would have to make room for me. Then, drifting on the edge of sleep, she would clasp me to her breast, entwine her naked legs with mine. Where the nightgown had slipped open, the flesh was hot, as if with fever.

Before long, this had become my nightly pleasure, until finally I myself no longer knew whether I was waking up because I needed to go to the toilet, or going to the toilet was an excuse to be held by my mother. Surely, when she held me, the feeling that came through my skin was not just my own pleasure, but the jagged restlessness of my mother's flesh, and the sinful awareness that I had thrust myself into the void left by my father and was enjoying her greedily.

Yes, a third person not actually present could well have been part of that night scene on the hill. And was it not my father? Some unusual circumstance must have been responsible for my mother's being there at that strange time and having me with her.

They had quarrelled, perhaps, and the repercussions had come to me. I do seem to remember something that happened between them just before the war.

My father was warming one hand over the charcoal brazier and commanding my mother, sitting on the matted floor opposite him, to 'Go, I said! Go now!'

The ringing of the copper kettle made the silence that followed seem horribly long and suffocating.

'I'm telling you, go and settle it properly, once and for all,' he said, his authority overwhelming. My mother hung her head in silence. He turned away.

'But it's so late . . .' she murmured in desperation.

'I don't give a damn. You go,' he said and looked away again.

'Please, not tonight. I'll go in the morning. I swear I will.'

'I said tonight and I meant it.'

Their confrontation went on, and eventually my mother seemed to be crying.

'Oh, please forgive me,' she sobbed. 'Forgive your wife!'

She reached for the hand he held over the brazier, but he swept her hand away as if it were something vile, knocking the fire tongs into the ashes. As they fell, she crumpled before him, clinging to his knees.

Perhaps he had only been trying to avoid her touch, but his hand had struck hers, and this filled me with terror. Now it was my turn to burst into tears, I suspect, and my mother, resigned to what she must do, probably led me out into the night.

The failing for which my mother was being blamed that night may have amounted to nothing at all. Obstinate military man that he was, my father often tormented her this way, and she submitted meekly.

That scene, too, ends abruptly, and I have no idea where it leads, no way of knowing what came of it. But even now I can hear my mother in tears at my father's knee: 'Oh, please forgive me. Forgive your wife!' Her cry rings through the darkness, caressing, seductive. I do not doubt that my father heard the almost unseemly erotic appeal in her voice, the soft, clinging tones of the Osaka woman. And he did not succumb to her sexual onslaught because I was there, watching.

Was not *this* my cold winter night? And if it was, then my mother had taken me to the neighbouring town not to buy anything, but to accomplish something far more important – or at least, something far more painful. But the further I pursue this line of reasoning, the more confused I become, for another part of me clings stubbornly to the memory of pushing the old pram down the hill with my mother through the winter moonlight, our breath white in the cold.

After wandering thus in endless circles, I feel as though I have been hurled once again on to the hill on the road that – today as then – links our town with the next.

I know that my mother and I passed that place wheeling a pram – but does all certainty end there?

Having retreated fifty paces, let me fall back a hundred: perhaps I was merely *riding* in that pram? Or, yielding another hundred paces: perhaps the dark hill – the one place that seemed more eerily unknown than any other to my boyhood imagination – perhaps this setting could be an image that stayed with me from a time when I passed there alone several years later? And through some weird manipulation of memory, I may have been arbitrarily throwing into this setting an image of myself in the pram wrapped in my mother's shawl, or an image of myself on another road on another night that I passed asleep and only heard about later, or yet a wholly different scene of my mother and me pushing something in the pram.

What emerges from this is the arcane spectacle of me as a boy, wheeling a pram that holds my infant self.

OGAWA YŌKO

The Tale of the House of Physics

Translated by Ted Goossen

On my last day at the publishing house, I jotted down the authors' names and titles of the many volumes I had worked on during my thirty-two years as a book editor. This was no exercise in self-congratulation – a 'Gosh, look how much I got done!' kind of thing. Rather, quite on the spur of the moment, I listed the names and titles as they came back to me from long ago, scribbling on the thick brown manila envelope I'd just received from the company (filled with complicated documents concerning my pension and health-insurance plans as well as membership information from the retirees' association, the Can't Hear Ya Club). Yet I must confess that, as I sat alone in my study that evening reflecting on the career I had just safely concluded, surrounded by piles of books overflowing their shelves, I did grow rather sentimental.

Once I started making the list, I was amazed at how easily the individual books came back to me. If I wasn't sure about something, a quick glance at my notebooks was all it took to set me straight. Strangely, the writers and poets I remembered most vividly were those who had died long before, or had disappeared, or had broken off with me over some trivial misunderstanding. The conversations we had shared, their gestures, how they held their liquor, their voices on the phone, their red-inked edits on the galleys: along with these came clear images of the books themselves, from their cover designs to the blurbs on their belly bands, as I filled in my list on the back of the manila envelope.

I was not an editor whose name ever inspired adjectives like *popular, gifted* or *dynamic*. Indeed, I was worlds removed from editors who tend a flock of best-selling authors while orchestrating brilliant debuts for their up-and-coming talent. No, my redeeming points were my steadiness and my dogged determination – apart from those, I had nothing to boast about.

Although most of my writers were strangers to the best-seller lists, their aims were high. The fact that these aims went largely unrecognized, however, left the writers prone to bouts of lethargy and despair. Whenever I saw them being sucked down into that silent swamp, it was my role to send them the message that everything was fine, that they were heading in the right direction, that there was nothing to worry about. My unspoken message was: if you give up now, your work will never come out.

There are editors who stand as beacons to light the way for writers to follow. And others who lash their wrists to those of their writers in order to lead them like sightless runners in a long-distance race. The role that I took upon myself, I must confess, was far less ambitious. My chief fear was that I would become a hindrance to my writers' work. Sometimes that scared me even more than the thought of a misprint on the cover.

'Don't get in the way' was the watchword that defined my career as an editor. The more deeply I admired a writer, the more care I took not to draw too close: rather, I occupied the most inconspicuous corner I could find. Yet that corner had to possess a secret path to the writer's inner ear for me to fulfil my primary responsibility. My challenge was to discover how to access that path, so that my whispers would rise to my author's mind like drops of water carrying nutrients from the soil through the capillaries to the pistil of a plant. If I could but secure that conduit, the writer would apprehend my words of reassurance as if they came not from me but from within, and thus be emboldened to pick up the pen to write the first line.

My list of books quickly surpassed a hundred volumes, crowding the back of the manila envelope. The familiar books surrounding me became even quieter; the darkness outside my window (I had neglected to draw the curtains) deepened. Strewn about my desk were objects that had fallen out of my notebooks – business cards, obscure notes to myself, loose pages from colour-sample books.

Whenever I bade farewell to my writers, I always watched them until they disappeared from sight, whether their mode of departure was taxi, lift or train. This did not stem so much from social etiquette as it did from my compulsion to study their retreating backs. Those who live by the pen, a fragile instrument that can easily be snapped in two, are themselves equally vulnerable; yet that vulnerability can only be perceived when one views their departure from the rear. This is as true for the first-time novelist as it is for the literary lion.

I loved to watch them as they walked away, though my shoulders might be soaking in a sudden shower or my body crying out with fatigue in the dim, pre-dawn light. Their postures revealed the depth of their fragility, which I could then take in my hands and read, as one might a holy book. I think I was not bidding them farewell so much as I was praying for them. Praying that the weight of their burden would not drive them to their knees and send the pen flying from their hands.

To be honest, some writers made me want to direct a curse in their direction, not a prayer. More than a few times I was forced to ponder how someone who wrote such a beautiful novel could be such a jerk. A writer's character, however, lies outside the part of the field that an editor can be expected to cover. I at least stuck to that policy. When a writer of mine wrote a book that delighted its readers, I was able to love it unconditionally, however nasty its author might be, and I could offer up a prayer to his or her back upon parting.

By now my list filled one whole side of the manila envelope. Title (author's name); title (author's name); title (author's name) – just a succession of meaningless signs to an outsider, perhaps, but to me a long lyric poem bestowed by a galaxy of writers.

When I reached the end, I checked for omissions and corrected any characters I had miswritten or left out. Finally, to give my list some added panache, I inserted a bullet point before each entry. When I was done, I went back to the space I had left at the top of the list and added a single line, the name of the very first book I had ever edited:

- *The Tale of the House of Physics* (author's name unknown)

Directly across the lane from the house that I grew up in sat an antiquated building called the Information Management Office of the Institute for Advanced Studies in Particle Physics. Despite the imposing sign attached to the vitrified brick columns of its gate, its days as a functioning administrative office were long past. Indeed, moss and mould had so deformed the characters on the sign they could barely be made out. No one locally knew what purpose the place had served.

It was a Western building totally out of sync with the rest of the neighbourhood, built in a style that might be called colonial, and rendered all the stranger by its green but riotously unkempt tree-shaded garden. If you looked closely at the features of the building – the gambrel roof curving gracefully to the eaves, the white-painted clapboard walls in bright contrast with the green of the trees, the scalloped arch framing an entranceway that bathed the front porch in quiet shadow – you could see it had once been a magnificent structure, but long years of neglect had left all that beauty in disarray. Vines ate away at the roof's curves, peeled paint created a weird patchwork on the walls, and the porch housed countless bats, which emerged at dusk to fly about the garden, squeaking their disapproval. The hanging wisteria had once been so thick that the wind never ruffled its petals, and so heavy that the trellis had finally collapsed; the pungent fumes from the fermenting algae in the garden pond had grown so worrisome one summer that the fire brigade was called in to investigate.

People in the neighbourhood feared and hated what they called the House of Physics, but it was such a convenient landmark that they always mentioned it when giving directions to their homes from the train station.

The House of Physics was home to one person, a single woman. No one believed she was there legally, but neither were they about to snitch on her to city hall in those more laid-back times, and since the rightful owners never complained, things were allowed to remain ambiguous.

She was a thin woman with long arms and legs, two plaits that hung past her waist and thick glasses. Whatever the season, she wore a thin dress and sandals on her bare feet. She seemed strongly averse to people. When she walked to the market near the station, she always hugged the far side of the street, teetering precariously on the edge of the roadside ditch like a gymnast on a balance beam. Her swinging plaits made her look as if she had four arms as she struggled to maintain her balance.

People in the neighbourhood kept their distance from her, mainly because of the way she was constantly muttering incomprehensible things to herself. In shops, she would just point to whatever she wanted to buy, and if someone tried to direct a kind word to her, all they heard in reply was a stream of meaningless syllables. The eyes behind her glasses were constantly moving to avoid meeting anyone's gaze. Every community had its resident eccentric in those days, an outcast despised by all, and she was certainly ours.

No one knew anything about her – her name, or where she came from. There was no shortage of wild theories, though, when the local women gathered to gossip. Some said she had been a girl Friday at the Research Institute; others said, no, she was actually the daughter of the university administrator who had once run the place; while still others scoffed, saying that she was just a homeless vagrant.

Yet there was a side to the woman from the House of Physics grownups never saw. With my friends and me, she was always bragging about herself. True, her boasts were so transparent even we could see right through them, but, unlike her babble, they were at least framed in proper sentences.

'I used to be a writer,' she told us in a voice made hoarse by incessant muttering.

'What the heck is that?'

There was no place more fun for us than the House of Physics. We sneaked in to play our war games in the garden, and when we were tired, we hung out on the steps at the entranceway. This usually drew the woman out to join us and indulge in her bragging.

'A writer is someone who writes books. Don't you know that much?'

We responded to her challenge.

'Sure we do.'

'Yeah.'

'We learn all that stuff at school.'

Just as the garden was the perfect place to play, the woman was the perfect playmate – or, if you can excuse the cruelty of the expression, the perfect toy. A peculiar, unpredictable toy that provided fun without complications.

'Now pay attention. Some writers write novels. Novels, get it? That's what a novelist is. Someone like me.'

The woman thumped her flat chest with her hand. Yet even then her eyes would not meet ours. We could see the hollow of her breastbone through the sagging neck of her dress. The legs draped over the porch steps were covered with scabs.

'Writers are supposed to be great, aren't they? What's so great about you?'

'Yeah, that's right.'

'Sounds like a big fib to me.'

We knocked bats down from the porch ceiling with sticks, clambered up the drain pipe, pulled long weeds out of the pond and swung them around. If one of us was hurling acorns against the roof, another was yanking on the woman's long plaits, which were so caked in grease and dirt they never came undone, no matter how hard you tried. We behaved as badly as we could in the knowledge that, at the House of Physics, all would be forgiven. We knew the woman would never get angry with us. She was too busy bragging.

'It's not that great people become writers. It's that writing important books makes us great. Look, this is how we scoop the air . . .' she said, cupping her hands and raising them to the level of her forehead. 'It looks empty, but a story is hiding there, waiting to be heard. You ordinary people can't see or hear anything, right? But a writer is different. We know the story's there. It's just waiting for someone it can really trust to show its true form. Stories are timid, bashful things, you see.'

'That looks weird – you can't write like that. You have to sit at a desk with a fountain pen.'

'If you're a real writer, show us your book!'

'Yeah, bring it here and show it to us!'

'Bring it here! Bring it here!' we chanted.

'Everything was burnt up in the war. Really . . . everything,' she answered, her cupped hands still held high. 'You can't imagine my joy when I saw my book on a bookshop shelf for the first time. Just an inch-wide bundle of paper, but it sparkled like a newborn jewel, like the crystallization of cosmic rays. Readers from far away sent piles of grateful letters. I felt your story was meant for me, they wrote, thank you so very much. But their letters all went up in flames. Where, oh where, have they gone?'

Just then a drop of bat shit landed squarely on the woman's outstretched palms.

'Yuck, now your hands are full of germs!'

'That'll teach you to tell fibs!'

'Hooray! Hooray!'

The timing had been too perfect. Singing madly, we danced around the porch, stamped across the grounds and exited the House of Physics. As we passed through the gate, I looked back and saw the woman in the same position, her shit-smeared hands raised like a chalice to the sky.

My mother didn't believe me when I said the woman could speak normally. And she found the notion that she had once been a writer preposterous.

'I don't want you talking to that person!' she snapped whenever I mentioned the woman from the House of Physics.

I was on my way home from an errand at the market near the station one day when I saw the woman passing along the narrow alley that runs parallel to the main street. As always, she was tiptoeing along the edge of the ditch on the far side of the path, but this time she was dragging a thin stalk of bamboo behind her. Then I remembered – today was Tanabata, the seventh day of the seventh month, when the Weaver Star and the Cowherd Star have their annual lovers' rendezvous in the sky. The market had been giving out bamboo stalks and slips of coloured paper to write wishes on, and the woman seldom passed up anything free.

The swishing of the bamboo on the ground blended in my ears with the woman's mumbling. Usually her balance on the very edge of the ditch was perfect, but this time, perhaps because she was dragging an unfamiliar object, her bony legs, no thicker than the bamboo, looked unsteady. The hem of her dress swayed along with the bending branch.

Just as I was about to overtake her, I noticed the branch was shedding its coloured paper slips one after another on to the ground. I picked one up and read it.

May my book appear in bookshops.

The characters looked like a traced silhouette of the woman's spindly body. Written in a trembling, tentative hand, they drooped in sad isolation from one another. The character for 'book' (本) in particular had elongated sides that resembled the woman's arm-length plaits as seen from behind. The roughly cut pieces of coloured paper were limp and tattered from their contact with the ground.

May my novel become a book.

She and I were the only ones in the alley. Not wishing to overtake her, I slowed my pace. A hazy moon had risen in the sky, which was dyed red by the setting sun. Our two shadows connected at her feet, forming a line that extended to the far side of the alley.

May someone read my book.

The woman was having too much difficulty dragging the long stalk of bamboo to notice the loss of the paper wishes. Instead of soaring to heaven along the flowing Milky Way, her prayers fluttered briefly in the breeze, then fell to languish on the ground.

May I write a good novel.

I picked up the pieces of paper one by one but had no idea what to do with them. I couldn't throw them away, nor could I stop her and hand them over, so I just silently stuffed them in my pocket. What else could I do?

The games we boys played grew wilder with the start of the summer holidays. The House of Physics was in its liveliest season: black stag beetles fought their duels and mayflies mated as the cicadas' shrill cries echoed through the garden. Seeds that had blown in from elsewhere invaded even the smallest spaces with their leaves and flowers and vines. They too seemed to realize that everything was permitted at the House of Physics.

The incident began with our discovery of a dead weasel in the tall pampas grass next to the river. We could find no wounds on the body, but the animal had obviously died in agony. Its fur stood on end, its tail stuck straight out and its legs were splayed at strange angles. Its small black eyes glistened with moisture, as if staring too long at a single spot had left them starting out of its head. Maggots squirmed around the edges, trying to burrow their way inside.

We stood there at a loss for words, just staring at the weasel. It was no bigger than a cat, but being dead made it look much larger.

'Let's bury it at the House of Physics.'

I can't remember which of us said that, but the proposal met with immediate and unanimous support. We couldn't bear prolonging our silent vigil; we had to find a way – any way – to turn things in a livelier direction. For that the House of Physics was clearly the most appropriate setting.

Reinvigorated, we began putting our plans into action. To shake off the pall the weasel's carcass had cast over us, we threw ourselves into the work, each of us excited by our own marvellous ideas for action: one would look for a plank to be the weasel's stretcher; another would flick away the maggots with the end of a twig; while yet another would requisition a shovel from home.

We stopped sweating when we stepped into the cool green air of the grounds of the House of Physics, where the sun's glare could never reach. The sounds of the outside world receded into the distance, replaced by the insistent presence of the plant and animal life around us. Walking quietly so as not to alert the woman to our presence, we crept through the trees and along the garden wall. The two boys carrying the plank were especially vigilant, petrified that the weasel might fall to the ground. It had been no easy task to get the body on top of the board in the first place. Since no one had been brave enough to touch it, in the end we had pushed and prodded it into place with short sticks. The woman was nowhere to be seen, all the windows being either shuttered or covered with tattered curtains.

We decided the best place for the burial was under the collapsed wisteria trellis. The few vines that had survived there were tightly entangled, creating just the atmosphere we were looking for.

At first the dirt was soft and moist. The boy who was our leader shovelled, while the rest of us pitched in with trowels. Beneath the dead leaves and mulch, however, we ran into clay soil the colour of lead, which forced us to step up our efforts. We unearthed everything imaginable – earthworms, slugs, centipedes, a chrysalis of some kind, eggs, snail shells, tree roots, seashells, teeth, bones, nails, screws, buttons, but nobody said anything. All we could hear were the sounds of pitched soil and our increasingly ragged breathing. With no wind and the sun still high in the sky, we worked in a motionless, dappled world. Only when a bird launched itself from a tree branch did the dapples tremble momentarily. An alley cat was lying on its belly on the moss nearby. From time to time, it would open its slit-like eyes to watch us.

Intent as we were on making the hole a little deeper, then a little deeper again, we lost track of why we were digging. None of us even glanced at the dead weasel beside us. It waited patiently, its barely attached eyes still fixed on a single point.

'Okay, that should do it!' the boy with the shovel finally announced, to our relief. We were all sweaty, but remembering the purpose of our effort excited us again.

No one had wanted to touch the dead weasel before, but now that the time had come to slide it into the hole, everyone wanted to play a part, so we picked up the makeshift stretcher together.

'One, two, three,' we chanted in our schoolboy English, and dumped the body into the pit. It was over all too soon, given the trouble it had taken. The weasel's eyes dropped out on impact. What faced the sky now were two tiny hollows.

The summer holidays ended and the autumn rains began. They fell quietly but steadily, bringing a temporary truce to our war games in the House of Physics.

I don't know what made me so uneasy when I glanced at the House of Physics that day on my way home from school, but something bothered me about the place. I stood there with my back to my own house, my backpack growing wetter and wetter, staring at the garden. For a change, I was alone – none of my friends were with me. The sign over the gate, the porch steps, the pond, everything was soaking wet. All I could hear was the falling rain.

When I stepped through the gate, I felt the first pang of fear. My boots sank further in the mud with each step, and the dripping leaves made it seem as if the rain had picked up. I found myself tightening my grip on my umbrella. The cracked steps where the woman always sat were black with bat shit or perhaps the woman's own grime.

Then it hit me – where were the bats? They should have been hanging from the arched entranceway waiting for the sun to set, yet not one was there.

I could feel the black goo sticking to my boots as I walked up the steps. A window beside the door was wide open, the curtains poking through. When I lifted them up with my hand and peered inside, my eyes met those of the woman for a split second.

She lay on an iron cot wrapped in a thin blanket, and though I was just a child, I could tell she was in very bad shape. Once inside the room, I could see that her face was pale and bloodless, her forehead oily with sweat, and the feet peeking out from beneath the blanket were quivering. She stared fixedly into the air as if to blink would be to invite the end.

Her thick glasses lay half buried in the wrinkled sheets. The only proof she was still alive was the white drool trickling down her cheek and the blood oozing from her cracked lips.

'Is something wrong?' I asked, suddenly fearful that her heart might stop at the sound of my voice. She didn't answer. The only hopeful sign was that, despite her condition, her two plaits had preserved their shape – they lay neatly on the blanket with not a hair out of place.

'Are you sick?'

At last she blinked, although, as always, she refused to look in my direction. Gathering my courage, I reached out to touch her forehead with the tip of one finger. At first it just seemed sticky, but then I felt the abnormal heat.

The room was dark and gloomy, with high ceilings. Despite the count-less days I had spent playing in its garden, this was my first time inside the building. Its mantelpiece and doorknobs, not to mention the lattice pattern of its windowpanes, gave it a Western feel, yet vestiges of its for-mer identity as the Information Management Office of the Institute for Advanced Studies in Particle Physics were apparent in the binder-stuffed cabinet and the massive office desk with the typewriter perched on top. As with the exterior, however, all was neglected and run down. The woman's bed occupied the centre of the room, as if it had pushed every-thing else aside.

I had to find some way to cool her off. I put down my backpack and looked around for a towel. A dirty-looking cloth – a dishrag or handkerchief – was draped over the railing of the bed. That'll do, I thought. As I reached out to grab it, however, I noticed a plate of food on the desk just beyond the typewriter.

Whatever was on the plate looked greasy and gelatinous. It smelled bad, too. I could make out what appeared to be the flat, broad tops of several large mushrooms. They had crimson speckles. Was that because they had gone bad, or were they . . . ?

'Did you eat these?' I burst out. 'Couldn't you tell they were poisonous?'

Tossing the cloth away, I ran from the room and down the steps, leav-ing my backpack behind. This wasn't something a cool cloth on the forehead could cure – I had to find help, and quickly. Immediately. With this single thought in mind, I moved too fast, tripped over a tree root and fell so hard I lost a boot. I pitched face first into the mud. It tasted foul, as if I had taken a bite of the mushrooms.

I had fallen precisely where we had buried the weasel under the collapsed wisteria trellis that summer. There should have been a mound there, but at some point the earth had sunk so much that I feared the weasel's rotting carcass might reveal itself. Huddled together there in the depression was a cluster of mushrooms. Mushrooms with crimson speckles on their crowns.

I think the Thermos flask full of my mother's vegetable soup that I took to the House of Physics each evening thereafter was the outward manifestation of the guilt I felt. As it turned out, the incident was resolved much more neatly than I had imagined: the woman was driven to the hospital in the car owned by the head of our neighbourhood association, treated and then returned home the same day for what was determined to be nothing worse than a common case of food poisoning.

I told no one the secret of the mushrooms. It was not that I feared the adults' anger. No, I think I wanted to bear sole responsibility as a kind of solitary penance for what had been caused by the weasel we had buried in the garden. Then again, I may have felt sharing the secret with the woman would comfort her in her isolation.

'I'm leaving your soup here,' I said, placing the Thermos, a mug and a spoon on the desk next to what appeared to be donations from members of the neighbourhood association: an apple, a bottle of cod-liver oil and a hot-water bottle.

'Try a mouthful of the soup,' I coaxed. 'It's good for you.'

Day by day, the woman's condition improved. She was even thinner than before, a painful sight beneath the blanket, but her face had regained some of its vitality, and she was able to blink normally again.

'Now let's see if your temperature's down,' I said, leaning over the bed and placing a hand on her forehead. The woman was mumbling to herself. 'Good, good. Talking to yourself proves how much better you are.' Her forehead was cool and dry, almost parched – the oily sweat had disappeared. 'See,' I said. 'Your fever's gone.'

She was speaking so quietly she seemed to be breathing the words. It was as if she were convinced that only if she spoke in a whisper could the message pouring from her barely parted lips reach its faraway recipient.

Then it hit me – these were not incoherent ramblings at all; they had a definite meaning. The problem was they were virtually inaudible. That was why no one had ever paid attention.

I opened one of the desk drawers, pulled out a pencil stub and a few documents left from when the place had been a working office, and approached the head of the bed, where I could manage to make out what she was saying. The documents were covered with indecipherable formulae and symbols, but they were blank on the back, so taking up the pencil, I began committing her words to paper.

The story she told was like none I had encountered before. Its hero was a fragment from an expired world, an atomic particle flung out into the universe by an exploding star. Borne along on gravitational waves, he (she referred to the particle this way) had wandered through realms of darkness, slipping between stars, planets and comets. Because he was the tiniest particle in the universe, he couldn't get anyone to notice him. His lot was to pass through the cracks in the world entirely alone. He had but one modest wish – to bump into some other entity. He spent his long nights entranced by thoughts of what that encounter might feel like. The woman described the darkness vividly: it was a place she seemed to know well, stretched out before her very eyes. She spoke in the particle's words. Using his tiny voice.

I recorded everything I could make out, although, to be honest, there were many words I didn't understand. Focusing intently on her lips, I tried not to miss a single word of the many that gushed out. I had never written so much; in fact, I began to worry that the pencil would wear down before I could finish. Her delivery didn't change at all with me listening. It was exactly the same as when she had dragged the bamboo stalk along the narrow lane, shedding the paper wishes. I took great care not to disrupt her rhythm with a cough or a sniffle. Instinctively, I understood that recording her story meant not getting in the way.

The particle was aware he would turn into light the moment he bumped into something else. Nothing in the universe was more beautiful; yet there would be no one to exclaim in wonder as that light faded into nothingness. The particle was forever falling from the sky, sometimes here, other times there, seeking contact with someone as it passed through. The woman's story spun and circled, rolled and swelled. The particle's voyage continued on without beginning or end. On occasion, phlegm would catch in her throat and her voice would quaver. At such times, I would help her through the difficulty by whispering in her ear, 'Don't worry, it's all right' – a phrase I would often repeat to myself in the years to come.

The garden's trees watched us expectantly, holding their breath, as the sun went down. The woman's glasses lay by her bedside, a distorted image of the black garden reflected on their surface. My earlobes tingled with her faint breath.

As the woman recovered, life returned to normal. We saw her walking along the edge of ditches with her two plaits swinging, scaring those she met with her perpetual monologue. We resumed our war games and our mockery of the woman's boasts. Yet, however absorbed I was in racing about the garden, I always froze in my tracks when I caught sight of the weasel's grave. The mushrooms were gone. And the bats too failed to return.

When I got home that night, I made a clean copy of what I had jotted down on the back of the documents, added a cardboard cover and bound the whole thing with string. I chose the title *The Tale of the House of Physics*, carefully calculated the precise centre of the page with a ruler, and then, heart pounding lest I make a mistake, wrote the six Japanese characters (BUTSU-RI-NO-YAKATA-MONO-GATARI) with a fat-tipped Magic Marker. It was a thin book, and far from elegant, but it was a book nonetheless. The first book I ever made.

I lacked the courage to hand the book to the woman myself, so I sneaked into the building when she had gone to market and placed it in the cabinet where all the binders were lined up, standing it in the very centre of the shelf where she could not fail to notice it. Sandwiched among the thick, serious binders, it stood proudly, secure in its privileged position.

The woman left the House of Physics the spring I left primary school. No one could tell us if she had been evicted or if she had moved by choice. Nor did anyone seem to know where she had gone. People were slow to notice that she had left but quick to believe the rumour, totally unfounded, that she would suddenly reappear. As time passed, however, they grew used to her absence, until in the end, hardly anyone remembered she had ever existed.

I stepped inside the doors of the House of Physics only once after her disappearance. By then, our season of feverish war games had long since passed. The iron cot and the typewriter rested under a thick coat of dust in the same space they had occupied before. Then my eyes moved to the cabinet. Sure enough, there was a narrow empty space where *The Tale of the House of Physics* had once stood.

I pictured the back of the woman as she slipped unnoticed through the cracks of the world like an atomic particle. I recalled her sitting there with her cupped hands raised to the heavens as if to catch the particles raining down, and I thought about her wish to see their light, the most beautiful in the universe.

The Tale of the House of Physics sits close by her side. It alone will keep her company. Watching her depart, I clasp my hands in prayer.

KUNIKIDA DOPPO

Unforgettable People

Translated by Jay Rubin

Just beyond the Futago landing, where the ferry from Tokyo crosses the Tama River, lies the old post town of Mizonokuchi. Midway through the long, narrow town stands an inn, the Kameya.

It was early March. The sky was overcast, and a strong wind blew from the north. Always bleak, the town seemed colder and more desolate than usual. Yesterday's snow remained on the thatched roofs that formed uneven lines down both sides of the roadway, and from the edges of the southern eaves, drops of snowmelt fell dancing in the wind. Even the rippling muddy water in sandal tracks seemed to be shivering with the cold. The sun went down, and soon most of the shops closed for the night. The town lay silent, huddled along the dark road. As an inn, the Kameya remained open, its paper windows aglow, though few travellers had stopped to spend the night, it seemed. The only sound from within was the occasional rapping of a heavy metal pipe against the wooden edge of a charcoal brazier.

All at once the sliding door shot back and a large man eased himself across the threshold. The innkeeper was still leaning against the brazier, mulling over the day's receipts, and before he could look up the man had taken three long strides across the dirt-floored entryway and planted himself before him. The newcomer looked somewhat less than thirty years of age. He wore a Western-style suit and cloth cap, but his straw sandals and gaiters left his feet exposed like those of any Japanese traveller. He carried an umbrella in his right hand, and he hugged a small satchel under his left arm.

'I'd like a room for the night.'

Still absorbed in examining his guest's outfit, the innkeeper said nothing. Just then a handclap sounded from the back.

'Take care of number six!' the innkeeper bellowed. Then, still leaning against the brazier, he asked, 'And you, sir, are from . . . ?'

The man's shoulders stiffened, and a scowl crossed his face. But then, with the hint of a smile, he answered, 'Me? I'm from Tokyo.'

'And you are on your way to . . . ?'

'Hachiōji.'

The traveller sat down on the raised wooden floor and began to untie his gaiters.

'Hmm, Tokyo to Hachiōji, is it? This is an odd way to be going, don't you think?'

The innkeeper's suspicions seemed to have been aroused – he looked as though he had more to say.

Sensing this, the traveller spoke first. 'I live in Tokyo, but that's not where I'm coming from today. I got a late start from Kawasaki, and before I knew it the sun was down. Let me have some hot water, please.'

'Bring some hot water right away!' the innkeeper shouted. 'It must have been cold on the road today. Hachiōji is probably even colder.'

His words were friendly enough, but the innkeeper's overall manner was far from welcoming. He was about sixty years old. Over his stout frame he wore a heavily quilted jacket, which made his broad head jut out as though attached directly to his shoulders. His eyes, set into a wide, fleshy face, drooped at the corners. There was something tough and inflexible about him, but he impressed the traveller at once as a straightforward old fellow.

The traveller had washed his feet and was still drying them when the innkeeper shouted, 'Show the gentleman to number seven!'

To the gentleman himself he had nothing more to say. Nor did he glance at him again as he retired to his room. A black cat appeared from the kitchen, crept on to the master's lap and curled up there. The old man might have been unaware of this. His eyes were shut tight. Soon his right hand edged towards his tobacco holder, and his stubby fingers began to roll some tobacco into a little ball.

'When number six is through with the tub, take care of number seven!'

Startled, the cat leaped down.

'Not you, stupid!'

The cat scurried into the kitchen. A wall clock struck eight slow gongs.

'Grandma, Kichizō must be tired. Put the warmer in his bed and let him go to sleep, poor fellow.' The old man himself sounded sleepy.

'He's in here,' came the voice of an old woman from the kitchen. 'But he's still studying.'

'He is? Go to bed now, Kichizō. You can get up early tomorrow and do that. Put the warmer in his bed now, Grandma.'

'Yes, right away.'

In the kitchen, the old woman and the maid looked at each other and tittered. There was a loud yawn out front.

'He's the tired one,' the old woman muttered as she put coals into a sooty bed warmer. She was a small woman, perhaps in her late fifties.

Out front the paper door rattled in the wind as a light shower of rain swept past.

'Close the shutters for the night!' the old man shouted. With an exasperated click of the tongue, he muttered, 'Rain again, damn it!'

He was right. The wind had picked up, and now it was really beginning to pour. Spring was on its way, but a freezing cold wind, bearing rain and sleet, tore across the broad Musashi Plain. All night long it raged over the dark little town of Mizonokuchi.

Midnight had come and gone, but the lamp in room seven burned brightly. Everyone in the Kameya was asleep except the two guests who sat facing each other in the middle of the room. Outside, the storm raged on. The shutters sent up a constant rattle.

'If this keeps up, you won't be able to leave tomorrow,' said the man from room six.

'I wouldn't mind spending the day here. I'm in no hurry.'

Both men were flushed, their noses bright red. Three freshly warmed bottles of sake stood on the low table next to them, and sake remained in their cups. They sat comfortably cross-legged on the matted floor with the brazier between them as warmer and ashtray. The visitor from room six would puff on his cigarette now and then and reach out from his loose padded sleeping robe, baring his arm to the elbow to shake off the ashes. They spoke without reserve, but it was clear the two had met that night. Perhaps something had led to a remark or two through the sliding door between their rooms. The man in number six, feeling lonely, would have made the first move, followed by an exchange of business cards. An order of sake, formalities dispensed with, and soon frank expressions were creeping into their polite speech.

'Ōtsu Benjirō' read the business card of the man in room seven. The other's was inscribed 'Akiyama Matsunosuke'. Neither card had the usual listing of titles and affiliations.

Ōtsu was the man in the Western suit who had arrived after sunset. His tall, thin frame and pale face contrasted with the other's appearance. Akiyama, in his mid-twenties, was round and ruddy, and the friendly look in his eyes made him appear to be smiling constantly. Ōtsu was an unknown writer, Akiyama an unknown painter. By some odd chance the two young unknown artists had come together in this rural inn.

'We probably ought to get to bed. There's no one left for us to tear apart.'

Their conversation had ranged from art to literature to religion. Absorbed in their scathing criticism of the day's noted artists and writers, they had not even noticed earlier when the clock struck eleven.

'It's still early,' said Akiyama, smiling. 'We can't leave tomorrow. We might as well talk all night.'

'What time is it anyway?' Ōtsu said, glancing at the watch beside him on the floor. 'It's after eleven!'

'Well, that's it, it's going to be an all-nighter,' Akiyama said, not at all bothered by the time. Staring at his sake cup, he added, 'But if you're sleepy, go ahead . . .'

'No, not at all. I thought *you* were sleepy. I left Kawasaki late today and walked less than ten miles, so I feel fine.'

'I'm not ready for bed, either. But I thought I'd just borrow this if you were.'

Akiyama picked up what looked like a manuscript of some ten pages. On the cover was the title 'Unforgettable People'.

'No, it's really no good,' said Ōtsu. 'It's like the pencil sketches you artists do – nothing that other people can appreciate.' But he made no attempt to retrieve the document. Akiyama glanced at a few pages.

'Sketches have their own special interest as sketches. I think I'd like to read this.'

'Let me see it a minute, will you?' Ōtsu took the sheets and leafed through them. Neither man said anything for a time. Only now did they seem to hear the storm outside. Ōtsu listened, rapt, as he stared at his manuscript.

'This kind of night is a writer's territory, don't you think?' Akiyama said. Ōtsu, silent, seemed unaware that he had spoken. Akiyama could not tell whether Ōtsu was listening to the storm or reading his manuscript, or whether, indeed, his thoughts had flown to someone far away. But he felt that Ōtsu's expression – his eyes – had entered a painter's territory.

Ōtsu turned to Akiyama with the look of one who has awakened from a dream. 'Rather than have you read this,' he said, 'it would make more sense for me to talk about what I have written. What do you say? This is just an outline. You wouldn't really understand it.'

'That would be even better – to hear all the details from you.' Akiyama saw that Ōtsu's eyes were moist and gave off a strange gleam.

'I'll tell you everything I can remember. If you find it dull, though, don't hesitate to tell me. Meanwhile, I won't hesitate to go on talking. It's odd, but suddenly I feel I'd like to have you hear this.'

Akiyama added charcoal to the fire and set the cooled bottles of sake into the warmer.

'"An unforgettable person is not of necessity one whom we dare not forget." Look, this is the first sentence I have written here.' Ōtsu showed Akiyama the manuscript. 'See? First, let me explain what I mean by it. That way you can understand the overall theme – though I'm sure you understand it already.'

'No, never mind that. Just go ahead. I'll listen like an ordinary reader. Pardon me if I lie down . . .'

Akiyama stretched out on the floor, a cigarette in his mouth. Resting his head on his right hand, he looked at Ōtsu with the trace of a smile in his eyes.

'We can't simply call parents and children or friends or the teachers and others to whom we are obligated "unforgettable people". These are people "whom we dare not forget". But then there are others – complete strangers – to whom we are bound by neither love nor duty. Forgetting them would imply neither neglect of duty nor want of compassion. Yet these are the very ones we cannot forget. I would not say that for everyone there are such unforgettable people, but for me there certainly are. Perhaps for you, too.'

Akiyama nodded in silence.

'It was the middle of spring, I remember, when I was nineteen years old. I was not feeling well and decided to leave school in Tokyo and go home for a rest, taking the Inland Sea steamer from Osaka. There was no wind that day, and the sea was calm. But all of this happened so long ago, I can remember nothing about the other passengers, or the captain, or the boy who served refreshments. No doubt there was some fellow passenger kind enough to pour my tea, and others with whom I chatted on deck, but none of this remains in my memory.

'Because of my poor health, I must have been in low spirits. I remember, at least, that I daydreamed about the future while roaming the deck and thought about the fate of man in this life – which all young people do at such times, of course. I watched the soft glow of the spring day melt into the sea's oil-smooth surface and listened to the pleasant sound of the ship's hull cutting through the water. As the ship advanced, one small island after another would rise out of the mist on either side of us and disappear. The islands, each draped in a thick brocade of yellow flowers and green barley leaves, seemed to be floating deep within the mist. Before long the ship passed no more than a few hundred yards from the beach of a small island off to the right, and I stepped to the rail, letting my eyes wander in that direction. There seemed to be no farmland or houses on the island, only groves of small, low pine trees scattered beneath the hillside. Where the tide had drawn back, the damp surface of the hushed, deserted beach glistened in the sun, and now and then a long streak – perhaps the playing of little waves at the water's edge – shone like a naked sword and then dissolved. From the faint call of a lark high over the hill, I could tell that the island was inhabited. I remembered my father's haiku –

> A soaring lark!
> Ah, now I know the island
> Has a farm

– and found myself thinking that there must certainly be houses somewhere on the far side of the hill. Just then, I caught sight of a lone figure on the sunlit beach. I could tell it was a man and not a woman or a child. He seemed to be picking things up repeatedly and putting them into a basket or pail. He would take a few steps, squat down and retrieve something from the sand. I kept my gaze fixed on this person foraging along the deserted little beach beneath the hill. As the ship drew further away, the man's form became a black dot, and soon the beach, the hill and the entire island faded into the mist. Nearly ten years have gone by, yet how many times have I thought of this man on the island, a man whose face I do not know! This is one of my "unforgettable people".

'The next one I saw five years ago on a walking trip. My younger brother and I had celebrated New Year's Day with my parents and then immediately set out for Kyushu, crossing the island from Kumamoto to Ōita.

'We left Kumamoto early in the morning, prepared for our trek with sandals and gaiters – and high spirits. We walked as far as Tateno, arriving well before sunset, and there we spent the night. We left the next day before sunrise and headed for Mount Aso, whose famed white plume of volcanic smoke I had always wanted to see. Trudging along the frosty ground, crossing bridges suspended among the rocks, losing our way now and then, we were nearly at the summit of Aso by noon and probably reached the lip of the crater some time after one o'clock. The whole Kumamoto area is warm, of course, and that day it was clear and windless. Even near the top of the mountain, five thousand feet up in midwinter, we hardly felt the cold. Steam poured out of the crater and drifted up to the highest peak, Takadake, where it froze, gleaming white. There was hardly any snow on the mountain, just some dead white grass stirring in the breeze. Sharp cliffs burnt red and black were all that remained of the vast ancient crater that once gaped fifteen miles across. I could never capture the desolation in words – written or spoken. This is more your territory.

'We climbed to the edge of the crater and for a while stood looking into the terrible pit and enjoying the vast panorama that stretched out in all directions. Up that high, to be sure, the wind was unbearably cold. Soon we retreated to the little hut next to Aso Shrine, just below the crater rim, which offered tea and rice balls. Invigorated, we climbed again to the crater.

'By that time, the sun was sinking, and the fog that enveloped the Higo Plain below us had caught its reddish glow, turning the same colour as the charred cliff that formed the western edge of the old crater. The cone of Mount Kujū soared high above the flock of hills to the north. The plateau at its base, a carpet of withered grass that stretched for miles, also caught the glow of the setting sun. The air there was so clear, one might have caught sight of a horse and rider despite the great distance. The earth and sky seemed like a single vast enclosure. The ground shook beneath us and a thick column of white smoke shot straight up, angled off sharply, grazing Takadake, and dissolved into the distance. What could one call such a spectacle? Magnificent? Beautiful? Awe-inspiring? We stood, silent as stone figures. These are the moments when one cannot help but sense the vastness of the universe and the mystery of man's existence.

'What most enthralled us was the great basin that lay between distant Mount Kujū and Mount Aso, where we stood. I had always heard that this was the remains of the world's largest volcanic crater. Now with my own eyes I could see how the plateau beneath Kujū dropped suddenly away to form the sheer cliff that continued for miles along the northern and western rim of the basin. Unlike the Nantai crater in Nikkō, which had changed into the beautiful, secluded Lake Chūzenji, this enormous crater had, through the ages, become a vast garden of grain. The villages, forests and wheat fields in the basin now caught the slanting rays of the setting sun. Down there, too, was the little post town of Miyaji and the promise it held out to us of a night of restful, untroubled sleep.

'We talked for a while of sleeping in the mountain hut that night to see the glowing crater in the dark, but we needed to press on towards Ōita, so we started our descent to Miyaji. The downward slope was much gentler than the climb had been. We hurried along a path that snaked its way through the dry grass of the ridges and ravines. As we neared the villages, we overtook more and more horses laden with bales of hay. All around us on the paths down the mountain were men leading horses. Everything was bathed in the light of the setting sun, the air filled with the tinkling of harness bells. To every horse was strapped a load of hay. Near as the foot of the mountain had appeared from above, we seemed to be making no headway towards the villages. The sun was almost gone. We walked faster and faster, and finally broke into a run.

'When we entered the nearest village, the sun was down and the twilight fading. The activity there was remarkable. Grown-ups were hurrying about, finishing up the day's work. Children were gathered in the shade of fences or under eaves within sight of kitchen fires, laughing, singing, crying. It was the same here as in any country town at dusk, but I had never been so struck with such a scene, having raced down from Aso's desolation to plunge into the midst of this humanity. We two dragged ourselves along, knowing how far the road still stretched before us in the dark but looking forward to our night's lodging in Miyaji almost as if we were heading home.

'We had not gone far beyond the village into woods and fields when the twilight gave way to darkness and our shadows stood out clearly on the ground. I turned to see the full moon rising beside a lesser peak of Aso, casting its clear, bluish rays upon the villages in the basin like a lord viewing his prized possessions. Directly overhead, we saw how the volcanic smoke that in the daylight had risen in white billows now shone silvery grey in the light of the moon. It seemed to strike against the opaque blue-green sky, an awesome and beautiful sight. We came to a short bridge – broader than it was long – and, glad for the chance to rest our feet, leaned for a while against the railing, watching the changing shape of the smoke in the sky and half listening to the far-off voices of the village people. Just then the sound of an empty cart came echoing from the woods through which we had passed. It drew nearer, resounding in the stillness.

'Soon, along with the rattle of the empty cart, we could hear the clear, ringing tone of a teamster's song. Still gazing at the stream of smoke, I listened for the song and half consciously waited for its singer to reach us.

'A human shape appeared in the darkness, and a man's stirring voice resounded, drawing out each note of a country tune – "Miyaji's a fine old place under Mount Aso" – until the singer reached the bridge where we were standing. How moving it was – the spirit of the song, the strong, plaintive voice! A sturdy young man in his mid-twenties passed by, leading his horse, without so much as a glance in our direction. I kept my gaze fixed on his passing shadow, but with the rising moon at his back, I could hardly make out his profile. Even now, though, I can see the black silhouette of his powerful body.

'I watched him disappear into the darkness, then looked up once again at the smoke of Mount Aso. The young man is another one of my "unforgettable people".

'This next one I happened upon when I had spent a night in Mitsugahama, Shikoku, and was waiting for a steamship. I recall that it was the beginning of summer. I left the inn first thing in the morning, and when

I heard that the ship would be arriving in the afternoon, I decided to take a stroll along the waterfront. Mitsugahama is a thriving harbour town because of its location near Matsuyama in the interior. The fish market, which operates in the morning, was especially busy. The sky was bright and cloudless. The morning sun shone gloriously. Everything sparkled in its light. Colours seemed more vibrant, and the bustling scene took on added gaiety. Shouting and laughter, curses and cheers erupted from every corner. Buyers and sellers, young and old, men and women, hurried back and forth, all looking absorbed and happy in their work. A row of food stalls waited for customers, who would eat standing up. The food they offered hardly bears description. Only sailors and boat hands were eating there. Scattered all around were sea bream and flounder, eels and octopus. The sleeves and skirts of people rushing by fanned the harsh odour of raw fish.

'I was a total stranger in the town – a mere traveller. There was not a face in the crowd that I knew, not a bald spot that looked familiar. My anonymity amid these sights aroused a strange emotion in me, and I felt I was seeing the world with a new clarity. All but forgetting my own existence, I strolled through the milling crowd until I came to the end of a quiet street.

'The first thing I heard at that point was music. An itinerant monk stood in front of a shop, playing a lute. He might have been in his midforties, a short, heavy man with a broad, square face. The look on his face, the light in his eyes seemed perfectly suited to the mournful sound of the lute. His low, heavy voice followed sluggishly behind the muffled wail of the strings. No one on the street took notice of the monk, and no one appeared from the houses to listen to his music. The morning sun shone. The world went about its business.

'But I watched the monk and listened to his playing. The narrow yet busy street with its ramshackle dwellings had little in common with the monk and the lute, but somewhere, I felt, there was a deep understanding between them. The lute's sobbing tones drifted between the rows of houses on either side, mingling with the bold cries of peddlers and the ringing of an anvil nearby. When I heard the music, flowing like a current of pure springwater through a muddy pond, I felt as though the heartstrings of all these busy, happy, excited people on the street were playing a tune of nature. The monk, then, with his lute, is one of my "unforgettable people".'

At this point, Ōtsu laid his manuscript aside and sank into his thoughts. Outside, the storm roared on as before. Akiyama sat up.

'And then . . . ?'

'I think I'll make that the last one. It's getting late. There are so many left – a miner in Utashinai, Hokkaido; a young fisherman I saw on the shore of Dalian Bay in China; a boatman on the Banjō River in Kyushu with a wen on his face. We'd be up till morning if I told you everything there was to tell about them. But more important is why I can never forget them, why they appear to me again and again. That is what I want to make clear to you.

'To tell you the truth, I am not a happy man. I am constantly plagued by life's great questions and oppressed by my own ambitions for the future.

'In the deepening hours of a night such as this, alone, facing the lamp, I feel the isolation in which men live, and I experience unbearable sorrow. At these times my brittle egoism seems to shatter, and the thought of others touches me deeply. I think of my friends and of days long past. But more than anything else, images of these people I have described to you come streaming into my mind. No, I see not the people themselves: I see them as figures within a much larger scene. They are part of their surroundings, part of a moment. I remember these people and from deep within me the thought wells up: How am I different from anyone else? Don't we all receive this life of ours in a place between heaven and earth, only to return, hand in hand, along the same eternal track, to that infinite heaven? And when this feeling strikes me, I find myself in tears, for in truth there is then no self, no other. I am touched by thoughts of each and every one.

'Only at these times do I feel such peace, such liberation, such sympathy towards all things. Only then do worldly thoughts of fame and the struggle for fortune utterly disappear.

'I want very much to write on this theme and express exactly what I have in mind. I believe that somewhere in this world there must be those who feel as I do.'

Two years passed. Circumstances had brought Ōtsu to make his home in Tōhoku. His acquaintance with the man Akiyama, whom he had met at the inn in Mizonokuchi, had long since ended. The time of year was what it had been then in Mizonokuchi. It was a rainy night. Ōtsu sat alone at his desk, sunk in thought. On his desk was the manuscript of 'Unforgettable People' that he had shown to Akiyama two years before. A new chapter had been added: 'The Innkeeper of the Kameya'.

There was no chapter called 'Akiyama'.

MURAKAMI HARUKI

The 1963/1982 Girl from Ipanema

Translated by Jay Rubin

Tall and tan and young and lovely,
The girl from Ipanema goes walking.
When she walks, it's like a samba
That swings so cool and sways so gently.
How can I tell her I love her?
Yes, I would give my heart gladly.
But each day when she walks to the sea,
She looks straight ahead, not at me.

This was how the girl from Ipanema looked at the sea back then, in 1963. And that's how she keeps looking at the sea now, in 1982. She hasn't aged. Sealed in her image, she drifts through the ocean of time. If she had continued to age, she'd probably be close to forty by now. Or maybe not. But at least she wouldn't have her slim figure any more, and she wouldn't be so tan. She might retain some of her old loveliness, but she'd have three children, and too much sun would damage her skin.

Inside my record, of course, she hasn't grown any older. Wrapped in the velvet of Stan Getz's tenor sax, she's as cool as ever, the gently swaying girl from Ipanema. I put the record on the turntable, set the needle in the groove, and there she is.

How can I tell her I love her?

Yes, I would give my heart gladly.

The tune always brings back memories of the corridor in my high school – a dark, damp high-school corridor. Whenever you walked along the concrete floor, your footsteps would echo off the high ceiling. It had a few windows on the north side, but these were pressed against the mountain, which is why the corridor was always dark. And it was almost always silent. In my memory, at least.

I'm not exactly sure why 'The Girl from Ipanema' reminds me of the corridor in my high school. The two have absolutely nothing to do with each other. I wonder what kind of pebbles the 1963 girl from Ipanema threw into the well of my consciousness.

When I think of the corridor in my high school, I think of mixed salads: lettuce, tomatoes, cucumbers, green peppers, asparagus, onion rings and pink Thousand Island dressing. Not that there was a salad shop at the end of the corridor. No, there was just a door, and beyond the door a drab twenty-five-metre pool.

So why does that corridor in my old high school remind me of mixed salads? These two don't have anything to do with each other, either. They just happened to come together, like an unlucky lady who finds herself sitting on a freshly painted bench.

Mixed salads remind me of a girl I sort of knew back then. Now, this connection is a logical one, because all this girl ever ate was salads.

'How about that (munch munch) English assignment (munch munch)? Finished it yet?'

'Not quite (munch munch). Still got to (munch munch) do some reading.'

I was pretty fond of salads myself, so whenever I was with her, we had these salad-filled conversations. She was a girl of strong convictions, one of which was that if you ate a well-balanced diet, with plenty of vegetables, everything would be all right. As long as everyone ate vegetables, the world would be a place of beauty and peace, filled to overflowing with love and good health. Kind of like *The Strawberry Statement*.

'Long, long ago,' wrote a certain philosopher, 'there was a time when matter and memory were separated by a metaphysical abyss.'

The 1963/1982 girl from Ipanema continues to walk silently along the hot sands of a metaphysical beach. It's a very long beach, lapped by gentle white waves. There's no wind, nothing to be seen on the horizon. Just the smell of the sea. And the sun is burning hot.

Sprawled under a beach umbrella, I take a can of beer from the cooler and pull the tab. She's still walking by, a primary-coloured bikini clinging to her tall, tanned body.

I give it a try: 'Hi, how's it goin'?'

'Oh, hello,' she says.

'How 'bout a beer?'

She hesitates. But after all, she's tired of walking, and she's thirsty. 'I'd like that,' she says.

And together we drink beer beneath my beach umbrella.

'By the way,' I venture, 'I'm sure we met in 1963. Same time. Same place.'

'That must have been a *long* time ago,' she says, cocking her head just a bit.

'Yeah,' I say. 'It was.'

She empties half the beer can in one gulp, then stares at the hole in the top. It's just an ordinary can of beer with an ordinary hole, but the way she stares at the opening, it seems to take on a special significance – as if the entire world were going to slip inside.

'Maybe we did meet – 1963, was it? Hmmm . . . 1963. Maybe we did meet.'

'You haven't aged at all.'

'Of course not. I'm a metaphysical girl.'

I nod. 'Back then, you didn't know I existed. You looked at the ocean, never at me.'

'Could be,' she says. Then she smiles. A wonderful smile, but a little sad. 'Maybe I did keep looking at the ocean. Maybe I didn't see anything else.'

I open another beer for myself and offer her one. She just shakes her head. 'I can't drink so much beer,' she says. 'I have to keep walking and walking. But thanks.'

'Don't the soles of your feet get hot?' I ask.

'Not at all,' she says. 'They're completely metaphysical. Want to see?'

'Okay.'

She stretches a long, slim leg towards me and shows me the sole of her foot. She's right: it's a wonderfully metaphysical sole. I touch it with my finger. Not hot, not cold. There's a faint sound of waves when my finger touches her sole. A metaphysical sound.

I close my eyes for a moment, and then I open them and slug down a whole can of cold beer. The sun hasn't shifted at all. Time itself has stopped, as if it has been sucked into a mirror.

'Whenever I think of you, I think of the corridor in my high school,' I decide to tell her. 'I wonder why.'

'The human essence lies in complexity,' she replies. 'The objects of scientific investigation lie not in the object, you know, but in the subject contained within the human body.'

'Yeah?'

'In any case, you must live. Live! Live! Live! That's all. The most important thing is to go on living. That's all I can say. Really, that's all. I'm just a girl with metaphysical soles.'

The 1963/1982 girl from Ipanema brushes the sand from her thighs and stands up. 'Thank you for the beer.'

'Don't mention it.'

Every once in a while – every long once in a while – I see her on the subway. I recognize her and she recognizes me. She always sends me a little 'Thanks for the beer' smile. We haven't spoken since that day on the beach, but I can tell there is some sort of connection linking our hearts. I'm not sure just what the connection is. The link is probably in a strange place in a far-off world.

I try to imagine that link – a link in my consciousness spread out in silence across a dark hallway down which no one comes. When I think about it like this, all kinds of happenings, all kinds of things, begin to fill me with nostalgia, bit by bit. Somewhere in there, I'm sure, is the link joining me with myself. Some day, too, I'm sure, I'll meet myself in a strange place in a far-off world. And if I have anything to say about it, I'd like that place to be a warm one. And if I've got a few cold beers there as well, who could ask for anything more? In that place, I am myself and myself is me. Subject is object and object is subject. All gaps gone. A perfect union. There must be a strange place like this somewhere in the world.

The 1963 1982 girl from Ipanema continues to walk along the hot beach. And she'll continue to walk without resting until the last record wears out.

SHIBATA MOTOYUKI

Cambridge Circus

Translated by Jay Rubin

Thirty years ago, when you were twenty, you took a break from the university and lived in London for six months. You worked in a hotel part time and went to a language school to improve your English. At the six-month point, your mother needed cancer surgery, so you went home to Japan and returned to the university.

You went by bus a lot while you were in London. Buses were slower than the Underground, they rarely ran on schedule and when they finally did reach your stop, two or three buses running the same route would arrive at once like beads on a string. But still, you loved sitting in the front seat upstairs in those double-decker buses, watching the city roll by. You had all the time you needed, so you would take a bus to work, take one to the language school, and go by bus everywhere to get maximum value out of your four-pound-a-month pass.

Traditional double-decker London buses had no doors in the back where passengers would enter and exit. As long as the bus was not going fast, you could get on or off even if you weren't at a bus stop. You especially enjoyed hopping off before your stop, along with all the other Londoners, when a bus was stuck in traffic.

One midwinter afternoon, you were heading for the used bookshops on Charing Cross Road on your way to work when you stepped off at Cambridge Circus. The bus was rounding the curve in front of the theatre and you were pleased to think of yourself as an honest-to-goodness Londoner hopping down to the street. Just then, however, the traffic was not very backed up and the bus had not slowed down much. As soon as one foot hit the road, you lost your balance and fell headlong, rolling over three times in the street.

Fortunately, the impact was cushioned by the (for you) rather luxurious duffle coat you had bought with your last pennies to ward off the cold, and though you had some pain in your shoulders and knees, you were pretty sure you had not caused yourself any injury. That, and your embarrassment at being stared at by passers-by, who, you could tell, were trying not to laugh, prompted you to dust yourself off and stride away towards the bookshops up the road.

Thirty years have gone by, my work has brought me to London, and here I am again, standing in Cambridge Circus. The curve of the road has been altered somewhat (not necessitated, I'm sure, by a spate of bus passengers rolling on the street), but the feel of the place has hardly changed. The same old double-decker buses roar past me without slowing down very much.

Before my eyes, my former self stands on the open platform at the rear of a bus. I release my grip on the pole and, with a self-satisfied look on my face, I hop down right in front of the theatre. I lose my balance, plop down on the road and roll over three times.

The old me tries hard to look unfazed. I stand up, dust myself off and start walking in the direction of the bookshops towards the thirty years of life to come.

Hey, wait there, Shibata, don't be in such a hurry, I feel the urge to shout. *Have a cup of tea somewhere nearby, and calm down.*

Of course, the old me can't hear such mental mutterings of a ghost from the future. He just strides away pretending he's not in any pain. But the ghost is free to imagine whatever he likes.

In the ghost's imagination, you change your mind and go into the nearest café for a cup of tea to regain your poise.

And during the fifteen minutes you're in the café, your life changes irrevocably.

By which I don't mean that you meet someone and fall in love or that the book you've been reading provides you with some enormous revelation. You just sit there sipping your tea and staring at a faded Pepsi-Cola sign while discreetly rubbing your knee. And while you're there, the ghost imagines, something inside you changes – subtly but irrevocably. Two months later, your father writes to you about your mother's cancer, but you don't go back to Japan and you don't re-enrol at the university.

Thirty years later, you're still in London. It would be nice to say that you've had all kinds of exciting experiences in the meantime, but that's not what happens. The time just creeps along as you go from one odd job to another – washing dishes at hotels, cleaning buildings, working at discount shops – and when you stop to notice, thirty years have gone by. Now you're doing office chores at the language school and you pass through Cambridge Circus almost every day, but you have no special feeling for the place.

Today, though, you happen to be standing in Cambridge Circus with nothing much in mind, happy to have some free time until you meet a friend and to feel the winter sunshine on your back. The big, red body of a double-decker bus enters your field of vision from beyond the intersection. You know that short young Japanese fellow in the brown duffle coat who is standing on the open boarding platform, clutching the pole and wearing a silly grin.

He jumps down, falls over and rolls. Then he stands up with a look of feigned detachment on his face and starts walking towards the used book-shops but changes his mind and turns to enter a café.

Don't go in there! the ghost from the future silently shouts now that he knows the irreversible change that will happen during those fifteen minutes inside. His imagination tells him: the young man changes his mind again, does *not* go into the café and starts walking towards the used bookshop – towards a different life.

That young man thirty years later, it seems, will turn out to be me. My work has brought me to London today and I'm standing in Cambridge Circus, where I've arranged to meet an old friend from my college days who lives in London now. It's summer, everyone is wearing short-sleeved shirts, and the double-decker buses are running as always, but I don't have to worry about spotting a short Japanese fellow in a duffle coat. There's no fear today of my becoming anyone's future ghost. I live in the real world, teach at a real university and translate contemporary American literature on the side. I have a wife and friends and colleagues and students. I'm me now, just me myself.

Well, I guess you're free to think that, someone says. *Everybody has the right to think they are themselves, and your right to think such a thought is not significantly less than anyone else's. But aren't you forgetting one thing – that on that day thirty years ago, when you jumped down from the bus and fell, rolling over* four *times in the street, the next bus in the string came along?*

MODERN LIFE AND
OTHER NONSENSE

UNO KŌJI

Closet LLB

Translated by Jay Rubin

Five years have gone by since Otsukotsu Sansaku received his Bachelor of Laws degree from the university and became known as Otsukotsu Sansaku, LLB, but he still has no fixed occupation. Almost nine years have gone by since he first arrived in Tokyo from the provinces, but he still spreads his bedding in the same room of the same boarding house he chose at the beginning (while ownership of the boarding house itself has changed hands thirteen times).

As an undergraduate, Sansaku was, in fact, present on at least two-thirds of the days his college was open for classes – perhaps because the rules prohibited anything less – and his grades were on the high side. At university, however, he averaged ten days a year, passing through the campus gate no more than forty times in four years, as a result of which he graduated second from the bottom in his class.

Back in the third or fourth year of primary school, Sansaku became obsessed with boys' magazines and fairy tales, and he aspired, if somewhat vaguely, to become a children's author like Iwaya Sazanami.[1]

His father died when Sansaku was three, leaving Sansaku and his mother enough money to live on for the rest of their lives. His mother took the extra precaution of entrusting the property to an influential relative, but this had the reverse effect of plunging them into misfortune when, unexpectedly, the relative went bankrupt, losing not only his own property but theirs as well. This happened the year Sansaku entered middle school.

At that point another relative, a man named Ōike, stepped forward to pay his school fees. Ōike was a cousin of Sansaku's father whom the father had aided monetarily and in other ways and who, unexpectedly, had succeeded in business and become a millionaire. When the fourteen-year-old Sansaku finished his first year of middle school, Ōike brought him to live in the Ōike household and insisted that he take an examination to transfer into a prestigious business school. Try as he might, Sansaku could not make himself study for the exam, and two days before the appointed date he ran away from the Ōikes' to his own house (or, rather, to the house of his mother's parents, who had taken them in after the bankruptcy).

Ōike then gave up on his plans for Sansaku and resigned himself to paying the boy's tuition and letting him continue through the full five years of middle school. Sansaku had had excellent grades all the way through primary and middle school, which is not to say that he was working especially hard in middle school. Far from it. Indeed, he was already completely immersed in magazines and fiction. But the ambition Iwaya Sazanami had sparked in his earliest years had been evolving bit by bit: first, Sansaku found himself wanting to be a staff writer at a magazine, and then, from the third year of middle school, he embraced the unshakeable goal of becoming a novelist. To this very day, that has not changed. Which only goes to prove that we are dealing here with someone who was once a childhood prodigy.

Yet another problem arose when Sansaku graduated from middle school at the age of eighteen. Ōike, convinced that this was the time for him to take action, again pressed Sansaku to study business, but Sansaku insisted that his future lay in literature. The two clashed repeatedly until it was decided (through the offices of a third party) that Sansaku should take the middle path and study law at college. Not even the gifted Otsukotsu Sansaku was able to grasp exactly how law was the 'middle path' between business and literature, but he did see that any further resistance to the wishes of the relative who was paying for his education would be both futile and against his better interests, and in the end he resigned himself to entering the college's pre-law programme. Thus it came about that, through the three years of college and four more at university, Sansaku steeped himself exclusively in literature while supposedly settled in law. He managed to squeeze through his university law exams at least, and five years ago became, if in name only, a Bachelor of Laws: Otsukotsu Sansaku, LLB.

Just about the time he graduated from university, Ōike died. This did not spell the end of the Ōike line, however, since Mr Ōike had a perfectly fine heir to carry on his name. But the payments to Sansaku came to a halt the moment he graduated, almost as if Ōike's debt to Sansaku's father had now been settled once and for all. As noted earlier, Sansaku is a Bachelor of Laws, but he knows almost nothing about the law. Not one of his relatives, who felt only antipathy towards him, offered to help him find employment. Nor did he, in his strange arrogance, bother to approach any of his senior law colleagues in search of an opening. None of them liked Sansaku, either.

In this way did our poor Bachelor of Laws suddenly find himself pressed to make ends meet. While at university, most of his friends had been in the literature department rather than law, and it was through those friends that Sansaku was able to live from one poverty-stricken day to the next by doing the occasional cut-rate translation or writing fairy tales, though even so he has run up a sizeable debt at his boarding house. In addition, once he graduated he found that he was expected to send fifteen yen every month to his elderly mother in the country.

Over the past year or two, Sansaku has fallen into ever-deepening poverty. There has never been enough translation work, and he has run out of ideas for fairy tales. Still, visiting literary friends to beg for work has been just as hard for him as calling upon his senior colleagues in law. (In other words, though arrogant, he is also a man of great diffidence.) Before he knew it, then, his payments to his mother fell further and further behind. Once that happened, it ceased to bother him, and he gradually stopped sending anything at all. In the end, he could toss her urgent letters aside with hardly a twinge of conscience.

Then, just a month ago, a letter arrived from the country. As we have seen, Sansaku might allow two or three days to go by before reading his mother's letters, and some he never read at all; but this one, fortunately, he opened and read immediately – 'fortunately' because it brought him excellent news. Since he had so often been late sending money to her, his mother said, their relatives had begun to hear of her difficulties, and several of them who, like Ōike, had been aided by Sansaku's late father and had since done especially well for themselves, had got together and collected ten thousand yen, enabling her to open a small but dependable shop.

This news brought Sansaku such a tremendous sense of relief from the cares of day-to-day living that he felt quite drained.

'What was that again?' he muttered to himself, recalling the last part of his mother's letter. '"Our relatives say they pooled their resources and helped me open a shop because you have failed to support me the way you ought to, Sansaku, so under no circumstances should you even *dream* of pestering your mother" – "not that we are in a position to say such a thing," said the hypocritical bastards! – "for a loan." A loan? Who the hell's asking for a loan? But wait a minute,' he went on, trying to make sense of the situation. 'If they gave it to her, it's hers. And besides, it's not as if I'm some prodigal son planning to "pester" his mother for money to support his dissolute lifestyle. This will be my chance to sit down and do some serious work. Which means . . . and so . . .

'All right, then, let me just set all thought of money aside and take the time to apply myself to a grown-up novel.' (Having written so many fairy tales over the years, this is how Sansaku refers to standard novels.)

'Because I've had to send out fifteen yen or so every month until now, I've been compelled to keep taking stupid jobs I absolutely detested, but now that my mother's livelihood is assured . . .'

No sooner had his thoughts brought him this far than Sansaku felt that sudden, draining sense of relief, like a traveller who remains unconscious of his fatigue as long as he keeps hurrying down the road but who collapses in a heap from exhaustion the moment he realizes he has reached his destination (though in fact, as stated earlier, Sansaku had by no means been making regular monthly remittances to his mother). Once he felt it was no longer necessary for him to act, the will to act simply vanished. Although he did at least feel an occasional urge to write a grown-up novel – after all, it was an ambition he had often harboured to the point of ignoring everything else, including his studies for a time – it occurred to him that, even if he managed to finish one, far from earning him easy money like his fairy tales, just getting it accepted would require enormous effort on his part. And so he flung his pen away.

Every single day since then he has spent either visiting friends or sleeping. Sansaku's style of sleeping deserves special mention. His small tatami-matted room has the standard tall, deep closet divided by a sturdy shelf into upper and lower compartments for storing his futon and covers behind a pair of sliding paper doors, but Sansaku long ago decided that it was too much trouble to open the closet door and pull the bedding out every day to spread it on the tatami. Instead he cleared out the upper compartment and now keeps his futon spread out permanently on the shelf. He sleeps in the closet with the doors open and never has to make his bed.

'This is it! This is the answer!' he cried in delight at his own discovery. 'I may have been born in the sticks, but I'm different from the typical farmer or merchant's son. I'm delicately built, so I can't sleep just anywhere with a pile of magazines or a folded cushion for a pillow. This is it!'

Lazy as he was, Sansaku still managed to wake up early every morning, wash his face and eat breakfast. After an hour or two, however, he would crawl back into his bed on the closet shelf. Usually he would be awakened by the maid when she brought his lunch on a tray, which she would set on the tatami. He would slip down from the shelf, sit cross-legged on the floor to finish his lunch and then immediately burrow his way back into the bedding on the closet shelf. Then, in the evening, he would be awakened yet again by the maid when she arrived with his dinner on the usual tray. While he slept, of course, Sansaku was unconscious, so it seemed as if his three meals – breakfast, lunch and dinner – were delivered to him in rapid succession the way a waiter in a Western restaurant brings one dish after another to the table. He spent most evenings strolling around the city or visiting friends to talk about nothing in particular. Bedtime was two o'clock in the morning for him most days. Still, it was Sansaku more than anyone who was amazed at how much he could sleep.

'On the other hand, I never sleep without dreaming,' he would often think to himself. 'Which may mean that the amount of time I am actually asleep is short. If ordinary people dream a little while sleeping, in my case it's more that I sleep a little while dreaming.'

Now, the boarding house in which Otsukotsu Sansaku, LLB, lives is halfway up a hill, and it stands on a plot of land that is two feet lower than the street level, as a result of which, even though his room is on the upper floor facing the street (that is, the hill), the faces of people passing by are at virtually the same height as his when he is sitting on his tatami floor. This means that when he leaves his window open and keeps the door of his closet slid back, he can lie amid the bedding on his closet shelf, watching the street and closely observing the passers-by – none of whom, of course, can imagine that there is a person in the closet watching them and who must consequently pass by unconcerned about what they assume to be an empty room.

This way, from among the folds of his bedding, Sansaku can spend certain intervals – the five or ten minutes between the time his eyes have tired of reading magazines and the time he drifts into his morning or afternoon nap – watching the people climbing or descending the hill as if he were seeing them in a play. He has developed the ability to pick out local residents even if he has never spoken a word to them, saying to himself, 'Aha! That's so-and-so from such-and-such a house.' Quite often, while lying in bed and watching the passers-by in this way, he will eventually slip into a dream while muttering something like 'Oh, I'm glad to see *him* out walking all the time again: he must have got over his sickness' or 'My goodness, look at that girl! She's really decked out today!'

In his student days, Sansaku had been terribly dissatisfied with the law as an academic discipline. Now he has the LLB attached to his name, but he still lives like a literature student, albeit one to whom current literature and literary people have come to seem just as dissatisfying and contemptible. Before, he (and perhaps only he) had believed that a literary man was someone who possessed keen powers of appreciation for all things in this world. Now, however, how did those literary people he had grown familiar with appear to him?

'To take an example close at hand,' thought Otsukotsu Sansaku, LLB, while observing the street from his closet bed as usual, 'the face of that woman passing by: among the writers I know' (and in fact, many of the literature-student friends he had while he was in law school were already well-known men of letters) 'is there even one who would be capable of composing a decent critique of how beautiful – or *not* beautiful – her face is, or her figure, or the way she wears her kimono, or her whole outfit?'

As a child, Sansaku tended to be smug and arrogant, always ready to show off his slightest ability. He was, in a word, vaguely contemptuous of just about everything and everyone. The tendency only increased with age to the point where now even he has come to find it somewhat abnormal. His sense of dissatisfaction has increased over the past two or three years such that all works of art – not only fiction but critical essays, dramatic texts, theatrical performances, paintings – are remarkable to him only for their innumerable shortcomings. He has come to feel that he is the only one who can perceive their flaws and virtues (if, indeed, they possess any virtues), that he alone truly understands them. He has gone so far as to think he should therefore provide models for other writers, write works that would serve to guide them to increasingly greater accomplishments; but in the end nothing has ever materialized.

Say, he goes out to eat, or to a performance of *gidayū* or *rakugo* or *kōdan* or *naniwabushi*, or perhaps *ongyoku* or *buyō*, or down a notch to comic *teodori* or a *shinpa* tragedy: there is absolutely nothing about them that he does not know how to appreciate. He believes himself capable of discovering points of beauty in things that everyone else dismisses, and equally able to find bad points in things that everyone else admires, which makes him very pleased with himself.

'Had I become a sumo wrestler, I'm sure I would have numbered among the champions.' This was one of the more far-fetched thoughts that came to Sansaku one day as he was lying in his closet. 'Take that Ōarashi Tatsugorō, for example. Everybody is calling him unbeatable, but I knew him in middle school. At first, he and I were in the same class, but he was what they called a "backward" student and failed his exams twice in two years, ending up two grades behind me. Now you look at the sumo coverage in the paper and they're calling him an unusually smart wrestler. Well, I used to face him in judo all the time. I never had the physical strength, but my body was as unresisting as noodles, so the other guy could come at me with all his might, but I was like a willow in the wind – sure, it's an old figure of speech, but that's how I was – and nobody could ever knock me down. After a while, when the other guy started pressing, I'd see an opening and use his strength against him. I always won. Old Ōarashi was fairly strong back then (though nothing special), but he never once beat me. If I had been training all this time like Ōarashi, I'd be great by now, or at least a damn good – if unusual – wrestler.'

The thought made Otsukotsu Sansaku feel he couldn't lose against Ōarashi even now. As he lay there in his closet imagining himself going up against each of the current sumo wrestlers, a big grin crossed his face.

'I wonder why I never put more of myself into studying the law,' thought Sansaku one day. 'I mean, think of that stiff-brained, tongue-tied, unimpressive-looking classmate of mine, Kakii: I see in today's paper they're calling him one of the up-and-coming hot young lawyers for some stupid case he's managed to win. The public is so damn easy to fool.' (Sansaku finds fault only with other people and forgets how hard the public is – and has been – for *him* to fool.) 'With my intelligence and my eloquence . . .' More than once, such thoughts inspired him to resolve to hit the law books and apply to be a judge or public prosecutor, but the inspiration never lasted more than an hour.

Ultimately, Sansaku lacked the most important elements for making a go of it in this world: perseverance, courage and common sense. To him, everything was 'stupid', everything was 'boring', everything he saw and heard filled him with displeasure and sometimes even anger. He was especially repulsed by his landlady's modern, swept-back hairstyle, to which she added an extra swirl by placing a black-lacquered wire frame against her scalp and covering it as best she could with her thinning hair, each strand stuck in place with pomade. She also appeared to spend her days in eager anticipation of being called 'madam' not only by the maids but by her lodgers as well; she was trying to hide the fact that she was the mistress of an old country gentleman who visited her once or twice a week.

Only Sansaku made a point of calling her 'Mistress Proprietor', to which she never once deigned to reply. In spite of her refusal to respond, he would always ask her, 'How much fun are you getting out of life?'

'How much fun are you getting out of life?' was a pet phrase of Sansaku's.

'And you?' he once asked a friend. 'Are you enjoying life?'

The friend's only answer was a couple of non-committal grunts.

Another friend answered the question with a straight-out 'Not at all', to which Sansaku responded with his second pet phrase, 'Don't you want to die?'

'I'd like to be killed without knowing it,' the friend answered.

'Oh, oh, I can't take it any longer. I think I'll just find myself an aeroplane. I was one of the best gymnasts in middle school, so I'm sure I'd make a great pilot.' Sansaku's own special delusions of grandeur were taking flight. 'Too bad I don't have the one thing you really need for that . . . guts.' And soon he was drifting into his usual dream world in his closet bed.

Otsukotsu Sansaku had been an excellent long-jumper in middle school. He would take a twenty-foot run, plant his left foot on the line and sail into the air with his legs still rotating, as if swimming. As he neared the end of his jump, he would flip his body forwards, beginning a second arc and lengthening his distance, and then twist himself to make still another arc the moment before he touched down, forming three arcs in all. This way, he managed to jump much further than the other jumpers, who could only execute a single arc. Now, in his mind, he found himself using this technique to send his body aloft until he was sailing through the air without the aid of machinery. 'This is so much fun! And so easy for me! Oh, look! I'm flying over pine trees and all those people down there! Strange how no one seems amazed by this. But they'll realize it soon enough. I'll show them! They'll see how great my work is! Oh, I'm coming to the far bank of the river. But so what? River, ocean, they're all the same to me. Just go, go, it doesn't matter. See? It's nothing, I'm across the river now!' This was all in his dream, of course. He didn't know when he awoke, but the one thing he knew for sure was that the dream didn't end, as they so often did, in failure.

Otsukotsu Sansaku was not the least bit surprised when he opened his eyes. He really had been an excellent long-jumper at school, and he could clearly remember being able to propel his body further in mid-jump.

'Why haven't I tried that all this time? Sprinting to the line is the same as a plane accelerating for a take-off, and planting the foot is probably the take-off itself. Sure, that's it, I know I can do it! But . . .' Of course he started having second thoughts in the midst of his enthusiasm. 'But . . .' he thought to himself again.

He climbed out of his closet and gave it a try in his narrow six-mat room, but he could not even rise a foot above the tatami. In fact, he fell back so heavily and clumsily that he suspected he must have gained weight. 'No, I can't be this bad,' he told himself, his initial failure spurring him on to a more determined attempt. He stepped out into the corridor. Fortunately, there was no one present. It so happened that the house had undergone a major clean a month earlier, and a layer of oiled paper soaked with some kind of new chemical and varnish that had been put down to improve appearances and protect against bed bugs was still spread out over the floor. It was very slippery, and Sansaku enjoyed skating on it in his slippers whenever he was bored.

Now, using the aeronautical skills suggested by his dream, Sansaku gave himself over to running down the corridor and leaping through the air, but he could not make a tenth of the distance he used to cover at school. When he tried to plant his foot for the take-off on his fourth run down the corridor, he slipped and fell, slamming his shin against the banister and landing on his bottom. He was sitting there on the floor, scowling with pain, when the landlady with her hard-pomaded backswept hairdo came climbing up the stairs.

'My goodness!' the woman cried with wide-open eyes. 'Mr Otsukotsu!'

'Madam!' Sansaku responded with the title he preferred not to use for her. He chose it because he had recalled something that made it necessary to call her 'madam', something that even made him forget about the pain in his shin.

'Madam, I expect to receive a small payment tomorrow, so I will be able to . . .'

After he said this, he sighed from the pain in his leg and from the imagined consequences of his lie. Feeling a need for further words to cover his embarrassment, he came out with his habitual: 'Life is not much fun, is it, madam?'

'Not much,' she replied resolutely. 'For either of us.' Without so much as a smile, she headed back down the stairs.

'Not for either of us, is it? I see, I see,' Otsukotsu Sansaku, LLB, still flat on his backside, mumbled to himself as he watched her go.

GENJI KEITA

Mr English

Translated by Jay Rubin

I

The day after it happened, word spread through the company that 'Mr English', Mogi Soichirō, and the Assistant Director's assistant Oda Yoshirō, had slugged it out at the conclusion of a heated argument in the bar Heiroku.

'So they finally did it!' somebody shouted with a loud clap.

But Mogi was fifty-seven, Oda fifty-two. At the very least, this was no way for mature men to behave. Everybody found the whole thing ridiculous, especially when they heard that Mogi not only had to be rushed to a nearby hospital with blood gushing from his wound, but that he also went home with layer upon layer of white bandaging around his head. Nobody needed a witness to tell them who was at fault: it had to be Mogi.

Mogi was a temporary employee, as he had been ever since joining the company twenty years earlier. This seemed to be the chief source of pain in his life, but he had at least stopped complaining about it in recent years because a company rule gave temp status even to regular employees who stayed on past the mandatory retirement age of fifty-five. It would be hasty to conclude, however, that just because he was no longer grumbling, Mogi had managed to sweep away the deep-seated dissatisfaction he felt towards the company for having kept him on temporary status up until the age of fifty-five. Not only was the difference like night and day between regular and temporary staff with regard to both bonus size and severance pay, but each day Mogi reported to work, he had to press his seal in the attendance register below the name of even the most recently hired office girl.

'Humph! What do they take me for?' Mogi would mutter each morning when he pressed his seal in the register, after which he would make a point of tossing the book to the far end of the table. It turned his stomach to see the untroubled faces of those youngsters fresh from college who glided into the top ranks of the registry, contemptuous of his twenty years of hard work. He had to find a way to amaze each one with a show of his outstanding abilities.

'Hey, young fella, they tell me you're a college graduate,' he would accost a newcomer – usually in the company lounge.

'Yes, I am,' the young man would reply with a proud swelling of the chest, though of course all the other newcomers were college graduates, too.

'Then your English is probably pretty good. No, excuse me, it *must* be good. So let me ask you a question.'

At this point the typical newcomer would fasten a suspicious gaze on the short, scrawny – and obviously nasty – old Mogi, who, despite his advanced age, did not appear to be either a department manager or a general manager, much less a company director.

'How do you say *"Keigun no ikkaku"* in English?'

'Huh? That sounds more like Chinese than Japanese. What's *"keigun"*?'

'A flock of chickens.'

'And *"ikkaku"*?'

'A crane, of course.'

'A crane in a flock of chickens?'

'Exactly. So how would you translate that into English?'

'Come on . . .'

'You don't know, eh? Too bad. Here's an easier one: *"Abata mo ekubo."*'

'"Even her pockmarks are dimples to him"? You want an English phrase for that? That's too hard.'

'Too hard? It couldn't be any easier! *"Rabu izu buraindo"*!'

'"Love . . . is . . . blind"? Oh, I get it.'

'You *should* get it. You're a college graduate, after all, but you don't know a thing. What good are you? You'd better hit the books.'

'I guess I should.'

The bewildered newcomer could only scratch his head and blush to think the first thing he had done on entering the company was to embarrass himself before the veteran members of staff who usually gathered around. Once Mogi had marched off in triumph, though, one of the older men would snicker, 'He got you,' and explain that Mogi was the temp who worked as the company's English consultant, which only made the new man feel worse. Far from winning Mogi the respect he thought he deserved, this technique only succeeded in convincing newcomers that he was a hateful old man.

Mogi was not a college graduate. In fact, his only education after primary school was the training he received at Dr Saitō's English Academy. Nothing much is known about his subsequent efforts to learn English, but he presented himself as an expert, and was in fact quite good at the language. As long as they had Mogi, the company was never at a loss in its negotiations with foreigners. That a man of such ability could never convince them to raise his status from temporary to permanent was certainly due in part to his truncated academic career, but the main reason should be made clear by the following episode.

On this occasion, Mogi had put a newcomer in his place as usual. He had done it that time not with 'Even her pockmarks are dimples to him' but *'Bancha mo debana'* ('The bloom of youth makes even the plainest girl attractive'). Mogi was walking off, pleased with himself, when this particular young man vented his frustration by yelling at him from behind, 'Hey, you *paypah doggu*, you!'

Mogi whirled around in shock. With his English expertise, he was well prepared to deal with something like *hotto doggu*, but this *paypah doggu* was new.

'What did you say to me?' he demanded.

'Paypah doggu!'

'Paypah doggu?'

Even the great Mr English could only cock his head in puzzlement.

'Don't get it, eh? Well that is too bad!' the young man declared, obviously mocking Mogi's earlier tone with him. 'You *do* know what *paypah* is, don't you?'

Mogi could do little more than reply, *'Paypah* is paper.'

'Yes, that's *kami* in Japanese, for your information. So how about *doggu?'*

'Doggu is dog,' Mogi answered with annoyance.

'Excellent! And "dog" in Japanese is *inu*. Or perhaps you knew that already. So *paypah doggu* should be translated *kami-inu* in Japanese, wouldn't you say?'

'*Kami-inu?*'

'Yes – or perhaps I should say that in English for you: *iesu*. And since *kami* can mean "biting" as well as "paper", a *kami-inu* is a yappy little dog that bites everybody and anybody: a biting dog. I'm sure you get it. They call you "Mr English", but you don't know a thing, do you? You'll have to do better than that!'

'You son of a –'

Mogi, now livid, sprang at the newcomer, but a moment later he found himself sitting on the floor. The young man had been a sumo wrestler at college. Mogi looked up at his beefy adversary, aware that he had chosen to tangle with the wrong person. He left the building then and there, which later gave rise to considerable ridicule.

When Kazama Kyōta dropped by the Heiroku that evening, he found Mogi there.

'The bastard called me a *paypah doggu*! He was making fun of me!' Mogi whined to the landlady as he drowned his sorrows in sake, eventually slumping to the table in a drunken stupor. Kyōta still thought of Mogi as a nasty old man, but he found the sight of Mogi, lying there fast asleep, so sad and lonely that what should have been the pleasant effect of a night-time drink was obliterated by a deep sense of the transitory nature of all human life.

It later came out that the young newcomer had been put on guard against Mogi by the Assistant Director's assistant, Oda Yoshirō. The news made Mogi so furious he tried to bite Oda's head off. Though Oda was too big-hearted to take him seriously, from that day onwards he became the object of Mogi's smouldering resentment.

Paypah doggu! Everyone at the company was delighted that the young man had nailed Mogi so perfectly. A true 'biting dog', he was always trying to sink his fangs into people. He scattered curses everywhere he went, angry at the world. Quite naturally, people kept their distance from him, the company directors being no exception. Surely it made perfect sense that they had never promoted Mogi from temporary to full time.

This no doubt encouraged his inborn nasty personality to develop ever more *paypah doggu*-like tendencies; yet the bosses never went so far as to fire him, probably because they recognized the true value of his work as 'Mr English'.

2

Kazama Kyōta first began to suspect that he should see Mogi in a new light after Mogi was called upon to translate a draft application he had written under the Corporate Rehabilitation and Reorganization Law. When it became necessary to explain the gist of the application to the Occupation authorities, Mogi went with one of the directors and Kyōta and translated for them into fluent English. It was a thrill to watch him cross swords with the American officer, never backing down an inch. He was magnificent.

Whether or not Mogi fully grasped the contents of the application, he seemed to double everything the Director said. If the Director spoke for five minutes, Mogi stretched it out to ten. He was clearly exceeding his authority, but Kyōta had never seen him perform with such gusto, and he realized that Mogi's thick-skinned approach was the only way to make the other side fully grasp what the company wanted. Of course, such a brash attitude on the part of a mere interpreter might have backfired, but the application was accepted and Kyōta came out of the deal looking good.

'Now, *this* has given me a whole new appreciation for your abilities,' Kyōta said to Mogi.

'Hey, what are you talking about? You've got some nerve, making fun of an old man.'

'No, seriously, I'm very grateful for what you've done.'

'Humph.'

Mogi made as if to pass off Kyōta's praise with a snort, but he was obviously very pleased by it. In fact, he soon came up with an outlandish suggestion.

'If you're really so grateful, why don't you become my apprentice?'

'Don't be ridiculous.'

'No, really. I was just thinking I'd like to have an apprentice.'

'What a terrible idea!' Kyōta said with a feeble smile, hoping this was just a one-time joke, but Mogi, perhaps because he was kept at a distance by everyone else, started dropping by Kyōta's desk at least once a day to proclaim for all to hear that he wanted the younger man to become his apprentice. Kyōta was floored by this, especially when some of the other men began calling him 'Mr Apprentice'.

Needless to say, Mogi had none of the dignity of an apprentice's master. Whenever he called Kyōta his apprentice, Kyōta would think of the sad face of the sleeping drunken Mogi he had seen that night in the Heiroku. Maybe it was that loneliness that caused Mogi to give the 'apprentice' label to someone who had shown him the slightest kindness. Kyōta thought he could understand what Mogi was feeling.

One day, however, Kyōta decided he had had enough. 'I want you to stop calling me your "apprentice",' he declared. 'You have never once given me the special consideration that a true master should show his apprentice.'

'You've got some nerve picking a fight with your master!'

'My master? We've never formally shared a cup of sake to seal the bond. The least you should do is treat me to some major drinking!'

'Now you're trying to twist my arm!'

'You bet I am!'

Kyōta had more or less forgotten this confrontation when, a few days later, Mogi announced, 'Get ready for some heavy drinking tonight, Apprentice!'

'No no no, I was just joking,' Kyōta said, flustered.

'Too late for that now,' Mogi declared. 'I'm not letting you get away.'

And, indeed, that night Mogi dragged the protesting Kyōta to the Heiroku.

Located in Osaka's lively Umeda district, Heiroku was an absolutely ordinary bar, but it was the one most often frequented by employees of the company. It had disappeared for a time after the bombing flattened the city centre, but the landlady had reopened a year earlier near the original spot. Her husband, Heiroku, had been drafted and killed in the war, and she was apparently still a widow. If anything, she had put on new curves after losing her husband, and at thirty-seven or thirty-eight was sexier than ever. The men from the office often said what a waste it would be to leave her a widow, and talked among themselves about who might be the first to win her, but what really attested to her character was her policy of never overcharging her customers.

Mogi announced to the landlady straight off: 'This fellow is going to become my apprentice tonight – my first one! If I'm Robin Hood, he'll be my Little John. Be nice to him!'

'Oh, my goodness!' she exclaimed with a look of amazement. 'Is that true, Mr Kazama?'

'Well, ma'am, I wasn't really planning on this, but you know how you can get yourself in trouble just by opening your mouth. I feel like a prisoner of war tonight.'

Kyōta's sullen scowl only seemed to energize Mogi. 'Too late for that!' he crowed. 'Bring the sake right away, ma'am, please!'

'Yes, sir!'

As soon as the hot sake arrived, Mogi lifted the ceramic bottle and held it out, ready to pour for Kyōta.

'All right, Apprentice. Here comes our ceremonial cup.'

Kyōta had no choice but to lift his sake cup for Mogi to fill.

'As soon as you're done, hand the cup to me.'

'All right. Here it is.'

Kyōta handed the empty cup to Mogi and filled it for him.

'That does it,' Mogi said after draining the cup. 'Now you're my apprentice.'

In high spirits, Mogi drank a lot that night. And, most unusually for him, he talked a lot about the past. He had been born into a poor family in the old Tamatsukuri district of Osaka, and between the ages of thirteen and sixteen had spent four hard years in service to a dry-goods store in Kita-Kyūhōjimachi. Recognizing that this was leading nowhere, he left for Tokyo with high hopes. There, while studying at the English Academy, he served as a student houseboy at the office of the prominent party politician Hoshi Tōru, which was in the area where the NHK Broadcasting headquarters now stand. In his houseboy position, he had been preceded by such important politicians as Akita Kiyoshi and Maeda Yonezō. Next he boarded a ship to China, where he worked as a newspaper reporter, then quickly joined that small band of Japanese adventurers who wandered the continent, involving themselves behind the scenes in politically and diplomatically sensitive issues. All the while, he worked on polishing his English. Eventually he returned to Japan and went to work for the company on a temporary basis. Oda Yoshirō was another temporary hire from around that time.

'That damned Oda is a clever bastard the way he got them to hire him full time in his fifth year,' Mogi growled.

Twenty years had gone by since the company had linked capital and technical forces with the top-flight American company IES; Mogi had been hired to help with those negotiations. Once they were completed, however, Mogi found himself being chewed out by the Director.

'All you're supposed to do is give an honest translation of whatever I say. Today, though, you were not only getting involved where you shouldn't have but offering your own opinions. And you call yourself an interpreter?'

Then, when the war was coming and Japan strengthened the Foreign Exchange Control Law, the company was ordered by the army to increase the number of its shares, which necessitated some difficult discussions with IES as chief stockholder. That time, too, Mogi found himself being reprimanded after the negotiations.

'Are you Japanese? Is some other company paying your salary? In today's negotiations, you were clearly taking the side of an enemy country. Do you see what I'm saying?'

Kyōta immediately recognized that this was the very kind of thing for which Mogi would be likely to be admonished, but he could also easily picture a mortified Mogi glaring back at the boss all the while.

Once the war was under way, the company no longer needed English, and rumour suggested that they would never need it again. Instead, the study of Malay took off. Understandably, it must have been a stressful time for Mogi. Under normal circumstances, a 'Mr English' might have been fired as a useless luxury. Yet Mogi was kept on, thanks less to the Director's foresight, in all probability, than to the sort of paternalism that prevails at large companies. Mogi must have sensed this. At least, it is not hard to imagine that he felt a good deal of anguish, knowing how dim his prospects of finding a new job were at his age. Still, although he never went so far as to say that Japan was going to lose the war, he earned ever greater disapproval in the company by circulating his outrageous view that America would never lose.

In the end, of course, Japan did lose, ushering in the age of English Almighty. The only thing this did for Mogi was vastly increase the amount of work he had to do. He still remained the temp they called 'Mr English', a *paypah doggu*, as lonely after the war as he had been before.

The more he heard Mogi's stories of the old days, the less inclined Kyōta felt to resist being called 'apprentice' by him.

'Shut up, Apprentice! Look here, Apprentice! Hey you, Apprentice!' The obvious joy with which he yelled at Kyōta revealed how completely Mogi had let his guard down. If Mogi was going to call him 'Apprentice' so affectionately, Kyōta was willing to let him get away with it.

Mogi's knowledge of English never showed up in the form of affected Americanisms. When drunk enough to start singing, he never sang English songs but traditional Japanese shrine-pilgrimage songs or the standard lively drinking tunes. In any case, tonight he had drunk too much. 'You'd better stop,' the landlady said, worried.

He instantly complied with her suggestion, but just as quickly started begging for 'just one more'. As a result, when it was time for him to go home he was totally intoxicated – so woozy that there was no question of sending him off alone. They managed to load him into a cab, but he simply lay there unconscious. Kyōta wanted to ride with him, but he didn't know Mogi's address.

'Well, then, I'll go with you,' the landlady said, climbing right in as soon as she had put a barmaid in charge. 'I know where he lives.' This seemed like more than simple kindness on the part of a landlady, but once the cab started moving, she mumbled an explanation to the effect that she had seen him home the night he drank himself into oblivion after being called a *paypah doggu*.

3

Mogi lived in Jūsō, a ten-minute ride from Umeda, in a little four-room, two-storey house below the Yodo River dike. He snored the whole way there, leaning all his weight against the landlady's shoulder, but he miraculously awoke when she ordered the taxi driver to stop.

'What? I'm home? I was just dreaming I was at the Arima Hot Springs with you,' he said to her.

'Don't be ridiculous! Come on, get out of the cab.'

'Sure, sure. You, too, Apprentice, as long as you've come this far. Have a cup of tea. You wouldn't disobey your master, would you?'

He wouldn't take no for an answer.

Mogi's wife had died during the war. They had a son, a total wastrel according to Mogi, who almost never came home. So, despite his advanced age, Mogi lived alone and cooked for himself. He had hired several maids over the years, but they had apparently all quit, unwilling to put up with his nagging.

Having demanded that his two guests stay, Mogi seemed to find their presence so calming that he promptly collapsed snoring on the tatami.

Kyōta and the landlady looked at each other with resigned smiles.

'He doesn't need us here,' Kyōta said.

'Let's just accept our fate and put him to bed,' the landlady said, pulling Mogi's bedding out of the closet and laying out the mattress.

Kyōta lifted Mogi's shoulders and the landlady took his feet. Together, they just about managed to dump him on to the thin mattress before covering him with a quilt. Mogi mumbled something incoherent and started snoring again.

'He thinks he's got servants here,' she said with a touch of annoyance, yet she tenderly patted down the four corners of the quilt.

Having escaped the bombing, the house was well kitted out with ageing furniture, and Mogi seemed to keep the place neat and clean.

'Time to go, I guess,' the landlady said, casting a melancholy glance around the room.

'Yes,' Kyōta said. 'Well, then, Master, we'll be going.'

There was no reply, of course.

They stepped outside to find the moon glowing in the early autumn sky. There was time, still, until the last train. The two strolled atop the Yodo River dike towards Hankyū Station. Kyōta thought he could hear the flow of the river below. Walking beside the landlady like this deep at night gave Kyōta a special feeling, one not at all unpleasant.

The landlady giggled as though suddenly recalling something.

'Mr Mogi once asked me to come and live with him in that house, you know, just after the war.'

'Oh, really?'

'I lost my house in the bombing, I lost my husband, I had no way to start up the business again, my daughter and I were squeezed in with a relative in Takarazuka: things looked hopeless.'

The landlady had bumped into Mogi when she was walking along Shinsaibashi Street, lost in dark thoughts about the future. He had piped up as usual, 'How are you doing, ma'am? I hope you'll be opening the bar soon. Better not delay or it'll be too late! And besides, I don't know where else to go!'

He took her to a nearby café, where he said the same things to her all over again. She gave him a moving account of her current difficulties.

'I see,' he said. 'It must be tough, living with relatives like that. Why don't you come to my place instead?'

With some hesitation, she told him that she had a seven-year-old daughter to care for.

'That's no problem, bring her along,' he said.

'Thank you so much,' she replied, then gave the invitation some careful thought. Mogi must be a widower, so when he suggested she come and live with him, was it just a matter of offering her a place to live, or was there a deeper meaning to it? This was not merely an abstract question to ponder but a possible turning point in her life. She blushed like a schoolgirl and toyed with her coffee spoon all the while she was mulling things over.

Before she could say anything, Mogi suddenly asked, 'What is O-Kiyo doing these days?'

O-Kiyo was a barmaid who had worked in the Heiroku. The landlady replied that O-Kiyo was also in great distress with nowhere to go.

'All right, then, it doesn't have to be you,' he said breezily, taking a whole new tack. 'Why don't you send her to see me?'

'Well . . .'

'I can put up with either of you; it doesn't matter to me.'

The landlady felt let down at first, then angry. If Mogi had merely been offering her a place to live, she could hardly object to his easy switch from one woman to another, but 'put up with'? And he finally tried to appeal to her sympathies with 'I'm lonely living by myself', which was enough to make her want to call him a horny old goat.

Instead, she said, 'Thank you very much. Let me give it some thought,' and walked out of the café wearing an understandably morose expression, leaving Mogi behind.

After that, the landlady succeeded in opening her present bar, but to this day, she said, she had been unable to repress the mixed feelings of gratitude and anger towards Mogi she experienced whenever she thought of her misery in those early days after the war.

'This is the first I've heard of that,' Kyōta said with a smile. 'But at least Mogi liked you best and O-Kiyo second best.'

The landlady chuckled softly and said with a little pout, 'He probably would have been fine with whichever of us he could get first.' Soon the dim glow of the station lights could be seen in the distance.

'I'll bet Mr Mogi is still snoring,' she said, looking back, but Mogi's little house was no longer visible.

4

Mogi missed work the day after the rumoured fight. He was probably in bed in his Jūsō house, his head bandaged as it had been the night before. Kyōta thought of dropping by to look in on him after work. Otherwise, Mogi was likely to accuse him of coldness. Kyōta was thinking about visiting Mogi when along came Oda, the colleague with whom Mogi had scuffled.

'Look here, Mr Oda,' Kyōta said, 'I can't have you fighting with my master any more. It reflects badly on me as his apprentice.'

'Well, he's the one who started it,' Oda said with an easy smile. 'That *paypah doggu* is just too much for me.'

'But why did someone of your standing have to go and punch him? Both of you are way too old to be getting involved in fisticuffs.'

'Fisticuffs? I never laid a hand on him. He got all worked up and fell off his barstool.'

'You mean he just fell off by himself?'

'Sure. And he caught his head on the corner of a table. He's such a loser. I'm kind of worried about him, though. Could you drop in and see how he's doing?'

'Yes, of course.'

'Thanks, I'm counting on you.'

Oda wandered off towards his desk.

Even supposing that Mogi was jealous of Oda for having been pro-moted over the years, there was no one in the company who found this unfair. They all viewed Oda as someone special, forgetting that he had ever been a temp. This was due entirely to the fine figure he had cut when he was evacuated from Dalian after Japan lost the war.

The company had sent him to China and made him chief of the Dalian branch. Most people who were evacuated from China following Japan's surrender came back looking like beggars, but Oda walked into the office wearing a 100-per-cent-wool suit and London-made hat and carrying a snakewood walking stick, like some kind of fine British gentleman. You hardly ever saw such a well-dressed chap in the Japanese homeland in those days, let alone in the far-flung corners of the now-defunct empire.

'What's with the suit?' the Director asked.

'I wore this all the way back from Dalian.'

'Oh, come on, Oda, you –'

'Please, sir,' Oda stopped him in order to announce, as though he had been looking forward to this moment, 'if I may say so, Oda Yoshirō made quite a name for himself representing our company in Dalian. Japan may have lost the war, but that is no excuse for people to come back dressed like beggars. I decided that there should be at least one evacuee displaying the dignity of a proper Japanese. Of course I disdained anything so abject as wearing a backpack. This is what it means to be a man.'

'Magnificent, Oda!' the Director cried. 'I couldn't have said it better myself.' He added, 'You are the honour and glory of our company.' Oda was immediately elevated to Assistant to the Assistant Director.

Everyone thought it a near miracle that Oda had escaped in such style from the desperation and chaos on the Chinese mainland. The whole company sensed in him the heroism of Japan's old Restoration patriots, and indeed, he carried himself with a dignity and composure one would expect from such men.

Mogi never should have tangled with an opponent of Oda's calibre. When people heard that Mr English had received a bloody head wound, rather than asking what had caused it, they said, 'Maybe he's learned his lesson' or 'He should know better at his age.'

Kyōta dropped by Mogi's house on his way home from work that day. Mogi was alone, lying on his mattress in the room facing the garden.

'Oh, thanks for coming,' Mogi said with obvious pleasure, as if he had been waiting all day for Kyōta to visit.

'I'm afraid you cut a sorry figure last night, Master.'

'I should never have let my guard down.'

'I hear you got all worked up and fell off your barstool. You really made a fool of yourself. Oda told me about it.'

'Oh, really? Now he's sunk to a new low. He saw me getting up and kicked my barstool out from under me. Here, let me tell you what *really* happened.'

Mogi had been drinking at the Heiroku the night before. The landlady was keeping him company and he was fairly drunk when Oda showed up.

'That son of a bitch has his eye on the landlady,' Mogi said to Kyōta, 'and he's been coming to the bar a lot lately. Anyhow, I never liked him.'

Kyōta heard this as a virtual confession that the two men were rivals in love.

Oda had given Mogi a grunt and sat down on the barstool next to his. Mogi just glared back at him without replying, which obviously annoyed Oda. The two started drinking almost back to back, deliberately ignoring each other while each man watched the other's alcohol consumption.

'Ma'am, more sake!' Mogi waved his now-empty sake bottle in the air for her to see.

'Ma'am, more sake, please!' Oda said a moment later and shook his own sake bottle. It made a hollow splash, revealing that it was far from empty. Not even the heroic Oda could help but be embarrassed by the revelation, and he blushed slightly as he set his bottle down. Then quickly, as if to hide his embarrassment, he called out, 'Ma'am, beef strips fried in butter, please!'

Not to be outdone, Mogi called, 'Beef strips in butter, ma'am, superior cut.'

'Make mine the best quality, and *extra large*,' Oda countered.

The landlady looked back and forth between the two men in disbelief.

'The only butter-fried beef we have is normal grade. We're all out of "superior cut" and "best quality" and "extra large" today!'

To Mogi she served wasabi fish cakes and to Oda miso cucumbers. 'You'll have to make do with these,' she said, her show of equal treatment eliciting stifled laughter from her other customers. Oda had the good sense to join in the lightened mood, but Mogi was still fuming.

Stealing a glance at the stubborn Mogi, Oda said to the landlady, 'I gather you had a very difficult time after your first place was bombed. A tough time with men, too. I heard that one man tried to seduce you, using his house as bait.'

A shiver seemed to run through the fingers with which Mogi held his sake cup, but Oda went on to the shocked-looking landlady as if chatting about everyday things: 'And the way I heard it, when you didn't answer him, the fellow said he could "put up with" O-Kiyo instead of you. I saw O-Kiyo the other day, and let me tell you, she was mad! "For him to say something like that – he can 'put up with O-Kiyo' – just goes to show what a horny old goat he is! What nerve!" she said. I don't blame her for being mad. I don't suppose the fellow comes here any more, does he? If he does, I'd like to see what he looks like. Or maybe I'm wrong – maybe he's somewhere close by. But what an idiot!'

Following this little speech, Oda ostentatiously sipped his sake amid a second wave of stifled laughter.

Then it was Mogi's turn to address the landlady. 'Here's a little scoop for you I've never told anyone before.'

Now the others pricked up their ears in anticipation of a third wave.

'A few years ago, I just happened to be passing Osaka Station when I saw a group of evacuees from Dalian. One of them was a man I knew well. It made me so happy to see he had found his way back from the Chinese mainland safe and sound! But he was very impressive. While all the others were dressed in rags, he was a veritable crane among chickens, wearing a suit and carrying a stick like a fine English gentleman. "Japan may have lost the war," he said, "but as a true Japanese I didn't want to evacuate to the homeland looking shabby." This was the genuine samurai spirit. The samurai flaunts his toothpick even when starving. Of course, this particular "samurai" came from a long line of Kyushu farmers.'

Mogi took a slug of sake. The landlady glanced at Oda, who was looking rather proud of himself.

'So anyway, standing behind this preening peacock was his wife. And was she dressed in a gorgeous kimono to match his suit? No, she had on a hideous pair of farm trousers, a towel wrapped around her head, and the pack on her back looked big enough to snap her in two.'

'I've never heard of anything so ridiculous!' the landlady said, fuming.

'In other words, this fellow had travelled all the way from China, letting his wife carry a gigantic pack while he himself wore a fancy suit, sported a walking stick and carried on as if he was the one true Japanese. The poor woman! This turned me against him then and there. "You call yourself a man, treating her like that?" I said to him. "No no," he says as if it was nothing at all. "She wanted to do this. She's a model wife." And maybe he was right about his own wife, but to me, in that precious suit of his, he looked like some black marketeer making a show of his fancy clothes. It was like catching some big, famous guy with a snot ball hanging from his nose.'

'Hey,' Oda said.

'What?' Mogi answered.

'"Black marketeer"? "Snot ball"?'

'"Horny old goat"?'

Both men ran out of things to say after that, glaring as if ready to bite each other's head off. To be sure, they did not start throwing punches, but the longer Mogi focused on Oda's face, the more his accumulated resentment boiled up until, almost without thinking, he emptied his sake cup on to Oda's suit. Certain that Oda would strike back, Mogi started to get up from his barstool to brace himself, but in the next instant, he and the barstool clattered to the floor.

5

'There's no way someone like me would just fall off his chair like that. Oda kicked it out from under me, no question,' Mogi insisted again.

Kyōta struggled to keep from laughing. 'So it was two old fellows in a love feud,' he said.

'Well, I suppose it boils down to that,' Mogi admitted with surprising ease. 'But hey, I'm not such an old fellow.'

The two men fell silent at that point. Kyōta looked outside towards the corner of the garden, where a white flower glowed softly in the darkness.

'You know, Kazama, it's lonely sleeping alone like this.'

'I know.'

'Hey, do you think the Heiroku landlady could ever fall for me?'

Mogi said that the Heiroku landlady looked a lot like the young daughter of the family who ran the dry-goods shop where he worked as a boy. This meant she looked like his first love of forty years earlier, whose memory he had carried with him in his travels around the Chinese mainland. Whether or not it was actually possible to remember a woman's face for forty years, Mogi believed he did.

'Even if she does like you, nothing's ever going to come of it,' Kyōta said.

'Well, that's a mean thing to say. What proof do you have?'

'It's just a guess, but I suspect the landlady found herself a patron who helped her open her new bar. And I also imagine that even if he decided not to make any demands on her at first, it's becoming harder and harder for him to control himself. The landlady is very attractive even to us, and all *we* can do is look at her, so you can imagine how worked up this patron of hers is getting. And with that special kindness of hers, she's bound to respond to his passion. In fact, I imagine she has already responded.'

'You've got a pretty ugly imagination.'

'No, just an imagination.'

'So how about Oda?'

'It's probably the same for him, I imagine, but –'

'Well, if you imagine it's the same for him, there was no point in us fighting, was there? So I got hurt for nothing?'

'I guess I'd have to say that.'

'And O-Kiyo's out of the question, too. It's a hopeless situation.'

Mogi seemed to have resigned himself to losing both women. Just then the front door slid open.

'Good evening, Father,' said a young voice, instantaneously transforming Mogi's newly softened expression into a stern mask. In walked a young man in his mid-twenties. Kyōta knew at a glance that this had to be Mogi's son, the 'great playboy' who never came to visit him, but this shameless profligate had a remarkably clear gaze, and he had a lovely young thing with him who was perhaps twenty years old.

Kyōta seized the moment. 'Well, then, I guess I'll be going,' he announced, getting to his feet.

He stepped outside and lit a cigarette. He was starting to walk away when he heard Mogi shout at the top of his lungs, 'Get the hell out of here! You've got some nerve coming here to tell me that!'

Kyōta stopped dead in his tracks.

'But Father –'

'Don't "But Father" me! You never come to see me, and now all of a sudden you show up with a girl and ask me to let you marry her? You selfish little twerp!'

'We want to get married and take care of you.'

'Ridiculous! I can take care of myself perfectly well, thank you! I don't want to become beholden to some unfilial idiot who thinks he's going to "take care" of me all of a sudden!'

'But Father, I only left the house because you wouldn't stop nagging me. You never tried to understand me.'

'What are you talking about? I nagged you *because* I understood you! Now listen to me. The only reason I have had to endure the shame of being a mere temp all these years is that I didn't have a college education – because I never went beyond primary school. I wanted to make sure I put you through college so you wouldn't have to experience the pain I've lived with. I was willing to do anything to make you into a college-educated company man. That was my dream!'

Mogi's voice seethed with righteous indignation. Kyōta couldn't help believing that, deep in his heart, Mogi was almost certainly crying.

'As soon as you finished middle school, though, you started saying you didn't want to go to school any more. I finally managed to get you into high school, but they called me in and told me you hadn't been attending at all. That's when I found out you had been studying drawing – that you wanted to become an artist! Well, let me tell you, mister, it's not that easy to make your living as an artist. I had to put my foot down. I threatened to stop paying your rent to try to convince you to abandon that dream, but you gave me all this big talk about making your own way in life, and then walked right out of here. Do you have any idea how that made me feel? And after bragging how you're going to become this big artist, what do you end up doing? Painting posters!'

'But Father, that's what I wanted to tell you: I've had a work accepted in an exhibition.'

'You what?'

'This is the time for me to come home and take care of you and –'

'You idiot!'

Mogi's ferocious shout seemed to shake the air around Kyōta.

'So you think getting one picture accepted in an exhibition makes you an artist? Well, let me tell you how I got to where I am today. I have unshakeable confidence that my English is second to none – and I've never been anywhere outside this country but China! I got that confidence with sheer hard work, pouring every ounce of my strength into studying. That's how I made it my calling, my life's work – and I'm just talking about English. To become a real artist, you have to work even harder than I did on English. You have to give it everything you've got. But here you are, walking on air because you had one lousy painting accepted, all pleased with yourself as if you've got it made.'

'No, Father, I don't feel that way at all.'

'You've got to do better than that! I don't want to be "taken care of" by some dreamy-eyed son who wants to play filial piety games with me all of a sudden. If you really want to practise filial piety, come back to me after you've established yourself as a full-fledged artist. I'll stick it out here by myself as long as it takes – ten years, twenty years, a lifetime.'

With that, the house fell silent.

Kyōta peeked through a knothole in the fence to see the son and his girlfriend kneeling on the matted floor, their heads hanging down. Beside them knelt Mogi, his head still wrapped in bandages, staring with gritted teeth at a spot in the garden. In the lamplight, Kyōta thought he saw a glistening tear glide down from Mogi's eye.

6

Mogi stayed away from work for three days. On the fourth day, he removed his bandages and went in to the office. Kyōta had been sent to Kobe that day, but as soon as he returned to the office at two o'clock, he went to see Mogi, who was just then engaged in a verbal tug of war with the errand boy.

'I don't want this,' Mogi was saying. 'Give it back to the Director.'

'But –' The young man stood there in confusion, holding a sheet of paper.

'What's that?' Kyōta asked.

'Here, sir, have a look.'

Kyōta saw that it was a notice of dismissal for Mogi.

'What's this all about?'

'The Director says I'm fired, damn him. He thinks I'm worthless.'

As soon as he arrived at the office, Mogi said, the Director had called him in and growled at him, 'I hear you got into a bar fight, a man of your age. Don't you see what tremendous harm something like that can do to the company's reputation?'

Mogi, unbowed, shot back, 'The company's reputation? Come on, it was just a little bar fight. Don't make such a big deal about it.'

'So you've decided to be insubordinate, huh? It's that rash attitude that makes everybody here hate you.'

'I do my job the way I'm supposed to do it.'

'The problem is with your humanity. Humanity is everything.'

'And my English ability is nothing?'

'Your level of English is nothing special any more. Everybody can speak as well as you these days, especially the younger employees. I've been thinking for a while it's about time to have you hand in your resignation.'

'I will never resign.'

'And why not?'

'It's the rule: temps stay on until they turn sixty.'

'Unless the company no longer needs them. Then it only makes sense for us to have you resign.'

The Director had probably not intended to go that far, but both men were worked up, and one remark led to another.

'Not me. I will not resign.'

'I'll see to it that you do.'

'No, never.'

With that, Mogi had stalked out of the Director's office. At that point, Oda came strolling along.

'What happened? Did the boss give you a dressing down? I got mine the other day.'

'Oh, really? You, too?'

If that was the case, Mogi concluded, there had been no favouritism involved.

'I don't suppose he fired you, though.'

'No, of course not.'

'He says he's going to fire me.'

'That's crazy.'

'I know. So I refused to quit.'

'That's the spirit!'

'You think so? Even you?'

'I do.'

'That's great. I'm surprised: we see eye to eye.'

'What are you talking about? Back when I was the hit of Dalian –'

'Oh, shut up! You make me sick to my stomach with that stuff.'

'What the hell – you *paypah doggu*, you!'

'You had to go and say it, huh? Snot ball!'

'All right, enough of this. It's just going to lower my dignity. Let's stop the fighting for now,' Oda said, calling for compromise.

That afternoon, however, the Director had reached boiling point, it seemed. He sent the errand boy to deliver the notice of dismissal. Mogi refused to accept it and sent the boy back. A short time later, the boy brought the notice again, 'on orders from the Director'. Kyōta came in at that point, and so did Oda.

'Mark my words,' Mogi said, 'if I resign now, the company is going to have big problems. Negotiations with IES will be starting soon. It's totally presumptuous to think some rookie can take my place at a time like this. That's how much confidence I have in my own English. It kills me to think that so little value is placed on my English skills that I can be fired for a mere bar fight. I refuse to resign. I will come to work every day. I couldn't ask for a better opponent than the Director. And why is that? Because I'm the one and only *paypah doggu*.'

After delivering this speech to Kyōta, Mogi said to the boy, 'Hey, snap out of it! Take that notice back to the Director immediately and tell him I don't want it. That's what your job is all about.'

'Yes, but –'

The boy was at a total loss and finally blurted out, 'I feel like Taira no Shigemori.'

'What the hell are you talking about? Shigemori lived eight hundred years ago – you're nothing like him!' Mogi barked.

'Well, kind of . . . evil general's son . . . tried to be a good guy . . .'

'Hey, errand boy Shigemori,' Oda interjected, 'nobody's going to take that scrap of paper from you, so just leave it in your desk drawer for a while.'

'Oh, all right,' the young man said with a sigh as if he had finally found a way out of his predicament. 'I'll do that,' he added as he left.

'Do you really think that's all right?' Kyōta asked. 'Wouldn't the safest thing be to take the humble approach and apologize?'

But Mogi said he absolutely refused to apologize.

Even Oda egged him on: 'No, you really shouldn't apologize.'

True to his word, from the following day on, Mogi came to work as usual. All the office gossip suddenly focused on him, much of it in his favour:

'This is the strangest thing that's ever happened in the company's history.'

'You have to hand it to Mr English. He's not all bad.'

Employees always had to worry about being let go. If Mogi's high-handed tactics worked, they should be taken as a model of the best way to respond to a firing. No, Mogi was probably the only one who could get away with such a thing. If someone else tried it, he might be in for a rude awakening. The Director who fired Mogi was acting grumpy these days, as if his authority had been slighted. But what was most likely preventing him from adopting a more decisive attitude was his unease about the approaching negotiations with IES. Mogi was undoubtedly aware of the Director's nervousness, but a young employee in Administration had already been chosen to do the interpreting. The fellow could be depended upon to handle ordinary interpreting, but when it came to negotiations like these, which presented major problems involving the introduction of both technology and foreign capital, the interpreter had to have a commensurate amount of sheer guts.

The negotiations started. If they proceeded smoothly without Mogi, his reputation would be ruined. Not surprisingly, even Mogi appeared nervous that day. He came and sat by Kyōta's desk first thing in the morning. Kyōta deliberately avoided mentioning the negotiations. 'So, what did you do about your son?' he asked.

'The rascal! Of course I sent him packing that night.'

'Sounds cold-hearted to me.'

'Cold-hearted? It was the only thing to do.'

'No, it was cold-hearted, even cruel. I'm not going to call you "Master" any more.'

'Hey, wait a minute now, Apprentice, don't be so hasty. To tell you the truth . . .'

'The truth? About what?'

A look of embarrassment came over Mogi such as he had rarely, if ever, displayed.

'Tarō told me he had worked hard and made himself into a real artist, so I figured I had to light one last fire under his tail. And that young bride of his wouldn't have been able to stand me nagging her from morning to night. Let's call it a father's love at work.'

'Very impressive, Master.'

'Hey, enough with the flattery. I can see right through you,' Mogi said shyly.

'Doesn't this mean you're going to go on being lonely?' Kyōta asked.

'I'm used to being by myself. If I get lonely, I can just take aim at the Heiroku's landlady. I'm still full of energy, and I will be for a while yet. Hey, what do you say we invite Oda along and go to the Heiroku tonight?'

Mogi gave him a big smile, but Kyōta was thinking about Mogi's face as he had seen it through the knothole in the fence.

The errand boy came running up to them at that point. 'Mr Mogi,' he said, 'the Director wants you in the reception room right away.'

'What for?' Mogi asked, playing dumb, but his face was suddenly brimming with life.

'I don't know, but he says you'd better hurry.'

'No, first I want you to go ask what this is about.'

A moment or two later, the Director himself came running in.

'Mogi, come *now*!'

'Oh my, what could this be about?'

'It's your old friend Mr O'Brien from IES. He says he misses you. Come and say hello to him.'

'If it's just a matter of saying hello, I can do that later.'

'Look, don't needle me at a time like this. Mr O'Brien wants you to interpret.'

'But I thought you fired me.'

'Yes, but you wouldn't accept the notice, would you? That makes us even. It's still your duty to follow company orders. Come *now!*'

'Go ahead, Mogi,' Kyōta said from the side.

'Well, then, I suppose I ought to go . . .'

Mogi rose up with a lordly air, the eyes of the entire office focused on him. Never before had the countenance – indeed, the whole physique – of Mr English, Soichirō Mogi, shone with such splendid vigour, like a fish that has finally found its way back into water.

BETSUYAKU MINORU

Factory Town

Translated by Royall Tyler

One day, just like that, a small factory appeared on the outskirts of the town. Its chimney began puffing out great billows of black smoke.

'Goodness!' some townsfolk exclaimed when they happened by. 'What's going on here?'

'Looks like a factory to me, with all that smoke coming out of the chimney.'

'Fine, but what's it *making*?'

'I wonder.'

So they stole up to the factory and one man peeked in through a knot-hole in the fence.

'What's that going thunka-thunka-thunka?'

'Must be the machine. There's a huge, black machine in there going round and round. But what can it be making?'

'Come on, now, give me a look! Yes, it's the machine, all right. A *big* one! Oh – I see some men working!'

'What are they like?'

'There are three of them. The older one must be the father and the two younger ones his sons.'

'So – a family.'

'They're covered with grease, and they're certainly going at it!'

'Can you tell what they're making?'

'I wish I could.'

Anyway, the news about the factory spread that day by word of mouth through the whole town. Mothers back from shopping, fathers strolling in the park, sisters and brothers sipping tea in the coffee shop – everyone was talking about it.

'Pots and pans, that's what they're making, if you ask me. Our town has a serious shortage of both, you know.'

'I'll go for sickles and hoes. Tools like that wear out right away. You keep needing new ones.'

'I'd say they're baking bread. We do have a baker, but he's always so slow getting the bread out.'

The baker thought otherwise.

'No, it's not bread. Must be charcoal briquettes. That black smoke isn't from baking. It's from making briquettes.

The briquette-maker disagreed, of course.

'No, not briquettes. The smell's wrong. That's a brick factory. They're making bricks.

'Bricks? Not a chance!' the brick-maker roared, red in the face. 'I'm damned if I'll have them coming around here, making bricks! No, no, it's something else. Must be glass. They're making bottles and glasses.'

Day after day the talk went on, but there was still no sign of the product. Not that the men at the factory were slacking off. Black smoke billowed daily from the chimney, and through the knothole you could see the two sons and the father, black with grease, working away like mad. You had only to stroll past the place to hear the machine's endless thunka-thunka-thunka.

'When do those people *rest?*' the townspeople wondered whenever they peeked through the knothole.

'What incredible workers!'

'I've never seen anyone work like that!

'I want my son to see this!'

'I'm going to tell my husband he needs to do better!'

All the people in this town much preferred relaxing to working. And why not? The crops in the fields grew by themselves, the sea yielded more fish than they could eat, and you could work hard and save all the money you liked, but there was still nothing to spend it on.

Once the factory turned up, though, people's ideas began to change. That black smoke billowing up so bravely from the little factory stirred everyone deeply. From the hilltop you could see the whole town, sleepily nestled in green. The factory alone looked sturdy, like a steam locomotive chugging through the fields.

'That's what I call *bold*!' the boys looking down from up there exclaimed to one another.

'That's what I call *macho*!'

Meanwhile, their mothers and big sisters kept egging them on.

'The factory starts work at 7 a.m., you know.'

'They take only ten-minute breaks.'

'They work with the lights on after dark.'

The boys pulled themselves together and tried getting up early and going to bed late. They still had no work to do, though. They could only wander around town looking busy and end up at the factory fence. They took turns at the knothole, sighing with envy.

'Their eyes are so bright!'

'Look at that sweat! He doesn't even wipe it off!'

'And those arms! He picked up that heavy hammer like nothing!'

The factory kept at it, but there was still no sign of a product.

'They're really working, though. It'll be fantastic, whatever they're making.'

'Absolutely! Look what a big machine they have!'

The townspeople kept picturing this product or that, and they could hardly wait for it to come on sale.

'Still, don't you think there's a little too much smoke coming from that chimney?'

'Actually, yes, I suppose there is. The sky always seems kind of cloudy.'

The black smoke kept boiling up from the factory chimney. Day after day the sky over the town, once blue, stayed grey.

'They can't help it, though. It's such a big machine!'

'I just know they're racing to get the product out as soon as they can.'

'It's got to be something good.'

'Yes, indeed.'

One of the boys who got up early one morning let out a great shout in front of his house.

'Hey! Look! The factory's got *two* chimneys!'

Everyone within earshot came out to see, rubbing their sleepy eyes. The sight was impressive. Two great smokestacks now towered over the little factory, spewing two thick columns of black smoke into the dawn sky. The smoke drifted heavily, lazily towards the town. You could just make out tiny black specks glittering down from it.

'That's awesome!'

'That smoke makes me feel a sort of power rising up inside me.'

'They must've reached the last stage. That's why they've added another stack. They know how much we look forward to what they're making, and they're rushing to get it done.'

'What's it going to be?'

'Something amazing, something we can really use.'

'I'm sure you're right.'

Every day after that the twin stacks belched out twin columns of smoke. What with the soot, the people could no longer walk about with their eyes open. Their throats were so sore that they coughed every minute or two. Laundry hanging on the line, their clothing, even their faces turned black. Still, they put up with it all patiently, sure that the product would be something truly special.

At last one day, though, they couldn't take it any more. They went to talk things over with the mayor.

'We're wondering what to do. The smoke is so bad now. We hate to complain to such hard workers, but couldn't we at least get them to tell us when they'll have their product ready and what it'll be?'

'I see what you mean. We can hold out a little longer if they're making something really good. All right, let's go and hear what they have to say.'

The mayor and the townspeople trooped out to the factory, coughing and brushing off the soot as they went.

'Hello, gentlemen of the factory!'

Out came the hard-working factory chief, his blackened face beaming.

'Hello! So it's you, Mr Mayor! And everyone else, too? What's up?'

'You see, the people of the town would like to know when your product will be out.'

'Oh, is *that* it? Then, I have good news. It's finally ready.'

'Really? It *is*?'

'Yes. Come right in. I'll show you. You will all be very pleased.'

Cheering, the townsfolk followed the chief inside. He and his sons welcomed them with smiles.

'Now, have a look at this!'

He pointed to a shiny little machine next to the great big one they'd seen through the knothole. Pearl-like beads were popping out one end and dropping into a hopper.

The chief handed the mayor a bead. The mayor stared at it in his hand.

'Umm, what is this?'

'Put it in your mouth! It's a cough drop.'

'A cough drop?'

The people cheered loudly again. Just then, you see, they were coughing so much that they could hardly breathe.

'Yes, indeed. Ladies and gentlemen, our product is cough drops. They are a little expensive, but they really work!'

'So you *have* been making something wonderful!'

'It's exactly what we need right now!'

'I'll take one this minute!'

They bought the drops straight from the hands of the smiling chief and his sons and began taking them, right there in the factory. Meanwhile the mayor asked his burning question.

'Excuse me, Mr Factory Chief, I understand that the little machine makes cough drops. But what does the big one make?' He gestured towards the big machine that the townsfolk had seen through the knothole. 'It has two smokestacks, after all. It must make something even better.'

'Oh, that one?' the chief asked, still beaming. 'That one doesn't make anything.'

'It doesn't make *anything*?'

'No. Just smoke. We had quite a time, you know, putting up that second stack. Still, when you get right down to it, two stacks put out a lot more smoke than one.'

KAWAKAMI MIEKO

Dreams of Love, Etc.

Translated by Hitomi Yoshio

I don't know what these particular roses are called – there are hundreds of different species in the world, after all. But roses they are, for certain. Under the cloudy June sky, I see the buds on the new green stems that stretch out left and right, some still small and tight and some about to bloom, and I sometimes wonder what it is that makes them so obviously roses. Is it the thorns, the petals, or something else? Somewhere in the world, there must be roses that have shapes and colours and clusters that I could never imagine, and if I were to encounter them unexpectedly, perhaps on a journey – in Edinburgh or maybe Macedonia – what then? Yet, even if I had never laid eyes on them before, I would know . . . right. As I water my flowers with an insanely long hose that leaks at the nozzle – it must be torn or rotten or something – I let my thoughts wander this morning, the way they do every morning.

There is one decent flower shop in the arcade near the train station. By decent, I mean you can pop in, give them a price and count on them to make a nice bouquet. That day, I saw they had some with white flowers and tiny dark green leaves, and, wanting to, in a way, celebrate the beautiful weather, I said to the shopkeeper, Could I have three of those rose bushes please?

As I was paying, I added, I've never bought flowers that weren't pre-cut, and the overly plump girl said with an overly large smile, This one here, it'll bloom all year long if you take good care of it. Buoyed by her swelling presence, I returned the girl's smile and said with a wave, I'll take good care of it.

The big earthquake[1] hit two months after we bought a house near the river, and for a while I felt depressed and out of sorts. My husband has

278

always maintained that there's nothing to worry about in Tokyo – who knows if he really believes that or if he's just fooling himself? A month after the earthquake, though, my tension and anxiety were starting to wear off, and then before I knew it spring had passed by in a daze. That's how I ended up buying the roses. I recall the flower shop that day was crowded with local housewives and mothers. One practically shoved her face into the bushy pots of ivy and olive, pointed to the colourful flowers in the back of the cool glass case and said, Could I have more of those? Others said things like, You'll call me when new ones come in, won't you? or, Actually, I'll have some of these too. They bustled back and forth in the narrow shop with armloads of plants as if in some kind of competition. I remember thinking how tasteless one woman's oversized purse was with its pimply grey ostrich leather.

That evening, I asked my husband when he came home from work, Do you think people buy flowers and things because it makes them feel safer to pretend that everything is back to normal?

Yeah, there's probably something to that.

So much for that topic.

Oh, that reminds me of a story I heard – or maybe read somewhere. You know some mixed couples, they apparently fight over whether to leave Japan or not. They get caught between the Japanese partner saying they shouldn't leave no matter what and the foreign partner saying they'd be crazy not to leave in such an emergency. They have so much trouble putting those feelings into words, a lot of them have ended up divorcing. That's what I read.

Hmm, well it's true that people are dealing with a lot these days, my husband said before slipping from my sight as usual.

But I had been hoping to say more. At the very least we're both Japanese, you and me – I don't know, who knows what will happen, maybe there'll be a big explosion and we'll all die – but still don't you think we're better off than they are? Because we're inherently the same, even if that means we're just resigned to our fate. And maybe that's not such a bad thing? That was what I wanted to say.

My husband comes home late. Usually I try not to think about how I fill my days when I'm alone, and when I do, it depresses me. I don't work. I'm not pregnant. Housework for two, washing and cleaning, takes two hours at most, even now that we live in a proper house. I don't watch TV. I don't read books. Come to think of it, I don't do anything. I don't take lessons, and I don't have the skills or the patience to cook a fancy meal. I really don't do anything at all. Stretched out on the sofa, I would hear a piano trilling away somewhere every day. It sounded so good I thought it was a recording at first, but sometimes it would break off or repeat a passage so I knew it was someone practising. Or maybe that was part of the interpretation? In any case, it would start at random hours. Sometimes at nine in the morning, sometimes in the evening, sometimes as late as ten o'clock at night. So someone is playing a piano somewhere, but that someone is not me. Whenever I start thinking about how I do absolutely nothing at all, these pairs of white doors slide open behind my forehead, one after another, and once I dozed off and had a really pointless dream. I want to avoid things like that. But I can't help thinking about it sometimes, so the other day I sat down at the dining table and wrote the Chinese character for *what*. It felt like a totally useless exercise, until I discovered that the character for *what* looks exactly like my face when you examine it closely.

So that's how I go about my days, doing nothing, but since buying the roses I started picking up some potted plants when I was in the mood, and now I have quite a collection. We don't have a garden, so they're all laid out around the edge of the front porch. I set a pot of ivy on top of the lamp post attached to the mailbox and let the leaves dangle like hair. I put a potted olive tree next to it, and underneath a row of maidenhair ferns, violets, eucalyptus and those robust little blue flowers that I can never remember the name of. And some chocolate cosmos too, so they looked just so, like the entrance of a café. I transplanted those first roses into larger pots, and to my surprise, they expanded so shamelessly that their size almost doubled. The buds kept multiplying like rabbits. I visited online forums to learn how to plant different varieties in a single pot, and while I was there bought all sorts of things, like a shovel, fertilizer and those little pebbles that you line the bottom of pots with. I bought special scissors and started snipping off the yellow and black leaves that were no longer healthy. That made me feel good, like I was giving someone a haircut.

The more I got into it, the more I started to wonder about other people's gardens and flower beds, and so I began going for walks every morning. You could easily tell which plants were being well taken care of and which were not. Seeing neglected flowers or trees always reminded me of my childhood. I saw countless camellias – one of the few flowers I could identify – growing straight and sober. They seemed to be popular around here. Their thick, oily petals had always struck me as artificial, and I wondered why so many people planted these walls of camellias around their houses. Well, apparently camellias prevent fire, and come to think of it they really do look impervious to flames, so I guess it's a good thing.

I sometimes fantasize about our house being broken into. Of course it wouldn't be an ordinary burglary. It would be really gory and ghoulish – I'd be torn to shreds and whatnot – and then reporters with nothing better to do would swarm like flies to our house from all over and interview the neighbours, pointing mics at them and asking the usual, What was the victim like? And they would probably answer, Well, yes, we never talked or anything, but I got the impression that she was very fond of gardening. I'd see her taking really good care of her plants in the morning and afternoon, and even at night. These thoughts made me feel a little better as I unravelled the ever-expanding ivy tangles.

One afternoon, I was trimming the overgrown roots of my wild strawberries when I heard the garage door rumble up lazily next door and a Mercedes stuck its nose out. A big car, round and dull. A woman with her arms crossed came out to see the car speed off, though the driver remained in the shadows from where I stood. Noticing me, the woman gave me a very friendly smile and said, Hello there, your flowers always look so lovely, then smiled again.

Oh, not at all, I just buy them and stick them here. I smiled back, just as friendly.

Her face suggested that she was in her early sixties, but the rest of her said seventy. Her hair was almost entirely white, as if the thought of dyeing it had never occurred to her. Her face was no longer firm; devoid of make-up, it had an eerily transparent quality. It reminded me of an old woman I once saw in a sauna or at a hot-springs resort, whose nipples had completely lost their pigment and looked like a child's.

When we first moved here, I had paid courtesy calls around the neighbourhood with boxes of sweets. Since her house had remained silent no matter how many times I rang the doorbell, this was the first time I had had a chance to speak to her.

You have such an eye for flowers. I always enjoy looking at them.

Thank you for saying that. By the way, is there someone who plays the piano in your home? Someone who plays extremely well?

Oh my! That's me – I'm the one playing.

Really! How wonderful. I enjoy listening to it so much. You're a terrific pianist.

Not at all. I played for about ten years when I was growing up, then stopped. I'm embarrassed to say that I only started fooling around with it again in my old age.

That's so nice. I don't know . . . I really envy that you can play for yourself. I think it's wonderful.

The car that left just now, he's the piano tuner. I asked him to sit down and listen to me play, but oh my, I couldn't play at all. When I'm all alone, I somehow manage to play a piece through till the end, but with someone listening I always make mistakes.

But I really thought it was a CD at first.

I wonder which piece that was?

I couldn't say, but I'm sure it's famous since even I recognized it. It goes duum, da, dum in the beginning and then repeats the same notes.

Oh, that's Liszt. Liszt's *Liebestraum*. Dream of Love.

Yes, that sounds right. The melody does sound like it might have a title like that. It's such a pretty piece.

Why don't you come over one of these days? My piano is nothing to listen to, but I could offer you a cup of tea at the very least.

So the day after the day after next, I bought a pile of colourful macarons at the macaron shop in the arcade, stopped at the Takashimaya department store nearby to pick up the second most expensive box of cherries, and rang her doorbell. It was two o'clock in the afternoon – that most vacant time of the day when the laundry is done and the vacuum put away, but it's still too early to go food shopping. The time when you feel most keenly that you are useless and the world is silently laughing at you from afar. No matter how hard you try to inflate your fantasies, mobilizing all the memories, imaginings and gossip you can muster, you just can't seem to fill up the space. It was right then, when one is stupidly waiting for anything to happen, that I rang the doorbell and soon heard her voice over the intercom. Why hello!

Hello, a friend gave me a big box of cherries – I thought you might like some.

Hold on just a moment, I'll open the door.

Her house seemed much more spacious than mine. It was spotlessly clean and the furniture went together perfectly. Every single piece seemed expensive, every curve had its own particular sheen. There was that distinctive smell that always lingers in other people's homes, which I found pleasing. The large, superbly soft leather couch felt cold on my thighs, but after a few seconds it warmed up. I placed the boxes of macarons and cherries on the coffee table with a polite bow. Thanking me with a smile, she took the two boxes to the kitchen and soon returned with some coffee and the macarons neatly arranged on a plate. I had half expected to see a maid walk in. I sipped the coffee and took a tiny bite of a macaron. It's such a peculiar feeling, buying macarons. You feel like a complete idiot, and yet that very absurdity makes it somehow satisfying. They're unbearably sweet, and the outer shell never fails to stick to the roof of your mouth, and besides the name is so silly. It's infuriating how overpriced they are, only because people think they're something special. They only remind you that you've never once thought they tasted good.

I'll have the pink one, if you don't mind.

Please. This yellow one is quite exquisite too.

After a while, she began to tell me the history of her relationship with the piano. Her first teacher, her first recital. Bach's Inventions and the effects of age on one's hands and one's ear, etc., etc. I was more curious about what her husband did for a living, or her family members, or about so-and-so in the neighbourhood, or whether property values had really fallen in our area because of the earthquake, or anything that would pass the time – frivolous topics perfect for occasions such as this – but she seemed uninterested in small talk and never asked me about such things either. As I listened to her, remembering to nod from time to time, I began to recognize something familiar hidden in the tone of her voice, or maybe in her way of speaking. I didn't know what it was exactly. It felt as if a piece of fabric was fluttering at the edge of my vision. I couldn't tell its colour or size. All I could catch was the fluttering movement. And as I sat listening to this unfamiliar woman tell unfamiliar stories while sitting on an unfamiliar sofa in an unfamiliar house, I felt something loosen up somewhere between my throat and my belly button. It was a kind of aimless, gentle feeling, like someone holding my hand and tracing my palm with their fingers, reminding me of the unsurprising fact that I too was a complete stranger to someone else. But it wasn't the sort of gentle feeling that I could simply surrender myself to. It also reminded me of all the anxieties, jealousies, impulses and passions that had once made me, and those around me, suffer so irrationally – stupid as it sounds as I write about it now – and of the fact that those things have left without a trace, and that what I see now, what I can touch and smell from here onwards, are only remnants of all that once was.

Having talked and nodded and let a certain amount of time go by, we both realized we had nothing more to offer one another, and probably had nothing to begin with. I should be going soon, I said, I had such a wonderful time. As I smiled and gestured to leave, she asked, hesitantly, if I wouldn't mind listening to her play just one piece on the piano. Of course, I replied with a reassuring smile, following her into the room with the piano.

The piano was in her bedroom, a spacious room of about fifteen tatami mats; here too, expensive furniture lined the walls with the heavy forthrightness of a coffin for a bear that had lived an admirably ascetic life. Sitting down on the ottoman, I said, What a lovely bedroom. Tell me, Ms . . . I realized that I couldn't remember her name. What was it? What was the name of this woman standing before me? No matter how many times I wiped my imaginary mind with an imaginary cloth, nothing revealed itself. I could have just let it go, but, flustered by the fact that I had completely blanked on her name, I blurted out the question, What should I call you?

Terry, if you will.

Looking me straight in the eye, she said once again: Terry, if you will.

Terry?

Yes, I'd like to be called Terry.

I wondered for a moment whether her real name was Teruko or Teruyo, but I refrained from asking. I should call you Terry, just like that? Yes, I'd like that. Okay. I managed to answer with a smile, but an awkward silence ensued. It occurred to me that I should follow this exchange by saying with a straight face, So Terry, play me something – but I obviously lacked the nerve to do so. All I could muster was an awkward smile, gesturing with my hands to urge her to go ahead.

She looked at me intently and asked, with a smile, What should I call you?

Me? All I had to do was remember my own name, but for some reason, I couldn't answer right away. She waited for me patiently, while I sat silent. I began to feel desperate, trying to grasp any name that came to mind, but naturally, I hesitated choosing a name that wasn't mine. It didn't matter what I chose, yet it did matter somehow. Every name that popped into my head sounded wrong. Not that there was right or wrong in any of this.

Please call me Bianca.

Bianca. What a beautiful name.

I felt my face turn bright red. Bianca? I had no idea why that name of all names popped out of my mouth. Where did it come from? It was probably a character from some comic book I had read as a child, nothing more. But Bianca! As I called myself that in my mind, one part of me felt strangely liberated, while another part began to melt into a deep slumber.

Bianca, will you listen to me play?

Yes, of course.

Realizing she was waiting for me to say more, I quickly added, Terry. Terry smiled contentedly and began playing her usual duum, da, dum piece. But she stumbled almost right away, and kept stumbling over the same spot. Starting over again and again, Terry eventually shook her head and turned towards me, sighing deeply.

See, Bianca, I told you. I can't play when I know someone is listening.

But it's so beautiful. I'm completely drawn in by the sound – it's as if the whole landscape changes with a single note. Isn't it just a matter of getting used to? I mean . . . oh, I'm sorry, I really don't know what I'm talking about.

No, you're right. It's probably just that. You know, it really made me happy the other day, Bianca, when you told me that you liked listening to me play the piano. It made me so happy to hear that you were touched. And today, you kindly came to my house. I have such bad memories attached to playing the piano, so for me, this is like a fresh new start. Liszt's *Liebestraum* brings back such bittersweet . . . no . . . truly awful memories. So if I can play it all the way through without making a mistake in front of you, Bianca, I feel very strongly that . . . that I could be a whole new person.

I think I understand how you feel.

I had a sense, you know, when I talked to you the other day – a kind of intuition.

I know exactly what you mean.

Terry continued to play the *Liebestraum* for two hours straight – I know because I kept looking at the antique clock on the wall. I sat still and erect on the backless ottoman, letting my attention wander from Terry's back to the shiny furniture, then to jumbled landscapes in my memory and to words exchanged with a certain someone somewhere. Whenever I remembered to focus on the melody, I would hear Terry stumbling. After playing for a full two hours, Terry finally got up, saying, That's enough for today. I gave an enormous mental sigh of relief, larger than anything I'd ever seen or touched, and stood up, nodding vigorously. My hips were as stiff as if a metal plate had been inserted into them, and my eyes felt stuffed with cotton wool. We descended the stairs in silence, but as I put on my shoes in the entranceway, Terry said:

Bianca, won't you come twice a week, whenever you're free? Until I complete my Dream of Love?

How about Tuesdays and Thursdays?

And so it was decided that every Tuesday and Thursday, I would spend the afternoon listening to Terry play the piano.

Is it possible to be utterly unable to play a piece that one used to play smoothly, however many years ago? And after practising every single day? It must be. Maybe that's how difficult and profound and complex playing an instrument is, but still it was bewildering how slowly Terry progressed. She would unfailingly stumble at the beginning, and just when I thought she had finally got into the flow, she would stop again at a familiar spot. It made me wonder if she was doing it on purpose. This piece, with its sugary title that made me want to squirm in my seat, Dream of Love, could not be much more than four minutes long, and yet Terry could never play those four minutes straight through. Whether the piece was for beginners or for really advanced players, who knows, but its overdramatic progression – the way it built up to a climax felt so over the top, going up or coming down or both – always made me queasy. Just when you thought the piece was ending, a series of hysterically high notes would soar up, only to trail off as if to excuse itself, Dear me, did that come off as hysterical? It's just that I'm so terribly pleased with myself. Then the lower notes would follow with an oh-so-convincing air, pulling the listener back into the piece only to end abruptly, as if everything that had taken place had suddenly been abandoned. What was that about?

Terry, however, seemed to be emotionally attached to the music and continued to play it on Tuesdays and Thursdays for two hours straight without a break. Glancing at her in profile one time, I noticed that she was so consumed by her Dream of Love that sweat appeared to be dripping from every pore. It was all I could do to keep a straight face. When the time came for me to leave, Terry would always apologize. Bianca, I'm so sorry. Next time, next time for sure, I'll knock it out of the park. It made me smile to hear the phrase 'knock it out of the park' from someone like Terry, whose body was inhabited by a sixty-year-old and a seventy-year-old.

I thought meeting regularly like that would lead to an exchange of personal stories or gossip, but no such thing occurred. Terry had no idea what my husband did for a living, and I had no idea what her husband did either. What's your family like? Where were you born? How old are you? What do you do every day? How long have you lived here? Do you even *have* a husband? Do you have children? Do I have any intention of having children? What kind of life do you lead? Those questions never passed our lips.

Terry would just play, saying nothing. During our brief teatime before each session, she would reflect on her mistakes from the last session and lay out her goals for that day, all sober and serious. I couldn't tell whether Terry was an unhappy woman. I have a habit of imagining how unhappy a woman is every time I see one. Of course, nothing comes of it since I can't ask a woman flat out, So are you unhappy or not? Terry was earnestness itself. But her eyes were timid when she looked at me. I would say every time, You're going to be great today, I have a feeling . . . Terry, I would hastily add.

Really, Bianca? It makes me so happy to hear you say that.

And yet, Terry still couldn't play the piece to the end without stumbling. Two weeks passed, then three weeks, like slowly walking down a long, empty corridor.

Sitting at home doing nothing, I could hear Terry practising her usual *Liebestraum*. I hummed along to the now utterly familiar melody, tracing the notes as I brought in the laundry and wiped the dishes. My husband, who happened to be at home, seemed surprised to hear me humming and asked me what the matter was. He seemed oblivious to the sound of Terry's piano.

It's nothing . . . hey, what do you think of the name Bianca?

Bianca? What's that about?

Don't you think Bianca is a great name?

I don't know . . . is it Italian? I guess it's not bad. But then, I don't know what makes a name great either.

Sometimes, when I heard the faint sound of a piano – while watching a news item about the nuclear meltdown, for example – I would turn off the TV and softly approach the wall. If I noticed it while vacuuming, I would flip the switch and open the window. And sometimes I would sit at the dining table very straight and take a deep breath. Then I would place my hands on the table and move them at random along with Terry's music. Even though I was just tapping away haphazardly – the last time I touched a piano was probably during a music lesson at primary school – when the music ended and my fingers stopped moving, an unfamiliar elation would fall upon me like golden rain, maybe from the back of my throat or somewhere high in the air. It would be so intense that my heart would ache. And I felt, vaguely, how wonderful it must be to be able to do something like that with one's fingers and eyes and body. Then, a feeling of anxiety would rush over me. What exactly is 'something like that'? Touching a piano? Reading, memorizing and managing to play a piece through? What is it? Or, is it related to all that, but something else entirely? The more I thought about it, the more confused I became. All I knew was that it wasn't just about the satisfaction I gained by moving my fingers randomly to the sound of music that someone else had spent ages practising.

On my thirteenth visit, Terry finally succeeded in playing the entire *Liebestraum* without making a single mistake. It happened quite suddenly. By that time, I had given up wondering whether she would ever get through the piece. Terry's performance was simply magnificent. With tremendous concentration, she played as if marking something unrepeatable on something irretrievable, tenderly drawing the keyboard down to some soft place buried within her heart, then abruptly pulling it upwards. Each breath enveloped her fingers, her arms – enveloped Terry herself. The notes were tied together by an invisible string, and yet they were so free. The glimmering tremolo in the middle of the piece made it feel as if the world itself was quivering under its inconceivable brilliance. I pressed my hand over my heart. Please never end – I almost spoke the words out loud.

When the echoes of the last note disappeared from the room, Terry turned to me quietly and whispered, I did it. Then, she said in a slightly louder voice, Bianca, I did it, Bianca. Were you listening?

Yes, Terry, I was listening. You did it, I said.

Terry flared her nostrils in excitement, her mouth closed. I stood up, raised my hands up to my face and clapped as hard as I could. I even raised my hands above my head and clapped. I clapped until my hands grew numb. Terry clapped too, as if competing with me. The room filled with our clapping, which made the two of us happy all over again. We kept on clapping for one another. To a stranger, we were nothing more than a white-haired old lady and a scrawny pale-faced woman in her forties – but at that moment, I was Bianca and she was Terry. And – I don't know how it happened – we pressed our lips together, quite naturally. It was just that, a pressing of the lips, but we did it with all our heart.

I stopped going to Terry's house after that. I stopped seeing her altogether, just as it had been before. That's how it is, even among neighbours. I would sometimes hear the garage door open and watch from my kitchen window upstairs as a car left, but I could never see who was inside. I spent my days as aimlessly as before, watering the ivy pots, chocolate cosmos and violets that bordered the front porch, clipping the overgrown leaves, spraying insect repellent and adding fertilizer to the soil. The sound of the piano had ceased entirely, and before I knew it, it was August. All the roses had withered, the ones that during the rainy season I had feared might overtake the house with millions of blossoms. With their flowers gone, leaves were all that remained of the rosebushes. Yet, there were still some small white petals scattered beneath the deep green leaves. I put the petals in my palm, one by one. With no particular celebration or ceremony in mind, I placed the petals next to one another on the sunny windowsill.

HOSHI SHIN'ICHI

Shoulder-Top Secretary

Translated by Jay Rubin

Gliding down the plastic-paved street on his automatic rollerskates, Zame glances at his watch.

4.30. Hmm, maybe I'll try one more place before I go back to the office. Zame slows his skates and stops in front of a house.

Zame is a salesman. In his left hand he carries a big case full of merchandise. Perched on his right shoulder is a parrot with beautiful wings. Such parrots ride atop the shoulders of everyone in this era.

He presses the doorbell and waits. Eventually the door opens and the woman of the house appears.

'Hi,' Zame mumbles, and immediately the parrot on his shoulder begins to declaim: 'Madam, please be so kind as to forgive me for intruding on you at this busy time.'

The parrot is a robot. It is equipped with a precise electronic brain, a recorder and a speaker, and is designed to elaborate on the mutterings of its owner in conversations.

After a brief pause, the parrot on the woman's shoulder replies, 'Oh, thank you very much for coming today. Please forgive me, though. My memory is so bad, I can't quite recall your name . . .'

Zame's parrot leans close to his ear and whispers, ' "Who're you?" she's asking.'

These robotic parrots also function to summarize and report the speech of the other person.

'I'm from the New Electro Company,' Zame mutters. 'Buy this electric spider.'

The parrot then interprets with the utmost politeness: 'Actually, madam, I am a sales representative of the New Electro Company. I believe you probably know that we as a company pride ourselves on our long tradition and reliability. I am here today to show you a new product that our research division has finally managed to perfect after many years of experimentation. It is none other than this magnificent electric spider . . .'

At this point, Zame opens his case and pulls out a small metal device that looks like a shiny golden spider. His parrot continues: 'And here it is. When, for example, your back becomes itchy, you slip this under your clothes. Then the spider automatically finds its way to the itchy spot and gives it a delightful scratching with these little legs. I'm sure you will agree that it is a marvellously convenient invention. I have made a special point of bringing it with me today because I am sure that an elegant household such as yours should be equipped with one.'

When Zame's parrot stops speaking, the parrot on the housewife's shoulder whispers into her ear too quietly for Zame to hear: 'He says, "Buy this automatic backscratcher."'

She mutters back to her parrot, 'Don't wannit,' which her parrot expands for her as follows: 'Oh, how marvellous! Your company makes one new product after another! Unfortunately, however, we simply do not have the means to outfit our home with such a superb mechanism.'

Zame's parrot reports to him, 'She says, "Don't wannit."'

Zame mutters, 'Aw, c'mon!' His parrot proclaims with increased warmth: 'But you see, madam, what a marvellously convenient product this is. It enables you to scratch where your hand is unable to reach, and it can be used in the presence of guests without their ever suspecting. Not to mention the drudgery it saves! And we have outdone ourselves in setting the price as low as possible.'

'He says, "*Please* buy it."'

'What a pain.'

After this exchange with its owner, the woman's parrot answers, 'To tell you the truth, I never buy anything without consulting my husband. Unfortunately, he hasn't come home from work yet, and so I can't possibly make such an important decision. Perhaps I can discuss it with him tonight, and then, possibly the next time you're in the area, you might be so good as to stop by again. I would love to buy it, but it really is out of the question. I'm terribly sorry.'

Zame's parrot summarizes this for him: 'She says, "Get lost."'

Zame resigns himself, and as he is returning the electric spider to his case, he mutters, 'So long, babe.'

The parrot on his shoulder announces his departure with the utmost politeness. 'Oh, well, it truly is a shame. All right, then, if you don't mind, I will call on you again at some point in the near future. I am sorry for having taken up so much of your valuable time. Please give my regards to your husband.'

Zame steps outside. With the parrot still clinging to his shoulder, he revs up his roller skates again and goes back to the office.

He is seated at his desk, adding up the day's receipts on his calculator, when the parrot on the department chief's shoulder calls out to him: 'Hey, Zame!'

'Oh, great, another lecture,' Zame mutters to himself, whereupon his parrot responds: 'Right away, sir! Just let me finish straightening up here . . .'

Soon Zame is standing before the chief's desk. The chief releases a cloud of tobacco smoke, from the depths of which the parrot on his shoulder says with authority, 'Now see here, Zame, these are critical times for the company. We are being called upon to make a great leap forward. I believe you know this as well as anyone. And yet, when I look at your results, I can't help feeling that you could do better. This is a deplorable situation. I want you to understand what I'm saying here. You need to buckle down.'

Zame's parrot whispers to him: 'He says, "Sell more."'

'Yeah,' Zame mutters back, 'like it's so easy.' His parrot meekly responds, 'Yes, sir, I understand completely, and I am determined to increase my sales volume yet again. Our competitors, however, are using all kinds of new techniques. Selling is not as easy as it used to be. I will of course increase my efforts, but I would be most grateful, sir, if you would ask Research and Development to create more and more new products.'

The bell sounds the end of the workday at New Electro. *Over at last! It's exhausting to run around all day like that. Gotta have a drink.*

Zame pushes open the door of the Galaxy, a bar he often visits on his way home. Spotting him, the landlady's parrot calls out to him in a sexy voice: 'Oh, it's you, Mr Zame! Please come in. It's been ages since I last saw you. Without a handsome man like you here, this place can be *so* depressing . . .'

For Zame, this is the most enjoyable part of the day.

DREAD

AKUTAGAWA RYŪNOSUKE

Hell Screen

Translated by Jay Rubin

I

I am certain there has never been anyone like our great Lord of Horikawa, and I doubt there ever will be another.[1] In a dream before His Lordship was born, Her Maternal Ladyship saw the awesomely armed Guardian Deity of the West – or so people say. In any case, His Lordship seemed to have innate qualities that distinguished him from ordinary human beings. And because of this, his accomplishments never ceased to amaze us. You need only glance at his mansion in the Capital's Horikawa district to sense the boldness of its conception. Its – how shall I put it? – its grandeur, its heroic scale are beyond the reach of our mediocre minds. Some have questioned the wisdom of His Lordship's undertaking such a project, comparing him to China's First Emperor, whose subjects were forced to build the Great Wall, or to the Sui Emperor Yang, who made his people erect lofty palaces;[2] but such critics might be likened to the proverbial blind men who described the elephant according only to the parts they could feel. It was never His Lordship's intention to seek splendour and glory for himself alone. He was always a man of great magnanimity who shared his joys with the wider world, so to speak, and kept in mind even the lowliest of his subjects.

Surely this is why he was left unscathed by his encounter with that midnight procession of goblins so often seen at the lonely intersection of Nijō-Ōmiya in the Capital;[3] it is also why, when rumour had it that the ghost of Tōru, Minister of the Left, was appearing night after night at the site of his ruined mansion by the river at Higashi-Sanjō (you must know it: where the minister had recreated the famous seascape of Shiogama in his garden), it took only a simple rebuke from His Lordship to make the spirit vanish.[4] In the face of such resplendent majesty, no wonder all residents of the Capital – old and young, men and women – revered His Lordship as a reincarnation of the Buddha. One time, it is said, His Lordship was returning from a plum-blossom banquet at the palace when the ox pulling his carriage broke loose and injured an old man who happened to be passing by. The old fellow knelt and clasped his hands in prayerful thanks for having been caught on the horns of His Lordship's own ox!

So many, many stories about His Lordship have been handed down. His Imperial Majesty himself once presented His Lordship with thirty pure white horses on the occasion of a New Year's banquet. Another time, when construction of the Nagara Bridge seemed to be running counter to the will of the local deity, His Lordship offered up a favourite boy attendant as a human sacrifice to be buried at the foot of a pillar.[5] And then there was the time when, to have a growth cut from his thigh, he summoned the Chinese monk who had brought the art of surgery to our country. Oh, there's no end to the tales! For sheer horror, though, none of them measures up to the story of the screen depicting scenes of hell which is now a prized family heirloom. Even His Lordship, normally so imperturbable, was horrified by what happened, and those of us who waited upon him – well, it goes without saying that we were shocked out of our minds. I myself had served as one of His Lordship's men for a full twenty years, but what I witnessed then was more terrible than anything I had ever – or *have* ever – experienced.

In order to tell you the story of the hell screen, however, I must first tell you about the painter who created it. His name was Yoshihide.[6]

2

I suspect that even now there are ladies and gentlemen who would recognize the name 'Yoshihide'. He was famous back then as the greatest painter in the land, but he had reached the age of perhaps fifty, and he looked like nothing more than a thoroughly unpleasant little old man, all skin and bones. He dressed normally enough for his appearances at His Lordship's mansion – in a reddish brown, broad-sleeved silk robe and a tall black hat with a soft bend to the right – but as a person he was anything but normal. You could see he had a mean streak, and his lips, unnaturally red for such an old man, gave a disturbing, bestial impression. Some people said the redness came from moistening his paint brush with his lips, but I wonder about that. Crueller tongues used to say that he looked and moved like a monkey, and they went so far as to give Yoshihide the nickname 'Monkeyhide'.[7]

Ah, that nickname reminds me of a particular episode. Yoshihide had a daughter, his only child – a sweet, lovely girl of fifteen, utterly unlike her father. She had been taken into the Horikawa mansion as a junior lady-in-waiting for His Lordship's own daughter, the Young Mistress. Perhaps because she lost her mother at a tender age, she had an unusually mature and deeply sympathetic nature and a cleverness beyond her years, and everyone from Her Ladyship on down loved the girl for her quickness to notice others' every need.

Around that time someone from the province of Tamba presented His Lordship with a tame monkey, and His Lordship's son, the Young Master, who was then at the height of his boyish naughtiness, decided to name it 'Yoshihide'. The monkey was a funny-looking little creature as it was, but capping it with that name gave everyone in the household a hearty laugh. Oh, if only they had been satisfied just to laugh! But whatever the monkey did – whether climbing to the top of a garden pine, or soiling the mats of a staff member's room – people would find a reason to torment it, and always with a shout of 'Yoshihide!'

Then one day, as Yoshihide's daughter was gliding down a long outdoor corridor to deliver a note gaily knotted on a branch of red winter plum, the monkey Yoshihide darted in through the sliding door at the far end, in full flight from something. The animal was running with a limp and seemed unable to escape up a post as it often did when frightened. Then who should appear chasing after it but the Young Master, brandishing a switch and shouting, 'Come back here, you tangerine thief! Come back here!' Yoshihide's daughter drew up short at the sight, and the monkey clung to her skirts with a pitiful cry. This must have aroused her compassion, for, still holding the plum branch in one hand, she swept the monkey up in the soft folds of her lavender sleeve. Then, giving a little bow to the Young Master, she said with cool clarity, 'Forgive me for interfering, my young lord, but he is just an animal. Please pardon him.'

Temper still up from the chase, the Young Master scowled and stamped his foot several times. 'Why are you protecting him?' he demanded. 'He stole my tangerine!'

'He is just an animal,' she repeated. 'He doesn't know any better.' And then, smiling sadly, she added, 'His name is Yoshihide, after all. I can't just stand by and watch "my father" being punished.' This bold stroke was apparently enough to break the Young Master's will.

'All right, then,' he said with obvious reluctance. 'If you're pleading for your father's life, I'll let him off this time.'

The Young Master flung his switch into the garden and stalked back out through the sliding door.

3

After this incident, Yoshihide's daughter and the little monkey grew close. The girl had a golden bell that her young mistress had given her, which she hung from the monkey's neck on a pretty crimson cord. And he, for his part, would almost never leave her side. Once, when she was in bed with a cold, the monkey spent hours by her pillow, biting its nails, and I swear it had a worried look on its face.

People stopped teasing the monkey after that, strangely enough. In fact, they began treating it with special kindness, until even the Young Master would occasionally throw it a persimmon or a chestnut, and I heard he once flew into a rage when one of the samurai kicked the animal. Soon after that, His Lordship himself ordered the girl to appear before him with the monkey in her arms – all because, in hearing about the Young Master's tantrum, I am told, he naturally also heard about how the girl had come to care for the monkey.

'I admire your filial behaviour,' His Lordship said. 'Here, take this.' And he presented her with a fine scarlet under-robe. They tell me that His Lordship was especially pleased when the monkey, imitating the girl's expression of gratitude, bowed low before him, holding the robe aloft. And so His Lordship's partiality for the girl was born entirely from his wish to commend her filial devotion to her father and not, as rumour had it, from any physical attraction he might have felt for her. Not that such suspicions were entirely groundless, but there will be time for me to tell you about that later. For now, suffice it to say that His Lordship was not the sort of person to lavish his affections on the daughter of a mere painter, however beautiful she might be.

Well, then, having been singled out for praise this way, Yoshihide's daughter withdrew from His Lordship's presence, but she knew how to avoid provoking the envy of the household's other, less modest, ladies-in-waiting. Indeed, people grew fonder than ever of her and the monkey, and the Young Mistress almost never let them leave her side, even bringing them with her in her ox-drawn carriage when she went to observe shrine rituals and the like.

But enough about the girl for now. Let me continue with my story of her father, Yoshihide. As I have said, the monkey Yoshihide quickly became everyone's little darling, but Yoshihide himself remained an object of universal scorn, reviled as 'Monkeyhide' by everyone behind his back. And not only in the Horikawa mansion. Even such an eminent Buddhist prelate as the Abbot of Yokawa hated Yoshihide so much that the very mention of his name was enough to make him turn purple as if he had seen a devil. (Some said this was because Yoshihide had drawn a caricature ridiculing certain aspects of the abbot's behaviour, but this was merely a rumour that circulated among the lower classes and as such can hardly be credited.) In any case, Yoshihide's reputation was so bad that anyone you asked would have told you the same thing. If there were those who spoke kindly of Yoshihide, they were either a handful of the brotherhood of painters or else people who knew his work but not the man himself.

His appearance was not the only thing that people hated about Yoshihide. In fact, he had many evil traits that repelled them even more, and for which he had only himself to blame.

4

For one thing, Yoshihide was a terrible miser; he was harsh in his dealings with people; he had no shame; he was lazy and greedy. But worst of all, he was insolent and arrogant. He never let you forget that he was 'the greatest painter in the land'. Nor was his arrogance limited to painting.

He could not be satisfied till he displayed his contempt for every custom and convention that ordinary people practised. A man who was his apprentice for many years once told me this story. Yoshihide was present one day in the mansion of a certain gentleman when the celebrated Shamaness of the Cypress Enclosure was there, undergoing spirit possession. The woman delivered a horrifying message from the spirit, but Yoshihide was unimpressed. He took up a handy ink brush and did a detailed sketch of her wild expression as if he viewed spirit possession as mere trickery.

No wonder, then, that such a man would commit acts of sacrilege in his work: in painting the lovely goddess Kisshōten, he used the face of a common harlot, and to portray the mighty flame-draped deity Fudō, his model was a criminal released to do chores in the magistrate's office. If you tried to warn him that he was flirting with danger, he would respond with feigned innocence. '*I'm* the one who painted them, after all,' he would say. 'Are you trying to tell me that my own Buddhas and gods are going to punish me?' Even his apprentices were shocked by this. I myself knew several of them who, fearing for their own punishment in the afterlife, wasted no time in leaving his employ. The man's arrogance simply knew no bounds. He was convinced that he was the greatest human being under heaven.

It goes without saying that Yoshihide lorded it over the other painters of his time. True, his brushwork and colours were utterly different from theirs, and so the many painters with whom he was on bad terms tended to speak of him as a charlatan. They rhapsodized over the work of old masters such as Kawanari or Kanaoka[8] ('On moonlit nights you could actually *smell* the plum blossoms painted on that wooden door' or 'You could actually *hear* the courtier on that screen playing his flute'), but all they had to say about Yoshihide's work was how eerie and unsettling they found it. Take his *Five Levels of Rebirth* on the Ryūgaiji Temple gate, for example.[9] 'When I passed the gate late at night,' one said, 'I could hear the dying celestials sighing and sobbing.' 'That's nothing,' another claimed. 'I could smell the flesh of the dead rotting.' 'And how about the portraits of the household's ladies-in-waiting that His Lordship ordered from Yoshihide? Every single woman he painted fell ill and died within three years. It was as if he had snatched their very souls from them.' According to one of his harshest critics, this was the final proof that Yoshihide practised the Devil's Art.

But Yoshihide was so perverse, as I've said, that remarks like this only filled him with pride. When His Lordship joked to him one time, 'For you, it seems, the uglier the better,' old Yoshihide's far-too-red lips spread in an eerie grin and he replied imperiously, 'Yes, My Lord, it's true. Other painters are such mediocrities, they cannot appreciate the beauty of ugliness.' I must say, 'greatest painter in the land' or not, it was incredible that he could spout such self-congratulatory nonsense in His Lordship's presence! No wonder his apprentices called him Chira Eiju behind his back! You know: Chira Eiju, the long-nosed goblin who crossed over from China long ago to spread the sin of arrogance.

But still, even Yoshihide, in all his incredible perversity – yes, even Yoshihide displayed human tenderness when it came to one thing.

5

By this I mean that Yoshihide was truly mad about his only daughter, the young lady-in-waiting. The girl was, as I said before, a wonderfully kind-hearted young creature, deeply devoted to her father, and his love for her was no less strong than hers for him. I gather that he provided for her every need – every robe, every hair ornament – without the slightest objection. Don't you find this incredible for a man who had never made a single contribution to a temple?

Yoshihide's love for his daughter, however, remained just that: love. It never occurred to him that he should be trying to find her a good husband some day. Far from it: he was not above hiring street thugs to beat up anyone who might make improper advances to her. So even when His Lordship honoured her with the position of junior lady-in-waiting in his own household, Yoshihide was far from happy about it, and for a while he always wore a sour expression whenever he was in His Lordship's presence. I have no doubt that people who witnessed this display were the ones who began speculating that His Lordship had been attracted to the girl's beauty when he ordered her into service despite her father's objections.

Such rumours were entirely false, of course. It was nothing but Yoshihide's obsessive love for his daughter that kept him wishing to have her step down from service, that is certain. I remember the time His Lordship ordered Yoshihide to do a painting of Monju[10] as a child, and Yoshihide pleased him greatly with a marvellous work that used one of His Lordship's own boy favourites as a model. 'You can have anything you want as your reward,' said His Lordship. 'Anything at all.'

Yoshihide should have been awestruck to hear such praise from His Lordship's own lips, and he did in fact prostrate himself in thanks before him, but can you imagine what he asked? 'If it please Your Lordship, I beg you to return my daughter to her former lowly state.' The impudence of the man! This was no ordinary household, after all. No matter how much he loved his daughter, to beg for her release from service in privileged proximity to the great Lord of Horikawa himself – where in the world does one find such audacity? Not even a man as grandly magnanimous as His Lordship could help feeling some small annoyance at such a request, as was evident from the way he stared at Yoshihide for a while in silence.

Presently he spoke: 'That will not happen,' he said, all but spitting out the words, and he abruptly withdrew.

This was not the first nor the last such incident: I think there might have been four or five in all. And with each repetition, it now seems to me, His Lordship gazed on Yoshihide with increasing coldness. The girl, for her part, seemed to fear for her father's welfare. Often she could be seen sobbing quietly to herself in her room, teeth clamped on her sleeve. All this only reinforced the rumour that His Lordship was enamoured of the girl. People also said that the command to paint the screen had something to do with her rejection of His Lordship's advances, but that, of course, could not be so.

As I see it, it was entirely out of pity for the girl's situation that His Lordship refused to let her go. I am certain he believed, with great generosity, that she would be far better off if he were to keep her in his mansion and enable her to live without care than if he sent her back to her hard-headed old father. That he was partial to her, of course, there could be no doubt: she was such a sweet-tempered young thing. But to assert that he took his lustful pleasure with her is a view that springs from twisted reasoning. No, I would have to call it a groundless falsehood.

At any rate, owing to these matters regarding his daughter, this was a period when Yoshihide was in great disfavour with His Lordship. Then suddenly one day, for whatever reason, His Lordship summoned Yoshihide and ordered him to paint a folding screen portraying scenes from the eight Buddhist hells.

6

Oh, that screen! I can almost see its terrifying images of hell before me now!

Other artists painted what they called images of hell, but their compositions were nothing like Yoshihide's. He had the Ten Kings of Hell and their minions over in one small corner, and everything else – the entire screen – was enveloped in a firestorm so terrible you thought the swirling flames were going to melt the Mountain of Sabres and the Forest of Swords. Aside from the vaguely Chinese costumes of the Judges of the Dark, with their swatches of yellow and indigo, all you saw was the searing colour of flames and, dancing wildly among them, black smoke clouds of hurled India ink and flying sparks of blown-on gold dust.

These alone were enough to shock and amaze any viewer, but the sinners writhing in the hellfire of Yoshihide's powerful brush had nothing in common with those to be seen in ordinary pictures of hell. For Yoshihide had included sinners from all stations in life, from the most brilliant luminary of His Majesty's exalted circle to the basest beggar and outcast. A courtier in magnificent ceremonial vestments, a nubile lady-in-waiting in five-layered robes, a rosary-clutching priest intoning the holy name of Amida, a samurai student on high wooden clogs, an aristocratic little girl in a simple shift, a Yin-Yang diviner swishing his paper wand through the air: I could never name them all. But there they were, human beings of every kind, inundated by smoke and flame, tormented by wardens of hell with their heads of bulls and horses, and driven in all directions like autumn leaves scattering before a great wind. 'Oh, look at that one,' you would say, 'the one with her hair all tangled up in a forked lance and her arms and legs drawn in tighter than a spider's: could she be one of those shrine maidens who perform for the gods? And, oh, *that* fellow there, hanging upside down like a bat, his breast pierced by a short lance: surely he is supposed to be a novice provincial governor.' And the kinds of torture were as numberless as the sinners themselves – flogging with an iron scourge, crushing under a gigantic rock, pecking by a monstrous bird, grinding in the jaws of a poisonous serpent . . .

But surely the single most horrifying image of all was that of a carriage plummeting through space. As it fell, it grazed the upper boughs of a sword tree, where clumps of corpses were skewered on fang-like branches. Blasts of hell wind swept up the carriage curtains to reveal a court lady so gorgeously apparelled she might have been one of His Imperial Majesty's own consorts or intimates, her straight black hip-length hair flying upwards in the flames, the full whiteness of her throat laid bare as she writhed in agony. Every detail of the woman's form and the blazing carriage filled the viewer with an appalling sense of the hideous torments to be found in the Hell of Searing Heat. I felt – how can I put it? – as though the sheer horror of the entire screen were concentrated in this one figure. It had been executed with such inspired workmanship, you'd think that all who saw it could hear the woman's dreadful screams.

Oh yes, this was it: for the sake of painting this one image, the terrible event occurred. Otherwise, how could even the great Yoshihide have painted hell's torments so vividly? It was his cruel fate to lose his life in exchange for completing the screen. In a sense, the hell in his painting was the hell into which Yoshihide himself, the greatest painter in the realm, was doomed one day to fall.

I am afraid that, in my haste to speak of the screen with its unusual images of hell, I may have reversed the order of my story. Now let me continue with the part about Yoshihide when he received His Lordship's command to do a painting of hell.

7

For nearly six months after the commission, Yoshihide poured all his energy into the screen, never once calling at His Lordship's residence. Don't you find it strange that such a doting father should abandon all thought of seeing his daughter once he had started on a painting? According to the apprentice I mentioned earlier, Yoshihide always approached his work like a man possessed by a fox spirit.[11] In fact, people used to say that the only reason Yoshihide was able to make such a name for himself in art was that he had pledged his soul to one of the great gods of fortune; what proved it was that if you peeked in on him when he was painting, you could always see shadowy fox spirits swarming all around him. What this means, I suspect, is that, once he picked up his brush, Yoshihide thought of nothing else but completing the painting before him. He would spend all day and night shut up in his studio out of sight. His concentration seems to have been especially intense when he was working on this particular screen with its images of hell.

This is not merely to say that he would keep the latticed shutters pulled down and spend all day by the tripod oil lamp, mixing secret combinations of paint or posing his apprentices in various costumes for him to sketch. No, that was normal behaviour for the working Yoshihide, even before this screen. Remember, this was the man who, when he was painting his *Five Levels of Rebirth* on the Ryūgaiji Temple gate, went out specially to inspect a corpse lying on the roadside – the kind of sight from which any ordinary person would recoil – and spent hours sitting before it, sketching its rotting face and limbs without missing a hair. I don't blame you, then, if you are among those who cannot imagine what I mean when I say that his concentration during his work on the hell screen was especially intense. I haven't time now to explain this in detail, but I can at least tell you the most important things.

One day an apprentice of Yoshihide's (the one I've mentioned a few times already) was busy dissolving pigments when the master suddenly said to him, 'I'm planning to take a nap but, I don't know, I've been having bad dreams lately.'

There was nothing strange about this, so the apprentice merely answered, 'I see, Master,' and continued with his work.

Yoshihide, however, was not his usual self. Somewhat hesitantly, and with a doleful look on his face, he made a surprising request: 'I want you to sit and work beside me while I sleep.'

The apprentice thought it rather odd that his master should be worrying about dreams, but it was a simple enough request and he promptly agreed to it.

'All right, then,' Yoshihide said, still looking worried, 'come inside right away.' He hesitated. 'And when the other apprentices arrive,' he added, 'don't let any of them in where I am sleeping.'

'Inside' meant the room where the master actually did his painting, and as usual on this day, the apprentice told me, its doors and windows were shut as tightly as at night. In the dull glow of an oil lamp, its panels arranged in a semicircle, stood the large folding screen, which was still only sketched out in charcoal. Yoshihide lay down with his head pillowed on his forearm and slipped into the deep sleep of an utterly exhausted man. Hardly any time had gone by, however, when the apprentice began to hear a sound that he had no way of describing. It was a voice, he told me, but a strange and eerie one.

8

At first, it was just a sound, but soon, in snatches, the voice began to form words that came to him as if under water, like the muffled cries of a drowning man. 'Wha-a-a-t?' the voice said. 'You want me to come with you? . . . Where? Where are you taking me? To hell, you say. To the Hell of Searing Heat, you say. Who . . . who are you, damn you? Who can you be but –'

The apprentice, dissolving pigments, felt his hands stop of their own accord. He peered fearfully through the gloom at his master's face. Not only had the furrowed skin gone stark white, but fat beads of sweat oozed from it, and the dry-lipped, snaggle-toothed mouth strained wide open as if gasping for breath. The youth saw something moving in his master's mouth with dizzying speed, like an object being yanked by a cord, but then – imagine! – he realized the thing was Yoshihide's tongue. The fragmented speech had been coming from that tongue of his.

'Who could it be but – *you*, damn you. It *is* you! I thought so! What's that? You've come to show me the way there? You want me to follow you. To hell! My daughter is waiting for me in hell!'

The apprentice told me that an uncanny feeling overcame him at that point – his eyes seemed to make out vague, misshapen shadows that slid over the surface of the screen and flooded down upon the two of them. Naturally, he immediately reached over and shook Yoshihide as hard as he could; but rather than waking, the master, in a dreamlike state, went on talking to himself and showed no sign of regaining consciousness. Desperate now, the apprentice grabbed the jar for washing brushes and splashed all its water into Yoshihide's face.

'I'm waiting for you,' Yoshihide was saying, 'so hurry and get into the cart. Come along to hell!' But the moment the water hit him his words turned to a strangled moan. At last he opened his eyes, and he sprang up more wildly than if he had been jabbed with a needle. But the misshapen creatures must have been with him still, for he stared into space, with mouth agape and with terrified eyes. At length he returned to himself and, without a hint of gratitude, barked at the poor apprentice, 'I'm all right now. Get out of here.'

The apprentice knew he would be scolded if he resisted his master at a time like this, so he hurried out of the room, but he told me that when he saw the sunlight again he felt as relieved as if he were waking from his own nightmare.

This was by no means Yoshihide at his worst, however. A month later he called another apprentice into the inner room. The young man found Yoshihide standing in the dim light of the oil lamp biting the end of his paintbrush. Without a moment's hesitation, Yoshihide turned to him and said, 'Sorry, but I want you to get naked again.' The master had ordered such things in the past, so the apprentice quickly stripped off his clothes, but now Yoshihide said with a strange scowl, 'I want to see a person in chains, so do what I tell you. Sorry about this, but it will just take a little while.' Yoshihide could mouth apologetic phrases, but he issued his cold commands without the least show of sympathy. This particular apprentice was a well-built lad who looked more suited to wielding a sword than a paintbrush, but even he must have been shocked by what happened. 'I figured the master had gone crazy and was going to kill me,' he told people again and again for long afterwards. Yoshihide was apparently annoyed by the young man's slow preparations. Instead of waiting, he dragged out a narrow iron chain from heaven knows where and all but pounced on the apprentice's back, wrenching the man's arms behind him and winding him in the chain. Then he gave the end of the chain a cruel yank and sent the young man crashing down on the floor.

9

The apprentice lay there like – what? – like a keg of sake that someone had knocked over. Legs and arms mercilessly contorted, he could move only his head. And with the chain cutting off the circulation of his blood, you know, his skin became red and swollen – face, torso, everywhere. Yoshihide, though, was apparently not the least bit concerned to see him like this; he circled this sake keg of a body, observing it from every angle and drawing sketch after sketch. I am certain that, without my spelling it out, you can imagine what torture this must have been for the poor apprentice.

If nothing had interrupted it, the young man's ordeal would almost surely have lasted even longer, but fortunately (or perhaps unfortunately) a narrow, winding streak of black oil, or so it seemed, began to flow from behind a large jar in the corner of the room. At first it moved slowly, like a thick liquid, but then it began to slide along the floor more smoothly, glinting in the darkness until it was almost touching the apprentice's nose. He took a good look at it, gasped and screamed, 'A snake! A snake!' The way he described the moment to me, he felt as if every drop of blood in his body would freeze, which I can well understand, for in fact the snake's cold tongue was just about to touch the flesh of his neck where the chain was biting. Even Yoshihide, for all his perversity, must have felt a rush of horror at this unforeseen occurrence. Flinging his brush down, he bent and gripped the snake by the tail, dangling it upside down. The snake raised its head and began to coil upwards around its own body, but it could not reach Yoshihide's hand.

'You cost me a good brushstroke, damn you,' he growled at the snake, flinging it into the corner jar. Then, with obvious reluctance, he loosened the chains that bound the apprentice's body. In fact, loosening the chains was as far as he was willing to go: to the youth himself he spared not a word of sympathy. I suspect he was more enraged at having botched a single brush stroke than concerned that his apprentice might have been bitten by a snake. I heard afterwards that he had been keeping the snake to sketch from.

I imagine that what little you have heard is enough for you to grasp the fanatic intensity with which Yoshihide approached his work. But let me give you one last, terrible example concerning a young apprentice – no more than thirteen or fourteen years old – who could have lost his life for the hell screen. It happened one night when the boy, whose skin was fair as a girl's, was called into the master's studio. There he found Yoshihide by the tripod lamp balancing a piece of raw meat on his palm and feeding it to a bird the likes of which he had never seen before. The bird was the size of a cat, and in fact, with its two feather tufts sticking out from its head like ears and its big, round, amber-coloured eyes, it did look very much like a cat.

10

Yoshihide was a man who simply hated to have anyone pry into his business, and – the snake I told you about was one such case – he would never let his apprentices know what kinds of things he had in his studio. Depending on the subject he happened to be painting at the time, he might have a human skull perched on his table, or rows of silver bowls and gold-lacquered stands – you never knew. And his helpers told me they had no idea where he kept such things when he was not using them. This was surely one reason for the rumour that Yoshihide was the beneficiary of miraculous aid from a god of fortune.

Well, then: the young apprentice, assuming that the strange bird on the table was a model Yoshihide needed for the hell screen, knelt before the painter and asked in all humility, 'How can I help you, Master?'

Almost as if he had not heard the boy speak, Yoshihide licked his red lips and jerked his chin towards the bird. 'Not bad, eh? Look how tame it is.'

'Please tell me, Master, what is it? I have never seen anything like it before,' the boy said, keeping his wary gaze fixed on the cat-like bird with ears.

'What? Never seen anything like it?' Yoshihide responded with his familiar scornful laugh. 'That's what you get for growing up in the Capital! It's a bird. A horned owl. A hunter brought it to me a few days ago from Mount Kurama. Only, you don't usually find them so tame.'

As he spoke, Yoshihide slowly raised his hand and gave a soft upward stroke to the feathers of the owl's back just as the bird finished swallowing the chunk of meat. Instantly the bird emitted a shriek and leaped from the table top, aiming its outstretched talons at the apprentice's face. Had the boy not shot his arm out to protect himself, I have no doubt that he would

311

have ended up with more than a gash or two on his face. He cried out and shook his sleeve in an attempt to sweep the bird away, which only added to the fury of the attack. Beak clattering, the owl came in for another thrust. Disregarding Yoshihide's presence, the apprentice ran wildly around the cramped room, now standing to defend himself, now crouching to drive the bird away. The monster, of course, stuck with him, flying up when he stood up and down when he crouched down, and using any opening to go straight for his eyes. With each lunge came a tremendous flapping of wings that filled the boy with dread. He felt so lost, he said later, that the familiar studio seemed like a haunted valley deep in the mountains, with the smell of rotting leaves, the spray of a waterfall, the sour fumes of fruit stashed away by a monkey; even the dim glow of the master's oil lamp on its tripod looked to him like misty moonlight in the hills.

Being attacked by the owl, however, was not what most frightened the lad. What really made his flesh crawl was the way the master Yoshihide followed the commotion with his cold stare, taking his time to spread out a piece of paper, lick his brush and then set about capturing the terrible image of a delicate boy being tormented by a hideous bird. At the sight, the apprentice was overcome by an inexpressible terror. For a time, he says, he even thought his master might kill him.

II

And you actually couldn't say that such a thing was out of the question. For it did seem that Yoshihide's sole purpose in calling the apprentice to his studio that night had been to set the owl on him and draw him trying to escape. Thus, when the apprentice caught that glimpse of his master at work, he instinctively put both arms up to protect his head and an incoherent scream escaped his throat as he slumped down against the sliding door in the corner of the room. In that same instant, Yoshihide himself cried out and jumped to his feet, whereupon the beating of the owl's wings grew faster and louder and there came the clatter of something falling over and a tearing sound. Having covered his head in terror, the apprentice now lowered his arms and looked around to find that the room had gone pitch dark, and he heard Yoshihide's angry voice calling to the other apprentices.

Eventually there was a far-off cry in response, and soon an apprentice rushed in with a lantern held high. In its sooty-smelling glow, the boy saw the tripod collapsed on the floor and the mats and planking soaked in the oil of the overturned lamp. He saw the owl, too, beating one wing in apparent pain as it flopped around the room. On the far side of the table, looking stunned, Yoshihide was raising himself from the floor and muttering something incomprehensible. And no wonder! The black snake was tightly coiled around the owl from neck to tail and over one wing. The apprentice had probably knocked the jar over as he slumped to the floor, and when the snake crawled out, the owl must have made the mistake of trying to grab it with its talons, only to give rise to this struggle. The two apprentices gaped at the bizarre scene and at each other until, with a silent bow to the master, they slipped out of the room. What happened to the owl and snake after that, no one knows.

This was by no means the only such incident. I forgot to mention that it was the beginning of autumn when His Lordship commanded Yoshihide to paint the hell screen; from then until the end of winter the apprentices were continually subjected to their master's frightening behaviour. At that point, however, something seemed to interfere with Yoshihide's work on the screen. An even deeper layer of gloom came to settle over him, and he spoke to his assistants in markedly harsher tones. The screen was perhaps four-fifths finished, but it showed no further signs of progress. Indeed, Yoshihide occasionally seemed to be on the verge of painting over those parts that he had already completed.

No one knew why he was having such difficulty with the screen, and what's more, no one tried to find out. Stung by those earlier incidents, his apprentices felt as if they were locked in a cage with a tiger or a wolf, and they found every way they could to keep their distance from the master.

12

For that reason, I have little to tell you about that period. The only unusual thing I can think of is that the hard-headed old man suddenly turned weepy; people would often see him shedding tears when he was alone. An apprentice told me that one day he walked into the garden and saw the master standing on the veranda, gazing blankly at the sky with its promise of spring, his eyes full of tears. Embarrassed for the old man, the apprentice said, he silently withdrew. Don't you find it odd that this arrogant man, who went so far as to sketch a corpse on the roadside for his *Five Levels of Rebirth*, would cry like an infant just because the painting of the screen wasn't going as well as he wanted it to?

In any case, while Yoshihide was madly absorbed in his work on the screen, his daughter began to show increasing signs of melancholy, until the rest of us could see that she was often fighting back her tears. A pale, reserved, sad-faced girl to begin with, she took on a genuinely mournful aspect as her lashes grew heavy and shadows began to form around her eyes. This gave rise to all sorts of speculation – that she was worried about her father, or that she was suffering the pangs of love – but soon people were saying that it was all because His Lordship was trying to bend her to his will. Then the gossiping ground to a halt, as though everyone had suddenly forgotten about her.

A certain event occurred at that time. Well after the first watch of the night, I was walking down an outdoor corridor when the monkey Yoshihide came flying at me from out of nowhere and started tugging at the skirts of my *hakama*. As I recall it, this was one of those warm early spring nights when you expect at any time to be catching the sweet fragrance of plum blossoms in the pale moonlight. But what did I see in the moon's faint glow? It was the monkey baring its white fangs, wrinkling up its nose and shrieking with almost manic intensity. An eerie chill was only three parts of what I felt: the other seven parts were anger at having my new *hakama* yanked at like that, and I considered kicking the beast aside and continuing on my way. I quickly changed my mind, however, recalling the case of the samurai who had earned the Young Master's displeasure by tormenting the monkey. And besides, the way the monkey was behaving, there was obviously something wrong. I therefore gave up trying to resist and allowed myself to be pulled several paces further.

Where the corridor turned a corner, the pale surface of His Lordship's pond could be seen stretching off through the darkness beyond a gently drooping pine. When the animal led me to that point, my ears were assaulted by the frantic yet strangely muffled sounds of what I took to be a struggle in a nearby room. All else was hushed. I heard no voices, no sounds but the splash of a fish leaping in the mingled moonlight and fog. The sound of the struggle brought me up short. If this was an intruder, I resolved, I would teach him a lesson, and, holding my breath, I edged closer to the sliding door.

13

My approach, however, was obviously too slow and cautious for the monkey. Yoshihide scampered around me in circles – once, twice, three times – then bounded up to my shoulder with a strangled cry. Instinctively, I jerked my head aside to avoid being scratched. The monkey dug its claws into my sleeve to keep from slipping down. This sent me staggering, and I stumbled backwards, slamming against the door. Now I could no longer hesitate. I shot the door open and crouched to spring in beyond the moonlight's edge. At that very moment something rose up to block my view. With a start I realized it was a woman. She flew towards me as if someone had flung her out of the room. She nearly hit me but instead she tumbled forwards and – why, I could not tell – went down on one knee before me, trembling and breathless, and staring up at me as if at some terrifying sight.

I am sure I need not tell you it was Yoshihide's daughter. That night, however, my eyes beheld her with a new vividness, as though she were an utterly different person. Her eyes were huge and shining. And her cheeks seemed to be burning red. Her dishevelled clothes gave her an erotic allure that contrasted sharply with her usual childish innocence. Could this actually be the daughter of Yoshihide, I wondered – that frail-looking girl so modest and self-effacing in all things? Leaning against the sliding wooden door, I stared at this beautiful girl in the moonlight and then, as if they were capable of pointing, I flicked my eyes in the direction of hurried footsteps that could be heard receding into the distance, as if to ask her soundlessly, *Who was that?*

The girl bit her lip and shook her head in silence. I could see she felt deeply mortified.

I bent over her and, speaking softly next to her ear, now put my question into words: 'Who was that?' But again she refused to answer and would only shake her head. Indeed, she bit her lip harder than ever as tears gathered on her long lashes.

Born stupid, I can never understand anything that isn't perfectly obvious, and so I had no idea what to say to her. I could do nothing but stand there, feeling as if my only purpose was to listen to the wild beating of her heart. Of course, one thing that kept me silent was the conviction that it would be wrong of me to question her any further.

How long this went on, I do not know, but eventually I slid shut the door and gently told the girl, 'Go to your room now.' Her agitation seemed to have subsided somewhat. Assailed by an uneasy feeling that I had seen something I was not meant to see, and a sense of shame towards anyone and no one in particular, I began to pad my way back up the corridor. I had hardly gone ten paces, however, when again I felt a tug – a timid one – at the skirts of my *hakama*. I whirled around, startled, but what do you think it was?

I looked down to find the monkey Yoshihide prostrating himself at my feet, hands on the floor like a human being, bowing over and over in thanks, his golden bell ringing.

14

Perhaps a fortnight went by after that night's incident. All of a sudden, Yoshihide arrived at the mansion to beg a personal audience with His Lordship. He probably dared do such a thing despite his humble station because he had long been in His Lordship's special favour. His Lordship rarely allowed anyone to come into his presence, but that day, as so often before, he assented readily to Yoshihide's request and had him shown in without a moment's delay. The man wore his usual reddish-brown robe and tall black soft hat. His face revealed a new level of sullenness, but he went down on all fours before His Lordship and at length, eyes down, he began to speak in husky tones:

'I come into your honoured presence this day, My Lord, regarding the screen bearing images of hell which His Lordship ordered me to paint. I have applied myself to it day and night – outdone myself – such that my efforts have begun to bear fruit, and it is largely finished.'

'This is excellent news. I am very pleased.'

Even as His Lordship spoke these words, however, his voice seemed oddly lacking in power and vitality.

'No, My Lord, I am afraid the news is anything but excellent,' said Yoshihide, his eyes still fastened on the floor in a way that hinted at anger. 'The work may be largely finished, but there is still a part that I am unable to paint.'

'What? Unable to paint?'

'Indeed, sir. As a rule, I can only paint what I have seen. Or even if I succeed in painting something unknown to me, I myself cannot be satisfied with it. This is the same as not being able to paint it, does His Lordship not agree?'

As His Lordship listened to Yoshihide's words, his face gradually took on a mocking smile.

'Which would mean that if you wanted to paint a screen depicting hell, you would have to have seen hell itself.'

'Exactly, My Lord. In the great fire some years ago, though, I saw flames with my own eyes that I could use for those of the Hell of Searing Heat. In fact, I succeeded with my *Fudō of Twisting Flames* only because I experienced that fire. I believe My Lord is familiar with the painting.'

'What about sinners, though? And hell wardens – you have never seen those, have you?' His Lordship challenged Yoshihide with one question after another as though he had not heard Yoshihide's words.

'I have seen a person bound in iron chains,' said Yoshihide. 'And I have done a detailed sketch of someone being tormented by a monstrous bird. No, I think it cannot be said that I have never seen sinners being tortured. And as for hell wardens,' said Yoshihide, breaking into an eerie smile, 'my eyes have beheld them any number of times as I drift between sleeping and waking. The bull-headed ones, the horse-headed ones, the three-faced, six-armed devils: almost every night they come to torture me with their soundless clapping hands, their voiceless gaping mouths. No, they are not the ones I am having so much difficulty painting.'

I suspect this shocked even His Lordship. For a long while he only glared at Yoshihide until, with an angry twitch of the brow, he spat out, 'All right, then. What is it that you say you are unable to paint?'

15

'In the centre of the screen, falling from the sky, I want to paint an aristocrat's carriage, its enclosure woven of the finest split palm leaf.' As he spoke, Yoshihide raised himself to look directly at His Lordship for the first time – and with a penetrating gaze. I had heard that Yoshihide could be like a madman where painting was concerned; to me the look in his eyes at that moment was terrifying in that very way.

'In the carriage, a voluptuous noblewoman writhes in agony, her long, black hair tossing in the ferocious flames. Her face . . . well, perhaps she contorts her brows and casts her gaze skyward towards the ceiling of the enclosure as she chokes on the rising clouds of smoke. Her hands might tear at the cloth streamers of the carriage blinds in her struggle to ward off the shower of sparks raining down upon her. Around her swarm fierce, carnivorous birds, perhaps a dozen or more, snapping their beaks in anticipation – oh, My Lord, it is this, this image of the noblewoman in the carriage, that I am unable to paint.'

'And therefore . . . ?'

His Lordship seemed to be deriving an odd sort of pleasure from this as he urged Yoshihide to continue, but Yoshihide himself, red lips trembling as with a fever, could only repeat, as if in a dream, 'This is what I am unable to paint.'

Then suddenly, all but biting into his own words, he cried, 'I beg you, My Lord: have your men set a carriage on fire. Let me watch the flames devour its frame and its woven enclosure. And, if possible –'

A dark cloud crossed His Lordship's face, but no sooner had it passed than he broke into a loud cackle. He was still choking with laughter when he spoke: '"Possible"? I'll do whatever you want. Don't waste time worrying about what is "possible".'

His Lordship's words filled me with a terrible foreboding. And in fact his appearance at that moment was anything but ordinary. White foam gathered at the corners of his mouth. His eyebrows convulsed into jagged bolts of lightning. It was as if His Lordship himself had become infused with Yoshihide's madness. And no sooner had he finished speaking than laughter – endless laughter – exploded from his throat once again.

'I'll burn a carriage for you,' he said. 'And I'll have a voluptuous woman inside it, dressed in a noblewoman's robes. She will die writhing with agony in flames and black smoke. I have to salute you, Yoshihide. Who could have thought of such a thing but the greatest painter in the land?'

Yoshihide went pale when he heard this, and for a time the only part of him that moved was his lips: he seemed to be gasping for breath. Then, as though all the muscles of his body had gone limp at once, he crumpled forward with his hands on the matted floor again.

'A thousand thanks to you, My Lord,' Yoshihide said with rare humility, his voice barely audible. Perhaps the full horror of his own plan had come all too clear to him as he heard it spelled out in His Lordship's words. Only this once in my life did I ever think of Yoshihide as a man to be pitied.

16

Two or three nights later, His Lordship summoned Yoshihide as promised to witness the burning of the carriage. He held the event not at the Horikawa mansion, but outside the Capital, at his late younger sister's mountain retreat, widely known as the 'Palace of the Melting Snows'.

No one had lived at this 'palace' for a very long time. Its broad gardens had gone wild, and the desolate sight must have given rise to all sorts of rumours, many about His Lordship's sister, who had actually died there. People used to say that on moonless nights Her Ladyship's broad-skirted scarlet *hakama* would glide eerily along the outdoor corridor, never touching the floor. And no wonder there were such stories! The palace was lonely enough in the daytime, but once the sun set it became downright unnerving. The garden stream would murmur ominously in the darkness and herons would look like monstrous creatures swooping in the starlight.

As it happened, the carriage burning took place on one of those pitch-dark, moonless nights. Oil lamps revealed His Lordship seated in cross-legged ease on the veranda. Beneath a turquoise robe he wore patterned *hakama* in a deep lavender colour. On a thick, round mat edged in white brocade, his position was of course elevated above the half-dozen or so attendants who surrounded him. One among them appeared most eager to be of service to His Lordship, a burly samurai who had distinguished himself in the campaign against the northern barbarians some years earlier. He was said to have survived starvation by eating human flesh, after which he had the strength to tear out the antlers of a living stag with his bare hands. On this night he knelt in stern readiness below the veranda, in the scabbard at his armour-clad waist a sword tipped up and back like a gull's tail, ready to draw at a moment's notice. These men presented a strangely terrifying, almost dreamlike spectacle. The lamplight flickering in the night wind turned them all dark one moment, bright the next.

And then there was the carriage itself. Even without an ox attached to its long, black shafts, their ends resting on the usual low bench that tilted the whole slightly forward, it stood out against the night, its tall enclosure woven of the finest split palm leaf, exactly as Yoshihide had requested: truly, a conveyance worthy of His Imperial Majesty or the most powerful ministers of state. When I saw its gold fittings gleaming like stars in the sky, and considered what was soon to happen to this lavishly appointed vehicle, a shiver went through me in spite of the warm spring night. As for what might be inside the carriage, there was no way to tell: its lovely blinds, woven of still-green bamboo and edged in patterned cloth, had been rolled down tight, and around it alert-looking conscripts stood guard, holding flaming torches and seeming to worry that too much smoke might be drifting towards His Lordship on the veranda.

Yoshihide himself was situated at some remove, kneeling on the ground directly opposite the veranda. He wore what seemed to be his usual reddish-brown robe and tall black soft hat, and he looked especially small and shabby, as though the star-filled sky were a weight pressing down upon him. Behind him knelt another person in an outfit like his – probably an apprentice he had brought along. With them crouching down low in the darkness like that, I could not make out the colour of their robes from my place below the veranda.

17

Midnight was approaching, I believe. I felt as if the darkness enveloping the garden were silently watching us all breathing, the only sound an occasional rush of night wind, each gust wafting towards us the resinous smell of the torches' pine smoke. His Lordship remained silent for some moments, observing the mysterious scene, but then, edging forward where he sat, he cried sharply:

'Yoshihide!'

Yoshihide may have said some word in response, but to my ears it sounded like nothing so much as a moan.

'Tonight, Yoshihide, I am going to burn a carriage for you, as you requested.'

When he said this, His Lordship glanced at the men around him. I thought I saw a meaningful smile pass between him and certain of them. Of course, it could have been my imagination. Now Yoshihide seemed to be timidly raising his head and looking up towards the veranda, but still he waited, saying nothing.

'I want you to look at this,' His Lordship said. 'This is *my* carriage, the one I use every day. You know it well, I'm sure. I will now have it set on fire in order that you may see the Hell of Searing Heat here on earth before your eyes.'

His Lordship reverted to silence and his eyes flashed another signal to his men. Then, with sudden vehemence, he cried, 'Chained inside the carriage is a sinful woman. When we set the carriage afire, her flesh will be roasted, her bones will be charred: she will die an agonizing death. Never again will you have such a perfect model for the screen. Do not fail to watch as her snow-white flesh erupts in flames. See and remember her long, black hair dancing in a whirl of sparks!'

His Lordship sank into silence for yet a third time, but – whatever could have been in his mind? – now all he did was laugh soundlessly, his shoulders quaking.

'Never again will there be a sight like this, Yoshihide! I shall join you in observing it. All right, men, raise the blind. Let Yoshihide see the woman inside!'

On hearing this command, one of the conscripts, torch held high, strode up to the carriage, stretched out his free hand, and whipped the blind up. The torch crackled and flickered and cast its red gleam inside. On the carriage's matted floor, cruelly chained, sat a woman – and, oh, who could have failed to recognize her? Her long, black hair flowed in a voluptuous band across a gorgeous robe embroidered in cherry blossoms, and the golden hairpins atop her downcast head sparkled beautifully in the firelight. For all the differences in costuming, there was no mistaking that girlish frame, that graceful neck (where now a gag was fastened), that touchingly modest profile: they belonged to none other than Yoshihide's daughter. I could hardly keep from crying out.

Just then the samurai kneeling across from me sprang to his feet and, pressing threateningly on his sword hilt, glared at Yoshihide. Startled by this sudden movement, I turned my gaze towards Yoshihide. He looked as if this spectacle were driving him half mad. Where he had been crouching until then, he was on his feet now and poised – arms outstretched – to run towards the carriage. Unfortunately, though, as I said before, he was in the shadows far away from me, and so I did not have a clear view of his face. My frustration lasted but a moment, however. For, drained of colour though it was, Yoshihide's face – or, should I say, Yoshihide's entire form, raised aloft now by some invisible power – appeared before me with such clarity it seemed to have cut its way through the surrounding darkness. For in that instant, His Lordship cried, 'Burn it!', the conscripts flung their torches and the carriage, with Yoshihide's daughter inside, had burst into flame.

18

The fire engulfed the entire carriage. The purple roof tassels blew aside, then clouds of smoke swirled aloft, stark white against the blackness of the night, and finally a shower of sparks spurted upwards with such terrifying force that in a single instant the blinds, the side panels and the roof's metal fittings were ripped off in the blast and sent flying. Still more horrible was the colour of the flames that licked the latticed cabin vents before shooting skywards, as though – might I say? – the sun itself had crashed to earth, spewing its heavenly fire in all directions. As close as I had come to crying out before, now I could only gape in mute awe at the horrifying spectacle.

But what of the girl's father?

I will never forget the look on Yoshihide's face at that instant. He had started towards the carriage on impulse but halted when the flames flared up. He then stood there with arms outstretched, eyes devouring the smoke and flames that enveloped the carriage. In the firelight that bathed him from head to toe, I could see every feature of his ugly, wrinkled face. His wide-staring eyes, his contorted lips, the twitching flesh of his cheeks: all drew a vivid picture of the shock, the terror and the sorrow that traversed Yoshihide's heart by turns. Such anguish, I suspect, would not be seen even on the face of a convicted thief about to have his head cut off or the guiltiest sinner about to face the judgement of the Ten Kings of Hell. Even the powerful samurai went pale at the sight and stole a fearful glance at His Lordship above him.

But what of His Lordship himself? Biting his lip and smiling strangely now and then, he stared straight ahead, never taking his eyes off the carriage. And the girl in the carriage – ah, I don't think I have the courage to describe in detail what she looked like then. The pale whiteness of her upturned face as she choked on the smoke; the tangled length of her hair as she tried to shake the flames from it; the beauty of her cherry blossom robe as it burst into flame: it was all so cruel, so terrible! Especially at one point when the night wind rushed down from the mountain to sweep away the smoke: the sight of her against a flaming background of red flecked with gold dust, gnawing at her gag, writhing as if to snap the chains that bound her – it was enough to make our flesh creep, not only mine but the powerful samurai's as well, as if the tortures of hell were being pictured right there before our eyes.

Just then the night wind gusted once more, rustling the branches of the garden's trees – or so it seemed to me and, I am sure, to everyone else. Such a sound seemed to race through the dark sky, and in that instant some black thing shot from the palace roof into the blazing carriage. It travelled in a perfectly straight line like a ball that has been kicked, neither touching the earth nor arcing through space. And as the carriage's burning side lattices collapsed inwards, glowing as if coated in crimson lacquer, the thing grasped the girl's straining shoulders and hurled a long, piercing and inexpressibly anguished scream out beyond the billowing smoke. Another scream followed, and then a third, until we all found ourselves crying out with it. For though it had been left tethered back at the Horikawa mansion, what we saw now clinging to the girl's shoulders against a flaming backdrop was the monkey Yoshihide.

19

We could see the monkey for only the briefest moment, though. A fountain of sparks shot up to the sky like gold dust in black lacquer, and then not only the monkey but the girl, too, was shrouded in black smoke. Now in the middle of the garden there was only a carriage of fire seething in flames with a terrible roar. No – 'pillar of fire' might better describe this horrific conflagration boiling up to the starry heavens.

But, oh, how strange it was to see the painter now, standing absolutely rigid before the pillar of fire! Yoshihide – who only a few moments earlier had seemed to be suffering the torments of hell – stood there with his arms locked across his chest as if he had forgotten even the presence of His Lordship, his whole wrinkled face suffused now with an inexpressible radiance – the radiance of religious ecstasy. I could have sworn that the man's eyes were no longer watching his daughter dying in agony, that instead the gorgeous colours of flames and the sight of a woman suffering in them were giving him joy beyond measure.

The most wondrous thing was not just that he watched his only daughter's death throes with apparent joy, but also that Yoshihide at that moment possessed a strange, inhuman majesty that resembled the rage of the King of Beasts himself as you might see him in a dream. For this reason – although I might have been imagining it – the countless night birds that flew around us squawking in alarm at each new eruption of flames seemed to keep their distance from Yoshihide's tall black hat. Perhaps even these insentient birds could see the mysterious grandeur that hung above Yoshihide like a radiant aura.

If the birds could see it, how much more so the rest of us, down to the lowly conscripts. Trembling inwardly, scarcely breathing and filled with a bizarre sense of adoration, we kept our eyes fastened on Yoshihide as if we were present at the decisive moment when a lump of stone or wood becomes a holy image of the Buddha. The carriage flames that filled the heavens with a roar; Yoshihide under the spell of the flames, transfixed: what sublimity! what rapture! But among us only one, His Lordship, looked on as if transformed into another person, his noble countenance drained of colour, the corners of his mouth flecked with foam, hands clutching his knees through his lavender *hakama* as he panted like a beast in need of water . . .

20

Word soon spread that His Lordship had burnt the carriage that night in the Palace of the Melting Snows, and there seem to have been many who were highly critical of the event. First of all came the question of Yoshihide's daughter: why had His Lordship chosen to burn her alive? The rumour most often heard was that he had done it out of spite for her rejection of his love. I am certain, however, that he did it to punish the twisted personality of an artist who would go so far as to burn a carriage and kill a human being to complete the painting of a screen. In fact, I overheard His Lordship saying as much himself.

And then there was Yoshihide, whose stony heart was also apparently the topic of much negative commentary. How, after seeing his own daughter burned alive, could he want to finish the screen painting? Some cursed him as a beast in human guise who had forgotten a father's love for the sake of a picture. One who allied himself with this opinion was His Reverence the Abbot of Yokawa, who always used to say, 'Excel in his art though he might, if a man does not know the Five Virtues,[12] he can only end up in hell.'

A month went by, and the screen with its images of hell was finished at last. Yoshihide brought it to the mansion that very day and humbly presented it for His Lordship's inspection. His Reverence happened to be visiting at the time, and I am certain that he was shocked at the sight of the horrible firestorm blasting through it. Until he actually saw the screen, he was glowering at Yoshihide, but then he slapped his knee and exclaimed, 'What magnificent work!' I can still see the bitter smile on His Lordship's face when he heard those words.

Almost no one spoke ill of Yoshihide after that – at least not in the mansion. Could it be because all who saw the screen – even those who had always hated him – were struck by strangely solemn feelings when they witnessed the tortures of the Hell of Searing Heat in all their reality?

By then, however, Yoshihide numbered among those who are no longer of this world. The night after he finished the screen, he tied a rope to a beam in his room and hanged himself. I suspect that, having sent his daughter on ahead to the other world, he could not bear to go on living here as if nothing had happened. His body lies buried in the ruins of his home. The little stone marker is probably so cloaked in moss now, after decades of exposure to the wind and rain, that no one can tell whose grave it is any more.

SAWANISHI YŪTEN

Filling Up with Sugar

Translated by Jay Rubin

The vagina was the first part of her mother's body that turned to sugar – probably because it was the one organ for which her mother no longer had any use. Yukiko had never asked directly, but she had never sensed a male presence about her mother after her father had died early in Yukiko's first year of high school. Her mother must have passed through meno-pause long before then, too. The uterus and the dark channel that extended from it had quietly dried up and changed to sugar.

A vague and childish thought had crossed Yukiko's mind long ago when she first learned that an illness existed in which the cells of the body turn to sugar: *Filling up with sugar – what a lovely way to die!* She imagined it must feel something like Hansel and Gretel's joy on discovering the gingerbread house combined with the witch's elation at the appearance of her long-awaited victims.

Yukiko once took a day off to meet her mother in town. Ordinarily, her mother would visit one shop after another without a break, but that day she complained of an odd feeling in her lower abdomen, and the two had withdrawn to a café to rest.

Neither of them had realized at the time what changes were occurring deep inside her mother's body. But the illness was incurable, which meant that even if they had become aware of it at that stage, the most they could have done was face the impending threat of death that much earlier.

But six months after the shopping trip, Yukiko learned that it was her own mother being ravaged by the 'lovely' illness. She found herself unable to form an image in her mind on hearing the news, as if she were watch-ing an out-of-focus movie. The doctor explained that the disease advanced slowly, beginning with such unused parts of the body as the uterus or the

327

ear canals. Only then did she picture her mother on their shopping day, and like a projectionist who rushes to correct the blurred image on the screen, she began to see it all with vivid clarity.

Yukiko decided to devote herself to caring for her mother, and submitted her resignation to the tourist bureau where she had worked as a temporary employee for seven years since graduating from junior college. She did this out of neither sentiment nor self-sacrifice. She had recently failed the exam that would have made her a fully fledged staff member, and when she weighed her father's life insurance money against the income she would receive if she remained in her job, the scales did not incline significantly in either direction. The insurance money was not enough to continue supporting her mother in her old age, but it was plenty to keep two women alive for two years or so. Her boss advised against making any sudden moves, but before Yukiko could decide whether or not to tell him about her mother's illness, he assured her that his reason for failing her had not been to prompt her resignation. Such crass considerations hardly weighed against the most important thing: knowing that her mother had perhaps two years to live. That took care of any lingering attachment she might have had for the job and made her glad she had not said anything about her mother.

Moving out of her apartment, Yukiko left the city by train, transferring to the single-track electric line that led to the country town of her youth. She had not announced the time of her arrival, but her mother was there to greet her partway, wearing a black coat and standing against a telegraph pole, alone and still. After an uncertain interval between the time they spotted each other and the moment they were face to face, her mother embraced her with a firm 'Welcome home'.

'I'm glad to be back,' Yukiko responded, putting her arms around her mother gently as if drawing towards herself a delicate creation of spun sugar. The sour body odour she caught from her mother's neck was faintly sweet.

'What are you doing here, standing by the road like this?' Yukiko asked, less in the hope of an answer than to comfort her mother, as if to say, 'I'm here now. You won't be alone any more.'

'I wanted to welcome you,' her mother said without further explanation. Together, they began their slow walk home.

The house was shockingly neat. It felt hushed and empty, like a new house whose owners have not had time to buy all their furnishings. When Yukiko openly expressed surprise, her mother explained, almost apologetically, that she had been slowly getting rid of things while still able to move. The little house had been handed down, with repeated renovation, from her grandfather's time, and now it, too, seemed to be on the verge of taking its final breath. Gone were her mother's amateur watercolours and the decorative cards autographed by favourite mystery writers. In their place on the walls hung family photographs that had always been kept in albums.

'The place seems more cheerful this way, don't you think?' her mother said, now with a touch of pride. 'Photos will be easier for you all to divide up later.'

Yukiko recognized most of the photographs, but there were two less familiar ones in the bedroom: pictures from her parents' wedding. Both were in lovely white frames, the one on the left a group shot of the extended family, and the one on the right the bride and groom: she in pure white, and he in traditional *haori* and *hakama*. Yukiko's mother looked very happy, in contrast to the rather tense expression on her father's face. Yes, this was her father as she remembered him.

'We had our troubles, but this was the beginning of my happiness.'

Yukiko turned away from the pictures, not sure she could stand any more shy pronouncements from her mother. This had always been a Japanese bedroom, with futon spread on the matted floor at night, but now an electric reclining bed stood in the very centre of the room.

Her mother became confined to that bed, as she had feared, not long after Yukiko's arrival. Perhaps she had been willing herself to remain active until now and had already reached her limits.

In this progressive illness, systemic saccharification syndrome, after the unused internal organs turn to sugar, the skin (more precisely, the dermis, quickly followed by the epidermis) changes also. The cells can be clearly seen beneath the surface of fully transformed skin, and these cause the patient terrible pain whenever the skin happens to peel off or bump against objects. After a bath, especially, the sugar begins to melt, leaving white wounds open and exposed. Yukiko quickly gave up the idea of bathing her mother, resorting instead to gentle wipe-downs.

By the time the epidermis turns entirely to sugar, the saccharification process of the lower half of the body is complete. Most patients can only lie in bed, waiting for the approach of death. The one saving grace is that the disease affects the nerves as well, which alleviates the pain.

Yukiko might spend hours at her mother's side, but she could not suffer the pain in her mother's place or take on even a part of it for her. Here her mother was, losing one physical function after another and turning into sucrose, while Yukiko felt only frustration at her inability to touch her mother's suffering.

In Yukiko's presence, however, her mother did not complain. Had her own husband been the one in attendance, she might have been able to voice her pain more openly, but to Yukiko she said only, 'I'm so glad you're here for me.' Yukiko pretended not to notice the note of apology in her words.

Yukiko's two elder sisters had held off on making their first sick calls, but her mother acted unconcerned. Both sisters lived in the Tokyo suburbs, and both had their hands full with work, childcare and looking after their husbands. They had already left the family by the time their father died and Yukiko and her mother moved into their grandfather's little house. And so, the few times they did come to visit, they would not linger in this place for which they evidenced little attachment. Besides, they had always been closer to their father than their mother. Nevertheless, at weekends they would phone Yukiko to ask how their mother was doing.

Couldn't Yukiko put their mother into some facility that was not so hard to get to? they would ask, but Yukiko let these suggestions pass in silence. 'If you ever need anything, just let me know. I've got a little something put away,' each sister would say in the same tone as if she had worked it out with the other one. It was more than Yukiko could bear; she would hang up without a word. Her sisters were like each other in every way – both had their mother's soft white skin and open features, her edgy speech patterns.

Their mother wanted to see her grandchildren, but the sisters never brought them, perhaps afraid that a child might accidentally injure her brittle sugar flesh or say something cruel. Only once after a visit by the eldest sister did Yukiko catch her mother grumbling about the sisters' coldness.

Now and then, Yukiko would find herself deep in thought as she studied her sleeping mother's face. What were those clear, youthful eyes of hers doing behind their still-lovely lids – chasing after the remnants of her memories? She raised a little prayer that her mother might – if only for a short time – fall under the spell of some beautiful recollection.

Often, too, she recalled the time between high school and her graduation from junior college when she and her mother were the only two living in this house. Because her sisters had already left, and her mother held multiple part-time jobs, she always came home to an empty house. She still had vivid recollections of the gloomy chill of the place, its only light the few rays entering through the windows, and of how unsettled her feelings remained until she had gone from room to room pressing switches, ending with the round white lamp on the living-room ceiling. This memory overlapped with another memory of the living room, which was where her mother would place calls to her sisters when she was worried about them at college: then Yukiko would often turn away and climb the stairs to her own unlit room.

Yukiko took her mother out in a wheelchair from time to time. Following the doctor's advice, she had bent her mother's legs into a sitting position while they were still movable, and waited for them to harden. She would wrap her mother in a blanket and carry her to the wheelchair, taking great care to prevent any shocks from cracking the saccharified skin. Her mother's body felt strangely light. The life inside it had been gradually changing into sugar. 'You're so light,' Yukiko said. 'Like a little girl.' She immediately regretted the offhand remark.

Yukiko handled her mother with a care that no one could imitate. Not even the prince who found Snow White asleep from eating the poison apple could have matched the gentle way she assisted her mother to prevent cracking.

She had to exercise great caution with the room's humidity. If the air became too dry, the surface of the sugar became easily cracked, and once that happened, the saccharified skin would never heal. The transparent surface layer, which had shown the crimson dermis beneath, changed to a milky white. Whenever she saw such an apparent impact wound on her mother's skin, Yukiko would blame herself for having caused irreparable damage, often remaining in an agitated state until well after she was under the covers of the futon beside her mother's bed. How could she have let such a thing happen?

Aside from brief trips to the local shops, Yukiko left the house only two days a month for meetings of a readers' group. At first her sole reason for leaving her mother with a carer for the day was to collect medicine from a town two hours away by train, but the helper became concerned for Yukiko and suggested that, for a change of pace, she attend one of the hospital's carer workshops or support groups. Yukiko resisted at first, but when even her mother began pushing her to do it, she decided to ask for details at the hospital's reception desk. They gave her a sheet of paper with a calendar of events for carers.

Few items on the list caught her eye – most were things like nappy changing or simple massage – but there was one that did arouse her interest: a group that read books aloud. The listing in the little square on the calendar gave no information beyond a book's title and author and the location of the meetings, which were intended for those engaged in caring for victims of her mother's disease. The twice-monthly meetings coincided exactly with the days that Yukiko had to visit the hospital.

The readers' group met on the second and fourth Thursdays of the month at 2.30 p.m. Meetings were scheduled to end at four o'clock, but attendees could leave early, and extension was also a possibility. The important thing was that participants derive some satisfaction from the meetings and that they regain some of their zest for life.

The gatherings were rather odd. Yukiko attended the first with some misgivings, imagining that people would take turns reading aloud from the assigned book. Instead, she found a number of armchairs arranged in a circle so that participants could hear each other clearly, and people listening quietly to the speaker. People did not have to read the entire book in advance. They could just read passages they happened to like, and if they didn't find any such passages, that was all right, too.

Each participant had his or her own way of reading the chosen passage aloud. Some read with powerful intonations that suggested they had practised the section repeatedly. Others would stumble over the pronunciation of certain characters; the members would encourage them and reward them with extra-loud applause at the end. Some read with resonant tones that told you the person must have been a drama club member at college, while others mumbled so badly in embarrassment that you couldn't tell what section they were reading. All briefly offered their impressions of the passages they had read before resuming their seats, and applause followed each presentation. Some chatting would begin after a reading, and when the remarks ran out, another person would then take over.

Books read at the meetings included such immediately relevant works as Elisabeth Kübler-Ross's *On Death and Dying*, which traced the psychological changes of dying people, and Rebecca Brown's *Excerpts from a Family Medical Dictionary*, which was based on the author's own experience as a carer, but also books with sugar or sweetness in the title such as Richard Brautigan's *In Watermelon Sugar*, Ogawa Yōko's *Sugartime* and Mori Mari's *Room of Sweet Nectar*.

Yukiko at first looked forward to the others' earnest readings, but gradually she, too, began to find pleasure in raising her own voice. Once she had chosen a passage, she would read precisely that, neither more nor less. She found that this gave her the same kind of pleasure as wiping her mother's hands, carefully, one finger at a time.

The book that Yukiko liked best was *An Invisible Sign of My Own* by Aimee Bender. It tells the story of Mona, who started 'to quit' things from the time her father fell ill when she was ten years old, but who now, at the age of twenty, is able to get something she truly wants for the first time in her life. The thing is an axe. Yukiko read the scene aloud to herself over and over:

'"Will you look at this!" I said out loud to the world. "Just what I've always wanted!"'

As if raising the sharp axe, Yukiko tightened her grip on the book as she read. It made her strangely calm whenever she did this. (She was also fond of a passage six pages later, but that one she could not bring herself to read aloud.)

She made it a habit to read the assigned book while her mother was sleeping. If the television was on, she would lower the volume and pick up where she had left off. She and her mother had a tacit understanding that she would not turn the television off at such times. Sleep liberated her mother from the reality of her saccharification and gave her a moment's peace, but that moment had to end. Her mother had to wake and realize that her interrupted world was still there, unchanged. Television was good for masking this cruel moment of confusion. Television gently told them that her mother had not moved in her sleep, and it let them know, too, how much time had gone by. 'Awake?' Yukiko would ask when she heard the change in her mother's breathing, by which time she would have stashed the bookmarked volume beneath the foot of the bed out of her mother's sight.

She would wipe the sweat that had oozed from her mother's saccharified skin in her sleep, daubing with enormous care to prevent the epidermis, which had now turned almost entirely to sugar, from cracking or from melting in the sweat and peeling off. She worked with unbroken attention, allowing not the slightest bit of dirt to escape the movement of her hands. It was almost as if she believed that, by so doing, she could restore her mother's skin to its original whiteness and lustre. Even after the job was done, Yukiko would continue staring at her mother's skin until she was satisfied that she had missed nothing. She always made sure to use a thin Japanese facecloth. A thick towel might shed fibres that would adhere to the skin.

The other members of the reading group had family members who were either visiting the hospital regularly or had been admitted there.

The discussions were lively. All participants would be losing family members before long, and talking about it helped them to prepare for it emotionally. They were resigned to the fact that they could do nothing to postpone the deaths of their family members, but there was no telling exactly how or when any single loved one's death would arrive. The readings themselves often prompted discussions of death, more often with respect to characters in a book than anyone's actual family members.

Yukiko could not forget the story of a traffic accident told by one of the women participants. It had involved her husband's uncle, whose disease was well advanced. The family had gone to visit him and were strolling with him in his wheelchair when the one pushing the chair took his hands off at the top of a slope. It happened in an instant when everyone was looking away from the uncle. The tyres smoothly and quickly traced the curve of the hill, plunging downwards and flinging the uncle on to the road in the path of a car that happened along at that exact moment. The whole family watched, mesmerized, as the uncle's body was shattered from the impact. The pieces of sugar flesh soaked up the blood, turning the colour of death before their eyes, then quickly dissolved into the puddled blood to form a red mud patch on the road.

From that day onwards, whenever she took her mother out for a walk, her hands would sweat on the wheelchair handles. Caught in the narrow space between a death that was sure to come soon and a death that could happen at any moment, Yukiko was determined to keep a firm grip on her mother's life and not let go.

One time, someone talked about a human trafficker who bought and sold tiny children afflicted with the disease. No one responded well to the story, and for several awkward minutes the group almost seemed to be offering a silent prayer for the victimized children. Some members might even have been hearing the children's cries during the tense, wordless interval. There had never been anything like this before, but something very different occupied Yukiko's mind while it was happening. The previous night, she had found it impossible to resist a certain impulse that came over her as she lay on the floor beside her mother. She crept to the foot of the bed and gazed at her mother's toes, which she had just finished wiping. Fully transformed into sugar, the tips softly inhaled the moonlight spilling in through the pale green curtains, glowing faintly as if to hint at their presence in the darkness. All five toes were there where they had always been, beautifully aligned on each foot, from the rounded, drop-like big toe on the inside, down to the small toe on the outside. Unlike those of patients Yukiko had glimpsed in their hospital rooms, her mother's feet were not missing any parts. Neither had they taken on that milky opacity but instead wore the light with the dull sheen of a crystal.

After checking to be sure that her mother was asleep, Yukiko softly extended her tongue, over which spread the sensation of the foot's melting. Was it the sugar that made her tongue feel hot, or the perversion? She was dreamily recalling the sweet sensation when the topic seemed to swerve in a new direction and she found herself amid the readers' group once again.

The silence had yielded to a heated exchange of opinions regarding ways to memorialize the dead. One person was saying she had heard that some people wrap the corpse in silver foil and slowly roast it, afterwards letting the melted sugar harden and using the crystals as amulets.

Such mutilation of the dead was out of the question, someone immediately objected, but since cremation was no different in its inflicting of injury on the corpse, that must not have been the point of the criticism. Which was the more direct confrontation with death – burying the corpse in the earth, or making it into crystals and carrying it around? And what was a funeral, anyhow – a service for the dead or a ceremony for the living? Some people delivered cogent, well-argued opinions, while others tried to cut down their opponents' views with emotion. Their confusion appeared to Yukiko as evidence that they were not fully prepared to accept death.

'I gather you have decided how you will memorialize your loved one?' a man named Kajiura said to Yukiko after the end of the meeting. He always wore a somewhat oversized blue jacket, and he apparently owned a delivery company. Yukiko knew his name and face because he was one of the very few men in the group. She was surprised to be addressed – and surprised by the question itself – but she smiled back without hesitation.

'No, what makes you think so?'

'Because you didn't say anything on the subject.'

'Well, that's true, but I wasn't the only one.'

'No, but you were the only one looking straight at every speaker.'

Yukiko did not reply to this.

'I was hoping to hear what you had to say,' Kajiura continued. 'I'm sorry, though, I didn't mean to pry.'

He bowed deeply to Yukiko and hurried away. She liked his baggy shoulders, which seemed to go with his polite manner. She watched him shrink into the distance and disappear.

From then on, Yukiko made sure to take a place near Kajiura in order to avoid sitting opposite him, uneasy lest he see inside her again. She had not noticed before, but his style of reading was different from the others'. Not that it was especially polished, but the voice with which he carefully read the text aloud could make a very different impression depending on the place of the listener. She never felt drawn to him when he sat across from her, but at his side she became aware of soft reverberations from his deep voice that seemed to caress her ears, and the closer she sat, the nicer the reverberations felt. This was the voice of a man who handled objects with care and delivered them reliably, she thought.

Before she knew it, the seat beside Kajiura had become reserved for her. He would speak to her in the natural course of things while they were putting the chairs away after meetings, and on several occasions he invited her for a chat at a nearby café. At such times they talked only about their impressions of the meeting or their family members' medical conditions or Kajiura's work, but never anything as involved as what he had first broached to her.

One evening, a call came from him. He had made a delivery nearby, he said, and wondered if she might have time for a chat. Because she never left the house for anything but shopping and the reading group, she hesitated at first, and then asked him to wait for her at the station. There was still time before she had to prepare dinner, and her mother's condition was stable. When she announced that she would be stepping out for a moment, her mother gave her a questioning glance but only said, 'Don't be gone too long' with her usual smile.

She applied a touch of make-up to her face, but she had not bothered to fix her hair since morning, and now it refused to behave. Yukiko borrowed the white knitted hat that her mother wore on their walks. It made her feel protected by her mother, like a little girl excited to be going out to play. Kajiura was waiting at the station, wearing his blue jacket. They drove to the Jazzlin Café near her old school. The area was exactly as it had always been, and the café's owner was still going strong. Yukiko chattered cheerfully about her memories of school, and Kajiura joined in with impressions of the neighbourhood he had noticed along the way.

She was much later getting home than she had planned to be, and the surrounding area was pitch dark. The house felt cold inside. She must have forgotten to close the small kitchen window she had opened for ventilation. Her mother was probably asleep – the place was utterly still. As Yukiko pressed the switch, creating a circle of light in the darkness, she ventured a soft 'I'm home' and heard a voice calling her name. It was a strangled, trembling cry. She hurried down the hall, switching on lights as she went. When she turned on the bedroom light, she let out a scream. Her mother was swarming with ants, unable to shake them off.

Yukiko swept the ants from her mother's body and crushed them when they hit the floor. She worked with feverish urgency. She had been given repeated warnings about this in summer and had kept fierce guard against such an eventuality. But this was winter! There shouldn't be ants now! She smashed them with her fists, frantic, not caring that their crushed corpses were sticking to the straw floor mats. She went on crushing them one by one, as if by so doing she could be forgiven for having taken her eyes off her mother, or she could stop death from carrying her mother away bit by bit.

It was after midnight by the time she finished crushing every single ant. She then set about picking off the little ant corpses that littered her mother's body and wiping the indentation that each had left behind. They were everywhere – in the grooves beside her nose, on her cheeks, the back of her neck, her upper arms, between her toes. Yukiko learned afterward at the hospital that these were a species of ant that had been introduced from Argentina which remained active in winter. How frightening it must have been to have thousands of ants crawling over her and to be able to do nothing with her immovable body but lie there and bear it! Her flowing tears had eroded little lines in the saccharified skin leading away from the outer corners of her eyes. Yukiko did all she could to prevent her tears from falling on her mother's body. 'I'm sorry, so sorry,' she said over and over as she worked.

Yukiko stopped attending the readers' group after that, returning straight from the hospital instead. Her mother soon lost her voice, and then all expression in her face. The endless tension of the days that followed was almost unbearable. Yukiko felt as if she were slowly moving through a dense fog, knowing all the while that a steep cliff lay before her yet having no choice but to keep moving towards it, feeling a chill of fear whenever her feet slipped or she bumped into a tree.

The day her mother's eyes ceased to open, Yukiko set about her morning duties on the assumption that her mother was still asleep. Even after she had finished a bowl of fruit and yogurt for breakfast and hung the laundry out to dry, there was still no sign her mother's eyes were going to open, and she finally realized that they would never open again. The doctor had told her that her mother's eyes would continue roaming through a pure white visual field for two or three days after the lids became sealed. The saccharified skin would then become moist, and when it began to dry again, that would indicate that her mother's life had ended. At some point in that interval, the disease reached the heart and the entire body would have changed to sugar. All Yukiko could do was pray that her mother would not suffer. She stayed by her side, holding her hand, never letting go.

When all water was gone from her mother's body and Yukiko had checked repeatedly to be sure that the disease had run its course, she telephoned Kajiura. He sounded concerned that she might have stopped attending the meetings because of him.

'Our next book will be Kawabata Yasunari's *House of the Sleeping* –'

'My mother died,' Yukiko said, quietly but clearly.

'Oh. I'm –'

But before he could finish expressing his condolences, Yukiko said there was something she wanted him to bring her.

The day of the wake, the Shinkansen train schedule was thrown off by a major snowstorm, and her sisters arrived late. This time they brought their children and husbands to see their mother's body wrapped – quite literally wrapped like a package, legs and arms removed – in her white shroud. It was the perfect funeral garb for her, fully crystallized as she was now into white sugar. The two sisters held each other, shedding tears, to see their mother so totally transformed. The children seemed to understand that they should not be doing anything playful, but they peered into the coffin with obvious fascination. The sisters' husbands were discussing the funeral arrangements. Kajiura was among the mourners.

'You must be hungry,' Yukiko said to the children, leading them into the kitchen. She moved aside the cardboard box that Kajiura had brought, now empty and placed by the door, and she sat the children down at the table where she and her mother had always eaten dinner together. She slowly stirred the contents of the larger pot on the stove, revealing red adzuki beans in the thick, black liquid and spreading a sweet aroma through the kitchen. Rice-flour dumplings floated to the surface of the other pot as it boiled. She swished some dumplings through cold water to firm them up, dropped them into the first pot, stirred them once and then served them, in the sweet adzuki soup, to the children.

'Yum! Zenzai!' they cried.

Yukiko had made the zenzai for tonight's family dinner but she spooned some into a lacquer bowl for herself and sat down with the children. It suddenly occurred to her that she had not eaten anything since her mother died. The sweet aroma sent a painful spasm through her empty stomach. Her hands trembled as she lifted her bowl, but she knew she must not spill a drop of the precious liquid: her mother was dead now. The tears she had been holding back poured out of her. The rough skins of the adzuki beans from Kajiura grazed her tongue as she tasted the warm sugar that was filling her stomach.

UCHIDA HYAKKEN

Kudan

Translated by Rachel DiNitto

A large yellow moon hung in the distance, all colour, no light. Was this night time? Probably not. Was the pale blue streak of light in the sky behind me from a setting or a rising sun? A dragonfly floated across the moon's yellow surface, but when its silhouette left the moon, I lost sight of it. The field around me extended as far as the eye could see. I stood soaking wet, water dripping from the end of my tail. As a child, I'd heard stories about the *kudan*, never thinking I would turn into such a pathetic monster myself. But now here I was, a cow with a human face. What should I do in this vast, empty field? Why had I been put here? Where was the cow that had spawned me?

At some point, the moon turned blue. The sky darkened, leaving only a thin band of light on the horizon. The band grew even thinner, and just when it seemed about to disappear, small black dots began to show up in it. They increased in number, and by the time they formed a line on the horizon, the band of light was gone and the sky was dark. Then the moon began to glow. This was when I knew that it was nightfall and that the fading light had been coming from the west. My body dried off, and each time the wind blew across my back, my short fur stirred in the breeze. As the moon grew smaller, its blue light flowed in all directions. Here in the middle of this field, which seemed as if it were under water, I recalled things about my human past with regret. But the sequence was a blur: try as I might, I couldn't tell at which point my life as a human being had ceased. Folding my front legs, I tried lying down. But I didn't like the sand sticking to my hairless chin and got up again. As the night deepened, I wandered aimlessly or stood still in a daze. The moon descended into the western sky. As dawn approached, a gust of wind rose from the west like a giant wave, carrying the smell of sand, and I understood that my first day as a *kudan* was beginning. Then the terrifying thought I'd let slip from my memory suddenly returned. The *kudan* lives only three days, and before it dies it reveals a prophecy in human language. Having been reborn in this form, I didn't care how long I might live, so it didn't bother me that I'd be dead in three days, but the part about the prophecy was troubling. I had no idea what prophecy to make. For the moment I didn't need to worry. Here in the middle of the field with nobody around, I could keep my mouth shut and wait for death. Just then the wind picked up and I could hear the clamour of human voices. Frightened, I gazed into the distance, and as the wind blew, I heard the voices again: 'Over there! Over there!' The voices seemed vaguely familiar.

That was when I realized that the black dots on the horizon the evening before had been people, that they'd crossed the field in the night to hear my prophecy. I had to escape – as soon as possible. I fled eastwards. A pale blue light filtered into the eastern sky, turning white as the sky lightened. Across the field I could see a terrifying crowd approaching like the ominous shadow of a cloud. A wind rose up from the east, carrying their shouts of 'Over there! Over there!' Their voices were now definitely familiar, and they sounded nearby. In a panic I fled north, but the north wind blew and their shouts rode back to me on the breeze. The same thing happened when I ran south. The wind changed direction and the mass of people closed in on me. I was trapped. The huge crowd was coming to hear the prophecy from my mouth. If they knew I had nothing to say even though I was a *kudan*, they'd be furious. I didn't mind dying on the third day, but the torment before that would be unbearable. I stamped my feet in vexation, ready to flee. The yellow moon hung hazily in the western sky, growing larger. The scenery was the same as last night's. I gazed at the moon, bewildered.

The day had fully dawned.

The crowd encircled me in the middle of the vast field. The frightening mass of people must have numbered in the thousands, perhaps tens of thousands. Several dozens of them stepped forwards and quickly got to work. They brought in timber and constructed a large fenced-in area around me. They erected scaffolding and made a grandstand. Time passed, and before long it was noon. Unable to do anything, I watched them work.

Their activity could only mean that they intended to sit and wait three days for my prophecy. They were surrounding me like this, even though I had nothing to say. I needed to escape, but there was no way out. People filled the upper reaches of the gallery, which grew dark with the crowd. The overflow stood below the grandstand or crouched by the fence. After a while, a man in a white kimono appeared from below the western stands holding up a ceremonial vessel and approaching me in silence. The crowd went quiet. The man advanced with great solemnity and stopped when he was very close to me. Then he placed the vessel on the ground and retreated. The vessel was filled with clean water. Sure that he meant it for me, I approached and drank it.

The crowd suddenly came to life. 'He drank it!' someone said.

'Finally. It won't be long now!' another said.

I was caught off guard and looked around. Apparently, they thought I would speak the prophecy after I drank the water. But I had nothing to say. I turned away and took a few steps at random. Dusk seemed to be approaching. If only night would come faster!

'Hey, he's turned his back on us,' someone said, as though surprised.

'It may not happen today.'

'Then the prophecy is bound to be important.'

I was sure I had heard all their voices somewhere before. I spun around and saw the familiar face of a man who was crouching by the fence and staring hard at me. At first I couldn't recall with any clarity, but slowly I began to remember, and soon I recognized the faces of my friends, my relatives, my teachers, my students. I hated the way they were elbowing their way forward to get a better look at me.

'Hey,' someone said, 'this *kudan* looks familiar.'

'I don't know. I'm not so sure,' someone else replied.

'He does look like somebody, but I can't remember who.'

This talk threw me further into confusion. I couldn't bear to have my friends know I'd become this hairy beast. I thought I'd better hide my face and tried not to look in their direction.

Before I knew it, the sun had set and a dim yellow moon hung in the sky. As it slowly took on a blue tinge, the stands and fence dissolved into the gloom, and night fell.

In the darkness, the crowd lit bonfires around the fence. All night long the flames leaped into the moonlit sky. The crowd stayed awake, waiting for a word from me. The deep red smoke of the bonfire drifted up and darkened as it crossed the face of the moon, whose brightness faded, and the wind of dawn began to blow. Day broke once again. Thousands more must have crossed the field over the course of the night. The area around the fence was even more raucous than the day before. Faces in the crowd kept changing. They grew more and more threatening, and I was full of fear.

The man in the white kimono approached once again, reverently offering me the vessel, and then he withdrew. As before, the vessel was filled with water. I wasn't thirsty and knew I'd be expected to speak if I drank, so I didn't even look at it.

'He's not going to drink,' someone said.

'Shut up. You shouldn't be talking at a time like this.'

'It must be one hell of a prophecy. The fact that he's taking so long must mean something.'

The crowd grew noisy again as people came and went. The man in the white kimono kept bringing me water. The crowd fell silent each time he offered me the vessel, but as soon as they saw I wasn't drinking from it, the noise got worse. He brought water more frequently, putting it closer to me each time. I found this annoying and became angry. Then another man, carrying another vessel, walked up to me and stared at me. He shoved the vessel up under my face. I recognized him. I couldn't say exactly who he was, but the sight of him only increased my anger.

When he saw that I had no intention of drinking the water, he clicked his tongue impatiently. 'Come on, drink it, will you?'

'No, I don't want to,' I replied in anger.

The crowd went crazy. I looked around and saw to my shock that people in the stands were jumping down and those behind the fence were climbing over it. They ran towards me, shouting terrifying curses at one another.

'He spoke.'

'He finally said something.'

'What'd he say?'

'Who cares? It's what he's *going* to say.'

When I looked up, I saw the yellow moon again. The light over the field was growing dim. The sun was setting on my second day. I was still unable to prophesy anything, but I didn't think I would die, either.

Perhaps the prophecy itself would cause my death, which meant that if I didn't say anything, I might not die at the end of three days. In that case I'd rather live, I thought. At that moment, the ones at the front of the crowd reached my side. Those behind kept pushing forward, admonishing each other, 'Quiet, quiet.' Who knew what would become of me if I were grabbed by this angry, disappointed mob? I wanted desperately to get out, but I was trapped by the human fence. The crowd grew more unruly; shrieks could be heard over the din. The human fence grew tighter and tighter around me. I was paralysed with fear. Without thinking, I drank the water in the vessel. In that instant the crowd fell silent. I was stunned when I realized what I'd done, but there was no way to undo it. The look of anticipation on their faces was even more frightening. I broke out in a cold sweat. As I remained silent, the crowd slowly came back to life.

'What happened? Something's wrong.'

'No, it's coming, an absolutely amazing prophecy.'

I heard this much, but otherwise the commotion around me was not too bad. There seemed to be a new uneasiness in the crowd. I relaxed a little and looked at the faces of the ones who'd formed the human fence, realizing that I knew every one of those in front. A strange anxiety and fear registered on each of their faces. As I watched this happen, my own fear dissipated and I was able to relax. I suddenly felt thirsty and took a sip from the vessel in front of me. This time nobody spoke. The shadow of fear deepened, and everyone seemed to be holding their breath. It was like that for a while, until someone broke the silence: 'I'm scared.' The voice was soft but echoed across the crowd.

The circle around me widened. The crowd was slowly backing off.

'Now I'm afraid to hear the prophecy. By the looks of this *kudan*, who knows what terrible thing he'll say?'

'Good or bad, it's best not to know. Let's kill him quickly before he has a chance to say anything.'

I was shocked at the threat to kill me, but the voice was what took me by surprise. It belonged to my son, my own human son. The other voices had sounded familiar, but I was unable to place them; yet the voice of my son I recognized. In an effort to see him I stood on my hind legs.

'The *kudan* is lifting its front legs.'

'He's going to make his prophecy,' I heard someone say in a panicked voice. The tightly packed human enclosure began to break down, and without another word the crowd scattered in all directions. Jumping the wooden fence and ducking under the stands, they ran as fast as they could. In their wake, night once again approached and the moon began to cast its hazy yellow light. With great relief, I stretched out my front legs and yawned three or four times. Perhaps I wouldn't die after all.

DISASTERS, NATURAL AND MAN-MADE

AKUTAGAWA RYŪNOSUKE

The Great Earthquake
and
General Kim

Translated by Jay Rubin

The Great Earthquake[1]
(1923)

The odour was something like that of overripe apricots. Catching a hint of it as he walked through the charred ruins, he found himself thinking such thoughts as these: *The smell of corpses rotting in the sun is not as bad as I would have expected*. When he stood before a pond where bodies were piled upon bodies, however, he discovered that the old Chinese expression 'burning the nose' was no mere sensory exaggeration of grief and horror. What especially moved him was the corpse of a child of twelve or thirteen. He felt something like envy as he looked at it, recalling such expressions as 'Those whom the gods love die young'. Both his sister and his half-brother had lost their houses to fire. His sister's husband, though, was on a suspended sentence for perjury.

Too bad we didn't all die.

Standing in the charred ruins, he could hardly keep from feeling this way.

General Kim
(1592)

Their faces concealed by deep straw hats, two saffron-robed monks were walking down a country road one summer day in the village of Dong-u in the county of Ryonggang, in Korea's South P'yŏng'an Province. The pair were no ordinary mendicants, however. Indeed, they were none other than Katō Kiyomasa, Lord of Higo, and Konishi Yukinaga, Lord of Settsu,[2] two powerful Japanese generals, who had crossed the sea to assess military conditions in the neighbouring kingdom of Korea.

The two trod the paths among the green paddy fields, observing their surroundings. Suddenly they came upon the sleeping figure of what appeared to be a farm boy, his head pillowed on a round stone. Kiyomasa studied the youth from beneath the low-hanging brim of his hat.

'I don't like the looks of this young knave.'

Without another word, the Demon General kicked the stone away. Instead of falling to earth, however, the young boy's head remained pillowed on the space the stone had occupied, its owner still sound asleep.

'Now I know for certain this is no ordinary boy,' Kiyomasa said. He grasped the hilt of the dagger hidden beneath his robe, thinking to nip this threat to his country in the bud. But Yukinaga, laughing derisively, held his hand in check.

'What can this mere stripling do to us? It is wrong to take life for no purpose.'

The two monks continued on down the path among the rice paddies, but the tiger-whiskered Demon General continued to look back at the boy from time to time . . .

Thirty years later, the men who had been disguised as monks back then, Kiyomasa and Yukinaga, invaded the eight provinces of Korea with a gigantic army. The people of the eight provinces, their houses set afire by the warriors from Wa (the 'Dwarf Kingdom', as they called Japan), fled in all directions, parents losing children, wives snatched from husbands. Hanseong had already fallen. Pyongyang was no longer a royal city. King Seonjo[3] had barely managed to flee across the border to Ŭiju and now was anxiously waiting for the Chinese Ming Empire to send him reinforcements. If the people had merely stood by and let the forces of Wa run roughshod over them, they would have witnessed their eight beautiful provinces being transformed into one vast stretch of scorched earth. Fortunately, however, Heaven had not yet abandoned Korea. Which is to say that it entrusted the task of saving the country to Eung-seo[4] – the boy who had demonstrated his miraculous power on that path among the green paddy fields so long ago.

Kim Eung-seo hastened to the Tonggun Pavilion in Ŭiju, where he was allowed into the presence of His Majesty, King Seonjo, whose worn royal countenance revealed his utter exhaustion.

'Now that I am here,' Kim Eung-seo said, 'His Majesty may set his mind at ease.'

King Seonjo smiled sadly. 'They say that the Wa are stronger than demons. Bring me the head of a Wa general if you can.'

One of those Wa generals, Konishi Yukinaga, kept his longtime favourite *kisaeng*, Kye Wol-hyang,[5] in Pyongyang's Daedong Hall. None of the eight thousand other *kisaeng* was a match for her beauty. But just as she would never forget to put a jewelled pin in her hair each day, not one day passed in her service to the foreign general when Kye Wol-hyang failed to grieve for her beloved country. Even when her eyes sparkled with laughter, a tinge of sadness showed beneath their long, dark lashes.

One winter night, Kye Wol-hyang knelt by Yukinaga, pouring sake for him and his drinking companion, her pale, handsome elder brother. She kept pressing Yukinaga to drink, lavishing her charms on him with special warmth, for in the sake she had secreted a sleeping potion.

Once Yukinaga had drunk himself to sleep, Kye Wol-hyang and her brother tiptoed out of the room. Yukinaga slept on in utter oblivion, his miraculous sword perched where he had left it on the rack outside the surrounding green-and-gold curtains. Nor was this entirely a matter of Yukinaga's carelessness. The small curtained area was known as a 'belled encampment'. If anyone were to attempt to enter the narrow enclosure, the surrounding bells would set up a noisy clanging that would rouse him. Yukinaga did not know, however, that Kye Wol-hyang had stuffed the bells with cotton to keep them from ringing.

Kye Wol-hyang and her brother came back into the room. Tonight she had concealed cooking ashes in the hem of her trailing embroidered robe. And her brother – no, this man with his sleeve pushed high up his bared arm was not in fact her brother but Kim Eung-seo, who, in pursuit of the king's orders, carried a long-handled Chinese green-dragon sword. They crept ever closer to the curtained enclosure when suddenly Yukinaga's wondrous sword leaped from its scabbard as if it had sprouted wings and flew straight at General Kim. Unperturbed, General Kim launched a gob of spit at the sword, which seemed to lose its magic powers when smeared by the saliva and crashed to the floor.

With a huge cry, General Kim swung his green-dragon sword and lopped off the head of the fearsome Wa general. Fangs slashing in rage, the head struggled to reattach itself to the body. When she witnessed this stupefying sight, Kye Wol-hyang reached into her robe and threw handfuls of ash on the haemorrhaging neck stump. The head leaped up again and again, but was unable to settle on to the ash-smeared wound.

Yukinaga's headless body, however, groped for its master's sword on the floor, picked it up and hurled it at General Kim. Taken by surprise, General Kim lifted Kye Wol-hyang under one arm and jumped up to a high roof beam, but as it sailed through the air, Yukinaga's sword managed to slice off the vaulting General Kim's little toe.

Dawn had still not broken as General Kim, bearing Kye Wol-hyang on his back, was running across a deserted plain. At the distant edge of the plain, the last traces of the moon were sinking behind a dark hill. At that moment General Kim recalled that Kye Wol-hyang was pregnant. The child of a Wa general was no different from a poisonous viper. If he did not kill it now, there was no telling what evil it could foment. General Kim reached the same conclusion that Kiyomasa had arrived at thirty years earlier: he would have to kill the child.

Heroes have always been monsters who crushed sentimentalism underfoot. Without a moment's hesitation, General Kim killed Kye Wol-hyang and ripped the child from her belly. In the fading moonlight the child was no more than a shapeless, gory lump, but it shuddered and raised a cry like that of a full-grown human being: 'If only you had waited three months longer, I would have avenged my father's death!'

As the voice reverberated across the dusky open field like the bellowing of a water buffalo, the last traces of the moon disappeared behind the hill.

Such is the story of the death of Konishi Yukinaga as it has been handed down in Korea. We know, of course, that Yukinaga did not lose his life in the Korean campaign. But Korea is not the only country to embellish its history. The history we Japanese teach our children – and our men, who are not much different from children – is full of such legends. When, for example, has a Japanese history textbook ever contained an account of a losing battle like this one from the *Chronicles of Japan*[6] between the Chinese Tang and the Japanese Yamato?

> The Tang general, leading 170 ships, made his camp at the Baekchon River. On the twenty-seventh day, the Yamato captain first arrived and fought with the Tang captain. Yamato could not win and retreated . . . On the twenty-eighth day, the generals of Yamato . . . leading the unorganized soldiers of Yamato's middle army . . . advanced and attacked the Tang army at their fortified encampment. The Tang then came with ships on the left and right and surrounded them, and they fought. After a short time, the Yamato army had lost. Many went into the water and died. Their boats could also not be turned around.

To any nation's people, their history is glorious. The legend of General Kim is by no means the only one worth a laugh.

ŌTA YŌKO

Hiroshima, City of Doom

Translated by Richard H. Minear

People who never saw Hiroshima before the bomb must wonder what the city used to be like.

In the distant past it was called not Hiroshima, 'broad island', but Ashihara, 'reed plain'. It was a broad, reed-covered delta. In the Warring States Era, some four hundred years ago, the powerful Mōri Motonari built a castle here. Driven out by the Tokugawa shogun, Motonari moved west to Hagi in present-day Yamaguchi Prefecture. He was succeeded in Hiroshima by Fukushima Masanori,[1] who expanded the castle and made it his seat.

But the house of Fukushima, too, lasted only one generation. Its successor, the Asano, flourished for thirteen generations before its long rule came to an end in the Meiji Restoration; Lord Asano Nagakoto[2] of the Loyalist faction was the last of the line. In that era of revolution, neighbouring Chōshū rose to a position of great power, but Hiroshima was unable to display similar brilliance. Although Lord Nagakoto was granted the new aristocratic title of marquis and was himself a fine and noble individual, those who served him were said to be wanting in ardour. This fact can be useful in understanding the psychology of Hiroshima people in modern times.

The Hiroshima personality can be as bright as the scenery, but it can also be irresponsible and unsociable. In the local dialect, words are spoken lightly at the tip of the tongue, in stark contrast to the heaviness of the Tōhoku accent of north-eastern Japan. Still, as long as you didn't take things too seriously or become too deeply involved, Hiroshima remained a bright and cheerful town with a good climate and material riches: a good place to live.

In terms of its topography, Hiroshima fanned out between the mountain range to the north and the Inland Sea to the south. Seven branches of the Ōta River flowed gently among the delta's various neighbourhoods, spanned by countless bridges, all of them modern, clean, broad, white and long.

White-sailed fishing boats and small passenger boats would navigate well up into the river branches from Ujina Bay. Upstream, the river offered vivid reflections of the mountains.

The rivers of Hiroshima were beautiful – beautiful in a way that made you feel sleepy. The blue rivers themselves could have been asleep as they spread across the broad, even landscape. You couldn't see that they were flowing or hear the pleasant sound of rapids or spend time gazing at gentle shallows. Even on freezing winter days, when snow blanketed the area, the sight of the rivers could induce that sleepy mood.

I liked Hiroshima's rivers best on days when a heavy snow fell. The snow sealed off the various parts of town from each other and turned the city into a silent and uniformly silver world. Yet the seven rivers still flowed, unhurried, the water so clear that the white sand and greenish pebbles on the bottom gleamed through as always. The fine sand of the dry river banks was white, the pebbles white and brown and dark green. On occasion, there would be one that looked as if it had been dyed a pale red.

The surface of the water was a quiet pale blue, like that of a lake deep in the mountains. In winter it appeared to be covered with a thin, blue sheet of smoky glass or overspread with a delicate layer of waxed silken gauze. Each flake of snow pouring down on to it was gently absorbed and disappeared.

The map shows Hiroshima lying towards the west, but the city had a southern warmth, a languid and carefree air, due no doubt to the rivers and to the way its neighbourhoods spread towards the south like an open fan. With the exception of that southern side facing the water, the city was surrounded by mountains. Low and gently rolling, the mountains ran from one into another like the humps of a sleeping camel. Wherever you looked, the mountains were right there, visible even from the middle of the bustling city centre. I had not always lived in Hiroshima, and the nearness of the mountains surprised me.

Hiroshima Castle, too, seemed very near viewed from all parts of the city, rising up on its crumbling stone foundations in bold relief against the mountains. In its quiet tones of white, black and grey, the tall old castle provided the flat city with one sort of variation.

The young women of Hiroshima do not have the white skin and bold faces of mountain women; their colouring is generally dark. Some say the rivers tan their skin. The tide comes straight into the rivers from nearby Ujina Bay, ebbing and flowing several times a day, so it may make sense to speak of 'river burn'.

Most of the young women are stocky. With their black hair and white teeth, they brim with youth, but they have an odd way of swaying when they walk, they run when they don't need to, they avert their vacant eyes as if making fun of people, and on the bus they let their mouths hang open.

Occasionally you do see a tall girl with a bold and beautiful face, but the sound of her soft chatter – using only the tip of the tongue, as I mentioned earlier – can put people off.

Including such easy-to-be-with young women as these, the population of Hiroshima was said to be 400,000. One also used to hear 300,000 and 500,000. The wartime evacuation to the countryside appears to have reduced the figure greatly. Meanwhile, large numbers of military men had poured into the city from all parts of the nation. On 6 August there were, I think, about 400,000 people here.

Using a conservative estimate of one house for every four people, Hiroshima had about 100,000 houses. Before the 6 August attack, houses in every quarter – even historic buildings – had been torn down ruthlessly to create firebreaks. Yet as I looked at the city from the roof of the four-storey Red Cross Hospital just before 6 August, the houses were crammed together so haphazardly I had to wonder where the firebreaks could be.

This was the city above which, one morning at the height of summer, without warning, an eerie blue flash came from the sky.

I was staying in the house where my mother and younger sister lived in Hakushima Kukenchō. Situated on the north-eastern edge of the city, Hakushima was an old, established residential area. Many military men and office workers lived in this very middle-class neighbourhood, which meant that during the day it was full of housewives keeping to themselves behind closed doors.

Ours was an all-female household: my mother, my sister, her baby daughter and myself. My sister's husband had been called up for the second time at the end of June, and we had no idea where he was.

I had come back from Tokyo at New Year's, intending to wait until March and then take someone with me to dispose of my Tokyo house. Until the weather warmed up a bit, it was impossible to accomplish anything in Tokyo, where day and night you had to hide underground from the constant air raids.

The very first bombing of Tokyo had taken place on the rainy night of 30 October. Hit repeatedly by bombs and firebombs, Nishi-Kanda and the Nihonbashi area burned from eleven at night until after five in the morning. In the next raid, on 2 November, seventy planes appeared suddenly in the sky over Nerima, where I was living, and scattered bombs and firebombs here and there over the Musashi Plain stretching off to the west, where the houses were spaced more sparsely. People said two hundred bombs were dropped, one per one and a half city blocks. All around me, houses I knew well went up in smoke or were demolished.

I often used to joke with a female friend who lived nearby, another writer, about Admiral Tōgō Heihachirō's[3] dictum, 'The enemy will come when you least expect him.' Exhausted by the round-the-clock bombing of Tokyo and the shortage of food, I had come back to Hiroshima.

I never thought of Hiroshima as a safe place to live during the war, but I couldn't come back to my home town empty-handed, either, so I was planning to retrieve the belongings I had left in Tokyo. March came and went, April came, and the danger of travelling to Tokyo only increased. From Tokyo to the west as far as Osaka and Kobe, eastern Japan was being subjected to ferocious bombing without a day's let-up.

In May I suddenly took sick and was admitted to the Red Cross Hospital. I was there until 26 July. While in the hospital, I rented a house in the country, but factors like these delayed my departure.

On the morning of 6 August, I was sound asleep. On the night of the fifth, virtually all night long, repeated waves of bombers had hit Ube in Yamaguchi Prefecture. As I listened to the radio reports, the flames seemed to rise up before my eyes.

To the west of us in Yamaguchi Prefecture, one city after another had burnt: Hikari, Kudamatsu, Ube. That very night, Hiroshima too might be turned into a sea of flames. The radio also reported that Fukuyama, on the other side of Hiroshima from Ube, was undergoing its own fire-bomb attack, although the announcer later retracted the report as erroneous.

The air-raid alarm sounded in Hiroshima, too, and the neighbourhood group sent around a warning to be ready to flee at any moment. So, on the night of the fifth, sleep was out of the question.

At daybreak the red alert was lifted, and shortly after seven o'clock the yellow alert was lifted too. I went back to sleep. I usually slept late any-way, and since I had just been discharged from the hospital, I often slept till close to noon, which is why the others left me alone until that bright blue light flashed.

I was sound asleep inside the mosquito net. Some say the bomb fell at 8.10; some say 8.30. In any case, I dreamed that I was enveloped by a blue flash, like lightning at the bottom of the sea. Immediately afterwards came a terrible sound, loud enough to shake the earth. It was like an indescribably huge roll of thunder, and at the same moment the roof came crashing down with such force it was as if a gigantic boulder had broken from the mountaintop and fallen on the house. When I came to, I was standing in a cloud of plaster dust from the smashed walls around me, utterly dazed, struck dumb. I felt neither pain nor fear but only a strange, almost light-headed sort of calm. The bright early morning sunlight had been replaced by a gloom like that of a rainy-season evening.

The air raid on Kure came to mind, where the firebombs were said to have fallen like large, fluffy snowflakes. Wide-eyed, I searched in vain for firebombs amid the bare skeleton of the dark upper floor, where the window glass, the walls, the sliding paper doors separating my room from the next, and the roof had all been blasted away.

I imagined that forty or fifty firebombs had dropped next to me where I lay. Yet there was no flame, no smoke. And I was alive. How could I still be alive? It was too strange. I looked all around me, half expecting to see my dead body stretched out somewhere.

But in this upstairs room there was nothing to be seen, just a little pile of dirt with dust rising from it, shattered glass fragments and a small mound of roof-tile chunks, but no sign of my mosquito net or bedding or my bedside possessions – my air-raid jacket and hat, my watch, my books. There was no trace of the twelve pieces of luggage we had packed for the countryside and stored in the next room, as if someone had made off with them. The several large glass-doored bookcases holding the 3,000 volumes of the library of my sister's husband: I had no idea where they had flown off to.

Inside the house, there was nothing to be seen, but outside, as far as the eye could see – which was much further than usual – there stretched one ruined house after another. The same was true of far-off parts of town. The headquarters of the *Chūgoku shinbun* newspaper in Hatchōbori and the radio station in Nagarekawa looked to me like silhouettes, deserted and empty.

All that was left of the house across the street was its stone gate. The house itself had been ruthlessly flattened. A young girl stood in the gate, looking dazed and drained of energy. She stared up at me, in full view on the upper floor, and exclaimed, 'Oh!' Then, in a subdued voice, she said, 'You should come down from there right away!'

But there was no way I could get down. The front and back staircases were still intact, but both were blocked partway down by piles of debris taller than I was: boards, tiles, bamboo.

I asked the girl to summon the other members of my family, but even as I pinned my hopes on them, I felt certain that no one would ever come up to get me.

Smeared with blood, her face monstrously transformed, my sister came climbing partway up the stairs. Her white dress had turned bright red as if she had dyed it. Her jaw was held up by a white cloth wrapping, and her face was as purple and swollen as a pumpkin.

'Is Mother alive?' I asked at once.

'Yes, she's fine. She's looking at you from the cemetery out back. The baby's alive, too. Quick, come down.'

'How am I supposed to do that? It looks impossible.'

Hearing that my mother was alive was such a relief, I felt the strength go out of me. My sister tried pushing at the stuff blocking the staircase, but she closed her eyes and seemed about to collapse against it.

'Never mind,' I called to her. 'Go ahead, I'll be right down.'

'You're probably not injured as badly as I am,' she said. 'Get yourself out of there if you can.'

As she said this, I noticed for the first time that the collar of my kimono was drenched in blood. The blood was dripping from my shoulder to my chest. As I left the room, this room I would never enter again, this ten-mat room that had been home to me for several months, I took one last look around. There was not even a single handkerchief to be seen. Where the bed might have been, I finally made out our Singer sewing machine, lying on its side in pieces.

On the stairs, I made an opening in the pile of debris that was just big enough for me to crawl through. The ground floor was not as much of a mess as the upper storey. The chests and trunks and boxes that my sister had packed only two days ago to take with her when she left for the countryside were piled impossibly on top of each other. In the garden behind the house, my large trunk and my mother's wicker trunk lay half buried, as if they had been hurled down with great force. The night before, we had set them out on the edge of the upper-floor concrete balcony, planning to throw them down to the cemetery at the back in case there was a fire-bomb attack.

The cemetery lay beyond the board fence that enclosed the back yard. A wattle gate led from our property to the large cemetery, on the edge of which we had dug an air-raid shelter and made a small vegetable garden. Now that the fence had been blown away, I could see the whole cemetery. My mother was going back and forth between the cemetery and the house.

The cemetery led to a raised stone embankment, and around the stone embankment stretched a board fence. That fence, too, was gone. Normally I could not see the stone steps of the embankment, but now they were clearly visible, and I could also see that my stepbrother's shrine had been flattened, leaving only its torii gate standing.

I joined my mother and sister in the cemetery.

'Could they have been aiming at the shrine?' my mother whispered to me as if sharing a secret. But despite the fact that so many houses had been destroyed, there were no fires, so it couldn't have been firebombs. Ordinary bombs were unthinkable as well. I had experienced both in Tokyo, and this was different. For one thing, no air-raid alarm had sounded, and we had not heard any planes.

How could everything in our vicinity have been so utterly transformed in an instant? I toyed vaguely with the idea that it might not have been an air raid but something quite different, something unconnected with the war, something that occurs at the end of the world when the globe disintegrates, as we read about in children's books.

A hush had fallen over everything. (The newspaper later said there was 'instant pandemonium', but that was the writer's preconceived notion. In fact, an eerie stillness descended as if people, trees and plants had all died at once.)

'We kept calling to you from down here,' my mother said. 'Didn't you hear us? We heard a scream, and then nothing. We called to you over and over, but when you didn't answer, we thought you must be done for.'

I had no recollection of having cried out.

'I was so happy when I looked up from the cemetery and saw you standing there looking around!'

'Really?' I replied. 'We were lucky, weren't we? All of us survived.'

Sitting on a gravestone, her face in her hands, my sister was barely staving off collapse. My mother handed me the sleeping baby. She went back into the house, which looked as if it might fall over at any moment, to get water. She walked through our house, through the house across the street, and kept going, receding into the distance.

The people from next door and other nearby houses gathered in the cemetery. Most were barefoot, and every single one of them was drenched in blood. Heavily wooded, the cemetery was a large and pleasant space. Curiously, not a single gravestone had been knocked over. Everyone was strangely calm. Their faces were still and expressionless, and they talked among themselves as they always did – 'Did you all get out?', 'You were lucky you weren't hurt badly' and so forth. Everyone kept silent about bombs or firebombs, which were not permissible topics of conversation for loyal subjects of the empire.

Soon the large girl from next door started shouting, 'Mother! Mother! Let's get out of here now! The fires are coming. We'll die if we start looking for stuff in the house. It's no time to be greedy. That's what's been happening in all the other towns. Let's get out of here now!'

She was right, we realized. It was too dangerous to just stay there hoping for the best. If we took our time, our mother would be like this girl's, she'd keep going back inside to search for things. We should leave soon, if only to stop Mother from doing that.

Thin smoke started to issue from the eastern end of the flattened neighbourhood, creeping along the ground. I wanted to store the partially buried trunk and wicker suitcase in the air-raid shelter, but I didn't have the strength to move them. And if I gave the baby to my sister to hold, the little thing would be smeared with blood. I gave up on the luggage.

My mother, who had no bloody wounds, brought out some cotton trousers for me and I pulled them on. Then I put on some old straw sandals we used for going out into the fields and shouldered my pack. Each evening we set all our packs in the entryway. Only the things in the entryway were undamaged. Each of us carried a bucket. I used a dark green umbrella for a cane, like an old woman. The shaft of the umbrella was bent in the middle, like the house. My mother had thrown several items out into the cemetery for me – a few pairs of shoes I valued, a summer overcoat and the like. I saw them as I fled, but I did not reach for them, as if I were beyond such desires.

It would be more accurate to say that I had lost interest in anything at all, rather than that I had given up on the luggage. For the same reason, even people who were normally attached to their possessions abandoned things they might well have carried. This numb emptiness lasted a long time, remaining almost unchanged thirty or forty days afterwards.

In the shrine compound, we caught sight of my stepbrother's wife. She was wandering back and forth between the flattened shrine and her demolished house. Her husband had been called up for the third time in June and was now serving with the Hiroshima First Detachment, leaving his young wife alone.

By the time we got out on to the road in front of the shrine, fire was already crawling towards us from across the road on the right. Nearby on the left, where the embankment was visible, we saw five or six people walking along the railway tracks on top. They seemed in no rush. Seeing this, we figured the fire couldn't be all that fierce yet.

We were walking through a neighbourhood that had been demolished, but it still aroused no feeling in us. As if this were an ordinary occurrence on an ordinary day, we felt no surprise, we did not cry, we were in no particular hurry as we followed people on to the nearby embankment. On one side of the embankment was a block of government-owned homes for officials. It, too, was part of the Hakushima district in which we lived, but the houses here were of far higher quality, far more grand and beautiful, than the ones in our Kukenchō neighbourhood. Every single one of these houses had been levelled as if flattened by a powerful force. My old friend Saeki Ayako lived here, but her house was one of those destroyed without a trace. What had become of Saeki Ayako herself? The question flashed through my mind and I looked around, but here, too, it was hushed, without any sign of people.

Each of the beautiful homes on the embankment had stone steps leading down from the back garden to the riverbed. There were vegetable gardens on the parts of the riverbed above the water line, with hedges separating one plot from the next. We walked between demolished houses and down the stone steps to the riverbed. It was about three blocks from our house to the riverbed. Perhaps forty minutes had gone by since we had experienced the blue flash, during which time we milled around, disoriented, in the cemetery before walking there. Only long afterwards did I manage to estimate the time it had taken.

The tide had ebbed. A band of blue water was flowing gently on the other side of the white sand. Here and there on the broad stretch of white grew clumps of weeds, while bundles of straw and such lay where they had come floating up the river at high tide.

We had managed to flee more quickly than those who had been pinned under their houses, and there were still a few flames rising from the ruins, so the river banks did not appear to be very crowded. People wandered about, searching for places to sit, like spectators at an open-air theatre. Individuals made seats for themselves as they wished – beneath the hedges' lush foliage or beside trees that stood between the garden patches, or on the bank very close to the river itself. We chose a spot beneath a fig tree on the edge of Saeki Ayako's garden. It was quite far from the water.

More and more refugees crowded into the area. Soon there were no more good places left, such as beneath a tree, where you could avoid the sun. Everyone who flocked to the riverbed bore wounds, as if only the injured were permitted to come here. Judging from the faces, hands and legs protruding from their clothing, it was impossible to tell what had given them their lacerations. But each person had a half dozen or more cuts, and they were covered in blood.

Some people had streaks of dried blood on their faces and limbs, while others still had fresh blood dripping everywhere on their bodies. All their faces had been hideously transformed. The number of people on the riverbed increased minute by minute, many of them now with severe burns. At first we didn't realize that their injuries were burns. There were no fires, so where and how could they have been burnt so badly? Strange, grotesque, they were more pathetic than frightening. They had all been burnt in the same way, as if the men who bake rice crackers had roasted them all in those iron ovens. Normal burns are part red and part white, but these were ash-coloured, as if the skin had been grilled rather than burnt. Ash-coloured skin hung from their flesh, peeling off in strips like the skins of roast potatoes.

Virtually everyone was naked to the waist. Their trousers were tattered, and some people wore only underpants. Their bodies were puffy and swollen, like those of drowning victims. Their faces were ponderously swollen. Their eyes were swollen shut, the skin around the edges pink and split. They held their puffy, swollen arms out, bent at the elbows, like crabs holding up their two claws. Grey skin hung down from both arms like rags. On their heads some appeared to be wearing bowls; the black hair on top was still there, having been protected by their field caps, but from the ears down the hair had disappeared, leaving a dividing line as sharp as if the hair had been shaved off. Those who looked like this, we knew, were members of a unit of young soldiers, well built, with broad chests and shoulders.

With their strange injuries, these victims were soon lying down on the hot, sunbaked sand of the riverbed. Most of them had been blinded. Even though they were in such frightful shape, nowhere did pandemonium arise. Nor did the term 'ghastly' apply. This had partly to do with the fact that no one said a word. The soldiers, too, were silent. No one called out in pain or complained of the heat or spoke of their fear. As we watched, the broad riverbed filled up with wounded people.

Here and there on the hot white sand, people were sitting or standing or lying stretched out as if dead. The burnt ones vomited continually, a nerve-wracking sound. Saeki Ayako's German shepherd prowled the riverbed. With people arriving all the while, the human mass on the riverbed grew still larger.

Each new arrival would quickly find a little spot and settle in.

In any situation, human beings are always impatient to find a place to call their own, it seemed. Even when the sky is their only roof, they prefer not to be jumbled together but instead want to take possession of a seat that is unambiguously theirs. Soon fires began to break out all over the city. Even then, people still did not dream that the whole city of Hiroshima had been set ablaze all at once. Each thought that only his or her own part of town – for me, it was Hakushima – had been hit by a major disaster.

One after another, pillars of fire rose up in our Kukenchō neighbourhood. Then the grand homes on the embankment, the residences of officials, began to burn. The houses on the opposite bank of the river burst into flames, and beyond a white fence over there, in Nigitsu Park, tall pillars of flame suddenly shot up. From out of the flames came terrible, loud reports of things exploding. Always short-tempered, I was now starting to get really angry and said to my mother and sister, 'Why are they letting these fires start everywhere? Don't they know it's the end when that happens? Didn't we go through all that training to put out fires? This is not from firebombs, so it must be carelessness. If only people had put out their stove and charcoal fires before they fled!'

My mother and sister kept silent as if to say that nothing could be done.

Resignation was an attitude I detested. As if blaming the two of them for not getting angry, I went on: 'These fires are a disgrace for the people of Hiroshima. Now everyone will be making fun of us. We should never have let this happen.'

The sky was still as dark as at dusk. The roar of aeroplane engines had been audible up there for some time now, and word spread through the crowd to watch out for strafing. People rushed to conceal everything white or red. Some stuck their heads into the hedges while those who planned to jump into the river moved closer to the edge of the riverbed. The sparks and flames from the row of houses burning on the embankment were so hot we couldn't stay by our fig tree and went out on to the sandy bank.

What with the heat of both the sun and the flames, we soon found ourselves at the water's edge. The area was full of soldiers with burns, lying face up. Time and again they asked us to soak towels in the water for them. We made the towels sopping wet and spread them as asked on their chests, but soon the towels were bone dry once more.

'What happened to you?' my mother asked a soldier.

'We were on a labour detail at the primary school. I don't know what it was, but we heard this enormous noise, and the next thing we knew we were burnt like this.'

His whole face was swollen and torn as if with some kind of grey leprosy. The contrast with his broad, rugged chest and with the youthfulness of his well-built, handsome body was all too pathetic.

The fires spread fiercely, with irresistible force. Flames even began to spurt from the engine of the freight train stopped in the middle of the railway bridge close by on the right. One after another, the train's black carriages burst into flame, and when the fire reached the end carriage, it showered sparks and belched powerful flames as if it had been crammed full of gunpowder. With each explosion, it spat fire, as if molten iron were gushing out of a tunnel. Below the bridge, we could see the shore of the elegant park, the Asano Izumi Villa, where demonic deep red flames were crawling on the other side of the river. Soon the surface of the river itself started to burn, and we could see groups of people crossing to the other side. Now the river was burning fiercely. The people around us on the bank tried to flee upriver. Overhead, the familiar incessant roar of circling B-29s told us that at any moment strafing, firebombs or conventional bombs might pour down on our dark gathering.

People felt certain that a second wave of attacks would be coming. But surely there was no need to drop any more of those things on us, a part of me was thinking.

While we hid in the grass or squatted beside the river in fear of a strafing, up in the sky they were taking photographs. Out in the open as we were, we were having our pictures taken from overhead, as was the entire devastated city.

Some sort of typhoon seemed to be blowing nearby, and we were getting the less direct gusts followed by large raindrops. I had heard that the burning of Osaka had also caused wind and rain and that people had emerged from their shelters carrying umbrellas even though the sun was shining. So I opened my green umbrella. The rain was a watery black colour, and along with it countless sparks poured out of the sky.

These 'sparks' that I assumed to be small grains of fire were actually bits of rag and scraps of wood glowing bright red as they were swept along by the high wind. The sky became darker still, as if night had come, and the red ball of the sun appeared to be plunging down out of a mass of black clouds.

My sister leaned against me, whispering, 'Look, way up there in the sky, a firebomb! A firebomb!'

'What are you talking about? Can't you see it's the sun?' We tittered nervously, our first bit of laughter in all this. But by then neither she nor I could open our mouths easily.

'We may not be able to eat anything for another day or more,' I said to her. 'Let's drink some river water now and scoop some up for later.' I filled the bucket, thinking that any time now dead bodies might come floating down the river. Still, there was a pale rainbow hanging in the distant sky. The rain had just let up. There was something eerie about that faintly coloured rainbow.

'Water! Water! Let me have a drink!' the burnt soldiers pleaded incessantly.

'Burn victims die if you give them water. Don't do it!'

The faint shadow of death could already be seen between those warning against giving water to the soldiers and the soldiers themselves, who went on pleading for it.

The fires swelled into hills of flame, beat back everything before them, and proceeded to destroy the city block by block. The heat was unbearable. We could see the fires spreading through distant neighbourhoods and hear endless violent explosions from all directions. Not one Japanese plane showed itself in the sky.

We could not conceive of the day's events as being related in any way to the war. We were being crushed by a sheer force – an intense and one-sided force – that had nothing to do with war. Neither did we as fellow Japanese encourage one another or console one another. We behaved submissively and said nothing. No one came to tend the injured, no one came to tell us where or how to pass the night. We were simply on our own.

Saeki Ayako's German shepherd was still wandering among the crowds of wounded on the riverbed, never making a sound. It was widely known in Hiroshima as one of the fiercer dogs of the city, but the way it came and went with its tail hanging down, it was like a human being in misery, having lost all powers of resistance. Saeki Ayako was nowhere to be seen.

Since coming to the riverbed, I had been half consciously looking for her or for the mother-in-law or the sixteen-year-old daughter, Yuriko, who shared her home, but even after dusk, I saw no sign of them.

Night fell, but I was not sure when. The day itself had been so dark there was no clear break between day and night. When night did come, however, both city and riverbed were red from the reflection of the fires. We ate nothing during the day or the night, but we did not feel hungry. Each of us had taken pains to fashion a place for ourselves during the day, but we were unable to stay put for long. The sparks, the rain and the sound of enemy planes chased us away. People said that the tide would rise after dark, so we gathered in the vegetable gardens and by the clumps of trees below the gardens on the way down to the sandy riverbed. We fashioned a place to lie down in front of the hedge facing the riverbed.

Pulling up lots of weeds and spreading them out, we covered them with straw that the river had carried to the sandy bank and on top of that laid the coat that my mother had worn over the baby on her back. The four of us took our places on this makeshift theatre box. A chubby eight months old, the baby had slept all day and did not wake at night. My sister and I removed the kerchiefs that had protected our necks and faces through the day. This was the first good look we had had of each other's angry faces, but smiling was an impossibility.

We couldn't see our own faces, but looking at each other gave us the idea. My sister's face was puffed up like a round loaf of bread, and her eyes, normally large, black and uncannily clear, had become mere slits, their edges dark as blue-black ink. A cross-shaped cut extended from the right edge of her lip into her cheek, twisting her whole mouth into a sideways inverted letter L, a sight so ugly I could not look at it for long. Her hair was caked with blood and the red clay of our house's walls, as if she had been on the streets, begging, for years. Both of us had bound our wounds with odd bits of fabric. I can't recall where we found it, but three or four days earlier, in preparation for autumn and winter, my mother had dyed a piece of crêpe – the broad collar of an old kimono. We had each wrapped the cloth under our chins and knotted it on top of our heads. I had a deep cut from the middle of my left ear, opening like a valley to a spot below the ear.

Our injuries were covered over with strands of hair caked with blood. Our mouths were swollen shut and difficult to open, not so much because of the pain as the feeling that they had been glued in place and locked.

'What were you two doing yesterday morning?' I asked, barely able to move my lips.

'Yesterday? It was *this* morning!' my sister said with a smile, her lips puckered as if she were trying to whistle.

My mother remembered what she was doing at the time and said with regret, 'This morning I got out the salted bamboo shoots I had been saving for a special occasion. I boiled them in soy sauce with carrots and potatoes I had grown out back. It was delicious! I had just eaten a mouthful with rice when there was that blue flash.'

'What did you think it was?' I asked. 'A bomb? A firebomb?'

'That huge bang happened before I even had time to think what it was, and the cupboard fell over. I threw myself down when the flash hit, and the cupboard fell on top of me, but fortunately the closet behind me kept the cupboard from falling all the way. I was bent over in a kind of cave like being curled up under a desk or something, so nothing happened to me. Then I heard you give a shriek.'

My sister had been sitting across from my mother in the family room. She, too, had just eaten a mouthful of breakfast. When she saw the flash, she rushed to the baby in the next room. Because there were mosquitoes about even in the morning, she had put the baby to sleep under a mosquito net. She threw herself down on top of the baby, who was sound asleep but, thinking that a lot of firebombs must have fallen on the family room, she turned to look in that direction. At that moment there was a sudden gust of wind, and she immediately started bleeding.

'The blue flash lasted only an instant, but I must have flown to the baby in the first instant of that instant. Still, I have no memory of ducking under the mosquito net.'

My mother spoke again: 'That breakfast this morning – what a waste!'

I said, 'So, what do you think happened this morning? I have no idea what that was. My umbrella shaft had no bend in it before.'

My sister seemed to think she had to say something. 'Maybe it was *iperitto*.'

'*Iperitto*? What's that?'

'Mustard gas. Poison gas.'

'That's it, for sure. But poison gas couldn't have knocked the houses down.'

'They combined it – with conventional bombs.'

Having no clear idea what had happened, we talked nonsense. The fires continued to burn fiercely in the distance, soaring up into the sky. In the space of one night, all of Hakushima had burnt itself out: Kukenchō, nearby Higashimachi, Nakamachi, Kitamachi, the houses on the embankment, everything there had dimmed to an ashen grey. Two or three houses on the opposite river bank continued to burn out of control. Their wild flames writhed like giant snakes. The Ushita area had been on fire during the day, and when night came, the flames moved from peak to peak along the low, wavy range of hills, looking like lights in a far-off town. Chunks of flame flew continually across the space between one peak and the next like shooting stars, and then the second peak would start a new fire.

After night fell, we started hearing dull groans from the distance. The low, monotonous groans echoed all around us.

At around that time, someone brought word that food was going to be distributed. We hadn't given the slightest thought to supper, so we responded with happy cries.

The energetic voice of someone passing among us, probably a soldier, called to those of us lined up along the hedges: 'All those who can walk, please go to the East Parade Ground to pick up food.' Everyone began to chatter, and for the first time you could tell that the silhouettes moving along the riverbed were in fact flesh-and-blood human beings. Of our little group, both my sister and I ached all over and were unable to stand or walk. My mother went, helped by the young woman next to her. It was a mile or more to the East Parade Ground. She came back with four white, triangular rice balls that were still warm, wrapped up in a square of cloth. She also received four bags of hardtack.

'A feast!'

We gladly took hold of the rice balls and found them heavy to the touch. But neither my sister nor I could open our mouths wide enough to eat. Like a dentist, I forced my paralysed mouth open with the thumb and index finger of my left hand while, with my right hand, I pressed the rice through my lips a few grains at a time.

'Is Tokiwa Bridge still there?'

'Both railings were burnt away, but the road itself is still there, all bulged out. Things are really pretty bad everywhere. There's nothing left unburnt.'

Listening to the conversations of people sitting lined up in front of the hedge facing the river, it became clear to us that today's conflagration had consumed the entire city of Hiroshima, leaving no part of town untouched. This was no minor fire caused by some individuals' carelessness; enemy planes had scattered sparks over the whole city.

'They scattered sparks? No wonder the whole place burned! With bombs, it would have taken a hundred or two, even five hundred or a thousand. They didn't just "drop" bombs – they sprayed the place.'

In the local dialect, 'spraying' meant they had rained bombs down in clusters, like a waterfall. There was not a single crater anywhere, though. People still didn't realize it meant there had been no bombs. They had so little idea what had happened, they didn't have a lot to say.

We stretched out on the ground. Owing to the surrounding forest fires and the conflagration on the other shore of the river, it was bright and warm. We heard groans from far and near like mournful musical instruments, and these were joined by the cries of insects. It was all so very sad.

My entire body numb with the sadness and pain, my tangled thoughts gave way to a somewhat clear idea: this numb feeling, this intensely odd numb feeling from an external shock, was my body's direct physical response to the moment when the morning's strange blue flash and powerful noise became one with the total destruction of the city. It crossed my mind that some kind of colourless, odourless intangible substance might have burnt up the air in a process involving physics or physical chemistry, not something that would stink or be visible or have a smell such as a poison gas. Out of a desire to pin something down, I tried to find it based on that physical sense of mine.

I fell easily, naturally, into a primitive mode of thought. Like a child, I recalled the nitrogen, oxygen and carbon dioxide gases in the air. Perhaps the enemy planes had sent electrons, via very high-frequency radio waves, into these things invisible to the human eye. Without giving off any sound or smell or exhibiting any colour, these airborne radio waves must have turned into huge, white flames. Unless I drew a mental picture of a new mystery world like that, I couldn't conceive of how there could have been so many victims with such strange burns. I thought it fairly remarkable that I was able to formulate such thoughts – or perhaps I should say such instinctive feelings – before descending into an unbearably painful sense of defeat.

'The war's over,' I whispered to my sister on the ground beside me.

'What are you saying?' she demanded.

'There's nothing more we can do,' I muttered. 'Japan's got two months at the most.'

The fires in the mountains continued to burn spectacularly, spreading from peak to peak. The night deepened, but no one came to tend to the injured. We heard the cries of the insects among the low, heavy human groans that welled up all around us.

SEIRAI YŪICHI

Insects

Translated by Paul Warham

The bright green grasshopper comes crawling up my bloodstained calf, its square jaws munching at the skin that flaps there like a leaf. It turns its long narrow face towards me and examines me with its expressionless compound eyes. 'Are you still alive?' it asks. I wake up screaming.

From the silence around me, I realize it must still be the middle of the night. I want to throw myself into somebody's arms. I shut my eyes but it's no use – I'm awake. A surge of images from the past comes back to life, vivid and unstoppable.

What a miserable business it is, getting old!

'Are you still alive?'

Sixty years have passed since I was asked that question. At the time, I had no idea who was talking. I couldn't even tell if it was a man or a woman. I can hear the voice even now – 'Are you still alive?' – calling to me like a grasshopper, a fly or one of the creatures that crawl upon the earth. There's no sense of desperation or panic in the question. It isn't saying, 'Are you hurt? Don't die!' The tone is more like someone asking, 'Are you still awake?' There's something dopey and amiable about it.

I had just paused to catch my breath after crawling out of the rubble on my hands and knees when I saw the grasshopper flitting, apparently unscathed, among the ruins. It must have been carried here by the blast of the explosion. This must be the thing that was speaking to me, I thought: a crackbrained idea that would never have occurred to me normally. I think I may even have replied, 'Yes, thanks, I'm still alive.'

After that, I lost consciousness again. I have no idea how much time passed. My next memory is of being picked up in someone's arms and then moving as if swept downstream, to the shelter of a brick wall that had escaped destruction.

I don't recall much else about that day. One thing I do remember is ants – swarms of black ants scurrying back and forth between pools of blood scattered among the shards of brick and glass. The strange thought occurred to me that this great army of ants had carried or dragged me along.

I saw a body that had split open at the abdomen. Who was it? I was too scared to look at the face. Gooey white intestines spilled out like noodles. A knot of what might have been a tapeworm squirmed around the open wound.

I was fifteen years old and training to be a nurse. Trembling, I saw with my own eyes the reality that insects and creepy-crawlies are everywhere around us: in the trees and bushes, under the eaves of houses, in the earth beneath our feet – and even inside our bodies.

All around me were the faces of people crushed in the rubble. But my first emotion wasn't exactly sadness. The human world was over, I thought, and the world of the insects was about to take its place.

It was the arrival of another postcard from Reiko that had made me dream of the green insect again. I reached up and felt for the light switch by the pillow. The sleeve of my nightgown fell to my shoulder, and a whiff of body odour rose from my armpit. I remembered the faint smell of mildew my grandmother used to give off long ago.

If I rub at the back of my hand, I can feel a hard strand of narrow sinewy bone. The skeleton is beginning to emerge from beneath my skin, and the blotches and blemishes are spreading. I am an old woman now, and I don't have much time left. But death, I feel, is still some distance away. My periods came to an end long ago, but a warm-blooded woman still lurks inside this decrepit body, threatening to come crawling to the surface.

Rolling on to my stomach, I switched on the light and picked up Reiko's postcard from the tatami where I had left it the night before.

Dear Michiko,

I hope this finds you well. Last month I spent another enjoyable week at the hot spring in Kannawa. It's been fifteen years since I moved here, and I know a lot of the people at the resort by now. We sit and soak for hours, chatting away and quite forgetting the time.

There's nothing like a long refreshing soak on a hot day – and that first sip of beer after a long bath! It's heaven when the evening sun glints on the surface of the water.

Why don't you come out and visit? We could have a good soak together and talk about the past. It's fifteen years now since he died, and there aren't many friends left with whom I can share memories of the good old times. Maybe you could tell me about a side of him I never knew.

Best wishes,

Reiko

What a peaceful old age she's having! How can she be so relaxed and cheerful?

Anger welled up inside me. I poured some water from the jug and gulped it down, still lying on my stomach. The timer had switched off the air conditioner, and the house felt hot and humid. The blood had rushed to my head. I threw the thin blanket off the futon and sat up in bed. 'Leave me alone!' I shouted, brushing away the grey hair clinging to my cheeks.

Things are not over between him and me. There *is* such a thing as never-ending love. Even fifteen years after his death, the longing for him still burns inside me. Most of the time it's just a small flickering light, like the dying embers in the ruins of a burnt-out city. But sometimes, late at night, it still bursts into flame and scorches my heart.

Tell me, Holy Mother: why was I the only one who didn't die that day, buried under the rubble? Of the five trainee nurses in the hospital, why was I the only one to survive? Why did my parents and my four brothers and sisters have to die? Did no one ask them the same question I was asked: 'Are you still alive?' If only a grasshopper or an ant or a tapeworm had been on hand to speak to them, maybe they, too, would have made it out alive.

I heard the low whine of a mosquito by my ear, drawn by the sweat that coated my skin. I'll brush them off if they're buzzing near my cheek, but I can't bring myself to swat them or kill them with coils.

Every living thing on this earth – however insignificant – has had to struggle to survive. I find it moving to think of all they've endured to get this far. Sometimes I even feel like saying a little prayer for them, though it's unlikely Our Lady or Jesus would care much about a lowly mosquito.

I was wide awake now, with a dull headache somewhere deep inside my skull. I turned on the air conditioning and sat with my hands in my lap and my eyes closed, arching my back like a cat and letting the cool air blow into my face. It was no good – sleep was out of the question. I got up and went to sit in front of my little altar to the Virgin Mary.

No light came in through the curtains. Morning was still some time off. I struck a match and lit the two large candles on the altar.

I love the soft light of the candles, warmer than a light bulb but not as bright as sunlight. It's a mellow kind of light – like a small beacon between this world and the next. In candlelight, sharp edges are soothed, softened. Mary's round cheeks and the folds in the veil of blue fabric that covered her hair stood out in the subtle light.

Our Father, who art in Heaven . . . calm this anger in my heart! Take away the jealous thoughts that make me hate Reiko.

I put my hands together and prayed. I felt the darkness wash over me – the same darkness in which our ancestors spent their lives for so many generations. It brought me a little peace of mind.

Tell me, Holy Mother: did they struggle like this against hatred and anger when they prayed to you in secret? Did they, too, suffer from the sin of envy?

A chain of prayers joins me to those people. We are all linked together like the beads on a rosary. It won't be long now before I take my place on the chain.

I moved my face closer and saw what looked like some lint under Mary's lower eyelid. My eyesight has never really recovered from the operation I had for cataracts. Without my glasses, everything is blurred. It's like being underwater. Most of the time, it doesn't bother me; I have seen enough of this world already. I rarely watch TV and don't read the papers either. Often I don't even use my glasses when I'm at home. But I needed them now.

I took a pair out of the drawer of the simple desk I use as an altar. When I looked again with them on, I could see a mosquito perched quite still under one of Mary's eyes. Despite the slippery surface of the porcelain, it seemed to have no trouble staying put. It was probably the same mosquito

I'd heard buzzing in the dark a few minutes earlier. I watched it stretching out its hindmost legs – first the left, then the right – as if trying to shake the numbness out of them. Its belly was red and swollen.

Suddenly, it fell from there on to the white cloth that covered the altar. Maybe it had sucked out too much blood and couldn't support its own weight. Or it had been stunned by the thin smoke from the candles. The mosquito lay there upside down for a moment, then kicked its legs and flew off into the darkness.

I offered a prayer of thanks to Our Lady and as I crossed myself I felt a slight itch in my right arm. I looked down to find a red bump there and impressed the sign of the cross on it with a fingernail.

If I had remained buried under the debris like Noshita and Kino and all the others, I would have been spared things like this sixty years later: being roused in the middle of the night and battling mosquitoes. But then I would never have met him either. I would never have experienced that moment of sinfulness when I blazed up, briefly but brilliantly, as a woman. Am I glad I survived, or would it have been better to have perished along with everyone else? I honestly can't say.

I remember crawling from under the rubble and losing consciousness. When I came to, I was in a clearing of bamboo that, by some accident of geography, had escaped the heat rays and the blast of the atomic bomb. Green bamboo sighed in the breeze, and a spider with vivid yellow-and-black stripes waited patiently in an unbroken web. I must have spent two days and nights there.

The wounded lay in the clearing. Most of them died during the first night. The stench of death was heavy in the air. I lay half covered by withered bamboo leaves, staring into the blurry bright light.

I felt no sadness. I was exhausted. My body weighed a ton. Everything seemed to fall apart in the summer sunlight. The line between life and death was gone. Apart from lethargy, I felt nothing at all.

On the morning of the second day, I watched a fly crawl across the cheek of the middle-aged woman, probably an office worker, lying next to me. It moved up her cheekbone to her temple, stopping now and then to rub its front legs as though performing a ritual.

A jagged tear ran down the leg of her dark blue work trousers, but the white calf it revealed was miraculously unscathed. The woman lay still. Probably dead, I assumed. After a while, the fly got on to her eyelid. Suddenly, she reached up and brushed it away, opening the eye. There was still a moist light inside.

Old people would probably remember the flypapers that used to hang overhead in fish shops. Sometimes I would see them so thick with flies they looked like solid black sticks. We may owe our lives to insects, yet we hardly ever stop to consider their little lives at all. I can't help feeling we're unforgivable in some ways.

One time, I saw a fly crawling across the pale bony chest of Jesus in the cathedral. Maybe a fly was there with Him at Golgotha and asked Him: 'Are you still alive?' Is it too much to imagine that, with his head feebly hanging down, Our Lord opened His blackened eyelids for a moment and glimpsed the people gathered at His feet?

Ever since I was a little girl, I've been fascinated by the idea of Noah's Ark. There can't have been just horses and oxen, cats and dogs on board. All kinds of other stowaways must have fled on to the Ark, undetected by God: fleas and lice sheltering in the coats of the horses and cattle, beautiful green grasshoppers lurking in the bales of hay.

Flies must have laid their eggs in the dung of the cattle, and the seeds of flowers and grasses would have been carried in the mud that caked the animals' hooves. The Ark must have been full of life – and dirt, and smells! And all these creatures had a part to play in bringing the world back to life after the waters receded. I read somewhere that it takes hundreds of millions of invisible living things to support the life of one human being.

Only once have I mentioned my belief in the sacredness of all life – including even the insects – to someone else. To him. Sasaki-san was a devout Christian, from a family of secret Christians who had fled from Sotome to the Gotō Islands during the years when the faith was outlawed.

'You're a sweet girl, Hirose-san,' he said when I told him. 'But the thing you're suggesting . . . I don't know: I'm not sure it could be considered Christianity any more, actually.'

It was an ambiguous response. He hadn't really agreed or disagreed. After the war, he went back to the Gotō Islands for a while but reappeared in Nagasaki soon after. He worked at a printing company while he finished his teacher training. I was in my early twenties then – just one year younger than he was.

The neat arrangement of his features was enough to make you wonder if he had the blood of foreign missionaries in his veins. It may have been this neatness that made it so difficult to bring his face to mind when I tried to remember him later on. In those early days, he struck me as almost too perfect – a bit lacking in individuality.

I had heard bits and pieces about Sasaki's experience during the war. I knew that he had been with the Special Attack Forces in Chiran and had received his orders for a final kamikaze mission. But engine trouble grounded his plane, and the war ended with him still waiting for an opportunity to attack.

I asked him once if he had really been ready to be worshipped with all the other war dead at Yasukuni Shrine, but he didn't reply. After that, we never spoke again about what had happened.

Maybe it was these experiences that had trimmed the flab from his faith and concentrated his mind on God. I was young and naive and respected him for what he'd gone through. Love was already beginning to stir in my heart. When I first met him, of course, Reiko wasn't yet on the scene.

Sasaki used to carry batches of printed paper from the warehouse to the truck outside. I limped behind him with a stub of pencil, totting up the number of hymn books and bibles and making sure they tallied with what I had on the form in front of me. Again and again we did this, back and forth between the warehouse and the truck. The low-grade pulp we used was beginning to improve in quality around that time. The difference wasn't that obvious if you had only ten or a hundred volumes. But when you were dealing with thousands at once, the batches were quite heavy, and shifting them was serious work. I remember how he used to gulp water from the tap next to the warehouse during his breaks, dripping with sweat.

Please don't be angry with me, Holy Mother. I'm merely telling you what happened.

I was already starting to feel the ache of physical desire. Never have I been so struck by the sheer attractiveness of a man as I was then. I remember the way the water splashed from his bared gums, the shining drops that ran down his Adam's apple and chin. I longed to throw my arms around him, to embrace the sweat-soaked muscles on his neck as he towelled himself dry around the open collar of his shirt. The bomb had made me ugly, and I had spent most of my later teenage years indoors – but even an unlovely specimen like me wasn't immune to the flood of emotions that comes sweeping over you.

I couldn't help the way my voice rose in pitch whenever I spoke to him. Ozaki was always giving us dirty looks.

Ozaki was the same age as Sasaki, but his face had been shattered by metal fragments in the atomic blast. Far from having a chiselled jawline for water to drip from, in Ozaki's case the neck seemed to start immediately below his lips.

Perhaps because he was ashamed of his appearance, Ozaki was a man of very few words, and I can hardly remember the sound of his voice. But I haven't forgotten the things he did say. Like me, he lost his parents and all five siblings in the blast. Once in a while, he would talk to me tearfully about what had happened.

'The bones came jumbled together from the kitchen . . . there was no way of telling my parents from my brothers and sisters. I put them all in the same urn. Sometimes, late at night, I hold them in my hands and cry.'

Ozaki glanced at my leg, as if appealing to me for sympathy. After all, hadn't we both been scarred by the same thing? I knew exactly what he was trying to say. There were two types of people now: those whose lives had been affected by the bomb and those who hadn't suffered.

There was no denying the mark on my cheek – you know all about it, Holy Mother. I used to try to hide it under heavy make-up, but even then it would show up blue in the glare of a fluorescent light. And I still drag my left leg behind me when I walk. So I, too, have every reason to feel ashamed of my body and the traces it carries of that day.

And yet here I was, infatuated with beautiful, healthy Sasaki. Was that wrong of me, Holy Mother? I don't think any woman could have resisted him as he was then – with his faith, his strength and his idealism.

Ozaki got on my nerves, and I tried to brush him off. He had three operations to fix his jaw while he was still in his twenties. Eventually, the miseries of radiation sickness on top of everything else were more than he could bear, and he hanged himself in the forests on Mount Konpira.

Tell me, Mother Mary, how can such terrible things happen? Wasn't it possible to save him? Or was he released and called home to God?

Sometimes I can feel him staring at me even now – his eyes crawling across my breasts, down my back and across my cheeks. My scar tingles as I imagine his eyes on my skin.

I sensed his desire. His glaring eyes sent a chill through me. They were like an insect's eyes. Even beetles and cicadas and snails become aroused when summer arrives and males and females reach out to satisfy themselves. Even the smallest insects feel the insistent hum of desire thrumming inside them.

Why didn't I just give him my body to do with as he wished? The thought makes me feel tearful now. If he and I had lived our lives together, leaning on each other for support and nursing one another's spiritual and physical scars . . . Who knows, I might have enjoyed a peaceful old age and never had sleepless nights like this, kept awake by anger and jealousy.

How soft and soothing candlelight can be for the soul, Mother Mary.

The night deepens, and the insects fall silent until there's no sound at all. A small stabbing pain runs down my left leg. Ever since that day, I have had to keep the leg stretched out in front of me when I sit on the floor. The pain comes most often in winter, but even on summer mornings when there's a chill in the air, it hurts as if a sliver of ice has fallen on my leg. I imagine the shards of glass still inside me, grating against the nerves.

I hitch up the bottom of my pyjamas and look at the discoloured thing that has been part of my life since I was fifteen. The leg can't support my weight, and the muscles atrophied long ago, leaving a thin, wizened husk like a piece of wood. All that remains of the surface wound is a reddish-brown discoloration on the skin.

I can still remember the shock I felt when I saw the leg for the first time in that clearing sixty years ago. My left leg was completely covered in sharp fragments of glass, as if they had been sucked in by a magnet. A distant relative from Mitsuyama who had come looking for her daughter stumbled on me lying there.

We barely knew each other, but she took me home, stripped off my torn trousers and disinfected my cuts with iodine, using a pair of chopsticks to pick out the glass slivers from my legs.

Towards evening that day, an eight-year-old girl was carried to the house on a wooden screen door. It was my relative's granddaughter. She was wrapped up like a mummy, with just a few sprigs of hair sprouting from her head, and two holes cut into the cloth for her eyes and another for her mouth. They set her down next to me. From time to time, she stirred and let out a low moan that disturbed my sleep.

I awoke to the sharp sound of a man's voice during the night.

'It's no good. Her breathing's getting weaker.'

'Maybe we should have her baptized,' I heard my relative say.

'There's no priest,' another man's voice replied.

'In an emergency, any person of faith can do it. That's how they used to do it in the old days. Fetch some fresh water. I'll baptize her.'

There was the sound of a whispered prayer and a faint splashing of water as the man wet his fingers to make the sign of the cross on the girl's forehead. A feeling of calm came over me. It was as though our ancestors were in the room beside us.

'I baptize you in the name of the Father, and of the Son, and of the Holy Ghost.'

After a while, I felt that something had come to an end, and I heard my relative's tearful voice. 'It's all right, Michiyo. You can go to Heaven now.' No sound came from the girl. To this day, I can't say for sure whether any of this really happened. Was it just another of my feverish dreams?

It was around noon the next day when my grandfather came to collect me, pulling a two-wheeled handcart behind him.

'You're alive!'

He knelt by my side and wept, all but rocking back and forth as his cracked voice honked like a sea lion. The body of the young girl still lay beside me. My grandfather made the sign of the cross and hung his head.

'Come on, let's take you home. Your grandmother's waiting. If you at least don't get better, I don't know what we'll do.'

My grandparents lived in an old house that backed on to the mountains upriver, close to the source of the Urakami, an area where the faith had been kept alive for generations.

'What about Mummy and Daddy?'

There was no reply.

'And Toki? And Shin'ichirō? And Fuji-chan and Sanae-chan?'

Again, nothing.

'We'll look after you and make you better. No point taking you to the hospital. There's no medicine anyway. Let's go home,' he said, lifting my light body easily in his arms.

The skin on my left leg was peeling. I moaned in pain. I didn't ask again about the rest of the family. His silence told me all I needed to know.

Not a trace was left of the house in Matsuyama. My parents and my four brothers and sisters must all have been home at the time, but we never even found their bones. We ended up just putting white ash in their graves.

My grandfather loaded me on to the cart and wrapped me in a blanket, then bowed repeatedly in thanks to our relative.

'You get better, now, you hear?' she said to me. 'You have to live for Michiyo too now.' She was crying. I lay in the cart and watched blankly as her silhouette got smaller and smaller and faded into the distance. I remember watching the wheels of the cart as they turned. The cart's framework was red with rust and smelled of iron. Slowly and carefully, my grandfather made his way down the long winding slope from Mitsuyama. Occasionally he would stop and look back to check on me.

'You all right back there, Mitsuko?'

All along the way, we passed people heading into the mountains. They were like soot-black shadows. Almost no one was dressed in normal clothes.

At the top of a small hill, my grandfather stopped to rest in the shade of a tree.

'Why did this have to happen?' he muttered.

He wheeled the cart around so that I could see the scorched earth where Urakami used to be.

'Look at that,' he said, wiping his forehead with a cloth he wore at his waist. 'Even the church is gone.'

For the first time, tears welled up in my eyes. There was nothing left. Everything was gone. Our house, the iron foundry, the tofu shop . . .

Of the church that had stood on the hill, only the foundations and a few fragments of the walls remained. It looked like a mouth ravaged by tooth decay. The houses in Matsuyama had been completely destroyed. Trails of smoke rose from the blasted landscape. The rubble stretched on without end.

The next instant, a green grasshopper flitted up from a clump of grass and settled on my bloodstained big toe. Once I got over my surprise, I realized somehow that I wasn't going to die. The insect was my guardian angel.

We used to see them in the fields all the time back then. They made a distinctive sound. As summer drew to a close, you would hear them singing in the grass: su-wee chon, su-wee chon, su-wee chon. It could get quite loud at times. My sister always used to make the same joke whenever she heard it. 'The grasshopper's in love,' she would say. 'Why's that?' I would ask – even though I already knew the answer. 'Because he's always singing about his sweet-one, sweet-one, sweet-one!' she said with a laugh.

The grasshopper moved its long legs silently and made its way slowly up my damaged leg. The insect looked quite unharmed. It seemed so pure and clean. Never have I felt the beauty of insects as powerfully as at that moment.

Then it spread its thin brown inner wings and flew off towards the wasteland.

'Why did this have to happen?' my grandfather kept saying. Bloodied bodies lay in the shade of the tree. 'Water. Please, give me some water,' they cried out to no one in particular. Their voices were like sighs. Occasionally one of them would raise a thin black arm into the air. After a while I couldn't bear to look and kept my eyes shut tight.

My grandfather spat into his palms and roused himself with a grunt. We started downhill again. Eventually, back on level ground, we reached the ruins of the cathedral, where a number of people had been seated in prayer. Their bodies were charred black; it was impossible to tell the men from the women. The skin had started to fester and crawled with flies. I was struck by the thought that the flies stood in the way of their slipping away, that they were holding them back, asking, 'Are you still alive?' In my heart I told them to leave the people alone. 'Let them be. Let them sleep.'

A few of the wooden houses behind the cathedral had survived the blaze. My grandfather trundled the cart down the deserted alleys through the heat. We met no one.

My grandparents' house was out of town, close to the head of the Urakami River. The site has been built over since then and where the old house used to stand is part of a big housing complex today. But even now, if I close my eyes and listen to the sound of the river, all the old memories soon come flooding back. My younger brothers and sisters had spent most of that summer out there with our grandparents, away from the city with its hunger and air raids. But on 8 August, they travelled home to be with our father, who was on furlough from his posting in Moji. At our first family meal in months, we had white rice – a rare treat in those days – along with some dried Inland Sea fish he'd brought back with him.

Our father had a beaky nose and big eyes. When he glared at us with those big eyes, it scared us stiff. But that night we all were delighted to be together again, and it was a relaxed, happy summer evening.

The river ran in front of the house. Through the gaps in the trees, you could make out the red brick walls of a small prison. Today, it's part of the Peace Park – the small hill with the big peace statue. On the adjacent hill was Urakami Cathedral. We always used to hear the bells.

That evening, we were able to forget the misery of the war for a moment and enjoy the cool breeze on our sweaty skin. It was the last meal we ever ate together.

'What happened to the house?' I couldn't help asking, even though I could see with my own eyes that most of the area around the church was nothing but scorched earth.

'Everything burned down,' my grandfather said in a whisper. Stooping forward, he somehow managed to pull the cart behind him one step at a time. I still feel a pang when I remember my cruel question. It must have taken all his reserves of strength not to break down and sob as he tugged me through the ruins.

Once we escaped the blackened remains of the city and moved upstream, the greenery around us grew richer, and I heard the sound of running water. The unspoiled scenery had a calming effect on me, and I fell into a deep sleep. Even now, I sometimes feel as if I'm still slumbering in the cart, adrift in dreams as my grandfather pulls me along behind him.

'Easy does it . . .' Supporting my bad leg with my hands, I shuffled over to the low desk by the window and settled on to the floor cushion in front of it. I switched on the fluorescent light and read through the postcard again. 'Tell me about a side of him I never knew . . .' All right, I thought. If that's what you really want, I'll tell you. You know what I mean, don't you, Holy Mother? We saw a side of him that Reiko knows nothing about . . . But forgive me, Mother Mary! Help me control this anger that rolls in like a tide and blurs the world in front of my eyes.

Reiko came to work in the printing firm about two years after I joined. Everyone still bore the scars of the war in those days. Even Sasaki wasn't immune. He was studying to become a teacher, and a look of exhaustion would sometimes cloud his symmetrical features – a reminder that the shadow of the war still hung over us. It was probably my first glimpse of the emptiness he carried inside.

But Reiko was seven years younger and had grown up in the country-side. She had hardly known real hunger. This, along with the fact that none of her family had even been wounded in the war, probably explained why she was so untouched by the deprivation and depression that weighed so heavily on the rest of us. Maybe it was simply that she had been a little girl during the war years and didn't remember much about them. Or she just had a naturally cheerful, confident personality. Perhaps it was a combination of these things. She was one of those happy-go-lucky young women who started to crop up everywhere in the years that followed.

I remember clearly the moment when Sasaki first laid eyes on her. She bowed formally and flashed her charming smile. 'Pleased to meet you,' she said in a sweet, slightly nasal voice. Something responded in his eyes, and I felt a rush of anxiety and jealousy.

As I feared, they soon grew close. In no time at all, she had his heart right where she wanted it, pliable as putty in those soft hands of hers. All I could do was look on in silence.

One day, I was watching them eating lunch together under a pink-flowering chestnut tree in the courtyard of the company building, when Ozaki suddenly turned to me as if he had finally figured something out. I suppose the resentment on my face was plain to see.

'Jealous?' he said.

Hopelessly, I tried to laugh it off. 'Not at all. Two good-looking people like that . . . they make a lovely couple.'

'Out of your league,' he said.

I was so upset that I let fly at him. I can still remember the way he bit down on his malformed lip. He seemed to wilt. How could I have said such awful things? But I wasn't myself in those days, Holy Mother.

Not long after that, Sasaki had an offer from his old middle school, and left to return to the Gotō Islands. Reiko followed two months later. They were engaged to be married.

I was tormented by jealousy, day and night. Why had he chosen her over me? Now I realize that it was only natural, but at the time it felt like the cruellest, most unfair thing in the world. How I used to bother you, Holy Mother – nagging away with the same questions every night in my prayers.

Show me a side of him I never knew. What could I possibly say in my reply? How could she be so naive? A side of him she never knew! Would she be able to face the truth?

Unlike Reiko, I can't dash off a letter just like that, and I hated the idea that anyone else might read what I was about to write – so a postcard was out of the question. I went so far as to spread open a sheet of writing paper, but the pen stopped in my hand as soon as I put down the standard greeting. My mind churned with things I wanted to say but couldn't find the words to express. More than half a century had passed, yet in my heart I was still a jealous young woman.

Reiko sends me one of her chatty postcards about once a month, keeping me abreast of her life, apparently oblivious to my real feelings. Probably she's just not very sensitive to these things. At times, though, it occurs to me that she might be playing a tricky kind of game. Maybe forcing me to write an inoffensive reply every month is her way of rubbing my nose in it.

My feelings didn't change even after they were married. I have never known anyone else in my life who seemed as decent and attractive as he was then. I simply refused to believe that he could live happily with anyone but me. Even when they'd been married for ten years and had three children, my love didn't fade.

I grew older. He did too, of course – but age never seemed to spoil him. If anything, he only grew even better looking and more impressive, like a tree reaching maturity. His back was as straight as ever, while his hair acquired a touch of silver and the lines on his face were more sharply defined. But his eyes remained soft and clear – until the day he was suddenly brought down, like an old tree felled by lightning. A cluster of wire-thin blood vessels in his brain abruptly burst, and he died of a haemorrhage. The fifteen years since then have passed in the blink of an eye. He still lives on inside me, Holy Mother.

How ashamed I would feel if he could see me now that I have passed him in years. My fingernails have yellowed, and there are dark blotches on my skin. White hairs sprout from my nose and arms. My body is practically ash already. But when I close my eyes and remember him, my skin seems to regain the bloom and softness it once had. My hair becomes long and black, and I feel the dying embers inside me begin to spark and flare.

My hatred and jealousy haven't faded, either. I can't help it. I still resent Reiko for taking him away from me. The way she basks in her memories makes me want to scream. What a mean-spirited person I am. Forgive me, Holy Mother. But I can't stand the way she has consigned everything to the past. In my heart, he's still alive.

If they had vanished completely from my life after they moved to the Gotō Islands, things might have been different. But no, they refused to disappear. They always got in touch when they returned to Nagasaki and asked me to dinner. After the children were born, I was invited to join them for family meals.

The three children came to accept me as part of the extended family. They called me their 'Nagasaki auntie', and sometimes when I joined in the fun, I found a kind of consolation in it, as though these moments were an extension of the times I'd spent with my own family before I lost everything when the bomb fell.

Reiko and I were almost like sisters. I think she must have been at least dimly aware of my feelings for her husband. Sometimes I wonder if the kindness she showed me stemmed from pity. She must have sensed how lonely I was without a family of my own. Or perhaps, it occurs to me now, letting me see her happy family life was a way of warning me to stay in line. But if that was her intention, it failed. My love for him didn't die away. I ached with envy, and my feelings grew stronger than ever.

And then the mistake happened, almost as though by prior agreement.

He had turned forty; I was nearing the end of my thirties. He was back in Nagasaki on his own for the first time in years, on a summer training programme. He asked me out, and we had dinner in Chinatown.

I was a little tipsy from the Chinese wine we had drunk, sweetened with lumps of rock sugar. Noticing that I was unsteady on my feet, he offered to see me home.

You saw it all, Holy Mother. In the flickering light of the candles, you witnessed everything.

The first thing I do when I get home always is to light the candles on the altar to thank Our Lady for seeing me safely through the day. But he tried to stop me.

'Better not light them now – not after you've been drinking,' he said.

'I don't sleep properly unless I say my prayers.'

'So pious. I'm impressed,' he said. 'Just be careful you don't knock them over.' As he spoke, he reached out from behind and cupped his soft hands around my neck. I twisted my body and tried to wriggle free.

'No. Don't. Our Lady will . . .'

'That? It's just a porcelain doll. There's nothing inside,' he muttered roughly. I could hardly believe what I was hearing. I had always thought of him as devout.

'God is watching.'

'No he isn't. There's no one there.'

'Sasaki-san! How can you say that?'

'Anyone who lived through the war knows it. You, too – you survived the atomic bomb, didn't you?'

'By the grace of God.'

'By the grace of pure luck is more like it.'

'Luck?'

'We're like your insects. Eat, mate, reproduce. Who lives, who dies? It's just luck, and that's all there is to it.'

'It was part of God's plan, I think, that I was the only one to survive in my family. He must have had something in mind.'

'God doesn't spend his time watching over every little person in the world. He doesn't remember our faces and names. There are too many of us. We cover the land everywhere you look. Like insects. God doesn't keep an eye out for every insect that's born or dies. They don't even have names. Their faces are all the same. And they don't give a damn about him, either. What makes you think people are any better than bugs?'

He wrapped his long arms around me with brutal strength. I had no way to resist.

Holy Mother, you saw everything. He tore off my blouse and grabbed my trembling breasts in his sweaty palms. Then we coupled in front of you, as though you weren't even there. It was my first time – but I was longing for it. I burned with passion, panting and moaning shamelessly, not caring who might hear.

The candlelight must have cast our shadows on the walls, our long thin arms entwined, like a pair of huge insects locked together.

When the moment was over, we simply returned to the same relationship we'd had before. From the way he looked at me whenever we met, you would never have suspected a thing. And I continued to have dinner with them all – with him and Reiko and the children.

But after hearing the things he told me that night, I couldn't understand how he could go on working at the Gotō parish school. What did the Bible mean to him? How was he able to pass on the message of the Gospels to the young people he taught? He seemed so empty, so unreadable! I don't think I ever met anyone as hard to understand. Were his prayers nothing more than a daily habit? And did he perform his duties merely out of respect for the centuries-old traditions of the place?

We never spoke a word about what had happened. He kept the secret locked inside him until his dying day some twenty years later, just before his sixtieth birthday. Never was there a hint from him that we might sin again in the same way.

Reiko is always eager to talk about him whenever we meet. She still sees him not just as a man with film-star looks but as a devout and hardworking husband. She's so shallow, she just projects herself on to the unknown part of him. She doesn't understand him at all, does she, Holy Mother?

Who knows what lay at the bottom of his heart . . . what feelings he had as a survivor of the Special Attack Forces. Perhaps he wasn't quite human, but a beautiful, faithless insect, spreading its wings in the empty blue sky.

Oh, Holy Mother, what sinful mistakes we humans commit!

When they dropped the bomb, people rejected God and became one with the insects. That's what I think. For sixty years now I too have lived like an insect in fear and confusion. My life has been a blank, unthinking stretch of time. I regret the mistake I committed with him – truly I do.

But I still savour the memory of the pleasure that surged through my body that night.

I still sometimes imagine myself lying on the cart behind my grandfather, daydreaming as I'm shunted gently from side to side.

After crossing the wasteland, we headed upstream. When we came close to the head of the river, my grandmother came out to meet us, her hair bound in a white kerchief, her mouth open wide so that I could see her teeth as she wept and wailed. Sometimes that open mouth of hers appears in my dreams, like the gateway to another world.

She carried me, wrapped in my blanket, into the tatami room at the back of the house. For a while she just wept. Then, still sobbing, she said the same thing my grandfather had said: 'We'll look after you. We'll make sure you get better.' Using some of her precious stock of white rice and eggs, she made me some warm congee, but I was overcome with nausea and couldn't swallow. The white gruel was dyed with the blood that oozed from my gums, as though mixed with red perilla. I felt as if the red ash of the flattened city was spreading through me, like a disease I'd caught from what I'd seen there.

'You have to eat. Think of it as medicine.' With my grandmother's encouragement, I eventually managed to swallow some of the food – but all I got was a taste of iron, and I threw up again almost immediately. My body seemed to be on fire. The thirst was unbearable and unrelenting. For several days I lived on water alone, dozing and waking, sinking repeatedly and floating to the surface again.

At one stage, she brought in a small watermelon – heaven only knows where she'd found such a thing in those days. 'This should be easier to get down. Plenty of water in this. You must try to eat something. Your body needs the fuel. I'll leave it here for you.'

I have a vague memory of her voice as I floated in and out of consciousness. When the body is weak, one's sight and hearing grow faint as well, though the other senses, smell and touch, can become sharper than usual.

What I do remember is how the sweet, gentle scent of the watermelon by my pillow intensified a thirst that seemed to well up from the depths of the earth, making me lift myself, still barely conscious, and suck the watermelon down, all but burying my face in it.

I suppose it was a simple will to live, an instinct that made me cling to a life that hung in the balance. I don't retain many memories of those days, but the sense of rapture as the sweet juice trickled down my throat has remained with me to this day.

'She looks like a little grasshopper,' my grandmother apparently whispered when she saw me. A grasshopper, of all things! I don't know what strange coincidence made her compare me to a grasshopper rather than a cricket or a beetle, but perhaps there always was something insect-like about me even from those early days.

They say she was still sniffling when she called in my grandfather. 'Look at her. Just like a little grasshopper,' she said, tearful and smiling at the same time.

I often woke up in the middle of the night convinced that I had heard voices asking, 'Are you still alive?' In my dreams, I saw severed hands and feet and heads with eyeballs torn from their sockets on the ground. They all grew legs and gaping mouths, spread their wings and flew away. The voices would continue to sound in my sleepy ears after I awoke – but whether they were countless human voices or merely the babble of river and mountain spirits, I was never sure.

There was a military supplies factory on the middle reaches of the Urakami River and a row of houses nearby, but almost no one lived this far upstream. At night, the area was as quiet and dark as the bottom of a well. A small mountain stream ran close by the house, and there were paddy fields where frogs and toads came to mate in the summer. They laid their spawn like transparent piles of droppings in the puddles on the ridges and paths between the fields.

It was the frogs that woke me late at night – countless frogs calling out to one another in the darkness. The noise would build to a crescendo, like monks chanting in a temple, and then abruptly stop as if on cue. When the frogs fell silent, another voice would make itself heard. Su-wee chon, su-wee chon, su-wee chon. 'Who is your sweet-one? Who do you love?' I answered back, with tears in my eyes. Then one or two frogs would begin croaking, and soon the whole chorus would start up again, drowning out the insects' song.

My hair began to fall out. It came out in clumps when I combed it, and before long I was totally bald from my forehead to the back of my scalp. I looked like a backwoods samurai whose topknot had come undone. My grandmother hid the mirrors, but feeling with my fingers gave me a clear enough idea of how I must look. I didn't want to live my life like this. Sometimes I wished I could turn into a toad or a lizard or some kind of insect devoid of religious faith.

Physically, my condition was wretched. I still couldn't hold down any solid food. The only thing that kept me alive was the watermelon my grandmother somehow managed to get her hands on.

It must have been in late September that my grandfather came to tell me about the Kunchi festival.[1] We'd assumed there would be no festival this year, but it was going on as usual, he said, and all the young men were already running in the streets. I was surprised to see him so happy about a pagan celebration.

Little by little, I clawed my way back to normal life. Slowly, my appetite improved, and eventually I was just about strong enough to walk. The wounds on my leg healed over, although smooth bits of glass still emerged from time to time, coated in blood and fat. I began to spend whole days out on the cool veranda, idling my time away. Sometimes I felt that my heart would burst with sadness. Shadowy memories of my parents, or of Toki, Shin'ichirō, Fuji and Sanae, would press against my chest until I thought I'd suffocate.

Sanae had just turned five at the time and referred to me in her childish lisp as her 'big thithter'. When she saw me coming home at the end of the day, she would run out of the house calling my name. She used to jump into my arms and rub her plump red cheeks against mine. I had practically raised her myself. Without ever becoming a mother, I knew the anguish of losing a child – just as you did, Holy Mother.

When autumn arrived, a few friends who had survived the bomb came to visit, but my grandmother just thanked them politely at the door and wouldn't let them in to see me.

As winter approached, the loneliness seeped deep into my bones. I found it hard to sleep and would lie listening to the moaning and creaking of the oak trees on the hills behind the house as they bent under the force of the north wind. Alone in my room, I often woke up screaming. After a while, my grandparents took to sleeping near me.

One cold night, I awoke to hear my grandmother talking in a small, trembly voice.

'We should never have let the children go that day.'

'There's no sense in thinking like that. They were happy to go. They were excited to see their parents again.'

I heard her tearful whisper again, and the sound of sniffling.

'Why did it happen?'

'What?'

'Why did such a terrible thing have to happen? They were just innocent children. They had no idea.'

'I don't know. How should I know?'

There was a catch in my grandfather's voice, too.

'It must all be part of God's plan.'

'What could He have been thinking?'

'No one can know that.'

'But I want Him to explain Himself. The whole family was wiped out, Hiromitsu. I can't understand it. I almost want to blame Our Lady for letting this happen to us.'

'The family wasn't completely destroyed. There's still Mitsuko . . .'

'She'll never have any children. No one will marry her the way she looks now. She'll be the last of the family line. And our faith will die out with her, too.'

'All right, that's enough. You'll wake her up,' my grandfather said in a whisper. For a while her voice fell silent. I could feel her looking at me in the darkness.

'Can you hear the water?'

It was the middle of the night, in deep midwinter. The frogs had long since fallen silent. When the groaning of the trees on the hillsides stopped, there was a moment of stillness, broken only by the gurgling of one of the small streams that flowed into the Urakami River.

'You can always hear water wherever you are in this house,' my grand-father said.

'Our ancestors must have lived their whole lives with that sound in their ears, day in, day out, year after year . . .'

'What about it?'

'The way we believe in God hasn't changed at all. Our faith is as pure as ever. It's been handed down through the generations. We haven't done anything wrong. No matter how hard things got, even when we were persecuted, our faith kept running like a clear stream. It never stopped once. Think of that magnificent church we built here.'

'What are you trying to say?'

'Maybe we did something to make God angry with us.'

'Don't be stupid. It wasn't our fault the country went to war.'

'Are we being tested again? Does God still not trust us, even after all this time? Even though our ancestors were burnt at the stake for their faith? Why was the whole family destroyed like this? Why can't He believe in us, the way we believe in Him?'

'I don't know. All we can do is pray,' my grandfather said brusquely. But she wouldn't let it rest.

'We were at war. America and England were the enemy. So there were air raids . . . maybe that couldn't be helped. But the people in those countries have the same religion as us. How could they do such a thing? They even destroyed the church. Why did God allow His people in Urakami to be killed by their fellow Christians?'

'Look. God's intentions are too deep for us to understand. I've made up my mind not to think about it. The world's full of things we'll never understand. All we can do is trust Him and pray.'

'I just want someone to tell me why.'

'Come on, now go to sleep. You'll wake her up.'

There was a rustling as he turned over in bed. I shut my eyes and pulled the covers over my face to stifle my sobs. Everything fell silent, and before long I heard them snoring, occasionally grinding their teeth. Left alone in the darkness, I prayed to Our Lady with all my heart.

Despite everything, spring eventually arrived as it always does. With the change of season, I could feel rough bristles whenever I happened to rub the palm of my hand across my scalp. At last, my hair had started to grow back. I wasn't going to spend my life as bald as an egg after all.

'Granny! Grandpa! My hair's growing back!'

They were both moved to tears by the news. 'What a relief! We thought you might not pull through,' they said. We still didn't understand what was causing the hair loss at that stage. All we knew was that in many cases, people who suddenly lost their hair died soon afterwards. My grandparents had heard the rumours and feared the worst.

Gradually, day by day, my scalp darkened in colour until eventually it was covered in thick black hair. It was almost the first time I had felt any happiness since the bomb. A couple of months later, no hint of my baldness remained, and a little light began to shine into my life again. I was walking by then, too, albeit with a limp in my left leg.

One day that spring, as I walked toward the hospital through a still mostly derelict part of the city, I came to a place where a confusion of shepherd's purse and speedwell was in bloom by the river. The embankments had not been repaired yet, and the air was heavy with the smell of the earth. Along the banks, scattered with rubble, grew lush green grass, and there were white and yellow and purple flowers everywhere.

A big wooden cartwheel had sunk in the middle of the river. The water was clear, and a school of killifish darted in and out of the wheel. Most of the city was still a wasteland, but here and there shacks and temporary housing stood out against the desolation, and people's laundry fluttered in the breeze. I stood and hummed the 'Apple Song', a popular tune that played constantly on the radio in those days. I often found myself staring up into a clear blue sky, just like in the song.

Under my grandparents' care, I was recuperating. I began to help with the housework. When harvest time arrived, I tried to help in the fields, too. My body began to regain its strength, and there was talk of my going back to nursing school. But after everything that had happened, the prospect of coping with other people's wounds was terrifying. Splintered fingertips, perforated skulls, festering skin – I had seen enough of these things.

I hardly ever went out, but people from our church started to make suggestions. It wasn't good for me to be cooped up indoors all the time, they said. On top of that, it wasn't easy for two old people to keep the household going on what they made from the farm alone. So, shortly after my nineteenth birthday, I started work at a printing company that dealt mainly with religious materials.

Sasaki and Ozaki were my co-workers. Of the six employees, five were atomic bomb survivors. Sasaki was the only exception. We all had injuries or disfigurements of one kind or another, and I found it easy to relax when

I was around them. It did us good to share our troubles. He alone stood out; he alone bore no scars from the bomb.

All of us felt uneasy and resentful around Sasaki, me included. But in retrospect, it occurs to me the presence of Ozaki may have helped allay these feelings somewhat. His injuries were much worse than anyone else's. I think the horrendous condition of his jaw brought the rest of us a cruel kind of comfort. It's an awful thing to admit, Holy Mother, but somewhere inside me lurked the hard-hearted thought that, compared with him, I wasn't so badly off.

Maybe . . . A dark shadow passed through me, and the candles on the altar guttered suddenly. Your smile seemed to freeze, Holy Mother. Maybe that's why Reiko was so keen to have me tell her my memories of Sasaki-san. Maybe a glimpse of my miserable old age would make her feel better about the way her own life had turned out. 'Compared with her,' she might think, 'I should consider myself lucky.' Perhaps that's what all those postcards were about – part of a cruel game she was playing with me.

Maybe that innocent, sunny manner of hers was just a front. Deep down inside her was something else, faceless and horrible, some parasite like a tapeworm coiled white in her black guts.

Why don't you come out and visit? We could have a good soak together and talk about the past. It's fifteen years now since he died, and there aren't many friends left with whom I can share memories of the good old times. Maybe you could tell me about a side of him I never knew.

I ran my eyes over Reiko's brisk, flowing handwriting again. I had to tell her the truth. I couldn't keep up this pretence of friendliness any longer. I had to confess the truth about what he and I had done together.

I wrote a greeting on a fresh piece of stationery. My pen felt a little unsteady as I pressed down on the smooth surface of the paper. My revenge. I was going to have my revenge at last on this thieving creature.

If you really want to hear about the past, there is one thing that remains especially clear in my memory. Once – just once – he and I slept together. We betrayed you, one summer's night thirty-five years ago.

I always meant to take the secret with me to the grave. But I decided that after all the time you two spent together, I wanted you to know about this other side of him.

What we did was a sin, something shameful. But perhaps sin and shame don't really exist if they aren't exposed. I've always believed that God knows everything. But if – just if – God doesn't exist, then who would retain any memory of the mistake that happened between us?

I breathed out softly and touched the top end of the pen to my cheek, a habit that had been with me since I was a schoolgirl. I heaved a heavy sigh. The sensations I'd had with him that night came back to me now with sudden force. His lips brushing the blue disfiguration on my cheek, his hot, sweaty hands grabbing at my blackened leg, the strength with which he pried my knees apart . . . How could I forget? My cheek and my bad leg were the parts of my body that shamed me most. I tried to twist away, tried to resist . . . But it was useless. He pressed too hard. He was too insistent. I was powerless to resist. And above all, I welcomed it.

Holy Mother: you saw everything, you watched unblinking through the flames of the candles.

He pressed his lips to my ugly leg. I told him to stop. 'Our Lady . . .' I'd muttered, but he had cackled in my ear and said, 'It's just a hollow doll.' He told me we were like insects, that God had no special interest in us. That insects had no faith, no God.

And with him I became an insect, too. An insect that mates with the wet tip of its body.

You speak so blithely, so innocently of the past, Reiko, that I'm forced to assume your memories of him are fading. It's only when a person is truly present to us that we feel the whole range of emotions. Hatred. Resentment. Irritation . . . To you, perhaps, he seems far away. But not to me. He still lives on inside me. I've never forgotten the weight of him, the touch of him against me.

I'm old now, and my body feels like cold ash. But when I think of him, my heart warms and sparks into flame. Even now, I love him very much.

But I hate him, too – that man who toyed with me and used me for his pleasure that one single night. He branded me with his hands, his lips, his skin.

Maybe when you read these words, you'll find him coming to life again inside you too. In fact, maybe you're seething with anger and hatred at this very moment. You may feel like killing me. And you'll want to pay him back for what he did – even though he is already dead.

I imagine after you read this you won't find it quite so easy to soak happily in your precious hot-spring bath again. But that's what happens when people reminisce. Things come crawling out from under the rubble inside them . . . resurrected, if that's the right word.

So here it is, Reiko: the side of him you never knew. Tell me – can you still live with him happily after all these years?

Before I knew what I was doing, my blue ink had filled the page. So I signed off, squeezing in my name at the bottom of the page. I then read over what I had written. It was too much. I couldn't send this. The only thing to do was tear the letter up and toss it away. But I couldn't bring myself to do that either.

I took another sheet of paper and started to write a routine letter – seasonal greeting, recent news, all the usual stuff . . . But suddenly my pen stopped still. I couldn't go on.

I've never forgotten his dismissive laugh. 'It's just a hollow doll,' he said. But you saw everything, Holy Mother, didn't you?

Why does that episode still shine so vividly in my memory? If the moment when I regained consciousness under the rubble ('Are you still alive?') was the low point of my life, the brief time I spent with him was the peak. Sometimes I feel as though I crawled out of the rubble simply for that moment of pleasure in his embrace.

I wrote a postscript on a separate sheet of paper.

P.S. Reiko: Let me tell you about another side of him you never knew. You can't possibly imagine what he really was, but I know. He was an insect. A grasshopper that fell short and landed in the epicentre after the bomb fell. A godless insect.

When summer comes, that whole area is filled with insects: cicadas, ants, flies and grasshoppers. Here and there, an occasional lizard darts among the shadows. These are the creatures that hid away on Noah's Ark and have survived all the cataclysms of the world. When autumn comes, their front legs twitch together as if in prayer, and they wither and die. Maybe they also long for faith, like us.

That's what he was, Reiko – one of those insects.

Someone like Reiko probably wouldn't understand a word of what I'd written, but I added a blank sheet to the letter, stuck the doubled paper in an envelope and addressed it. Then I carefully pasted the envelope shut and stuck on a stamp. Finally, I put the letter away in the drawer of the altar, with its carved roses.

Why are you always smiling, Holy Mother? I extinguished the candles and crawled back under the quilt. A pale streak of light floated up to meet my eyes, now grown used to the dark. Daylight was starting to show through the gap in the curtains. The night was slowly giving way. I would doze for a while, then go out while it was still cool and put the letter in the old red postbox near the epicentre.

Soon the translucent white cicada larvae would come out of the ground and crawl up the trunks of the magnolia trees in the garden, twitching and squirming as they emerged and spread their wings. Their sloughed-off husks must be clinging to the trees already. Insects were stirring deep within the earth, hidden under the grass, or lying in wait in the hollows of ancient tree trunks. Soon it would be time for them to emerge all together.

But of course: summer was here again.

I'm lying in the wobbly cart pulled by my grandfather, watching the wheels turn and breathing in the smell of iron. I'm wrapped in a rough blanket, and as I feel the burning in my leg, from the shallows of my sleep I see *his* empty incarnation.

Out of the sky above the wasteland, a huge green grasshopper lands on my damaged leg and crawls towards my buttocks. With a laugh, it asks: 'Are you still alive?' Then it thrusts the moistened tip of its tail into my belly and shoots its seed like a million glittering glass shards, thick with the smell of green grass.

KAWABATA YASUNARI

The Silver Fifty-Sen Pieces

Translated by Lane Dunlop

I

It was a custom that the two-yen allowance she received at the start of each month be placed in Yoshiko's purse by her mother's own hand in the form of four silver fifty-sen pieces.

The number of these coins in circulation had been declining in those days. They looked light but felt heavy, and they seemed to Yoshiko to fill her red leather string purse with a solid dignity. Careful not to waste her allowance, Yoshiko often kept the coins in the purse in her handbag until the end of the month. She did not actively spurn such girlish pleasures as taking in a movie or going to a coffee shop with her friends from work, but she simply saw those diversions as being outside her life. Never having experienced them, she was never tempted by them.

Once a week, on her way back from the office, she would stop off at a department store and spend ten sen on a loaf of the salted French bread she liked so much. Other than that, there was nothing she particularly wanted for herself.

One day, though, in the stationery department at Mitsukoshi's, a glass paperweight caught her eye. Hexagonal, it had a dog carved on it in relief. Charmed by the dog, Yoshiko took the paperweight in her hand. Its thrilling coolness, its unexpected weightiness gave her a sudden pleasure. She loved this kind of delicately accomplished work and found herself captivated. She weighed it in her palm, looked at it from every angle, and then, reluctantly, she placed it back in its box. It cost forty sen.

She came back the next day and examined the paperweight again the same way. She came and looked at it again the day after that. After ten days of this, she finally made up her mind.

'I'll take this,' she said to the shop assistant, her heart beating fast.

When she got home, her mother and elder sister laughed at her.

'How could you spend your money on such a toy?'

But when each of them had taken it in her hand and looked at it, they said, 'You're right, it *is* rather pretty. And it's so well made.'

They held it up to the light. The polished clear glass surface harmonized delicately with the misty frosted glass of the relief, and there was an exquisite rightness in the hexagonal facets. To Yoshiko, it was a lovely work of art.

Having taken seven days, eight days and more to determine that the paperweight was an object worth making her possession, Yoshiko didn't care what anyone else might have to say about it, but still she felt some pride in receiving this recognition of her good taste from her mother and sister.

Even if she was laughed at for her exaggerated carefulness – taking those ten days to buy something for a mere forty sen – Yoshiko could not have done it any other way. She would not have to regret having bought something on the spur of the moment. The seventeen-year-old Yoshiko did not possess such meticulous discrimination that she had spent so many days looking and thinking before arriving at her decision. She was simply afraid of carelessly spending the silver fifty-sen pieces that had taken on such deep-seated importance in her mind.

When the story of the paperweight came up three years later and everyone burst out laughing, her mother said with real feeling, 'I thought you were so lovable that time.'

An amusing anecdote like this was attached to every single one of Yoshiko's possessions.

2

They started by taking the lift to Mitsukoshi's fifth floor because it was easier to shop from the top storey down. Yoshiko had agreed to accompany her mother on a Sunday shopping trip for a change.

The day's shopping should have been over when they reached ground level, but her mother continued down to the bargain basement as though it were a matter of course for her.

'It's so crowded, Mother. I hate that place,' Yoshiko grumbled, but her mother was already immersed in the basement's competitive atmosphere, it seemed, and didn't hear her.

The bargain basement was a place set up for the sole purpose of making people waste their money, but perhaps her mother would find something. Yoshiko followed her at a distance to keep an eye on her. It was air-conditioned so not oppressively hot.

First her mother bought three packs of stationery for twenty-five sen, then turned to look at Yoshiko. They shared a grin. Lately her mother had been using her stationery, much to Yoshiko's annoyance. Now we can rest easy, their looks seemed to say.

Drawn towards the counters for kitchen utensils and underwear, her mother was not bold enough to thrust her way through the mobs they attracted. She stood on tiptoe, peering over people's shoulders, or reached between their sleeves, but didn't buy anything, heading instead towards the exit, moving hesitantly as if not entirely convinced she should give up.

'Oh, these are just ninety-five sen? My . . .' Her mother picked up one of the umbrellas for sale near the exit. Surprised to find that every umbrella she dug out of the pile bore the same ninety-five-sen price tag, she said with suddenly regained energy, 'They're so cheap, aren't they, Yoshiko? Aren't they cheap?' as if her reluctance to leave had found an outlet. 'Well, don't you think they're cheap?'

'They really are.' Yoshiko picked one up, too. Her mother took it and opened it alongside her own.

'The ribs alone would be cheap at the price,' her mother said. 'The fabric – well, it's rayon, but it's well made, don't you think?'

How was it possible to sell such a decent item at this price? No sooner had the thought flashed through Yoshiko's mind than a strange resentment welled up inside her of being tricked into taking a defective product. Her mother rummaged through the pile, opening one umbrella after another in a grim search for one suitable to her age. Yoshiko waited several minutes before saying, 'Mother, don't you have one for everyday use at home?'

'Yes, I do, but that one . . .' She glanced at Yoshiko. 'It's ten years, no, more. I've had it fifteen years. It's worn out and old-fashioned. Or if I passed this one on to somebody, think how happy they would be.'

'True. It's all right if you're buying it as a gift.'

'Anybody would be delighted to get this, I'm sure.'

Yoshiko smiled, but she wondered if her mother was really choosing umbrellas with someone else in mind. Certainly, it could not have been any-one close to them. If it were, her mother would not have said 'anybody'.

'How about this one, Yoshiko?'

'Hmm, I wonder.'

Yoshiko couldn't drum up much enthusiasm, but she stepped closer to join in the search, hoping to find an umbrella that would be suitable for her mother.

Other shoppers, wearing thin summer rayon dresses, streamed past, quickly snapping up umbrellas as they remarked on the items' cheapness.

Yoshiko felt a little sorry – and angry at herself – for having hesitated to help her flushed and tense-looking mother.

Yoshiko turned towards her, prepared to say, 'Why not just buy one, any one, quickly?'

'Let's stop this, Yoshiko.'

'What?'

Her mother smiled weakly, placed her hand on Yoshiko's shoulder as if to brush something off and moved away from the counter. Now it was Yoshiko's turn to want more, but five or six steps were all it took for her to feel relief.

Taking hold of her mother's hand on her shoulder, she squeezed it hard and gave it one big swing, the two of them shoulder to shoulder as they hurried towards the exit.

This had happened seven years before, in 1939.

3

When the rain pounded against the roof of her scorched sheet-metal shack, Yoshiko found herself wishing they had bought an umbrella that time, and that she could joke with her mother about the one or two hundred yen such an umbrella would cost now, but her mother had died in the firebombing of their Kanda, Tokyo, neighbourhood.

Even if they had bought an umbrella, it probably would have been consumed in the flames.

By chance, the glass paperweight had survived. When her in-laws' house had burnt down in Yokohama, the paperweight was among those things that she'd frantically stuffed into an emergency bag, and now it was her only souvenir of life in her girlhood home.

From evening on, in the alley, she could hear the strange cries of the neighbourhood girls. Rumour had it that they could make a thousand yen in a single night. Now and then she would find herself holding the forty-sen paperweight she had bought after ten days of indecision when she was these girls' age, and as she studied the sweet little dog in relief, she would realize with a shock that there was not a single dog left in the whole burnt-out neighbourhood.

NOSAKA AKIYUKI

American Hijiki

Translated by Jay Rubin

A white spot out of nowhere in the burning sky – and look! – it puffs out round and in the middle of the round a kernel swaying like a pendulum aimed straight above me. It has to be a parachute, but in the sky no sight no sound no nothing of a plane and before I can think how weird this is the chute glides down into the garden's crazy glut of loquat, birch, persimmon, beech, myrtle, hydrangea, never catching on a branch, never tearing off a leaf. 'Hello, how are you?' this skinny foreign devil says with a grin. Wait a minute, he looks just like General Percival. The white chute falls around his shoulders like a cape, slips down and covers the garden in a blanket of snow. All right, the man said hello. You've got to answer him. 'I am very glad to see you'? No, that would be funny for an unexpected guest – if that's what this foreigner is. 'Who are you?' would sound like a grilling. 'Look, you son of a bitch, who are you? Who are you? Who are you?' Three times and if he doesn't answer, bang! let him have it. Wait, what are you thinking? First you've got to talk to him. 'How . . . how . . . how . . .' comes crawling up from my belly and gets stuck in my mouth. This has happened to me before, this desperate, cornered feeling. When could it have been now, let me see . . .

And searching for the answer, Toshio woke from his dream pressed flat against the wall by the buttocks of his wife, Kyoko, curled up, shrimp-like, beside him. A mean push sent her back to her side of the bed and knocked something to the floor.

Aha, the English conversation book Kyoko was mumbling over before they fell asleep. That explained to Toshio where his weird dream had come from.

An old American couple that Toshio had never met were coming tonight to stay with them. A month ago Kyoko, all excited and waving a red-white-and-blue-bordered airmail envelope, had said to him, 'Papa,

406

the Higginses are coming to Japan! Let's have them stay here.' She had met Mr and Mrs Higgins that spring in Hawaii.

It was a small operation, true enough, but Toshio ran a studio that produced TV commercials, and hoping to make up for the irregular hours he kept, meeting sponsors and overseeing film sessions, he had sent Kyoko and their three-year-old son, Keiichi, to Hawaii – not without a twinge of conscience at this unwonted luxury, but he had been able to get a break on the tickets through a connection with an airline and had hit on the small businessman's happy expedient of charging it to the company. Kyoko, who, for all her past study of English conversation, might well have been nervous about travelling alone with a child, if anything, took advantage of being a woman and boldly spread her wings, making many friends over there, Higgins among them. Retired from the State Department and living on a pension, he had married off his three daughters and – whatever his former rank might have been – he and his wife were now pursuing the enviable task of travelling around the world on a second honeymoon.

'Americans are so cold-hearted. Once the children get married, the parents might as well be strangers,' said Kyoko, conveniently forgetting the way she treated her own parents. 'It wouldn't hurt to be nice to them, I decided, and I did them a few little favours. You wouldn't believe how happy it made them. They said they liked me better than their very own daughters.' And they treated her to meals in fancy hotels that she could never have afforded on her $500 budget, took her island-hopping in a chartered plane, and sent chocolates for Keiichi's birthday that July, in return for which she mailed them a mat of woven straw. Then letters went flying back and forth across the Pacific at least once a week, culminating in the announcement that the Higginses were coming to Japan.

'They're really lovely people. You'll be going to America some day, too, Papa. Think of the confidence it will give you to have someone there that you know. And Mr Higgins says he's going to get Keiichi into an American college.'

A good bit of Kyoko's interest in the Higginses sounded like self-interest, he was tempted to say. Supposing three-year-old Keiichi went to college at all, it would be fifteen years from now. What made her think a retired official could last that long? But Kyoko's calculations, after all, were merely a way to justify all the money they would have to spend if they were going to entertain Mr and Mrs Higgins. And she was carried away with the honour of having an American house guest.

'They always said they wanted to see where I live. And they want to meet you.' She had assumed his consent before Toshio could say a word. 'Grandma and Grandpa Higgins are coming to see us, Keiichi. You remember them, don't you? Grandpa always used to say "Hello" to you, and you'd wave to him and answer, "Ba-ha-hye,"' she twittered.

So now it's Hello-Ba-ha-hye Japan–American friendship, is it? Twenty-two years ago, it was Q–Q Japan–American friendship.

'America is a country of gentlemen. They all respect ladies. "Ladies first" is the motto. And they're all polite. Well, you fellows won't have to think about "Ladies first" for a while, but politeness is another thing. What worries me is you're going to be rude and make the Americans think Japan is full of barbarians.' All of a sudden the war was over and after four years of persistent, rat-like picking on the students to console himself for having to teach an enemy language, the English teacher (he was such a coward he used to sit quivering in the air-raid shelter chanting sutras) walked into his first class and started in on us like this. Then he wrote 'THANK YOU' and 'EXCUSE ME' across the blackboard, surveyed us all with a look of contempt, and said: 'Anyone know how to pronounce these? No, of course not. This one is "San-Q" and this one is "Ekusu-Q-zu-mee". Got that? The accent is on the Q.' He underlined the Q with a forceful stroke that snapped the chalk and sent it flying. Grim smiles filled the classroom. (Here we go again. Until two months ago, the Chinese-classics teacher had stopped teaching and spent all his time lecturing on the war. 'In the final battle for Japan, Heaven shall be with us.' And whenever he'd write the characters for 'American and English Devil-Brutes' on the board, he would be so overcome with loathing that the chalk would always screech and crack in two.)

'All you have to do is smile and say "Q" and America-san will understand. Got that?'

The class ended with this 'Q–Q' and we went out to fill in the bomb shelter that had been dug around the edge of the schoolyard. If you hit someone with a rock, it was 'Q'. When you asked someone to take the other end of a beam, it was 'Q'. Soon we were using it for everything.

It's no wonder we don't know English. After three years of middle school, the only words I could spell were 'Black' and 'Love'. About the only thing I learned to say that seemed like real English was 'Umbrerra'. And nobody understood the difference between 'I', 'my' and 'me'. The first thing I learned when I started middle school in 1943 was how to read Japanese written in Roman letters. At home I found a butter container that said 'Hokkaidō Kōnō Kōsha' and I realized it was the name of the dairy. That was the first time I had ever deciphered the 'horizontal writing'. Before I had a chance to perfect 'Dis izu a pen', though, military drill took the place of English classes, and all we got from the English teacher on rainy days were hymns to the glory of college boys who went to the front.

'American college students do nothing but enjoy themselves, going to dance parties at the weekend, that kind of thing. Compared to them, Japanese college students . . . etc., etc. The only English you kids have to know is "Yes or no?" When we took Singapore, General Yamashita said to the enemy general, Percival' – and here he pounded on the desk, his cheek distorted in a nervous spasm, his eyeballs bulging – '"Yes or no!" What fighting spirit!'

We had an exam, all right, but on the translation problem you could get full credit for 'she's house'.

Struggling in pictures to shoulder a Union Jack and a white flag of surrender furled together, skinny shanks protruding from his shorts, the defeated General Percival stood for all the foreign devils that Japan was going to whip into submission. 'The foreign dogs may be tall,' shouted the judo instructor, 'but they're weak from the waist down. This comes from sitting in chairs. We Japanese have strong legs and hips because we squat on floor mats.' A plaque reading 'Reflect on That Which Lies Underfoot' hung above him. 'So all you've got to do with a foreigner is hit him low, use a hip throw, trip him from the inside, trip him from the outside, just work on his legs and he'll go down easy. Right? Now, everybody up!' During the free-for-all, everyone would imagine he was fighting Percival, throw the poor old guy down, jump on his back and get him in a headlock. 'Yes or no! Yes or no!'

In the second year of middle school, we went out to the farming villages to do labour service. After the fall of Saipan, this meant what they called the 'decongestion of dwellings'. The floor mats, the sliding doors and paper windows, the storm shutters of a house would all be loaded into a big wagon and taken to the nearest wartime 'people's' primary school. When the house was just a shell, the firemen would throw a rope around the central pillar and yank it down. You could see signs of how the people had rushed to get out: the bathtub full of water, old nappies hanging under the toilet eaves, a Hotei scroll, a three-pronged spear from feudal times, an empty coin bank (this was 'booty' we hid in the hedge and took home afterwards) and a big, thick book filled with nothing but English. 'Maybe they were spies.' 'It could be some kind of code.' We flipped through it as if on a treasure hunt, everyone straining to find a word he knew. Finally, the head of the class found 'silk hat' and said, 'It means a hat made of silk.' In that instant, the bare floorboards, the old calendar, the pillar with the mark of a torn-off amulet all disappeared to be replaced by the scene of a ball and men in silk hats. We had always known the words shiruku hatto, *but the class-head's translation came as a revelation. 'That's amazing,' said one boy, 'I never knew* shiruku hatto *meant "silk hat".' And even now, when I hear the words* shiruku hatto, *as a matter of reflex I think, 'A hat made of silk.'*

When he saw the first letter from Higgins displayed conspicuously on the dinner table like a flower straight from Kyoko's heart, the airmail envelope's garish border caused an unpleasant commotion in Toshio's chest. Not that he was worried about looking bad if Kyoko asked him to read it to her: it was the simple shock of getting a letter from an American. But Kyoko, overjoyed, had managed to read it and told him what Higgins had to say.

'I'll have to answer him. Can somebody at the company translate a letter for me?'

'Well, sure, I suppose so.'

'Here, I've got it all written.'

Toshio found the letter a schoolgirlish string of pretty clichés. For the moment, he was willing to give it to one of the young men at the office who were hard at work on English in the unshakeable belief that a trip to America had been ordained for the future. But on careful rereading, the sentence 'My husband joins me in expressing our sincerest gratitude for your many kindnesses' didn't sit well with him and he tore this part out before submitting it to the translator. Higgins' second letter, however, came hard on the heels of the first with the assurance that Kyoko could send her 'delightful' letters in Japanese because Higgins had a Japanese neighbour to read them to him. Moved by this show of consideration, Kyoko wrote a long letter on the fancy stationery that Toshio had brought her from Kyoto. Toshio did not ask what was in the letter, but she had apparently sent an open-hearted – and somewhat ostentatious – account of just about everything concerning the family.

'Mr Higgins says making TV films is the most promising profession in America, too. He says you must be very busy, so be careful not to over-tax yourself. Papa, are you listening? This is for you.'

Some TV film companies were the kind that bought Hollywood studios, and then there were those like Toshio's that produced a lot of five- or at best fifteen-second commercials at low profit. True, if you looked in the telephone directory, they would both be under the same heading, but Toshio was not in the mood to start explaining the difference between them to Kyoko, who was becoming annoyed at his inattention.

'Papa, you ought to go to America, too. It would enhance your image.'

'No, it's too late for me. Anyhow, the way everybody and his brother is going overseas these days, people who've never gone once may have a certain scarcity value. We're the only ones uncontaminated by superficial exposure to foreign countries.'

'That's just sour grapes. And as far as the language goes, you manage one way or another when you get there.'

Once it had been decided that Kyoko would be going to Hawaii, she had bought some English conversation records and practised phrases she would need for going through customs, words for shopping and such, as a result of which she discovered that 'They don't say "Papa" and "Mama" in America, it says. They use "Daddy" and "Mommy". A "Mama" is supposed to be a vulgar woman.' She proceeded to teach the new words to Keiichi. Toshio had allowed himself to be called 'Papa' now that '*Otōchan*' was too old-fashioned, but 'Daddy' was more than he could stomach, and after a spirited argument, he maintained with a finality rare for him, 'I don't care what you do in Hawaii, but in Japan I am to be called "Papa".'

Until we lost the war, any English we managed to learn was written English. Afterwards, it was spoken English, as symbolized by new lyrics like 'Comu, comu, eburybody' for traditional children's songs. The English–Speaking Society got started when I was in my fourth year of middle school, attracting the student elite. 'Oowat-tsumara-izyoo?' one of them, an older boy, said to me in the sunny place outside the wrestling (formerly judo) gym. I thought, maybe 'tsumara' means 'tomorrow' and he's asking me what I plan to do. Before I could make sense of it, though, he jeered at me and said: 'They won't understand you if you say it the old way, "Howatto izu matah ooizu yoo?" You've got to say, "Oowat-tsumara-izyoo?" Anyhow, habagoot-taimu.' He went off laughing with his friends.

I left school after the fourth year. My father was killed in the war, my mother was an invalid and my little sister (in her second year at girls' school) ran the house. To feed the three of us I went from a stocking factory to a battery factory to being an ad-taker for the Kyoto-Osaka Daily.

I don't know if it was my appearance that won her confidence – steady-looking for that time, with the bottom two buttons of my seven-button cadet jacket smashed, and for trousers, cotton jodhpurs narrow at the shins – but one day when I had skipped work and was walking around Nakanoshima Park, a girl came over to me and said, 'Are you a schoolboy? If you are, there's something I want you to do.' She wanted to get to know an American soldier and asked me to introduce her. Sure enough, where she was looking there stood a soldier staring idly at the boats on the river.

'I'll pay you. Just meet me here tomorrow.'

I knew well enough that 'How ah you' was the right thing to say, but I had never tried using it on one of them. The soldier, maybe sensing what was going on, came over to us. 'Sukueezu,' I thought he said, holding out a thick hand to me. For a second, I didn't understand, then remembered the English teacher, who doubled as manager of the baseball team, explaining to a dumbfounded player: 'Sukueezu means wring, press, tighten – squeeze. Don't you remember? You learned if you sukueezu snow, you get a snowball.'

When I timidly grasped the soldier's hand, he looked at me as if to say 'Is that the best you can do?' and squeezed me back as easily as crumpling up a scrap of paper. I almost jumped with the pain. Maybe he just wanted to look good in front of the girl, but she started laughing when she saw me wince, and the soldier immediately started talking to her. She panicked and looked to me for help, but while I could catch a few fragments – 'name', 'friend' – I had no idea what he was saying.

Real classwork had only started for me in the fourth year, but there were not enough English teachers and I had this old guy who worked part time and specialized in onomatopoeic words. 'In Japan, we say that tram bells ring "chin-chin", but in America they say "ding-dong".' Nyao was 'meow', kokekokkō was 'cockadoodle-doo'. Some kids, deadly serious, would make vocabulary cards that said 'chin-chin' on the front and 'ding-dong' on the back. The next thing you knew, the teacher would come up with a sentence like 'He cannot be cornered' that you felt couldn't possibly be real English even if you didn't know what it meant. After learning English from teachers like this, what the soldier said to me could have been a Chinaman talking in his sleep.

I knew I had to say something, started pointing back and forth between the soldier and the girl, when this totally unexpected shout of 'Daburu, daburu' came out of me. 'Okay, okay,' he said, looking satisfied and putting his arm around the girl. 'Taxi,' he ordered. True, there were these humped-over-looking cabs running past now and then, but the problem for me was getting one to stop. When he saw me looking baffled, the soldier ripped out a sheet of paper and wrote 'TAXI' in great big letters with a ballpoint pen, then shoved it under my nose, whining and urging me to get a cab. Probably realizing it was hopeless, he signalled for the girl to follow and started walking. I looked at the word 'TAXI' written in genuine English, then put it in my breast pocket, handling it as carefully as if it had been a movie star's autograph, and murmuring the word to myself in imitation of the soldier's pronunciation. The next day, expecting nothing, I went back to the same place and there she was, holding a half-pound can of MJB coffee and a can of Hershey's cocoa powder. She looked almost proud of herself. 'Know somebody that'll buy this stuff?' I told her about a coffee house in Nakanoshima Park, a hangout for GI whores, where this Korean handled the coffee, chocolate, cheese and cigarettes that the soldiers used for money. 'You take care of it,' she pleaded. 'I'll give you a cut.' When I went to the coffee house (they had second-rate pastries for ten yen, coffee for five), the Korean was out, but the minute she saw what I had, this fat lady who also must have been a dealer said, 'I'll take them off your hands.' She pulled a roll of notes out of a big, black purse like the ones the bus conductors use and gave me four hundred yen without batting an eyelash. 'You got cigarettes? I'll give ya twelve hundred yen a carton.' Another woman in the place, obviously a GI whore, was singing 'Only five minutes more, give me five minutes more' in a surprisingly pretty voice. I knew my share of songs in English.

Debates, protests, band and baseball seemed to take up our whole middle-school education. The biggest loudmouth would represent the class in the debates. 'Student Uniforms: For and Against' was one, but not half the students, whether for or against, could afford the luxury of a uniform. The girls, though, all had nice sailor dresses. I guess it was around December the year after the war ended. I stood staring open-mouthed at five or six Otemae girls who came almost dancing out of nowhere, pleated skirts fluttering before my eyes, along the moat of bombed-out Osaka Castle. My little sister was still wearing wartime farm trousers then. Before the old higher primary schools were upgraded to middle schools, it was normal for all students, girls included, to dress as they had during the war. Band was something that the rich kids with uniforms had asked for, and for their first recital they played – *without sheet music but with a decent collection of instruments – 'You Are My Sunshine', 'There's a Lamp Shinin' Bright in a Cabin', 'Moonlight on the River Colorado' and the big showpiece, 'La Comparsita'. A fifth-year student (a local landowner's son who, it was rumoured, had already bought women in the Hashimoto red-light district) was master of ceremonies, and when he announced the tango as 'Rodriguez's "La Comparsita"', the weighty ring of that 'Rodriguez's' just bowled us over. Even the Crown Prince used to sing 'Twinkle, Twinkle, Little Star', according to the newspapers.*

The souvenir photographer in Nakanoshima was a part-time student at the Foreign Language School and good at spoken English, so I used to go to his place when he was free and get English lessons in exchange for cigarette butts. I needed English for my pimping – if you can call getting one or two women a day for soldiers pimping. The girls were all pale, bony-shouldered aspiring whores who had got word that they could meet America-san and get chocolate if they came here, the soldiers all sad-faced boys who stood watching what was then the swift, clear flow of the Dōjima River, maybe thinking of home, but not over here in Nakanoshima because it was supposed to be girl-hunting territory. Amateurs, the girls had no idea how to turn their nicely bagged spoils into cash. My daily cut from selling the stuff to the Korean came to a hundred yen anyhow, which was a lot more profitable than the door-to-door selling of photo magazines and newspaper delivery boxes I did when not taking ads. I gave this job everything I had and started entertaining the soldiers with 'I hohpu you hahbu a good-doh taimu' or, leering, 'Watto kind ob pojishon do you rike?' – whether or not I understood exactly what I was saying. Kyoko is right – I managed the language one way or another. I guess one school friend who happened by was less shocked at my miserable clothing than the sight of me trading English with the soldiers, because word got round that I was an interpreter ('You should hear that guy's English!') and a lot of the kids I hadn't seen since I left school started showing up to watch me work.

Once it was certain that Higgins would be coming to Japan, Kyoko got excited about English conversation again, even teaching some to Kei-ichi. 'Goom-mohneen. When you wake up, you say, "Goom-mohneen". Go ahead, try it.' And: 'How about you, Papa? You ought to practise a little. You'll have to show them around – to kabuki, Tokyo Tower. They were so nice to me in Hawaii.'

'It's out of the question. I'm much too busy.'

'I'm sure you can manage two or three days. Husband and wife are a single unit in America. People in Hawaii used to ask me where you were. I covered up by saying you'd be coming later.'

What the hell are you talking about? The only reason you got to go to Hawaii was because I stayed here and worked! But what really gets me down is the thought of having to show them around Tokyo. The building on the right is the tallest in Japan. 'Rooku atto za righto beerudingu, zatto izu za highesto.' Why should I have to start playing the Nakanoshima pimp all over again? It amazes me to see anybody grinning and talking to Americans without the slightest hesitation. Walking along the Ginza, I see these young guys happily chattering away to Americans, the really shameless ones strolling down the avenue arm in arm with American girls like it was the most normal thing in the world. Sure, there were some in our day who talked to them, too, I remember. Once, on a crowded tram a tense college student got up the nerve to ask some soldiers: 'Ho-what-toh do you sheenku ob Japahn?' One of them shrugged, the other fixed him with a stare and said: 'Half good, half bad.' The student nodded gravely as though he had just had some profound philosophy explained to him. He took the stick of gum held out to him by the one who shrugged, rolled it like a cigarette and popped it into his mouth, much to the envy of the other passengers. Why was it? A soldier just had to look at you in those days and he was ready to give you chewing gum, cigarettes. Were they frightened to be in a place that had only just ceased being enemy territory? Did our hunger make them pity us?

But you can't get full on chewing gum. In the summer of 1946 we were living in Ohmiyamachi on the outskirts of Osaka, near a farm – which may have been why the food rations for our particular area were often late or never came at all. My sister would go several times a day to look at the blackboard outside the rice shop and come back crushed when she found nothing posted. Once, we turned the house upside down but found only rock salt and baking powder. We were so desperate we dissolved them in water and drank it, but this tastes bad, no matter how hungry you are. Just then the barber's wife, her big, bovine breasts hanging out, came to tell us, 'There's been a delivery. Seven days' rations!' This was it! I grabbed the bean-paste strainer and started out. The strainer wasn't going to be big enough for seven days' worth, though. We'd need the sack. The strainer had become a habit because we had only been getting two or three days' provisions at a time, just a fistful for a household of three, which made a big sack embarrassing. We ran out to the rice shop, where a couple of housewives were standing near the stacks of olive-drab US Army cartons. 'My old man hasn't been able to do it to me since he got back from Manchuria.' 'Ain't you the lucky one! Mine comes at me every time I've had a bath and finally got cooled off. Then I'm hot and sweaty all over again.' And they laughed obscenely while they waited for their share. I understood what they were talking about and told my sister to go and wait for me at home. Her navel always stuck out a little and once a sharp-eyed housewife who used to be a nurse saw her walking around without a top because she had nothing to wear. 'Oh, what a cute little outie! But it's going to be kind of embarrassing when you get undressed for your husband,' she said right to her face.

What would it be this time? Cheese? Apricots? I was used to these olive-drab cartons and knew we weren't getting rice but American provisions. The sugar-cured apricots had nothing to them, but you felt you were getting some nourishment from the cheese, which tasted pretty good in miso soup. We all watched as the rice man split open a carton with a big kitchen knife and came out with these little packets wrapped in dazzling red-and-green paper. As if to keep our curiosity in check, he said: 'A substitute rice ration – a seven-day supply of chewing gum. That's what these cartons are.' He pulled out something like a jewel case. This was a three-day supply.

I carried off nine of these little boxes, each containing fifty five-stick packs, a week's ration for the three of us. It was a good, heavy load that had the feel of luxury. 'What is it? What is it?' My sister came flying at me and screeching for joy when she heard it was gum. My mother placed a box on the crude, little altar of plain wood. The local carpenter had made it in exchange for the fancy kimono she had taken with her when we evacuated the city. She dedicated the gum to my father's spirit with a ding of the prayer bell, and our joyful little evening repast was under way, each of us peeling his gum wrappers and chewing in silence. At twenty-five sticks each per meal, it would have been exhausting to chew them one at a time. We would throw in a new stick whenever the sweetness began to fade. Anyone who saw our mouths working would swear they were stuffed with doughy pastry. Then my sister, holding a brown lump of chewed gum in her fingertips, said: 'I guess we have to spit this out when we're through.' The second I answered 'Sure', I realized we had to live for seven days on this gum, this stuff that made not the slightest dent in our hunger. Anything is better than nothing, they say, but this anything was our own saliva, and when the hunger pangs attacked again, my eyes filled with tears of anger and self-pity. In the end, I sold it on the black market – which was on the verge of being closed down – and bought some cornflour to keep us from starving. So I have no reason to be bitter. One thing is sure, though: you can't get full on chewing gum.

Gibu me shigaretto, chocoreto, san-Q. No one who's had the experience of begging from a GI could carry on a free-and-easy conversation with an American, that's for sure. Look at those guys with their monkey faces, and the Americans with their high-bridged noses and deep-set eyes. Nowadays you hear people saying the Japanese have interesting faces, beautiful skin – can they be serious? Often in a beer hall I'll see a sailor at a nearby table, or some foreigner who seems shabby if you just look at his clothes, but his face is all civilization and I catch myself staring at his three-dimensional features. Compared with the Japanese all around him, he's a shining star. Look at those muscular arms, the massive chest. How can you not feel ashamed next to him?

'Mr Higgins' ancestors come from England, he says. He has a white beard, just like some famous stage actor.' Yes, Toshio knew well enough what Higgins looked like from those colour snapshots of him in a bathing suit against Black Sand Beach or Diamond Head, the chest muscles sagging, of course, but the belly good and firm, and Mrs Higgins standing by in a bikini-like thing despite her age. 'He's so white he gets sunburnt immediately. And he's hairy, but the texture of the hair is different from ours – soft, with a golden glow, very handsome.' Probably it was the food, and for a while after they got back, she fed Keiichi nothing but meat. That hadn't lasted long, but she had started in again recently. 'Americans are very fond of steak, you know. Japanese beef is so good, I'm sure I can make something they'll like.' For practice, she started keeping big, American-style chunks of beef in the refrigerator, making steaks every night and serving them with lectures on 'rare' and 'medium' like some overzealous hotel waiter.

Kyoko put a pink towelling cover on the toilet seat, no doubt thinking it a point of etiquette because she had seen it done in Hawaii. Their Japanese-style bath worried her: could the Higginses manage to wash and rinse before they got in to soak? She took special pains in killing cockroaches. She bought a mattress for herself and Toshio, deciding that the Higginses would sleep in their bedroom. Vinyl flowers in the living room were bad enough, but she enlarged and framed their wedding photo and a snapshot of herself and Keiichi in Hawaii. This, he was pretty sure, was something she had picked up from an American TV drama. He complained at first, but it was easier to let Kyoko handle everything in her own way. He decided to be above it all and observe the progress of the changing cheap decor from the sidelines.

Once, while I was an imitation pimp in Nakanoshima, one of my old classmates, a Shinsaibashi butcher's son, asked me to bring an American to their house for dinner. 'What for?' I asked him. The way he told it, his old man had made so much money selling beef it scared him to have the cash around. He had built a new house with doors that opened and closed electrically, but he still didn't know what to do with his money. He liked to have a good time and gave a lot of parties and now he wanted to have an America-san over 'to thank him for the trouble we've caused him, making him take a special trip all the way to Japan'. I agreed to find somebody, figuring there might be a good chunk of beef in it for me, and brought along a twenty-one-year-old Texan soldier named Kenneth after doing my best to explain to him what this was all about. They sat him crosslegged on a tiger skin before the tokonoma *of their luxurious villa and put two miniature lacquered tables in front of him, serving one tiny dish after another of the purest Japanese-style catered cuisine. Kenneth didn't know what to do with his long legs, there was no hope of his liking the carp boiled in bean soup or the raw slices of sea bream, and all he did was drink glass after glass of beer. Finally, the kids started to do this terrible dancing and miming of a Japanese folk song. I was climbing the walls with embarrassment, but the butcher looked enormously satisfied with all this, kept puffing on his long, skinny pipe and repeating the only English he knew: 'Japahn pye-pu, Japahn pye-pu.'*

They could never have a repeat performance of that fiasco, but if Higgins made a face and refused Kyoko's cooking, and if Kyoko encouraged Keiichi, who had been happily imitating those awful singers on TV, 'Sing for Grandpa Higgins now, Keiichi, rettsu shingu.' Just imagining the scene, Toshio felt the blood rush to his head.

'Do you think this will fit him?' Kyoko tore off the department-store wrapping and showed him a maroon bathrobe. 'I bought the largest size they had. Here, try it on, Papa.' She had him into it before Toshio could say a word. His five-foot-nine-inch frame was big for a Japanese and the robe fit him perfectly. 'Let's see, he must be about this much taller than you.' She stretched out a hand to indicate the difference between Higgins and himself. 'I suppose we'll have to ask him to make do with this. Mrs Higgins can wear a yukata.'

'Look at the Americans. Their average height is five feet ten inches. For us, it's only five foot three. This difference of seven inches figures in everything, and I believe that's why we lost the war. A basic difference in physical strength is invariably manifested in national strength,' said the social studies (formerly just 'history') teacher. This fellow might be talking off the top of his head or spouting sheer nonsense, but he was so good at it, you never knew how seriously to take him. Maybe this was just his way of covering up the embarrassment he felt at suddenly having to preach Democratic Japan after Holy Japan from textbooks filled with the censors' black blottings, but at the time of America's first post-war atomic bomb test on Eniwetok Atoll, he scared us with prophetic pronouncements like 'If the chain reaction is infinite, the earth will be blown to bits' and 'Do you know why the Americans are making us hand over the lead pipes that are found in the burnt-out ruins? So they can send them home as material to block radiation! The Third World War is at hand. America and Russia are bound to fight it out.' But he didn't have to tell me about a difference in physical strength making for a difference in national strength. I knew it all too well from experience.

The twenty-fifth of September 1945 was a fantastically clear day. It seems as if there was never a cloud in the burning sky from summer into autumn that year – which is not true, of course. I have heart-withering memories as well of an early typhoon and the rice plants in the paddies falling in swirls, the very footprints of the wind. This tied in perfectly with expectations of a bad crop. But on 25 September, in any case (as had been true of 15 August, the day the war ended), we had what would have been a 'Japanese beauty' of a day if it had not been the day everyone said the American army was finally coming. We were let out of school – not that we had any classes to speak of, since most of our time was spent cleaning up the fire-bombed ruins. For no very good reason, I had always thought the Americans would be coming in planes or boats, but when I walked towards the ocean from the shelter we were living in there in the ruins of Kobe's Shinzaike, a motorcycle with a sidecar came roaring down the highway carrying a tense-looking policeman who wore a hat with a chin-strap, and following a hundred yards or so behind him in majestic silence was a winding column of what I later realized were jeeps and canvas-hooded troop trucks. I watched in a daze as one car after another sped past my eyes, travelling much faster than they had appeared to be at a distance.

Six years earlier, I had watched the same sort of truck detachment going down the highway, except then it had been at night and the soldiers were Japanese. The troops had put up with families near Kobe Harbour, waiting nearly three full weeks for their ship to come. Two men stayed at our house, which was great fun for me. When their orders arrived all of a sudden, it was close to nine at night. I went with my mother to see the soldiers piling silently into truck after truck on the highway, heard orders ringing now and then like the cries of some strange bird, but we looked in vain for the two men who had stayed with us, swallowed up now in the darkness. It seems to me that eventually a victory song welled up, but this must be a trick of the memory. I do remember that the tears were pouring out of me. The trucks moved off down the highway, heading west, and searchlights sent two unwavering beams aloft, picking clouds out of the night sky.

The Americans also went from east to west down the highway. At first I chased them with my eyes like counting wagons in a freight train, but there was no end to them. 'Look, they brought along fishing rods,' shouted a boy with his bulbous head exposed. He was one of the few bare-headed people in the crowd that quickly formed along the road, most still wearing gaiters and army caps. He was right: all the jeeps had long, flexible objects like fishing rods that swayed with each bump. 'The Chinks went to war with umbrellas, the Americans take fishing rods. They are different,' said an old man. I don't know what was supposed to be so 'different', but it did seem odd to think of American soldiers fishing just like us for the same fish from the same beaches. But then a young fellow who looked like an already demobilized soldier answered: 'That's an antenna, a radio antenna.' In all innocence, I had to admire them: so the Americans took radios along when they went to war!

All at once, without an order or a shout of any kind, the column came to a halt and the soldiers, who until then had looked like part of the machinery with their uniforms the same colour as the trucks, sprang out – almost as if they had been shot out – holding rifles. Once on the ground, they leaned casually against the vehicles, looking at us, their cheeks as red as devils'. 'Who says they're white? They're red devils!' said one frightened boy of my age as if my thoughts had been his own. A couple of hundred yards east down the wall of people, a cry arose that could have been a cheer or a scream. I looked over to see two American soldiers who stood a head – no, a head and shoulders – above the crowd that surrounded them. As I was about to step into the road to see what was happening, three big men came up before I knew it and, standing six feet from me, their mouths working constantly, started opening packs of gum and throwing the sticks in our direction. They were so offhand about it, we were all too startled to move. The soldiers started gesturing for us to pick up the gum, and I suspect the first one to take a stick did so less out of a willingness to accept charity than a fear of being punished if he refused. This was a man in a crêpe undershirt and knee-length drawers, brown shoes and garters to hold up his socks, who timidly stretched out his hand and showed not the least pleasure at having received a stick of chewing gum. The rest were like pigeons flocking for beans.

I had never thought much about it until then, but the second I saw the American soldiers I remembered the judo teacher's spirited lecture on how easy it would be to knock down the hairy beasts if you got them below the waist, where they were weak. Half seriously, I looked them over – and my illusions died on the spot. Maybe General Percival was an exception, because the soldiers I was looking at now had arms like roof beams and hips like millstones, and underneath trousers that glowed with a sheen our civilian uniforms never had, you could see their big, powerful buttocks. I had been granted beginner's status in the Martial Arts Society and I knew how to trip up the biggest lugs in school, but I could never do a thing to these American soldiers. What a magnificent build they had! No wonder Japan lost the war. Why were we fighting these giants to begin with? If you went after these guys with the wooden rifles we used in bayonet drill, they'd snap in two. Feeding us like pigeons began to bore them after a while, I suppose, and the soldiers climbed back into their trucks. A few people ran after them, as though sorry to see them go, but a soldier grabbed his rifle and scared the daylights out of them. The soldier laughed, and jeering laughter rose in the crowd as well.

Next day, there was labour service at the customs house. We had to throw all the papers in the building out of the windows. Everything was to be burnt, supposedly as part of a 'major clean-up', but whatever they didn't want the Occupation Army to find had certainly been taken care of long ago. This was sheer madness inspired by an overdose of fear, because the most these papers had on them was lines. If they're going to burn these, I might as well take them, I decided, because all I had for notepaper then was the backs of old cash memos from the stationer's. I stuffed some in my shirt, but this was not the customs house for nothing. My smuggling was uncovered in no time and the papers were burnt to ashes.

Just three months earlier, we had gathered in front of the customs house and walked to the beach at Onohama, weaving in and out of the Mitsui and Mit-subishi warehouses crammed into the area, to build a protective wall for Japan's latest piece of weaponry, a 125-mm anti-aircraft gun they said could pierce steel plating at an altitude of 45,000 feet. 'Coupled with radar, this gun is capable of firing at planes that are approaching, overhead, and going – all three,' explained the platoon leader. Kobe was thus protected by a veritable wall of iron, he said, but there were only six of these guns. He also let us look through his binoculars. You could see Jupiter perfectly even though it was broad daylight.

The B-29s that made a straight line across Osaka Bay and attacked the city on 1 June met with a savage barrage of fire from these 125-mm guns that failed to down a single plane. I tried to be encouraging. 'What fantastic guns! They really spit fire!' But the soldiers, unfazed, answered matter-of-factly: 'That is why they're called spitfires.'

Then, I had been helping the army shoot back at the Americans. Three months later, I was cleaning up to receive them as guests. The only difference was that work on the gun emplacement got me a loaf of bread, while for labour service after we lost I always got money – one yen fifty sen a day. Once, during the lunch break at the customs house, I went down to the beach. Both the anti-aircraft gun and the radar antenna (it looked like a fish grill) had disappeared without a trace. The only things on the beach were a few dozen concrete pipes, and in the water a line of small warships, American minesweepers cleaning up the mines the Americans themselves had planted.

'How old is Mr Higgins?' it suddenly occurred to Toshio to ask.

'I'm not sure. Sixty-two? Sixty-three? Why?'

'Did he ever say he fought in the war?'

'No, of course not. Who'd go to Hawaii for a holiday and talk about such awful things?' Then Kyoko added, 'Except you.' She hurriedly went on: 'Please don't start talking about the war, even if he did fight in it. It won't make him feel very good to hear that your father was killed.'

Whenever Toshio brought a friend his own age home for a drink, the liquor at its height would call forth war songs, stories of experiences in the war effort, and Kyoko, feeling left out, would grumble, 'It's so stupid, the same old stories over and over,' which was probably why she had included this warning in Higgins' case. She need not have feared, how-ever: Toshio did not know enough English to share war stories with an American.

'You just have to forget these terrible things. Every summer they come out with new war stories, more memoirs – well, I just hate it. I mean, I remember my mother carrying me piggyback into the air-raid shelter, I ate those starchy wartime foods, but I hate the way they dig up the war and bring back memories of 15 August year after year after year. It's as though they're proud of having suffered so much.'

In the face of Kyoko's increasingly earnest appeal, Toshio could only remain silent. At the company, whenever he would let slip a remark or two on the air raids or the black market, the younger men would smile faintly as if to say, 'Here we go again.' The fear would suddenly come over him that the others were seeing through a tale that grew more exaggerated with each telling, and he would cut himself short with a pang of emotion. This coming 15 August would be the twenty-second anniversary, after all: why shouldn't his stories be taken as an old man's senile prattling?

On 15 August, I had my mother and sister with me in our shelter in the Shin-zaike ruins. It might sound funny to say that they were with me, a fourteen-year-old boy, but fourteen-year-olds were the only ones left in Japan by then who could be called upon to do a man's work. I was the only one who could bail out the shelter when it rained or go to the well when the pipes failed. My mother was practically an invalid with her asthma and neuralgia. I can't be sure now whether it was the day before or that morning, but the word was passed that some important news was coming. I probably heard it from one of our neighbours. (The neighbourhood council building had been destroyed, but we still had a council. We had lots of neighbours living in shacks of galvanized sheeting put up where a wall had been left standing, or in underground air-raid shelters with roofs that stuck up three feet above ground.) I went to join the group of thirty or so who gathered in front of the still intact Young Men's Association. 'I'm telling you, they're going to declare martial law.' 'Maybe His Majesty himself is going to take command of the army?' There had been a major air raid on Osaka on the fourteenth, and Kobe itself had been strafed by carrier planes; none of us had the slightest idea that the war would end the next day. We heard the strangely disembodied voice saying, '. . . and thus am torn asunder . . . to bear the unbearable, endure the unendurable . . .' but we were more mystified than anything else. The announcer solemnly reread the emperor's proclamation, and the broadcast was over. Everyone probably realized in a vague sort of way that the war had ended, but nobody wanted to risk being the first to let it slip out. 'Harmony has been restored, that's what it means,' said the head of the neighbourhood council, the white hairs conspicuous on his long-unshaven head. His choice of words brought to mind the 'restoration of harmony' between Ieyasu and Hideyori after the Summer Siege (or was it the Winter Siege?) of Osaka Castle over three hundred years ago, but it conveyed no immediate sense of our having lost the war. I suppose I was in a state of excitement, because for a while I didn't notice the streams of sweat that had come from standing under the burning sky, but then I walked straight back to the shelter. 'I think there's no more war, Mama.' My little sister, combing the lice from her hair, was the first to answer. 'You mean Father's coming home?' My mother went on silently rubbing her skinny knees with talcum powder, and after a while said only, 'We'll have to be careful.'

'Look! The B-29s are dropping something,' my sister shouted. At the time, I was trying to get what little coolness was available in the hot, steamy shelter by blowing into my shirt. 'Get back in here, stupid!' They might have been more bombs. 'It's all right, they're just parachutes.' When I timidly stuck my head out, the sun was on its way down, casting its red glow on Mount Rokkō, and the three-plane formation of B-29s had already flown so far that they were beginning to blend into the contrasting deep blue of the sky above the ocean. In a long band that started directly overhead, countless numbers of billowing, overlapping parachutes were streaming westwards at a slight incline, almost as if they had a will of their own. My sister clung to me, afraid, and I held her close, ducking down again just in case. 'What could they have dropped?' My voice quavered. The new bomb they dropped on Hiroshima was an atomic bomb, and that was supposed to have had a parachute, but certainly they would never drop so many – and not here, where there was nothing but burnt-out ruins as far as you could see. The parachutes fell more slowly as they neared the ground, then glided in and collapsed sideways when they hit. It was the hour of the evening calm and absolutely windless. The parachutes never moved.

An old man holding his shovel like a rifle and an old woman wearing a scarf on her head in spite of the sweltering heat kept going in and out of their shack and pointing at the parachutes. Amid the strange silence, the first one to start running was a shirtless boy of about first-year middle-school age. I started walking, too, frightened and fascinated to see what the things could be. The first one I came to was in a tennis-court-turned-potato-field. The white cloth of the chute was draped over its cargo – a bomb or something – but nobody wanted to go near it. 'Stay away! Move! Get away!' a policeman shouted through a megaphone, walking over with his bicycle. I climbed a tree that had escaped burning, to get a better view. All along the highway to the west were white clumps that looked like the puddles that formed in bomb craters. 'Waah! There's hundreds of them!' I immediately announced my discovery. Some of the white clumps were surrounded by crowds, while others between the highway and the ocean had still not been noticed. An old woman appeared, looking for help. 'One of them fell right next to my shelter.' 'Did you see what it was?' Everyone had watched the parachutes sailing to the ground, but nobody had got a clear look at what they carried. 'I don't know, it's some kind of big barrel. I have eggs in my shelter – do you think it's safe to go and get them?' The fear of duds and time bombs was too deeply ingrained. No one was willing to offer his assurances. We just stood there looking fearfully at the white ghost that would suddenly come alive now and then when the almost imperceptible breeze filled the chute.

Their boots crunching on the earth, some soldiers came running in our direction. At last! The dud squad! But no, there were only ten shirtless, unarmed men. They set to work on the chute without order or hesitation. The crowd pressed forward, tightening the circle. When the chute was stripped off, an olive-drab metal drum emerged. I had seen plenty of old, scorched oil drums, but this one had the gloss of newness, and there were small English letters and some numbers on it. Three soldiers pushed it over and started rolling it, crushing the thick growth of potato leaves in furrows. 'What is it?' someone finally dared to ask. 'Isn't it a bomb?' 'They dropped stuff for the prisoners. The Americans take good care of their men.'

There was a prisoner-of-war camp at Wakihama, and the prisoners often used to carry freight on the pier, but could these things really be for them? 'Well, we're the prisoners as of today,' one man said good-humouredly and took out a pack of cigarettes. 'These are good smokes, from Roosevelt – no, Truman.' He gave one to an old civil corpsman. 'They've got everything in these barrels!' When they finally got the barrel to the roadside, they kicked it along, then rolled it up into a wagon. As soon as they went rattling off with it, the crowd dispersed in all directions. I ran for those white clumps I had seen on the beach side of the highway. Hell, if they were going to give these treasure cans that had 'everything' in them to the POWs, I'd take one for myself, I thought, driven more by hunger than hatred for the enemy. The sun was down, the burnt-out ruins on the verge of darkness. Just as I had run around looking for a shelter in the 5 June air raid, the black smoke enveloping me and turning the afternoon into evening,

I ran towards the white chutes, now seeking out what had fallen from the sky instead of fleeing from it, as we had until yesterday.

Every one of the drums was an anthill crawling with grown-ups in a sweat to get the things open with hammers and crowbars. I got yelled at for just looking at them from a distance. On the way back to the shelter, I heard the voice of the old woman who had been worrying about her eggs, now screeching through the darkness: 'No! No! This thing fell on our land, so it's ours! I don't care what you say, I'm not giving it up! Get out of here! Get out!'

The army took charge of the situation. There was too much stuff to give it all to the POWs, so each neighbourhood council would take the responsibility of dividing it up evenly – and quickly, because there was no telling when the American army might show up. If there were something in a drum besides food, this had to be reported immediately, and if someone were found to have taken possession of any such thing, he might be immediately executed. Sending along sufficient threats, they allotted two drums to each block, though of course anyone who had taken anything from the drums got to keep it. The contents of the drums were ready to be parcelled out next afternoon in front of the Young Men's Association, but everything was wrapped in green and it was impossible to tell what was what. 'Can anybody here read English?' the head of the neighbourhood council asked, trying to smile, but intellectuals like that had been smart enough to evacuate long ago. It was the people who belonged to the place that stayed behind – the tinsmith, the carpenter, the tailor, the tobacconist, the grocer, the Golden Light priest, the primary-school teacher. I was an air-raid drillmaster and well used to looking clever in front of grown-ups, but not when it came to English. 'How about opening all the packages so everything gets distributed fairly?' Each barrel had been filled with a single product – nothing but shoes, say, or all cigarettes – and these the neighbourhood councils had divided up evenly. Now the first thing we opened were some long, narrow boxes. They were packed full like a child's lunchbox with cheese, tinned beans, green toilet paper, three cigarettes, chewing gum, bars of chocolate, hardtack, soap, matches, jam, marmalade and three white pills. These were distributed, two boxes per household. Then we opened some round cans that were stuffed full of cheese or bacon, ham, beans, sugar. I felt like taking everything for myself, even if it meant killing everybody there, and I suppose everybody else felt the same. Sighs went up when the sugar can was poured into a cardboard box. 'Luxury Is the Enemy.' 'We Desire Nothing – Until Victory Is Won.' Whenever I had seen these slogans, it had seemed to me they were talking about sugar. Luxury is sugar; when victory is won, we can eat as much as we like. So on the day we lost, what came falling out of the sky but sugar, along with a load of other treasures, including some wrinkled black stuff like little pieces of thread. This was distributed loose, each family getting what could be scooped up in both hands. It was the only thing we didn't recognize, but nobody had time to worry about that. Anything that came out of the green boxes, even if it had been sand, you would have carefully stowed away, checking your share against what everyone else got. There was even some cotton wool, and when a middle-aged lady in glasses asked that it be distributed to the women, the civil corpsman turned her down flat. 'No favours for anybody!' he shouted, red with anger. I had a vague idea what the women wanted cotton wool for. A little after we were burnt out, my mother went to the pharmacy for advice. 'My period is awfully late this time.' 'So's mine,' said another customer about her age. The pharmacist joined in and an embarrassing conversation ensued, ending with: 'Still, it's a lot less trouble this way as long as you can't get cotton wool.' Apparently a lot of women stopped having their periods after the bombing started.

'We don't know when the Americans are going to come here. This is a special ration we stole from the prisoners, so get rid of it as soon as you can. Let's not take any chances,' the head of the council warned us, and the first thing I did when I got back to the shelter was repeat this emphatically. We had got into the habit of stretching everything to the limit, so if my mother had said to me, 'Let's just have the beans today,' I would have looked long and hard at our portion and then cried like a little kid watching his mother put away his favourite sweets 'for later'. The only reason I hadn't started eating the sugar on the way was my excitement: all I wanted to do was hurry back and show off the food as if I had got it through some daring exploit.

My mother did as I said and offered a piece of hardtack and cigarettes before my father's picture in a corner of our shelter. It only occurred to me after I had sampled most of this special ration from America, but if my father's spirit was alive somewhere, what would he have thought of all this? It was so strange – helping yourself to something that belonged to the 'American and English Devil-Brutes' who had killed your father and then offering it up before his spirit!

'What is this?' I asked, once things had calmed down. The stringy, black stuff was the only thing that seemed to need cooking, but we couldn't tell what it was from either the taste or the smell. 'I'll go ask somebody,' I said. Desperate to eat,

I ran out and asked the laundry woman. 'I don't know,' she said, as puzzled as the rest of us, 'Maybe you have to soften it in water and boil it. It looks a lot like hijiki.' *Could it be another kind of seaweed like* hijiki? *I had heard they used to cook* hijiki *with fried bean curd, a favourite of the Osaka merchants' apprentices. Our cracked earthenware brazier was held together by wire, but I immediately got a fire going and set a pot on it that we had saved from the bombing. When I started boiling the stuff as the laundry woman had suggested, the water turned an increasingly dark, rusty brown colour. 'Is* hijiki *supposed to be like this?' I asked my mother. She came over to look, dragging her bad leg. 'The bitterness is coming out. American* hijiki *has a lot of bitterness!' I tried draining it and changing the water, but still couldn't get rid of the rusty brown. The fourth change of water stayed clear, so I flavoured the stuff with rock salt and took a taste after boiling it down. It turned out to be this sticky, absolutely tasteless stuff like the black ersatz noodles they made from seaweed – only worse. Chewing did no good. It just seemed to stick to the inside of my mouth. And swallowing it was impossible. 'That's funny – maybe I boiled it too long.' My mother and sister both made faces when they tried it. 'The Americans eat some pretty awful things, too,' my mother grumbled, but we certainly couldn't throw it out. Having been boiled, it would probably keep for a while. We left it in the pot and refreshed our mouths with chewing gum. Nobody ever did figure out how to cook this American* hijiki. *The head of the neighbourhood council asked a soldier about it three days later and told us: 'He says it was something called "black tea", the tea leaves they use in America.' But by then, there was not a speck of it left in any of the shelters.*

The narrow lanes between the burnt-out houses were filled with discarded silver chewing-gum wrappers. One of the first men to grab a drum for himself had found it filled with chewing gum. As much as he chewed, he couldn't get rid of it all. He was afraid the Americans might show up at any time and, besides, his jaw was getting tired, so he handed it all out to the children, who chewed it like cinnamon bark and threw it away as soon as the flavour was gone. At first, everybody smoothed the wrinkles out of the silver papers and saved them for origami, but there were so many they ceased to have any value and soon the streets were covered with silver-paper snow glittering in the summer sun. This was like hiding your head and leaving your tail exposed. If the Americans saw it, they would know immediately that the drums had been stolen. But nobody worried about that. The special ration was gone soon enough, except

the sugar, which we kept nibbling at, but even after we had gone back to the
old boiled miscellanies and starchy soups, the silver chewing-gum wrappers, like
the colourful rubbish spread around a shrine after a festival, kept the special
ration of dreams from America alive in the yellow-brown landscape.

'America' for Toshio meant American *hijiki*, summer snow in the burnt-
out ruins, big hips under glossy gabardine, a thick hand held out for him
to sukueezu, seven days' rice rations of chewing gum, habagoot-taimu,
General MacArthur with the emperor just up to his shoulders, Q-Q and
Japan–American friendship, half-pound cans of MJB coffee, DDT doused
on him in the station by a black soldier, a lone bulldozer smoothing over
the burnt-out ruins, jeeps with fishing rods, and a Christmas tree in an
American civilian's house, its only decorations electric lights blinking
silently on and off.

In response to Kyoko's entreaties, Toshio agreed to have the company
car take them to meet the Higginses at Haneda Airport. 'You'll be coming,
too, won't you, Papa?' she pressed, in answer to which a busy schedule would
have been too obvious an excuse. But worse, he hated the thought of being
seen through ('What are you afraid of?') if he refused. And so, on to the
chaos of the airport and Kyoko flaunting her one-time experience of foreign
travel, gliding into International Arrivals with: 'Oh, look, Keiichi, remember we got on the plane over there? And customs is way over there.'

'I'll be in the bar.'

There was still time until the plane arrived. Toshio took the escalator
upstairs. 'Straight whisky, double.' He gulped it down like an alcoholic.
'I will *not* speak to him in English,' had been his first firm resolve on
waking this morning, not that he could have done so had he wanted to,
but the fragments of conversation he had used back then in Nakanoshima might suddenly come to life again and start pouring out under
pressure to use English. 'No, right from the start I'll give him the old
standard "*Yaa, irasshai*" or "*Konnichi wa*", and if he doesn't understand me,
to hell with him. You come to Japan, speak Japanese. I won't even say
"goon-nighto" to him.' As he drank, the fluttering in the chest that had
been with him since lunch gradually subsided and he began to sense the
thrill of striking back at the enemy.

The crowd came pouring through the gate: a bearded American student
wearing cotton trousers and flip-flops and looking as if he were on a trip

to the nearest town, a horrifyingly tall couple, a middle-aged man who walked with the quick, high-strung steps of the successful businessman in familiar territory, beaming Japanese travellers who really did have slanted eyes and muddy-looking skin when you saw them like this mixed in with foreigners, Hawaiian Nisei all round-faced with thick heads of hair. 'Hi, Higgins-san!' screeched Kyoko, and there he was in blue blazer, grey trousers, leather necktie and the white beard that Toshio knew so well, and with him a little old lady wearing bright red lipstick and looking smaller than she had in the snapshots. Shaking his head 'Yes, yes', Higgins walked over to them, hugged Kyoko and patted Keiichi on the head. Even Kyoko seemed at a loss to produce English right away, flagging after 'How ah you' and trying to overcome her awkwardness by gesturing towards Toshio with 'My husband'. Toshio threw out his chest, extended his hand and said, '*Yaa, irasshai*' somewhat hoarsely, to which Higgins responded in faltering but correct Japanese, '*Konnichi wa, hajimemashite.*' So utterly unprepared for this was Toshio that whatever composure he had mustered up gave way to a hurried scraping together of vocabulary fragments that would enable him to answer in English, which he felt he must by all means do. 'Werucome, berry good-do.' Higgins received these disconnected bits with a smile and said in his shaky Japanese: 'We could come Japan, I am very glad.' Toshio could think of nothing for this but a few polite groans. Meanwhile, Kyoko and Mrs Higgins were managing to communicate with English and sign language. To Toshio, Mrs Higgins said the usual 'How are you', and he answered by echoing the phrase, his firm resolve by now having floated off somewhere.

Using 'Ladies first' as an excuse, Toshio got Kyoko into the back seat with Mr and Mrs Higgins and sat next to the driver with Keiichi.

'You're just terrible, Mr Higgins. You didn't tell me in Hawaii that you knew Japanese.'

'Yes, then I was without confidence. But when we decided to come Japan, I tried hard to remember.' During the war, he said, he had studied conversational Japanese at the University of Michigan's Japanese language school and then come to Japan for six months in 1946 with the Occupation forces. Toshio recalled the rumour going around back then that there were Americans walking the streets pretending not to know Japanese, and when they heard someone criticizing America they would send him off to Okinawa to do hard labour. Higgins said he had been doing newspaper work in Japan. If it was 1946, everything had still been a pile of rubble. Speeding along the expressway from the airport, Toshio thought several times of asking with pride: 'Japan has changed quite a lot, don't you think?' Higgins should have been the one to show surprise, but he kept silent while his wife chimed in with 'Wonderful, wonderful' each time Kyoko pointed out Tokyo Tower strung with lights or the panorama of high-rise buildings.

'Do you like to drink, Mr Higgins?'

'Yes, I do,' he nodded happily and handed a cigar to Toshio, who had turned to face him.

'San-Q,' said Toshio, no longer hesitant about speaking English. But the cigar was another matter: weren't you supposed to snip one end off before you smoked it? American officers used to bite the end off and spit it out. All right, then . . . but it was more than he could manage. When he looked up, Higgins was carefully running his big tongue all over his cigar, which seemed to be absorbing his full attention. He looked like some kind of animal. When he started feeling for a match, Toshio quickly proffered his lighter.

They left the expressway, heading for home in Yotsuya, and as they approached the famous Ginza Yonchōme intersection, Toshio, unable to resist the role of guide any longer, said: 'This is the Ginza.' Higgins would have to be surprised at the glut of neon here. It was supposed to be more spectacular than that of New York or Hollywood.

'The Ginza, I know. The PX was here.'

They passed the Wakō building where the PX had been, before there was time to point it out.

'If you like, we can have dinner here instead of going straight home,' Toshio suggested. Kyoko had made preparations for dinner, but she went along with him, and Higgins, apparently willing to leave everything up to Toshio, stepped gleefully from the car.

Toshio could not decide whether to take them to a restaurant with a foreign chef, or to one serving sukiyaki and tempura. But Higgins asked: 'Is sushi here?'

'You eat sushi, Mr Higgins? It has raw fish, you know.'

'Yes, there are sushi restaurants in America. Kame-zushi, Kiyo-zushi, very good.'

Mrs Higgins, apparently startled at the tidal wave of people, kept pressing her husband for information.

'My lovely wife is asking me this a festival?' he said to Toshio, smiling.

Toshio wanted to follow Higgins' reasonably workable Japanese with something clever in English, but the best he could do was, 'Oar-ways rush-shu, ne,' an explanation for Mrs Higgins in strict GI-whore style. It seemed to have got through to her, though, because she nodded and started yammering at him in incomprehensible English. He nodded back and gave her the famous Japahnese sumairu.

Holding their chopsticks in what should have been an unusable position, Mr and Mrs Higgins deftly picked up the bits of raw fish and vinegared rice balls plopped before them by the sushi chef. 'In America, too, the different kinds of sushi they call *toro, kohada, kappa-maki*,' said Higgins, drinking green tea and looking as if he and his wife had been in Japan for years.

'Mr Higgins and I are going to have a drink together, Kyoko, so you take Mrs Higgins home. Right, Mr Higgins?'

'Fi-ine,' Higgins nodded, smiling.

'But they must be so tired,' Kyoko objected. 'And it's not very nice for Mrs Higgins.'

But Mrs Higgins seemed satisfied with her husband's explanation, to which Toshio added the wholly unnecessary 'Stag-gu pahtee'.

'Well, all right, maybe we can do a little shopping,' Kyoko said, then awkwardly repeated this in English for Mrs Higgins.

'Don't come home too late,' she reminded Toshio as usual, and started off with Mrs Higgins and Keiichi.

'Your son is up until late. Is it all right?' Higgins volunteered a sort of admonition.

True, the children usually stayed home when the husband and wife went out in America, Toshio recalled with some embarrassment. He was pretty sure he had seen that in a 'Blondie' comic strip.

They went to a nightclub where Toshio often entertained important sponsors.

'What's this? Are you doing business with foreigners now?'

'No, no,' Toshio hurried to explain. 'He's been to Japan before and his Japanese is *very* good.' He was taking no chances on Higgins' catching some rude remark. But the manager had his wits about him and quickly got two English-speaking bar hostesses for Toshio and his foreign guest. Toshio felt a little awkward with the unfamiliar girls, but Higgins seemed relieved at having been liberated from Japanese and started chattering away, turning to Toshio now and then with a bit of flattery. 'Young ladies speak wonderful English.' Soon he was hugging them and holding hands.

Aha, this old dog likes the girls, I see, thought Toshio, convinced that he would be providing inadequate service if he failed to find Higgins a woman. Perhaps a call girl tomorrow night? He thought of an agent in that particular field with whom he had had some dealings in connection with work.

'Mr Higgins, do you have anything planned for tomorrow?'

Higgins produced a memo book, which he showed to Toshio. 'Three o'clock, Press Club. Five o'clock, I see a friend at CBS, have dinner. Why?'

Toshio, almost annoyed that Higgins should have so many acquaintances in Japan, said: 'That's all right, the evening will be just as good. I was thinking of introducing you to a nice gahru.'

'Thank you.' Higgins did not seem especially pleased.

'How about after you have dinner with your CBS friend?'

'What time?'

'Eight o'clock should be all right.'

'Okay.'

Toshio darted from the table as if he had important business to expedite and telephoned the call-girl agent.

'He's a foreigner, now, an old guy. I think he'd probably like a really young girl.' It would be 50 per cent extra for foreigners, the agent said, but the girl would be absolutely stacked. Toshio ordered a girl for himself and they arranged to meet in a hotel in Sugamo.

Higgins was having the girls fill old-fashioned glasses half full of straight whisky for him and drinking them down in a single gulp. He was not the least bit drunk, however, and from the one bag he refused to part with when the company car took the luggage home, he produced a cardboard-lined envelope. 'Nude photos, I took them,' he said, and displayed a series of explicit spread-leg standing poses among the hors d'oeuvres and fruit on the table, obviously enjoying the commotion raised by the shrieking hostesses. 'My camera work. Pretty good, isn't it? I took lots the time I in Japan, too.'

For a second, Toshio was ready to pick a fight – I suppose you gave young girls chewing gum, chocolate, stockings, and forced them to get undressed for your camera? – but the feeling quickly passed as he began to get interested in the near-obscene photographs of blonde girls. Suddenly a little blob of something went shooting past him and he looked up to find Higgins pulling a narrow rubber band through the spaces between his teeth. He was flicking whatever food was lodged there in any direction it happened to fly, along with trailing bits of stuff that could have been saliva or tartar but was in any case disturbing to the hostesses, who wiped themselves but did not object openly to Higgins' bad manners.

They went to two more places after that, Higgins totally unaffected by the alcohol he kept gulping down, the two of them harmonizing on 'You Are My Sunshine' in the cab and arriving home at 3 a.m. Toshio showed Higgins upstairs, then crawled in next to Kyoko and Keiichi, who were sleeping amid a jumble of what must have been presents from the Higginses – chewing gum, cookies, perfume, brandy and the kind of cheap muumuu the Hawaiian natives wear.

He woke with a terrible hangover, called to say he would be late for work, and was still munching painkillers when he said good morning to the Higginses, who had been up for some time. Higgins, showing no trace of last night's drinking, stood looking out at the lawn and said: 'It needs a little mowing.' Kyoko had done a thorough job on the inside of the house but had not got to the back garden, which was to be sure an overgrown jungle, punctuated here and there with bits of dried dog shit. Toshio thought it rather considerate of them to serve Higgins iced coffee, but this he curtly refused, asking instead for green tea. He ate only a single slice of bread, never touching the salad or the fried eggs, then asked: 'Do they sell English-language newspapers around here?' They ought to have them at the local distributor's, Toshio answered, still in too deep a fog to go out and buy one for his guest.

'I'm taking Mrs Higgins to the kabuki theatre today,' said Kyoko. 'She says her husband is going to be busy. We'll be eating out, so what will you do?' Toshio could hardly say he was going to buy a couple of women with Higgins, and Higgins, who could certainly overhear this conversation, was busy licking another cigar and never said a word. 'That's all right, I'll find something to do,' said Toshio.

Mrs Higgins had got hold of Keiichi and was trying to make him learn English pronunciation. 'Good morning, how are you?' He kept responding with sheer nonsense, obviously wanting to be left alone, but she would not give up.

'Why don't you leave Keiichi with your mother?' Toshio suggested quietly in the kitchen.

'She's not feeling well. Why?'

'You're sure to be coming home late tonight, and spending all that time with grown-ups will just tire him out. Besides, he'll get into the habit of staying up late.'

'Don't worry, he gets along beautifully with Mrs Higgins, and he can learn a little English from her, too.' Kyoko may have thought Toshio was finding fault with her for leaving the house like that with Mrs Higgins, and she added sulkily: 'Here's a better idea. Why don't you come home early and babysit? I don't see why you're so worried about him developing new habits. He never goes to bed until you get home, no matter how late. He says he's "waiting up for Papa".' With this unfavourable shift in wind direction, Toshio left the kitchen. Keiichi's happy twittering attracted his attention to the garden, where Higgins, cigar in mouth, was slowly pushing the lawnmower they had bought when the lawn was first planted and left thereafter in the storage shed. His form was a perfect replica of an advertising poster's.

'Oh, please, Mr Higgins,' shouted Kyoko, 'please don't do that.' And to Toshio: 'I asked you to mow the lawn, didn't I? That thing is too heavy for me. I'm so embarrassed.'

The ladies were going to the beauty parlour and then on to kabuki, they said, departing with Keiichi after lunch. Toshio's hangover had passed, but he could not leave Higgins at home alone and, for something to do, suggested a beer after Higgins had finished mowing and had rinsed himself off in the bath. 'Have you got whisky?' Toshio found himself keeping Higgins company in an authentic drinking bout with the sun still high and pouring himself a whisky and water even after Higgins had left for his three o'clock appointment, when it was too late to go to work. Having nothing better to do, he peeked into the bedroom upstairs and found it littered with Mrs Higgins' clothing. Inspection of a suitcase revealed a dozen or more gaudily coloured panties that he could not conceive of as belonging to that little old lady.

Toshio was good and drunk by the time they met at Hotel N at seven o'clock. 'What do you say?' he started in playfully on Higgins. 'You can take both girls and I'll keep out of your way. You've got a numbah one gahru tonight, old boy. Caviar. Yoo noh? Caviar inside.' Higgins did not understand. 'In a word, cunt. Yoo noh? Eets rike caviar inside.' Higgins, it appeared, had fooled around quite a bit in his day, because he recognized this and laughed aloud when he heard 'octopus trap'. 'I know "string purse",' he volunteered.

They found the agent alone in the Sugamo hotel, his attitude wholly changed from what it had been last night when he was so quick to make promises. 'There's just a limited number of girls who are willing to take foreigners. And you didn't give me enough time. I did manage something, but she's not so young. I absolutely guarantee her technique, though.' She was thirty-two, he said, and used to work the American base at Tachikawa.

'How about mine?'

'For you, I've got a real nice one. Practically untouched.'

'Look, wouldn't she take him if I doubled her fee? This guy is an important client.' What if Higgins decided he didn't like the thirty-two-year-old? Toshio couldn't give him inferior goods after his promise of a numbah one. He was getting frantic.

'I'm afraid I can't force the girl,' the agent said almost loftily, 'but I will talk to her and see.'

'Please try. Money is no object.'

He found Higgins in the next room, sitting in the *tokonoma* to avoid the bedding spread all over the matted floor, and fiddling with his camera.

'Is all right to take pictures the young lady?' he asked.

Face shots would be no problem, but if they were going to be obscene photos like last night's, Toshio could not be sure. 'Okay, I'll try negotiating,' he said, now the compleat pimp.

Twenty minutes later the two girls arrived. The agent motioned Toshio aside. 'I got it all worked out. It looks okay for a double fee.'

'How about photos?'

'By which you mean . . . ?'

'Nudes. There's nothing to worry about. He's going straight back to America.'

'Well, the girl will have to decide for herself. You'd better talk to her,' he said, as if he expected her to refuse.

The young one was a slender beauty who could pass for a fashion model. The graduate GI whore – sitting slouchy and sullen – was a tough-looking woman with a square jaw. The two seemed not to know each other. Higgins stayed quiet in his *tokonoma* seat. This called for a little pimping.

'What's your name, honey?'

'Miyuki,' said the younger one.

'Meet Mistah Higgins-san,' he said, figuring there was no need to use a pseudonym. 'Your room is over here.' He showed them the way, letting Higgins into the room first and explaining to the girl, 'This American likes cameras and he wants to take your picture. He'll be going straight home, and you'll be in his album to represent Japanese womanhood. Of course there'll be some money –'

'Not me, mister. No deal.' She glared at him as if he had been the one with the camera.

Dragging himself back to his room, he found the graduate in a black slip, and though his heart wasn't in it, he gave himself up to his drunkenness and took his clothes off. He had no idea what it was supposed to mean, but the minute he lay down she purred, 'Baby, I'm a widow,' and stretched out on top of him, whining. Her famous 'technique' was strictly for her own satisfaction. Maybe this was what she had learned to do for foreigners. She started kissing him all over and digging her nails in, while Toshio struggled to keep the brand of infidelity from being impressed on his skin. His only stimulus the exact opposite kind of scene that he vividly imagined must be taking place in the next room between Higgins and Miyuki, who could justly be called a beautiful girl, Toshio eventually climaxed and went to take a bath, there to discover himself splotched with sickening red love bites on the side, the upper arm, close to a nipple – and suddenly he was sober.

He sent the graduate away and started drinking beer from the fridge, but still there was no sign of Higgins. Lying down, he dozed off for a while and woke with a start just as the two of them were coming into the room, Miyuki clinging to Higgins without a trace of her former venom.

'Oh, Higgins-san, your Japanese is so good!' Now she was paying him compliments.

'Thank you very much,' said Higgins, rewinding the film in his camera. So he had managed to get his pictures, too.

The agent called to ask how everything had gone. 'All right,' said Toshio.

'What I'm really calling about is this first-class *shiro-kuro* couple I'm handling. How do you think your foreign friend would like them? I doubt if you can see a show like this anywhere else.' It would be thirty thousand yen, complete with a blue film, he said. The man had been a big hit in the Asakusa entertainment district, had stopped performing for a while and now was making a comeback. His thing was truly magnificent and well worth a look.

'Higgins-san, yoo noh what they call *shiro-kuro*?'

'No, I don't.'

'Eh, obsheen show, ne. Fahcking show.'

'I understand,' he grinned.

'Fine,' he said to the agent, 'make it tomorrow, six o'clock.' And to Higgins: 'They'll do it here, toomohrow, Japahnese numbah one penis.'

Higgins nodded.

Again they went from one Ginza bar to another, Higgins in no way hesitant about being treated. Of course, if he *had* taken out his wallet, Toshio would have indignantly stopped him. Kyoko was still up when they got home after one last stop in Roppongi for sushi.

'I wish you had told me you were going to be with Mr Higgins,' she said resentfully. 'I started worrying when you were so late. Mrs Higgins told me you were out together drinking again. I was awfully embarrassed.' Was it all right for Toshio to stay out every night? Didn't he have to go to work? There had been several calls from the office, she said pointedly.

'What's the difference? He's your guest, isn't he? I'm providing all this service, so what are you complaining about?'

'Service doesn't have to mean drinking every night until three and four in the morning. He can't take that kind of pace. He's an old man.'

Who's an old man? he wanted to say, but that was out of the question.

'And that old lady could learn some manners, too, the way she goes poking into everything. She was inspecting the fridge!' Was the mother-in-law impulse something they had in America, too? she wondered aloud. Unable to pick a fight with Toshio over the guests she had inflicted on herself, Kyoko snuggled up to him. But if this was going to lead to love-making, Toshio had the evening's event to worry about. It would be too strange for him to stay in his underwear in this hot weather, but if he got undressed, she'd see the love bites.

'I'll take a bath.' He pressed her back nonchalantly.

'You can't,' she snapped. 'Mrs Higgins washed herself inside the tub and drained the dirty water.' It would have been so much trouble to clean the tub, fill it again and wait for the water to heat up that she and Keiichi had gone without bathing. 'And you can put up with it, too!' She turned angrily away, and he lay down again, relieved.

Aware of the fatigue that follows a binge, that sensation of being dragged into darkness, Toshio was still wide awake in another part of his mind.

What is it that makes me perform such service for this old man? When I'm around him, what makes me feel I have to give everything I've got to make him happy? He comes from the country that killed my father, but I don't resent him at all. Far from it, I feel nostalgically close to him. What am I doing when I buy him drinks and women? Trying to cancel out a fourteen-year-old's terror at the sight of those huge Occupation soldiers? Paying him back for the food they sent when we were so hungry we couldn't bear it – the parachuted special rations, the consignments of soya bean dregs that were nothing but animal feed to the Americans? Maybe it's true they were just getting rid of their agricultural surplus on us, but how many thousands and thousands of people would have starved to death if the Americans hadn't sent corn when they did? Still, this doesn't explain why I feel so close to Higgins. Maybe he feels that same nostalgia, recalling the days when he was here with the Occupation. Considering his age, the time he spent in Japan might have been the fullest period of his life, something he had been missing and reverted to the minute he came back here. That might explain his almost insulting behaviour, his serene willingness to let me go on buying him drinks. That's not hard to understand. But the question is, why should I go along with it? Why should I be so happy to play the pimp the way the grown-ups did back then? No blessing is bestowed on me for drinking booze with some lousy Yankee. Could it be that I'm feeling nostalgic for those days, too? No, that shouldn't be. Those were miserable times, when you were so hungry you learned to chew your cud like a cow, bringing the food back for a second, a third taste. Swimming out from the beach at Kōroen and being chased by an American boat and almost drowning; getting beaten up in Naka-no-shima by an angry American soldier whose girl had run out on him: no, however you looked at it, there were no happy memories. It was the bombing, after all, that ruined my mother's health and finally killed her; it was America, you could say, that put my sister's life in my hands and caused us so much suffering. Why, then, should the sight of Higgins make me want to do such service? Is this like the virgin who can never forget the repulsive man who raped her?

The new day brought back Kyoko's good spirits. They would be taking a bus tour of Tokyo, something Mrs Higgins wanted very much to do. 'If it weren't for an opportunity like this, I'd never take Keiichi to see the Sengakuji Temple,' she said, Kyoko herself far from lacking in enthusiasm. 'What are you going to do today? With Mr Higgins again?'

'Um.'

'Come home early tonight. I'm making dinner for them.'

Higgins had got up early and gone out for a stroll, undaunted by his ignorance of the area. 'There is a nice church,' he said with satisfaction, drinking a whisky. Toshio, usually confident of his capacity, was unable to join him. He could not ignore work completely, and he invited Higgins to leave with him. But Higgins answered simply, 'I will relax a little more. Feel free.' There was nothing Toshio could do but hand over the key and ask him to lock the door when he went out. Higgins assented as easily as if he had been sponging off them for years.

When Toshio explained to his staff somewhat apologetically that he had a guest from America, the total absence of any hint from him until then of contact with foreigners made their unanimous surprise that much greater. 'Are we going to move in on the US market? Japanese animation techniques have a good reputation over there.' Toshio did not feel like explaining how far off the mark that was. 'If you need an interpreter, I'd be glad to offer my services,' said another young man, his eyes sparkling.

'No, he's just a rich American here for a visit.'

'Wow, that's terrific. An old friend of yours?'

'Uh-huh, from the Occupation.' This almost had the feel of truth for Toshio himself. To him, all Americans were Occupation soldiers, and an American child was just a small Occupation soldier. This was something his young staff could never understand. For them, America was a place you had to visit once, like a famous temple, a place where something holy rubbed off on you, a place that enhanced your image, a traveller's paradise where you could get by for next to nothing if you used your connections cleverly.

They went to the Sugamo hotel again as arranged, Toshio asking on the way how things had gone yesterday. Higgins winked. 'She had a very lovely body. But my models in America have better curves,' he said, boasting of the obvious. All right, brother, hold on to your hat, now you're going to see the *shiro-kuro* show and numbah one penis, the pride of Japan. Let not their magnificence astound you. Toshio was eager to get started. Soon the agent appeared with the couple, the man on the small side, about Toshio's age, the woman in her mid-twenties. They bowed with exaggerated formality and withdrew to change their clothes.

'This is his first performance for a Foreigner-san, he tells me. Anyhow, he's got an amazing thing there. I get a complex just looking at it, it's so huge,' the agent expressed his earlier opinion. Eventually, the couple appeared in light robes and lay on the floor mattress. Unable to get a good view, Higgins pointed towards the head of the mattress and signalled that he would like to change his seat. 'Please, by all means, get as close as you like. Take a good look at Japan's Forty-Eight Holds.'

'Fohty-eighto pojishon,' Toshio explained, eliciting a nod from Higgins.

The man started by plastering the girl with passionate kisses on the lips, the neck, down to the breasts, and then she was panting, her robe opening bit by bit, revealing more and more flesh, when suddenly there was a loud 'Thump!' and Toshio saw that Higgins, engrossed in the spectacle, had fallen over sideways from his low pile of floor cushions near the couple's pillow. He reseated himself calmly, without embarrassment. That'll teach you, thought Toshio, and suddenly he realized:

The reason I'm doing all this service for Higgins is that somehow, one way or another, I want to bring him to his knees. I don't care if it's by drinking him unconscious or driving him crazy over a woman, I want to turn this grinning, maddeningly self-possessed son of a bitch on to something – anything – Japanese and make him knuckle under. That's what I'm after!

Soon the woman was completely naked and obviously no longer acting in response to the seemingly endless foreplay. She was truly dying for the man, who now spread her legs and, poised before her on his knees, opened the front of his robe. Indeed, his was equipment worthy of a veteran, for even now it had yet to attain its full heroic stature but rose, ever dark and coiling, in defiance of the coming storm. The man spat into his palm and began to massage himself slowly. Higgins stretched his neck forward, staring intently. The woman by now was frantic, wrapping her legs around the man and pulling him closer. He continued with his prayer-like manipulation, which did result in some additional upthrust, but he was far from ready to come to grips with anything. He went on like this with his right hand, caressing the woman's body with his left, and after he had taken several steps that were familiar to Toshio from occasions when performance failed to match desire after heavy drinking, he simply lay on top of her. The woman moaned, but clearly union had not taken place. Was this part of the act? But no, the man wore a look of exasperation. He returned to his knees and started massaging himself again, having shrunk in the meantime to something far short of numbah one. Aware at last of what was happening, the woman got on top and used her mouth, but there was no sign of recovery.

Toshio glanced at the agent, who wore a twisted smile and looked very puzzled. The man now had his face down near Higgins' feet and, bathed in sweat, he knit his brow and closed his eyes as if in intense meditation. Every now and then he would spread his legs wide like a woman and stretch them out, while the woman ran her fingers over his chest, his thighs, the desperate valour of her efforts clear to all. Before he knew it, Toshio was straining as if he himself had been struck impotent.

What the hell are you doing? You're numbah one, aren't you? Come on, show this American. That huge thing of yours is the pride of Japan. Knock him out with it! Scare the shit out of him!

It was a matter of pecker nationalism: his thing had to stand, or it would mean dishonour to the race. Toshio almost wanted to take the man's place, his own thing now taut and ready. Noticing this, he glanced at Higgins' crotch, but nothing was happening there.

'Yoshi-chan, what's wrong?' the agent cried out, unable to contain himself after nearly half an hour's struggle.

Lying on his back, too exhausted even to sit up, the man answered hoarsely, 'I'm sorry, this has never happened before. I don't know what to say.'

The woman, too, was at a loss. 'Maybe he's tired. This never happens.'

'Well, take a break, have a beer,' said Toshio, less discomfited before Higgins than sorry for this man who had drained all his energy trying to achieve erection.

Refusing the beer, the man said with extreme formality: 'This has been terribly embarrassing. I will return your money, and I hope to have an opportunity to perform for you as a complimentary service.'

'No, not at all, don't let it worry you. This happens to men all the time. Come on, have a drink,' Toshio tried to comfort him, but the man fled from the room. Higgins was silently licking another cigar.

'This was a totally unheard-of occurrence. To think that Yoshi-chan could have failed!' said the agent, recounting tales of the prowess of that magnificent organ. 'I'm sure this didn't happen just because a Foreigner-san was here!' he concluded, turning to Higgins with a laugh.

This man they call Yoshi-chan must be in his mid-thirties, and if so, Higgins might well have been the cause of his sudden impotence. If Yoshi-chan had the same sort of experience that I did in the Occupation – and he must have, whatever the differences between Tokyo and Osaka-Kobe – if he has memories of 'Gibu me chewingamu', if he can recall being frightened by the soldiers' huge builds, then it's no wonder he shrivelled up like that. Yoshi-chan might have been in a state of perfect professional detachment, but when Higgins sat down over him like a ton of bricks, inside his head the jeeps started rolling, the strains of 'Comu, comu, eburybody' began to echo again, and he recalled, as clearly as if it were yesterday, the hopeless feeling when there was no more fleet, no more Zero fighters, recalled the emptiness of the blinding, burning sky above the burnt-out ruins, and in that instant the impotence overtook him. Higgins could never understand that. No Japanese can understand it, probably, if he's not my age. No Japanese who can have an ordinary conversation with an American, who can go to America and have Americans all around him without going crazy, who can see an American enter his field of vision and feel no need to brace himself, who can speak English without embarrassment, who condemns Americans, who applauds Americans, no Japanese like this can understand the America inside Yoshi-chan – inside me.

Exhausted, Toshio said to Higgins, 'We ought to go home now. Kyoko's making a sukiyaki party.'

'I must excuse myself. Am going to see a friend at the embassy.' And after a 'Thank you very much' to the agent that sounded like pure sarcasm, he walked away with a brisk at-homeness unthinkable after a twenty-year absence from the country.

Toshio found Kyoko in a rage. 'The nerve of the woman! She knew I was making dinner for them. All of a sudden she says she's going to stay with friends in Yokohama tonight!' On the table stood a large platter of the finest Matsuzaka beef and enormous quantities of all the other sukiyaki ingredients in anticipation of large American appetites. 'Anyhow, the three of us will eat it. And you'd better have a lot!' Then Kyoko started in on Mrs Higgins. 'I couldn't do enough for that old lady, but she never noticed. I was explaining everything on the tour bus, but she just kept reading her English guidebook. And she's so stingy! I saw the things she picked out when we went shopping – all cheap. The toys she bought for Keiichi are like what the street vendors sell. That doesn't stop her from opening her big mouth, though. I can be standing right there when she gets mad at Keiichi and she'll scold him without a nod to me, his mother. I've never seen such rudeness. They come in here and expect us to do everything for them. All right, they were nice to me in Hawaii, so to show my appreciation I invited them to stay with us, but how long do they plan to stay here? Did he tell you? How long do they think they're going to stay here?'

'Who knows? A month?'

'Never! I won't have it! I'll tell them outright they have to leave!'

Higgins will go back sooner or later, I suppose. But it won't make any difference. As long as I live, there will be an American sitting inside me like a ton of bricks, and every now and then this American inside me, my American, will drag me around by the nose and make me scream, 'Gibu me chewingamu, Q-Q,' because what I have is an incurable disease, the Great American Allergy.

'Toshio, what are you going to do tomorrow? Just let them take care of themselves.'

I suppose I'll get him a geisha next time, for variety. Japahnese geisha gahru, courtesy of Toshio the pimp.

And from a mound that never diminished, however quickly he moved his chopsticks, Toshio went on stuffing his already full stomach with the prized cuts of beef, eating and eating in joyless abandonment as if it had been American *hijiki*.

HOSHINO TOMOYUKI

Pink

Translated by Brian Bergstrom

The sixth of August marked the start of the nine-day streak of blistering heat. Just after one in the afternoon, Tokyo registered forty degrees Celsius. It was the highest temperature on record, and the heat kept rising, reaching 42.7 degrees two hours later. The humidity never dropped below 80 per cent, and the sky, though cloudless, was thick with a pale mist. Older people greeted each other, laughing, with lines like *Next week is the Bon festival, but the dead might go back early – it's too hot even for them!* Perhaps because age had numbed their senses, they seemed unbothered by the heat, and several of these very senior citizens were content to stand talking in the sunshine that beat down on Tokyo's Kaki-no-ike Park. It seemed to Naomi, as she listened to two old biddies go on while she watched her niece play in the sandpit, that it might be a good idea if they thought about their own welfare rather than that of the dead. Or maybe they *were* the dead, having returned for Bon, but without realizing it they were chattering away thinking they were still alive. Though why the dead would want to come back to this prison called life – just because it was that time of year again – was beyond her. *If I had the chance to end it all,* muttered Naomi to herself, *I'd leave this world in an instant and never look back.* What was her problem? Why was she so irritated, she didn't even know these women, why was she getting so carried away? It was the heat, the goddamn heat, and it was her goddamn stupid sister, who insisted that Naomi take her daughter outside to play at least once a day – for her health – even in this toxic weather. *Why don't you take her outside?* thought Naomi, but she nonetheless did as her sister asked, the promise of a thousand yen for her trouble pushing her out the door.

Naomi's two-year-old niece Pink (*what a stupid name to give a kid*) was

445

absorbed with her playmates in some sort of sandpit public-works project, and so, seeing that other mothers were keeping an eye on things, Naomi left the play area and walked over to the edge of the pond to have a smoke. There were no trees to filter the sunlight, which poured down from the yellow sun like sulphurous gas. Even the cicadas, whose tinny drone was usually inescapable, were silent. The hot air oozed with humidity, sticking to Naomi like a swarm of insects. It felt less as though she was sweating than that her skin was melting and running down her body. Everything around her seemed not entirely solid, a series of colours running together like so many abandoned scoops of ice cream. *When the temperature gets high enough, even the landscape melts*, thought Naomi.

Little bodies began to fall one by one from above. They were birds, dropping down for a dip in the pond. They gathered at the edge, splashing themselves with water. Sparrows and white-eyes, starlings and bulbuls: there were so many of them. A few birds actually immersed themselves in the water – ducks, Naomi thought, but when they broke the surface, she could see they were sparrows. She saw some dive straight into the water. Naomi counted the seconds – one . . . two . . . – and then, flapping their wings, the birds emerged and flew up into the sky.

It wasn't just sparrows. The white-eyes, the bulbuls, the starlings: they all began to dive into the water, as if imitating the sparrows. At one point, the oversized body of a crow crashed into the water, causing the smaller birds to fly off. Only the pigeons, perhaps unable to dive, scuttled back and forth at the water's edge.

The crow finally left, and the sparrows returned. They dived into the water again and again, twisting their bodies and spinning in the air. Had sparrows always been waterfowl? It began to seem so to Naomi. As they emerged from the pond, water spraying, the wet sparrows gleamed in the sun. Suddenly, in their midst, shiny things began to leap from the pond. They were fish! Similar in colour and size to the sparrows, the fish were flying alongside the birds just above the surface of the water.

Naomi crouched down and dipped a finger into the pond. As expected, the water was warm – too warm. The fish were suffering. They were throwing themselves into the air for the same reason the birds were plunging into the water. Seeming to follow the sparrows' lead, the fish twisted and somersaulted in the air. Were they trying to fan themselves? Birds have wings; humans have hands; fish have only their bodies to twist and turn if they want to generate a breeze.

Fish were jumping and twirling all across the surface of the pond. The pond was alive with the spray they produced, a silver mist that, carried by the hot wind, cooled Naomi's face.

Naomi was gripped with a sudden joy. This place was a living hell. No creatures were dead, but they felt closer to death than the dead. Assaulted by such unbearable conditions, they longed to flee their existence. Birds wished to stop being birds and become fish, fish longed to stop being fish and become birds, cats wanted to be people, people longed to become anything but people. And so they all went crazy, flailing and flopping, spinning and twirling. But wasn't it fun too? To spin, to twirl?

A crowd gathered to watch the leaping fish, but Naomi broke away from them and began twirling slowly by herself, arms outstretched like a ballerina. She spun clockwise as viewed from above, her body the axis of the clock, arms tracing a circle parallel to the ground. The soft breeze produced by her twirling touched the sweat on her skin, cooling it. Slowly, gently, so as not to get dizzy, she twirled her way back to the sandpit where Pink was playing.

Naomi raised her head to look up, which gave her the illusion the sky was drawing closer, as if she were floating up into space as she spun. Spiralling like a drill or a shuttlecock, she bored her way upwards through the layers of air. To spin and spin until you moved like the wind itself – would that make her a tornado? Well, nothing so strong as a tornado – a whirlwind? That's it, I'm a whirlwind. If she became a whirlwind, she'd stay cool. Light. She could fly.

Naomi lost track of where her feet were carrying her. She brought her eyes down from the sky and stopped spinning. She was near the sandpit, and just about to run into a metal post. Now the heat pressed in on her from all sides, and sweat poured from her like water from a spring. She felt wobbly, and her head ached. She should never have done this. Once you start to twirl, you can't stop, because if you do, it'll be even worse than before you began. The only way out was to spin and spin forever.

Naomi walked over to Pink, saying, 'Time to go home!' as she grabbed the child's hands. The moment she did this, she was struck by a feeling that something wasn't right. Naomi looked around, inspected Pink from head to toe, but nothing seemed out of place. Still, Naomi couldn't shake the feeling that some unknown had been introduced into the world around her, something that created a subtle but inescapable dissonance. It was as if everything around her had been replaced by an exquisite fake.

In order to collect herself, Naomi, still hand in hand with Pink, spread her arms to create a circle between them and began to spin with the child, singing softly. *Bird in the cage, bird in the ca-a-age* . . . Pink danced happily even when her legs tangled up as they spun. Naomi didn't want Pink to get dizzy, so every few spins they would walk side by side for a bit until Pink said, 'Let's play bird-in-the-cage again!' They'd re-form the circle between them, repeating the pattern again and again until they reached home. Exhausted by the heat and the excitement, Pink fell asleep at once. Not long after, Naomi was asleep too.

That evening, they watched the television news over dinner; it was all about the heatwave. Not only Tokyo but all of Japan had seen temperatures exceeding forty degrees, with 392 people hospitalized and 56 dead, mostly elderly. But the story that really grabbed people's attention was that of a seventeen-year-old schoolgirl in Fukui who'd spun and spun under the blazing sun until she succumbed to heatstroke and died. According to friends who were with her, the girl had said, *Hey, what if we spin like fans – wouldn't that cool us off?* And so she tried it, and it worked so well she invited her friends to join her – *Oh, it feels so good! Try it, try it!* – and they did, but soon, dizzy and nauseated, they lay down to rest, and, after a while, the girl lay down beside them; when it came time to get up, she was still, and when they tried to rouse her they realized she was gone. A so-called expert compared her to someone trapped on the top floor of a burning high-rise choosing to jump out of a window rather than face the flames; it was a perfectly logical choice for that person, not abnormal in the least.

'Things are so fucking awful they're going to die either way. Let's not beat about the bush,' Naomi carped at the television.

'Could you not use that kind of language in front of Pink?' her sister objected. 'As it is, all she does is imitate everything you do.'

'It's only natural. I'm the daddy around here. She's a daddy's girl.'

'No one asked you to be her daddy. She's better off without one. All I asked was for you to be her big sister.'

Appalled at the utter immaturity of Pink's father, Naomi's sister had dumped him and kept Pink. It was like throwing away a box of sweets and keeping the prize that came with it. She was working at a nursing home to make ends meet, and had invited Naomi, who had graduated from university but was without a job, to look after Pink in exchange for a place to live. Naomi had accepted the invitation without a moment's hesitation. She'd been stuck in the couch-surfing life and, nearing the limits of her friends' patience, she'd been on the verge of signing up with the Self-Defence Forces anyway. The truth was that Naomi had been fixated on the SDF since she was little; she had the feeling that her sister's offer was, at least in part, an effort to stop her from enlisting.

After he was dumped by Naomi's sister, Pink's father thought he would 'toughen himself up' by participating in right-wing demonstrations, and about a year later he showed up on her doorstep, the fashionable street style that had been his sole redeeming feature replaced by a tired old kimono that clung to his thickening frame. *I'm an adult now. Give me another chance!* When Naomi's sister had asked what he meant by 'adult', he replied that he could now state his beliefs without fear even as the world looked unkindly upon him, that he could remain cool and resolute even as he was blasted by the harsh winds of public opinion, that he had learned how to stand his ground even if it meant putting his body on the line and that he would put everything on the line to protect himself and his family. Naomi's sister had heard enough, and she told him to get out. But he refused, saying that he was no longer the weakling who gives up and leaves just because a woman tells him to.

As the confrontation escalated, Naomi returned with Pink from one of their customary trips to the park and couldn't help breaking in. She'd once seen Pink's father in action – on a street corner with a group yelling into megaphones for revival of the colonial policy of Five Races Under One Union.[1] 'You joined the right-wingers to find yourself – what do you think you're going to find here? There's nothing for you here, not yourself or anything else.'

Enraged by Naomi's ridicule, Pink's father began yelling, though it wasn't clear exactly what he was saying. Naomi cut him off: 'This is you being an adult? All you've done is learned how to yell! Everything else is the same; you're still a little boy begging for attention: *Mummy, Mummy, listen to me, Mummy, please!* A real adult would start by asking my sister what she needs!' Pink's father slunk away, swearing they would get what was coming to them.

Naomi's sister was left feeling uneasy, worried that he would try to get revenge. But ever since then, Pink had stuck to Naomi like glue, from the beginning of every day to its end.

'Naomi was smoking!'

'Telltale!'

Naomi took Pink's cheeks in her hands and squeezed them, rubbing them up and down. Delighted, Pink shouted, 'You were smoking! You were smoking!' in the hope of prolonging the cheek squeezing. As she dutifully complied, Naomi noticed that the small bruise Pink had got earlier in the day – she'd bumped into the doorknob while playing around as they got ready to go to the park – had disappeared without a trace.

Starting the next day, Naomi's sister insisted that Pink be out of the house so she could have some time to herself, if only in the morning or evening when the temperature fell below forty degrees. Each day, Pink would rush to the door, ready to start playing bird-in-the-cage. Her body plastered with cooling patches, Naomi would do as she was told.

There were now – several days into the heatwave – endless reports of people sustaining burn injuries from cars and rocks that had heated up during the day. What with streets and buildings and the humid air holding stored-up heat, the temperature failed to dip below thirty-five at night, and hot winds blew continuously from the outdoor units of cranked-up air conditioners as if they were clothes dryers. Day after day, the number of people dying from the heat reached triple digits, and anywhere you went, you'd encounter the corpses of small animals. On the fifth day of the heatwave, the city of Kōfu saw temperatures reach 50.2 degrees. It was a new record for the country. Where Naomi lived with her sister and niece, the temperature soared above forty-five by noon. When things 'cooled off', dropping down to forty in the late afternoon, Naomi would leave the house with Pink. Almost no one was outside, the area a ghost town, the streets like vacant sets. Pink and Naomi made their way to the park, spinning and sweating all the while. Naomi drank bottles of Pocari Sweat in an attempt to replace the liquid draining from her body. By the time they reached the park, she looked as if she'd emerged from a soak in a hot spring.

All signs of life had disappeared from Kaki-no-ike Park, and a terrible stench rose from the pond. The water level was low, the surface oily and lumpy with dead fish. Not just dead fish – dead birds were mixed in with them – and some sort of larger striped animal, part of its bulk sticking up out of the water. Naomi didn't want to know what it might be.

She took Pink into the shade beneath a huge zelkova tree, and they began to play bird-in-the-cage. The ground was pitted and uneven, not only because the earth had hardened and cracked in the heat, but also because the tree's roots, seeking water, were extending crazily in all directions. If a tree concentrates its energy in its roots, it can displace the earth. Most plants in conditions like these might wither and die, but a tree that was strong enough could fight for what water there was.

On the other side of the pond was a large camphor tree. Someone over there had tied a rope around a branch and was twirling in mid-air from it. *So, somebody else had the same idea!* Naomi thought appreciatively as she and Pink went to take a closer look.

'It doesn't hurt, hanging like that?' Naomi asked the young man.

'Not at all, it's nice and cool!' he replied. 'Gives me goosebumps.'

'So you're doing what the fish do?'

'Fish? No, no. I saw it on TV! You can spin like this and feel cool – and you can get dizzy enough to forget everything!'

'The other day the fish in the pond were jumping and spinning in the air, trying to get cool too.'

'But they're all dead now, right?'

The young man grabbed the rope and nimbly pulled himself up its length to sit on the branch. 'I'm not just cooling off, you know,' he said as he untied the rope from his waist. 'I discovered that if I really let myself spin, it was like I was getting . . . purified. If I was feeling depressed, I'd feel better, as if the depression flew off somewhere while I was going around and around. Like I was in a salad spinner. So I began to spin faster and faster. Pushing the limit, you know? I would get sick and vomit. And I would sweat, really sweat. It was like detox. Like bidding farewell to parts of me that were bad. And as I got rid of more and more toxins, I could spin as much as I wanted without getting sick. It was the most amazing feeling. Like it wasn't me who was spinning, but some larger force that was spinning me. It felt good giving myself up to this great force I'd never noticed before. I don't know how to put it. Maybe it's like life taking over, so you can just go with it, naturally. Like letting go and feeling easy, feeling . . . peace.'

The young man had descended from the tree and was now standing in front of Naomi and Pink.

'Huh. Well,' Naomi said, 'I've been spinning a little these days, but I've never felt anything like that.'

'It's not just me. I mean, there're a lot of people who feel this way. They begin by just spinning, but then they have some kind of awakening. And they realize that the spinning is really a kind of prayer.'

Naomi felt irritation bubble up within her. 'Prayer?' she said, her voice rising. 'To whom? For what? I don't get it.'

'A prayer to a larger force, or power, kind of. Asking it to make us suffer less. Like a prayer to the heat, even. Or a prayer for rain.'

'I take it this *larger power* hasn't heard our prayers yet?'

'Maybe the prayer isn't powerful enough yet. I believe that if enough people come together and unite their feelings, something will happen. It's like a prophecy.'

'So, after prayer comes a prophecy?'

'It's not just wishful thinking on my part. There's really something to this, I know it. And I'm not the only one. When you're spinning, you get this feeling that, I don't know, you're getting stronger, you're growing. You really feel it. Everyone feels this way, so we've started to believe that if we can gather all this power together, we can really make something happen.'

'I've never felt anything like that.'

'Maybe it's rude of me to say, but I think your spinning must be inadequate. You have to do it more, devote half a day or more to it, and you'll see. The feeling will come, and it will be real.'

'I haven't been spinning all day every day or anything, but I've been doing it pretty regularly for five days now, and all I've noticed is that it feels good while I'm going around and around, but once I stop I feel exhausted. Isn't that normal?'

'Five days? You're more experienced than me! You started the first day of the heatwave then, right? That makes you one of the first to be enlightened! Don't you think it's strange? That so many people began spinning that day – not just you but people all over Japan? Nobody was copying anybody else – they just started doing it naturally.'

'You mean like that girl who died?'

'Yes! Our first martyr. I myself only began spinning when I heard about her on the news – I'm just a wannabe! Who am I to say anything to you – you're the real deal, starting spontaneously like that. What made you do it?'

'I told you, I was watching the fish jump and twist in the air and imitated them. It wasn't some revelation from above.'

'If you see fish jumping and twisting, do you always start doing it too? Did anyone else watching the fish start spinning?'

Naomi shook her head. All she knew was that she had separated herself from the crowd that had gathered around the pond and started twirling, off on her own. She had separated herself from the others because she knew she'd be behaving differently from them.

'So I'm right. The fish might have been the inspiration, but it was a larger force that moved you.'

Naomi was shaken. She began to doubt that her spinning was a result of her own intention. But she didn't agree with the young man that some higher force had possessed her, either. That wasn't how it felt. It just seemed as if the only way to respond to such crazy heat was to do something she would never normally do.

'What about tornadoes or whirlwinds? They're touched off by forces larger than themselves, right? Natural forces, like gravity and atmospheric pressure. But no matter how hard you pray to the atmosphere or to gravity, they won't make the heat go down.'

'Do you think it was gravity or the atmosphere that made you start spinning?'

'Well, no, but –'

'Were all the people who started spinning that day moved by the same force that produces a whirlwind?'

'I don't know anything about anybody else. All I know is that I thought if I became a whirlwind I might cool off.'

'Most of the people who started spinning that day describe it like that.

They thought if they could become a whirlwind, or become a breeze, or become a fan, then they'd finally get cool.'

'It doesn't seem so strange that people who are all subjected to the same unusual heat would end up having similar thoughts.'

'We could stand here and debate all day, but what's the point? We should go where the others are and see for ourselves. Even if you don't end up agreeing with me, you'll at least see what I'm talking about.'

'Where the others are? Where's that?'

'Just over this way, at Kumano Shrine.'

The young man spun around as he led the way to the shrine. Naomi and Pink began to spin too. Before long, the three of them formed a big circle as they continued on their way. Pink shrank shyly away from the young man at first, but gradually relaxed and began to return his smiles.

Even before they entered the grounds of Kumano Shrine, they could sense a force emanating from inside. And once they passed through the torii gate, they found the place packed with people, their body heat and moisture rising like steam from an internal combustion engine. They were twirling, all of them, as if intoxicated. All in the same direction too: clockwise. Completely silent, their heads slightly tilted, staring into space through half-lidded eyes as if near sleep, their arms spread like butterfly wings, they spun around and around in the same direction at the same speed. It was so quiet, as if the shrine were sucking the sound from the air, while the energy the twirling crowd exuded was so strong it seemed able to blast any onlooker into the air.

The first to join them was Pink. She began awkwardly, losing her footing and bumping into one of the twirlers. As if drawn in by Pink, Naomi too started to move. Out of the corner of her eye, she saw the young man walking away.

Naomi closed her eyes completely and felt her own self-generated wave of energy coursing through her body. If she could just ride that wave, she could spin and spin forever. She let herself go with it, her arms rising of their own accord, like the wings of a bird. She tried to spin a bit faster and felt resistance in her body, as if it were putting on brakes. Before long, she realized that this resistance, like walking against a strong wind, came from the wave of energy produced by the people spinning around her. The wave she was riding came not just from her own movements but everyone else's too. The waves produced by the spinning of each individual interacted in complex ways, rippling the air within the shrine's grounds, and Naomi rode the waves with great skill. Everyone around her was riding these complex rippling waves, moving with them and putting up not the least resistance, lost in the motion. It was like music. Like dancing to music. Soon Naomi felt her consciousness on the verge of leaving her completely. She had the feeling that if she passed out, she would ascend to another level and be able to spin furiously, on and on, even unconsciously. Her insides would grow transparent, her self subsumed entirely by the trance. Surely more than half the people around her were spinning in such a state.

I might as well let go completely, thought Naomi, but as she did she became aware that the crowd had thinned significantly, and that there was only a smattering of fellow spinners left around her. The wave grew weak, depriving Naomi of the force that had been driving her, and she stopped. The heat descended once again upon her, and, pouring with sweat, Naomi took Pink by the hand and headed away from the shrine.

'It hurts, I said! Why aren't you listening to me?' yelled Pink, pulling her hand from Naomi's grasp. It was only then that Naomi realized she had been yanking Pink along.

'You're not respecting my will!'

What? Naomi looked hard at Pink. *Why is she talking like that?* Pink was clearly parroting the exact words that Naomi said to her sister all the time. But this was the first time Pink had said anything like that herself.

'I'm so sorry. Do you still feel sick?'

'My legs hurt.'

'We spun around too much, huh? That guy really got us going . . .' This last bit was addressed more to herself, but Pink replied nonetheless. 'Yeah, he's really cool.'

Pink kept complaining that her knees hurt, so they stopped to rest again and again as they made their way home, finally arriving only after night had fallen.

As soon as they walked into the house, Naomi's sister glared at Pink and sighed, 'Those clothes are already too tight for you, aren't they? We're going to have to get you some new ones.' Shaking her head, she added, 'It would be nice if you could take a break from growing once in a while, you know.'

Naomi, who didn't remember Pink's clothes being too small when she'd helped her get dressed that morning, dubiously pulled at a sleeve. It was indeed tight as a drum.

The next evening, Pink and Naomi found the young man spinning from the camphor tree again.

'I didn't think I'd see you here today!' he exclaimed.

'The kid kept pestering me, saying she wanted to go back to the shrine,' Naomi said, pointing at Pink.

'So why aren't you there?'

'I wanted to spin by myself,' Naomi replied, almost angrily.

The young man looked intently at Naomi from where he hung suspended in mid-air. 'Every day more people show up, so it's getting a bit hard to find room over at Kumano – maybe we should try Sampin Temple. It has bigger grounds.'

'I told you – I want to spin by myself. And anyway, why are *you* out here all by yourself?'

'I can't really handle crowds.'

'What? You were the one going on and on about everyone uniting in feeling and all that crap! Do as you say and not as you do – is that it?'

'I can pray here all by myself and still be united in feeling with everyone else.'

'There's a term for that, you know. Delusion.'

'It's like I said yesterday. It's a real feeling I have. And so I'm just fine out here all alone. But it's different for people like you. I really am someone who can't handle crowds, and so I know how people are when they truly want to be left alone. They're not like you. It's so obvious to me that all you really want is to melt completely into a crowd. Besides, I saw how you were yesterday.'

There was no denying it. Naomi hadn't gone back to the shrine because she was afraid of her desire to do it all again. Maybe this guy had her figured out, and that's why he was tempting her now with Sampin.

'But enough about me. What I want to know is why you can't stand being around other people.'

The young man clambered easily back up his rope and, standing on the branch, undid the knot at his waist before shimmying down to the ground.

'Have you heard of the Greater East Asian Friendship Society?'[2]

'Yeah. They're the Five Races Under One Union guys.'

This was the right-wing group Naomi's sister's ex had joined. Their idea was that, instead of East Asian countries squabbling all the time, they'd form an East Asian Union – like the European Union – and that East Asia would become a free economic zone. The headquarters would be in northern Kyushu, and a free-trade zone would be established in Kyushu or Okinawa or Hokkaido, where people from the union would be able to move in and out freely. The standard currency would be the Japanese yen and the standard language would be Japanese, with a major effort to spread the study of Japanese to all nations that were likely to participate. The government would strive to establish harmony with neighbouring countries and promote the doctrine of the Five Races Under One Union, in addition to which they would establish a strong military. Even now the society was staging monthly demonstrations advocating these positions.

'I wasn't bright enough to get into anything but a local vocational school no matter how hard I studied,' the young man said. 'I wasn't the kind to join a gang, so I wasn't popular with girls. My sport was gymnastics, and while I got pretty good at the rings and parallel bars, I was never better than anyone else who practised a lot. In other words, I was completely unremarkable – maybe below average. I never thought I'd be able to find a good job when I graduated, and sure enough, I didn't. Objectively speaking, I was disposable. But I wanted to improve myself, even just a little, and ended up getting interested in history. I joined a history group. Groups studying Japanese history, they're full of losers like me. Below average, socially awkward: they don't fit in anywhere and they're desperate not to feel like losers. These groups are hangouts for the serious-minded but mediocre. I joined one, and then, along with another guy from the group, joined the Greater East Asian Friendship Society.'

Naomi had seen enough of her sister's ex to understand exactly the kind of feeling the young man was describing. Come to think of it, this story wasn't so different from her own trajectory either, graduating from a third-rate university and applying to 108 companies only to be hired by none.

'And you know, I felt great when I did things with them. I could respect myself. We were serious, maybe not so bright, but committed to debating important things and doing something about them, unlike the thoughtless, lazy people all around us who went about their lives with no sense of urgency. That this pride might lead to arrogance was maybe inevitable; after all, I was only about twenty. But I had a strong sense that I was working on behalf of Japan. The group gave me responsibilities, I worked with the police and got permits, I was put in charge of a platoon of demonstrators.'

'*Platoon?*'

'Yeah, the society was organized into different levels, and each level had its captains and lieutenants and other borrowed military titles. They made me a sergeant major, and I led a platoon. The idea was that if the Japanese military did get re-established as the society hoped, a period of military experience was going to be required for membership.'

'Why?'

'So that we could defend ourselves without help. Self-reliance was a big thing in the society. We had slogans like *Rely not on others – let others rely on you!* Anyway, one day one of the demonstrations I was leading got into a clash with some anti-foreign group. Those guys are idiots – they think that Japan will benefit by picking fights with its neighbours. The basest, most thuggish way of thinking. The Greater East Asian Friendship Society was about establishing Japan's leadership of East Asia at a much higher level – we didn't want to dwell on petty differences. They never understood that. So they saw us as the enemy, and they targeted us that day. They were screaming stuff like *You want to sell out Japan! You're just a bunch of Koreans!* Some of my guys wanted to rise to their challenge, but I tried to keep everyone calm. The police trusted me, so they were on our side too. But the rookies in our group who wanted to fight started shouting me down and yelling that there was a government mole in the society. The anti-foreign idiots joined in, and soon all hell broke loose. Later, at a society meeting, I tried to explain what happened as calmly and clearly as I could. I thought that in a group focused on the big picture, reason would prevail over tough-guy talk, and so I couldn't believe what happened next. I was accused of being the mole, a traitor working for a government that was selling out its people, an agent provocateur causing division within the group, an enemy of the Japan that was to be, an anti-patriot. I was kicked out of the society. And you know who the leader of the charge against me was? My friend from the history group! To see friends turn on me before my eyes, willing to string me up in front of a group I was devoted to – it was like I died, really died, in that moment.'

'And so now crowds are a source of trauma for you.'

'That all these believers in self-reliance could suddenly turn into a mob like that . . . but now I understand what it was about. We thought we were using reason to bring about a revolution in society, but all we really wanted was to feel that our lives weren't useless, that we had purpose, had value; we were each trying to find ourselves but instead we ended up finding an "us". The content of the things we said or did didn't really matter. What was important was the feeling of "us".'

'You said it was obvious I wanted to melt into a crowd. Are you telling me I'm a candidate for something like the Greater East Asian Friendship Society?'

'I might have said that before. But not now. Because this "tornado dance" thing is pure. You don't do it to please anyone, even yourself. The joy and satisfaction are in the spinning itself, and all the unnecessary parts of the self fall away. There's no gap between one dancer's intentions and another's. That's why it's a kind of prayer. It's different from an ideology or a political position. It's a shared suffering and a shared attempt to overcome that suffering. A plea, from the simple basis of being alive. There's no difference between people at that level. Of course, some might not experience this suffering. But they're relatively few; most begin spinning purely from a desire to ease their discomfort, and everything else just flows from that.'

Naomi remembered the curious joy that had burst within her as she watched the fish leap and spin in the pond. They had spun in the air because their world had become a living hell, because they wanted to become anything else besides what they were, as if they believed that to spin was to be reborn. If that joy was what this young man meant by 'purity', she understood what he was saying perfectly.

'You called it a "tornado dance"?'

'Yeah, I heard it on the news yesterday. They call it that.'

'Who does?'

'There's supposedly a little village up north of Tokyo that had a traditional dance they called the "tornado dance". Tornadoes would hit the area every few years, killing villagers and destroying crops, and so, to contain the tornado god's wrath, the whole village began whirling themselves around in the opposite direction, clockwise. The area became depopulated over the years, and the tradition disappeared, and now the people left there say that's why the whole Tokyo area has had all these tornadoes lately.'

'Well, do you want to come with us to tornado-dance over at Sampin Temple, then? But if you're going to slip away again, you might as well stay here. Pink and I will be fine on our own.'

'All right, I'll stay.' The young man began to climb back up his rope to the tree branch.

'I wonder – do you think there are more people like you, spinning and spinning on their own somewhere?'

'I bet there are. There must be plenty of people around with stories like mine.' The young man said this with a smile that seemed to come from the bottom of his heart.

'Scary!' It was Pink who said this. Naomi looked back at the young man. He was concentrating on suspending himself from the tree again, now that Naomi and Pink were out of sight and thus, it seemed, out of mind. 'Let's go,' said Naomi, tugging Pink by the hand.

Sampin Temple turned out to be already filled to bursting with spinners. All was silent, even the cicadas; the air held only the smell of hot bodies, wafting from the temple in clouds. If Pink hadn't been there to lead her by the hand, Naomi might not have ventured in. But sure enough, her hesitation and unease faded away as she began to move. Surprisingly, Pink no longer clung to her as they spun, but rather went off to twirl alone. She took rests from time to time, but she spun just fine by herself, becoming as intoxicated in the trance as anyone else. She didn't seem to be stifling any nausea either.

An hour passed this way, and Naomi could no longer deny it. Pink was growing, and quickly. Her body was getting bigger, and the look in her eyes showed that her mind was maturing as well. Which meant that Naomi had to be ageing faster too. If she didn't want to chew up the time she had left, she had to stop spinning, right? But she didn't have the impression that time grew slower when she stopped. In fact, it was during her twirling that it seemed to slow down. Enough that it was a reason she kept spinning.

A chill went through Naomi. This unseen larger power, was it deceiving them, compelling them towards unspeakable acts? Were they unknowingly speeding time up? Was it a conspiracy? Was the young man in the tree sending people to these shrines and temples to do this 'tornado dance' for him? He said there were others like him all over. Were they a coordinated group inciting a movement? Were people like her, who longed to become one with something larger than herself, unwittingly becoming slaves?

Don't be stupid! I started spinning all on my own. It was only after however many days of it that I met that guy, there's no reason to think there's a conspiracy. Conspiracy theories are just illusions conjured by uneasy hearts. I'm totally at ease when I spin. If I do feel uneasy, all I have to do to feel better is spin more. Spinning makes all that is illusory fall away. The things that remain – those are the things that are real. That are true. Things like Pink growing up so quickly, for instance.

Naomi began to spin faster. She twirled fast enough that the landscape around her melted into a colourful blur. Now she was so good at spinning that no matter how fast she went around, she didn't feel sick. Spurred on by her, the dancers around Naomi began spinning faster as well. At this speed, it seemed as if they would be lifting off the ground before long. She could feel her consciousness begin to detach itself again, somewhere in the back of her mind. *Let go*, she thought. *It's time.*

She spun. She flew. Gravity disappeared, and she floated in the air for a moment, only to gently come back down to earth when it returned. Her body still felt light. The rush of grey in front of her resolved into distinct shapes. She concentrated her gaze. A figure began to rise before her. The grey became transparent. The figure was Pink. Now a teenager, she had become pretty, even sexy. She was spinning as fast as Naomi, but she appeared still as she returned her aunt's gaze. And not just Pink. Everyone around Naomi moved so fast that the movement disappeared, leaving their still figures to emerge from the blur. It was like a zoetrope or the frames of a film, images revealed through high-speed revolution. But they were not just images; she could reach out and touch them. 'It's getting late, we should get back before dark,' said Pink, but when Naomi took her by the hand, Pink shook her off. 'I'm not a kid any more.'

Even as they continued to spin at such high speeds, they found that they could walk normally as they made their way home, as if it were a day like any other. When they reached the house, Naomi's sister greeted them at the door waving an envelope watermarked with cherry blossoms. 'It arrived!' she exclaimed. The back of the envelope bore a Ministry of Defence insignia, and the letter informed Naomi that although she was just finishing the last vacation period of her military service, she was being deployed; and so, in the time it took to say, *Off I go!*, Naomi became a crew member on the destroyer *Sakimori*. Because it was a battle to defend some islands, the fighting took place almost entirely at sea, with threats and displays of force exchanged almost as if choreographed in advance, but Naomi's unit, under cover of the crossfire, was commanded to make a landing using ultra-mini, single-passenger submarines, and just as Naomi was thinking she'd succeeded, it turned out to be a trap, torpedoes coming at them from three sides within the confines of the bay, and while she managed to eject herself from the submarine right away, she was hit in the back by shrapnel from the explosion, which immobilized her, and she drifted out to sea, only to be picked up by a passing cruiser and given a hero's welcome upon her return home, but even as she spent her time in the hospital working diligently at rehabilitation, she never rid herself of a lingering paralysis in her arms and legs, and she grew depressed with the passage of day after listless day, while her sister, who was a nurse after all, did her best to take care of her; her depression expressed itself as resentment, resentment spewed at her sister and the world. *It can just go to hell for all I care!* she would say and say again, and soon the islands were all snatched away, Japan's supposed allies declaring that they wouldn't intervene, and thus the East Asian Union dissolved, leaving Japan isolated, its food supply rapidly diminishing, the country finally paying the price for opening its food markets so completely to foreign goods, the domestic agricultural industry woefully behind the times, unable to increase production to meet demand, and even in Naomi's household, meals dwindled to two servings of thin potato gruel a day, and Pink, having once so idolized Naomi and being now so disgusted by her current state, left home to live in a dormitory while she attended technical college, volunteering for the army right after graduation and ending up on the front lines near Kyushu, where she became a casualty of war at twenty-one, taken out by an unmanned stealth-fighter strike, leaving Naomi overwhelmed with guilt as if she had been the one to do the killing, the heaviness of her heart paralysing the rest of her body completely, but even as she imagined her own death again and again, she couldn't bring herself to abandon her sister to what had become a life dark with tragedy, a life her sister strove every day to keep herself from abandoning completely, and thus it was that August came again as rumours swirled that the war had reached Japan's main island at last, and the sun, as if driven mad, poured heat mercilessly down upon the land, Tokyo's temperatures breaking forty for the first time in nineteen years. Weakened and hungry, the residents of the archipelago, reduced to mere shimmers in the hot air, winked out one by one, and it dawned on Naomi as she watched her sister unable to cope, languishing before her on the tatami, that she could become a fan herself and create a breeze to revive her, and so, taking a small fan in each hand, she wrestled with her stiffened body, forcing it into motion, and as she slowly began to revolve, she remembered how she had spun like this to battle the heat nineteen years before, how Pink, so young then, had clamoured to play bird-in-the-cage and spin, and as she shared these memories with her sister, they revitalized her enough that she joined Naomi in her spinning, a spinning that somehow made them both feel newly strong, and newly hungry too, enough to want to leave the house for food, and so out they went as the sun went down, and in the park they encountered a crowd of people gathered at the edge of the pond, spinning slowly all in unison, and Naomi found herself joining them, looking up into the sky just as she had before, but this time she felt she was falling, and she noticed she was spinning left, counter to the clockwise revolutions of nineteen years ago, perhaps this meant that time could reverse direction too, could unbind her from this past that so entangled and constrained her, and perhaps Pink could come back to life as well, and together they could go back to before they'd twisted their bodies in wicked prayer and find some other way to free themselves from a world become a living hell, and so she vowed that once they'd wound the world back a full nineteen years, they would take it in their hands again and make it theirs at last; on and on she spun, every revolution a prayer in reverse.

MURAKAMI HARUKI

UFO in Kushiro

Translated by Jay Rubin

Five straight days she spent in front of the television, staring at crumbled banks and hospitals, whole blocks of shops in flames, severed railway lines and motorways. She never said a word. Sunk deep in the cushions of the sofa, her mouth clamped shut, she wouldn't answer when Komura spoke to her. She wouldn't shake her head or nod. Komura could not be sure the sound of his voice was even getting through to her.

Komura's wife came from way up north in Yamagata, and, as far as he knew, she had no friends or relatives who could have been hurt in Kobe.[1] Yet she stayed rooted in front of the television from morning to night. In his presence, at least, she ate nothing and drank nothing and never went to the toilet. Aside from an occasional flick of the remote control to change the channel, she hardly moved a muscle.

Komura would make his own toast and coffee, and head off to work. When he came home in the evening, he'd fix himself a snack with whatever he found in the fridge and eat alone. She'd still be glaring at the late news when he dropped off to sleep. A stone wall of silence surrounded her. Komura gave up trying to break through.

When he came home from work on Sunday, the sixth day, his wife had disappeared.

Komura was a salesman at one of the oldest audio equipment specialty stores in Tokyo's Akihabara 'Electronics Town'. He handled top-of-the-line stuff and earned a sizeable commission whenever he made a sale. Most of his clients were doctors, wealthy independent businessmen and rich provincials. He had been doing this for eight years and had a decent income right from the start. The economy was healthy, property prices were rising and Japan was overflowing with money. People's wallets were bursting with ten-thousand-yen bills, and everyone was dying to spend them. The most expensive items were the first to sell out.

Komura was tall and slim and a stylish dresser. He was good with people. In his bachelor days he had dated a lot of women. But after getting married, at twenty-six, he found that his desire for sexual adventures simply – and mysteriously – vanished. He hadn't slept with any woman but his wife during the five years of their marriage. Not that the opportunity had never presented itself – but he had lost all interest in fleeting affairs and one-night stands. He much preferred to come home early, have a relaxed meal with his wife, talk with her for a while on the sofa, then go to bed and make love. This was everything he wanted.

Komura's friends and colleagues were puzzled by his marriage. Alongside him with his clean, classic good looks, his wife could not have seemed more ordinary. She was short with thick arms, and she had a dull, even stolid, appearance. And it wasn't just physical: there was nothing attractive about her personality, either. She rarely spoke and always wore a sullen expression.

Still, though he did not quite understand why, Komura always felt his tension dissipate when he and his wife were together under one roof; it was the only time he could truly relax. He slept well with her, undisturbed by the strange dreams that had troubled him in the past. His erections were hard; his sex life was warm. He no longer had to worry about death or venereal disease or the vastness of the universe.

His wife, on the other hand, disliked Tokyo's crowds and longed for Yamagata. She missed her parents and her two elder sisters, and she would go home to see them whenever she felt the need. Her parents ran a successful inn, which kept them financially comfortable. Her father was crazy about his youngest daughter and happily paid her return fares. Several times, Komura had come home from work to find his wife gone and a note on the kitchen table telling him that she would be visiting her parents for a while. He never objected. He just waited for her to come back, and she always did, after a week or ten days, in a good mood.

But the letter his wife left for him when she vanished five days after the earthquake was different: *I am never coming back*, she had written, then went on to explain, simply but clearly, why she no longer wanted to live with him.

The problem is that you never give me anything, she wrote. *Or, to put it more precisely, you have nothing inside you that you can give me. You are good and kind and handsome, but living with you is like living with a chunk of air. It's not your fault, though. There are lots of women who will fall in love with you. But please don't call me. Just get rid of all the stuff I'm leaving behind.*

In fact, she hadn't left much of anything behind. Her clothes, her shoes, her umbrella, her coffee mug, her hair dryer: all were gone. She must have packed them in boxes and shipped them out after he left for work that morning. The only things still in the house that could be called 'her stuff' were the bike she used for shopping and a few books. The Beatles and Bill Evans CDs that Komura had been collecting since his bachelor days had also vanished.

The next day, he tried calling his wife's parents in Yamagata. His mother-in-law answered the phone and told him that his wife didn't want to talk to him. She sounded somewhat apologetic. She also told him that they would be sending him the necessary forms soon and that he should put his seal on them and send them back right away.

Komura answered that he might not be able to send them 'right away'. This was an important matter, and he wanted time to think it over.

'You can think it over all you want, but I know it won't change anything,' his mother-in-law said.

She was probably right, Komura told himself. No matter how much he thought or waited, things would never be the same. He was sure of that.

Shortly after he had sent the papers back with his seal stamped on them, Komura asked for a week's paid leave. His boss had a general idea of what had been happening, and February was a slow time of the year, so he let Komura go without a fuss. He seemed on the verge of saying something to Komura, but finally said nothing.

Sasaki, a colleague of Komura's, came over to him at lunch and said, 'I hear you're taking time off. Are you planning to do something?'

'I don't know,' Komura said. 'What *should* I do?'

Sasaki was a bachelor, three years younger than Komura. He had a delicate build and short hair, and he wore round, gold-rimmed glasses. A lot of people thought he talked too much and had a rather arrogant air, but he got along well enough with the easy-going Komura.

'What the hell – as long as you're taking the time off, why not make a nice trip out of it?'

'Not a bad idea,' Komura said.

Wiping his glasses with his handkerchief, Sasaki peered at Komura as if looking for some kind of clue.

'Have you ever been to Hokkaido?' he asked.

'Never,' Komura said.

'Would you like to go?'

'Why do you ask?'

Sasaki narrowed his eyes and cleared his throat. 'To tell you the truth, I've got a small package I'd like to send to Kushiro, and I'm hoping you'll take it there for me. You'd be doing me a big favour, and I'd be glad to pay for the return airfare. I could cover your hotel in Kushiro, too.'

'A small package?'

'Like this,' Sasaki said, shaping a four-inch cube with his hands. 'Nothing heavy.'

'Something to do with work?'

Sasaki shook his head. 'Not at all,' he said. 'Strictly personal. I just don't want it to get knocked around, which is why I can't mail it. I'd like somebody I know to deliver it by hand, if possible. I really ought to do it myself, but I haven't been able to find the time to fly all the way to Hokkaido.'

'Is it something important?'

His closed lips curling slightly, Sasaki nodded. 'It's nothing fragile, and there are no "hazardous materials". There's no need to worry about it. They're not going to stop you when they X-ray it at the airport. I promise I'm not going to get you into trouble. And it weighs practically nothing. All I'm asking is that you take it along just as you'd take anything else. The only reason I'm not mailing it is I just don't *feel* like mailing it.'

Hokkaido in February would be freezing cold, Komura knew, but, cold or hot, it was all the same to him.

'So who do I give the package to?'

'My sister. My younger sister. She lives up there.'

Komura decided to accept Sasaki's offer. He hadn't thought about how to spend his week off, and making plans now would have been too much trouble. Besides, he had no reason for not wanting to go to Hokkaido. Sasaki called the airline then and there, reserving a ticket to Kushiro. The flight would leave two days later, in the afternoon.

At work the next day, Sasaki handed Komura a box like the ones used for human ashes, only smaller, wrapped in brown paper. Judging from the feel, it was made of wood. As Sasaki had said, it weighed practically nothing. Broad strips of clear adhesive tape went all around the package over the paper. Komura held it in his hands and studied it a few seconds. He gave it a little shake, but he couldn't feel or hear anything moving inside.

'My sister will pick you up at the airport. And she'll be arranging a room for you,' Sasaki said. 'All you have to do is stand outside the gate with the package in your hands where she can see it. Don't worry, the airport's not very big.'

Komura left home with the box in his suitcase, wrapped in a thick thermal undershirt. The plane was far more crowded than he had expected. Why were all these people going from Tokyo to Kushiro in the middle of winter? he wondered.

The morning paper was full of earthquake reports. He read it from beginning to end on the plane. The number of dead was rising. Many areas were still without water or electricity, and countless people had lost their homes. Each article reported some new tragedy, but to Komura the details seemed oddly lacking in depth. All sounds reached him as far-off, monotonous echoes. The only thing he could give any serious thought to was his wife as she retreated ever further into the distance.

Mechanically he ran his eyes over the earthquake reports, stopped now and then to think about his wife, then went back to the paper. When he grew tired of this, he closed his eyes and napped. And when he woke, he thought about his wife again. Why had she followed the TV earthquake reports with such intensity, from morning to night, without eating or sleeping? What could she have seen in them?

Two young women wearing overcoats of similar design and colour approached Komura at the airport. One was fair-skinned and maybe five foot six, with short hair. The area from her nose to her full upper lip was oddly extended in a way that made Komura think of short-haired ungulates. Her companion was more like five foot one and would have been quite pretty if her nose hadn't been so small. Her long hair fell straight to her shoulders. Her ears were exposed, and there were two moles on her right earlobe which were emphasized by the earrings she wore. Both women looked to be in their mid-twenties. They took Komura to a café in the airport.

'I'm Sasaki Keiko,' the taller woman said. 'My brother told me how helpful you've been to him. This is my friend Shimao.'

'Nice to meet you,' Komura said.

'Hi,' Shimao said.

'My brother tells me your wife recently passed away,' Sasaki Keiko said with a respectful expression.

Komura waited a moment before answering, 'No, she didn't die.'

'I just talked to my brother the day before yesterday. I'm sure he said quite clearly that you'd lost your wife.'

'I did. She divorced me. But as far as I know she's alive and well.'

'That's odd. I couldn't possibly have misheard something so important.' She gave him an injured look. Komura put a small amount of sugar in his coffee and gave it a gentle stir before taking a sip. The liquid was thin, with no taste to speak of, more sign than substance. *What the hell am I doing here?* he wondered.

'Well, I guess I did mishear it. I can't imagine how else to explain the mistake,' Sasaki Keiko said, apparently satisfied now. She drew in a deep breath and chewed her lower lip. 'Please forgive me. I was very rude.'

'Don't worry about it. Either way, she's gone.'

Shimao said nothing while Komura and Keiko spoke, but she smiled and kept her eyes on Komura. She seemed to like him. He could tell from her expression and her subtle body language. A brief silence fell over the three of them.

'Anyway, let me give you the important package I brought,' Komura said. He unzipped his suitcase and pulled the box out of the folds of the thick ski undershirt he had wrapped it in. The thought struck him then: *I was supposed to be holding this when I got off the plane. That's how they were going to recognize me. How did they know who I was?*

Sasaki Keiko stretched her hands across the table, her expressionless eyes fixed on the package. After testing its weight, she did as Komura had done and gave it a few shakes by her ear. She flashed him a smile as if to signal that everything was fine, and slipped the box into her oversized shoulder bag.

'I have to make a call,' she said. 'Do you mind if I excuse myself for a moment?'

'Not at all,' Komura said. 'Feel free.'

Keiko slung the bag over her shoulder and walked off towards a distant phone booth. Komura studied the way she walked. The upper half of her body was still, while everything from the hips down made large, smooth, mechanical movements. He had the strange impression that he was witnessing some moment from the past, shoved with random suddenness into the present.

'Have you been to Hokkaido before?' Shimao asked.

Komura shook his head.

'Yeah, I know. It's a long way to come.'

Komura nodded, then turned to survey his surroundings. 'Funny,' he said, 'sitting here like this, it doesn't feel as if I've come all that far.'

'Because you flew. Those planes are too damn fast. Your mind can't keep up with your body.'

'You may be right.'

'Did you want to make such a long trip?'

'I guess so,' Komura said.

'Because your wife left?'

Komura nodded.

'No matter how far you travel, you can never get away from yourself,' Shimao said.

Komura was staring at the sugar bowl on the table as she spoke, but then he raised his eyes to hers.

'It's true,' he said. 'No matter how far you travel, you can never get away from yourself. It's like your shadow. It follows you everywhere.'

Shimao looked hard at Komura. 'I'll bet you loved her, didn't you?'

Komura dodged the question. 'You're a friend of Sasaki Keiko's?'

'Right. We do stuff together.'

'What kind of stuff?'

Instead of answering him, Shimao asked, 'Are you hungry?'

'I don't know,' Komura said. 'I feel kind of hungry and kind of not.'

'Let's go and have something warm, the three of us. It'll help you relax.'

Shimao drove a small four-wheel-drive Subaru. It had to have done way over a hundred thousand miles, judging by how battered it was. The rear bumper had a huge dent in it. Sasaki Keiko sat next to Shimao, and Komura had the cramped rear seat to himself. There was nothing particularly wrong with Shimao's driving, but the noise in the back was terrible, and the suspension was nearly shot. The automatic transmission slammed into gear whenever it downshifted, and the heater blew hot and cold. Shutting his eyes, Komura felt as if he had been imprisoned in a washing machine.

No snow had been allowed to accumulate on the streets in Kushiro, but dirty, icy mounds stood at random intervals on both sides of the road. Dense clouds hung low, and although it was not yet sunset, everything was dark and desolate. The wind tore through the city in sharp squeals. There were hardly any pedestrians. Even the traffic lights looked frozen.

'This is one part of Hokkaido that doesn't get much snow,' Sasaki Keiko explained in a loud voice, glancing back at Komura. 'We're on the coast and the wind is strong, so whatever piles up gets blown away. It's cold, though, *freezing* cold. Sometimes it feels like it's taking your ears off.'

'You hear about drunks who freeze to death sleeping on the street,' Shimao said.

'Do you get bears around here?' Komura asked.

Keiko giggled and turned to Shimao. 'Bears, he says.'

Shimao gave the same kind of giggle.

'I don't know much about Hokkaido,' Komura said by way of explanation.

'I know a good story about bears,' Keiko said. 'Right, Shimao?'

'A *great* story!' Shimao said.

But their talk broke off at that point, and neither of them told the bear story. Komura didn't ask to hear it. Soon they reached their destination, a big noodle shop on the highway. They stopped in the car park and went inside. Komura had a beer and a hot bowl of ramen noodles. The place was dirty and empty, and the chairs and tables were rickety, but the ramen was excellent, and when he had finished eating, Komura did, in fact, feel somewhat more relaxed.

'Tell me, Mr Komura,' Sasaki Keiko said, 'do you have something you want to do in Hokkaido? My brother tells me you're going to spend a week here.'

Komura thought about it for a moment but couldn't come up with anything he wanted to do.

'How about a hot spring? Would you like a nice, long soak in a tub? I know a little country place not far from here.'

'Not a bad idea,' Komura said.

'I'm sure you'd like it. It's really nice. No bears or anything.'

The two women looked at each other and laughed again.

'Do you mind if I ask you about your wife?' Keiko asked.

'I don't mind.'

'When did she leave?'

'Hmm . . . five days after the earthquake, so that's more than two weeks ago now.'

'Did it have something to do with the earthquake?'

Komura shook his head. 'Probably not. I don't think so.'

'Still, I wonder if things like that aren't connected somehow,' Shimao said with a tilt of the head.

'Yeah,' Keiko said. 'It's just that you can't see how.'

'Right,' Shimao said. 'Stuff like that happens all the time.'

'Stuff like what?' Komura asked.

'Like, say, what happened with somebody I know,' Keiko said.

'You mean Mr Saeki?' Shimao asked.

'Exactly,' Keiko said. 'There's this guy – Saeki. He lives in Kushiro. He's about forty. A hairdresser. His wife saw a UFO last year, in the autumn. She was driving on the edge of town all by herself in the middle of the night and she saw a huge UFO land in a field. *Whoosh!* Like in *Close Encounters*. A week later, she left home. They weren't having any domestic problems or anything. She just disappeared and never came back.'

'Into thin air,' Shimao said.

'And it was because of the UFO?' Komura asked.

'I don't know why,' Keiko said. 'She just walked out. No note or anything. She had two kids at primary school, too. The whole week before she left, all she'd do was tell people about the UFO. You couldn't get her to stop. She'd go on and on about how big and beautiful it was.'

She paused to let the story sink in.

'My wife left a note,' Komura said. 'And we don't have any kids.'

'So your situation's a little better than Saeki's,' Keiko said.

'Yeah. Kids make a big difference,' Shimao said, nodding.

'Shimao's father left home when she was seven,' Keiko explained with a frown. 'Ran off with his wife's younger sister.'

'All of a sudden. One day,' Shimao said, smiling.

A silence settled over the group.

'Maybe Mr Saeki's wife didn't run away but was captured by aliens from the UFO,' Komura said to smooth things over.

'It's possible,' Shimao said with a sombre expression. 'You hear stories like that all the time.'

'You mean like you're-walking-along-the-street-and-a-bear-eats-you kind of thing?' Keiko asked. The two women laughed again.

The three of them left the noodle shop and went to a nearby love hotel. It was on the edge of town, in a street where love hotels alternated with gravestone dealers. The hotel Shimao had chosen was an odd building, constructed to look like a European castle. A triangular red flag flew on its highest tower.

Keiko got the key at the front desk, and the three of them took the lift to the room. The windows were tiny, compared with the absurdly big bed. Komura hung his down jacket on a hanger and went into the toilet. During the few minutes he was in there, the two women managed to run a bath, dim the lights, check the heat, turn on the television, examine the delivery menus from local restaurants, test the light switches at the head of the bed, and check the contents of the minibar.

'The owners are friends of mine,' Keiko said. 'I had them get their biggest room ready. It *is* a love hotel, but don't let that bother you. You're not bothered, are you?'

'Not at all,' Komura said.

'I thought this would make a lot more sense than sticking you in a cramped, little room in some cheap business hotel by the station.'

'You may be right,' Komura said.

'Why don't you take a bath? I filled the tub.'

Komura did as he was told. The tub was huge. He felt uneasy soaking in it alone. The couples who came to this hotel probably took baths together.

When he emerged from the bathroom, Komura was surprised to find that Sasaki Keiko had left. Shimao was still there, drinking beer and watching TV.

'Keiko went home,' Shimao said. 'She wanted me to apologize and tell you that she'll be back tomorrow morning. Do you mind if I stay here a little while and have a beer?'

'Fine,' Komura said.

'You're sure it's no problem? Like, you want to be alone, or you can't relax if somebody else is around or something?'

Komura insisted that it was no problem. Drinking his beer and drying his hair with a towel, he watched TV with Shimao. It was a news special on the Kobe earthquake. The usual images appeared again and again: tilted buildings, buckled streets, old women weeping, confusion and aimless anger. When a commercial came on, Shimao used the remote to switch off the TV.

'Let's talk,' she said, 'as long as we're here.'

'Fine,' Komura said.

'Hmm, what should we talk about?'

'In the car, you and Keiko said something about a bear, remember? You said it was a great story.'

'Oh, yeah,' she said, nodding. 'The bear story.'

'You want to tell it to me?'

'Sure, why not?'

Shimao got a fresh beer from the fridge and filled both their glasses.

'It's a little raunchy,' she said. 'You don't mind?'

Komura shook his head.

'I mean, some men don't like hearing a woman tell certain kinds of stories.'

'I'm not like that.'

'It's something that actually happened to me, so it's a little embarrassing.'

'I'd like to hear it if you're okay with it.'

'I'm okay,' Shimao said, 'if you're okay.'

'I'm okay,' Komura said.

'Three years ago – back around the time I entered junior college – I was dating this guy. He was a year older than me, a university student. He was the first man I had sex with. One day the two of us were out hiking – in the mountains way up north.'

Shimao took a sip of beer.

'It was autumn, and the hills were full of bears. That's the time of year when the bears are getting ready to hibernate, so they're out looking for food and they're really dangerous. Sometimes they attack people. They did an awful job on one hiker just three days before we went out. So somebody gave us a bell to carry – about as big as a wind bell. You're supposed to shake it when you walk so the bears know there are people around and won't come out. Bears don't attack people on purpose. I mean, they're pretty much vegetarians. They don't *have* to attack people. What happens is they suddenly bump into people in their territory and they get surprised or angry and they attack out of reflex. So if you walk along ringing your bell, they'll avoid you. Get it?'

'I get it.'

'So that's what we were doing, walking along and ringing the bell. We got to this place where there was nobody else around, and all of a sudden he said he wanted to . . . do it. I kind of liked the idea, too, so I said okay and we went into this bushy place off the trail where nobody could see us, and we spread out a plastic sheet. But I was afraid of the bears. I mean, think how awful it would be to have some bear attack you from behind and kill you when you're having sex! I would never want to die that way. Would you?'

Komura agreed that he would not want to die that way.

'So there we were, shaking the bell with one hand and having sex. Kept it up from start to finish. *Ding-a-ling! Ding-a-ling!*'

'Which one of you shook the bell?'

'We took turns. We'd trade off when our hands got tired. It was so weird, shaking this bell the whole time we were doing it! I think about it sometimes even now, when I'm having sex, and I start laughing.'

Komura gave a little laugh, too.

Shimao clapped her hands. 'Oh, that's wonderful,' she said. 'You *can* laugh after all!'

'Of course I can laugh,' Komura said, but, come to think of it, this was the first time he had laughed in quite a while. When was the last time?

'Do you mind if I take a bath, too?' Shimao asked.

'Fine,' Komura said.

While she was bathing, Komura watched a variety show presented by some comedian with a loud voice. He didn't find it the least bit funny, but he couldn't tell whether that was the show's fault or his own. He drank a beer and opened a packet of nuts from the minibar. Shimao stayed in the bath for a very long time. Finally, she came out wearing nothing but a towel and sat on the edge of the bed. Dropping the towel, she slid in between the sheets like a cat and lay there looking straight at Komura.

'When was the last time you did it with your wife?' she asked.

'At the end of December, I think.'

'And nothing since?'

'Nothing.'

'Not with anybody?'

Komura closed his eyes and shook his head.

'You know what *I* think,' Shimao said. 'You need to lighten up and learn to enjoy life a little more. I mean, think about it: tomorrow there could be an earthquake; you could be kidnapped by aliens; you could be eaten by a bear. Nobody knows what's going to happen.'

'Nobody knows what's going to happen,' Komura echoed.

'*Ding-a-ling*,' Shimao said.

After several failed attempts to have sex with Shimao, Komura gave up. This had never happened to him before.

'You must have been thinking about your wife,' Shimao said.

'Yup,' Komura said, but in fact what he had been thinking about was the earthquake. Images of it had come to him one after another, as if in a slide show, flashing on the screen and fading away. Motorways, flames, smoke, piles of rubble, cracks in streets. He couldn't break the chain of silent images.

Shimao pressed her ear against his naked chest.

'These things happen,' she said.

'Uh-huh.'

'You shouldn't let it bother you.'

'I'll try not to,' Komura said.

'Men always let it bother them, though.'

Komura said nothing.

Shimao played with his nipple.

'You said your wife left a note, didn't you?'

'I did.'

'What did it say?'

'That living with me was like living with a chunk of air.'

'A chunk of air?' Shimao tilted her head back to look up at Komura. 'What does *that* mean?'

'That there's nothing inside me, I guess.'

'Is it true?'

'Could be,' Komura said. 'I'm not sure, though. I may have nothing inside me, but what would *something* be?'

'Yeah, really, come to think of it. What *would* something be? My mother was crazy about salmon skin. She always used to wish there were a kind of salmon made of nothing but skin. So there may be some cases when it's *better* to have nothing inside. Don't you think?'

Komura tried to imagine what a salmon made of nothing but skin would be like. But even supposing there were such a thing, wouldn't the skin itself be the *something* inside? Komura took a deep breath, raising and then lowering Shimao's head on his chest.

'I'll tell you this, though,' Shimao said. 'I don't know whether you've got nothing or something inside you, but I think you're terrific. I'll bet the world is full of women who would understand you and fall in love with you.'

'It said that, too.'

'What? Your wife's note?'

'Uh-huh.'

'No kidding,' Shimao said, lowering her head to Komura's chest again. He felt her earring against his skin like a secret object.

'Come to think of it,' Komura said, 'what's the *something* inside that box I brought up here?'

'Is it bothering you?'

'It wasn't bothering me before. But now, I don't know, it's starting to.'

'Since when?'

'Just now.'

'All of a sudden?'

'Yeah, once I started thinking about it, all of a sudden.'

'I wonder why it's started to bother you now, all of a sudden?'

Komura glared at the ceiling for a minute to think. 'I wonder.'

They listened to the moaning of the wind. The wind: it came from somewhere unknown to Komura, and it blew past to somewhere unknown to him.

'I'll tell you why,' Shimao said in a low voice. 'It's because that box contains the *something* that was inside you. You didn't know that when you carried it here and gave it to Keiko with your own hands. Now, you'll never get it back.'

Komura lifted himself from the mattress and looked down at the woman. Tiny nose, moles on the earlobe. In the room's deep silence, his heart beat with a loud, dry sound. His bones cracked as he leaned forward. For one split second, Komura realized that he was on the verge of committing an act of overwhelming violence.

'Just kidding,' Shimao said when she saw the look on his face. 'I said the first thing that popped into my head. It was a terrible joke. I'm sorry. Try not to let it bother you. I didn't mean to hurt you.'

Komura forced himself to calm down and, after a glance around the room, sank his head into his pillow again. He closed his eyes and took a deep breath. The huge bed stretched out around him like a nocturnal sea. He heard the freezing wind. The fierce pounding of his heart shook his bones.

'Are you starting to feel a *little* as if you've come a long way?' Shimao asked.

'Hmm. Now I feel as if I've come a *very* long way,' Komura answered honestly.

Shimao traced a complicated design on Komura's chest with her fingertip, as if casting a magic spell.

'But really,' she said, 'you're just at the beginning.'

SAEKI KAZUMI

Weather-Watching Hill

Translated by David Boyd

Beppu was just coming out of the school gym.

I held my hand up to get his attention. He saw me and walked right over.

Izawa called to tell me that, while Beppu had lost his home in the tsunami, he and his family were safe at the local primary-school gym, which had been converted into a shelter for evacuees. Izawa said on the phone that, when he and Beppu met, they hugged each other and cried. But when I saw Beppu outside the gym, we were calm – maybe because the reporter who gave me the ride to the shelter in his emergency vehicle was standing next to me. It was almost evening, and the air was filled with the smell of pork soup being cooked by Self-Defence Force troops in their camouflage fatigues.

A big fan of Yazawa Eikichi and Tom Waits, Beppu always dressed with a kind of rock-star flair, but his clothes that day were nondescript: he was wearing a grey-and-black-checked work shirt and jeans. His hair, typically slicked back with pomade, was greaseless. His chin was flecked with salt-and-pepper stubble. Still, I was relieved to find him looking better than I expected. It had been a week since the earthquake and tsunami on 11 March.

'They're all donations, these clothes,' Beppu said, as if he felt he had to explain. When I caught a glimpse of the red T-shirt under his overshirt, I couldn't help smiling.

'I'm just glad your family is safe,' I said. 'I was worried when I heard your house was hit in the tsunami. Izawa said he saw your name here by chance when he was volunteering with meals.'

'Yeah, I know. He was convinced I didn't make it. The second he saw me here, he started bawling – got me going, too . . .'

'Come on in,' Beppu said, as if he were trying to change the subject to something less embarrassing. He made it sound as though he were inviting me into his own home.

I didn't want to bother the other evacuees, so I hesitated a little. Beppu continued, 'Come on, Shigezaki-san – your reporter friend can come, too.' He walked on ahead of us.

'Weren't you heading out?'

'Just, you know,' Beppu said, holding up two fingers as if smoking a cigarette.

We took off our shoes and carried them into the gym. The whole place was covered with blankets and packed with people. The reporter asked, 'How many are staying here?' Beppu answered, 'Maybe three hundred.' The walls of the gym, the school building and the corridors connecting them were covered in missing-person notices.

It was freezing inside. Supplies had been cut off since the quake and kerosene was running short. I saw the elderly evacuees, wrapped in blankets to fight against the cold, and remembered the hypothermia warnings I'd seen on TV.

Beppu motioned towards a set of blankets in the middle of a row near the stage. 'This is my home now,' he said.

A gridded walkway ran between the blankets, drawn on the floor to help people navigate the gym. I looked down at the lines, impressed. 'Weird, isn't it?' Beppu said with a wry smile. 'Even in a place like this, it didn't take long to set up proper roads and zones. I guess this spot makes my address District One, Block Three? There's always someone who takes charge.'

Beppu's 'home' was a few blankets spread over an area of six tatami mats. He had six people in his family, which made me wonder if they'd been given one mat's space per person. I recognized Beppu's youngest boy, in his first year at school, sprawled out on the floor, playing with his Pokémon cards. The others didn't seem to be around.

'Make yourself comfortable,' Beppu said as we sat near the corner of a camel-coloured blanket.

'Now then, where's the tea . . . Would coffee be okay?' he asked, still half standing.

I shook my head in protest and waved him off. 'Don't bother, there's no need for that.'

'Come on. You're visiting my home. The least I can do is get you a cup of tea,' he pronounced theatrically, making his way towards the stage. Below the stage was a row of benches, on which sat cardboard boxes with emergency food supplies and Thermos flasks of hot water.

As I took a sip from the half-full mug of instant coffee, I noticed a copy of *Selected Tang Poetry* resting on one of the blankets. Beppu was a literature lover – he had turned his home into a cram school, where he taught primary- and middle-school students.

I had been living in the Tokyo area for years, working as an electrician and a writer, but had to move home to Sendai due to asbestos exposure. That was fifteen years ago. As soon as I came back, I started my own writing course; Beppu and Izawa were two of my students. When the class ended, the three of us became drinking companions.

'I thought it would help me calm down if I could read this. I had someone I know bring it over,' he said.

I recited the only line of Du Fu I knew by heart: *The realm is ruined, but the mountains and rivers remain* – right? Then I sighed and corrected myself: *The realm is ruined, and so are the mountains and rivers.* I had seen it on the drive over, when the reporter and I passed through the harbour town where Beppu's home had been; the Self-Defence Forces and the police were still searching for bodies there, and only emergency vehicles were allowed in.

Beppu nodded silently.

The reporter got up and started walking around the shelter with his SLR camera slung around his neck.

It's a miracle I'm still alive. Sometimes I find it hard to believe. Like, I wake up in the morning, asking myself if I'm dead – but I'm not. I'm still here.

Not that I really feel alive, though. More like I'm just pretending.

When the earthquake hit, I was home alone. The kids were at school and my wife was at the community centre, at a thank-you party with my eldest daughter's teacher. She finished middle school this spring.

Anyway, I've never felt anything like this earthquake before. The one off the coast of Miyagi Prefecture a couple of years ago was nothing compared to this. And this one just kept going. Seriously, I thought the house was about to fall on top of me.

*When the shaking finally stopped, I started cleaning up. The dressers and book-
shelves had all been tipped over. The cupboards were thrown wide open and our
dishes were smashed to pieces. The powerful aftershocks kept coming, but I didn't
stop. I just wanted to get rid of all the jagged pieces before the kids got home.*

*I was still cleaning when the sushi chef from next door came over. 'Beppu?
You're still here? Why aren't you going to the shelter?'*

'Shelter?' I asked.

'You never know. There could be a tsunami on the way,' he said.

*'What, like last year? That was a total waste of time,' I said. You remember
that? It was a Sunday, late last February. You and I had plans to go drinking,
but I backed out at the last minute because Chile had a giant earthquake and
everyone thought we were going to get hit with a tsunami here. Well, I thought
it would be the same thing this time. I'd go to the shelter at the community
centre, hole up there for a few hours while nothing happened, then head back
home. I told the chef I was going to pass – I'd rather stick around and clean up.
My wife had the car anyway, so I couldn't drive, and I hadn't heard any tsunami sirens, either. Now that I think about it, though, the power was out and
the whole system was probably down.*

*Anyway, the chef was insistent, which wasn't like him. He said he'd drive
me to the shelter. Then I remembered that my wife had called before the quake –
she left her mobile phone at home and wanted me to bring it to her at the
community centre when I had the chance. Okay, I thought, I might as well take
the ride.*

*You know how across the road from my house and the sushi place there's that
fish market – and the ocean's behind the market, right? I could see the ocean from
there, and it didn't look the least bit different. We got in the car and everything
was fine at first, but then we hit heavy traffic and came to a complete stop. 'We'll
have to walk from here,' I said. When I got out, I turned back to look the way
we came, for no particular reason. At the far end of the road, I saw an unbeliev-
ably tall, dark wave hurtling towards us. No way, I thought – a tsunami. I
panicked and told the chef to leave the car behind. We ran with everything we
had – but not to the community centre. We headed for another designated shelter,
the middle school, to get a little further away from the tsunami.*

*I was just about to reach the school gate when I tripped and fell flat on my
face. The tsunami was right behind me. I really thought I was done for.*

*

Beppu suddenly stopped and laughed a little, drawing a chuckle from me in spite of myself.

'But you played football throughout high school. I bet you're a good runner.'

'Not any more. And I was sprinting for more than five hundred metres. I swear, my heart was bursting and my legs were shaking.'

Then Beppu said, 'You probably think a tsunami comes at you from above – right?' I nodded, half remembering a surfing movie I'd seen once, where the crest of a giant wave rose up over a man like a shark baring its teeth.

'That's not what happens, though. It comes at you from behind, like it's taunting you. First it sweeps you off your feet, then as soon as you fall over backwards, the next surge comes to get you.'

Beppu went silent, as if the scene were coming back to him. I had my own rush of memories.

It was the morning of 13 March – two days after the giant, magnitude-9.0 earthquake.

I walked over to my living-room window, as I always do when I get up, to look at the ocean in the distance. For thirteen years, I had been living on the ground floor of an apartment block on the top of a hill that stood a hundred metres above sea level, but I couldn't believe what I was seeing out of my window that morning. The red-and-white-banded chimney of the waste-incineration plant rose in the foreground off to the left, the same as ever. The smoke that always billowed out – except for New Year's holidays – had been absent since the quake, but that wasn't what I found hard to believe.

When the dust clouds cleared and my vision finally came into focus, I saw the band of pines planted as a barrier along the coast – or what was left of it. I could count on my fingers the trees still standing. It was like one of those images of the African savanna that you see on TV or in magazines.

I had never really given much thought to those trees before, but as I stood there that morning, they came to me almost as a distant memory: a cluster of lush green pines clinging to the coastline, with the ocean shimmering over them. The beach was now as bare as a comb missing most of its teeth. With a pang, it occurred to me – there are some things you don't notice until they're gone.

The swollen sea, viewed through the remaining pines, appeared bigger and closer than before. Around the mouth of the river that ran between my town and the next were patches of boggy ground, reflecting the dull light of the sun.

Suddenly it hit me, that place . . . had been a village! In my mind, I could see the faces of friends and neighbours who had lived there.

I hurried to the bedroom to wake my wife.

We hadn't had power since the earthquake, so there was no TV. We learned everything we knew about the disaster from a hand-cranked emergency radio. Until that day, we were so busy getting the house in order and going out for water that we had no time to look out of the window.

I heard on the radio that a giant tsunami had ravaged the coast, that hundreds of bodies had washed ashore – but part of me didn't believe it. Looking out of the window that morning, I saw the first undeniable evidence that this had really happened.

A shiver ran down my back.

Three days later, the power came on. Watching images of the tsunami on TV, repeated over and over, I was finally able to grasp what the tsunami had actually been like, and I knew that if I had seen this footage right after the disaster – homes and cars being swallowed up and swept away by merciless waves – there was no way I could have handled it.

Then, when they started showing video footage of the nuclear reactors exploding in Fukushima, the next prefecture along, I grew even more anxious. Outside my window, Self-Defence Force helicopters flew back and forth, and the distant sirens of fire engines and ambulances wailed constantly.

'Look, sweetheart – you can get a good view of it from over here,' Beppu said to his eldest daughter, who wore a navy-blue school uniform and had her hair cut short. He pointed towards the coast. 'See the big bridge by the water? Just to the right of that.'

'Over there? Everything's gone,' the girl murmured.

Beppu had called me that afternoon, five days after we met at the shelter. 'I'm in the area – I came to check my daughter's exam results. Is it okay if I come by?' 'Of course,' I told him. Not ten minutes later, he was outside, in a car driven by one of his younger friends. He said that his daughter had taken the entrance exam for the high school at the bottom of my hill. I asked how she did, but he just walked over to the window without answering.

With his back to me, I couldn't tell if he was building up to announce that, happily, she had passed, or if he was steeling himself to reveal that, unfortunately, she had not.

We had electricity again, but no water or gas. On the living-room floor, we had lined up fifteen plastic bottles of drinking water and a couple of twenty-litre plastic tanks for cooking that we'd filled at the water-rationing station. There were also a couple of cardboard boxes loaded with emergency rations: pre-cooked rice in plastic packs, dried bread, canned goods, meals in sealed pouches – disaster supplies we had stocked up on before the earthquake because there had been warnings that there was a 99 per cent chance a major earthquake would hit the area in the next thirty years.

We were still getting powerful aftershocks, so we had laid our speakers and floor lamps on their sides, wrapped in blankets. On the living-room table, we were boiling water on a portable gas stove.

My wife made tea while we seated ourselves around the little *kotatsu*.

'Come on, Beppu! Don't keep us waiting,' my wife demanded. She was six years younger than me – the same age as Beppu – and they spoke to each other casually.

'You tell them, sweetheart,' Beppu said to his daughter, who blushed and made a small V-sign just over the surface of the *kotatsu*, breaking into a bashful smile.

'That's great!' my wife said warmly.

'She was the only one from her school to get in here,' Beppu said with a touch of pride. They lived in the next city from us, and most of her classmates were probably going to go to high school there.

'Congratulations,' I added belatedly. 'I'm sorry – I forgot your name.'

Beppu had brought her over a few times when she was little. She always seemed like a daddy's girl.

'It's Nozomi, written with the characters for *hope* and *ocean*.'

'Right, right,' I said. 'Nozomi . . . You came up with the name, didn't you, Beppu?'

'Sure did,' he said, with a proud thrust of his chin.

'Hold on,' said my wife, as if something had just occurred to her. She went to the kitchen and came back with milk tea and pound cake.

'It's just something a friend from Tokyo sent me in the emergency,' she said. 'But we should celebrate!'

Nozomi brushed aside her fringe and happily devoured her slice of cake.

'Here, have mine,' Beppu said as he handed his plate to his daughter.

I was with Nozomi the night of the tsunami.

By the time I made it to her school, the place was packed with evacuees. I tried going up the main stairs, but couldn't get past the people in wheelchairs from the local nursing home. When the water started to rush through the entrance, I remembered that there was an emergency stairwell in a corner of the building and ran there as fast as I could. I made it upstairs just in the nick of time. Good thing it was my old school and I knew the building so well.

I stayed on that floor for a while, but the water kept rising, so I went up another flight of stairs, before finally ending up on the landing to the roof, where I spent the night. It was so cold that day, it had snowed lightly. All the windows were shattered and everyone was soaking wet, shivering like mad. Once the water started to go down a little, I went around collecting curtains from the classrooms and shirts from the football club to help everyone stave off the cold.

At some point, Nozomi was there with me.

That night, our family was all over the place. My three other kids were at the primary school and my wife was at the community centre. I was worried sick, wondering if they were okay. I just sat there, unable to say anything, staring blankly at the dark floor. Then, in the middle of the night, Nozomi turned to me and said, 'Dad, look at how pretty the stars are.' Honestly, all I could think was: who cares about stars at a time like this? But I looked up and the sky was bright with them. Everything else around was pitch-black; the stars were all we could see. The earth had become this hell, but the stars were the same as ever . . .

'They really were beautiful,' my wife and I said, nodding.

I will never forget the beauty of the stars that night, when the whole city was blacked out. Those stars and the waxing moon were all we had.

One afternoon a little more than a month after the disaster, Beppu drove over to pick me up. Miraculously, they had discovered some raw sake, bottled just three days before the disaster, buried among the rubble of the local brewery, which was swept away in the tsunami. Alcohol wasn't allowed at the shelter, so Beppu wanted me to go for a drink with him.

'The head brewer's a former student of mine. He came all the way to the shelter to tell me about the find,' Beppu said. Under his unbuttoned light blue shirt, he was wearing a T-shirt with the face of Japan's King of Rock, Imawano Kiyoshirō.

'Where'd you get the car?'

'A friend from high school who transferred to Tokyo this spring. He said I could hold on to it while he's away.'

Beppu had always been quick to open up with people, so he had a lot of friends.

Beppu's own small car had been washed away in the tsunami. This was a seven-seat estate, which is probably why he had such a hard time steering it down the winding road where I lived. The cement-block walls lining the road had collapsed in places and the shoulder had been pushed up in the quake. The old inn on the opposite side had been obliterated in the earthquake, and the road running past it was still blocked to traffic.

'Were you okay the other night?' Beppu asked as we drove on to the highway. The road looked flat enough, but the quakes had opened hard-to-see gaps in the surface. The car bucked every time we hit one.

'The big aftershock? Yeah, that was intense,' I said as I grabbed the handle over the window to my left.

When it looked as though the aftershocks had started to die down, we put the furniture and bookshelves back and restored their contents. Then there was another big one: intensity six, magnitude 7.4; 11 March all over again. I felt as if somebody had pulled a ladder out from under me.

Many of the buildings that had survived the first quake were partially or completely destroyed by this one. The ground beneath my apartment building had sunk fifteen centimetres the first time, then dropped another ten with this one, exposing underground pipes and opening large cracks beneath the foundation, where moles had started to burrow.

The only good thing about this quake was that there was no tsunami.

'In the shelter, every time we get an aftershock, the basketball hoops overhead start to rattle like mad.'

'That's right,' I nodded as I remembered the gym. 'It has those back-boards that hang down from the ceiling, right?'

Yeah, and we have one of those damn things right over us, where we sleep.

Every time it rattles, I hold the kids tight to keep them from getting scared. Really, it's happened so many times I've lost count.

But that night, it wasn't just rattling. It was banging around like it was going to come crashing down at any second. To make matters worse, the power was out and the gym was completely dark. I half stood up to shield the kids with my body, in case it came down on us.

I heard a man shouting – 'It's a big one!' – and a woman screaming in terror.

Then the generator kicked in and we got the lights back – also right over my damn head.

The gym was hot that night. Everybody was running their portable heaters full blast, so I went to bed in just my underpants. There I was, under this spotlight, in front of everybody, in nothing but my underpants. You wouldn't believe the looks they were giving me, I swear.

'Check this out. It's like they haven't even touched the place.'
'Seriously.'
On the way to where the brewery had been, we went through the village across the river from the site of Beppu's house. We were close to the shore I had seen from my living-room window two mornings after the disaster – the coastline that had been picked clean of its pines.

I knew a few people who had lived around here. Someone told me about a woman who saw her husband swept away by the tsunami while he was parking the car near the shelter. I came by here with the reporter the day we went to the shelter to meet Beppu. The water had gone down somewhat, but the whole area looked pretty much the same as it had then.

It was a vast bog flooded by the tide. Some of the cars were twisted like origami. The ones that retained their original shape were marked by rescue squads: a white X meant that the passengers were alive, or the car was empty; a red X meant that the passengers were confirmed dead. I saw a decorative golden spoon on the ground; pines from the protective band that had been torn up by their roots; adult videos; an agricultural reference book; a framed photograph from a family altar; a box of onions with overgrown green sprouts; floor cushions; bedding; and a chair propped up in the middle of a paddy field, as if someone had been sitting in it a moment ago . . .

I felt as though daily life had been washed away.

'Not the best year for enjoying the cherry blossoms, was it?' Beppu said as he looked at the blossoms on a cherry tree branch that had been mowed down with the pines.

Here we are. The chef's place was over there and my house was right here. You remember coming to the chef's place with me, right? Must have been something like thirteen years ago. There was a kid on the tatami in the back, begging us to play with him and his toy trains, remember? He's at college now. Really bright, too. He got into the maths department at a national university last year. The chef told everyone at the shelter that he's determined to reopen the restaurant here, but I wonder. I hear the city isn't going to let anyone build this close to the water.

Me? My wife and kids are saying that they'd hate to come back to this place. But I honestly don't know what to do.

Just look at this – it's all gone, everything but the foundation. The entryway was right over here. You'd go inside and my classroom was right there. I had my blackboard set up over here and the kids' desks were over there. We lived in the back. My room was upstairs.

The only thing we found around here was one big platter – the kind you use for serving sashimi. I've got to say, though, part of me is relieved it's all gone. I've just been stuck in a rut for a while now.

I was stunned by the last thing Beppu said. I looked him in the eye, trying to figure out what he meant by that.

'Want to climb the *hiyoriyama*?' he suddenly asked.

Behind us, two hundred metres from the shore, was a small, man-made hill once used for weather-watching – a *hiyoriyama*. All the houses in the area were washed away in the tsunami, and now that hill was the only thing left.

Beppu coughed a few times on the way to the hill.

I looked around and muttered, 'There's a lot of asbestos in the air.'

Right after the tsunami, when everything was wet with seawater, the air was damp and relatively free of asbestos. Now that it was dry, the air appeared to be full of dust.

The bulldozers roared as they made mountains out of the rubble. The clean-up effort had been moving rapidly and what I saw now looked like an expanse of vacant lots. In a little more than a month, they had managed to clear away most of the debris – 'debris' that had only recently been a part of our lives. No matter how many times I saw it, I found it hard to watch those things being handled as if they were garbage.

'You know, I never dream about the time before the earthquake,' Beppu said. 'Not that I have nightmares about the tsunami or anything. Only what came after . . .'

'Same here, actually,' I said.

'Really, you too? It feels like everything is happening so fast, and I can't do anything about it. There's no time to stop and think clearly about things. I just wish I could make time stop flowing,' Beppu muttered.

When we reached the *hiyoriyama*, a large solitary pine was rising up from the back of the six-metre hill. There had been a small shrine at the top of the hill, about a metre square, with a few cherry trees around it, but they were all scraped away by the tsunami. Just this one tree remained stubbornly rooted to the soil.

'Someone who got caught in the tsunami and lived through it said the tsunami came clear over the top of this pine.'

I looked up as Beppu spoke. I figured the topmost branches had to be around ten metres high.

Beppu and I had actually come to this place before, thirteen years ago, when I was writing a travel piece for a magazine. According to what I found out then, Japan has more than eighty *hiyoriyama*. Each stands near a harbour that opens to the sea, and the highest of them tops out at around a hundred metres. In the old days, weather-watching experts would climb those hills to watch the movement of the clouds and changes in wind direction, then predict the weather. They probably followed the tides and flight patterns of birds, too. In times of disaster, they must have been the first ones to see the signs of a tsunami stirring at sea . . .

I thought I remembered seeing a stone memorial near the foot of the hill the first time we came here, with an inscription about a tsunami. I went looking for it, and found it on the other side of the hill, toppled over.

Beppu and I looked down at the words etched into the massive two-and-a-half-metre stone and read them out loud:

IN MEMORY OF THE 1933 SANRIKU DISASTER: BEWARE TSUNAMI FOLLOWING EARTHQUAKES

At 2.30 a.m. on 3 March 1933, a powerful earthquake suddenly struck. About forty minutes after it had settled down, there came a booming roar from the sea and the coast was hit with furious waves. A wall of water ten feet high surged up the Natori River. To the west, the water ran as far as the Enkō area; to the south, the stretch of land from Teizanbori to the Hiroura Inlet was flooded. More than twenty homes were inundated. Several thirty-ton motorized fishing boats moored outside the town, on the banks of the Natori River, were swept into the fields of the Yanagihara area. Many smaller vessels were also smashed to pieces. Fortunately, there was no loss of human or animal life. Damage to the region was minimal compared with the havoc wrought to the inland counties of Monō, Oshika and Motoyoshi, as well as parts of Iwate and Aomori prefectures. The epicentre of the earthquake was offshore, approximately 150 leagues east-northeast of Mount Kinka, sparing us from the full brunt of the tsunami, which was blocked by the Oshika Peninsula. What struck our shore were no more than secondary waves . . .

When we read the words 'Fortunately, there was no loss of human or animal life', Beppu moaned. 'They wrote it down. No one died and they still built this monument.'

From the top of the hill, we had a 360-degree view – a painful panorama.

The first time Beppu and I came here, the hill was surrounded by homes and we couldn't see the ocean at all. Now we saw white waves lapping against a shallow beach that seemed to run on forever. To the south, while Fukushima's nuclear power plant was out of view, I could see the chimneys of the thermal power plant just this side of it; to the north, I could make out the blurred shapes of the petrochemical complex on the industrial port and the peninsula behind it.

I doubt the view would have been that clear if the protective pine forest on the coast hadn't been mostly wiped out.

'Look,' Beppu said, pointing me in the opposite direction. I turned around and saw three television towers at the top of the hill where I lived. Every year from my place, we could see the summer fireworks going up at the beach here. I always looked forward to that.

Then it occurred to me, maybe my hill was a *hiyoriyama* in its own right.

At the top of the *hiyoriyama*, we saw a lot of handmade memorials, scraps of wood with messages written on them, nailed to posts that were painted white, and an elderly woman whose hands were clasped in prayer for the victims of the tsunami.

'Come on,' Beppu said. 'Let's head over to where the brewery was. Izawa should be there. He volunteered to wash the bottles.'

We started walking back to where we parked the car, where Beppu's house had been.

'At the shelter, Wataru heard some of us adults talking about "this world" and "that world", and . . .'

'Wataru – he's your youngest, right?' I asked as I remembered the boy playing with his cards on the floor of the shelter.

'Yeah, that's him. He was like, "Hey, Dad, what world are *we* in? Is it some world in between?"'

I didn't know what to say.

'He doesn't talk about it, but I know he saw a lot of people get washed away in the tsunami.'

I repeated the boy's words in my mind: *Some world in between . . .*

MATSUDA AOKO

Planting

Translated by Angus Turvill

Marguerite planted. She planted roses. She planted violets. She planted lilies of the valley. She planted clover. And, of course, she planted marguerites. When she found marguerites in the box, she would smile. 'We meet again!' she would say softly. The gentle curves etched lightly by the years around her mouth and eyes would dance. Marguerite planted. She planted balloons of pretty colours. She planted lip cream, its smell tingling in her nose. She planted thick ceramic mugs. She planted cashmere socks. It was Marguerite's job to plant. And so she planted. She planted lovely things, but nothing grand. She planted things one wouldn't tire of. She planted clothes that would make one feel happy all day. She planted soft, gentle colours. She planted soft, gentle textures. Marguerite planted every day. She planted a heart that knew each day was precious. She planted a heart that kept things it liked and used them time and again. She planted a heart that treated things with care. Marguerite didn't hurry. She planted slowly. It was fine to plant slowly here. How long had she been planting slowly? It was hard to say. Marguerite – her glasses unfashionable but delicate, cardigan and trousers of pure cotton, simple curls at the tips of her white-tinged, light brown hair. Marguerite and her garden, wrapped in the faint light of evening – to a passer-by it would have seemed like Heaven.

Marguerite was turning the pages of *Townwork*. She looked tired. Her clothes itched. She didn't care about them, didn't even notice the material was artificial. She was in a Doutor coffee shop, upstairs, in the seat nearest the toilet. Normally she drank her iced coffee quickly. If she waited for the ice to melt, the outside of the glass would become wet with

493

condensation and droplets would seep down through the thin paper napkin on which it rested and wet the table. She hated that. But on Mondays she let the water spread messily on the table. Goodness knows how many futile days she had spent like this, week after week, waiting for the next issue of *Townwork*. She picked up a copy at the FamilyMart convenience store every Monday, crossed the road to Doutor and started turning the pages. Before looking inside the thin magazine, she could never suppress a momentary hope – perhaps this week there would be the perfect job. But by the time she came to close the magazine, this hope had always turned to dejection, dejection mixed with resignation. Every single time. It was too much – Marguerite felt as though she might faint. The jobs were updated every week. There were always new positions advertised. What struck her most were the dental nurse ads. They gushed out of the pages like water from a spring – it was hard to believe there could be so many dental surgeries in the world. Looking through the ads in *Townwork* was interesting. But the fact was Marguerite never felt like applying for any of the jobs. 'A friendly workplace' – that was no good. She didn't think she could work with friendly people. 'We'll help your dream come true!' declared a restaurant manager beside a photograph of cheerful young staff, bandanas around their heads. That was no good. She didn't think that she could work with people who had dreams. And she couldn't work in a place where the staff would have to clap and sing if they found out it was a customer's birthday. 'Supportive colleagues' were no good either. Marguerite had never come across a colleague she could rely on. Basically, Marguerite was tired. She was tired of involvement with people, tired of working with people. But she didn't think she was yet tired of work itself. She wanted a job working alone, without having to speak to anyone. There had never been any jobs like that. But one week she found one – on a flimsy page in a small square-framed ad.

The first thing to come out of the box was a pure white shirt. Marguerite planted the shirt nervously, but in accordance with the manual. She was relieved when she had successfully planted it. And after that she planted, carefully, one by one, each of the other items that came out of the box. A box arrived every day. Some days from Yamato Transport, some days from Sagawa Express. Working time was nine to six – eight hours, allowing for breaks – nine hundred yen an hour. No work at weekends. At first, she thought the rate of pay was rather low, but she soon decided she couldn't help that. After all, the job was only planting. And she didn't have to meet anyone or speak to anyone apart from the deliverymen who gave her the boxes. There were no performance targets. If she couldn't plant everything from the box one day, she could plant them the next. So Marguerite planted slowly. Lovely tinkling ceramic bells. Macarons of many colours. Figurines of fighter girls. Band T-shirts. One after another they came out of the box. And Marguerite planted each one slowly, so that she would not forget any of the wonderful objects, beautiful objects that came to her. Marguerite cherished everything that came out of the box. That above all was what made her happy.

Marguerite was surprised to see the dead rat that came out of the box. She planted the dead rat, holding it away from her between forefinger and thumb. A crumpled handkerchief came out of the box. Marguerite planted the crumpled handkerchief. Muddy water came out. Marguerite planted the muddy water. She went to a nearby supermarket on her break and bought some rubber gloves. Rubber gloves on, she planted. She planted a soaking-wet cuddly toy. She planted shrivelled vegetables. She planted a bird with its wings pulled off. She planted a carpet stained red-black with blood. She could not bear to look directly at what came out of the box. She didn't understand what had happened. As soon as a thought came out of the box, the exact opposite thought would follow. As soon as a feeling came out, the exact opposite feeling would follow. Marguerite was confused. Confused, she planted. She planted a broken cup. She planted a tongue cut out of a mouth. She planted a heart that could love nobody. She planted hatred. She planted anger. She planted, though she wanted to bury. She wanted to bury everything that came out of the box. She wanted to bury them so deep in the earth that no shoot could ever reach the surface. It was only Marguerite who could bury them. But Marguerite had to plant, and so she planted. She wished what she planted would wither quickly away. 'Wither, wither, wither,' she muttered. That is what her job had become. She didn't plant slowly any more. Her heart sank when each new box arrived. She tried to deal with them as quickly as she could. But however many she dealt with, nothing wonderful now came out, nothing now to warm the heart. Marguerite planted sadness. She planted anxiety. She planted regret. She planted fear. She planted fear. She planted fear. She planted fear. She planted fear. Day after day she planted fear, as though in a game of forfeit. Instead of relaxing with a home-made lunch, she now ate as she worked, gnawing at a rice ball from a convenience store. Marguerite stopped breathing deeply. Her field of vision narrowed. She took fear from the box and it slipped from her hands. She gasped. As if waking from a trance, she picked up the fear and planted it quickly. She noticed she was sticky with sweat. It was uncomfortable. She felt sick. She took off her wig, releasing trapped heat and, with it, stiff black hair. She took off her non-prescription spectacles and rubbed her face. Her wrinkles, drawn in eyebrow pencil, smudged diagonally and disappeared. What do you mean 'Marguerite'? A stupid girl, not yet thirty, pretending to be washed out. A girl who can only plant what she wants to bury. A coward, incapable of anything. Makiko cried. Makiko stood crying stupidly in the middle of the garden.

Some time ago there was an author named Mori Mari, who called herself Maria. Makiko loved Mori Mari. She thought that if Mari could call herself Maria, then she, Makiko, could call herself Marguerite. It wouldn't harm anyone, would it? She knew that the men who delivered the boxes looked at her with mystified expressions, mystified feelings, but in this workplace she would be 'Marguerite'. She had decided this on the first day, when she planted the shirt.

Makiko looked around the garden as she cried. Fear hung low in the air, like fog. The pitch-black garden was like a mire, sucking Makiko down. Like a black hole. The place she stood was nowhere. Where is this? she thought. Then she realized – she had never had a choice. There is no way she could have chosen. Of course there wasn't. Makiko smiled faintly. Her tears stopped. She put her wig back on. She put on her glasses. She wiped her face with a handkerchief and took a make-up pouch from her bag. Looking in her hand mirror, she redrew the wrinkles. I will plant. I will plant, she thought. She put her hand in the box. Fear appeared. Marguerite did not look away. She fixed her gaze on fear. Then she slowly planted it. She planted it neatly. Marguerite resolved: I do not have the right to choose. But I can wait. If I carry on planting here like this, one day wonderful things may come out of the box again, things it warms the heart just to see. So I will wait here. Keep planting and wait. Marguerite planted fear. She planted fear. She took a deep breath. She planted fear. She stretched a little to relieve the tension in her body. She relaxed for a while with some nice-smelling herb tea from her flask. She planted fear. She planted fear. The man from Yamato Transport brought the next box. Marguerite took it, smiling. The man thought this was the first time he had seen her smile. What was in the box, she did not know. Her watch, a men's-style watch that would never go out of fashion, told her that her working hours were up. She decided she would open tomorrow's box tomorrow. Marguerite will be planting again tomorrow.

SATŌ YŪYA

Same as Always

Translated by Rachel DiNitto

I

Every time I saw it on the news it was a mystery to me. What kind of environment allowed for such a thing to happen? How could a mother get away with hitting a baby hard enough to bruise it or break its bones? Surely her husband would notice. Even if he were in on it, someone in the neighbourhood would notice – or a relative or a public official. I couldn't think of an environment in which you could get away with beating a baby to a pulp. People paid attention to and took even better care of babies than I had imagined.

I lived in an apartment with my husband, and with this blob that could only be called a baby, though at first glance you couldn't make out its face or sex. My mother-in-law would drop in all the time to see it, my parents pestered me to send them photos of their grandchild almost every day, and the apartment manager would peek into the pushchair and go on about how cute it was.

The whole world loves babies. How could you possibly find a chance to abuse one? I guess you could always shut everything out – lock the door, unplug the phone, close the curtains and beat the child to your heart's content, or at least until someone broke the door down. But in the end, you'd be caught. A little crying at night was all it took to be reported to the police. You'd be arrested, and your name and the dead baby's would be all over the news. I couldn't take that. What about those parents who beat their babies to death? What the hell were they thinking? All I could figure was they had no imagination.

It was different from bullying someone at school. You needed a plan if you were going to attack something as fragile as a baby.

But I could never hit a baby. Not because I'd feel sorry for it or because people weren't supposed to do things like that. It was for the same reason that I couldn't kill a bug. I hate bugs, but I can't kill them. When you killed one, even if you got it with a tissue, or used a rolled-up newspaper, there was no way to avoid that squishing sensation in your hand. If you killed it in the house, you had to clean it up – the ooze and broken body parts. For that reason, I gave up killing bugs. I hate them, but I'm through with killing them.

Given how traumatic it was for me to kill a bug, I knew I could never hit a child. I knew from the start that I couldn't bear the sensation of each punch or stand the sight of their messy, injured bodies. You could starve a child to death, but that wasn't an option for me either. Just the idea of an emaciated baby gave me the creeps. I got sick thinking about a thing like that hanging around the house.

There were other methods, like letting them die from neglect – never changing their nappy or bathing them – but I couldn't do that either. It would bother me long before the baby would mind. But even if my fastidiousness and aversion somehow disappeared, leaving me free to hit a baby, as I said before, society wouldn't let me get away with it. If I did happen to hurt the baby even a little, the evidence would be immediately found on its body, and I'd be arrested.

What about those parents who were in fact arrested? Their environment must have been exactly right for them to get away with beating the baby to death.

But in my case, my husband came home from the office like clockwork and loved me and the baby. Our relatives and even the apartment manager loved the baby. I loved everyone except the baby and didn't want to betray any of them. That's why I was relieved when I heard about the spread of the radiation.

2

I wasn't troubled at all when I saw the news about the huge earthquake and the explosion at the nuclear power plant that spewed radiation. The quake was fantastic, but after it passed, that was the end of it. The nuclear power plant was far enough away from where I lived that I felt little urgency. But everyone was making a big deal out of it. When I took the baby for a walk the next day, there was hardly a soul about; everyone was afraid to go outside because of the radiation. My usual pharmacy was closed due to the disaster, so I headed towards one of the chain stores near the train station. The streets were so quiet, it was the first time I'd ever heard the wheels spinning on the pushchair. I'd only gone a few hundred metres from my apartment, an area as familiar as my own garden, when I was seized by a sense of disorientation, like a child lost in an unknown place. It struck me that there should be others here at this time of day, not just a full-time housewife like me.

The issue of food safety came to the fore soon after the accident at the plant. When my husband saw the extensive news coverage of contaminated vegetables on the TV that night, he remarked on how terrible it was. 'I know,' I said as I spooned baby food into the child's mouth. It fussed as the food ran down its face. But the minute I heard the news, a deep feeling of relief ran through me, as if someone had assured me that everything would be okay. It's hard to put into words, but I felt encouragement spreading through my body. I didn't understand it at first myself. How could I feel this way when a foreign substance was covering the earth and contaminating the very food we put into our mouths? Only when I was boiling water to sterilize the baby's bottles did I realize the origins of my newfound ease. When the news reports warned us not to give tap water to infants, I embraced this new sense of security.

3

Spinach. Lotus root. Napa cabbage. Watercress. Sweet potatoes. Mizuna. Mustard greens. I went to a few different supermarkets, carefully choosing those vegetables we'd been warned to avoid, the ones with high radiation levels. I hurried home, the carrier bags stuffed with contaminated vegetables hanging from the hook on the pushchair, the baby sound asleep. My baby loves to go for walks, falling asleep as soon as I put it in the pushchair.

I got home, put the baby in the cot and headed into the kitchen. I threw away what baby food there was in the freezer. I heated the spinach and mustard greens in the microwave, added tap water, and ground them up. I flavoured the spinach paste and divided it up into small plastic bags. I accomplished all this without a tinge of emotion.

Then I heard a cry from the bedroom. The baby was sobbing, flailing its short arms and legs. I was filled with sadness and pity at the sight of this baby, its face bright red, its body writhing, eyelids full of tears. I don't know if you call this maternal instinct. I put the nursing cushion on my lap and pushed the baby's face to my breast. The round lump clamped on and sucked with tremendous force. In the half year since this thing had been born, I had never failed to perform my duty.

I burped the baby, prepared the bath, and while I was catching a few minutes of a TV drama repeat, my husband came home. As soon as he walked into the living room, his face lit up and he hugged the baby. The baby let out a high-pitched giggle. I loved to watch this more than anything. I was ready to burst with joy, wishing we could all die of happiness right then and there.

I prepped dinner while my husband bathed the baby. Today's menu was white rice, miso soup with plain and deep-fried tofu, squash boiled in soy sauce, dried daikon radish strips and amberjack teriyaki. I didn't dare use the contaminated vegetables. I wouldn't risk my or my husband's health by eating such horrifying things. My husband sipped his soup and watched the news, looking grim.

'Don't worry, I used mineral water,' I told him.

'We're fine, but they're saying not to give babies tap water,' he replied.

'I know,' I said as I fed the smooth, freshly bathed baby the food I'd made with contaminated vegetables and tap water. According to the news, when you boiled water its concentration of radioactive particles increased. Starting tomorrow, I'd stop breastfeeding and give the baby formula made with tap water.

4

From that point on, I poisoned the baby every day. I continued to feed it, allowing contaminated food and tap water to build up in that small body.

I don't know exactly why, but babies are more susceptible to radiation than children or adults, and they have increased rates of childhood cancer.

The national government keeps telling us that there is 'no immediate danger' from contaminated food or tap water, which amounts to them declaring that there is bound to be a danger at some point. So if I keep giving the baby contaminated food and water, it will die. I had the nation's word on that.

The baby showed no signs of change. No hair loss, no odour, no discolouring of the skin or clouding of the eyes. It grew like a weed. Which was lucky for me. Had the baby started showing symptoms, I couldn't possibly take care of it. Physical changes like that would really give me the creeps. Worse, though, people would find out that I had been filling the child's body with poison.

No, people finding out was not the issue where poisoning was concerned. Even if other mothers weren't doing it intentionally like I was, they were filling their children with poison, too. I wasn't the only guilty one. There was no real difference between what I was doing to my baby and what they were doing to theirs. Other mothers were supposedly stocking up on vegetables from distant areas and mineral water from overseas in an effort to protect their babies. But it was impossible to guard against radiation completely. A nuclear power plant had exploded in the middle of our country. Every day, little by little, radioactive material was building up inside those tiny bodies. No matter how careful you were, nothing could change that.

Giving them milk, feeding them, airing their rooms, hanging out the bedding, taking them for walks, bathing them, putting them to bed. These everyday chores – even those done to make them more comfortable – were fraught with danger. Radioactive particles would come in when you aired the room, you'd be showered with them when you went for a walk, they'd coat the bedding when you hung it out to dry, and they'd get mixed in with the bathwater. I made formula with tap water and baby food with contaminated vegetables, but other than that, I wasn't doing anything special. I aired the room, hung out the bedding, took the baby for walks, bathed it and put it to bed, that's all.

I was just like all the other mothers. All the other mothers were just like me.

Dosage and intentions aside, the minute they exposed their babies, even a little, the other mothers were no different from me. I did my best every day to contaminate my baby. The baby seemed to think it was being fussed over even more than normal, and cheerfully wrung that lovely voice from its throat. The sight of that face – round like a meat bun, opening its mouth in laughter to show off its two little front teeth – was so cute it ripped my heart out.

5

My mother-in-law came by one holiday, dropped some bottles of the now hard-to-get mineral water in the entryway, and announced that she planned to evacuate me and the baby to her ancestral home. Her birthplace was in the countryside, far from here and the power plant.

'This is so sudden, you're putting me in a difficult spot,' I said, but in fact it was no trouble at all. I was a housewife and the baby was not in pre-school, so if we decided to go, we could go right away.

When I looked to my husband for help, he said, 'It's a good idea. I've been worried too,' and, hugging the baby, he rubbed his nose against its head. The baby squealed with the tickle of it. The decision was made – the baby and I would leave in a week. My mother-in-law stayed late, so we ordered in sushi. As she cuddled the baby, she kept talking about the importance of going to a place where the nuclear accident wouldn't affect us as much. My husband nodded in agreement. 'I wish things would get back to normal soon,' he said. But I knew that was never going to happen.

I couldn't sleep that night so I surfed the internet as I nursed the baby. I was looking for information on the current state of radiation dispersal from the plant. Sure enough, I found it, plenty of it. Various countries, universities and organizations had taken measurements. There were so many maps comparing the readings against different standards using different instruments that I couldn't make sense of them all. I sat in the pale glow of the computer listening to the baby sucking on my breast and saving images of maps to help me figure out what I was going to do come next week. I found any number that showed the worst possible scenario.

6

My husband drove us out of town. My mother-in-law had gone ahead and was waiting for us. The baby seemed excited by the long drive. Lying in the car seat, it sucked on its fingers and cried out in delight. Sitting next to it, I rubbed the baby's belly. It was nice and warm. I wondered how much poison had already accumulated there.

'I'll be lonely, but I'll visit at weekends,' he said.

I thanked him, trying to imagine what kind of environment we were heading for. There was nothing I had to do. Keep nursing, changing nappies and following orders. Same as always. Which is why I had felt so relieved to learn that hell was spreading all around us.

Notes

TANIZAKI JUN'ICHIRŌ
The Story of Tomoda and Matsunaga

1. *fourth year*: Periods of time in this story are calculated using a traditional Japanese reckoning, in which the year of departure and the year of return are both counted as one even though each may be less than a full calendar year in length. Likewise, a child is counted as a year old in the year it is born and takes on another year each New Year's Day. Calculated this way, Japanese ages tend to be one or two years higher than when calculated from birthday to birthday.
2. *pilgrimage to the thirty-three Kannon temples*: As a religious austerity, it was customary to visit – usually on foot, dressed in white pilgrimage garb with a conical sedge hat and carrying a walking stick – thirty-three temples in western Japan enshrining images of Kannon, bodhisattva of compassion.
3. *waka poetry*: The most traditional form of Japanese verse, in five lines of 5-7-5-7-7 syllables.

NAGAI KAFŪ
Behind the Prison

1. *'Ah! let me . . . torrid summer!'*: William Aggeler, *The Flowers of Evil* (Fresno, CA: Academy Library Guild, 1954); online: http://fleursdumal.org/poem/208.
2. *the Japanese . . . in the future*: A reference to the Russo-Japanese War (1904–5); see 'Sanshirō', note 2.
3. *O my God . . . with love*: Translated from Kafū's Japanese. The original runs: 'Ô mon Dieu, vous m'avez blessé d'amour / Et la blessure est

encore vibrante, / Ô mon Dieu, vous m'avez blessé d'amour' – Paul Verlaine, *Sagesse* (1881), II.i.1–3.

NATSUME SŌSEKI
Sanshirō

1. *moxibustion*: A procedure used in traditional Chinese medicine, as practised in Japan, sometimes performed with acupuncture, wherein bits of the dried moxa plant (Japanese *mogusa*, or mugwort) are burned on the skin to stimulate the circulation in certain key locations of the body.
2. *the war*: The Russo-Japanese War (1904–5), fought to determine which of the two imperial powers would dominate parts of Manchuria and Korea, cost Japan over a hundred thousand fighting men's lives as they took such strategic Russian-occupied ports in Manchuria as Port Arthur in Dalian (Dairen in Japanese).
3. *the poet Shiki*: Masaoka Shiki (1867–1902), the modern haiku master, was a great friend of Sōseki's.

MORI ŌGAI
The Last Testament of Okitsu Yagoemon

1. *My ritual suicide today*: Mori Ōgai wrote 'The Last Testament of Okitsu Yagoemon' following the death by ritual suicide of General Nogi Maresuke (see the Introduction, p. xviii) and sent in his completed manuscript on 18 September, the day of Nogi's funeral. Obsessed with factual accuracy, Ōgai appended a note to his story naming his sources and enumerating the ways in which his fictional version departed from them. He also wrote a more heavily factual version of the story in 1913. See 'To the reader', dated October 1912, in Mori Ōgai, *The Incident at Sakai and Other Stories*, ed. David Dilworth and J. Thomas Rimer (Honolulu: University of Hawai'i Press, 1977), p. 22. See also pp. 23–33 for the 1913 version.

2. *province of Higo*: Higo was a province in central Kyushu, some five hundred miles from Yamashiro (present-day Kyoto).

MISHIMA YUKIO
Patriotism

1. *Incident of 26 February*: The coup staged in 1936 by a group of some hundred young Imperial Japanese Army officers fanatically loyal to the emperor who led nearly fifteen hundred troops in an uprising meant to cleanse the government of perceived foreign-inspired 'impurities'. They succeeded in taking over central Tokyo and assassinating several key government figures, but surrendered by 29 February in the face of united army opposition and the ire of the emperor himself.

NAKAGAMI KENJI
Remaining Flowers

1. *the alleyway*: In the unique fictional world of Nakagami Kenji, those who live in 'the alleyway' are members of Japan's outcaste Burakumin, the 'people of the village' historically linked with jobs that were considered defiling or demeaning: leather worker, undertaker, slaughterer, shoemaker. See Eve Zimmerman, *Out of the Alleyway: Nakagami Kenji and the Poetics of Outcaste Fiction* (Cambridge: Harvard University Press, 2007), pp. 1–9.

YOSHIMOTO BANANA
Bee Honey

1. *living under the junta . . . Peronists*: During the 'Dirty War' under junta rule in Argentina (1976–83), established following the overthrow of President Isabel Péron, thousands of students, intellectuals and labour

organizers were 'disappeared'. It was after travelling to Argentina that Yoshimoto published the volume containing this story, *Adultery and South America*, in 2000.

ENCHI FUMIKO
A Bond for Two Lifetimes – Gleanings

1. *Tales of Moonlight and Rain . . . Tales of Spring Rain*: See the Introduction, p. xxi.
2. *Tamakazura . . . Prince Genji's love interests*: In the eleventh-century *Tale of Genji*, Genji is attracted to the daughter (by another lover) of a woman he was briefly involved with.

UNO KŌJI
Closet LLB

1. *Iwaya Sazanami* (1870–1933): A writer, poet and editor known primarily for his children's literature.

KAWAKAMI MIEKO
Dreams of Love, Etc.

1. *The big earthquake*: A reference to the earthquake, tsunami and nuclear meltdown of 11 March 2011. Kawakami Mieko published this amusing and touching reflection on the challenge of nothingness in 2013, two years afterwards. (See also the Introduction, p. xxv.)

AKUTAGAWA RYŪNOSUKE
Hell Screen

1. *I am certain . . . be another*: Like many of Akutagawa's most successful stories, this tale, set in the late Heian period (794–1185), is based on a

medieval source. (See also the Introduction, pp. xxvi.) For an English translation of the much simpler thirteenth-century tale on which this story is based, see D. E. Mills, *A Collection of Tales from Uji: A Study and Translation of Uji Shūi monogatari* (Cambridge: Cambridge University Press, 1970), pp. 196–7.

2. *China's First Emperor . . . lofty palaces*: China's self-proclaimed 'First Emperor' (259–210 BC; r. 247–210) whose construction of the Great Wall, which began c.228 and was completed a few years after his death, cost the lives of many of his subjects. Yang, the second and last emperor of the Sui dynasty (AD 569–618; r. 604–18), was another ruler whose ambitious public works cost many lives and much treasure.

3. *procession of goblins . . . in the Capital*: Several eleventh- or twelfth-century stories marked this intersection outside the south-eastern corner of the Imperial Palace grounds as a place where one might encounter a procession of goblins. See, for example, Helen Craig McCullough, *Ōkagami: The Great Mirror* (Princeton, NJ: Princeton University Press, 1980), p. 136.

4. *ghost of Tōru . . . spirit vanish*: For the translation of a Noh play on the legend of Minamoto no Tōru (822–95), his lavish garden and his ghost, see Kenneth Yasuda, *Masterworks of the Nō Theatre* (Bloomington, IN: Indiana University Press, 1989), pp. 460–84.

5. *His Lordship offered . . . buried at the foot of a pillar*: This echoes an ancient legend which also inspired a fifteenth-century Noh play, *Nagara*, in which the spirit of the sacrificial victim returns to seek vengeance for his unjust death.

6. *Yoshihide*: This name has four evenly stressed syllables, pronounced: Yo-shee-hee-deh.

7. *'Monkeyhide'*: Like 'Yoshihide', 'Monkeyhide' has four syllables: Mon-key-hee-deh.

8. *Kawanari or Kanaoka*: Both artists, Kose no Kanaoka (*fl.* c.895) and Kudara no Kawanari (782–853), were noted for the uncanny realism of their works, none of which survive. A horse that Kanaoka painted on the Imperial Palace wall was said to escape at night and tear up nearby fields. See Yoshiko K. Dykstra, *The Konjaku Tales*, 3 vols (Osaka: Intercultural Research Institute, Kansai Gaidai University, 1998–2003), vol. 2, pp. 282–4, for a story about Kawanari.

9. *Five Levels of Rebirth on the Ryūgaiji Temple gate, for example*: In Buddhism, the five graduated realms to which the dead proceed depending on their virtue in past lives: heaven, human, animal, hungry ghost and hell. Ryūgaiji is a temple near Nara.

10. *Monju*: In Sanskrit, Manjusri, the bodhisattva of wisdom.

11. *fox spirit*: Japan is particularly rich in folklore about foxes as spiritual creatures with both threatening and nurturing aspects. See Karen A. Smyers, *The Fox and the Jewel: Shared and Private Meanings in Contemporary Japanese Inari Worship* (Honolulu: University of Hawai'i Press, 1998).

12. *Five Virtues*: The five Confucian virtues: benevolence, justice, courtesy, wisdom and fidelity.

AKUTAGAWA RYŪNOSUKE
The Great Earthquake and General Kim

1. *The Great Earthquake*: 'The Great Earthquake', written after the massive Kantō earthquake of 1923, was published as Section 31 of Akutagawa's episodic 'The Life of a Stupid Man' (1927). Akutagawa published 'General Kim' in January 1924, four months after he witnessed the 'upright citizens' of Tokyo committing mob violence against local Koreans in the aftermath of the earthquake. It is likely that he had these recent outrages in mind as he penned this brief but bloodthirsty tale. For full text and annotations of 'The Life of a Stupid Man', see Ryūnosuke Akutagawa, *Rashōmon and Seventeen Other Stories*, trans. Jay Rubin (London: Penguin Classics, 2006), pp. 186–205. For an annotated study of 'General Kim', see my translation in *Monkey Business*, vol. 3 (2013), pp. 213–17.

2. *Katō Kiyomasa . . . Konishi Yukinaga*: Katō Kiyomasa (1562–1611) and Konishi Yukinaga (1555–1600) were generals in the vanguard of Japan's well-organized, massive, but ultimately abortive invasion of Korea in 1592.

3. *King Seonjo* (1552–1608): Fourteenth king of the Joseon dynasty, who ruled Korea from 1567 to 1608.

4. *Kim Eung-seo* (1564–1624): Although the real General Kim could probably not have brought down a flying magic sword with a gob of spit,

he did exist, and he concluded a peace with the actual Yukinaga, who went home to die in Japan in 1600.

5. *kisaeng, Kye Wol-hyang*: Kye Wol-hyang (d. 1592?) was a *kisaeng* or Korean geisha – a highly trained female entertainer who was often also a courtesan.

6. *Chronicles of Japan*: The thirty-volume *Nihon shoki* (AD 720) was Japan's first official history.

ŌTA YŌKO
Hiroshima, City of Doom

1. *Mōri Motonari . . . Fukushima Masanori*: Mōri Motonari (1497–1571) and Fukushima Masanori (1561–1624).

2. *Lord Asano Nagakoto* (1842–1937).

3. *Admiral Tōgō Heihachirō* (1848–1934): Highly decorated naval hero who all but destroyed the enemy fleet in the Russo-Japanese War of 1904–5 (see 'Sanshirō', note 2).

SEIRAI YŪICHI
Insects

1. *Kunchi festival*: The Nagasaki Kunchi is an autumn festival held by a Shinto shrine to celebrate the harvest. During the Edo period (1603–1868), the authorities required a tour of homes to expose hidden Christians.

HOSHINO TOMOYUKI
Pink

1. *Five Races Under One Union*: Pre-war imperialist slogan (*Gozoku kyōwa*) calling for Japan's rule of the five East Asian 'races': Japanese, Chinese, Manchurian, Mongolian and Korean.

2. *Greater East Asian Friendship Society*: Meant to be reminiscent of another Japanese imperialist slogan, 'Greater East Asia Co-Prosperity Sphere'.

MURAKAMI HARUKI
UFO in Kushiro

1. *no friends or relatives . . . hurt in Kobe*: A reference to the 1995 Kobe earthquake. (See the Introduction, p. xxxi.)

Glossary

entryway   Japanese houses have a distinctly delineated area at ground level near the front door. You wear shoes into the tiled or stone-floored entryway but must change out of them before stepping up to the wooden floor.

hakama   In traditional Japanese dress, full-skirted trousers worn over a kimono.

haori   A traditional open-front jacket worn over a kimono, often paired with *hakama* on formal occasions.

kotatsu   A low wooden table frame set up in a **tatami**-matted room and covered by a quilt, upon which a table top rests. Underneath is a heat source, formerly a charcoal brazier but now electric, often built into the table itself. The *kotatsu* evokes nostalgic memories of the family huddled around it in winter, chatting and sharing hot tea and cold mandarin oranges.

mat   See **tatami**.

obi   A sash worn over a kimono. A somewhat simpler style first popularized in the city of Nagoya around 1918 is known as a Nagoya obi.

shoji   (or *shōji*). A sliding door or window covering made of translucent paper stretched over a wooden grid lattice.

tanzen   A winter kimono made with heavy cotton padding.

tatami   Except for utilitarian spaces, the floors of most rooms in Japanese homes are covered in densely woven straw mats called 'tatami', each mat measuring 1.8 x 0.9 metres (6 x 3 feet) and about 6.3cm (2½in) thick. Room size is designated by the number of mats on the floor. A six-mat room is about 3.6 metres (12 feet) square, for instance, and a more comfortable eight-mat room is about 4.5 x 3.6 metres (15 x 12 feet).

tokonoma   In a formal Japanese **tatami**-matted room, a *tokonoma* is a decorative alcove or recessed area edged by a pillar, in which a hanging scroll or other artwork is displayed. An honoured guest is always seated before (and facing away from) the *tokonoma*. A ceremonial space in which memorial tablets, samurai swords or other items of spiritual import are sometimes placed, the area is raised several inches above floor level and can be defiled by anyone thoughtless enough to sit on the raised edge, as old Higgins does in *American Hijiki*.

yukata　A light, unlined cotton kimono, often worn after a bath.

Acknowledgements

1. Tanizaki Jun'ichirō, 'The Story of Tomoda and Matsunaga'. Translation copyright © Paul Warham
2. Nagai Kafū, 'Behind the Prison'. Translation copyright © Jay Rubin
3. Natsume Sōseki, 'Sanshirō'. Translation copyright © Jay Rubin
4. Mori Ōgai, 'The Last Testament of Okitsu Yagoemon'. Translation copyright © UNESCO
5. Mishima Yukio, 'Patriotism', translated by Geoffrey W. Sargent, from *Death in Midsummer and Other Stories*, copyright © 1966 by New Directions Publishing Corp. Reprinted by permission of New Directions Publishing Corp.
6. Tsushima Yūko, 'Flames', copyright © the estate of Tsushima Yūko. Translation copyright © Geraldine Harcourt
7. Kōno Taeko, 'In the Box', copyright © Kōno Taeko. Translation copyright © Jay Rubin
8. Nakagami Kenji, 'Remaining Flowers', copyright © 1983/the Heirs of Kenji Nakagami, used by permission of the Wylie Agency (UK) Ltd. Translation copyright © Eve Zimmerman
9. Yoshimoto Banana, 'Bee Honey', copyright © 2000 by Yoshimoto Banana. The original Japanese edition of this work was published in *Furin to nanbei* by Gentōsha, Inc., in 2000. English translation rights arranged with Yoshimoto Banana through ZIPANGO, SS.L. Translation copyright © Michael Emmerich
10. Ohba Minako, 'The Smile of a Mountain Witch', copyright © 1976 by Yu Tani. English translation rights arranged with Yu Tani through Japan Foreign Rights Centre. Translation copyright © Noriko Mizuta
11. Enchi Fumiko, 'A Bond for Two Lifetimes – Gleanings', copyright © 1957 the Heirs of Enchi Fumiko, used by permission of the Wylie Agency (UK) Ltd. Translation copyright © Phyllis Birnbaum, from *Rabbits Crabs, Etc.: Stories by Japanese Women Writers*, the University of Hawai'i Press, 1982

12. Abe Akira, 'Peaches', copyright © the estate of Abe Akira. Translation copyright © Jay Rubin

13. Ogawa Yōko, 'The Tale of the House of Physics', copyright © Ogawa Yōko 2011. Translated by Ted Goossen, the story was first published in *Monkey Business: New Writing from Japan*, vol. 1 (2011)

14. Kunikida Doppo, 'Unforgettable People'. Translation copyright © Jay Rubin

15. Murakami Haruki, 'The 1963/1982 Girl from Ipanema', copyright © Murakami Haruki 1983. This story originally appeared in Japanese in *Kangarū biyori* in 1983 and was first published in English in Jay Rubin's *Haruki Murakami and the Music of Words* in 2002. Translation copyright © Murakami Haruki

'The Girl from Ipanema'. Music by Antonio Carlos Jobim. English words by Norman Gimbel. Original words by Vinicius De Moraes. Copyright © 1963 Antonio Carlos Jobim and Vinicius de Moraes, Brazil. Copyright renewed 1991 and assigned to Songs of Universal, Inc., and Words West LLC. English words renewed 1991 by Norman Gimbel for the world and assigned to Words West LLC (PO Box 15187, Beverly Hills, CA 90209 USA). All rights reserved used by permission. Reprinted by permission of Hal Leonard LLC

'The Girl from Ipanema' (Garota de Ipanema). Words by Norman Gimbel and Vinicius de Moraes. Music by Antonio Carlos Jobim © Copyright 1963 Universal Music Publishing Ltd/Hal Leonard LLC. All rights reserved. International copyright secured. Used by permission of Music Sales Ltd and Hal Leonard LLC

'The Girl from Ipanema' (Moraes/Jobim/Gimbel) © Songs of Universal, Inc./Universal Music Publishing Pty Ltd for Australia and New Zealand. All rights reserved. International copyright secured. Reprinted with permission

16. Shibata Motoyuki, 'Cambridge Circus'. Translation copyright © Jay Rubin

17. Uno Kōji, 'Closet LLB'. Translation copyright © Jay Rubin

18. Genji Keita, 'Mr English', copyright © the estate of Genji Keita. Translation copyright © Jay Rubin

19. Betsuyaku Minoru, 'Factory Town', copyright © Betsuyaku Minoru. Translation copyright © Royall Tyler

20. Kawakami Mieko, 'Dreams of Love, Etc.', copyright © Mieko Kawakami 2013. Translation copyright © Hitomi Yoshio

21. Hoshi Shin'ichi, 'Shoulder-Top Secretary', copyright © 1971 the Hoshi Library. First published in Japan in 1971 in *Bokko-chan* by Shinchōsha Publishing Company Ltd. English translation rights arranged with the Hoshi Library through Japan Foreign-Rights Centre. Translation copyright © Jay Rubin

22. Akutagawa Ryūnosuke, 'Hell Screen'. Translation copyright © Jay Rubin

23. Sawanishi Yūten, 'Filling Up with Sugar', copyright © Sawanishi Yūten. First published in *Granta 127: Japan*, 2014. Translation copyright © Jay Rubin

24. Uchida Hyakken, 'Kudan', copyright © the estate of Uchida Hyakken. Translation copyright © Rachel DiNitto

25. Akutagawa Ryūnosuke, 'The Great Earthquake'. Translation copyright © Jay Rubin

26. Akutagawa Ryūnosuke, 'General Kim'. Translation copyright © Jay Rubin

27. Ōta Yōko, 'Hiroshima, City of Doom', from *Hiroshima: Three Witnesses*, edited and translated by Richard H. Minear, copyright © 1990 by Princeton University Press. Reprinted by permission

28. Seirai Yūichi, 'Insects', copyright © Seirai Yūichi c/o the Japan Writers Association. Translation copyright © Paul Warham

29. Kawabata Yasunari, 'The Silver Fifty-Sen Pieces', from *Palm-of-the-Hand Stories* by Yasunari Kawabata, translated by Lane Dunlop and J. Martin Holman. Translation copyright © 1988 by Lane Dunlop and J. Martin Holman. Reprinted by permission of North Point Press, a division of Farrar, Straus and Giroux

30. Nosaka Akiyuki, 'American Hijiki', copyright © the estate of Akiyuki Nosaka. Translation copyright © Jay Rubin

31. Hoshino Tomoyuki, 'Pink', copyright © Hoshino Tomoyuki. Translation copyright © Brian Bergstrom. First published in in *Granta 127: Japan*, 2014

32. Murakami Haruki, 'UFO in Kushiro', copyright © Murakami Haruki 2001. English translation copyright © Murakami Haruki 2002. This story first appeared in the *New Yorker* in 2001. It was first published

in Great Britain in *after the quake* in 2002 by the Harvill Press and then in 2003 by Vintage; *after the quake* was originally published under the title *Kami no kodomo-tachi wa mina odoru* in 2000 by Shinchōsha Publishing Company Ltd, Tokyo

33. Saeki Kazumi, 'Weather-Watching Hill', copyright © Saeki Kazumi. Translation copyright © David Boyd

34. Matsuda Aoko, 'Planting', copyright © Matsuda Aoko. Translation copyright © Angus Turvill

35. Satō Yūya, 'Same as Always', translation by Rachel DiNitto, copyright © 2012 Satō Yūya. English language anthology rights arranged with the author c/o Shinchōsha Publishing Company Ltd through Tuttle-Mori Agency, Inc., Tokyo